The Furies

The Furies

A NOVEL

Fernanda Eberstadt

ALFRED A. KNOPF   NEW YORK   2003

THIS IS A BORZOI BOOK
PUBLISHED BY ALFRED A. KNOPF

Published in the United States by Alfred A. Knopf, a division of Random House, Inc.,
New York, and simultaneously in Canada by Random House of Canada Limited,
Toronto. Distributed by Random House, Inc., New York.
www.aaknopf.com

Knopf, Borzoi Books, and the colophon are registered trademarks of
Random House, Inc.

Library of Congress Cataloging-in-Publication Data
Eberstadt, Fernanda, [date]
The furies : a novel / Fernanda Eberstadt. – 1st ed.
p.   cm.
ISBN 0-375-41256-5 (alk. paper)
1. Married women–Fiction. 2. Manhattan (New York, N.Y.)–Fiction. 3. Inheritance
and succession–Fiction. 4. Interfaith marriage–Fiction. 5. Marital conflict–Fiction.
6. Puppeteers–Fiction. 7. Jewish men–Fiction. 8. Divorce–Fiction. I. Title.
PS3555.B484 F87 2003
813'.54–dc21   2002072990

Manufactured in the United States of America
First Edition

For Alastair

And you, harsh girl. You are looking for . . . absolution?

The Furies

BOOK ONE

Chapter One

I

Sunday in Central Park.

A raw gusty September afternoon, unseasonably cold. Wind ripping the browning leaves from the oaks and plane trees. Autumn in the air.

On this particular Sunday afternoon, middle of the 1990s, Gwendolen Lewis was sitting by the toy-boat pond, where she had arranged to meet a friend. Gwen, as was her habit, was early; her friend late.

She had ploughed through the remains of the Sunday papers (no news; just stupid *weekend* stories about how to spend your money); she had made notes on the next morning's business trip, picked up the messages on her voice mail—one from Constance, warning, redundantly, that she was late. She had bolted a cup of coffee, and now was reduced to restless waiting.

Glistening runners. Rollerbladers, colliding. Baby carriages with superstructures fanciful as Roman chariots, maneuvered by anxious parents. And dogs. Dogs sniffing, sparring, mounting; their owners jolly, self-exculpatory, resigned to this transient intimacy with strangers whose only point of commonality was that their dog just happened to be licking your dog's unprotesting asshole.

Damned Sundays. Late Constance. Loathsome park, with its neutered geometries, intended to placate creatures—dogs, small children, athletes—who shouldn't be living in a city to begin with.

Constance, an Englishwoman who lived in Singapore, was staying three blocks away at the Carlyle. So why couldn't she and Gwen have met instead downstairs in the Bemelmans Bar—a dark, confessional place which didn't welcome animals, or grown men on skates? Besides, it was about to pour.

And here, twenty-two minutes past the appointed hour, came Constance.

On the brow of the hill Gwen spotted her, and watched her descend through the crowd: long red-gold braid slapping one shoulder, schoolgirl-dishevelled in loose white corduroys, and something immeasurably provocative, derisive in the waggle of her bottom. A smiling obliviousness that declared, There are only twelve people in the universe I care about . . .

Long smooch, tight hug, faces buried in each other's hair, as if to obliterate the pity of their living eight thousand miles apart and only meeting three times a year.

"Why're you so late?"

Constance dropped beside her. "I made the mistake of calling the children. (They're staying with my parents.) Ruby wanted me to read her Noddy. I told her, 'My love, for some odd reason I didn't bring any Noddy books to New York with me.' She said, 'Here the book. Read it.' Rather difficult to explain to a two-year-old an instrument that enables you to hear but not see. What would you like—more coffee?"

The two women bought cappuccinos from the kiosk and strolled counterclockwise around the pond. Paused by the statue of Alice in Wonderland, on whom Gwen and her younger brother had climbed as children. Twenty million years ago. Grown Gwen eyed bronze Alice, impressed—despite herself—by the poised girth of the pinafored giantess. A vertical sphinx, with eyes the size of baseballs. Our Alice Who Art in Wonderland, live children hanging from her limbs, like the damned and the saved.

"Shall we sit?" Constance, evidently missing her own babies, wanting to watch other people's children play.

They sat. Next bench over, a bearded man was stretched out asleep, newspaper under his head. Homeless, or sleeping off a bender? Sleeping, Gwen decided. You no longer saw so many homeless people in the city. Giuliani had shipped them all out to . . . to where? To colonize some new Australia, maybe.

"So you're off to Russia tomorrow. I'm glad I caught you."

Gwen, mid-sip, nodded. "Me, too. I miss you; I don't seem to have any friends anymore. I find myself talking to the computer."

"How's work?"

"Hopping." Gwen was a director of an institute set up to help the former Soviet Union democratize. "We just found out our Moscow accountant—hired by me, naturally—has been embezzling funds."

"What a bore. Can you trace the money?"

"Oh, we'll never get it back. The money's not even the point. It's— what do you expect, the whole society has been this kleptocracy for *years*. It's no joke getting people to feel, This is your country now, you don't need to rape your wife, you could try making love to her for a change . . ."

"Do you still like it?"

"Russia? My job? Yeah, both of them. A lot. You know I've got this taste for dead-end streets. How about you, Constance? Are you getting used to the East? Don't you miss work?"

Constance was a lawyer who had specialized in mergers and acquisitions at a white-shoe London firm. For a few years she'd appeared a highflyer—till, burnt out on corporate hours, she had first shifted into human rights and then, after her second child, quit.

"You must be joking. I'm far too lazy for law; I'd much rather stay at home and gossip with the nannies." She paused. "You know, Singapore's hardly the East. Sadly. We live in international quarantine, like these sort of high-paid guest workers—you know how Singapore Chinese just despise *everybody*. But Roger swears we'll be back in London in a year . . ." She leaned forward, narrow shoulders hunched against the wind. Smiling, with an unfocused benevolence, at the boys and girls swarming over Alice's polished bestiary.

"You're homesick for your children." Gwen, jealous.

Constance, for reply, shifted her smile to her friend. "You don't want babies ever, do you? I mean, you think this mothery stuff is all unspeakably dreary and trivial, don't you?" Not accusing—on the contrary, vicariously enjoying her friend's lone freedom, her license to play the field. "The pleasures of small children—of one's own small children—are somehow impossible to convey."

Gwen considered (briefly) children's tyranny, their singsong voices too loud like deaf people's. The tedium of being expected to evince an interest in Noddy when all you wanted to do was read the paper, pay your bills.

"I guess so." Then, embarrassed, she launched into self-defense. "You know, I'm away a lot. Places without phones or . . . FAA regulations. I mean, nobody with a family could possibly justify setting foot on one of these rattraps they're flying out of . . . Murmansk. Sometimes I think if I could be the father—you know, just stop by once in a while to kiss the kid good night . . ."

"But you're happy . . ."

"Oh, come on. Happiness suggests an absence of self-loathing I can't quite pretend to, but let's say, I like my work. Then at the end of the day, I want to lock the door and be alone. Read a book, turn out the light whenever. There's something about two people in the bathroom at the same time, one of you trying to brush your teeth when the other one's pissing, that just makes me want to—"

"What about Campbell?"

"Campbell's great, but . . ."

"That sounds red-hot."

"What can I say? I'm an old maid. Am I going to wake up in ten, fifteen years, aghast that I forgot to have children? Maybe. I don't think that far ahead, I'm not ruling anything out, maybe I'll be that mother who orders her customized chick at seventy-three."

Not saying the obvious. That most of what she'd seen of marriage was lies, betrayal, destruction. At best, the slow erosion of whatever you'd once liked about yourself.

"Could you imagine spending your life with him?"

"Who, Campbell? I can't live with myself, let alone someone else. I mean, I guess that's what I'm saying—I'm just scraping by, there's not much margin of comfort to offer anybody else."

My husband—she'd heard women her age pronounce this pompous phrase as if the guy thus conjured were seven feet tall, shaved with a straight razor, and had fucked them to jelly that very morning. When in fact most husbands Gwen knew were snot-nosed squirts, needy, repetitive, cavilling. My husband? No.

"How's Roger doing?" Grudgingly. The irredentism creeping in, willy-nilly: I shared a bed with your wife back when she wore braces on her teeth and had to listen to Blondie's "Heart of Glass" five times before breakfast; I possess unstudied archives of her—age fifteen, seventeen, twenty-one, at the beach, shoplifting, on her first acid trip—that you would die for one peek at. When Constance was one of the few foreigners at a New England boarding school. An ugly duckling, all skinny legs and freckles. Like Gwen, a near-geek.

"Roger? He's a wonder," said Constance, ironically. "His bonuses are larger than the GNP of most Third World countries. I suppose that puts me off work, too: I can't very well pretend we need the money."

"I bet," said Gwen. "I remember when people used to go on about the eighties being this age of greed."

"Oh, the eighties were Hard Times compared to nowadays."

"This *is* the real thing, isn't it?"

The children swirling, swirling over Alice in Wonderland. Trampling the Dormouse, throttling the Mad Hatter and the Cheshire Cat. The children swirling, swirling, spilling over the edges like besiegers of a fortress.

On the bench next to Gwen and Constance's, the sleeping man turned over in his sleep. Tucked his long legs tighter under his butt. He was wearing a pair of red Converse All Stars, Gwen noted, his big toe poking out of a hole in one sneaker. Gwen intercepted her friend's unease: the danger-averting watchfulness of Constance-as-mother. What is this potential pervert doing here? I thought they didn't allow unaccompanied adults in the playgrounds. Maybe Constance had been living in Singapore too long . . .

Constance wasn't the only one watching their sleeping neighbor, Gwen noticed. A boy in a Braves shirt, scaling Alice's brawny shoulder, also kept glancing at the man.

High wind ruffling the leaves on the plane trees underside up, the clouds now dark and heavy-lidded with their burden, and a first grumble of thunder.

Gwen stood up. "We'd better split."

The parents, too, beginning to hustle their kids, pack up the strollers, slip windbreakers from knapsacks.

And now—as if everyone's eyes had finally bored him awake—the sleeper on the next-door bench sat up, stretched. Looked around. Taking in Constance, Gwen—who looked away too late.

The man yawned, stood up, glanced over at Alice. At the boy in the baseball shirt. "C'mon," said the man to the boy. "Time to go home."

And Gwen watched as he chucked his newspaper into a trash can and ambled over to the railings, where he unlocked a large rusty bicycle. Mounted, helped the boy onto its crossbar, and cycled away, wobbling.

Leaving Gwen feeling obscurely excluded. Not quite sure which it was she envied—the raffish ease of the cycler, or the trustfulness of the son nesting between those pedalling knees.

She and Constance also rose, hurrying up the hill and out onto

Fifth Avenue. The rain cascading now, surplusing in indented coveys in the octagonal paving. Lightning white-white in the sky's sullen darkness.

Gwen and Constance rushing across Madison Avenue in the pus-laden downpour, narrowly missed by a bus, splashing a group of people sheltering under the awning of the Carlyle.

"Do you want to come up to my room for some tea? Roger should be back any minute."

"I can't—I have to stop by the office."

"And tonight? We're supposed to meet Christopher at some new—"

"I know. Unfortunately, I've been summoned for dinner with my dad. The triannual dinner. He only calls up when Jacey's out of town."

"Count your blessings."

"I guess."

2

THE LAVRINSKY INSTITUTE was housed in a turn-of-the-century Gothic palace on the southeast corner of Seventy-ninth and Fifth. Gwen had wondered if her boss, Edward Lavrinsky, had not seen his own face in one of those crouching limestone monkey-men that dripped from each corner. Lavrinsky was an investor who had decided to translate his fortune into political philanthropy. Gwen, who had met his children, didn't much blame him.

In the late seventies and early eighties, Lavrinsky had funnelled money into the New York City public school system, of which he was a stellar graduate. But Lavrinsky had evidently been bored by education and its theoreticians: he was much more interested in shaping U.S. foreign policy—a job that in bolder days had been assumed by the U.S. government. With the end of the Cold War, Lavrinsky had founded an institute devoted to rehabilitating the former Soviet Union, whose southern reaches he himself had fled, long ago, as a small boy.

Half a billion dollars a year Lavrinsky spent on buying transmitters for independent television stations in Belarus; retraining biochemists in the warfare cities of Kazakhstan; vaccinating children against tuberculosis; reflooding the Aral Sea.

Gwen was in charge of their Russian portfolio. It was a sweet racy job, just subversive enough to keep her happy. Every year, like a medieval bishop spreading Christianity, she launched a new program in

Kazan or Stavropol or Arkhangel'sk; every few months she came round to check on her older parishes, manned by missionaries with bank accounts. She was often followed; their offices were bugged; their local employees were sometimes arrested while the foreign nationals got their visas revoked. Besides which, she sometimes knew in the worst way that their larger enterprise wasn't working, that Russia and its chickens were still a world apart. But it beat her previous job, working in the State Department.

Today, Gwen stayed at the office till seven, clearing her plate for the next three weeks' absence.

3

SNIP. SNIP. SNIP.

Steve was cutting Martin Lewis's hair. Slop-slop-slop of Steve's tea-colored fingers kneading the congealed knots of Martin Lewis's neck and shoulders. Sizzle of the gadget that singed the hairs in his nostrils and ears.

Gwen regarding, with reluctant fascination, the fuzz that grew on her father's pink ears. The head of crinkling auburn hair—now fading to ginger-gray—the only handsome thing on this short ruddy-freckly bull. Girly hair, Little Lord Fauntleroy hair, worn too long.

They were sitting in her father's new dressing room.

His current wife, Jacey, who was a decorator, had carved the room out of an adjoining bedroom and done it up like a London club—leather armchairs, a mahogany dressing table with tortoiseshell brush set, the mirrored walls so besmutted with instant age you could barely see yourself. New walk-in closets, disguised as library shelves with a trompe l'oeil of red-and-gold morocco volumes.

Gwen's father had spoiled the effect by moving in his StairMaster and a sixty-inch high-definition television set.

On the dressing table, family photos in silver frames. Martin on the terrace of their house in Connecticut—a snapshot Jacey had chosen because in it he looked uncustomarily trim and relaxed, not so quite so *Portrait of a Turn-of-the-Millennium Plutocrat on His Third Wife and Second Heart Attack.*

Jacey and their two children in a speedboat off the Greek islands: Alexander at the wheel, Serena looking seasick.

A now-discolored Polaroid of Gwen and Maddock, a quarter century ago, likewise nautical, taken by an onboard photographer in the dining room of a Caribbean cruise ship: the two children peering up from under the tablecloth like hungry puppies, Gwen miniskirted, Maddock in white bell-bottoms and a pageboy. Love-me grins shameless in their unanswered appeal.

Being sore about your childhood was part of the contemporary whininess Gwen objected to. Her father, who never mentioned his own upbringing—who thought it morbid to dwell on anything older than next week—doubtless agreed. Parents did their best; why beat a dead horse? When Gwen and Maddock were little, he had been a young lawyer, hustling to make sure they wanted *for nothing*. Because he believed in progress, it was only natural that Serena and Alexander got things better: the vacations jazzier, the schools more clued-in, their dad less busy.

Steve, an amateur astrologer, was reading Lewis's forecast. "Your moon moves into Scorpio on the twenty-sixth," Steve was saying. "That means you are going to be feeling super-super-dynamite these next couple of weeks. Anyone you look at is, like, going to pick up these real charismatic vibes from you. This should be a time of unrestrained sensuality . . ."

Her father caught Gwen's eye in the mirror. "I don't know what I pay this guy for—nothing but bad news. Steve is a famous practitioner of tantric sex."

Gwen, cell phone crooked between ear and shoulder, flicked through *The Economist*. Survey of Russia she supposed she ought to clip. Usual sloppy stats—as if *anybody* could assess the GDP of a country that worked half by barter, half by indentured servitude. Bleep-bleep-bleep, from her voice mail. You have four new messages. Remembered her father's second wife once telling her, semidrunk, self-justifying, that Gwen's parents' marriage had only fallen apart because Gwen's mother no longer wanted to sleep with Martin. When she repeated this to Maddock, her brother had replied, "I wouldn't let Pop fuck me, either: he's got a hairy back and he smells bad."

"I don't know much about tantric sex," she said, finally.

"I think it's where the guy is supposed to hang in there without shooting his wad—am I right, Steve? To me, it sounds like a hundred-dollar word for old age, but Steve swears women love it, and it makes you live forever."

"Ejaculation of the semen is, like, the worst thing you can do to your body," Steve confirmed. "Worse than smoking, worse than eating meat, worse than stress." Steve, a Chinese boy who was dressed in black martial-arts pajamas, wore his own hair long. Snip-snip-snip.

Steve, in his black pajamas and shoulder-length braid, believed that most of human woes were caused by diet. Nowadays you could meet sentient adults who subscribed to this reductivism. And character? Did you ever hear anymore of people simply being weak, let alone wicked? Did Trojan Paris have a sex addiction? Did Achilles suffer from attention deficit disorder?

"Speaking of stress, we"—he and Jacey, presumably—"were supposed to go to this fundraiser tonight."

"Oh yeah?" Gwen was listening to her messages.

Campbell, calling from Geneva, to say he missed her, call him if she got home in the next hour. Hotel Ambassade, Room 401. Constance, wanting to tell her the name of a book she'd blanked out on. *Le Rivage de Syrtes*. Her mother. Mikhail Becker, coming to New York next week, staying at the Helmsley Palace. Can she meet him for dinner? Beep. End of messages. Erase messages.

"Some theater group Suzy Goldfarb's on the board of. I got Melanie to cancel us out—Jacey's a sucker for these charity dos, but I'd rather eat at home."

"When's Jacey coming back?"

"When's she coming back? Last Wednesday's when she's coming back. Unfortunately, there was a problem with the pool house." Jacey, having turned their Manhattan duplex into a Wiltshire manor, was now busy turning their New England farmhouse into a Tuscan villa. That was the odd part, to Gwen's mind: that you busted your ass to make a fortune so that someone else could spend it in ways you didn't care for.

"What's wrong with the pool house?"

"The tiles," he explained, sardonically. "They showed up from Italy broken. She says. That's decoratorese for 'The contractor is a moron.' Gustave. I'm warning you—never do business with someone called Gustave . . ."

"Mmmm," said Gwen. Wondering which of her Filofax's genealogical tree of numbers for Mikhail Becker's various import firms, holding companies, and car phones was still current. She'd miss him, probably.

"So you're heading off for Russia again. I hear you gotta boil the water. Chandler always takes a jar of peanut butter with him when he goes, and an electric kettle. And he still comes back eight pounds thinner . . ."

Steve was sweeping up now, dusting her father's gristly shoulders.

"I can't be bothered with boiled water."

"You need to take care of yourself, Chugga. You're looking tired."

Women, in her father's view, needed husbands. If you lived alone, you sickened. Gwen said nothing. What her father didn't want to admit was that she was thirty-one (six years younger than her current step-mother) and looked it. Which was okay with her. She had no desire to appear fresh-faced, unmarked by experience; she'd had a full—a complicated—life, and was glad it showed.

"So I hear you're talking at the Council on Foreign Relations."

"Talking, well . . . I'm on a panel."

"Pretty sly, Chugga. When is it?"

"November the . . . fifteenth?"

"Call Melanie and give her the exact date, okay?"

What was this, the school play? "It's just a panel."

"I have a feeling I gotta be in L.A. that week. Remember I want to fix up that lunch with you and Jim Lawrence."

"I don't think I have time."

"Why not? Extra money never hurts." If she'd seen fit to go to law school, she'd be making buckets by now. As it was, nonprofit was a sector intended for men with trust funds or women with rich husbands. How's Campbell? (Fondly.)

Fine . . . Now Steve was wheeling her father around to admire the back view. The hair still a touch long, by today's taste. Goldilocks. Martin Lewis, back on his feet, pressed Steve's arm affectionately and slipped him a check. Gwen admired her father's choreography—left hand patting and massaging Steve's upper arm while right hand shimmied the check into Steve's tunic pocket. Waved the hairdresser good night as he ushered his daughter downstairs into the study. Blipping on the television, where Joe Pepitone was just warming up to discuss the evening's game. Atlanta versus the Blue Jays. Sadness versus anger.

"I thought we could watch this new Robin Williams movie Billy Guttman sent over." Martin Lewis had been one of the million lawyers briefly involved in Disney's acquisition of Miramax. Picked up the phone and buzzed for the housekeeper. "Sabine, could you serve us dinner in the library?"

And Gwen, irritated (she might have had dinner with Constance) to find that she had once again been summoned for a TV dinner. Because Jacey was out of town, because her father didn't feel like struggling into a dinner jacket and shlepping to Suzy Goldfarb's fundraiser all by himself. Irritation tempered by relief that she, too, could now relax from their customary game that both were people of the world, that each was happy and successful and had done well by the other, that it was all prizes and no regrets.

4

GWEN LEWIS LIVED in an Upper West Side luxury high-rise that, like an ocean liner, had a name.

Gwen's was called the Vanderveer.

The Vanderveer had brass revolving doors, a dark green polished marble lobby, doormen in gold braid, and a health club in the basement, which she'd never visited. She had bought her apartment on moving back to the city three years ago, and the place still looked barely lived in.

When she got back home that night, Gwen made her final preparations for the morning's flight. Ordered the car for the airport, left cash for the cleaning lady. Checked her tickets—international and, wedged between them, the internal death-flights: Aeroflots to St. Petersburg, Kazan, Novosibirsk.

Wondered what she'd forgotten—had she cancelled the newspapers while she was away? Each departure, no matter how much you travelled, a small death. Wondered if there would ever come a day she could see her father without being riven, afterwards, by pity, anger, grief.

At one, Gwen, who had drunk water all evening, crawled into bed with a shot of Jack Daniel's. An image, as she merged into sleep, of the bearded man in Central Park, bicycling uphill with his son between his knees—a figure shaggy and angular as a metropolitan hermit: John the Baptist on a rusting Raleigh. Why him? Some hint, maybe, that parenthood need not be all Noddy books and nannies, or the buying off of guilt with expensive toys. That you might after all be able to exert within its confines a sly autonomy . . .

Chapter Two

I

IT WAS A LAWLESS FRONTIER TOWN, ugly as sin, rotten-new, a deep-freeze Las Vegas with shackles at its ankles. Every month a deputy minister or a local gas boss or a foreign businessman was found dead in his ZIL; there were more bodyguards than schoolteachers. It was Novosibirsk four years After Communism (4 A.C.), and it was Gwen's favorite place on earth, her chosen no-man's-land.

When she'd first come to Russia, summer before her junior year in Moscow, Siberia is where she'd hightailed it to. Spent three weeks in Novosibirsk, getting to know the Russian East: harsh, generous, sick twin to the American West. A thousand miles of permafrost bog, inhabited by Baptists and Old Believers, aboriginal tribesmen, and ex-convicts. People who didn't believe in any institution larger than could be gathered in one kitchen, and who knew the only true equality is under the eye of God. An entire population on the lam. A place to swallow you alive, if you wanted. Back in the late eighties (the last days of empire, although you didn't know it then) Novosibirsk looked almost *flush*. The streets reeled with contraband from China and Korea, and every Saturday night black marketeers and party bosses had held court in the Hotel Sibirsk, drinking dollars, smoking dollars, fucking puking shooting dollars.

But illegality seemed to be as close as Russia got to freedom. For two centuries, Siberia had had a reputation for being the freest place in the Empire, this open-air nuthouse where being a third-generation prisoner made you aristocracy. You could see the difference, the (comparative) fearlessness in people's bearing: Gwen had met the descendant of a Decembrist who was married to the great-great-granddaughter of Poles deported here after the 1848 uprising, and it seemed to her that no beltway politician, no Boston Brahmin could ever match the arrogance of this couple whose families had been on the wrong side of power for a hundred and fifty years. What can you do to us, the joke ran, we're already in Siberia. That was certainly Algis's attitude.

Gwen had met Algis her second day in Novosibirsk.

She'd taken a bus out to the Museum of Aboriginal Peoples, and arrived just before closing time. Dark galleries of fish-skin robes and antlered masks, empty but for a cavernous-cheeked graying blond in a string undershirt who was swabbing the floor.

They struck up a conversation that lasted . . . years. He was a Lithuanian who had served eight years in Perm 36 for the twin crimes of Christianity and failed emigration: he had been caught crossing the border to Poland. When he was freed (Lavrinsky was now funding the camp's rebirth as a museum of the Gulag), he had got as far as Novosibirsk and stayed.

That Sunday, Algis invited her home—a basement room in an izba on the outskirts of town, with a patch of kitchen garden out back where he cultivated bees in a stacked hutch. She had noticed, learning Russia, how readily beekeeping consorted with Christianity: as if the hive were a more perfect conception of God's humankind, all humming, busyness, and order, with honey, not tyranny, slaughter, and terrifying scientific innovations the end product.

At the end of the summer, she'd watched Algis pickle and preserve his fruits, and promised she'd be back to eat them at New Year's. (Winter was when Siberia came into its own, those who loved it insisted.)

Ten years later, Gwen had returned to Novosibirsk on an expense account, commissioned to install democratic capitalism in this permafrost permadump that could teach the Cayman Islands a few tricks about hot money. She wasn't sure whether the new job told you more about her or about the ex–Soviet Union.

That visit, there were altogether too many exes. Algis had died the summer before. His landlady gave Gwen the shopping bag in which were stuffed his less perishable belongings: a Lithuanian Bible with pressed wildflowers between its pages, a set of false teeth, Maupassant in Russian. She tried to catch his smell on the nylon soccer shirt, the pajamas, but they only gave off mildew, as if this man she'd loved and been loved by had been dead a hundred years. Her letter to his son—a driving instructor in Kaunas—came back, Addressee Unknown. Life without traces.

That year—the year after the Fall—Gwen had rented a suite at the Hotel Sibirsk, and for two weeks she had tooled around Siberia. She had met with regional governors, environmentalists, legal scholars, filmmakers. Then—after negotiating a budget with the home office—she'd hired her staff. Rented three rooms in a downtown high-rise, in which she'd installed telephones, computers, fax machines. Opened an account at the Novosibirsk branch of the bank Lavrinsky—because he'd had dinner with its owner—had decided was the least likely to elope with your funds.

Twice a year Gwen came back, to check on who had stolen what. Hung out in the office, receiving petitioners, reviewing applications, going over programs, listening to her staff's complaints, trying to read between the lines—Vladimir Levin, their director, was a bully who got everybody's back up; Ira Grushinskaya no longer showed up for work although she was still being paid; ten thousand dollars of their textbook money had disappeared into a black hole; Tatiana Kuzlova was moonlighting for the mayor, who was rumored to have charged the city for his mistress's breast implants. And the Russian government's plans to convert Akademogoroduk to a Silicon Valley had, of course, utterly foundered.

Gwen listened, praised, scolded, took notes, and looked at her watch. Guilty/relieved that in another twenty-four hours she would be back in Moscow, under the thumbs of the Hotel Metropol's masseur, before dinner at Bill and Jamila's. Wasn't this one definition of "home"—a place you couldn't breathe?

Everything I love about Russia is going to disappear, she caught herself thinking, because capitalism—even pseudocapitalism, pyramid-scam capitalism, capitalism without capital—it turns out, is a far more effective eraser of cultural difference than Communism. And yet the apparent sameness will be spurious, since "They" in their haste to become "Us" are going to miss everything about us that is actually worth having . . .

2

SNOW IN THE AIR. Wild mushrooms in the farmers' market. Construction cranes like articulated church spires, already halted—soon to rust and die—for the winter. The local prosecutor with whom Gwen was lunching recounted the ironies of post-Communism, where the tin magnate he'd just charged with embezzling his factory's export profits also happened to be the most talented and articulate of the region's new "reformers." Next door, a table of boisterous German sportsmen on their way to the Altai Mountains to shoot mastodons, catch leviathans.

(Thus New Russia had reverted to its medieval economy: big game, honey, beeswax, slaves . . .)

Leaving the office, Gwen stopped by the market to say goodbye to her friend Lidia, a former ethnologist who now traded goods across the Chinese border.

3

THE PEROXIDE BLONDE was selling plaid bedroom slippers, a pair of Ping-Pong rackets, and an alarm clock; the woman with steel teeth was offering a pair of spectacles and a large pink teddy bear. A jostling crowd had gathered around a pale acned youth offering tiger-skin beach towels.

Gwen cruised, checking out the sideshows of this medieval fair. Eyeing the traders—dead-eyed stoics who knew in their sleep the day's exchange rates in four currencies, the weekend bus schedules between Khabarovsk and Harbin, narcoleptic itinerants whose homes were ferry terminals, train carriages, rent-by-the-hour hotel rooms in all the border towns of Turkey, Romania, Iran. And at the margins, the enforcers, mustached and puffy, in leather coats, who extorted the morning's collection plate for their bosses. Country, you are bleeding to death through every pore. Russia, who's to save you when your quickest talents are asleep on the concrete floor of a bus station in Bucharest?

Gwen caught sight of Lidia's teenage son, dressed in baggies, unlaced sneakers, and a backwards baseball cap, who was examining with several other boys a small silvery object—cigarette lighter? switchblade?—that disappeared as she approached. His mother was still on the road, Roman informed Gwen: she had been held up at the border and wasn't expected home till tomorrow.

"Will you give her a message from me?" Gwen, without much confidence, drew a hotel notepad from her bag: scribbled, while Roman, impassive, watched.

God, she was forgetting how to write, or was it that Russia was changing so fast—under such bursting pressure from the alien goods, values, systems, technologies being pumped into it—that you couldn't keep up, that you felt stymied somehow by the glib implausibility of its coinings. Gwen, after all, had been educated by Soviet dissidents—people who knew that they were fighting for freedom, but who didn't yet know that freedom would turn out to mean fifty brands of breakfast cereal to choose from. *Their* language—because it had no words for money and its placebos—now seemed as decorative as Church Slavonic.

At the far end of the market, a small crowd was gathered, craning over each other's shoulders. Chinese track suits? Then she heard an incongruous sound. Laughter.

What the spectators were laughing at, Gwen discovered, was a puppet show, being performed by an invisible puppeteer with a fairly primitive grasp of Russian. A travelling American, she guessed.

The story was semipolitical slapstick. The Devil visits a Siberian village, first in the guise of a Communist commissar, who poisons its river with nuclear plants and sends its shaman to the Gulag. Finally, the Devil appears as an IMF banker in an Uncle Sam hat, promising to make the villagers millionaires. Once bitten, twice shy: the newly freed shaman turns the Devil-banker into a rooster and eats him.

Appreciative roars from the audience. "Men and women," shouted the shaman, "there are enough devils in this country to put a chicken in every pot, so get your water boiling, and your knives sharp!"

The play was over: the puppeteer bobbed up from underneath his cardboard cage. He was long-limbed, bearded, vaguely hippieish, in a purple Grateful Dead T-shirt. The puppeteer took a bow and announced in memorized Russian that he hoped no one had been offended by his show, and that anyone who had enjoyed it should come to the Little Taiga that night, where they would be performing the world premiere of an original marionette play.

Gwen knew the Little Taiga. Its director, Ilya Rupnik, the son of a poetess who died in Magadan, was a wily operator who'd cottoned on quick to the New World Order of Corporate Sponsorship—chiefly, the Lavrinsky Institute, which now kicked in a yearly five grand for the Little Taiga's international puppet festival. (Such being their desperation to promote any cooperative venture not involving drugs, money laundering, extortion, or armed violence.)

The puppeteer made his last bow, and the crowd drifted. All except Gwen, who stayed, pretending to eye a tin cigarette case emblazoned with a picture of the Moscow radio tower, while the man packed up his theater.

There were two things that interested her. One was the swift practiced economy with which he collapsed the sides of his house, folding it away like a road map. Such handiness, as usual, making her feel by comparison—self-pitying woman!—clumsy, wonkish. The other was his shoes, which were a pair of red Converse high-tops with a hole in one toe. She had seen these same shoes before, not two weeks ago, on a bench in Central Park. It wasn't possible, Dr. Watson, but there it was. Our man from Alice, resurrected into a trans-Siberian puppeteer with a grudge out for the IMF. He caught her watching him.

"Zdrastvuchiye," he said in his joke Russian, winking hello. *He* comically now evinced an interest in *her* shoes, which were green crocodile-skin brogues. (You dressed, working in the New Russia. Portable wealth was what they listened to.)

Gestured, indicating bedazzlement. *"Haroshi tufli. Ochen zilyoni."* Shoes nice. Very green. Signalled that he would like to steal them for his puppet show, make the twin crocodiles dance a sailor's hornpipe. Trust an American never to recognize a fellow American.

"Thanks," she replied, laying down the cigarette case. "You can't have them."

His eyes were chestnut, swirly as kaleidoscopes. Funny face, nut-brown, crow's-feet expressing now a doggy amusement. He was younger than she'd taken him to be in Central Park. Not old, just bald.

"Well, blow me. It's a homegirl," he said. "I should have guessed from your Oz shoes. Where're you from?"

"New York."

"New York, New York? You don't sound like a New Yorker, sister. You sound like a debutante who got on the wrong train. What happened, your folks send you to finishing school in the Gulag?" His own New Yorkese raspy, a salt-sticky breeze off Coney Island, bringing scents of cotton candy and knishes.

She shrugged. "There are a lot of New Yorks."

"I wouldn't mind living in *yours.*" He lifted his collapsed theater now, ungainly big. Hauled it over to a white van, against whose back side he rested it, while searching his pockets for the keys.

"So let me guess. You work for . . . the World Bank? AID?" He'd obviously been bumping into his share of bankers abroad, the nineties equivalent of backpackers.

"Close," she said. "I work for the Lavrinsky Institute."

"Ha. The enemy."

"Why? What have you got against Lavrinsky? We probably helped send you over here."

"I liked it better under Communism. Frankly, they were a little more openhanded."

"You're kidding. Openhanded with what? With the recording devices? The KGB agents on your tail?"

"They *liked* theater. In the old days, I'd bring twenty actors here, we'd do eight cities, plane tickets, hotels, vodka dinners for forty, everything paid for. Now my Russian buddies tell me"—he mimicked a Russian accent—" 'Please, buy airplane ticket and come see us, you can sleep on floor. With other theater people from former Soviet Union.' "

She opened her mouth to *decimate* him—this willfully blind ignoramus—and stopped.

Mid-speech, the puppeteer had reached up, rising to unhook the inner latch of the van's back door. And as he stretched, his T-shirt hiked up, too, baring a good six inches of flat brown stomach (traversed, dear God, by a narrow river of glistening black hairs). And Gwen found herself . . . staring. Helpless. Put her in mind of spying, one long-ago summer on Plum Island, as her Cousin Rich skinned amid the bulrushes from wet bathing suit back to jeans. Remembering how her guts *melted,* reduced to solemn jelly by this first glimpse of male perfection, embodied in a sunburnt fifteen-year-old.

Now through the interval between jeans and T-shirt—mere bravado, as if it weren't already thirty-eight degrees Siberian time—she could see the puppeteer's lean stomach, the flesh honeyed, lustrous. So nothing changed, after all. Here she was, two decades later, half jaundiced, half ignorant, half burnt, half raw, the corroded sunlight squinting down at her from an ugly Siberian sky, and this dumb Communist who'd turned up in two funny places ten days and ten thousand miles apart, *annihilating* her with a flash of olive-brown belly. Well, blow me, sister.

Then he fell back on the balls of his feet, and she started breathing again. Held open the van door while he eased the folded puppet theater between cardboard boxes.

"Thanks, ma'am. There's one more load." Amused, clearly, by treating this lady in the reptilian shoes as his trusty. There were two of them, usually, he explained, but today his partner had stayed behind at the Little Taiga, there having been a power cut to deal with.

"You mind watching the van? These Russians are raccoons—they'll steal your *garbage.*"

Gwen, uncharacteristically docile, waited, while High-tops brought back another armful of equipment. A young drunk—pickled skin, no front teeth—seized the opportunity to talk, trying to sell them a pack of lighters commemorating the now-abandoned Baikal-Amur railroad.

Wheedling veering into menace. Gwen bought a lighter and told him to get lost.

Her companion sighed. "Man, you sound like a local fishwife. You got a Russian mom or something?"

"No. I like the language, that's all. You know—some girls go horse-crazy. I was this teen weirdo who spent my summer vacation learning Russian."

The puppeteer confessed that he had never known any girls who liked horses, although he had once seen an Elizabeth Taylor movie about one. "What's your name?"

"Gwen."

"Is that short for Guinevere? I'm Lancelot."

She made a Come-off-it gesture.

"You're right. I'm Gideon."

In the back of the van was a cardboard box loaded with puppets. At the top, a marionette—a wolf with a papier-mâché face, sharply expressive.

Gwen reached out. "May I take a look?"

The man untangled the wires, handed her the clutch. "Try."

She hesitated.

"This is one of the first puppets I ever made. Versatile mother. He's gonna be a Chechen gangster tonight. Try it." Noiselessly he was behind her, hands guiding hers, showing her how to manipulate the complex of wires, to make the puppet bow and caper. His breath toasty on the back of her neck.

She was thinking that she was too old for the flush that was creeping down her front. Because his hands—no wedding ring, she noted, so who was the munchkin riding his Central Park crossbars?—were holding hers. Because she could feel his body behind hers.

She swung around, thrust the puppet back at him. "I hate puppets."

Trying to regain her balance, to fend off that disabling warmth. To breathe. That's what male beauty—no, not even beauty—male *maleness* did to you, it was that pathetic.

"That's all right," said Gideon, agreeably. "I specialize in converting puppet-haters." He, meanwhile, had folded the marionette back into its box, and closed the back hatch. "You should come see our show at the Taiga tonight; it'll change your mind about puppets. They're not dolls, they're . . . spirits. In the right hands. God speaking through man. Devils. Us."

"I can't; I'm leaving for Moscow this afternoon."

He stared, visibly disappointed. "Lucky girl. Our next gig is a twelve-hour bus ride *east*."

"Where?"

"Some little nowheresville of loggers who supposedly like theater. Go figure. Tell Lavrinsky I want plane tickets next time. You think Lavrinsky would give us a grant, or does he only fork out for ex-Communists?"

"Why? You mean because you're *still* a Communist, fifty million murders later . . . ?"

He reached back into the van and handed her a pamphlet.

"Hey, someone's gotta mind the store. Nah, I'm just a wet—I don't know . . . I got some ideas about how the world should work—you know, those sappy old chestnuts about brotherhood that even the Commies fucked up. I don't like *anybody*."

She stood there, reading his flyer. Slowly, translating from Russian back to English.

"Flaming trousers?"

"Pants on Fire."

"Oh . . ." and then she caught the English version. Pants on Fire Puppet Theater of the Lower East Side . . . Gideon Wolkowitz—that was him. She looked up, glanced at her watch. Held out her hand for a brisk goodbye.

"Stay," he said. Taking her hand and not letting go.

"I have a plane leaving at—"

"I heard you already, I just wasn't impressed. Dump the plane; planes have no feelings. Come to our show tonight, in your emerald Oz shoes. You'll bring some class. And then we can go to Tonka-town together—you, me, my partners. You can translate for us: that way we won't have to get so sloshed over dinners."

So this was his life—picking up strangers on the road, a ragbag of interchangeable instant friends. She took one more look at his flyer, then handed it back to him. Irritated, suddenly. What did she think she was playing at, getting talked out of planes by Baldy who slept on park benches? "Thanks, it's a delicious offer—but I've got to get back to Moscow."

"All right, all right," the puppeteer said, now climbing into the driver's seat and reaching over to open the passenger door for her. "At least let me give you a ride to the airport."

Gwen hesitated. Thinking . . . well, she still had to pick up her suit-case and pay the hotel bill. Thinking . . . that she liked him, oddly, and felt—what? That there were things—his political ignorance being one—that she wanted still to discuss. Besides, she had a secret weapon.

"I've seen you before," she said, climbing into the van. "In Central Park."

He looked blank. "Come again?"

"I saw you at Alice in Wonderland, a couple of weeks ago. You were with your son."

A flicker of unease, of sexual paranoia, was purely male. That he who thought he was the pursuer had himself been pursued, unawares. That the woman he was glad-eyeing might actually be a psycho. Their anony-mous, ends-of-the-earth camaraderie brought uncomfortably home.

"I remember the sneakers," she explained, by way of reassurance.

Gideon started the engine with an uncomfortable roar, and stalled. "Shit. That wasn't my son. I don't have a son," he said. "These are my sons and daughters," he said, jerking a head back at the puppets.

The relief—she believed him—started in her stomach and surged down to the knees.

4

THERE IS A SCIENCE to who moves out. A science of cruelty and power.

When Martin Lewis decided that his first marriage was over, it was Gwen's mother who left, with the children. "On account of our sins, we were exiled . . ." But maybe it didn't seem that way to Katrina; maybe being the one to leave felt a first reassertion of control, after a husband who had barely trusted her with house keys. Later she told her daughter she'd always hated their apartment, with its poky bedrooms facing the air shaft, which Martin had chosen for its Upper East Side address.

Their Babylon was a suite in the Belleclaire Hotel, five blocks from home. That way Gwen and Maddock could still walk to school, while their mother figured out what to do next. Routine, apparently, was im-portant for children. More important than daddies, whose chief func-tion, Gwen's daddy maintained, was to pay the bills.

In the afternoons, Gwen and Maddock hid in the Belleclaire bar, sneaking peanuts and goldfish, finishing grown-ups' leftover drinks. Tall pillars of ice-melt, spiked with pink or caramel bitterness. They played

Nerf ball in the hotel corridors; they raided the chambermaids' trolleys for shoe polish kits and shower caps. Explored the service quarters and tried to climb onto the roof. Dinner also was a lark: takeout soup and sandwiches from the Olympic Deli. They ate in their pajamas, watching TV. Gwen didn't remember much about their mother from those days, except how early—and abruptly—she fell asleep.

Their own sleeping arrangements were trickier. At home—in their old apartment on East Ninety-third—Gwen and Maddock had shared a room. A bunk bed, she on top, he below. Maddock was a bed wetter. When he awoke, crying, sodden, Gwen used to strip him and airlift him to her bunk. White sticky tadpole-body clinging to hers, goosebump arms tight around her neck. They would talk themselves to sleep, pretending they were stowaways on an ocean liner. When they grew up, they were going to get married—to each other—and run a circus, with bears riding unicycles. That was the plan.

At the Belleclaire, however, Maddock slept in the sitting room while Gwen shared the bedroom with her mother. Pajamaed Maddock exiled to a sofa bed, Gwen in the twin separated from Katrina's by a bedside table. Sitting bolt upright in bed, hugging her knees, too scared to sleep. Listening to her mother's breathing, convinced that Katrina might at any moment slip across the border, irretrievably. Too gnawing-anxious to go check on Maddock.

Today Gwen spent most of her working life in hotels, it seemed. Yet each time she walked into a hotel lobby, bar, or bedroom, some complex olfactory whammy struck her with an almost insufferable dread. Catapulted her back into that most desolate passage—in reality, no more than six weeks—in their joint childhood, into afternoons of filching peanuts and sampling leftover cocktails in the Belleclaire bar, into nights of not knowing whether Maddock, next door, was awake needing her.

Each time, she had to stifle the same lunatic impulse to ask someone—anyone—to come sleep with her. But women, even single women on business trips, are not well advised to ask strangers to share their beds, so Gwen had found other ways of making her night-solitude tolerable. Even of welcoming it.

She had become, proudly so, the most solitary person in the world. For that was what you did: what you most feared, you hugged tightest. Racing to embrace your doom.

5

THEY WERE DRIVING along Lomonosov Boulevard.

Novosibirsk in the autumnal dusk, soot-gray, unquiet. Homegoing office workers huddled by the bus stops, drunks huddled by the kiosks that sold kvass. The first hookers of the evening in their patchwork furs and platforms. And then, as they turned off onto the highway leading to the airport, raw apartment blocks, flimsier than Gideon's pasteboard theater, unfinished but already rotting. What can you do to me, I'm already in Siberia.

In a couple of hours, Gwen would be flying westward, looking down on the taiga's trickly deltas of lit settlement, its vaster waste, its disused camps. Taiga, taiga, burning bright. That thrill of dislocated alienness—a Nobody-knows-I-am-here, This-could-be-anywhere, that was as close as she came to relief. And the man at the wheel, she suspected, someone similarly attuned to motion, surprise, the lure of mutable destiny.

They were continuing their conversation from the hotel.

She was telling him how she'd first come to the old Soviet Union and why Communism's poison would last a hundred years, and it seemed to her that after talking to this man she would never be able to talk to anyone again because—despite his clowning, his political half-bakedness—the receptivity and understanding seemed to be something intravenous, as if he didn't just know who she was, but *was* her. Her ideal self.

When they reached the airport and pulled up at the ramp where passengers were unloaded, Gideon leaned toward her. Laid his head on her shoulder, with a sweet sigh.

And she—petrified—soaked in his smell just a moment (woodsmoke, sweat, and some horsey-doggy smell from his T-shirt) before stammering, doltishly presumptuous, her last warning, last defense. "I have . . . I'm with somebody."

The puppeteer looked around. "Get out of here. Where's he hiding?"

"I mean, I have a boyfriend."

"I never woulda guessed. What's he see in you?"

He got out of the van now, came round to the passenger side to help her out, unloaded her bag. "Seriously—you look like a woman who needs a lot of upkeep. Is he nice? Attentive?"

"Very. He's a banker," she added, not sorry to make him wince.

"I hope he's not investing in Siberia." He examined her suitcase, whose zipper, under pressure of too many clothes, had ripped loose from its seam. "He could buy you a less crappy bag."

Ducked back into the van, and reemerged with a spool of masking tape. When he'd finished binding tight the suitcase, he looked up at her. Eyes infinitely amused.

"Maybe I'll come with you."

"To Moscow?" she said, laughing.

"Sure. Wherever, we could have a ball."

And they hung there, in the concrete throng of quarrelling taxi drivers, traders hauling plaid plastic sacks. Two foreigners, not wanting to part.

He held out his hand, mock-formal.

And she wanted, even then, not to shake his hand but to slip the jeans off his high butt, to cradle his balls in her hand, to lead him into her for damned eternity. To hide in his beard like a bird nesting.

Why? Was it ever more than liking someone's crooked nose, his dancing eyes, ever more than a bolt of lightning in the gut from the warm rightness of a palm in yours? The satisfaction of seeing the open guts of your suitcase sutured tight in his brown plastic swaddling. We are animals, really—we feel the touch and we either flick it off or shiver with pleasure.

Chapter Three

I

THE UNEASE OF REENTRY. Homecoming, after a significant absence: half satisfaction, half dismay. Was *this* her life, so perfunctory, so chill?

Pleased to see Mirko the super, alarmed by the piles of mail. Unable to remember who her friends were, or why she lived in this unamiable city. The apartment looking huffy from neglect: a place neither loved nor lived-in. Note from Mimi, requesting Windex, Murphy Oil Soap,

Lemon Pledge. A curled sheaf of thermal-paper faxes. A ceiling-high shipyard of roses sent by Campbell to commemorate their third anniversary, with a card saying "See you Saturday." A threat from Time Warner to disconnect her cable service. A made bed, its sheets shroud-cold.

The next morning, Gwen went out in the blackness before dawn, when only garbage trucks were cruising. Stocked up on groceries at the corner Korean—*amazed*, after Russia, by the profusion, the ingenuity, the high-gloss opulence of the fruit juices, the toilet rolls, the shampoos.

Came home and climbed back into bed with three newspapers. Watched the pale blue day break, the rust-red mourning doves on her balcony, the Empire State Building pushing its silvery nose skyward. Listened to the start-up of morning traffic, and began to remember why she had chosen this life, why this was where, more or less, she belonged.

After the second load of laundry, the third cup of coffee, she felt prepared once again to confront living flesh and voices.

2

BY EIGHT, Gwen was in the office. A debriefing by Gerald and Kalman, a morning of phone calls, mail. Sitting at a spare desk with her laptop, converting her travel notes into a more formal presentation for tomorrow's directors' meeting, at which Lavrinsky would be present.

Lunch at the Three Guys coffee shop with an old buddy from the State Department who was in town for a seminar on NATO expansion. Asked her if she had any hot Russian investment tips. I don't know, she said, something makes me nervous about a country whose most powerful businessmen keep asking you whether they've got a better chance of immigrating to the U.S. or to Canada . . .

After work, she stopped by the gallery of Christopher d'Aurilhac—her best friend, along with Constance, since prep school. Declined (too jet-lagged) to go on to dinner with a Japanese photographer who took pictures of empty movie theaters.

When Gwen got home that night, she ate takeout sushi at the kitchen counter while trying to wade through a proposal for the privatization of Russia's social security system, which was facing bankruptcy thanks in part to a retirement age even lower than life expectancy.

Struggling to stay awake till ten.

Thinking—trying not to think—about Gideon W., who was now taking his puppets on a two-week tour of the old Soviet bloc. Wondering if she showed up—at the marionette theater in Tbilisi, say—would he be pleased. Would he say, Let's run away, let's be prisoners of the Caucasus together, let's get lost in the camouflage drab of the steppes.

She could wonder. She was good at wondering. Her whole job was wondering (what were your best odds, for instance, of making a normal country out of an ex-Communist-imperial war machine with scorched earth and a population possessed of rotten livers, sticky fingers, and a collective fatalism bordering on death wish). Or, better yet, she could forget. It seemed to her that in their bare afternoon together, she had told the puppeteer things she had scarcely formulated even in the privacy of her own brain. Some part of her—a garrulous little gingerbread woman—had got away, decamped with that uneducated bald leftist. This gingerbread golem of her forbidden memories was now dancing for audiences across the old Russian Empire, and she wanted it back.

3

IN THE MEANTIME, there was the boyfriend.

The intermittent, good-for-you boyfriend, whose now three-year presence in her life she couldn't justify with any carrying enthusiasm. Except for that. He was good for her. He took her skiing in Sun Valley; they ran around the reservoir in Central Park; it amused him to accompany her shopping at Prada or Robert Clergerie; he could talk to both her parents (his father was on the board of a foundation with Gwen's stepfather). It comforted her to hear his even breathing through the night as she tossed, paced, cursed, as her noonday demons morphed into homicidal supervixens devouring the innards, counselling despair.

And yet something prevented them from joining their fates unequivocally: Campbell kept his pied-à-terre on Sixty-third, which he shared with a fellow banker who spent most of the week in the Far East; they each dined with their separate friends; their talk of children trailed off inconsequentially, as Campbell (one of five) wanted many, but not now, and she wanted none, ever.

Once or twice, discouraged by their own tepidness, they had broken it off—Campbell had taken up again with a previous girlfriend;

Gwen went off with a South African defense analyst. But invariably they rejoined.

At times, Gwen knew with absolute certainty that they would end up man and wife, and that it would be a lucky thing because he loved her, was kind, hale, rich, responsible—everything self-interest demanded—and because he would always leave the untouchable recesses of her respectfully unexamined.

So why stall?

Besides feeling that although he might be good for her, she without a doubt could only weaken him. Which itself was just a sanctimonious excuse for her own cold feet.

4

Eleven-ten Saturday morning.

Key rustling in the lock. The skid-shuffle of bags sliding across oak veneer parquet.

"Darling?"

And there he was. Good God. So white.

She had not remembered his being quite so white. Curly hair and eyelashes a chlorinated blond, anemic hands with veins standing out blue. Albino, practically. And *clean*. Nails manicured, pressed handkerchief in his blazer pocket. An East Coast sahib, home from the hunt, right off the runway from executive class, smelling of luggage and aftershave.

"Hello, little mouse," he began, sweeping her into his arms, smiling tenderly.

But although she recognized that in saner moments she had found him elegant, manly, today she did not even want to kiss him. Did not want his bags—his T. Anthony suitcase, his clutch of duty free goods—in her front hall.

She told her first whopper. "Campbell, I'm on a long-distance call. Do you mind—"

"Come find me when you're done," he said, hanging up his trench coat in the closet, and the self-confidence implicit in his tact—he was accustomed to her grumpiness, he was humoring her—only made her feel the more murderous.

5

IT WAS HELL, for both of them.

All he wanted was to plunge her into bed—they both were tired, both had had hard travels—all she wanted was to be alone.

He circled her waist, slid her onto his knee. She kissed him on the forehead as an old bachelor might peck a godchild and jumped up for an intensive watering of the trees on the balcony.

Campbell rose, too, took off his jacket, removed keys, ticket stub, passport, credit cards from his trousers pocket. As if he were intending to lie down. He did—and held out his arms to her in a gesture part command, part entreaty.

If she weren't made of quartz and impacted dirt she would have melted.

She stuttered. "Campbell—would you—I'm afraid something's come up—I'm going to have to stop by the office. Would you like to have a sleep, and we can meet later?"

He, being a banker-saint, smiled indulgently, as if her rebuff were just one more adorable quirk—such as her snitching his razors—or a genuine, if ill-timed, symptom of that enthusiasm for work which he shared.

6

CAMPBELL—WHO KNEW HOW to get the best tables at the right places—had made a reservation for Sunday lunch at Calico, which had opened that very week down on Greenwich Street.

They sat, impaled by rays of late afternoon sun, sipping Sauternes and eating pumpkin risotto with foie gras, served in tiny jack-o-lanterns. As Gwen tried to explain herself. There, in the russet-stippled room, the pint-sized pumpkins recalling the godly bounty her ancestors had come to America to enjoy. Outside, the golden glaze of autumnal sun fell on a TriBeCa warehouse, and the kind man held her hand as she tried to hurt and expel him.

She thought, I'm going to hate good food for the rest of my life . . .

Campbell finally spoke. Pressing his fingers together, beseechingly.

"There's so much pain in the world. Don't you realize how wanton it is, little mouse, to try and destroy what we've found together? Two people who have the same values, who make each other laugh, who have wonderful sex . . . You're not making sense. You say you love me; I can feel you love me. Do you want us to get married? Is that it?"

Then he sighed and beckoned for the check. Gwen thinking, in an unpardonable underthought, No chocolate juniper torte? Because after all, she was very used to him.

That night she awoke to find Campbell weeping in subdued gasps. They lay side by side, silent in the not-quite-darkness. Finally he buried his wet face in her shoulder.

7

AND THEN, more insistently, Did something happen to you in Russia? I.e., Whom did you meet? (Was it a gold-toothed mafia king who wooed you with the glamour of his imminent death? A Mongol herdsman, a teenage chess prodigy?)

The poisoned king wanting to know, Who is my successor? The long-term strategist calculating, If she's leaving me for nothing, I can wait it out; if she's leaving me for someone, then I'm sunk.

But people never leave you for nobody.

And she, having nothing to say, said nothing.

Chapter Four

I

THAT FALL, Gwen was swamped in work. A new crisis had broken, this time in Belarus, where the president was threatening to close down their Minsk office on phony charges of currency violations.

Belarus (along with Ukraine and Moldova) was Tim Greenstock's problem: all the more so since it was Tim, to Gwen's mind, who had provoked their ouster by pushing Lavrinsky into way too overtly funding the opposition. (It being the institute's high-minded M.O. to back processes, not personalities . . .) But Tim, a bullish swaggerer given to dangerous exploits, was out sick with hepatitis. Which meant that his problems had become Gwen's.

Eighteen million dollars the institute had spent on Belarus, and now they were threatened with eviction.

One morning, Gerald wandered over to Gwen's desk and said, "Hey Gwen, guess what I'm giving you for Christmas?"

"What?"

"Minsk pie."

"Ha-ha. I think I'd rather have a lump of coal in my stocking."

"Sweetheart, you keep us in business in Belarus and I promise you something *really* nice in your stocking. Remember, Eddie comes from that piss-hole; he'd take it hard to get kicked out of there twice."

"I always thought he came from Kishinev."

"Yeah, dumbo, and Kishinev—"

"Is in Bessarabia, now present-day Moldova."

"Oh, you unbearable pedant," Gerald groaned, making as if to bare his big bottom in her face. "Why'd I ever get mixed up with a girl whose idea of a turn-on is the fucking atlas? You know what I'm giving you for Christmas, I'm giving you one of those Playboy Bunny calendars, with a centerfold of the Carpathian Mountains dressed up in a Santa Claus hat . . ."

Gwen had a soft spot for Gerald. She had left a much more entertaining job at Radio Liberty to go work for him in the gutless Bush administration; she had left Washington (gladly) to follow him to Lavrinsky. He was this tall clumsy sour-shy southerner who had disappointed his daddy by becoming intellectual, and even after working for him long enough to discover what a slob he was, she didn't mind him a bit.

Long days of diplomacy, press releases, threats; short nights of staring at the luminous alarm clock.

In stray moments—in the back of a taxi, or half hypnotized by the computer screen's electric blue—she caught herself peeking at the frayed scrap of Hotel Sibirsk notepaper that she kept in a hidden fold of her wallet. Fingering it like a steerage passenger who's got family in the New World. Flimsy, by way of a founding document, but compulsive as gravity. A six-letter name in bold blocks, a seven-letter number she already knew by heart, an address on a street tucked midway in the bulge of Lower Manhattan, East River side—a region she knew only, glimpsed from the FDR Drive, as a drab beige landmass of union-worker projects.

Dreaming of crinkly beard, red sneaks, brown stomach. Wondering if Attorney Street could in any way be construed as being on her way somewhere.

One morning, calculating Gideon had now been back several days, she dialled the crumpled number.

A snatch of zither music from *The Third Man,* and then a woman's recorded voice—bouncy, Pants on Fire Puppet Theater, announcing Gwen's electronic options, none of which appealed. She left a stilted message, wondering why High-tops had fobbed her off with a work number. Perhaps because he, like her, was inclined to make heartfelt connections abroad—the Romanian importer-exporter you got drunk with on the train to Bologna, Andrei the gym teacher from Stavropol, Gwendolen Lewis from the Lavrinsky Institute—whom he didn't necessarily wish to bring home.

A guess confirmed when he didn't call back. Not for one day, not for two, not for three days, not for four. Gee, he must have *hated* her. She had already gotten two e-mails from Ilya Rupnik at the Little Taiga, why couldn't his colleague be equally on the ball?

Remember you loathe puppets, she told herself. Ever since Gail Lefever's fourth-grade birthday party. Who could respect a grown person who chose to wiggle his thumbs and talk in a squawky voice for a living? This, apparently, was the fate of women who became too mannish: the bifurcation of desire and respect.

In the meantime, she saw Campbell again—once, twice. Like adults, dating. Fucking, but no longer spending the night: those new rules by which you mark a break, an interregnum. The way you keep hurting someone not from malice but from indecisiveness.

In the meantime, she went to Vilnius to confront the Belarussians at a meeting of former Soviet republics.

In the meantime, she resumed reading *Wilhelm Meister* (a book she'd abandoned midway the previous spring, but which provided, Gwen now realized, vivid testimony to the captious triviality of all theater people).

In the meantime, she sold some stocks to pay her estimated taxes, took her half sister to the ballet, made plans to spend Christmas in Istanbul with her friend Christopher. In the meantime, she shut down a little more.

2

SOMETIMES THE TELEPHONE wrenches you out of sleep at an inhuman hour. And there is always a potential victim, a chronic menace you are carrying in the back of your head, an instant's superstitious knowledge of what the ring might tell you.

For Gwen, it was her brother Maddock, years after he had grown safe. Phone rang, too early or too late, and she just knew it was some stranger calling to say, He's been hit by a car, he's in jail. Not because Maddock was still dangerous, but because that's what she was till the end of days: his watcher, his slipshod guardian.

The digital clock mouthed 12:47 a.m., and she had not just answered the phone in her sleep but found herself already in the middle of a conversation. Campbell a blanketed bump beside her.

A raspy voice on the other end of the telephone. She was telling the voice about Moscow, about what she'd been doing since . . . No, no, of course, she wasn't asleep, she was just . . . She was telling a lie in her sleep! (Why would it have been so awful to admit he'd woken her up, what else are most people doing at home at 1 a.m.?) His voice and her voice, conjoined in a breathless mumble, strung like a frayed rope across the gulf of nocturnal airspace. The telephone, normally so antiseptic, so diminishing, had never seemed so terrifyingly intimate a receptacle. (Later on, Gideon would call her up and ask her to touch herself, to feel her clitoris, to imagine him touching himself as they talked. And even this would not seem as arousing, as *crucifying* as his voice now.) Him. Gideon. The one she had given up on. The one she didn't like. Who didn't interest her one bit.

He had been upstate, he informed her. Running a workshop with the man who'd taught him his trade. Jerome Drexler. The founder of Infernal Combustion.

"Of what?"

"Infernal Combustion."

She was supposed to have heard of it. Puppetry apparently had a lineage, proliferating schools, opposing tendencies, breakaway sects. Just as if it were a real field, like psychoanalysis or Marxism. Who knew?

"Oh," said Gwen. "Was it fun?"

"Fun? He's a perfectionist. You ever met one of them? Not fun."

Silence, during which she half dozed off again.

"So did you read the S. An-Ski book?"

"The what?"

"The *Dybbuk* guy I told you about."

This is it: the foundations of love, how you build it stone by stone. You tell each other the books you like, the other goes and reads. "I saw the Pasolini movie . . ." "I read *The Princesse de Clèves*." "No" means you don't care. "No" means you're not looking for any merging of souls.

She admitted it. She had. She'd gone straight to the Society Library, down the street from her office, and taken out a faded 1940s translation of the play Gideon said he was putting on this fall, trying to ingest his taste, to see if it comported with hers, to learn who he was from what he liked.

"You want to come see it?" said the voice.

"See what?"

"*The Dybbuk*. We're opening tomorrow night. You got a pen? I'm gonna give you the address."

Then the voice was gone, and she was hollow with foreboding.

Campbell, by her side, reaching out a sleepy arm to ask, "Who was that?"

"A puppeteer I met, wanting me to come see his show."

"A puppet show?"

"Yeah."

"Are you going to go?"

"I guess."

"When is it?"

"Tomorrow night. I mean—tonight. Why—do you want to come?"

"To a puppet show? I have a dinner with some clients."

3

THE RED VELVET CURTAIN rises on a shabby prayer house.

The singsong drone of Hebrew prayers.

The synagogue gossips—represented by three large soupspoons—are atwitter because Poor Boy, the village genius, having memorized half the Talmud, has now ventured into Kabala. Having tasted the fruit of the Tree of Forbidden Knowledge, he is become an angel-headed hipster who no longer eats or sleeps, but spends his nights experimenting with the letters of God's Holy Name. All his numerological speculations, we are told, are intended as magic to baffle the local merchant's plans to find a rich husband for his only daughter Queenie.

When Poor Boy learns that Queenie has been betrothed to Little Million, he drops dead at the girl's feet, the unholy texts spraying from his hand like a junkie's needle.

Wedding day. A live klezmer band marches through the theater: sinister tweedly music from two fiddlers, an accordionist, and a damsel with a dulcimer. Queenie invites to her wedding the ghosts of lovers who have died young.

The bridegroom's party arrives. Presented with Little Million, Queenie shouts in a terrible raspy baritone: "Satan!" She has been possessed by the spirit of Poor Boy, who declares her his eternal bride.

In the court of the Miracler Rebbe, an exorcism. But the demon-lover refuses to be expelled from the maiden's body. Queenie is his, he growls, all the angelic and secular orders are ranged against him, heaven and earth his enemy: he has nowhere else to go.

The merchant declares the marriage will proceed.

In the finale, as you hear the music of Little Million's wedding party once again approaching, the souls of Queenie and Poor Boy meet in a Chinese shadow play.

"Come to me, my bridegroom, my husband," breathes shadow Queenie.

"I am coming, I am coming," answers Poor Boy. "I have left your body in order to enter your soul."

"Come to me, my bridegroom, my destined one!"

As the groom's wedding party enters, Queenie drops to the floor. The shadow lovers soar together to heaven, and the play finishes with two Torah scrolls, dancing wildly.

It's not a bad production. The puppeteers have managed to convey Eastern European Jewry's dualism: this somber pogrom-haunted people who are materially so famished and yet mentally so rarefied, who are caught like rats in a trap, with nowhere to go but *up*.

The heroine is a Victorian wax doll in a brown velvet dress.

Her father is a centaur.

Little Richie is a pencil, with jiggly lead pop eyes.

The hero Poor Boy is a spindly punk marionette with purple sidelocks, dressed in black vinyl: a ghetto dreamer who, barred the straight path, tries to Bonnie-and-Clyde his way to paradise.

4

FORGIVE GWEN'S LITERAL-MINDEDNESS.

Gwen was this bookish, word-bound person who rarely looked at paintings or listened to music or went to the theater. Consequently, she watched Pants on Fire's *Dybbuk* as an enactment of the text she'd read, with no eye for how the puppeteers had turned their jerky inanimate medium to advantage. Although she was therefore unequipped to appreciate the production's cunning, she was nonetheless moved by the story. So much so that when the curtain came down and the lights went on, she found herself still rapt, immobilized.

The three operators emerged from behind their box theater and bowed: Gideon; a girl with dirty-blond dreadlocks; a fat woman. The musicians bowed. The fat woman then made a little speech explaining the current status of the city's efforts to close down their theater and asking any audience members who were not already Friends of La Merced to sign a petition to the mayor. A few announcements about forthcoming shows, and the audience rose, fumbled for coats, began to pile into the narrow aisles.

Now was the time when theatergoers moved on to bars or clubs, went home to bed. The play was over.

But Gwen still hesitated. She stretched her legs, she packed her manuscript into her briefcase. She lingered. There was a crowd of people waiting to greet the performers. Should she stand in line to say hello to Gideon? But she hardly knew him. No, better to telephone tomorrow, consign her congratulations to the bouncy answering machine.

She headed toward the exit, then—still infected by the sweet melancholy of the play—changed her mind once again and doubled back to join the clump of waiting well-wishers. She could see Gideon off to one side, talking to an older man. A surge in the crowd as somebody pushed past with a table. As before an ambulance's siren, the traffic parted to make way, and thrust her forward.

"Hey there," said Gideon, reaching out and clasping her to him in a sideways hug. He was wearing the purple Grateful Dead shirt he'd been wearing in Novosibirsk.

Gideon's interlocutor, a short man with whiskers, continued to lecture Gideon in a snuffly singsong. Vitebsk . . . Kishinev . . . Belistok . . . Berdichev . . . The forests . . . The whiskered speaker would not release

Gideon, or include Gwen in his harangue. He was talking about Abba Kovner, he was talking about YIVO, he was doing research, apparently, going through archives of oral histories of Jewish partisans in Poland during the Second World War. He wanted Gideon, it seemed, to recognize that Eastern European Jews had not all trotted meekly to the slaughter, that there had been a sizable contingent who had fought in the forests, alongside Polish resistance fighters, whose role had never been adequately acknowledged, postwar, not by Poland because they were Jews, and not by America because they were Communists.

Gwen, similarly unacknowledged, felt no obligation to pretend to listen. She daydreamed. Then her daydreams took a louche turn, and— once again—she found herself flushing. For Gideon, who had kept his arm around her waist, was pressing her to him while continuing to nod too fast, "Hmmm . . . Hmmmm . . . Hmmmm . . . mmmm . . ." an inappropriate grin on his face. Invisibly, they were locked together. A superglue fit, snug as two spoons, but an electric stirring below. Lightning, flame. As if his soul were poised to enter her body. As if they were about to fly off together into the blue velvet ether, the klezmer sky.

Then the movement of audience through the doors shifted, subsided, leaving an air bubble of space, and she was let loose.

Now Gwen was in the cold night air, on a dingy street of auto repair shops, empty lots jungly with sumac. She couldn't remember having said goodbye—only that he'd asked her (gliding beneath the radar of the Abba Kovner man) if she could find her way back to the theater by daylight. Our workshop's on the third floor, come back tomorrow, I'll give you lunch, and she'd said she couldn't come tomorrow, Well, how about the day after, Sure, Thursday was fine.

There was a line from the play, spoken by the wonder-working rebbe, that reverberated in her head. "Everything in the world has a heart, and the world too has a great heart of its own." All night, Gwen felt the world's great heart beating, like a sonic boom but regular.

The next day, over a drink at the Polo Bar, she told Campbell she no longer loved him. And this time Campbell didn't call her "little mouse" or protest. She sensed he was even quite relieved to be definitively rid of this woman who had no idea what she wanted—a luxury which meant hell for those around her—and she hadn't the heart to tell him that in fact she did know exactly what she wanted, she had seen all ten fingers of it dancing last night in a painted sky . . .

Chapter Five

I

GIDEON W. lived in an apartment over a Spanish Pentecostalist storefront church which he shared with a colleague, Dina Gribetz-Pinto, and Dina's eleven-year-old son Ethan.

The apartment—a three-room walk-up that cost a rent-controlled $695 a month—was part of the fallout from Dina's marriage: her exhusband's name was still on the lease, and although what in early years had felt spacious—the eat-in kitchen had served as Pants on Fire's first theater—now seemed cramped, neither Gideon nor Dina could afford to move somewhere more hospitable.

Dina fretted, occasionally, about the insalubriousness of a boy's sharing a bedroom with his mother; Gideon chafed, occasionally, at keeping such close quarters with a woman and child who were not his by blood or marriage; yet these inner revolts were generally quelled by a larger shame at their own bourgeois finickiness, because this after all was how most people lived, so why should they live any better?

Gideon had first met Dina and her brother Dan when they were all three interns at the Infernal Combustion Puppet Cooperative up in Lubeck, New York. The theater, founded by a sixties dropout called Jerome Drexler, operated on communal ideals. Everybody shared the work—lighting, sets, puppet-making, sound, booking tours. They raised ducks and a goat, baked their own bread, and chopped wood for the stove that heated the barn where the disciples slept, in a hayloft above the performance space.

For several years, Gideon and the Gribetzes ran the company together. Then, in one of the periodic ruptures between Jerome and his acolytes, first Dina and then Dan had quit. Dina went on to graduate school in social work, married a fellow student, and emigrated to Israel; Dan moved to Boston, where he taught violin and played in a bluegrass band.

Only Gideon stayed on in Lubeck, taking the company on tour each fall. Until he too clashed with Jerome. Spent six months in Jerusalem, then a couple of years drifting from upstate to Amherst to Portland, Maine. Doing carpentry jobs, teaching workshops, running after-school theater programs for disturbed youths. Prime among them, himself.

In the late eighties, he had sounded out Dina and Dan, who by then were both living in Manhattan, the most expensive city in the world: Shall we start our own puppet theater?

Dan, similarly in search of some anchoring cause, had agreed; Dina, now a divorced mother, had a counselling job at Kings County but volunteered her weekends and evenings, her computer, her sewing machine. Her big heart. The answer was Pants on Fire, dirt-cheap, vaguely Jewish, run out of Dina's Rivington Street walk-up—Gideon, Dan, Dina, and Dan's girlfriend Andrea, along with a changing crew of interns and volunteers, and Dina's son Ethan as resident mascot, collective child.

The others had day jobs, too: Andrea worked for Legal Aid; Dan was a manager at Tower Records. Gideon, who did carpentry jobs when he had to, looked after Ethan while Dina was at work.

Since their late teens, off and on, they had all lived together, and there was a mixture of jolliness and frustration in the arrangement, by which everybody worked for a higher purpose without quite getting what he or she alone needed. And meanwhile, the company grew. They performed in bars, churches, and schools around the city. They toured cross-country and abroad, appearing at many of the venues Gideon had first visited with Infernal Combustion; they acquired nonprofit status and found sufficiently reliable sponsors for Gideon to begin paying himself a salary.

Three years ago, Pants on Fire had found space in an old parochial school, Nuestra Señora de la Merced, an abandoned city property which a Lower East Side activist named Sancho Vazquez was running as an artists' squat. One large room, combined office/workshop/rehearsal space; free rent, free theater, free electricity, in exchange for Gideon and Dan's carpentry work, and the perpetual threat of imminent eviction . . .

Thus the company grew, ached, floundered, stagnated, grew. To everyone's mingled pride, anxiety, and fatigue. Next spring it would be eight years since their first Passion play in Dina's kitchen. Eight years is a long time for people to live together without money, privacy, or acclaim. Without knowing it, they—and in particular, Gideon—were each getting primed for a change.

2

SHE IS THE MOST STRIKING WOMAN he has ever seen.

Tall, broad-shouldered as a drag queen. Big bumpy nose. (Broken?) Big rib cage, guarding, doubtless, a big heart. (Broken?) Which he imagines an angry purple bird battering against the mini-rib cage of his cupped hands.

Square cleft chin jutting forward as she'd held forth—oh, delicious pedagogy—on the wonders of free markets, the evils of socialism. As he'd sidled up to her and sighed, almost ready to forgive demon capitalism, since it had produced the fabulous surplus of her long legs and back, the quadrupal-ply thickness of her dark gold hair.

Rich girl, upper-class girl. Money is *this* heedless surplus (he thinks disloyally of Dina's sparse mousy frizz). This golden-brown hair, these gray-blue eyes, this skin all one tawny taffeta, one shot-through-with-green-gray-hazel.

And yet, Gideon, you had not wanted to hear from her. You had not intended to see her again. You knew already that women in tweed coats who talked horses and dated bankers were not your kind, that you, who could play Punch in twelve languages, would find yourself mortally tone-deaf to her mother tongue's ambiguities. You wanted to dream of her, intensely, and then to shove those thoughts deep down inside yourself.

3

WHEN HE HEARD her voice on the machine, he had walked around with it in his head for days, afraid. It was as if you knew, Gideon, everything that would follow. And recognized from her uptight message—Gwen Lewis from the Lavrinsky Institute with a quick question for Gideon Wolkowitz—that she too felt trapped and exposed by the enormity, the irreversibility of her move. Days, marvelling. Afraid. And then he had decided, I'll ask her to the play, and if she comes I'll ask her to lunch—a meal he couldn't remember having sat down for since he was a little kid at his grandma's, circa 1974. Just to make it as difficult for them as possible.

Even then, Gideon, you understood that no matter how you fended it off with tablecloths or waiters or broad daylight, somewhere between two and three, Miss Gwendolen Lewis would be yours. Her lady-like clothes strewn across the floor. Her scarlet lipstick smeared. Her handbag quite akimbo. Her cell phone switched OFF. Her afternoon's appointments—would she make any, or would she clear her day for you?—DISREGARDED. And that this was an outcome at once better avoided and inevitable.

Thursday morning. Here was how you anticipated such eventualities, in a shudder of blood, nerves, lower intestines; as you soaped yourself extra-assiduously with the remaining sliver of Irish Spring, rummaged through your rat's-twist of dirty laundry. Recognizing that today might be the day not to choose the nicotine-yellow unravelling jockey shorts you resorted to when all your less vintage undergarments were incontrovertibly beyond the pale. Ashamed of your own worrywart triviality which was reducing the generosity of this girl's reaching out to you to an Oh shit, I forgot to go to the Laundromat. And then the real problem was not the underwear, but could you be certain that the workshop was going to be empty that afternoon, because you sure couldn't bring her back to Rivington Street, and what to do about Ethan.

Dialling Andrea's voice mail. Andy, I screwed up, is there any way you could possibly take Ethan to his karate class this afternoon . . . The excitement close to dread.

4

HE HEARD HER coming up the three flights to their workshop.

Heard the quick determined clatter of ascending toes on worn linoleum, and there she was, oh God in heaven, poised in the doorway like a gigantic butterfly, an avenging angel, even taller than he'd remembered, and dressed like some lady classics professor from Bryn Mawr, so frumpy it came out the other side, in tweed skirt and a cardigan and woollen stockings, all in a gray-green that made her tawniness look sallow, the only touch of provocative glamour the pair of gray ankle boots with silver buckles, polished star-bright. Who polishes your booties, big girl?

5

GWENDOLEN LEWIS was sitting on the edge of a sawhorse in the workshop of Gideon's puppet company—*why* was it called Pants on Fire, she wanted to know, was it he who was the liar?—trying to avoid the dirty plates of spaghetti they'd both been too nervous to eat.

"Want some coffee?" A pot on the hob, sizzling.

It was a large, high-ceilinged room. Cathedral windows, taped in plastic sheeting to keep out the cold.

On the west wall, floor-to-ceiling grids and cubbyholes containing hammers, wire, pliers, tape, brushes, jars of paint and glue. Overhead, storage racks stuffed with cartons labelled "Purimspiel" or "Dogman." On the north wall, a planing table with a wood-metal-cutting band saw, a table saw, a circular saw. A bucket full of scrap metal. On a trestle table—behind the computer—a row of daintily modelled heads and hands. Rolls of thick velvet, white gauze. (This was what she did when she got nervous: she logged inventories in her head, as if God on Judgment Day was going to ask her, And how many jars of woodworking glue were there in Gideon Wolkowitz's theater workshop? As if noticing were a compulsive disorder. Clocking the little so you could blot out the big . . .)

And this man in overalls, much too close to her as usual. She had expected to be disappointed when she saw Gideon back on home ground. Wrong. He was just as goofy-disarming, as disruptively intimate as she'd remembered. As she'd first seen him, sleeping on a park bench, under the Sunday parents' censorious eyes. Some voice inside her, crying, Yes, he's the one. Him in the OshKosh B'Goshes.

"Are you cold?"

"No . . ."

"Are you sure? Just tell me and I'll—"

"I'm fine."

"I thought you were going to bring your boyfriend."

"Did you, really?" she asked, a little mocking. Annoyed by this game. "Actually, we've . . . uh . . . we've decided to split up." Hoping he didn't think it was because of him.

He poured the coffee—Turkish ink—into two yellow cups already stained in tree-trunk rings of sludge.

His eyebrows hummocked. Worried. Or disapproving. "You've dumped that nice guy? The big earner?"

"How do you know he didn't dump me? He was nice. He is nice."

"Don't underestimate nice. Nice gets you through a lot of tricky shit."

"I know. That's what Campbell said. Somewhat more elegantly."

Sentence trailing off because while they were talking, he had gently removed her coffee cup, hiked up her skirt, and pulled down her woollen tights to her ankles. Took her bare thighs in his hands, eyeing them greedily, and squeezed them so tight she cried out.

And now he had parted her lips and was fingering her. Exploring, speculatively; then sniffed his own smeared fingers in an eyes-narrowed, private raptness that doubtless recalled a thousand million earlier such explorations. Those fingers that had been in who knew how many pies.

You were a pussy-eater, Gideon, that's what you did.

Hooking index and thumb around her, playing cat's cradle with her womb, like a rite performed solely for his own delectation, so that all she was supposed to do was lean back and let him.

Don't bother me, his frown said, this is what I live for. What was his job but fancy finger-work—a twiddling of hand puppets' innards, a jiggling and coaxing of his marionettes' struts till they begged, Enough.

That acquired dexterity, that blind man's nimbleness, that TIMING—the knowing to lull down, to let her breathe just when the excitement threatened to become high-pitch unbearable—this was Gwen's reward for the man's semicreepy profession. But when she—sloppy, blind from pleasure—reached for his overalls, searching for the unaccustomed buttons, he batted her away.

"Hold your horses, girl, I'm not done yet."

Softly, exultantly announcing his plans, ticklish in her ear. "I'm going to suck your little trumpet of a clitoris, like a bee sipping nectar. Come out, little sweetie."

And now he was hunkered down on his long haunches, her legs wrapped around his shoulders. Lapping her up, sucking tight the juice.

Talking not to her but to her clit, "My chinkatoo, my pemaquid, my quahog." Sucking till her lower lips were swollen shut and ringing like boxed ears.

Till she could no longer stay afloat, but was hauled under the depths, and the floods compassed her about, all thy billows and thy waves passed over her, O Lord, and the weeds were wrapped around her head.

6

A POOR HISPANIC NEIGHBORHOOD, made shabbier by autumn rain.

To the east, tall projects bordering the FDR Drive.

To the south and west, blocks of four-, five-story projects in pink brick.

On Clinton Street, a block of party supply stores, their neon signs dancing blearily in the wet haze. There are Jewish remnants here and there: a Romanian synagogue, funerary-monument stores with Yiddish signs, but they are outnumbered by Baptist Tabernacle churches with neon crosses. Templo Adventista del Séptimo Día. Bodegas that sell plaster saints and voodoo oils. Dominican coffee shops, Chinese takeout.

Poor, poor. Community gardens. An empty lot turned basketball court. Another one, where hot dog vendors store their wagons.

West, in the splattering rain—just before you reach the formerly Jewish, now Hispanic wholesale garment district—you hit the newly chic strip of Ludlow Street, a place much favored by recent college graduates, children of the suburbs playing ragamuffin.

Ludlow Street is where you might have found Gwendolen Lewis and Gideon Wolkowitz late Thursday afternoon, sitting in a booth at the Red Hen—a retro-grunge health food luncheonette, kitted out in turquoise vinyl armchairs, formica tables, mismatched furniture from a yard sale.

A bulletin board on the wall: handwritten strips offering bass guitars, almost-new futons, apartments to share; flyers, including one for Pants on Fire's *Dybbuk,* running two weeks at La Merced.

"Rum and Coca-Cola" on the jukebox, but no hard liquor served: these kids drank malted milk. Two sound engineers from Arlene Grocery playing Scrabble in the corner, and Wendy casting a nosy glance at Gwen as she took their order.

Gideon was wishing, mildly, he hadn't brought Gwen here. Any moment Hector or Sally or another of their interns was going to walk in, and it wouldn't be a catastrophe, it would just be too soon: he didn't want to have to explain Gwen, Day One. (Who knew anyway would there be a Day Two? This girl obviously could walk.) His manic bubble had burst and he felt depressed, suddenly, by the uncleverness of this venture. Too old and brittle for the complicated high jinks of a cross-class romance.

Gwen, having demolished her banana smoothie, was now galloping through an avocado-bean-sprouts-and-melted-Swiss-on-whole-grain. Yiddisher mama in Gideon, thinking, You didn't like my spaghetti? Wondering where Miss String Bean packed away all those calories.

"I have to go to Minsk on Saturday," she announced. Stabbing at the fractured ice at the bottom of her glass.

"Minsk?" Gideon repeated.

After all, she'd only just come back from what his mother used to refer to, mocking the old folks, as the Other Side. Not that Minsk was such a glamorous destination. Most of his ancestors had worked their fat little fingers to the bone trying to get *out* of Minsk and its less elevated environs.

What's playing in Minsk, he wanted to know, and she told him, but he wasn't really listening.

He was thinking of the lush live spring of her inside walls, of how the dripping silk clutch purse of her vulva—Gideon's favorite word maybe in the English-Latin language—had gripped his finger tight.

Wondering if he took her back once more to La Merced, could he count on nobody's walking in on them for one good hour. Cursing the collectivist ethic that had barred him from putting a lock on the door. Trying to remember when he'd called their run-through for tonight's performance. Was it five-thirty, or six? And he still had to pick up lights from J&M . . .

"I think I've fallen in love with you," she said, eyes glued downward.

And to this momentous confession, he replied, "Shush." As if to a fretting baby. Shush. Not so fast.

7

THE BOY ON GIDEON'S CROSSBAR in Central Park was the son of his partner. (Gwen quickly tried to resurrect the female puppeteers—was it the dreadlock blonde, she wondered, or the fatso?)

They all three lived together, him and the boy and the boy's mother; they had lived together since Ethan was practically a baby. This is what Gwen learned when she and Gideon met for lunch the next day at the Three Guys.

Two women her age with strollers and too many shopping bags were already hovering over their booth with that New-New-York vulturishness—the reigning shortage-complex, as if nowadays you had to put out a contract on someone just to sit down. Had everything been so overcrowded, so cutthroat when she was a kid? Didn't she and Maddock and their mom used to be able to go to the Nectar or Stark's or the Soup Burg, order their grilled cheese sandwiches, their black-and-white milk shakes, and zone out, counting the number 4's chugging up Madison? Back when coffee shops weren't the same price as lunch at the Carlyle, just because they were on the same block.

So Gideon lived with somebody. This gave Gwen a wrench in the gut, for sure. Gideon noticed her long face. Not romantic, he clarified, not even *ex*-romantic. They were colleagues—colleagues and roommates, finding their makeshift solution to a real estate crunch, a shark rental market.

Gwen, who had lived alone since she was twenty, tried to imagine herself sharing an apartment with Gerald and Alice and their two sons, or her father and Jacey doubling up with the Goldfarbs, but it didn't add up. Maybe in Soviet Russia, but that's what you overthrew governments for.

"Theater's different," Gideon explained. "I mean, we spend twelve months a year in a cardboard *box* together. Sometimes we gotta all jam into some dragon costume and *dance*? Me, Dan, Andrea. Dina. Whoever else we've hypnotized to come work for nothing. If one of us had garlic for lunch or forgot to change his socks, well, it's up your nose. We've been living this way since we were teenagers, three, four Houdinis in the same locked trunk. Sexually, you just turn off. You gotta be either married to each other or neuter. Otherwise, the spaces are too tight, and someone's gonna blow."

But it still meant that Gideon felt weird about spending nights out, and besides, he had to take Ethan to school in the morning.

"And you—which are you?"

"Which am I which?"

"Are you married or are you neuter?"

"Which do I look?"

"I can't really tell."

"No? You can't? Why not?" He gazed at her. "Aren't you going to eat your coleslaw?" Oblivious to the hovering mothers, who were actively allowing their little girl to dig her ladybird umbrella into Gwen's foot.

"I want you inside me." Didn't care who heard it.

"What's the matter, you don't like coleslaw?"

"I said, I want you inside me."

"I heard you the first time. You mind if I eat your coleslaw? I hate people who leave shit on their plate. Besides," he said, reaching over and harpooning a hunk of coleslaw, "I'm an expensive date. I need someone who can keep me in cigarillos and duct tape. I don't know if anybody can stand me but my partners."

"I think I could," she said. Looking at her watch, looking at the check, fishing to see if she had the exact change. She was used to being the difficult one, the one who let boys know in advance, You don't want to go out with me, I'm trouble. (And when they protested that they liked trouble, they realized too late that they had signed away their rights to bail out, or even just complain.) So this was Sadie Hawkins Day, her chance to be the calm body, the steady Pursuer. Her chance to learn that Turnabout was Turn-on.

BOOK TWO

Chapter One

I

WHEN GIDEON AWOKE, it was dark and her flank was warm against him, and he sunk back to sleep. And when he awoke, it was warm and her flank was dark against him and he fell back to sleep. And when he awoke a third time, it was dark and she was gone. Gone! with a startle of abandonment.

Then he realized that the darkness was a trick conjured by heavy bedroom curtains of dark red paisley, and that outside it was pale noon, the traffic was singing its workaday song, and the schoolchildren from P.S. 83 were playing on their lunch break.

Just as if he and Gwen had never met, as if he'd never sailed into that luxury high-rise, never entered the bronze gates of postmodern Ilium's topless towers, never rode the mirrored elevator to this room-of-no-return.

Eleven fifty-seven, said the red eyes of her digital radio clock. A moment's panic, then, Remember? Ethan was away at Bear Mountain, on a school camping trip. *Relax.*

He climbed out of the Guinevere's king-size bed—knocking over a pile of plastic-bound typescripts in Cyrillic—and wrapped her dark red cashmere dressing gown around him—dark red everything in this womb-apartment, like a skinned hare, like a skinned Gwen, which made him think once again of slipping into her blood-warm innards, into the hot wet sleeve of her. I could live and die in this woman.

It had been some time since Gideon had awoken in a strange Manhattan apartment. And Gwen's apartment was . . . strange. He felt baffled, rebuffed by the anonymous-expensive banality of this executive suite that was her home.

Pissing, he noted the cheesy opulence of her spa-like bathroom—one of two full bathrooms for this single woman!—the polished marble expanses, the floor-to-ceiling mirrors, the lighted cabinets showcasing a pharmacy-load of eucalyptus bath oils; orange-blossom scrubs; jelly from unborn babies, mud from the Dead Sea. He opened a jar, dabbed his nose in gray-black slime—amused that this girl's sole contact with the religion of his (and possibly her) fathers was an expensive face cream.

Nosed, guiltily, through the top drawer of her dressing room bureau, feeling like an as-yet-unpunished meddler from myth, an Acteon, a Pandora. Half searching for some trace of his predecessor, a billet-doux from the Upper East Coast paragon he didn't quite believe she'd shelved. For measly him? What greeted him instead were cirrous pyramids of underpants, camisoles, teddies—garments as ritually complex as a high priest's kittel, a knight's armor. Beginning to get a sense that keeping this girl on her feet provided full employment to a military-industrial complex of corsetieres, dressmakers, druggists.

Later, he confessed that he had been through her things.

"I know."

He must have looked surprised.

"Well, I figured it was either you or a raccoon," she said, amused.

2

PROCEEDING TO THE KITCHEN—hungry, from thwarted horniness at all that untenanted underwear—Gideon found the Sub-Zero as empty as the medicine chest was full.

Bison-grass vodka and a quart of Ben & Jerry's Chunky Monkey in the freezer, and above, condiments: mustard, pickles. Things that kept. It was the refrigerator that gave Gideon his first humanizing insight into Miss Gwendolen Lewis. Realized that this well-placed, overeducated girl with the ferociously *organized* lingerie, whom he had known a bare three weeks (less, not counting her trip to Belarus), was just as lonely as he—that whereas his loneliness was merely personal, a kind of aggravated intermittent mopeyness, hers was scabrous, unspeakable, gone cosmic the

way a sore turns septic. Decided, insanely purposeful, as one is sometimes, first thing in the morning, on a hangover and little sleep: I can
make it up to her, can fill her and heal her. I alone. A secret vow she
wouldn't know about.

Overcome, suddenly, by guilt at Dina. Another lonely-heart. Dialled her at work, and was half relieved to get her voice mail. Dialled La
Merced. Got Hector. "Say, Flyboy, is Carlos around? We need to talk to
him about the boiler."

Wishing Gwen would come back. Wishing she hadn't left. Wondering if it was okay to call her at the office. Dreamed of lying in bed beside
Gwen—an elongated bump under the covers—for the next forty years,
watching her sleeping mouth pucker, her dark-gold eyelashes laid out
heavy on the blond counterpane of her cheek. Wishing that they be
buried under one stone—two names on one stone, her name, his name.
One bed, one stone.

In those early days, the hunger to cement their destinies, to make it
up to her for what he already *knew* had been her amoral, unloved childhood, was always interchanging with an antsiness to be gone, a mistrust
of their differences that had to do with money, with not knowing her
money's language and its ethics. A fear of getting smushed.

The next night, Gideon, teasing Gwen about the empty refrigerator,
pointed out that there was a D'Agostino two blocks away. Maybe they
could just cruise over there one day and buy some *food*, so they didn't
have to get tapeworms ordering in sushi every night. And she—regarding
this sally as an assertion of the primal male drive to domesticize—said,
coolly, "I usually eat out."

To Gideon, in whose own life "eating out" meant a tuna fish sandwich and a can of Coke on a park bench, these words seemed to say, I
have the money; I make the rules.

And she did not yet know him well enough to realize that the
love-shining sweetness of his answering smile expressed nothing but a
sneakily invincible will to change all that.

Chapter Two

I

THAT FALL, Pants on Fire was putting on a Thanksgiving pageant, entitled *Thanks/No Thanks,* with students from a Lower East Side alternative high school; they were doing a skit for their friend Fran Neuhaus's Last-Sunday-in-Every-Month puppet night at the Aktion Room; and a revival of *Underground Man,* with Infernal Combustion and an actress from the Czech Marionette Theater, to be performed at the Theater for the New City.

Gwen worked days; evenings, Gideon was either rehearsing or performing. Which meant that—like vampires—the lovers only met after midnight, thus preserving the wrenchingly intimate illicitness of their first encounters. Sometimes, if Gwen had been out to dinner with friends or colleagues, they might reconnoiter in one of those midtown hotel bars—the Rialto, the Bedford—that a mere ten years ago had been frequented only by travelling salesmen or frugal tour groups, but which were once again fashionable. Teak panelling; a pianist playing "Miss Otis Regrets"; cocktails and canapés being consumed by murderously ambitious twenty-six-year-olds.

And G&G in a corner, drinking and smooching. Sharing a cigarillo, which Gideon smoked only on those rare occasions when he was very *very* happy.

Most nights, after work, Gideon biked up to Gwen's apartment at the Vanderveer. Locked up his mount, just as the night-shift doormen were ticking over. Hey Tony, hey Vlada, how you doing? Rang her bell, round about midnight. Gwen still sitting at the computer screen, in white satin pajamas, floating in Slavic cyberspace. And then they stayed up—talking, loving. Talking. Till the rat-gray dawn dawned on Manhattan—later each morning, as you burrowed deeper into the runty, stunted heart of winter.

At 6:30 a.m., they took a shower, soaped each other's eager-sleepy bodies, dressed, bolted coffee, and rode down in the mirrored elevator, picking up at each floor Wall Street's freshest suitors. Briefcased clones, the bunch of them, except for Gideon, who—in his shiny-shabby Chesterfield and holey All Stars—was riding downtown not for an eighty-fourth-floor office at Morgan Stanley, but to lug Ethan all the way back up to the Upper West Side, where he attended a progressive Jewish school.

Both of them—Gideon and Gwen—the walking dead by day. Gwen breezy at work. Her friends, neglected, leaving serial messages. And Gideon still unwilling to explain his tomcat absences to Dina, who cracked jokes but didn't ask.

2

AND YOU, Gwen, you never knew such happiness was to be found.

Sunday afternoon in late October, darkness at five-thirty, a day already gone when you'd not been out of doors, barely out of bed, the neon on the Hitachi building saying twenty-nine degrees out, Big Walter Horton on college radio singing "Kansas City Women."

You and your beloved riding the salt-white sheets. Happiness: when the brain stopped gerbilling and the heart overflowed. When he, rosy-fingered he, rose once more gasping from the depths, his beard and beaky nose silvered with your goo. This, then, was happiness: awakening three, four hours later, your arm pins-and-needled under his head, ravenous suddenly. Too cold to get out of bed.

And Gideon, quilt wrapped around his shoulders like a dimity superhero, brought back from the kitchen a tippy skyscraper of last night's takeout from Shun Lee, sizzling from the microwave. Yum, you said. Snow peas in the sheets and the eggplant tasting just like you. Just like your ginger-scallion pussy, he said.

"I'm gonna eat you with chopsticks and hoisin sauce," said Gideon, and he tried to, you fighting him off, weak with laughter.

"Too much hair," he complained. "Fingers are better."

And you both had slept through too much of the day to sleep now, although it was past midnight, so you sat up and talked. Sat up, legs entwined. You told him and he told you. Told him the story of your life which was a life without Gideon and how all your life you'd been waiting for him.

3

"I GOT BY," Gideon said. "I was kinda hollow-chested scrawny—you shoulda seen me back then, I had an *Afro*—but older girls took pity on me. My first girlfriend was two grades ahead of me. Jenny Randazzo—a smart girl, independent-minded, we started when I was fourteen, she took a lotta ragging for it, too, and we lasted five years. A lifetime. Jenny Randazzo."

They were sitting up in bed. Five o'clock in the morning, early November. His turn to jabber, and hers to listen, till the convulsion of confession passed.

"Jenny taught me to read—before her, I was a TV hound. She got me into Marxist doo-da, theater as political protest, we were scarfing down Strindberg and Gramsci, and we did after-school drama. Which is one of the few places teenage girls and boys can be normal together, can work like partners.

"I was a ham, I realized you could do anything with people if you made 'em laugh. Or cry. I remember telling Jenny my mom had cancer, just to get her to put out for me—boy, did I feel cheesy afterwards, but I couldn't help it, I was a born showman. Showmen got no self-respect.

"Why puppets? They're little, they're easy to boss around. People feel sorry for 'em. It's like dogs. You ever seen a dog show? You forgive a lot of bad acting, it's just a dog.

"Jenny's mom taught theater at Rutgers. She was really into masks, puppets, in a . . . anthropological sense. She got us writing our own plays. We put on our first puppet show in the Paramus Mall. Security got us outta *there* before Punch even bopped Judy. Now you know why I don't like malls, why screaming Reds like me bitch about the demise of public space. Jenny's mom helped us get summer jobs at Infernal Combustion; I never looked back. I was taking twenty-five crew and a school bus down to Central America, touring six countries, visiting villages three days' walk from paved roads. In Guatemala, we did an *Antigone* at night, with torches, down by the river, in this village where the army had just come in and massacred all the men, dumped 'em in an unmarked grave. I mean, talk about Can-I-please-give-my-brother-a-decent-burial . . . My home life was, like, pretty much scorched earth, but when you're sixteen, having a girlfriend and a job—and a school bus—is a lot more crucial determinant in your conscious state of well-being."

"Why—what was happening at home?"

"My mom was dying. And my sister was basically nuts."

Five-twenty a.m., an hour she hadn't seen crack open Manhattan since prep school days. Gideon was propped up against a pillow, naked, his body lean as pulled taffy, rivered in long flat muscles that came from sawing wood and hauling scenery, not pumped up in a gym or bulked out on carbo-fluids. High-visibility ribs, curving round from chest to spine, elegant as herringbone. He'll have a potbelly when he's old, and it will look good on him, she was thinking, and she wanted to be there. And the cock, now resting on his thigh—she watched him pull on it, absently. As a kid, he told her, he and his best friend had cut holes in their trousers pockets so they could feel themselves at school, see if they could come in class without anybody noticing. Could they? Yes. It was public school, remember, nobody notices anything. Wasn't it kind of sticky afterwards? Come on. Adolescent boys? That age you are crusted in one perpetual coating of jizm, it's like some kind of thermal insulation that gets you through the winter.

"What was she dying of?"

"Ovarian cancer," he said, rising to get a bottle of spring water from the kitchen.

4

AWAKENING INTO an infantine condition of unalloyed need. A frantic mouth rooting for the love-teat. Day, night reversed, negated. Light into darkness, the outside invisible, the invisible made all. Now the cock was rearing toward you again—a russet-brown arrow, lavender-tipped, with the shimmery luster of an oil spill. You took it in your hand, its texture like some super-new, space-invented fabric that was tensile yet softer than unborn lamb. A heat-seeking missile, blind but high-precisioned, a warm fleshly comet rimming the roof of your world, saying, Honey, I'm home.

And when, much later, he slipped out of you—because you'd coughed, because he'd sneezed—a stab of abandonment, a moment's unassuageable grief. The limbs entwining tighter, legs pretzelling in compensation for his (involuntary) withdrawal.

You had forgotten what it was like, Gwen (never known), how the world could disappear—no Gazprom no interest rates no Microsoft no

Duma no dead presidents no family. Only yearning inwardness—the hungry mirror of eyes, the blinding shelter of arms, the suffocating gulf of love. The gallop in your brain of Gideon-gideon-gideon-gid. The compulsion to tell everything, to pour your insides into each other's and mush them together, to be shriven and forgiven, to merge into one Siamese Gwideon soup.

You met your neighbors in the elevator, you hung out with your colleagues after work, you had lunch with your ex-dissident friends in midtown coffee shops and East Village health food restaurants, you went to the opera with Christopher, you chatted with the hygienist in the dentist's office, with your accountant and your broker, and you thought, Do they know about this, too?

5

OF COURSE, the home life Gideon had escaped from had been even sadder than he wished his new girlfriend to understand.

You don't know people like this, Gwen, or so Gideon thinks: families who skid from crummy town to town, as jobs go bad, as rent comes due. As their old ways catch up with them.

He'd been born with a different name. "Wolkowitz" was his stepfather; "Gideon" he'd taken later, in honor of a maternal great-uncle from Berdichev who'd been killed by the retreating German army. He didn't know his real dad, they hadn't heard of him in decades.

When his parents met, his father was a home appliance salesman at Whelan's Wharf in Harmsboro. Leonard Brager. You know the type: the dwindling frizz of black hair, the suave patter, the bottomless male vanity. A good dancer. A propensity for smacking women.

They met in a bar, Paula was with her girlfriends, Lenny with his buddies from work. General banter, a few rounds. And then the pairing off. I'll take the skinny one, he'd said.

(He's tried to piece together his parents' life, before he came along and wrecked it. She loved to dance, she was a night bird, she and Lenny had married, Gideon surmised, on the strength of sexual attraction and a shared taste for illegal substances—whatever trash-coke or industrial heroin people found in shit towns in the sixties, whatever amphetamines or barbiturates you could bribe a quack doctor to write you scrips for.)

Young marrieds, they had flitted across New Jersey, Pennsylvania, Delaware, Virginia—Paula worked in a hospital cafeteria, a Howard Johnson's, an airport restaurant, an IHOP; Lenny worked or didn't work or talked about going into business. About investment opportunities. He disappeared frequently before walking out for good, leaving his family in a summer rental in Rehoboth, when Gideon—then Gary—was a toddler; his sister Sheryl three. Gary's conception—his mom had once let slip—having been the final straw.

Perpetually pissed-off, was how Gideon remembered his mother. Equal parts bone-tired and fuming. Who wouldn't fume—two small children, several months' back rent owed, the car she thought she'd paid for repossessed while the neighbors watched?

She toughed it out. Got off pills. Sent the kids to live with her mother and enrolled in community college, where she trained—seven hundred hours!—to get her license as a therapeutical masseuse.

By the time Gideon started second grade, they were living together again in their own apartment in Passaic, but still not having too good a time. He remembered creeping into the kitchen late at night—a little boy with scary dreams or needing to pee—and finding his mom, smoking a cigarette and looking . . . bitter. Watching TV as if it were her worst enemy. Flicking the ash into her Diet Pepsi can, and sometimes forgetting and drinking the Pepsi.

If anger kills you—that's what the cancer doctors say—she wasn't much going to mind a swift exit. And his sister no better.

Which left Gary, the baby, his mama's little cutup, condemned to clowning in one Sisyphean effort to lighten these two angry females' load. (Three-quarters of the art in the world has been produced by men who grew up trying to make their mothers laugh.)

6

Gwen was surprised by how Gideon's voice sunk to an awed tear-thick mutter when he talked about his stepfather. She'd heard old sports fans talk of Ted Williams or Joe DiMaggio, heroes who were wry, humble, inimitably graceful: gentlemen. That, apparently, was Sonny. Mr. Solomon Wolkowitz, semi-retired owner of a sporting goods store.

"How'd they meet?"

"Muscle spasms. His doctor sent him to her clinic to get unkinked.

He walked in—hobbled in. Slab of furry back laid out on the table like *meat*."

"Romantic."

"You're telling me. And this was not a guy who woulda felt comfortable lying down naked in front of a strange woman."

They talked about their families, Gideon supposed; Sonny, a widower, had two grown daughters, one in St. Paul, one in Phoenix; they discovered they were both Yankees fans; he told her he had season tickets.

After the third, fourth session, he asked her if she'd like to go to a game. That was their first date, Sonny, Paula—and Gary, sulking to beat the band.

"How come?"

"I don't remember. But, you know, most boys aren't real into their moms dating . . ." (Some Telemachus-instinct that any moment your real father might show up and slaughter the suitors.)

They courted, slowly, as was Sonny's style; each visit, he brought toys from the store: a yo-yo that glowed in the dark for Gary, a bongo board for Sheryl.

They married. In good time, he adopted Paula's children.

Thus came future puppet master's preliminary sloughing-off of the slave name: from Gary Brager to Gary Wolkowitz.

And Sonny—treasurer of his synagogue, community do-gooder, an Abraham of Teaneck—had airlifted his new family from their sour ailing urban life, over the river and through the trees, into a colonial brick house where he'd already installed a basketball hoop over the garage door. Put a beanbag sofa and a record player in the finished basement: a place the kids could entertain their friends.

Can you conceive of what that meant, Gwen, to a city-rat hobbled by his cage? Space, light, respect. (Who, before Sonny, had ever assumed that Gary might *have* a friend to bring home?) Teachers who could spell, freedom from fear. Lawns with flowering trees. After-school plays.

Seeing his mother, in her black mink coat, her Florida winter tan, her new marmalade-colored permanent wave, sink back into the leather passenger seat of the Lincoln Continental, like a cat in the sun. (Is that what made you hate capitalism, Gideon, seeing how money, to your mother, meant love?)

It meant, later on, sitting in Jenny Randazzo's sunlit kitchen, wolfing Pepperidge Farm cookies, drinking in *her* mother's amiable bullshit about myth and ritual. You'd have to be much less starved than Gary was to be snotty about the burbs.

And as for Paula—oh, she lived probably a few years longer and millennially happier than she would have without Sonny's tender nursing. (You should have seen how these two lit up and gladdened at the sight of each other: how, toward the end, Paula's morphine-deadened eyes would flick to gladness, her yellow tanned-hide of a carcass *relax* when it was Sonny by her bedside, his warm square hand reaching for hers. How she panicked if he left the room to take a piss.)

It was from Sonny that Gideon had learned how a man could be gentler than a woman. Gentle and patient enough to win over nutso Sheryl and bratty Gary, who wasn't used to being told to take out the garbage or do his homework by some hairy-eared male who wore galoshes. And intuitive enough—since he was too stately, too sore-backed, too *old* to get out with a baseball mitt or football—to conceive of Judaism as a hobby that he and his stepson could do together.

Gary was eleven when his mother met Sonny, and a hospital circumcision had been his first/last glimpse of Judaism. The following year, Sonny enrolled him in Hebrew school. Together, on weekends, they practiced his bar mitzvah portion, hammering home the salty words, the notched flickery-flame totemic letters, each with its own tune. It was that smart of Sonny, to give him his Jewishness and his manhood all in one.

And when Paula finally died, these two men sent up their mourners' prayers like smoke signals into the New Jersey sky. By then, Gideon was more interested in the god of totem poles and shamans than in Sinai's I-am-what-I-am: more interested in prayer as a stamping of naked gospel-feet in the patterned dust. He had already chosen his career, but hadn't yet been shown by Dina and Dan how Jews and stringed demiurges might be reconciled behind one velvet curtain.

It was only years later—after Sonny, too, had "passed on"—that Gideon came to size up the solid extent of the man's gift: how he had cast the cloak of his good name over two soiled embezzled children, and lent them his faith, which was a way of being a man in the world. Of squaring your accounts. And then felt—oh, immeasurably bereaved. Lost. At sea.

But these were facts he wasn't ready to divulge: the story of his two-part transmutation from Gary Brager into Gideon Wolkowitz, impresario. How he had shed frightened skins, year by year, to end up this: antic, impecunious, borrowed (part Jenny Randazzo, part Sonny), self-created. Not ready to tell Gwen now, not yet, probably never. Some stories are just the wrong kind of sad; they make the listener want to flee.

7

"COME INTO ME, sweetheart, come into me, my soul, my queen, my golden calf," Gideon was murmuring, his face on the pillow, laughing up at her—chestnut eyes alight with pride at her triumph, at her bucking the waves of him like a sea rider, her pearly chariot coursing the waves, buck, buck, shout, a hard slap of surfy spray, till she was utterly dissolved, till she sank and subsided onto him again. All melted and pounded into a stunning nothingness of stilled ecstasy, melting into the divine and universal nihility of . . . God-the-surf-rider borne by sea horses back to His unknowable realm, and her washed up on the shore of Gideon's breast, emptied and shuddering with spent joy.

8

SHE SAID, "I think I've been in love with you all my life."

"You took your time finding me."

"I was waiting for *you* to find *me*."

"Doesn't sound like it. Not my idea of waiting," he said, jealously. She (big mistake) having told him about his predecessors. "We could have saved a lot of time. Back when you were seven and I was eight. I bet you didn't even know what New Jersey was back then." He shifted.

"Don't move."

"I gotta piss."

"So do I. In fact, I think my bladder's about to burst."

He pinned her tight between his thighs. "Who's stopping you?"

"I don't want to leave you."

"Can you pee with me inside? You don't think so? Well, I'll come, too."

She sat on the pot, legs splayed, while Gideon, laughing, pissed between them. Then, restless, fiddled with the dimmer on the vanity lights haloing her mirrored medicine cabinet. Peeked once again at its expensive contents. "Man, you must be one ugly witch without all this goo."

Gwen, still sprawled on the pot, had gone slack-jawed, daydreaming. Dreaming of what? ("Even Siberian tigresses when they dream, dream sometimes of harmless pleasures . . .")

"I thought you needed to pee."

"I do."

The pressure evidently too pent-up to release. This was a girl with a bladder forged in Stalingrad. The first lesson, evidently, that you learned at WASPy New England prep schools: how to hold your water.

"I don't hear you." Now he was crouched on the floor, between her thighs. "Come on, little Suzie. Let me hear you. Let it fly."

The giggles bubbling out of her like a *baby* when you threw it in the air. A vision of her in the Novosibirsk market, tall and scowling, in her violet tweed coat and green crocodile shoes. Looking like . . . what? A lady Sherlock Holmes. Grouchy, imperious. And something in him, blood-used to grumpy women, had perked up, felt right at home. *Knew* that inside the tall grouch was a little girl giggling too hard to pee.

9

SHE LIKED TO WATCH HIM as he worked, singing improvised snatches of old folk songs as he chopped onions or fixed her showerhead, as if he were a Neapolitan laborer, a Carpathian shepherd, and not Mr. Teaneck jostling the Third Millennium of Your Lord. She liked, too, perversely, to watch that tidal energy ebb. How he could suddenly deflate, mid-sentence.

When he was tired, used-up—or irritated beyond endurance by her class arrogance, her right-wing politics, he sunk into himself, looking suddenly a hundred years old. Defeated. Exuding blackness. Implying silently it was all your fault, that he'd given his everything trying to make you halfway human and it was no go, and now he was going to die, just waiting for you to go away.

Chapter Three

I

Lavrinsky! The glad tidings come over the loudspeakers, the news is piped into the office Muzak: Lavrinsky, whose *real* office is downtown, who no longer comes around quite so often to visit his own personal State Department, who—it is rumored—has been flirting with other, chic-er causes, like the creation of a Third Party in American Politics for whom he and the three other richest men in America are reputedly drafting potential runners, Lavrinsky, who has recently been all over the papers for having flown three hundred of his best friends to the Caribbean to celebrate his wife's fiftieth birthday, is HERE.

In the office. HERE!

Visiting Gerald, chatting with Kalman, and now he comes shimmying over to Gwen's desk, just as she is seeing out Oleksa Kirilenko, a journalist from Kiev.

He is resplendent, really. He is a practiced flatterer (she has never seen the famous temper tantrums), he uses your name in every sentence, like someone appearing on a talk show, he tosses back his head when he laughs at your clumsy half-jokes.

Once—running in Central Park—Gwen unexpectedly happened upon the Pope in his bulletproof Popemobile, radiant as God in white soutane, white cap. Lavrinsky, too, exudes just such a sidereal shininess: his hair is an improbable spun-gold, as if concocted by a pastry chef, his sleek skin is buffed to an improbable pink, his teeth are whiter than acrylic. Apollo in blue pinstripe and an aftershave she recognizes as . . . Guerlain?

He knows Martin and Jacey, who are his neighbors in Connecticut, and every now and then Gwen will bump into him at a party given by his daughter, who is an old friend of Christopher's, or once having dinner with Campbell at Le Bernardin, when Lavrinsky insisted on their coming and sitting down for a drink with him and his wife (an ex-opera singer from ex-Leningrad)—and this gives Gwen an "in" with Lavrinsky that she finds embarrassing—slightly demeaning to her professional independence—but that makes certain of her colleagues sick with envy.

He sits his flat bottom on her desk, plays with a rubber band and gazes out the window as if it's a mirror. "Nice view, Miss Lewis."

It's fine—Fifth Avenue, Dog Hill, but it's the second floor, and you get bus exhaust in your face if you try to open the paint-stuck window.

"Want to swap?" She has been once to his downtown office from which you see the Statue of Liberty, New Jersey, Staten Island, spread out like a whore's pussy . . .

"Ha-ha. I saw your esteemed papa at the Adlers' the other night."

"He told me."

"He scolded me for letting you run off to all these barbaric countries." They both laugh. Ha-ha-ha. An insider laugh, since these countries which normal people regard as barbaric they love.

"So what's going on over there?" Over there is Russia and Co.

"I have no idea," she says. "I haven't been back for a month. We're getting kicked out of Belarus, that's for sure."

(And the damned U.S. government wasn't going to do a thing about it. That's what killed her—the smug insularity. Not just this Congress, three-quarters of whom didn't even own passports, but the State Department, which was blinkered by the arrogant cowardice of short-term careerists. How come every branch of government, post-Cold War, had been subsumed into the Commerce Department, every founding American ideal replaced by the new lie that the country should be run like a business? Except that in business, the stakes were seen as higher.)

"I had dinner with the Rostropoviches," Lavrinsky is telling her. "You know, Gala still has family in Russia. She says the health situation is unbelievable—worse, if anything. She took her mother, who has heart trouble, to the hospital: this is Moscow, this is Rostropovich's *mother-in-law*, they-could-not-get-her-an-EKG. I told her, Why didn't you tell me, we've just given half a million dollars to Meditsina. I got the chief cardiologist to call her mother the next day."

(Lavrinsky likes names; like Gwen's father, he finds them reassuring. His conversation typically involves Mother Teresa or the Dalai Lama remarking it looks like rain, whereupon Lavrinsky says, Let me have my chauffeur send you over my special rain-resistant umbrella . . .)

"Yeah, the demographics are abysmal," Gwen agrees. "The smartest guy I know on Russia has just published this study on the correlation of health and economic power. He says with this drastic a health crisis—the deterioration across *every* age group is . . . unprecedented in peacetime; it looks like fourteenth-century Europe after the plague—in twenty-five years, the country's going to be about as significant a world power as Peru."

"Peru with nukes," points out Lavrinsky, who was looking ominously bored while she rabbited on about . . . demographics, for Christ's sake.

"Peru with nukes," he repeats. "Ha-ha-ha!"

"Ha-ha-ha," parrots Gwen.

That's the current game: you compare Russia to the most piddling country you can think of, and then you add, "Burkina Faso with nukes," "Afghanistan with nukes." Ha-ha-ha. Gwen and Lavrinsky laugh because they are both worldly-wise, but in reality neither of them finds this prospect very amusing, Lavrinsky because he's invested billions in the health of the Russian economy and state, Gwen because she loves this fucked-up country.

"Peru with nukes," repeats Lavrinsky. "Ha-ha-ha. Well, good thing we're buying their nukes from them."

(Another program Lavrinsky was putting more money into than the U.S. government. Curious, that this vain fidgety egomaniac should be so forward-looking, so patriotic.)

Ha-ha-ha, says Gwen. And she thinks, Maybe I should quit this job and do something useful, such as study Persian. Then I wouldn't have to sit around sucking up to men with gold hair and dentures. In the meantime, she scribbles a memo in her notebook. Russian Health. Call Morris Demblitz. She's been meaning for some time to put together a more systematic campaign—a conference here in the U.S., a book, maybe—about the Russian health crisis . . .

2

THE SYNAGOGUE is neo-Moorish: twisting bulbous pillars, brass chandeliers, red carpeting. You could be anywhere from Milan to Cincinnati, but in fact it's the synagogue adjoining Ethan's school, where Gideon—standing in for Dina—has shown up for a Thanksgiving Shabbos.

Ethan's school drives Gideon round the bend with its moneyed liberal pieties. (For Gideon, truth to tell, prefers his rich people forthrightly murderous.) But in Ethan's Upper West Side Jewish day school, where the parents are either two-mommy families or Wall Street investors, American History fast-forwards from slave narratives to My Lai (why should being "liberal," he wonders, mean having to feel ashamed), and every Friday the students serve meals to the homeless in penance for their folks' being so crawling-rich. All except Ethan's. Even with Eeth on scholarship, Dina can't figure how she's going to get him through the year, since Michael once again is defaulting on child support.

Ethan points out to Gideon his scattered enemies: Aaron Kirschbaum, Damian Horowitz, Jay Shatner, who like to trap Ethan in unfrequented corners of the stairwell in order to practice their half-nelsons—these bogey-men of Amalekite, Shivvite, Hunamite stature materializing into wispy eleven-year-olds in cardigans and hair slicked back, under the yarmulkes. So this is why you sent your kid to Jewish school: the inverse proportion of bucks to brawn.

Him and Ethan nudging each other like horses in a stall. Ethan, surreptitiously munching the martian-green pistachios he's brought back from last weekend with his paternal grandparents in Bay Ridge: Dina had dropped off the boy with the Pintos as a guilt-offering, a sin-offering, isn't your oldest grandson a doll, but just look at how his ribs stick out, wouldn't you like to contribute a little to his upkeep. Instead, Nissim and Sylvie had sent him home with a sack of pistachios and a photograph of Michael with his new baby, whom Ethan has never met. (An omission which is just one of a hundred reasons Gideon would like to murder Michael Pinto.) They wanted to know, once again, why Dina didn't remarry. Asked Ethan was she seeing anybody special.

Ethan is a runt, still—an almond-eyed squirt, subcontinent-dark (people figure he's Pakistani). A fancier of slick clothes. Today he is wearing the Uzbek skullcap that Gideon bought him in a Moscow market, which, tie-dyed and tiger-striped, looks like the kind of headgear favored by African dictators.

Dina has this theory that nowadays only poor people dress expensive—so that whereas Ethan's best friend Noah Liebman, whose dad is Park Avenue's favorite cosmetic surgeon, wears Old Navy sweats, Ethan—like her delinquent teen clients from the Brooklyn projects—fancies five-hundred-dollar North Face parkas and Phat Farm baggies. Fortunately, he's also got a talent (that Pinto merchant's blood) for ratting out cheap Chinatown knockoffs.

That's what he and his friends do after school, with someone's parent or big brother in tow: they hop the subway to Canal Street and *shop*.

These boys who have duplexes on Central Park West and summer houses in the Hamptons think Ethan's way cool to be living on the Lower East Side: he can go to the army-navy stores whenever he likes!

Is Ethan underprivileged? He bears his underprivilege lightly. In the land of two-mommies, the child of divorce is king.

Ethan offers Gideon a saline palmful of pistachios. They both try to pry open the shells one-handed, while juggling their prayer books, to pop the new-green sweetmeats into their mouths, chewing silently. *Haleb,* which means Aleppo, is the Hebrew word for pistachio.

The Pintos are Sephardic. Nissim, Ethan's granddaddy, was born in Syria, came to Brooklyn via some crappy settlement town in the Negev, and Gideon pictures Ethan's forebears Ottoman merchants dealing in Aleppo pistachios, olives, figs. Carpets from the Caucasus, Circassian slave girls. Yum.

Now they've reached the portion of the service that introduces the Torah reading, and Gideon, rising, cranes to peer into the opened ark. (This is the peep-show, puppet-theater side of Judaism.) The ark looks like a miniature Victorian toy store: parchment scrolls dressed in red velvet gold-embroidered coats, and trinkets jingling from the Trees of Life.

Doreen and Michael Shulevitz—parents of the twins Judah and Sam—are helping hoist the overdressed scrolls onto the shawled shoulders of rabbi and cantor, and the scrolls are then borne along the aisle in a triumphal march, the congregation—women in yarmulkes, men in blazers—reaching out to kiss them.

And even Gideon, raising his own voice in *"Kumah Adonai v'yafoot-zoo oyvaycha . . ."* (the sweetness of the tune in delicious counterpoint to the childishly vindictive paranoia of the words: Rise up, God, and let your enemies be scattered, and everyone who hates you run away), experiences a deep-soul wriggle of satisfaction at finding himself once again tossed and tumbled by the salt-fizzy tidal wave of the liturgy. For this is the great thing about shul, he has learned: no matter how repellent your fellow congregants, they can't screw up the words . . .

To Gideon, Jewishness has never been anything but an undeserved goodness. More than once, even, it's bailed him out. First Sonny; then Dan and Dina, who fled an Orthodox home in Toronto to become theater hippies in rural upstate, finally arriving at their own fusion Judaism, half Mishnah, half granola. Shabbos blessings over the anadama bread, Dan with *tzitzis* flying from underneath his Yah Rasta T-shirt. The long and the short of it being that these two traditions—puppets and Jews—

have become subliminally linked in Gideon's mind, big things in which you could simultaneously shine and lose yourself, quit popping the zit of your own existence, and remember before whom you stood.

Without this family, without these rites, he would be who knows where? Some kind of a basket case. More of a basket case.

He wonders could he ever manage to convey to Gwen, so vanilla-upper-crust-denatured-Episcopalian, what Judaism means to him, how when he thinks of one day, God willing, having children himself, it's because his understanding that the earth is criminally overpopulated by idiots is nonetheless overruled by genetic compulsion, a blind drive to help boost his perversely long-lived race.

What can Jewishness mean to Gwen—three generations, two trust funds, and a Mayflower mother away from the ghetto and its pariah superiorities, its history-haunted doublenesses? But this, after all, is Love's thrill—your chance to explain everything anew, to exonerate, to incriminate, to funnel yourself into the other's bloodstream and memory bank.

On brisk days—when he's among his own—it appears to Gideon almost a civic duty to instruct Miss Lewis—this piece of superdeluxe Manhattan flotsam—in the overmortgaged griefs, shames, and recreational joys of an average ethnic-American suburban youth. But when it comes down to it, on precious stolen nights, on wintry Saturday afternoons, he generally finds he'd rather kiss her every toe than reminisce about Zionist Youth groups and his spring on Kfar Blum.

Chapter Four

GWEN WAS SITTING in the auditorium of the Rigoberta Menchú High School, watching a rehearsal of *Thanks/No Thanks,* which was opening tomorrow night. A low-key way to meet Gideon's partners, a sneak peek at the part of Gideon he was almost proud of.

Onstage, backstage, in the lobby, there were scattered Pants on Fire-ites, each directing a separate section of the pageant. You could spot the puppeteers by their Jesus and his hill-country-apostles look: bandannas, matted hair, and hand-stitched work boots rough as clogs. (Whereas the high schoolers appeared techno-sharp, in leopard-skin velour bell-bottoms and platform sneakers . . .) There was Andrea, who was directing the Aztec priest chorus, a gap-toothed, husky-voiced young woman, sweaty and golden, dreads flying, big ass hanging out of her ripped patchwork jeans, tits and hairy armpits busting out of her tank top. (These people *sweated*, it wasn't like an office.)

In the lobby, Andrea's boyfriend Dan, pale with a wispy black goatee and a turquoise-blue embroidered cap, was rehearsing the brass band, which sounded, in bursts, like a Louisiana funeral procession, a gypsy wedding.

At center stage, Sally—one of their interns—in dirty bare feet, was directing the section where Moctezuma in a litter, accompanied by his priests and warriors, came to meet Lenin and Zapata and the Virgin of Guadalupe. The Aztec mob were life-size cardboard figures, with movable heads, arms, and legs. Lenin and Zapata and Moctezuma and Mary were giant mask puppets, ten feet tall.

Dina, in the rear, majestically fat in a purple peasant dress, was running through the dance of Quetzalcoatl, composed of Hester and Julio in a serpent costume.

And Gideon?

Gideon was everywhere, prowling, adjusting. Directing traffic. Moving bodies that were too clumped up, hiking at a robe that didn't cover the performer's shoes. Feline, sinuous, he kept up a steady gab of encouragement, correction.

"That's your cue, jaguar, that's where *you* come on. After they sing *'Ayudame!'* On that note, come in."

"Don't pile up by the ladder, because Julio has about twenty seconds to get backstage and out of his jaguar costume and up that ladder."

"Mob, you gotta zap offstage quicker, because the gods are too tall for the overhead beam, remember: they have to bow down"—he illustrated—"and be fed through the passageway one by one. Natalie, you be there to feed." Natalie, a Haitian girl, hefty, semiretarded, beamed assent.

The actors climbed back into their costumes—ankle-length patchwork robes, each with a small square mesh at eye level. The masks, Gwen saw, were stapled to long poles—tree trunks, actually, which rested in a coffee can tied by a rag halter around each actor's waist.

Among students and puppeteers, an excitement mingling with exhaustion. This was backbreaking labor, hauling weights for hours in contortionist stretches, and everything the Pants were asking their players to do represented some fluctuating accommodation, some compromise between physical bearability and a brisk clip. That your knees ached from squatting and either you were blinded by stage lights or you were blinded by the eyehole's slipping down to your nose, that your partner kept losing you or else kept stomping on your feet, dwindled to nothing, compared to the magnitude of their common enterprise, which appeared to inspire a giggly good-fellowship, a solicitude, a spirit of self-sacrifice that was halfway between getting high together and founding a new country.

"I smell coffee," said Julio.

"I smell a nice soft bed," said Hester.

"I smell a massage."

"You got a *good* sense of smell."

They ran through, worrying away at the trouble spots. Then Dina announced a fifteen-minute break, and the students dispersed. Milled around the lobby, went to phone their girlfriend/boyfriends, or to smoke a cigarette in the street.

Gideon was standing center stage, surrounded by actors, smiling through his beard. He was munching on a hunk of bread (baked by Andrea), he had taken a knife from a loop of his painter's pants and was sawing off more hunks, which he smeared with taramasalata and handed out.

The kids were whooping it up over the taramasalata. A boy wearing a fist-sized gold medallion of Jesus professed amazement that fish had eggs, he thought they just had little fish. His girlfriend reassured him, "It don't taste like fish, it taste like, what do you call it, like Russian dressing . . ."

Gideon was grinning, so they knew he was pleased with them, pleased with the show, they could feel he was having fun. His smile exploded in sunbursts of crow's-feet, and when he wheeled around, hand shielding his eyes from the stage lights, and looked for you, Gwen, you felt willing to follow him anywhere, just to catch a whiff of his barely suppressed elation, his sly doggy joy.

"You hungry, Gwen?" he called.

At his beckoning, she clambered up onstage.

"This is my friend Gwen."

"Howdy," said Dina, knowing/not knowing that the woman in the shearling coat was going to ruin her life.

"Are you a volunteer?"

"Hi Gwen, qué pasa?"

"Gwyn?"

"Gwen."

"Is that a Welsh name?"

"Are you a volunteer?" repeated Julio.

"No, I'm just—"

"Whatsa matter, you don't want to carry a fifteen-pound tree all night?"

"Anybody want some ginger tea?" asked Dina. "I'm going to make some ginger tea. Janina? This is a knockout for colds."

Now Ethan arrived—Gwen could piece him together, just barely, from Alice in Wonderland—pale, tired, knapsack over his shoulder. Dina poured him a cup of orange juice from a gallon carton, and he settled down to his homework in the back row of the auditorium.

They did one more run-through, without interruption, and you, Gwen, were somehow immensely touched by the play. The costumes, the masks, the sets were painted with a rough-hewn freedom, and there was a wild folkish beauty in the music, the a cappella chorus exuding a spirit holy as midnight mass in some Tyrolean mountain chapel. For the first time, you could understand why Gideon lambasted television puppetry's million-dollar special effects, its corporate tie-ins manipulating children into wanting junk their parents couldn't afford.

It wasn't just you who was affected. These students, too, you could see, these callous untaught teenagers from the surrounding projects and tenements had been sweetened up, turned simultaneously more child-like and more responsible by the company's ethic of everybody pitching in. These kids whose idea of music was trip-hop, techno, salsa, who had originally derided the hokiness of a live band, were now revelling in Dan's archaic instruments homemade from drainpipe and horsehair.

Gideon was holding one girl's arm as he talked, several other students piled onto him like puppies, and you thought, They all want to touch him. It's Gideon who sets the sweet tone, who makes everybody all giggly and companionable and semi-in-love. It was Gideon, your lanky archangel, your night visitor, who turned round just once to wink at you. "You cold? Not turned to ice yet?"

"I'm fine," you said, and what you meant was, You're fine.

Chapter Five

GWEN WAS STARING out the glass doors at the mirrored skyscrapers of mid-Manhattan. At the more intimate, chipped, and weather-beaten West Side foreground of brownstone roof gardens, wooden water towers. Dark gray clouds overhead. God in His heaven, New Jersey across the river.

She was in the study talking on the telephone to Christopher while Gideon, at her feet, drew pictures in his scrapbook. Gideon's drawings were messy but convincing. Today he was sketching hunters from Gwen's catalogue of the Museum of Aboriginal Peoples in Novosibirsk. (An early present from Algis, with a rather stilted inscription.) Turn-of-the-century photographs of Siberian tribesmen dressed like bears, or wearing reindeer antlers.

Gideon kept a scrapbook, stuffed with photographs, drawings, ideas for future projects. He scoured museums, libraries: he was always tooling up to the Jewish Museum or to MoMA, checking out some exhibition of Malevich's designs for a Soviet space magazine, Kubrick's sets for *2001*, calling her up from the Met saying he'd just stopped by to take a look at the African masks for a play they were doing about police brutality, and did she want to meet him in the park. Basically, Gwen suspected, he got itchy sitting alone in his workshop.

Next Wednesday, Gwen was going up to her mother's in Newburyport. Sad, uneasy at the separation to come—five days apart. This was the blackmail of family holidays: she'd already cancelled that fall a conference in Berlin, her routine swing through Russia, but Thanksgiving was inviolable—all year she'd said she'd come. Besides, Maddock was bringing his new girlfriend.

She hung up from Christopher, who was trying to decide whether to give himself a birthday party in his gallery space or at Balthazar. Bent over to kiss Gideon upside down. Upside down, his eyebrows looked like furry black caterpillars.

"How's the Marquis?"

He and Christopher had not yet met. Gideon hadn't met any of her friends—any of her glamour friends, that is—the Russians he consented to meet. When she suggested bringing him along to dinners with Christopher or cocktail parties at Gerald and Alice's, Gideon balked. He spent his whole day with people, he didn't need to meet more people. After work, he just wanted to hang with her, at home. This was his line, which she, for the time being, let pass. Happy still just to tell him about her friends, who were few but choice.

"I don't want to go to Newburyport."

"Isn't that where the flavor is?"

"What?"

"Come to Newburyport where the flavor is . . ."

"That's Newport." Fear of leaving Gideon transmuting, strangely, into fear of his leaving her. "I'm scared you're going to disappear. Couldn't I keep a guarantee?" Hand between his legs. "You don't need this, do you?"

"Me? I'm your ball and chain." (Your manacles, your burden and your curse.) "You wait and see; I'm not so easy to get rid of."

She moved over to the window seat. "It feels too good to be true. Did you know this existed?"

"I read about it. But I wasn't exactly expecting it, firsthand," said Gideon. (Liar. You'd dreamed of nothing else but blinding love, the merging into oneness, since you were old enough to look out a window and pray to the cold stars.) "You see couples who get along, who are, like, partners, but this? This is even better'n me and Dan. Almost as good as me 'n' Dina." (He liked to tease her about Dina, Gwen being so fish-in-a-barrel easy to get jealous.)

"Do you promise you're not going to disappear?" she persisted.

"Where would I disappear to? You're the one who's always hopping helicopters to the Arctic." Gideon seized her arm, twisted her watch face toward him. "Shit . . ."

"What's the matter?"

"I was supposed to call this lawyer friend of Andrea's. Looks like the mayor's getting serious about closing down La Merced."

"Can he do that?"

"It's city property. We annoy him enough." He flipped through his wallet. "Anyways, we need a new lawyer; the guy we've got isn't enough of a terrorist." He found the scrap of paper he was looking for, picked up the phone and dialled. "Shit—it's his voice mail." Dialled again, rolling his eyes at Gwen. Then, "Hey, Deen, I couldn't get through to Moskowitz, but I'll try him first thing in the morning. I'm uptown, I probably won't be back till late. See you in the a.m., sweetheart. Bye."

He plumped back down on the floor, but he was gloomy now, the thundercloud sitting cartoonish over his head.

Gwen, on her way to run a bath before dinner, paused. "What's wrong?"

"They're mad at me."

"Who?"

"My colleagues. They are hating me right now."

"Why? Do they know something I don't?"

"Plenty. Like what a smarmy fake I am."

"That's not true," she said. "I *do* know what a smarmy fake you are."

But Gideon was brooding, still. It was true. His colleagues—Dina, Dan, Andrea, even Sally and Hector—were acting funny with him, and who could blame them? He was absenting himself without explanation, and when he was there, he was not there. Underslept, screwing up because underslept. All of a sudden, nobody knew who to look to for the decisions that were Gideon's by custom. All of a sudden, he couldn't get it together to phone Moskowitz, who Andrea had carefully explained to him was leaving town for two weeks, but was expecting his call. Instead, he'd been sprawled on the floor, drawing pictures of bears, while his girlfriend prattled about birthday parties . . .

Feeling a moment's ungracious resentment of Gwen for making him a delinquent stranger to his own life.

Sunday morning (this was almost too painful to think about) Ethan had asked him for help with his Spanish homework, and Gideon, realizing he had an hour and a half in which to get uptown and squeeze Gwen before she headed out to brunch with the *Financial Times'* Moscow correspondent, had begged off. Asked him whether he couldn't run downstairs and ask Manny. To which Ethan, teasing-tentative smile behind the glittering orthodontistry his grandparents had finally forked out for, replied, "That's okay; I already knew you didn't like me anymore."

And Gideon had wanted to get down on the floor and kiss Ethan's smelly-stockinged feet, beg his forgiveness. But instead—on his way out the door—he'd cracked one of those fake-jocular deflecting jokes that make women and children hate the male race.

He'd sworn to himself that once Gwen left for her mom's, he'd make it up to Eeth. They would have one of their old weekends: dim sum at the Silver Phoenix, an afternoon movie. Maybe he'd even come up with the scratch to buy him a new pair of in-line skates.

So this was what love was like. There was a finite amount in the world, like gas or coal; your happiness subtracted from someone else's. Loving Gwen had meant less love for Ethan.

Chapter Six

I

THE DAY BEFORE THANKSGIVING, Gwen drove a rented car up to her mother's house. Maddock was bringing his new girlfriend; Gwen—just to rile her stepfather's stinginess, his class resentments—brought half a case of Châteauneuf du Pape.

Mind uncoiling as she left behind the frigid, miniature-glass cityscapes of Stamford, Bridgeport, Hartford, and crossed the Massachusetts border into forested hills that looked less populated than they would have been three hundred years ago, when her first New World forebears were shooting rabbits and hanging Quakers. (In Concord stood the Maddock House, now a home for assisted living: a white clapboard palace, filigreed as intricately as if pine were ivory, its gleaming girth attesting to the family's long cooniness at shuffling merchants and divines.)

Gideon, who chose to detect in Gwen some ongoing Manichean struggle between hedonist and prude, liked to tease her about her Puritan ancestry, but in reality this was only *one* portion of her bloodline, Gwen was quick to insist; the rest being Scotch-Irish strivers, illiterate Danes, and Russian Jews so bent on self-effacement she didn't even know from what unyieldy shnozz her surname had been bobbed. The Puritans just made a bigger noise, that's all: America's first pathological self-publicists.

You know, he had said, that just proves my point: self-punishing, hypocritical fire-and-brimstone repressives, the bunch of 'em. What you're missing is a little southern indolence, some Neapolitan sensualists. Gwen wondered haughtily was he missing Jenny Randazzo . . .

Stopped outside of Lowell for a cup of coffee, and tried Gideon on her cell phone. No answer; just the damned machine with damned Dina's damned voice sounding bossy and superior. Left no message. The missing-Gideon like a bad chemical reaction, a mosquito whine of grief. Driving *away* from him nonsensical, a rending of the flesh.

By nightfall, she had reached Newburyport. Sailed through the silent town, and past the airfield toward the Parker River Refuge. Looking out at Plum Island—a thin starry strip in the big night—she caught the first smell of the sea. Turned into her mother's driveway just before supper. Scarfing up the familiar scents of not-quite-home.

Katrina, a Bostonian herself, had moved up to Newburyport after the split. Why Newburyport? Because her sister-in-law had told her to. Not even her brother Richard, who would have considered Katrina an embarrassing liability, a failure who should be *punished* (now you're talking Puritan), but Richard's wife, square snaggletoothed homey Aunt Sue, a real estate agent who lived in a colonial farmhouse with dogs, husband, two horses, and one lean remote son. Katrina was lost, and Sue had said, I've got the perfect house for you; we'll have a blast. Had taken one look at Gwen (pudgy, bookish) and said, She needs to go to boarding school. Called up the admissions director at Milton where Uncle Richard was an alumnus and Cousin Rich (Gwen's first love) a senior. That was the seventies, where you could just call up in September and explain your niece needed to go to school, you didn't have to sleep with a trustee or pledge a new squash court.

Katrina, installed with Maddock in the house on Addison Road, had then cracked up in the most festive sort of way. (It having turned out, not unreasonably, that all she had been looking for, after Martin, was somewhere quiet to go nuts.) Burned holes in saucepans. Crashed the Oldsmobile. Swam naked in the churny October broth of the Atlantic. Learned, cockeyed, how to live without a man. What to do (after conquering the initial impulse to call Sue) when the lights blew, or the plumbing backed up, or Maddock got caught stealing an ax from the hardware store, because he said he needed to go ice fishing. Aunt Sue suggested Katrina get a dog to keep them company. Being Aunt Sue, she already had the pup lined up. (She was friends with its mother.) Thus, Snark.

For some time after the bust-up, Katrina had been unbearable. (Remember Uncle Richard's face the dinner she announced that she'd found real love with her yoga teacher, two-thirds her age and gay?) Then Martin had remarried—not to the former Miss Costa Rica who'd broken up their marriage, not to Jacey, but to the one in between, like one of those wives of Henry VIII or that Sixth Deadly Sin whose name slips through the memory hole—and that had settled her. No more just-like-old-times holiday reunions, no more Martin calling up to remind Katrina to file her tax returns. Over was over.

Gwen, newly teenage, newly released into the herd-freedom of a New England prep school, by then couldn't stand the sight of either parent. Let the messages to call home—both homes—pile up. Started getting good grades, a knack (a capitulation, really) she wasn't cynical enough to confuse with brains. Visited Addison Road—this house she'd never lived in—in the spirit of a caseworker, itching to get back to her real life, her books. Picking blond animal hairs off her dress. "Next time, Mom, couldn't you get a navy blue dog?"

One Christmas midnight, she had watched her kid brother, tanked up on Percodan and Southern Comfort, nearly sever his right index finger playing solo hockey on the pond below their house. Sitting in the emergency ward with the other drunks' waiting families, Gwen decided next vacation she wasn't coming back. Figured she'd rather stay at school, where they were urging her to apply to college a year early, or else with Constance, whose diplomat father said he could get her an internship at the UN. By then, too, Gwen had found Russian—a language almost as hard as calculus and boys, but maltier.

2

THANKSGIVING MORNING.

Waking in the cold bedroom Katrina had never wholeheartedly assigned to Gwen, although it did have certain items of furniture transported from her old room on Ninety-third Street.

Seven a.m. Her inner sleepometer rigged to workaday time, no use even trying to roll over and reinsert herself into that last dream about sneaking into Rivington Street to spy on Gideon with Dina and Ethan, realizing that they were actually his lawfully wedded wife and son. Pathetic, Miss Lewis. Don't you have enough guilts of your own that your sleeping mind must leech on to other people's?

Nineteen degrees, according to the thermometer outside the bathroom window. The window a thick sheet of snowflake-crystalled ice; Gwen's ass—wet from the lukewarm shower—practically freezing to the toilet seat. (Get Hal to crank up the *heat*.) The eastern sky gas-flame blue, with a low smudge of pink.

Downstairs, Maddock and his girlfriend were still asleep, and Hal was already holed up in his "office." Only her mother, padding about barefoot, watched Gwen rummage through the kitchen cabinets.

"Oh dear, I forgot you drank coffee."

"That's okay; I'll go buy some."

"Shall I come with you?" A chance . . . not to talk, but to be together, to rub shoulders. (Her mom was too fey, too frightened for intimacies: were you ever so cruel as to try to tell her something, she'd interrupt to wonder where she'd put the hedge-clippers, or start cooing baby talk to Snark.)

After picking up a cup of Green Mountain and some doughnuts from the gas station, they drove out to Plum Island so Gwen could see the ocean. The familiar rattle of wheels over the barrel bridge. Eerie, the early winter beauty: the shingle houses, the dimpled dunes, the rushes white-blond. They parked at a dead end and wandered down to the beach. The first view of the ocean, as always, got you by the gullet, electrifying.

On this calm morning, the Atlantic was churned silver, a continuous reel of metallurgical ripples. You could see the Isles of Shoals just barely, and the long thin line of Cape Ann lapping close around. Gwen and Katrina walked along the beach, slowly, Snark circling them. Ruinous cold, the sand frozen to a choppy porridge. Gwen admiring, as Katrina bent to find a stick for Snark, her mother's high round bottom, her long slim legs. A figure so luscious that at—what? not quite sixty—she looked like someone's kid sister in sneakers, an old army jacket of Hal's.

Curious how ripe for the picking she appeared, and yet each time you reached to kiss her, she somehow shrank or froze or swerved, decided at just that moment to make a brusque movement, so that your would-be embraces devolved into fumbled embarrassment, failure.

Now she was doubled over, examining odd wreckage: a tin colander, a pipe bowl fossilized from salt—the regurgitated bits from which she made her sculptures and collages. The sand a steel-blue-and-gold mosaic of baby mussel shells, shattered mother-of-pearl, razor clams, indigo-and-orange crab legs. Bleached driftwood branches like antlers.

Gwen, thwarted, threw a stick into the water and watched Snark plunge—powerful, stumpy body—into the winter ocean after it. Back on land, the dog shook herself.

"Oh honey, not on *us*."

Gwen had been a senior at Milton when Hal showed up. A bachelor, pin-neat as a Dutch housewife. Who bought powdered milk by the tub, because it was cheaper than fresh. Who baked his own bread, aggressively whole grain. Who dressed like a janitor, his work pants' cuffs several inches above the anklebone of his already short legs. (Funny, her mama's lech for men—bossy little terriers—who reached her armpit.) Who spent his vacations in a shack on Plum Island with no electricity or running water, but a very large picture window. Which was how he had spotted Gwen's mother, carousing through the autumnal undertow with her Lab. And thought, Here's a gal who doesn't need heating.

He was a neurobiologist who years before had done important work on eye-brain coordination. By the time he and Katrina met, he was head of a department at a research institute outside Boston. Gwen and Maddock united in their instant dislike of this nonmammalian control freak.

He, in turn (refusing to be drawn into quasi-parental discussions of What to do about Maddock), treated them to whimsical lectures on compost and septic tanks. When Gwen thought of Hal, this is what she pictured: his Plum Island cottage's gimcrack toilet opening into a bottomless pit of ordure. A man who'd started out thinking about the brain and ended up thinking about shit.

3

"WHY ARE THESE WETLANDS, these marshes so beautiful? Is it just because it's ours that we love it?"

"I don't know," said her mother. "I've never been anywhere else, I'm the least well-travelled person in the world."

"Where'd you go on your honeymoon with Pop?"

Only recent that you could mention Martin to her. (He, by contrast, never shut *up* about her—still bitching with proprietary fondness, as if she were an impossible great-aunt.)

"Paradise Island. Martin . . . Your daddy loved to gamble. I don't think I laid eyes on him midnight till breakfast."

(Not complaining: this is what men were like. Difficult. Your job was adapting. Katrina's father, a geologist married to a Danish woman, a different kind of difficult—harsh, distant, authoritarian. Martin, cuddly at first sight, must have looked a cinch.)

"But, well . . . the Caribbean. It just didn't thrill me. *Too* green. Too warm. Bathwater. Not like here." Her mother's staunchness, half Puritan, half painterly, that gray in fact was the loveliest color because it brought out other colors. "Remember how much sea glass there used to be on this beach? Blue, green. Brown was common as . . . Beer bottles. Now it's like striking gold. Everything's plastic."

"So Bonanno's closed." An inedible clam stand they used to frequent, in the years Katrina had refused to cook.

"Isn't that a shame? After Clay died, Dorothy just couldn't keep it going by herself. Then they had a fire . . . She's moved to Florida. Everybody has, except Hal and me."

Her mother stooped to pick up a mussel shell. Its mother-of-pearl insides soft as shale, dissolving between the fingers.

"How's Sue?"

"She's . . . coping. But it's taken a beating out of her."

Uncle Richard had died the year before, quickly, five, six months after a pain in his side was diagnosed as liver cancer.

"I told you she's down at Rich's for Thanksgiving this year."

"Yeah, is Rich there?"

"Is Rich where?"

Rich the teen beauty was now a laconic geologist like his granddad, prematurely gray, working for an oil company, with a chatterbox wife (efficient as Sue) and three sons. Geology, Gwen suspected, being just an excuse for Rich to slope off to Azerbaijan or Oman for several months at a stretch, leaving his family in Fairfax.

There was a male gene in the Maddock family for disappearing. For being there yet not there. And the women somehow didn't let themselves notice, didn't allow themselves to yearn for attachment, true communion. The women ratcheted up their conversation a little brighter, and considered themselves fortunate: a husband who paid the bills and left them alone.

"Did I tell you we saw Campbell's father at a party in Cambridge?"

"Yes, you did."

"At the Brookhisers'."

"Aha."

Would Mr. Gordon have mentioned to her mother and stepfather that the children had called it off? Hard to tell. Would Campbell have told his father? What did other people tell their parents? Hard to tell.

Katrina and Campbell had got along—two politely stoical people who understood a long game, sacrificing the small pieces to keep the big. Her mother would be genuinely stricken to hear that Gwen had given Campbell the boot. She herself would have been not all that much older than Gwen when Martin had left her, and that catastrophic abandonment by the man she'd loved had formed a kind of pox in the bone. To break up a comfortable ménage willingly would be just about beyond her sympathy. She'd side with Campbell, for sure.

"Here's another one for you, Mom," said Gwen, picking up a crab's blue claw. But didn't want either to spill the beans about Gideon or to have her mother worry about her only daughter's being over thirty and alone. This modern world where the parents did all the marrying, while the children stayed single. Mom and Marty's shotgun weddings, Maddock called them. Next time I'm the one bringing the shotgun.

After about two minutes, her mother's whimsical *vagueness*—that refusal to come out with it, to admit to knowing things, that was one side—the Danish side, maybe—of her blond mongrel blood—drove Gwen round the bend.

"Your front tooth needs fixing."

"Oh, I know. I cracked it on a piece of grit in the salad at your Aunt Sue's . . ."

"I remember. That was last summer. If you don't get it fixed, it'll chip more. You should get it capped properly. Doesn't Hal's insurance cover dentists?"

"Honey, I'm *old*. My teeth are old. Aren't I the one who's supposed to be nagging *you* to go to the doctor?"

4

GWEN DIDN'T GO to Harvard or Yale or Princeton or wherever the god of suitable destinies had planned for her.

She went straight from eleventh grade to Ann Arbor, Michigan, which had one of the best Russian programs in the country. Where a cache of Soviet émigrés—philologists, mathematicians, poets, professional dissidents, all—trained her as elaborately as if she were to be a

Cold War mole. Taught her how to drink vodka with sprats around the kitchen table and tell grim jokes. One summer she interned at a publishing house run by Slavophiles who translated into English the pungent raucous samizdat that got Russians years in prison. She met the greats, and she yearned to be one of them: felt silicone-glib not to be sixty years old, with emphysema and a pacemaker, and a thousand pages of police files back home.

Michigan was as far away from Newburyport as she could think of, yet. It took several years for Maddock to come find her. Her brother now a veteran pothead, flashing a blue front tooth from his lapsed career on ice.

By then Maddock had been kicked out of Abenaki Regional, and the two progressively more military boarding schools Sue had arranged, and Martin paid for. It was tenth grade, Maddock-time, and he had just called it quits. Was stopping to say hello on his way cross-country to San Francisco, where he planned to look up a girl he'd met. He had been sleeping in bus terminals en route, and he smelled as bad as a child can smell: some poisonous, sickly-sweet mixture of codeine cough syrup, puke, and menthol cigarettes. Gwen let him stay with her several weeks, then bought him a plane ticket to San Francisco.

Next time she laid eyes on him—at Katrina and Hal's wedding—Maddock had muttonchop whiskers and a glowery slur, and was working for a roofer near Hanover.

Nowadays he and his friend Buddy had their own roofing business, just across the New Hampshire border from Katrina's. Out back, golden marsh, where the two men hunted ducks all fall.

Gwen's Maddock—the skinny tadpole, perpetually runny-nosed, the bed wetter who couldn't get warm at night—now weighed 215 pounds of solid workingman flesh.

5

MADDOCK AND HIS GIRLFRIEND had arrived late the night before, in a badly dented Dodge Ram.

The girl was young—twenty-two. Pale blond, with a red velvet ribbon in her hair, and frighteningly self-possessed. Her name was Riley; her mother was a nurse, her father was a golf pro down on Fernandina Island, and who knows how—in the idiots' chess game of America-in-motion—she had ended up in Rye, New Hampshire, waitressing nights while getting her college degree at UNH.

Gwen, impressed despite herself by the valor of that red velvet band, thought, What's she want with my brother? Wondered, uncharitably, if Riley smelled the family money that skinflint Maddock had squirrelled away.

Maddock, who never went back to high school, liked to argue about biochemical warfare and the Asian economies. Maddock, it seemed to Gwen, was beginning underhandedly to resemble their father, minus the drive. Some cross between their father and the Unabomber. Riley had let drop, impassively, how nights—after picking her up from work—Maddock stayed up watching old war movies. Falling asleep in the La-Z-Boy to the sound of tommy guns.

Duck hunters on the marsh, fishermen by the river. When Gwen and Katrina got back home—after picking up more beer at the 7-Eleven—it was noon. Maddock was still asleep, Riley was in the kitchen ironing napkins and a tablecloth she'd found in a drawer, stowed with the lobster-shell crackers and the corn-on-the-cob holders.

And Hal—who had spent every daylit moment since his step-children's arrival sawing and stacking wood for the cast-iron stove that heated (yeah, right) the living room—daring Maddock not to join him, daring Gwen to sit like a lizard soaking up the unearned heat—Hal was now busy wrapping tiny quail (ordered by catalogue from North Carolina) in marinated vine leaves. Skewering them on a spit like so many socks hung up to dry. How attention-grabbing, how Hal-like hygienic even on Thanksgiving Day, to have ruled out one communal dish in favor of individually wrapped microbirds.

"It was a recipe from the *Globe*," explained Katrina, mildly. "It's Greek."

Maddock now wandered out of the downstairs bedroom wearing fatigues, one sock, and no shirt. Looking for a beer. Dirty-blond hair on end. He'd grown up barrel-chested, like their pop, but taller. Watched Katrina make a Caesar salad.

"I don't think the Pilgrims ate salad, Mom."

"No?" ventured Gwen, legs dangling from the kitchen table. "Doncha remember what Jesus said about rendering unto Caesar the salad?"

(And unto God the anchovies.)

"Would you like me to make pemmican? I didn't realize this was supposed to be a replica dinner."

"Pelican?"

At two, they sat down at the table—covered, thanks to Riley, in Katrina's mother's family linen. Gwen opening two bottles of Châteauneuf, Maddock opting for Coors.

"Isn't anybody going to say grace?" Riley inquired. Giving her boyfriend, already ear to ear in bird grease, a dirty look.

"Oh, so we've got a Godian in our midst." Hal, naturally, was an atheist. Most scientists Gwen had encountered were. Tetchily atheist as if religion were an insult to their own personal omnipotence. Only in Russia had she come across scientists with sufficient sense of mischief and awe to acknowledge a Creator. (Or was it rather the hope for someone big enough to erase their own unto-the-third-generational goofs?)

"You go ahead and say something, Riley," said Maddock. The suppressed gulp of male guilt. Not even *knowing* what he'd done wrong, but ready to be chastised.

"Yes, do. 'Abracadabra' might be more to the point. I thought all you advanced young ladies were Wiccans."

"What's a Wiccan?" asked Katrina.

"New Age for witch," said Gwen.

"Are you calling Riley a witch?" asked Maddock, ominously jovial.

"Not at all. I'd just read that goddess-worship was back in fashion."

6

Holidays need small children, to provide a ground cover of gaiety and chatter, to jolly along the lagging hours, to justify the trouble. Gwen and Maddock were grown-up, but still too infantile to have made their own families, to give their mother something new to love. Because this was the truth, Gwen saw: parents didn't *love* their grown children. Grown children irked you, they destabilized you, they showed up sullen, and silently and not-so-silently judged you. Blamed you for the mystifying hash they were making of their own lives. They came, they ate, they glowered, they picked fights with your husband, they were condescending about your work, your cooking, your friends, they made you feel small. Then they went away, leaving a mess and a gap. Their blame hanging over you. Unanswerable because unspoken.

Hal—equally childish—was monopolizing Katrina in his whispery voice, telling her about a molecular biologist from Stanford he hoped to lure to the institute, the man was coming east in December, they ought to take him and his wife to the theater or a concert. Where had she put the schedule from the Arena? Then, fake-facetious, needling Maddock about his facial hair.

Katrina obviously on the qui vive to fend off any talk of politics. (Had Hal noticed the antiabortion stickers on Maddock's bumper, Gwen wondered. Gratuitously aggressive, as if anybody was *for* killing unborn babies.) Relieved when the conversation moved on to local news: a fishing boat that had sunk off Gloucester.

"They musta been asleep," said Maddock. "They musta had the boat on automatic pilot. What else would all three of 'em be doing down below?"

"That still doesn't explain why the Coast Guard didn't get there faster," said Riley.

"Oh, the Coast Guards around here are far too busy hobnobbing with drug smugglers to notice who's drowning," said Hal.

"Here?" Katrina asked, incredulously. Drug smuggling surely was confined to the bathwater South, to waters less unimpeachably gray.

"Don't be naive. How do you think you make a living on this coast, the fishing's all fished out."

"It's so sad," Katrina confirmed to Gwen. "Cod's becoming practically this luxury item. You go to Shop 'n Save, all they've got is fake crab-stick, mahimahi flown in from the Pacific. A whole way of life's just disappearing. All those Portuguese and Italian fishing families in Gloucester—what's going to happen to them? I mean, I know we have to conserve our fisheries, but—"

"Everybody's going to go work at McDonald's, that's what. Welcome to the global economy," said Hal, looking around the table triumphantly.

"Nothing wrong with working at McDonald's," countered Maddock. "Beats getting drowned at thirty. I never saw what was so glamorous about a fisherman's life—I'd sure rather see any kid of mine flipping burgers."

Frighteningly possessive, the way he stared—glared almost—at the pale blond girl. Riley, meanwhile, bent on her quail, carving up its ragged grapeleaf into microscopic forkfuls as if feeding a baby.

Intercepted a glance between Maddock and Katrina, some silent interrogation spreading into a grin. Sometimes they still flashed that secret understanding that had nothing to do with speech, that came from those years alone together, in this house.

Katrina rose to get the pie (baked from last summer's blueberries) out of the icebox. It was Aunt Sue's recipe and it should have been okay, but Katrina had used whole grain flour for the dough, and somehow her pies always came out tasting like kindergarten art: cardboard with purple glue.

Gwen, going rigid, suddenly. "Shit. We never picked up any coffee . . ." I.e., Katrina had remembered to buy more of Maddock's favorite beer, but had once again neglected Gwen's needs. Gwen as out-of-the-blue livid as if the no-coffee were final proof she'd *never* been loved. Eventually discovered in the back of a kitchen cabinet a can of stale Chock full o' Nuts. But no filters. Hal getting bossy about how to make cowboy coffee by boiling the grounds. Home, home on the range.

Riley, more provident, had brought her own supply of peppermint tea, which she drank, her translucent, cold-reddened fingers wrapped around the Katrina-made mug.

Purple starfish on an ocher background, inspired by Roman mosaics. That had been Katrina's first stab at a cure, after moving up to Newburyport: weekly trips to the Heavenly Glaze to fire her own pottery. Streaky-smudged dishes, unutterably ugly, that Katrina and Maddock had broken quickly, like guests at a Greek wedding.

Looking at Riley sipping her tea, Gwen got a flash that this girl was here to stay. Will we someday love each other? That was what happened with in-laws, supposedly, the slow melding of unlikes. Remembered her mother telling her that when Uncle Richard first brought Sue home to meet his family, Katrina'd thought, God, why doesn't she do something about her *teeth*?

7

"ARE YOU FROZEN?" asks Gwen. More as a jibe at cheapo Hal than in genuine sympathy.

"No," says Riley. "This isn't half as cold as Maddock keeps our house." The flatness of her tone ruling out any antimale collusion.

"So you're finishing college?"

"I'm getting a joint degree in special education and computer science. Actually, that's what I'm interested in: seeing how you can use computers to teach children with learning disabilities."

"Aha," says Gwen vaguely. "When do you graduate?"

"June."

"Do you know what you're going to do after that?"

"Marry me," breaks in Maddock. "Bear my children." How has he managed to get sloshed so quick—a hefty guy like him, on a few beers?

"I've been offered a job in special ed by the Dover Christian Academy," Riley replies, casting Maddock a You-should-be-so-lucky look.

"She's a math whiz," says Maddock, proudly. "She does our books for us, got the business all computerized."

"Yeah, right, that's Maddock's idea of a math whiz," says Riley. "Is it really true he had to repeat algebra *three times*?"

"I don't know; I wasn't there."

"You come work for me and Bud," interrupts Maddock. Not looking at his sister. "We'll pay better than the Christian retards."

Another withering gaze. Then Riley returns to Gwen. "Anybody can do books nowadays," she explains. "All you need is the software."

"How's New York?" Maddock asks Gwen, abruptly. Challenging. "Last time I set foot in that hellhole was, like, eight years ago."

He is mad at Gwen. Still. He is mad at his sister for growing up and away into someone who wears high heels and works an office job. He is mad at her because he thinks—wrongly—living in Manhattan means siding with Martin. (And she despises him for hiding behind their mother.) He is so mad at her that he can't meet her eyes, so mad that he flushes red when he (reluctantly) addresses her.

Someday they are going to have to have a decent fight. He will yell, she will yell, they both will cry a little, and only after that will they be able to divulge something of what has happened to each in the years since they were coconspirators, partners-in-fear, but in the meantime they're stuck pretending they've grown up into adults who have nothing in common. Who have each chosen paths the other one, coincidentally, just happens to despise.

"It's changed since then. You should come visit," Gwen replies. "Both of you. I have a guest room."

"I don't even go to Boston anymore," Maddock says. "Sitting in traffic for two hours getting to Fenway? I'd rather watch the game at home. Is it true they got climbing walls all over Manhattan now so tax lawyers can pretend they're scaling some peak in the Rockies?"

"Darling?" intervenes Katrina. "Have you seen my new studio?" Hustles Gwen out to the studio Hal has made her, from a gardening shed. A damp cell, thinks Gwen uncharitably, its window facing not the garden but the laundry line.

8

AT TWILIGHT, Gwen drove too fast past the airfield and over the bridge. Hunkered down against a dune, and lit (hand cupped against the wind) one of Gideon's cigarillos from a pack she had found stowed in her pea-coat pocket as she pushed the memory button that dialled La Merced. Answering machine. Tried Rivington Street. Ring, ring. Let it not be Dina. Or Ethan's girlish peep.

Pickup. Crackle of bad connection. The harsh voice sounding a cagey "Hello," and she dissolved, not quite into tears of relief.

"Thank God it's you. I think I'm going to . . . drown."

"Is that the Atlantic I hear or is that static? Don't drown." And then, low-voiced, "Queen of heaven, you better not go away again. I can't get through another day of Gwenlessness. Tell me everything that's happened since I last . . . Is it cold up there, are they treating you okay? How's your headache? How's your pussy? How's the compost king?"

"You know, I can't even talk about it, it's too—grim. How about you?"

"Man, I don't know what's wrong with me. You shoulda seen me, dinner at Dan and Andrea's, surrounded by these people who are my asshole buddies, my chosen kin. Kids from Rigoberta Menchú—you remember Julio? Julio and his girlfriend and Janina came by . . . And I just wanted to fucking flee. I'm so crabby everybody thinks I'm sick. Is love supposed to make you hate the people you're supposed to love?"

She, in turn, tried/failed to tell him. The minginess of the life her stepfather had enforced on her mother, who used to have this capacity for unbridled *joy* that evidently scared him shitless. Her brother, whom she couldn't think about.

"You just hang in there, honey," he said. "In three days, we'll be back embedded deep inside each other, and I'm never going to let you go. I'm going to live and die in the heaped wheat of your belly. My only girl, my perfect one."

9

IN HER MIND Maddock is always eight, nine, ten, at most: white-faced; big dark circles under his eyes; a wide mouth, sardonic-crooked; a perpetual snuffle. They're still living in New York—their last year, though they don't know it.

And this is the defining image she carries of him, crisp as a dream: her class is returning to school from Central Park, and they cross *his* class, trailing along to soccer. There's Jennifer Kaplan teasing Jason Schwartzman, and there's Gilford Morrissey. She's looking for Maddock—and then she spots him, lagging far behind his classmates, his blue school T-shirt faded purple, his skinny ass unequal to the job of keeping his shorts from drooping.

He catches sight of her too now, and casts her a look that is ironical-resigned, yet infinitesimally expectant. Two prisoners in the jailyard. Who don't say anything because they don't need words. O my Maddock, she thinks, who was supposed to protect whom? She remembers their stealing sprees on Eighty-sixth Street, the Hungarian salamis and Hohner harmonica and bamboo fan from Azuma they squirrelled into down parkas. Remembers the time Maddock got caught palming a jade doorknob from an antique store on Third Avenue, and she, waiting outside, had had to go back in and claim him.

Thinks of Maddock and the hatchet-faced Plymouth Bay judges and merchants whose name he bears, the Danish Lutheran lay preachers and Russian-Jewish peddlers whose blood mingled to make him, and then of Maddock in his corrugated cottage on Route 1A, behind the storage lot of a travelling carnival. She thinks of Maddock (camouflaged by trailers emblazoned "Foot-Long Corn Dog!" "Fried Dough!" "Fiesta Fun!"), falling asleep every night in front of the television set, as if he's seventy-five years old, and she wants to die deep down.

The dark circles under the eyes, the skinny butt, the scabbed knees. O my kid, my monkey brother.

How they both resolved to do badly at Dalton, to get kicked out together. How she double-crossed him when she got sent to prep school and never came back. By deciding to get smart. By learning a language he didn't know.

While he kept true to their childhood pact, one-handed. Got picked up for burglary and sprung, thanks to Uncle Richard. Kicked out of Abenaki Regional on a false rape charge. Bumped from second-rate prep school to third-rate, fast and aimless. On Greyhound buses cross-country. Sucking off sad, angry married men for ten bucks in bus station toilets. Drying out in a San Francisco shelter for runaway teens. Phone calls after 2 a.m. Will you accept a call from . . . What was the worst thing you've ever done? Said No, I won't. Said, Take the ticket and go. Said . . . My Maddock.

IO

THIS IS WHAT they recited one by one, Julio and Hester and Janina in hushed voices echoing over the silent auditorium. Their communal *Thanks/No Thanks* psalm. Thank you for smallpox thank you for syphilis thank you for asphalt thank you for asbestos thank you for the Chrysler Building thank you for the diseases and the cures thank you for color coordination thank you for color consciousness thank you for law thank you for the Moseses, Robert, Grandma, and Rabeinu, thank you for greenbacks thank you for wetbacks thank you for the alphabet thank you for the Flintstones thank you for introducing the injustices and then taking them away thank you for the cello thank you for the minimization of destiny in human affairs thank you for Emily Dickinson and Walt Whitman and the Staten Island Ferry and the Brooklyn Bridge thank you for double-ledger accounting thank you for the Braves thank you for Rashida my little sister who fell out a window thank you for us and them thank you for the evening star.

BOOK THREE

Chapter One

December 1995. Lower East Side, Manhattan.

Here is a day in the life of a small-change, quick-change puppeteer. A quiet day, when his partners are at their day jobs and Gideon is wondering where to take the company next.

After the Ethan-run (his maniacal haul from West Seventy-ninth Street down to the Lower East Side, back up to West Eighty-third and down again to Delancey, his life-in-the-bowels-of-the-New-York-subway-system, condemned to phantom train lines like the B and the F, to changeovers at Thirty-fourth Street or Rockefeller Center), he stops by J&M to price out a space heater, Kinko's to pick up their latest mailing. Arrives at La Merced just before ten, wanders upstairs to see Sancho, who is being interviewed by a columnist from *El Pueblo* about the status of the mayor's plans to evict them. They shoot the breeze; discuss legal strategies. Then Gideon ducks back downstairs, slips into a pair of BVDs, his fingerless gloves to face the freeze. Makes himself a cup of coffee, zips through the downtown papers while he puts in a call to Abel Ibarra at the New Theater. Opening the mail while the New Theater's electronic secretary tells you the WINS temperature in midtown, heavy traffic on the Cross Bronx where a tractor-trailer's jackknifed . . . Thinking, It's just a *theater* for Christ's sake, it's not like you're trying to get the chairman of the Fed on the phone. "Hey Gideon, my man, what's happening?" "My man" is such a superciliously dated greeting it almost comes out the other side to retro-funk. Almost, Abel.

Now it's eleven, and his first appointment stands in the half-open door: a nineteen-year-old kibbutznik named Amnon, heavyset, churlish, who's worked as a technician on the Israeli-Palestinian *Sesame Street,* wants to volunteer for Pants on Fire, i.e., isn't allowed to work in the U.S. Fine, says Gideon, come and don't work for us. Gideon is probably the only person in the world, along with Dina, who actually likes Israelis, maybe because it's as close as either of them'll ever come to being made to feel like a dumb blonde.

Amnon overlaps with Emma, a Columbia grad student with a gorgeous bod who's doing her dissertation on Infernal Combustion, and has come to talk to him about Jerome in the eighties. Don't talk to me, talk to Caitlin, says Gideon. (Caitlin has this real analytical way of standing back and elucidating, like, these were Jerome's anti-Reagan years, when he finally gave up on the possibility of political dialogue in America, of there being any viable Left for generations, and got bitter.) They talk nonetheless, while Gideon flips through his various address books for Caitlin's current number, 914-783-... but he's blanked out the last four digits.

Just as Gideon finally finds the scrap of paper that's got Caitlin's number, in comes Carlos to inspect the window Sally broke. Gideon shows him the new pane he's put in himself; Carlos, evidently in one of his primal sulks, says Gideon used the wrong kind of caulking. Wants to stay and complain about Sancho. Gideon watching regretfully the girl from Columbia wave a wiggly-fingered Bye-bye. Next head around the door is a Slovak artist whose name he can't remember—Dushan? Duvar? Doo-wop?—who's in the building visiting Isaac Hooker, this big blond mountain-man who makes experimental movies, wants him and Dina to come to an exhibition at the Czech Arts Center.

Phone call from Joyce Glasher at NYU, who's bringing over the Ragusa family of Piccolo Teatro for an Italian arts festival. Phone call from Dina, saying has he seen the piece in this week's *New York Press* about the Lower East Side performance scene, the Little Green Men mentioned, that ubiquitous motormouth Hillary Katzenbach quoted, so why not them—oh here they are, in a sidebar on page 14, big deal—nonetheless, Gideon, who has the latest issue on his lap, highlights their name with his Day-Glo Yellow, and stows it away to Xerox for the press clippings that will accompany their next mailing. The *Press* journalist claiming that puppetry's going through some kind of N.Y. renaissance, a sure sign the gig's up and it's time to deal arms or raise alfalfa.

12. 30 mlaweh at the Red Sea with Elliott from the Klezmofunks, who lives on a cooperative in Northfield, Vermont.

After lunch, more phone calls. Grants, grants, grants. Calls up New York State Council on the Performing Arts, where is their application form? A Chillingworth—these are teensy, a thousand bucks, but easily obtainable. Calls up the Aurora Foundation, isn't it getting to be time for his annual lunch with the director? But Gebler's out of town, and his secretary says the grant applications won't be sent out till January. Gideon wonders aloud to nobody, What's the point of being a utopian socialist if I have to spend my entire life thinking about fucking money. Realizes that the only way *not* to spend your entire life thinking about fucking money is to be born a millionaire. Even a dinky little single-digit millionaire like Gwen—he guesses—just about never has to think about money, except for the five minutes four times a year when her accountant calls up and reminds her to send a check to the IRS.

At five, Gideon hops the subway up to Ethan's friend Noah's house to take Ethan over to his trumpet lesson at Mannes, calls Gwen to say, Why don't they meet for half an hour at Alice in Wonderland, chew over Old Times, but she's not in the office.

Grabs a slice of cappuccino cheesecake at Café Lalo while trying to concentrate on this Mandelstam poem Gwen's given him to read, then picks up Ethan from Mannes and takes him back downtown to La Merced, where the gang shows up at seven, minus Andrea, who's gone to visit her half sister in a drying-out clinic in the Berkshires.

Takes a broom and dustpan to sweep the room, which is filthy. Slices his finger on a splinter of broken glass. Blood and paper towels . . . Dan, red-cheeked from the cold, bearing a brown paper bag of knishes that is already splitting-soggy-dripping. Hot and greasy-yummy. No, I mustn't. Don't you even think of bleeding on my potato knish, says Dina. One eye on the clock thinking, Lansky's at midnight.

This was his life: bop till you drop. An overcaffeinated, underfunded babel of shmooze and hustle, a making-do, a monkeying around with telephone wire, milk cartons, handsaws. Improvising. Wasn't that how everybody on this planet lived, whether you were dictator of Congo or Stan Stan the garbageman? By improvisation. Wild guesswork, inspired lies, interspersed with just plain coasting. The best you did was get by. How'm I doing? Getting by. Fuck creativity or genius or fame, those instants of blinding recognition. What it came down to was hubcaps. Hubcaps and chicken wire getting transformed into musical instruments, or the time Dina had made a really cool Elizabethan bustle out of egg cartons. That was the rainy-day play-group side of low-budget theater. The flea market bike, the public library: that was the socialist side.

Little bits of Ethan sandwiched into his day when suddenly you had to slow down enough to read between the lines, practice that semi-parental telepathy of, Is he missing his dad, is he unhappy in school, or is everything in fact A-OK. Then back to zoom-time, phone calls, coffee, meetings, out to Williamsburg for a workshop, dropping by the Vulcan Lounge to watch Haide Gidelim's Katzenjammer Kids in rehearsal.

Spirits fluctuating. Dan, Andrea, they were pack mules, cheerful, steady. Dina, too, had stamina. But even them—this life which was half high school jolliness, half terror, wore them down. Dan broke out in eczema, Dina got migraines, when she crawled into bed and died for three days. You would catch Andrea popping vitamins, ginseng, antioxidants, flopped over in the yogic child-position, breathing out the toxins, glugging from a bottle of wild-cherry-flavored acidophilus like she was the school-yard dope pusher. But they never wigged.

Whereas Gideon's energy was some frantic, babbling, bluebottle buzziness, a trapeze artist's willful optimism that someone's going to catch him, and then suddenly it would crash. He would turn yellow the way olive-skinned types do in winter, get stomach cramps, lose weight. He'd go insomniac. You'd find him sitting in the kitchen at Rivington Street at 4 a.m., sorting quarters for the Laundromat or staring listlessly at his scrapbook, unable to decode its diagrams. He'd become short-tempered, messianic, accusatory. Announce to the Others they should disband. Tell Andrea and Dan to cut the crap and get married, Dina can make the bride's dress—for Dan. He would rail against big business, worry about the effects of eating genetically modified soybeans.

Nothing, his friends believed, a girlfriend wouldn't solve. No way, he insisted, the problem really *was* genetic engineering, didn't they realize that biotech companies were brainwashing farmers into using these monster seeds whose effects on the environment were *totally untested*? Gideon: he was a riot, a bundle of nerves, antic, scowling, dear (that was Dina's favorite word of the week: dear. It had that quaint, Anglo dowdiness she favored). He would scrunch up, knees to his chin, some striped knitted cap like an organ-grinder's monkey's warming his pate, forehead all wrinkly, wiry eyebrows vexed, and just not seeing the joke . . . Don't you understand the danger of living under a government that's completely in the thrall of big business, because big business writes the campaign checks? I mean, this affects what we eat and breathe, what we read or are not allowed to read in the newspaper, do you really *want* to be a citizen—no, not even a citizen, a subject—of Disney or Monsanto? Get a girlfriend, Gidele. A girlfriend, where? What, you want me to, like, carry off some Sabine woman? Don't you have any sense of history? We are living at the end of the Roman Empire. This is an age of dangerously decadent monoliths, our politics don't work, we have retreated into a private life whose most intimate recesses are determined and monitored by these same multinationals whose obsessive takeovers and conglomerations mean less and less freedom, and people are too lazy to exercise the democratic rights they've got left, "liberty" having been debased to "choice," which means unprincipled consumerism. Just think about it: when dance troupes are supported by cigarette companies, something's fucked. Get a girlfriend, Gidele. Am I Cassandra, here? Get a girl, Gid. I'm shocked at your ignorant indifference, doesn't it trouble you that never in the so-called free world has there been such a discrepancy in income between the richest and the poorest, when the upper five hundred have hogged such a humongous portion of the national wealth? Is it democracy when nobody votes, when you have neither taxation (if you're rich) nor representation (if you're poor)? When being a black man is, in the eyes of the police, a crime? Have a drink of water, Gideon, don't forget to breathe. You want to make nice art? Now is not the time. Now is the time for barricades. Here's the water, Gideon. Drink.

When he found the girl—when the woman found him—half of him didn't want to admit that she, the Megagwen, was what he had been (virtually) chaste for, unshackled, unhoused these last few years. Hoarded the secret of her to himself (how her pussy *melted* when he entered, like the soft center of a chocolate cream, and yet for all its yieldingness nonetheless clutched him tight with an instinct that was all the more moving for being purely physiological, then gave this kind of electrical jolt when she started coming that made it almost impossible for him not to come, too) while fending her off with dumb wisecracks, with masculine evasions. With his infernal, his Saint Vitus' dance of pointless activity, of anxious hustle. The company, Dina, Ethan. Whatever wasn't her. The poor shiny-junk shards of his former, his autonomous life. The things he believed in, the ideas he'd thought up himself or hijacked, heavily underlined, from brittle yellowed paperbacks found in secondhand bookstores across the Northeast, borrowed from the library, stolen from Jerome. Creeds laboriously self-evident as some bespectacled nursery schooler telling you, Did you know diplodocuses were extinct.

Breathe, Gideon. In and out. She's here at last, all five feet nine King Kong inches of her. Here to stay, real as buttered bialys, as Monday morning rush hour pouring into the IRT, Yours for the asking.

Breathe deep and count to ten and say it.

Know before whom you stand.

Know, Your alienation at being the end of an ethnic-ideological line is history.

Say it.

Say it.

Say, I want us to be buried under one stone.

Chapter Two

I

"CHRIS, I'VE GOT BAD NEWS. You're going to kill me . . ."

He raised an eyebrow, expectant.

Balthazar: brass railings, red banquettes, glistening platters of fruits de mer, the chatter and clatter of small crowded tables of artists and models. It might have been a café in Montmartre a hundred years ago, except the models—multiracial giantesses in jogging suits—were making as much money as bankers.

They'd come from a performance of the Wooster Group. Christopher scanning the other tables for famous people, colleagues. He was easily bored—by humans, that is. Music he could listen to forever, at museums he turned to stone.

Imagine these three: Gwen, Constance, Christopher, sophomore year at Milton. Christmas vacation in New York, 1979, Gwen staying at Constance's parents' apartment in the East Fifties. The cool kids their age are snorting cocaine in stretch limos on their way to Xenon or Studio 54. *Their* first date, Christopher takes the two girls to an Alfred

Brendel concert at Carnegie Hall. They sit in the highest circle; Christopher's mother is stingy with allowance (at twenty-one, he will become stunningly rich), but his point is pedagogic: it only takes six dollars for a chunk of aural paradise.

Constance and Gwen are already in love with him, like two women in a Shakespearean comedy who haven't yet discovered that the charming boy they adore is a girl. Constance and Gwen are depressed by the male race: boys, for them, having gone from being cretins interested only in firecrackers and whoopee cushions to cretins interested only in the sound of their own voices, with a minor sideline in women-below-the-waist. Here is one you can actually talk to, who will settle for nothing less than intimacy, affection, the exchange of ideas.

After the concert, they go back to Christopher's house for dinner. Where Constance, always shameless, poses the question over which the two girls have spent the previous night speculating (locked in Constance's bedroom wolfing butterscotch brownies, which they have calculated, according to *The Joy of Cooking*'s calorie counter, are less fattening than an egg salad sandwich): Is Christopher, like them, a virgin?

Funnily enough, he replies, he's just lost his virginity that fall. In a suite at the Paris Ritz, to a Belgian banker friend of his late father's. (Who else but a gay boy would have had the nerve to ask out on one date the two haughtiest girls in the school?)

"What? You haven't gotten back together again with Campbell—not *that* bad news, I hope."

"I'm going to have to bail out on Istanbul, after all . . ."

Christopher let go his langoustine shell. "Shit." He sucked his torn finger, then turned his full attention to her. "You'd better have a good excuse."

"I—"

"You know I had all these romantic excursions planned. Moonlight cruises up the Bosphorus, Christmas in the hamam, just the two of us, exchanging sweet nothings about irrigation canals in Kyrgyzstan and Belarus's sovereign debt. And you don't even look sorry."

"I *am* sorry. I'm devastated."

"I hope it's not work—you know I can't take your work very seriously. To me, you'd be much better off shopping and having ladies' lunches. Tell me at least I'm getting jilted for a lover."

Gwen stammered, speechless. Hunted under the table for her napkin.

"I see. Fill me in. You ditched the Royal Caledonian months ago now. (I must say, your well-wishers were *really* broken up over that one.) And the successor is . . . good in bed?" asked Christopher.

"What a cold-blooded question."

"Really?"

"Really. Isn't good in bed because you love each other?"

"No," said Christopher. "In my estimation, anybody who loves you becomes automatically *bad* in bed."

"Oh yeah?"

"Yeah. I have more than enough people to love—my mother, my sisters, my lifelong intimates, not Blondie I just picked up on the dance floor."

"That sounds a bit . . . diminishing."

"I don't find anything about sex diminishing. Except somebody asking me over breakfast, 'What are you thinking about?' when I'm trying to read the paper and pick my nose at the same time. What am I thinking about, I'm thinking about getting you out the door, sister-boy."

"Touching," said Gwen. Staring at this man who was beautiful in a medieval-knightly, *Chanson de Roland* sort of way: waves of golden-brown hair falling into golden-brown eyes, broad shoulders, slim wrists. Any notion of culture or friendship she possessed came from Christopher, but now the idea of passing two weeks with him in Turkey was purgatory. That was what love did to you, according to Gideon. It was a sickness, it turned you cold to all you'd formerly cherished.

"What do you care? You I'll love forever. You might as well take me as I am," he said. "You see, I've forgiven you already, and I'm not even asking any questions. I just hope he's a brighter spark than Campbell, whom I found rather milquetoasty. I'm sure he'll age well, but as I expect to be dead by then, the long view was never much comfort."

2

FAMILY VACATIONS, or How I Chose Old Slavonic as My Major. Under this heading, thanks to her father's glad wallet, there were entries abounding. (Less funded families give you only one place you never want to go back to: home. They don't imperialize the sun-and-snow portions of the globe with bad memories. For Gideon, it was hardly a handicap not wanting to set foot again in downtown Passaic.)

Perhaps her most instructive vacation being spring break in Vail:

Gwen, Martin, Martin's then girlfriend Lindsay, and Lindsay's daughter Tara—Gwen's age, which was thirteen. Two years before she was befriended by Constance and Christopher, taught to love Bach partitas and Scottish tweeds.

It was her first encounter with the etiquette of parents-and-their-new-lovers; it had come at an age when sex was still an aggravating mystery (she was late as a boy, sexually), and she'd muffed it big-time. Proved immeasurably dimmer than Tara, a semipro in white stretch ski suit and twin ponytails with pink pom-poms, whom Martin had already bawled out for having tried to call him "Dad."

Lindsay was organized: she'd hired for the week a handsome instructor to take the girls out on the slopes while she and Martin, who had phlebitis, remained in the chalet. Dumb Gwen, halfway through *The Brothers Karamazov,* had admitted Day One that she too would just as soon stay home. This, apparently, was merely the most egregious of Gwen's failures of courtesy and human understanding. Lindsay led her upstairs and explained, in a voice static with tears, that she and Martin needed a little private grown-up time together, and she wasn't having any spoiled brat ruining their vacation because she was too spoiled to GO OUT and SKI.

Gwen wasn't clear how she was ruining their vacation by reading Dostoevsky: if she'd insisted on reading it aloud to the loving couple, that well might have been a disincentive to relaxation. But all she wanted was to stay in her own room!

Later she discovered (from Tara, of course) that Lindsay was pregnant, and that Martin was refusing to do right by her, wondering why they needed to add one more unwanted mouth to an overpopulated world when abortion was cheap, safe, and legal. Tough man, her dad.

And Gwen was tough too in her own way. It took a bloody-mindedness verging on autism to remember this holiday not as the time Tara in her snow-bunny suit called Gwen's father "Dad," or Lindsay in tears called Gwen a spoiled brat, but as the birth of her decision to master Russian, of her introduction to Dmitri Karamazov's dictum that we bear responsibility for the commission of sins we have merely contemplated. (What sins did she herself contemplate, save celibacy?) That was what came of her Easter vacation in Vail, the unwillingness to let Constance Garnett any longer interpose her fusty Anglicisms between her and Fyodor Mikhailovich's fervid miasma of idiot bastards and society saints.

Was this what everybody's life was made up of, a succession of shameful relations with expendable partners, of memories too bad to cough up? How many "dads" had Tara ended up being disavowed by? How many babies, on average, got flushed before a marriage was made?

3

THE RIGHTNESS, the healing rightness of it. When his liquid eyes shined their tender love-light upon her, well, then she felt like a maimed person who wades out into a sacred river and rises . . . whole. He hadn't been joking when he'd told her, early days, that twaddling marionettes for him was faith healing. Gideon the Baptist's touch was a balm, his voice a creaky unguent, when he grinned or hooked his eyebrows, her bowels quivered and her womb leaped like a dolphin. That bad: phone rings at work, it's Wolkowitz and she nearly shits her pants from excitement.

Some days they couldn't last office hours: she'd cancel her lunch date; he'd mumble some lousy excuse to his crew and jump on his bike. They'd stroll, his hand up her skirt, her tongue in his mouth, through the Egyptian Wing, the Roman Hall, peeking at the golden long-dead, the togaed man and wife on their joint tomb, wondering, Did you know what we know? Once—their making-out gone haywire—he dragged her into the Ramble on a wintry noon and yanked down her briefs, bent her over as if they were unacquainted faggots, slid in, and rammed her with a concentrated savagery, her afterwards slathering away the trick-ling jizm with a laurel leaf, liking the small grunt with which he hiked himself back into his fatigues. Loving the urwald of black hair, the rib-bon from snail-shell belly button to pubis, that disappeared as he tucked in his T-shirt.

Yet touch—this whole female organism of hers he'd sprung into nervy juddering motion—wasn't all.

Suddenly, things didn't *exist* until she'd told them to Gideon. She'd never dreamed of an ideal interlocutor, someone who heart-yearningly needed to know had she had a good shit that morning, and what was she intending to order in for lunch, and what exactly made her think Gerald was mad at her, and what did the doctors say about Mandy's brother's leukemia.

The result was that she—this ruthlessly armored person—now could not order her BLT without his guidance. He had rendered her that in-fantile, that insatiable, that uncertain, that monstrous.

By telling her (not that she'd ever asked), No, she had never been loved, not by her mom not by her dad not by her uncle or aunt or cousins or dog, and not when she needed it, not when it mattered. By exposing this primal lack, he promised, But I who love you with the love of a mother the love of a father the love of God and the love of the Devil, I alone can make it up to you.

No wonder if his phone were busy, or if Dan told her Gideon was out and hadn't said when he'd be back, she lost it. No wonder she howled and battered her fists, like an infant whose mama's got up without a word and walked away . . .

4

"It's over," Gwen said.

Back home from ten days in Russia, where the question, as always, was, Is this working? Sometimes you'd felt optimistic, amazed that Russians had shed Communism so quickly, that there were regional politicians with guts and ambition, a younger generation of entrepreneurs supersonically attuned to capitalism's quick killings.

This trip, she'd looked around and thought, This revolution's taken a wrong turn. Nothing is being "created," nothing "produced," raw materials are merely being stolen. And Russians were educated enough to notice that once again they'd been royally screwed.

"I don't know what I'm doing there, Gideon. People *expect* something of us we are in no position to deliver."

Gideon shrugged. "You're trying to help."

"But it's not working. The operation's a failure, *and* the patient's going to die."

He was too generous to press his advantage. "Is there something else you'd rather do?"

"No. Maybe it's time to grow up and make some real money."

"Who are your heroes?"

She didn't know. Elena Bonner, maybe. That Canadian woman judge who was prosecuting Serbian war criminals. It was a very Gideonite question. Didn't he know they were living in a postheroic world? And yet she wanted him nonetheless to breathe some saving purpose into her day: say, Yes, you are a noble missionary, bringing civil institutions to an anarchic and sclerotic bandit-state, an ex–world menace. Yes, you will succeed and be vindicated, yes, you too are a healer, a country-healer.

Or maybe she wanted him to say, Forget about salary, forget about promotions and program officers, just be my love and come live with me under the poverty line. What he did instead was look at her with those love-eyes that, beaming approval, said, Whatever you want we'll do it. I am your source, your living waters, drink me and you will be mammothly big and infinitesimally little, and you will ride the winds and hear the salty stars sing.

Are you hungry, he asked. You want a bath before dinner?

She said, from the depths of her desire for him, she said, I want *you.*

Chapter Three

I

NEW YEAR, 1996.

The Bemelmans Bar on a weeknight.

Peanuts and goldfish in small bowls: nuggety salt-bombs to make you thirsty.

Piano player crooning "Blue Moon."

Tables of continental businessmen barking laughter.

A Japanese man sitting catercorner to them, a lonely executive traveller, sunk over his laptop in the candlelit darkness. Suddenly a Japanese woman in a yellow cocktail dress appears, and the man, grinning, purrs up at her salaciously, "Foxy Lady!"

Gwen trying to suppress the bad-good flashbacks to the Belleclaire.

Down the block, the dresses in Givenchy gleam phosphorescent in the violet dusk: pinks, oranges, greens floating disembodied in the dark; there is an opening at the Whitney, to which men in black tie and women in brocade coats and furs are swarming. Yellow taxis swim up Madison Avenue like barracudas.

In the Bemelmans Bar, she and Constance are snuggled together on a banquette. Their second round of bullshots: Gwen half deliberately setting out to get drunk enough to tell Constance about Gideon.

"So you ducked out of Istanbul . . ."

"Yeah, I couldn't face it. I'm sick of spending my life on planes."

"That's new."

"I guess." Pause. On the brink, then losing her nerve and rushing on. "Have you seen Christopher yet?"

"We're having lunch at his house tomorrow—he wants to show us his loot. It's pure atavism, isn't it? I'm sure some of those grasping little d'Aurilhacs must have been along for the sack of Constantinople."

"You think they brought back boys, too? He's told you about the—?"

Constance wiggled a hand in a yes-and-no gesture.

"It sounds pretty serious: he's going back to Istanbul at the end of the month. He wants the kid to move to New York."

"You must be joking—I can't remember Christopher *ever* having any sort of steady snog."

"Allah Akbar!"

"What do we know about him?"

"Nothing. Christopher met him in a nightclub. He lives with his parents, he's the youngest of seven children—what do you think that means in Turkey, that you're religious or just poor?"

"Pass. I don't imagine religious boys go to gay nightclubs, but how would I know? That *is* exciting. And what about you, my sweetheart? What did you do instead? You look very mischievous somehow . . ."

Gwen hesitated. On the point once again of spilling the beans. Then pulling back. "Well, I'd had this idea I was going to spend Christmas alone. You know: watch cartoons. Paint my toenails. Grab a hot dog at Papaya King. It seemed like one of the privileges of polygamous parents—you get to slip through the cracks at Christmas. And I did—kind of. It was great. But then Jacey put the screws on me—Martin's not so well, he's been kinda fluey all winter. So I drove out to Connecticut Christmas night."

"Rigid with resentment, I imagine. Was it hell?"

"It was Connecticut. This is the part of Connecticut that the megarich moved to when the Hamptons got too crowded. Compound country: see how much Outdoors you can regulate by remote control. Serena and Al howled the whole time because they hadn't gotten enough presents, or they didn't like their presents, or they wanted each other's presents; the only time they didn't howl was watching television. Which is all Martin does either, when he's not working. I gave the children handmade puppets. A dragon and a sailor." (Not mentioning it was Gideon's hands—actually, Dina's—who'd made them. Why couldn't you tell her, Gwen: your best friend?) "Serena screamed because she'd wanted an interactive Barbie. Martin forgot to tell me that's what she wanted. Did you know they still made Barbie dolls?"

"Did I KNOW?" Constance, ironical.

"Sixty-year-old men should be banned from having babies, it's that simple. Martin's soft in the head, and so are they. Plus it turned out he and Jacey weren't speaking, which I guess was why she'd wanted me to come to begin with. How was yours? You went back to England?"

"Fine, actually. We spent Christmas in Norfolk, with Roger's parents. Then we went to my friend Sophie's for New Year's Eve. We've got that division down rather well: Christmas is for the children, New Year's is for the grown-ups to crowd into someone's bathroom and take a lot of cocaine . . ."

"That sounds tempting. And I thought I was kinky hanging out at Papaya King. Was it fun?"

Constance had a way of pursuing her own train of thought, oblivious to any intervening questions. "Joe was there." Joe was Constance's boyfriend before Roger. "Have I told you he has hepatitis C? Everybody in London has hepatitis C—everyone who ever used a needle. He looks ghastly. I was terrified of what Roger would make of him."

"They never met?"

"No. I scarcely dare talk to him myself; I'm always scared one of us is going to absolutely horrify the other by bursting into tears or something equally unforgivable—" She was staring down at the table, shredding her cocktail napkin with an absentminded ferocity.

"And what happened?"

"When we were coming home in the cab, Roger said, Wasn't it fun. I asked—nervously—What did you make of Joe? Convinced he was going to say, My God, what a *creep*. But no, Roger thought he was fascinating. They talked all night about Lee Kwan Yew. He said, We must get him round next time we're in town. I said, Yes, but . . . And then he said, Do you know him well?"

"What?"

"He'd completely blanked it out. That this man had been the love of my life. He'd utterly forgotten."

"You're kidding. *Jesus.*"

They both burst out laughing.

"He has this idea of marriage as a friendship. He calls me his best friend."

Gwen stared, horrified. "Shit, that's depressing. Anyway, it's a pretty limp notion of best-friendship. If you forgot one of my exes, I'd fire you."

"Exactly."

Gwen, wondering what the import of the story was. Seven-year itch? Could you blame Constance? This glimpse into the slackness of other people's lives making her frantic, suddenly, to dive back into Gideon. The way their parched lips searched for each other's, seeking asphyxiation. We can die by it, if not live by love. Because living seemed so tepid, so mendacious compared to their nightly near-death experiences. Because living-in-love—domesticated, civilly sanctioned, long-haul love—evidently meant forgetting that the man with whom you were chatting at a party had nearly committed suicide when your wife left him.

"Excuse me, Con, I gotta make a call." Searching her handbag for the cell phone.

Constance's glance was affectionate. "Anybody I know?"

"Nah, but I guess you will, sooner or later."

"You always say that, and then you give them the boot before I get to meet them."

"You met Campbell plenty."

"Yes, the dull worthy ones you bring home. You look well, but too thin," said Constance, reaching over to stroke Gwen's hair. There, in the croony darkness, under the Bemelmans mural of elephants ice-skating in Central Park.

"That's family-Christmas, not love. Something about a dinner table where the adult at either end isn't speaking to the other . . . What can I tell you, I'm five at heart."

"Do I know this person?" repeated Constance, pushing Gwen's hair out of her eyes, tucking it behind her ears, with a smile so fond it made Gwen want to cry.

"You mean is it Gerald? No, thank God, I think I'm over that one . . ."

"Are you ready to tell?"

"God, do I ever want to tell," sighed Gwen, smiling and tears flooding her eyes at the same time . . .

2

WHEN SHE GOT HOME, drunk and ravenous—she and Constance had forgotten to eat; nothing in the refrigerator except a plastic tray of sprouts that were . . . sprouting—the apartment felt empty. Simultaneously empty and squalid. Mimi was back in the Philippines for a month, and the bedroom was strewn with old newspapers, stained coffee cups, yesterday's clothes. The sheets (where that morning they had . . .) twisted into a humid mop. But no Gideon. No trace of him. Not a T-shirt, not a dirty sock, even. She wanted him, badly. She wanted his clothes across a chair, his razor by her sink, his warm brown body in her bed, hand on the small of her back, like an old-fashioned dancing partner, as they waltzed through the sheets.

Twelve forty-five. Too late to call him at home. She tried La Merced, just on the off chance. Dan answered, and handed over Gid, hopped-up, impersonally friendly: his company self.

"I miss you," she said. "I've had three bullshots with Constance; I can't walk straight, but I miss you."

"Oh yeah? Can you weave your way into a taxicab?"

They were almost done, he said, but he had to spend the night on Rivington Street since Ethan was on his own—Dina was back in Toronto for a few days, helping her mother move house. "You want to meet me at the Sombrero?"

And Gwen felt pleased that they were past chivalry, that he was learning to assume she liked him enough to dredge one hundred blocks south at 1 a.m. in the howling cold for a plate of refried beans.

Chapter Four

I

SATURDAY MORNING. Gideon is lying in Gwen's bed, propped up on one elbow, watching Gwen polish her shoes. Not just one pair but five, six pairs of shoes, each in its cedarwood tree. A forest!

This is what the woman does on weekends—washes her sweaters by hand, balances her checkbook. Reads up on privatization schemes, the rise of sexually transmitted diseases in the ex-USSR, meets some documentary filmmaker who's got footage from the war in Chechnya, a liberal economist who's just been fired in the latest Yeltsin purge. Helps undeserving acquaintances get jobs or grants or assignments or green cards. Writes letters. Checks. Why not? She's got deep pockets. Why shouldn't she, as well as bigger fish, enjoy the buzz of altruism?

Nothing too chiliastic, too disruptive of society's current disposition, mostly seventy-five here, a hundred there, to your average yuppie-bluestocking charities—the Brooklyn Academy of Music or victims of land mines, spliced with her own weirdo right-wing sallies: the Salvation Army or some unforgivable Cuban exile group that's plotting to give Castro hemorrhoids. (He even caught her sending a check to Pants on Fire; Just make it out to me, he said.) Today it's the shoes she's spoiling rotten. Gwen in her white satin pajamas, cross-legged on the oak veneer floor, gear spread out like a child's model-train set. Scrub-scrub-scrub, goes the smear of Meltonian Neutral on flannel. Buff-buff-buff, goes the brush, it's only 9:55 a.m., and she's already been through "Arts & Leisure" and the Business section. A final swipe with a clean chamois cloth. And Gideon secretly *undone* because the shoe polish means she's leaving town next week, another two weeks in Russia, which it seems to him she's only just come back from, plus an utterly unnecessary junket in London, and the early morning alacrity of her drill means she's *excited* to be going back, the heartless bitch.

"Jesus," he complains from the bed she has deserted. "This isn't fetishism, this is fascism. I feel like I'm sleeping with a marine. What would happen if you *didn't* polish your shoes Saturday morning?"

She looks up. She thinks. Then laughs. That deep chuckle, a really guttural gurgle she gives out, like a stuffed bear you've accidentally pressed in the tummy. Which only aggravates him into *serious* though still subterfugitive hectoring.

"C'mon, tell me. Would you, like, go AWOL if you ever stopped polishing those shoes? Would you lie in a darkened room for the rest of your life, with a pillow over your head, howling at the horror of human existence?"

"Probably. Isn't that what you think? That between me and total annihilating world-hatred lies one can of shoe polish?" (She's evidently under the misapprehension he's *flattering* her.)

"What do *I* think? I think one can of shoe polish is pretty good, as buffers go. Most of us are working on slimmer protection than that. Most of us don't have so many shoes, either. You really are a world-class advertisement for Western consumerism, miss."

"What's consumerism?" she asks, smiling still. "You mean, buying things?"

Pleased, evidently, to let the conversation be diverted from her own execrable crotchets, her concealed nihilism. A dimple, chiselled deep in either cheek. She's *amused* by his politics.

"People buying garbage they don't need and can't afford in response to some marketing-induced social anxiety. Isn't that the Lavrinsky program, coercing three hundred million Russians into thinking they're flush enough to join the global spendfest? To buy his goodies?"

"There aren't three hundred million Russians. There *might* have been three hundred million Russians by now, if your favorite belief system hadn't murdered fifty million. Anyway, what goodies? He's not a candy store owner."

"Sweetheart, you know how big a chunk he owns of major U.S. corporations like—"

"You're too simplistic. Cynical, hence simplistic. You think you're the only person in the world with principles."

It's true. He genuinely *believes* the shit you read in *The Nation*: that Lavrinsky is an evil genius. That trying to turn ex-Commies into capitalists—human beings into consumers—is a shameful scam. (Here's the difference between them: Gwen thinks NATO expansion is a high-minded reward to brave Eastern Europeans for having fought for Western ideals of freedom and democracy; Gideon thinks it's a scam to blackmail small countries that should be spending their scarce revenues on health and education into buying fighter jets that even the Saudis know are crap.)

She is indulgent. She understands that he is knocking her job because he hates her going off and leaving him, because he worries when she's in remote parts without him.

They are kidnapping tourists in Tajikistan, beheading aid workers in Chechnya. Greater Russia, post-Communism, is hurtling backwards into Stone Age barbarism.

"I'm not going to Chechnya," she says.

"How do I know you're not? How do *you* know you're not? You're such a fucking hard-ass, somebody says to you, I got a military transport helicopter flying into Chechnya, wanna come, you'll be on it."

"Why don't you come, too?" (An image of Gideon in the Novosibirsk market, on the airport sidewalk, saying, Come with me to the taiga, I'm following you to Moscow. Saying, *We could have a ball anywhere*.)

He frowns. He can't. He is feeling broke and sour.

"C'mon, I'll buy you a ticket."

"I thought you were going to be working every moment of the day and night."

"Come on, I'll buy you a ticket. Or meet me in London, we can have a long weekend together."

"No can do."

"Why not? If you were the one with the money, I'd let you fly me round the world. Four days goofing around in London? Doesn't that sound good?"

"Come on, colonel," he says, finally. "Back to your boot polish."

2

"Hey there, Queenie. I miss you."

He was at work, she was at work. He said—in a different voice now—"Yo Hector, get me something sweet, okay? Like, a carrot muffin? There's a couple more bucks over there on the shelf." And to her, "*Mercy Unlimited* is making its first run of the day. Got any plans this evening, Miss Lewis?"

"I don't know—seeing you, I guess."

"Cool. I'm going to try to come over on the early side. I can't stay the night—I gotta leave by ten, latest."

"Oh really?" A chill in the heart. *Her* turn. The clutch, But we've only got two days left, before I go away . . .

"I said I'd pick up Ethan at a friend's house down the street from you. One of his penthouse pals—Morgan who lives in the Beresford, or is it Beresford who lives in the Morgan?"

Gwen said nothing. Pulse-pulse of another incoming call. Dr. Makover's secretary from the Institute of International Affairs wanting to fax her the flight reservations and the conference schedule and could she please check that the CV they'd provided for her was accurate . . . Click back to Gideon, sitting in a large freezing room on Attorney Street. What was he doing with his hands, she wondered, those long-fingered hands, nimble, olive-brown, their puckered knuckles ruddy. Pasting this, stapling that, rigging up that. Gideon, who couldn't sit still.

"I'm still here," said Gideon. Then, in an aside—"Ammo, don't use that roll—the white one's open already."

Gwen waited for his attention to return to her. Then, "Maybe we should skip tonight."

"No *way*. I'll get there as early as I can. What time you think you'll get off work? It sucks I can't stay, but I promised Dina I'd go get Ethan. I think she's not too pleased with me, never being around anymore." Pleading, conciliatory.

"Oh really? Aren't you a little old to have a landlady who doesn't like you to go out at night?" Words out, too sharp, before they could be tempered. You are no diplomat, Gwen. You close your eyes and slash. And Gideon is too wounded to consider that behind your massive contempt is jealousy that he is sharing a shoe box with a woman who is not you. Does she glimpse him early mornings, blowsy Dina, as he bounds into the shower with a hard-on like a coat peg? Does he strut around weekends naked as Patroclus sailing into battle? Does Dina too have the hots for him?

Gideon, stung, tried to justify what now seemed to him simultaneously a total drag and one last loyalty. Embattled, he went for the economic defense. "Do you have any idea what it's like out there for normal people, sugar pie? People who *don't* have trust funds? Of course, it's a total pain, having roommates. But Dina would be massacred if I moved out. And from my point of view, too, do I really want to spend half my income to live, where? Flatbush? Woodside? Two hours' commute each day? Yeah, I'd be more *comfortable* having my own suite at the Ritz, but . . ." The implication being, You're too busy running fucking Arkhangel'sk to realize how people in your own hometown live.

Cheap shot. Obvious. Ignore it, girl, answer instead the plea in his embattled voice. She tried. "I was thinking maybe you might move in with me," she said, faltering just a little. Hoping that nearby Tim really was fully occupied with his own phone call to Kiev.

"You? Doncha like your peace and quiet anymore—having your jars and lotions just so?" he teased. Affectionate, now.

"I think I like you better."

"I think you like the lotions. Ask me again in a year. You really want us to shack up together? This is all too sudden. I've never been proposed to before. I'm just an ingenue from Teaneck. You should see me—I'm blushing."

She steadied herself while Tim got off the phone, wandered over to her desk. Removed the phone from her ear. "Do you need me, Tim?"

"You got the *Index on Censorship*?"

"No, I left it at home. I'll try to remember to bring it tomorrow . . ." And thus having dispatched her neighbor, lapsed into despair. Really, she'd had no intention of asking Gideon to move in with her—on the contrary, his living arrangements had always seemed a shield against what might otherwise be a burdensome expectation of domesticity: if Gideon got sick of takeout sushi, he could always go home to Dina for a hot meal. But now, because she, almost accidentally, had asked, he must say yes—he must do it.

Quiet, once more, while Kalman walked by.

"Hold on," she told Gideon. Pause. "Is it that you—do you not trust me?"

"You don't trust you."

"I thought that was why I needed you to trust me."

"Checkmate. Is that Jesuitry or is that blackmail or what? Are you asking me to move *in* with you, or are you asking me to move *out* with the Family Gribetz?" came Gideon's raspy voice. Cheerful—he was enjoying her humiliation. "I think you like your apartment to yourself, miss. I don't see you as a sharer; I think you prefer me coming by for house calls once a month, like your banker boyfriend."

She listened, trying to keep her temper, not to *demolish* this insolent little posturer on the other end of the line.

"I like you. I've never liked anything so much in my life." Which, let's face it, was true. He was a creep, but she liked him. Through and through, long agile toes to fuzzy skull. She liked the clean radiant bore of his earholes, the bluish whites to his eyes, his warm horsey breath on the back of her neck at night.

"We'll see," said Gideon.

"That's what you say to a child."

And Gideon, out of patience suddenly, replied, "When I'm ready to live with you, I'll do the asking."

3

FORGIVE ME, forgive me, forgive me. Words running into a low murmur where meaning didn't matter, just the humming frequency, she was burning hot, burning. She had come home from work and fallen asleep just like that. No, she wasn't sick, she said, refusing to meet his eyes, just asleep. Forgive me . . . forgive me . . . For what? For waking me up? And the subject passed, unmentionable, of who lived where . . . She was going to Russia, she wasn't going to Russia, not until her temperature came down, it didn't matter where he lived, whose name was on what lease, which bathroom he kept his razors in, because he was hers and only hers, do you hear me, girl, arms tight-tight around her to stop the shivers damn I must be sick forgive me dove and time gather-gathering like a drop that never falls, gathering but not moving . . . I'm making some soup outta that barbecue chicken, said Gideon, chicken soup like my Grandma Bella used to make for me when I was sick. That sounds nice. Nah, she was a whiny old bitch.

4

January 1996. New York.

Icy and blue-skied, so blue there's not a cloud between here and Idaho, you feel, and the red-red and the blue-blue and the white-white of the American flags streaming from the forty-ninth floor of the hotels and office towers ripple in the crisp light like chromatic muscle, clean as jets.

You would think it took a different kind of oxygen, living at the bottom of Manhattan's silvery Alps, deep in the Valley of the Shadow of Success. And why, instead of dwarfing you, does it make you too soar up into the ether, blast off, feel, oh God in heaven, that everything is possible? Everything, if only Gwen weren't leaving town tomorrow . . .

5

He is holding her, just before the X-ray conveyor belt, the metal-detector doorframe that separates international travellers from the stay-at-home chaff. Beyond, a long beige marble slope upward out of sight, an elevated walkway to an antiseptic afterlife . . .

Guards. Inspectors. Uniformed personnel.

How many people have parted for the last time at this frontier, never to lay eyes on each other again.

Last weekend, Pants on Fire joined in a march on City Hall protesting U.S. immigration policies. (Open borders is the one political cause on which Gwen and Gideon are united.) After the rally, they went to an exhibition of photographs of illegal immigrants. There was this picture of a Chinese garment worker, lying dull-eyed on her bunk in the cell she shares with seven other workers. A babe is suckling at her breast, tiny hand gripping the other breast.

The sullen pockmarked mother is nursing her baby for *the last time,* the caption explains. She has kept him three months, delaying his departure day, kept him in this stationary cattle car that is her "home" between shifts, in this multistory garage in which she parks her carcass in the few dark hours it is not being driven. Now she has just paid a stranger a thousand dollars to fly her three-month-old infant back to China, because she can't afford to keep him in America while she works.

And you, the watcher, know something that that fiercely sucking infant does not yet know but is biologically programmed to fear worse than saber-toothed tigers—that in a few hours he will be ripped from his mama's warm flesh, her musky her-smell, her sweet life-source breast, into the metallic terror of international airspace and that he will never, never, never see his mother again, because the self he is at this moment and the self she is at this moment—their suckling flowing indissoluble oneness are about to be annihilated forever and ever. And that, really, is the only kind of forever you can count on.

The mother will still, long after he is gone, awaken every two hours of the night, her heavy aching breasts leaking-weeping milk for the babe who half a world away is screaming itself to sleep from want of her. Who will have to cure himself of that want, if he is ever to get older.

And Gideon too swallows his own wail, upon being forced to release Gwen into beige outer space. He is stroking her cheeks, her eyebrows, her nose, for the last time. Memorizing each fold and crease and bump. Forbidding himself to break down before she's out of sight. Thinking, This letting go is only bearable if I can have her *forever.*

Lovers, do you *believe* in your eternity? Or is it just a tease (the Rockies may crumble, Gibraltar may tumble), an ironical acknowledgment that the only certainty is rupture, dispossession? An absolute negation of everything we make. And even the more human time span of less boastful lovers (Agamemnon's declaring he had intended to see his Criseis one day a toothless granny mumbling at her loom), isn't this too a crying-for-the-moon?

So Gideon, humbler, more experienced at abandonment, lacks the vainglorious gall to invoke long vistas. Instead, Caitlin calls asking him to do a summer workshop up in Binghamton last two weeks of July, and he wonders, Will I still know Gwen by July? Will we still be one?

Some histrionic fame-seeker in him thinking, If her plane crashes over Finland–ptui, ptui, he spits–no one will ever know about our love. The superstitious bargainer in him thinking, If her plane doesn't crash, if you cherubim of the Upper Regions bring her home to me safe, that means we will stay together, that *this is it*. One last smooch on her curly lips sucking the caffeinated breath out of her, one last stroke of her heavy hair bound by a black velvet band, one frenzied murmured vow, and she is gone.

And though he stands staring after her in incredulous, crazed grief, as she, a reverse Eurydice revolving periodically to wave, mounts the seven-story mountain of departures, nonetheless he (the hysterically weeping infant who refuses to accept that he will have to grow up before he sees his mother again) wonders what really goes through her head after she has turned the corner into international airspace.

Chapter Five

I

THEY WERE PUTTING ON a Mardi Gras night in La Merced: Bux and Strange Days each performing a dance, along with the Karmanauts, an Argentine jazz clarinetist, and Isaac Hooker, who was going to screen a short called *Heliogabalus*.

Fifteen dollars at the door, proceeds to go to the Save La Merced fund. Gideon not feeling very bacchanalian, as Gwen was still overseas. Which made him not just cranky and glum but gummed-up-in-the-head, as if lovelornness were a particularly stupefying form of flu. Day of the show, and they were rehearsing a stripped-down version of the Passion play, him and Dan and Amnon and Andrea and Hector, with Ethan on the trumpet, and six kids from the neighborhood.

Wet dark afternoon—a kind of nagging slush-puppy crossbreed of rain and snow. Puddles from everybody's dripping coats and boots, the table laden with mayonnaise-soggy paper plates, scattered smithereens of barbecue-flavored chips, a gallon of Mountain Dew. Andrea tramping around in big boots with her accordion, Dina asking if anybody had an aspirin, Amnon and Hector trying for the sixtieth time to lower the cardboard Devil on a pulley, and the Devil, for the sixtieth time, falling off its hook. This time of year, everybody coughing-sneezing and he hadn't heard from Gwen in two days now.

"Let's roll," says Gideon.

The procession, chanting, starts; Gideon stops them; the procession starts; he stops them.

"Wait wait wait," he says. "Too much noise, people—the cries have to be real sporadic, otherwise it's awful. You have to listen to each other." They've put on this play a million times; they've done it in Costa Rica, Belgium, Czechoslovakia, and Stroudsburg, Pennsylvania. What is *wrong* with everybody today?

"The Devil's not supposed to move till the curtain's closed," he says.

"Hey Amnon," he says, "you took out the wrong lights. It's stage left. Did you just take down the master? Bring up the master, take it down again. Now bring back stage left. You can't bring it down any further than that.

"Wait, wait," he says. "There's too much slack in Fat Tuesday's robe. Andrea, can you take up some of that slack? Yeah, try and see."

They run through, they run through. And then they break, everyone plopping down for a communal self-criticism, Vietcong-style. "There's still a big problem with the Devil," Amnon maintains. "We need to relax the Devil, the Devil's coming down too stressed from last time it fell on top of us."

Is it Gideon's imagination or has something changed? Suddenly everybody's making decisions without him, and even Dina and Andrea seem to be looking to Amnon (this nineteen-year-old technician) for authority. The orientation of the company has shifted. While he wasn't looking. While he was in bed with Gwen.

"But I think it's getting there," Amnon concludes, encouragingly.

"I think it looks like shit," says Gideon, and they all look at him surprised, because usually he's the cheerleader.

2

BREAKFAST AT RIVINGTON STREET. A school morning. Winter darkness outside, drafty cold inside, Ethan whining, Dina puffy with sleep: mother-son locked in their eternal battle over Ethan's refusal to eat, and Gideon doesn't want to be there.

Imagines himself uptown, at the Vanderveer (where surely it would be warm and sunlit), feasting on brioches and black cherry jam and blond pussy. A million more days till she's home. Looking at his surroundings with a new censoriousness—do things have to be ugly just because they're cheap? Looking at Dina, in her drab nylon-quilted bathrobe, with a guilty distaste, as if she were an unloved wife. Thinking for the first time, Why is she so fat? Thinking, What kind of childhood is this for Ethan? Thinking, So what if he only wants to eat Doritos for breakfast, is it worth ruining everybody's day over?

At the bottom of his disaffection, a sneaky sense of undesired kinship—that he and Dina both are children of the Old World, begotten of the bitter depriving Pale. Him, Dina, Dan, even Ethan. Which means that each contains within himself—beneath the American gloss—this wary self-protective pessimism, a promise of accelerated decay. Because "They" are truly Gideon's Family, because they alone know him inside out, he is suddenly frantic to escape Them.

Whereas golden Gwen, all forward-jutting chin, all possibility, all ignorance, seems (despite her Plymouth Bay quarterings) to have sprung from the New: a steel-riveted skyscraper of a girl. And Gideon finds himself thinking, I want to be a flying buttress off her fortieth floor, a gargoyle spread-eagled from her chrome pinnacles; I want to live where the air is new-born thin, not lurk in dark cellars, forage for stunted roots. And this could only be done with Her.

A new mother-son fight erupting over Ethan's desire to go to a birthday party Friday night—Andre from karate class who lives out in Hoboken—and Dina says, No. Friday night is Shabbos, it's when you sit around the kitchen table singing haunting ancient Hebrew melodies about angels and exile, it's not when you haul across the Holland Tunnel to play Power Morphs in someone's basement. Ethan saying, It's a sleepover, I can go there *way* before sundown, I don't have to leave till the next evening. Dina: No means No. And Ethan getting a pinched look that said, Day I leave home, I'll be scarfing bacon cheeseburgers on Yom Kippur.

In the front parlor of his mind, Gideon thinks, I don't want to hurt Dina by moving out, she needs help with Ethan; while in the back, he is forced to acknowledge that for all Gwen's avowals and his, for all the perfection of their foreordained soul-twinnedness, he doesn't yet trust the woman with his fate. They don't come from the same neighborhood; he doesn't know her people (as Sonny Wolkowitz might have put it). It's something as atavistic as that, this mistrust which is a survival instinct he is not yet ready to overrule.

Chapter Six

I

"WHAT'S *our government* up to?" A rhetorical question from James Otis, an aide to the World Bank who was currently feeling no pain from Bill and Jamila's Armenian brandy. "Our government, as usual, is obsessed by propping up whatever dictator we happen already to have met. Out of, basically, social anxiety: God forbid the president should have to learn some totally new Russian president's unpronounceable name."

"Of course," said Jamila. "Which is why America's buying him the election with IMF money. On the *utterly* bankrupt line that we have to save this man's ass from the Communists. I did this interview with Stanley Fischer, who was just *so* bloody weaselly—" She growled, and made as if to strangle an imaginary throat.

Jamila and Bill Sachs, both foreign correspondents, have an open house for visiting Americans, which was how Gwen met them her first year at Lavrinsky: a scribbled telephone number on a torn piece of paper. Thus did God send her His deepest blessings. And indeed, there was something biblically hospitable about Jamila—a short square dynamo, half Egyptian, half English, fiercely in love with her husband and child—who, arriving home from the office at seven that evening, had cooked Georgian chicken with walnut sauce for their last-minute guests.

Bill was trying to tell Gwen about Luzhkov's birthday party, where . . . but James Otis's high sarcastic voice broke in. "Personally, I have nothing against Yeltsin except that the guy's half dead. He's a person who spends his time being either dead drunk or just plain dead. Maybe you guys could explain to me why this country's got such a predilection for being run by dead men."

"I don't think it does," Jamila protested. "I think the man is *desperately* unpopular. And it's frustrating, because there *are* genuinely decent, highly intelligent people out there, but there's simply not much incentive to be honest or civic-minded. If I were a young Russian today, I would be"—she pointed an index finger at her temple, pulled an imaginary trigger—"livid."

"What's going on with Yabloko?" Gwen asked. Last time she was in Moscow, Jamila and Bill had been having this love affair with Yavlinski's political party.

"Yabloko? It's just another piece of Western wishful thinking," said Bill. "You remember, like when your mom used to say, Why can't you be friends with little Arthur, because little Arthur wears bow ties and likes to practice the violin, but what your mom doesn't understand is he also likes to torture small animals in his spare time . . . So we keep on telling Yeltsin, If only you'll play with little Chubais or little Gaidar or little Yavlinski, we'll lend you unsupervised billions. The only problem is—all these so-called pro-Western reformers? Russians hate 'em. They hate 'em."

"I know, but why?"

"Because they're just as corrupt as the *anti*-Western *anti*reformers," said Jamila, laughing.

"Because they're all Jews," said Bill.

"Bill, that's not why," Jamila protested. "You could say that about half the—"

"You know, I remember this particular pathology back from *my* days in the State Department," Gwen remarked, "this kind of celebrity approach to foreign policy. Someone needs to explain to the American government, This isn't a Hollywood gossip column, forget Yeltsin and his—"

"Yeah, have you ever noticed how we go for the guys with the really good hair?" James Otis, a towhead himself, put in.

"—It doesn't really matter who's prime minister this week, this is about very large boring institutions that need to change, it's about tax collection, it's about regional governors out in Ufa, it's about rehauling social security, putting some kind of financial regulatory board in place. Remember the Raoul Hilberg school of Holocaust studies? It's not about Hitler, it's not about Göring, it's about some clerk at a desk writing out the order forms for more Zyklon B . . . I mean, I thought the whole point of Clinton was he was supposed to be a wonk."

"Not a wonk, unfortunately—a wank," Bill said, glumly.

"Mumma? Mumma? Me no sleep!"

The piping pronouncement came from a plump child peeking through a crack in the hall door.

"*Try* to sleep, my love," urged Jamila.

But the child, seeing her mother was not angry, hurtled across the living room parquet into Jamila's lap. And Jamila, stroking her daughter's dark gold curls, described to Jim Otis the philistinism of her editor, who, when she tried to pitch him a story about how the old Great Game was being replayed over Caspian gas fields, replied, "Did I hear Caspian? Now why don't you send us a nice story about *caviar* . . ." "I thought, Fine, if you're only interested in Lifestyle pieces, you might have sent me to Vienna." And Bill, meanwhile, was pumping Gwen to find out what she knew about Lavrinsky's investments in Russia . . .

"Mumma, me no sleep!" Tatiana repeated.

"I know, my darling, I know you no sleep," Jamila replied, soothingly. And sidelong to Gwen, "God, I *must* stop talking baby talk. Some nights Bill and I come home so tired we find ourselves parroting at each other, Me no hung-ee, me eat cake."

"It's abject," Bill confirmed, glumly. "Spending your life between Russian politicians and two-year-olds really does knock a couple of digits off the IQ."

"Bill, did I tell you what I heard from Tolya this afternoon?"

"No."

"About who paid for Luzhkov's birthday party?"

"No . . ."

Every time Gwen went to see Bill and Jamila—the only cloud in whose very happy life was that Jamila wanted badly to have a second child but kept miscarrying—she found herself thinking, Maybe I could stand being married. But unfortunately, you couldn't just look at the Sachses' marriage and say, I'll have one of those. It had obviously taken all Jamila's domestic-erotic genius to convert Bill, a sallow mournful fellow inclined to upset stomachs, into a model husband, a valorous companion.

And wasn't it strange, how Gwen's heart was aching, aching from missing Gideon, how her heart felt an indigestible lump in her chest? She sat, thinking, Two more weeks is too long; I'm going to have to cut this trip short. Thinking, with a kind of dread, Who is this man? Where is this heading? (As if love might be the fairy lights that led you over the cliff . . .)

But after another week on the road, Gwen's Gideon-sickness was past, and she had no more thoughts of coming home early. And that perhaps is what really should have worried you, Gwen: a week of mortal longing, and once you got past that hump, it was over.

2

ON HER LAST NIGHT in St. Petersburg, Gwen had dinner at the Tsarevich with Georgiy Semyonov, who was deputy to a liberal MP. Most of these "reformers" Gwen, like her friend Bill, found pretty suspect: intriguers, spoilers, prima donnas without a larger loyalty. Semyonov's boss, a former dissident mathematician, was different: she had backed Yeltsin during the storming of the White House, and now was an equally outspoken opponent of the various mafia/KGB/nationalist influences octopussing around Yeltsin's sclerotic throne.

Gwen had met her back in the eighties, when she was giving Gorbachev hell for not releasing political prisoners: a middle-aged woman who didn't look as if she'd make sixty: two bypasses, steel teeth, a bulldog's wheeze, her health broken by a diet of cigarettes and hunger strikes.

Georgiy—her subaltern—was twenty-eight years old. He was telling Gwen about death threats and attempted assassinations, a car bomb that had gone off too soon, he was telling her what a lousy gangster-state they were living in, how Yeltsin had become this sultan who each week threw his latest vizier into the sea in a sack full of stones. He had an angry little bark of a laugh.

"What can we do to help you?" Gwen asked. "Allow Lavrinsky to corrupt you—we can pay much more money than the lousy mafia. You know the lesson of the Cold War—the only way to beat the Enemy is to outspend it."

"What can you do for us?" said Georgiy. He laughed mirthlessly. "For a start, you could stop the war in Chechnya. You can get your president, the IMF, the World Bank, the leaders of the European Union, to tell Yeltsin, Pull your soldiers out of Chechnya, or else we will cut off the dollar pipeline, we will throw you out of the Council of Europe, we will—"

His recitation—checked off on slim fingers—was interrupted by a muffled bleating.

Whose phone? His? Hers? Unfortunately hers.

"And why do you think Chechnya is the heart of the problem?" Gwen asked. Ignoring the bleat.

He stared at her, his pale eyes inexpressive. "Are you familiar with Russian history?"

She made an impatient face, glanced at her phone.

"Russia, in its own mind, exists as a bulwark against Islam. There are two possibilities for countries today. Number One: You can get rich. Number Two: You can make holy war. Russia is failing at Number One, because we are too lazy, and because this mentality survives where we would rather everybody's cows die than the neighbor's cow gets fat, so now we choose Number Two. You have no idea how many of our enlightened colleagues are defending the war in Chechnya, saying the West should thank us for wiping out these dirty Muslim terrorists who are worming their way into European Christian civilization. Exactly as Serbs were saying in Bosnia: We are doing this for *you*. I don't know if you have been paying attention to the support the Russian Orthodox church gives to Milosevic: this is not an open tolerant religion with a good history of humanism—"

"Excuse me," Gwen said. Looked at her watch and realized it might be . . . "Alo?"

Gideon, voice pent-up hysterical. "Sweetheart? Can you hear me? I've been trying to get through since—can you talk?"

Impossible to say No. Impossible to tell that panicky voice, Try me again later. Sure, she said, but in fact she was constrained. There was no way round it: she was a tin woman just barely riveted together, not fluid or self-assured enough to fuse personae and time zones, to talk pillow talk on the job. (Scanning to see if there was a private place to escape to, but no, they'd already bagged the quietest corner of this noisy restaurant.)

"Excuse me," she said to Georgiy. "Home emergency."

And here came Gideon's voice, insect-buzzy. "You there, sweetheart? I miss you so badly I can't *breathe*."

"Me, too."

"I haven't slept since you left."

"I can't do anything *but* sleep," she replied, low. Dead ashamed to be cooing baby talk in front of this marked man who was ready to die for his political beliefs. Dead ashamed to be ashamed.

"I can't hear you, honey. Can you . . . I went over to your apartment just to . . . smell you, but it made it worse."

"MMmmmm. I'm sure."

Georgiy Semyonov, a busy man, was looking at his watch, searching for papers in his briefcase. He was too young to have a wife and children, too driven to entertain a love life that might interfere with his work. She signalled regret—one moment more and she'd be with him.

"Honey? Hello? You there, honey? It's kind of . . . fading in and out. Can you hear me?"

"Hello!"

"I just don't think I can hack ten more days . . ."

"Do you want to meet me in London?"

"What?"

"Do you—"

"I don't know. Maybe. Can you hear me? I don't know. Hello? Can you hear me? I don't know . . . We're pretty busy . . ."

She said, conscious of sounding fake, "Please do. Come to London. It would be wonderful. Will you let me buy you a ticket?" Sounding to her own ears tea-party insincere. Unable to handle the dissonance.

bruxsvzjsgifgftyteew3q34qxcxcf . . . Then the teeny humming voice again. *gfdrtertrfffxxxxsersdfxdxdsawaxdfxersreds.*

"What did you say? I can't hear you. Maybe we should talk later."

"I CAN'T."

"Can you hear me?"

He repeated, "I can't just hop on a plane to London—I've got a production to—"

Guilty relief when the connection broke for good.

She returned the phone to her briefcase. Looked up at Georgiy Semyonov, who put away his papers. Ambitious little throat-cutter. Speared a cold meatball in dill before the waiter took their plates away.

"That's a reminder," she said, smiling. "Why you want your country to become normal. So you can spend your evenings arranging your love life, instead of worrying about car bombs."

3

GIDEON LEFT LA MERCED after a meeting with Sancho and their new lawyer, and walked across town in the rain. Not going anywhere special. Just stretching his legs. Just thinking.

There was a mini-playground on East Houston, empty as usual of children. A couple of drunks arguing. People had gathered to watch as one of them—a tall skinny Rasta—broke the head off a bottle and, brandishing the jagged stub, ran at the other man. Amazing how fast a police car arrived. Gray day, darkness—never gotten light. Raining, sludging.

This was his life, he thought. East Houston Street, slush, wholesale lighting stores along the Bowery, murderous crazies in the playground. If he didn't watch out, that was how he'd end his days, too: a murderous crazy in the Bowery. He'd read that by 2050 people were no longer going to die of ill health, but in his family (the legacy of long poverty), they tended to punk out young. And suddenly he wanted—badly—to be transported into the glowing opulence that surrounded Gwen. The hotel bedrooms, the airport limousines, the saunas, the personnel paid to make her way smooth.

He was thinking about her so hard that he could smell her. Smell the new-washed cotton of her underpants, smell her thick gold hair, the toastiness of her naked blond skin, the milky-coffee on her breath, and underbitterness of nerves, that made up the olfactory complex of her.

Smelled deeper, imagined his nose burrowing into the underpants and got just the teeniest surge in his cock, which had been freeze-dried for the last two weeks, a geriatric he helped in and out of his pants only when it needed to pass water. Imagined his tongue searching out the tiny glutinous cherry-pink minnow of her clit and now felt his cock *awaken*. Like a dog from its sleep, shudder, rise on stiff legs, shake itself, and lunge into three-quarters alert, imparting to its owner a sudden spurious resolve.

Slicker pulled down over his still-poked-out jeans, he ran down the steps into a Spanish travel agent offering *Viajes! Viajes! Viajes!* Special deals to Santo Domingo. And bought a ticket to London; Air India, leaving Tuesday night, back on Sunday. That one unavailing hard-on had cost him four hundred dollars—four hundred dollars he didn't have, and he put it on the Visa card he'd made a New Year's resolution not to use. Four hundred dollars that if he did have, he would have put toward summer camp for Ethan.

4

Gideon held the ticket in his pocket for a day, while he gathered his nerve. Then he told the crew that next week he was going to England.

Kill me, his dog-eyes begged, flay me alive. I'm flying to London so I can canoodle with my girlfriend in a five-star hotel (their having flubbed their first chance at the Sibirsk last September) while you guys get chilblains in a Lower East Side squat.

But his mates appeared genuinely pleased.

"Cool," said Hector. "Bring me back a double-decker bus."

"Wow," said Andrea. "What's playing in London?"

Gideon hadn't been sure what he was going to say. "A woman I like."

"Is it Gwen?"

"It's Gwen."

Dina broke out into a congratulatory round of *"Siman tov oo-mazel tov!"* Encircled him in her arms, forcing him to dance along with her, forehead to forehead. Their Gid was in love!

And now everybody knew it, and what a relief to be unburdened of the aggravating mystery.

Chapter Seven

I

"YOU'RE ASLEEP AGAIN. I thought you had an afternoon panel."

He seated himself on the edge of the bed, switched on a sliver of halogen.

Gwen shielded her eyes, groaning. "I do. What time is it?" Not half so worried as she should have been. "Five-thirty? Jesus!"

She had slipped back upstairs to her hotel room at lunch break, in between sessions. Friday, last day of the conference. Feeling fluish. Taken a shower, popped some more vitamin C. Stretched out on the bed for a moment, and Holy shit . . . Five-thirty? She might still be able to catch the final half hour, but instead she sank into a deeper grogginess. Shit. As it was, there was already a dinner tonight she was crapping out of . . .

He stroked her cheek, pushed the heavy hair out of her eyes, worried. A little reproachful.

"What did you do this afternoon?" she asked, wishing he would leave so she could go back to sleep.

He cleared his throat, frowning. "I went to look at St. Paul's, and then I walked across the bridge and went to a show on the South Bank. Are you hungry?"

"No, just sleepy."

"Well, let's go out and get some air, otherwise you won't be able to sleep tonight."

2

HE WAS FULL OF IMPRESSIONS. He wanted to tell her everything he had seen these last few days, tramping around by himself. How powerfully this city had impressed him with its soot-darkened grandeur: domes, turrets, arcades pockmarked by war, and still . . . immensely suggestive of Imperium. How, when you crossed Waterloo Bridge in the early darkness, the Thames glimmered below like a black pearl—moist, melancholy, winding the town around its intestinal banks. And downstream rose the Tower where queens had been beheaded . . .

This place for centuries had been a center to things that Gideon loved. He had been to Marx's grave in Highgate, and the Bevis Marks synagogue in the City; he'd walked along the canal from Camden Town to the Isle of Dogs with an English puppeteer he'd met on tour last fall, who ran his theater out of a houseboat.

That the trip was his first "vacation" since high school made Gideon avid not to waste a moment. Admittedly, he had flown across the Atlantic not on purpose to see the Tower of London, but to see it with Gwen, to wander hand in hand through this old beautiful place which was immeasurably familiar, and yet where they knew no one. Turning the big beam of her intelligence on this fresh subject.

He had been cheerful enough about her professional duties, knowing the weekend stretched ahead. There were a million things Gideon intended them to do—fringe theater in upstairs rooms of pubs that was dirt-cheap, Brick Lane street market. He had even—and this was his shyest concession—offered to accompany her to the Burlington Arcade: a glass-hooped aviary in whose tiny astronomically expensive shops Gwen bought her Harris-tweed riding jackets and shetland sweaters. Taking Gwen shopping—rather, tagging along on her pursuit of the Ideal—was the most frightening prospect he had yet entertained in connection with this woman: certain social humiliation, joined with an unaccustomed irrelevance—being relegated to the ancillary position of husband, almost. (What were you supposed to *do* while a woman tried on clothes? Was bringing along a book considered uncompanionable?)

But Gwen from the moment he'd arrived at her hotel Wednesday morning had seemed a different person. Not her acute nervy self, but . . . dull. Remote. Perplexingly unresponsive. She was tired, she explained. She had flu, she thought. She'd had an exhausting time in Russia. She did not want to talk. She did not want to listen. She did not want to explore. She didn't even want (much) to fuck, making Gideon's massive hots for her seem like a semiannoyance. She only wanted to sleep.

And Gideon paced their hotel room, caged. Unwanted. Hiding his resentment in briskness, in activity. Came back bursting with all he'd seen and done without her, and then—enthusiasm fizzled out, under her heavy indifference.

Tonight, she had roused herself for an outing. Made a reservation (her treat, he was warned) at a fashionable restaurant up the Thames that Constance recommended.

3

Chintz-curtained darkness. Gideon is stroking Gwen's back. Gwen, who has just sicked up the evening's special of squid in black ink—a creepily delicious thing for which Gideon, too, has broken his highly frangible part-time dietary compunctions—lies, still shuddering.

"You know something, my queen?"

"MMMMMmmmmm . . . What?"

No answer.

She swivels. "What?" she repeats.

"I'm wild about you. You know what else?"

"No. What?"

"You're pregnant." His smile hides his terror.

"Oh, bullshit." Now she struggles upright. His Gwen, back fighting. "Get out of here, Gid, I'm a little fluey, that's all. You know what Russia's like nowadays? They have TB, they have cholera, they have bubonic plague floating around, they've got these futuristic diseases they spent the Cold War hatching in their science-cities. I mean, a little flu is like winning the lottery, Merry Christmas, it's only flu."

"You're with child, my girl."

"Give me a break."

"You're pregnant," he repeats.

"I just had a period—what, just before I left."

"No you didn't—you had your last period—remember, that night Annie Dolores came to my show. That was the first day of it. That was like the middle of December. You're two weeks . . . you're more than two weeks overdue."

"I'm not pregnant, I ate a bad squid, that's all."

"Bad squid, naughty squid." They are both laughing now. "Sure, you ate a bad squid, you got jet lag, the dog ate your period. You're having a baby, girl. You are knocked up. In the family way."

She lies back, giggling. Then she stops. "Jesus, this is . . . terrifying. How can I be pregnant?"

"They didn't teach biology at Milton?"

"They taught sex ed. What about that little whoopee cushion I've been using?"

"Diaphragms split. Unscrupulous pharmaceutical companies cutting corners."

"But I'm thirty-one years old. I've been using birth control since I was twenty, and I've never been pregnant before. I'm the only person I know who's never been pregnant in her entire . . ." She tails off, leaving unvoiced what had been her not-altogether-sorrowful assumption that she was probably infertile.

"Sweetheart, you're fertile as Nile mud; you could spontaneously generate. I've always known that about you. You just weren't in love before."

She reflects, grumpy bordering on semifurious. What about her work? You couldn't go around Russia pregnant; Russia quite justifiably was the land of five abortions for each live birth. A voice in her head saying, But I've never wanted children . . . "I don't believe you," she says, once again.

"You don't have to believe me, we'll go to the drugstore—what do they call it here, a chemist!—and buy a little kit."

"Let's give it a few more days." And then, inconsequently, "Why'd I have to get pregnant the one time we go away together?"

"We'll go other places. We'll take the baby."

She looks nervous. "What—do you—you want to have the child? I mean, if I did . . . if I were pregnant, you'd want to go ahead and have it?" Tears' sting of amazement making her gulp. *"Are you sure?"*

"My girl, I think you're the best idea God ever had. I want sixty children with you."

"I thought you wanted to spend your life with Dina on rent control."

"Who said anything about living with you? All I'm asking for is visitation rights, loosely exercised," he teases, then, seeing her scared face, "Oh sweetheart, you want me to get down on my knees? I will, gladly. Please Be Mine. Be my wife, be my ball and chain, my *ezer-k'neged*, my inspiration . . ."

But Gwen once again is looking unconvinced. If this indeed is pregnancy, why should it make you sick and stupid? Whose fucked-up design's responsible? No wonder people thought of God as male.

4

AFTER THEIR RETURN to New York, after the drugstore kit had delivered its pink-threaded Yes, after Gwen's first visit to her stepmother's Upper East Side ob-gyn, Gideon remained officially ecstatic. Why not?

He had always loved babies; what a thrill to be getting one of his own. He was proud of her, his expectant girlfriend: hadn't he known that behind her crocodile-skin defenses was a natural woman, fertile, tender?

He was happy when he was with Gwen, which was almost always. (Faith in her native competence coexisting with a certainty that once out of his sight, she'd miscarry.) But as soon as he turned the corner, dread set in.

It couldn't *not*. You couldn't be a child raised by a grandmother because your single mother, run ragged by debt, couldn't manage, you couldn't have watched all these years the dispiriting wrangles between Dina and Michael over who was going to pay Ethan's bus fare, without getting a little reactionary. Without concluding, Children need stability. Financial and moral. Sunlight. Space. A daddy on salary, a mother at home, health insurance. You take your consequences: he had picked a rackety, chronically unremunerative profession, conducted in a dangerous, dirty, and expensive city. He might *never* be in a position to have children. Or perhaps not until he was sixty, which, let's be cruelly honest, was a male prerogative.

When he thought of family life, it was the image of Jerome and

Bridey that guided him: an eighteenth-century farmhouse in a valley with a stream, raising your own goats, baking your own bread, teaching your children the names of the stars. He didn't want to raise his kid in a fly-by-night Manhattan high-rise, never knowing its neighbors, with the basement health club as its outdoors.

Again and again, the due date loomed in his mind, unnegotiable. And with it, an inadmissible resentment at having been forced into emergency-parenthood by Gwen's contraceptive incompetence—spoiled rich girl, so used to other people's taking care of her that she couldn't even look after her own diaphragm. In his flintiest moments, Gideon tried to imagine Gwen as his wife, a helpmeet, a succor in rough times, and drew a blank. Instead, he pictured her Sub-Zero, empty but for vodka and olives. (Then, guilty, he forced himself to recollect her surprising generosity; he pictured her reading the child Russian fairy stories of witches who lived in houses on stilts, and he thought, Maybe. Maybe she had just what it took, maybe it was just what she needed, to ripen and let loose.)

Chapter Eight

Rehearsal breaking up.

"Look, what is it—three forty-five? We'll take an hour break. How about another full run-through at five, okay?"

"I gotta run uptown," said Andrea. "But I'll be back by five-thirty."

"And Dan, when's Dan getting off work today? Andy, do you mind giving Dan a call? Okay, guys, I'm just going out to pick up those extension cords. So we'll go for a full run-through at five-thirty. That okay by you, Amnon?"

On the stairs he met Dina, umbrella dripping.

"Where you headed, pardner?"

"To Jem's. You wanna come mit? I need to talk . . ."

Dina, who had a rotten head cold, snuffled assent.

What was it with this *weather*? The rain no longer pretending to be something merry and festive—no, just a mean, snivelling drizzle. Dark as night along Delancey Street as they brushed past stores that sold lighted restaurant signs: lurid pictures of pepperoni pizza, sizzling spareribs, their reds and oranges and yellows runny in the rain. Clusters of home-bound Chinese schoolchildren skipping over the puddles in thin sneakers. Gideon dodging oncomers' umbrella spikes.

Underworld New York, bargain-basement New York. His New York, first stop for indigent immigrants for a century and a half. That you fled as soon as you'd saved ten cents. New York of narrow storefronts advertising Rapid Divorce, Tax Bankruptcy, Immigration. Or, alternatively, the Pentecostal Temple of Heavenly Radiance. His New York, cozy, cheap, substandard, unhealthy. Incubator of epidemics. Soggy-wet.

"It wasn't too smart of me to make you tramp around in the rain with a cold, huh?"

They ducked into Jem's, past Easter bunnies and twelve-packs of basketball socks, made their purchases, companionably silent as old marrieds.

"Shall we try the Hat?"

A.k.a. the Sombrero. They chose a booth at the back. Baby-fat waitress wearing lilac lipstick: the owner's daughter. Dina ordered a cup of tea; Gideon asked for huevos rancheros and coffee. Spanish soap opera on the television.

Four in the afternoon. Dark. Dina was still wearing her raincoat—a beige trench coat, dark with wet, half plastered to her skin.

"Take your coat off, Dina. You want to catch pneumonia?"

Dina looked beat. Defeated. She ran a program at Kings County Hospital for substance abusers and their families. She had been talking for years about quitting. Working with children, which was what interested her. Her boss was a passive-aggressive bitch, always going behind Dina's back or overruling her recommendations; their department was criminally understaffed; she spent three-quarters of her time doing paperwork. Gideon felt sorry, suddenly, for not having galvanized Dina into finding something more rewarding.

"Deen?" he said, gently. Interrupting her grumble about how Kinshasa had been bad-mouthing her to Mel. (If Gideon moved out, who would Dina complain to? Not Ethan. That's why people married: to have someone to soak up the low-frequency anxiety of can you afford a new sewing machine, and where are the paper towels you just bought, and how your boss just dumped a lot of extra work on you to take home, when she knows you're only getting paid part-time.) "Dina, you know my friend Gwen?"

Dina looked blank. Then she perked up. "Eh voilà, the mystery lady from Siberia. I can't say I know her, Gid. You haven't exactly been bringing her around."

"I'd like you to get to know her. It's getting serious."

Dina fished the Lipton tea bag from her cup. Regarded the tag's picture of an old salt. Then she placed the tea bag in the ashtray. They both watched it seep tannic juice into the volcanic residue of ash. Dirty restaurant, the Sombrero.

"Well, Andy and I, we figured either it was love or you were getting recruited by the CIA—like, phone calls from Central Asia, day trips to London. My pet theory? The CIA was trying to infiltrate the puppet world as a way of . . . No, seriously, tell me about her. Are you happy?"

"I'm . . . delirious."

He hemmed some more.

"Nu? Nu? Come on, Wolkowitz, spit it out. So you went to see her in London and . . . I've known you awhile, Wolkowitz. I recognize that squinty look, either you're trying to pass gas discreetly or you—"

He gave up. "Gwen's pregnant. We're going to have a baby."

And now Dina relented. Mimed amazement. Threw her arms around him wide, clutching him tight to her wet-raincoated bosom. (Gideon feeling a familial relief-irritation as he relaxed into that damp pneumatic embrace.)

"Caloo calay o frabjous day, she chortled in her joy," sang Dina. "A baaay-beee? My little Giddy-goo's gonna be a daddy? I can't hardly believe it."

"*You* can't believe it? I'm still reeling."

"Blessings upon you, and upon all the House of Gideon. Eons of happiness and health. We need more babies in this troupe: a second generation of little Pantaloons . . ." Now she had genuine tears in her eyes. Fumbled for a handkerchief, blew her nose. "I hope your example's going to encourage Dan and Andy to get moving, already. When's her due date?"

He told her; watched Dina do an instant's calculation of how long he must have known and kept it to himself. "A Libra, like me. You could use a little balance in your life. You know, I've got all Ethan's baby clothes saved away: Gwen'll flip. Gorgeous stuff I can give you: embroidered booties and hand-knitted sweaters. Those Pintos really came through when Eeth was a tot . . . And just think, you already know how to *do* all that diaper-changing, bottle-warming shit men spend the first two years of parenthood pretending is beyond their IQ capacity. Your bride owes me big-time . . ."

He listened to Dina's chatter, sopping up with ketchup-soaked toast the last of his huevos rancheros, and felt as if his stomach were full of stones. Dina was a diplomat. Who knew what she was really thinking, beneath her formal delight?

"So're you going to marry the maiden?"

"I'm hoping to," he replied, evasively.

She was full of practical questions Gideon hadn't thought of. How much maternity leave did Gwen get, was she going to keep on working full-time? Her dad was an entertainment lawyer? Did she have enough money from home *not* to work, or did she live entirely off her salary?

As Gideon answered, his discomfort eased. From Dina's perspective, he'd landed in the gravy, for sure. Gwen's trust fund, her salary, her five-room condo on the Upper West Side, were practical blessings unequivocal as good health. How jolly it would be for Gideon to have some margin of comfort, not to have to worry about being able to provide for his child.

"Have you met her folks yet? I don't need to tell you this, Gidele, right—liking your spouse is much less important than liking your in-laws. You gotta take a long hard look at your mother-in-law and say, Here in thirty years comes my bride . . ."

Was she Jewish? No? Dina trying to look neutral. Well, Gwen's dad was some kinda self-hating Jew who didn't want to talk about it; and her mom was this New England WASP, she had ancestors who'd . . .

Trying to get a feel for their intentions, Dina posed the kind of questions a family clergyman might ask: did, for instance, the happy couple intend this to be an old-timey marriage, one roof, joint account, Mr. and Mrs. Wolkowitz, and Baby Ditto, or were they envisaging some sort of bohemian-professional fudge, some hippie-yuppie truce where each kept his own name and apartment and they spent alternate weekends at the other's house?

Gideon replied, stammering with sincerity, that the issue to him wasn't marriage or no marriage, he didn't care who was called what, they could call themselves Fido or Shit-face, he could change his name a third time, the issue was love, and love, to his way of thinking, had nothing to do with bank accounts, it was an absolute. The love of a man and a woman, their vows to cleave to each other, forsaking all others, and that love's being embracing enough to sustain and nurture another human life, maybe several of 'em.

"Right on," said Dina, giving him a Can-the-boilerplate look.

(And as often happens, having made his speech, Gideon then believed it. Shame on him for his niggling bourgeois worries and covert want of faith.)

"Dina?"

"Gideon?"

"I hope you two'll like each other okay."

"Of course we'll like each other. Do we have a choice? *Te giuro,* we'll be old ladies in Florida together, complaining how our grandchildren never call."

He tried to down a last mouthful of cold hash browns. Couldn't swallow. Stomach surging against the unspeakable. What generous Dina was forbidding herself to feel, he knew, was the disparity in their lots: Gideon, glowing with his imminent marriage, his glamorous bride, while Dina, after the gruelling day's work, would still be stuck in the dim fluorescent tubing of their cruddy walk-up, cooking Ethan franks and beans that the kid wouldn't eat. And in not so many years, no more Ethan.

Why such a discrepancy in fates which had long been twinned? Because he was a man, which meant that his life lay before him, the field of desirable women wide-open. Whereas Dina, prematurely middle-aged from hauling a dismal shit-paying job and raising a son on her own, Dina statistically was more likely to get hijacked by Abu Nidal than find a fellow.

That was what no one wanted to admit, in this new world of unlimited sex and surgically perpetuated youth, Gideon reflected—that most people still weren't getting any. Guys who were too screwed up to ask. Ex-wives who were too saggy and discouraged to compete with twenty-year-olds with breasts like lilies.

"Dina?"

"What?"

"Are you going to be able to manage the rent on your own?"

"Of course," she said. Rolled eyes. "If Ethan gets into Stuyvesant next year, I'll have gazillions to spare. If he doesn't, you and Gwyn—"

"Gwen."

"—can adopt him."

BOOK FOUR

Chapter One

I

LUNCH AT LES HIRONDELLES, mid-Manhattan. Spring 1996.

A four-person slow-motion frieze. The older man pushes open the heavy glass door, ushering the women before him. The younger man (if this were an antique bas-relief, he would be child-sized) hesitates, hangs back, is rushed into the general sweep of females. The elder divests the women of their coats; the younger man is left to dispose of his own.

The older man then executes this rather biblical move—think patriarch Jacob greeting Esau—of sailing the two women forward, into the wide river of light—ahead of him, yet visibly still under his magical protection. Where they bob for a moment, conspicuous in the clamorous brightness, till they are met by a dark-suited hierophant, who manages to circle behind them in order to welcome the older man.

A welcome—handshakes, squeezes, jovial laughter, first names and last names: Gérard, Monsieur Lewis, jokes, inquiries after health, play insults—which is then extended, more deferentially, to the two women. (Teasing is male-to-male flirtation.) The younger man hangs behind, unintroduced.

The hierophant then ushers the women to a table where, once more, they stand waiting for the older man to tell them where to sit.

2

THE FIRST FAMILY MEETING.

Gwen, after neurotic procrastination, has finally devoted a morning to telephoning her family and friends, to inform them that she is about to marry a person she's never mentioned. Martin, caught on his car phone on the way to the airport, in his matching terror at once fobs her off on his secretary Melanie.

Jacey likes to joke that Martin divorced his second wife for dissing Melanie. It is true that Jacey, by contrast, instantly sized up this mynah-voiced frosted-blond grass widow as the person closest to Martin's essential being. (Even Gwen, as a little girl, had known it was Melanie she had to thank for the birthday roller skates or the toy soda fountain from FAO Schwarz, or for *ever* getting to see her father, usually on after-school visits to his office in Rockefeller Plaza.)

Thus it was Melanie who has offered, with much ribbing, the congratulations Martin flubbed, demanding that she be invited to Gwen's hen party at the male strip joint, and who—studying Martin's calendar—at once suggests a family get-together over lunch on the twenty-fifth at Les Hirondelles, which is two blocks from Martin's office. One of those grand French restaurants to which Gwen's friend Christopher, as a twenty-one-year-old show-off, used to take his friends, but which Martin Lewis no longer frequents because it is too time-consuming, too high-cholesterol, because in the new business environment people tend to have meetings rather than "lunch."

Gérard, the owner, returns to make more fuss over Martin. They chat about Gérard's plans to retire very soon to his farmhouse in the Auvergne. They talk about Martin and Jacey's recent trip to Paris, Martin rating in laborious detail all the restaurant meals they had consumed. Jacey compliments Gérard on his flowers. (It is his daughter-in-law who arranges them.) And Gwen, mid-nerves and mid-nausea, feels a surge of pleasure at the towers of lilies around the room, the starched white table linen, the staid florid waiters, the murals of cornucopia and nymphs, the moneyed hush. Really, how civilized these old-fashioned French restaurants are, compared to the brash frenzy of the garage spaces she and her friends frequent, with their heroin-chic waitresses, deafening sound systems, and menus offering tuna chirashi with mango salsa, as if food were invented yesterday and will be out of fashion tomorrow.

Gérard has given them a banquette at the front, from which Jacey can spot friends or clients. Jacey, who comes from Texas, has a professional interest in New York society.

"Look, there's Pamela Short," she nudges her stepdaughter. "You know how she stays so thin?"

"No, how?"

"Colonic irrigation."

"*Not* at mealtime," Jacey's husband intervenes.

"These, like, turbo-jet enemas? She says they're better than sex . . ."

"For what?"

"For staying thin."

"They might be better than sex with *her*," Martin concedes.

Gideon's eyebrows rocket in his first smile of the day. Gideon had refused any guidance in what to wear to lunch, and Gwen—hoping he would stun her dad with his Huckleberry-Finn-on-acid grunge-appeal—is disappointed by his choices.

He is wearing a suit which must originally have been bought for someone's graduation: beige permanent press, with a dejected-looking striped tie—no, she would never have believed he owned a tie, and especially not that tie. In this restaurant, he looks like what—a clergyman off-duty? And Martin has not yet addressed a word to him . . .

Jacey, as if making up for her husband's oversight, is talking to Gideon about vacation spots, they are thinking of taking the kids for Easter to St. Lucia, which some people don't like because the sand is black! (Gwen can see Gideon, nodding solemnly, is trying not to get the giggles.)

Martin, on the other hand, is too preoccupied by what he's going to eat and whether or not to order a bottle of wine to join the conversation. He is getting increasingly irritated by his guests' refusal to attend to business.

"Jacey, will you please be quiet a minute," he interrupts, finally. "Gérard is trying to tell us the day's specials."

They listen, Gwen lulled by the recitation of dishes that you never encountered anymore because they were too rich, too labor-intensive for modern people. Jacey and Martin embroiled in a supposedly humorous tussle over whether he's going to have the roast pork with gratin dauphinois or ask the chef to grill him a Dover sole, no sauce. (Guess who won?) Gwen, realizing too late that there isn't a single item on the menu that Gideon, even with his pick-and-choose approach to the Jewish dietary laws, can eat.

3

GIDEON HAS GONE STIFF, disapproving—a look Gwen has never seen before.

In truth, Gideon is confused by the discrepancy between his pre-conceptions about Martin Lewis—agent of the Entertainment Industry that is destroying Gideon's art, a blot upon the name of Israel, the source of most of Gwen's unhappiness—and the actual appearance of the man: short, freckly, evidently flustered. A Jewish redhead, with russet hair and furtive brown eyes. You feel almost sorry for him, pinned by these high-maintenance women—this man who, like it or not, is about to become the grandfather of Gideon's child.

Nor does Jacey—small, dark, with a pointed face clever and anxious as a fox terrier's—live up to his image of a Texan gold digger. She looks Jewish, which has never occurred to him. Which obviously has never occurred to Gwen, either. God help them all!

Martin and Jacey are quarrelling. It isn't the ideal moment, but they are evidently a scrappy couple—that's how their sexual energy runs, her goading, till he clamps her quiet—and a fight has blown up out of nowhere. Jacey has come from a meeting at Dalton where the school psychologist has recommended that they put Alexander on Ritalin. Jacey is livid.

Martin thinks she should consider the man's suggestion, why not try Ritalin, and if it doesn't work, no harm done.

"No harm?"

"I certainly think we should consider it. If the doctor—"

"He's not a doctor . . ."

"If the adviser—"

"No."

"Well, why don't you call Dr. Hattauer and see what he thinks?"

"Martin, I don't understand your exaggerated respect for authorities. For these, like, self-appointed experts."

Martin hikes an eyebrow at Gwen and Gideon. "This is my reward for marrying a child of the sixties."

"I just don't believe these flavor-of-the-month diagnostic labels are especially helpful. I mean, what does attention deficit disorder mean, besides fidgety? I mean, frankly, Martin, if somebody tried to sit *you* down at a teeny tiny desk and make *you* listen for forty-five minutes about, um, soil erosion in the Ozarks, I think you'd get a little . . . restless? I mean, Martin, you don't even have the attention span to go to these parent-teacher meetings, you want to stigmatize your only son?"

"He's not my only son." (Jacey biting her lip, briefly stricken.) "You mean I should take Ritalin? Fine, I'm happy to take Ritalin. Me and Alexander both, we'll take Ritalin."

"No. Not fine. Just because somebody's a so-called adviser or has a so-called degree in whatever doesn't mean you have to let them *sedate* your—"

"I thought Ritalin wasn't a sedative, it was—"

"That's right, it's a stimulant, it's a . . . a . . . a performance enhancer, like a steroid."

"I don't think either of us have enough information . . ."

"Maybe he should try colonic irrigation," Gwen suggests.

"Weight is *not* his problem."

"What is?" asks Gideon, in his most innocently interested voice.

"What? Nothing. Nothing is the problem. There is no problem. He's like a normal *active* nine-year-old who likes playing computer games and hates reading books. The school is the problem. We are paying this school, like, forty grand a year; I spend one day out of my week in a Day-Glo orange traffic warden's *apron* escorting children across the street; we are constantly going to these auctions and fundraisers and *potluck dinners,* is it too much to expect that they in return make some kind of commitment to educate our kids, to teach them some good learning habits? It's, like, beneath their dignity, beyond the school's capacity to tell a boy to sit still? I mean, it's such a selfish scumbag—"

"Jacey—"

"Excuse me. It's such a cop-out, your son distracts the other children, we're afraid he's gonna bring down our scores, so here's the deal, either *you* dope him into submission or *we* fire him—"

"Jacey, enough." Martin has assumed the cold, strong-arm look of when the long-forbearing riot police suddenly descend on the protesters. The fun is over, the subject closed, let's get back to black beaches. Jacey sighs, shoots him a dirty look, and is diverted into lower-decibel conversation with Gwen about other Dalton parents, whose truly quadrophonic wealth ("I mean it, they make Martin and I look like charity parents . . .") seems to inspire in her equal parts fascination, envy, revulsion, and respect.

4

MARTIN FOCUSES WEARILY on the young man opposite. Weedy. A lost soul. The beard obviously in compensation for his total baldness—Chugga never said the guy was bald. Gwen's husband-to-be? Something tells him that this marriage is not going to happen, that if he just stays quiet, this person's gonna go away.

"So Chugga tells me you're in the theater. You got your own company?"

"I'm a puppeteer."

"I used to know Jim Henson when I worked for public television. You ever come across Jim? That is some empire he created, for a guy who likes to play with dolls. Of course, since his death the company's made some bad calls, but there's still a lot of potential in the name. Chugga went to school with his daughter, didn't you, Chug?"

"She left in second grade," says Gwen.

"It's a boom business, children's entertainment. My good friend Mort Brenner is on the board of Nickelodeon, which our kids are nuts about. Remind me, Chug, to get you together sometime with Mort . . ."

Gideon is now sitting upright as a Buddha. Looking—for him—demure.

"Gideon's not into television," Gwen explains. "He doesn't even use recorded sound in his plays."

"What do you mean, not *into* television?"

"I'm that kind of a Luddite freak," confirms Gideon, agreeably.

"What's that mean?"

"Martin's a total addict," Jacey interposes.

"Well, I don't go firebombing ABC, but I wouldn't want a set in my house."

Martin nods, acknowledging the humorous tone with a grim Heh-heh. Yanking his head around to see where Gérard's got to. He's going to have to get back to the office. "How do you feel about, uh, electricity or . . . penicillin?"

"You mean, do I think television cures disease or—or lights up the house?"

"Wait till you have kids of your own—I promise you, you'll get a television," says Martin. (Is this, Gwen wonders, a lone reference to their intended union?) And now, after a prodding glance from Jacey, he resumes the friendly questioning. Where do you perform? What kind of audiences do you get? Where does your funding come from? He asks just enough to get a picture and this picture to him is obviously pathetic.

"Well, Gideon, your work sounds very . . . uh . . . what shall I say . . . very high-minded. I guess Gwen'll let us know when you've got something playing. But I don't know, I guess I belong to a different end of the industry. Jacey takes me out to Brooklyn—my partner's wife's on the board of BAM—and I say, Wake me up when it's over; this is too much like work. In my business, entertainment's entertainment. With you guys, it's gotta stop global warming or promote homosexuality or whatnot."

"That's me," replies Gideon, cheerfully. "My next show, in fact, is called *Be Gay or Die!*"

Heh-heh-heh, says Martin. Ha-ha, said Jacey.

Jacey, spying a potential ally, begins telling Gideon, in low conspiratorial tones, how much she loves new-wave performance art, how she's this longtime supporter of Bill T. Jones, but Martin's such a stick-in-the-mud. Unless there's a client involved, he's in bed by ten.

Martin, meanwhile, is telling Gwen about their trip to Paris—a business trip for Martin, in which he'd persuaded Jacey to meet him on her own for five days.

"Paris, to my way of thinking, is a city for adults. But you know Jacey, she's like this not-without-my-children, earth-mother type. I twisted her arm."

"Not *much*," smirks Jacey. "I'd been dreaming of Paris since I was . . . Serena's age. We had a ball," she informs Gideon, "and we brought back the cutest clothes for the kids. All the big French designers have kiddie sections now. Junior Dior."

"What a racket," sighs Martin, with satisfaction. "Two hundred dollars for a shirt they grow out of in three months."

Over coffee, he has one last go at his prospective son-in-law. "Is Wolkowitz a common name? W-O-L-K, right?"

"Right. Well, no, not very."

"I was in the army with a guy called Wolkowitz from Minneapolis. I guess that wasn't your dad?"

"My dad's name was Brager."

Seemingly casual questions—where did you grow up, where did you go to college. Martin himself went to Harvard, he'd thought Gwen was nuts not to apply, these colleges as far as he's concerned are a hundred grand of nothing, so why not go for the fancy name that gets you a job?

"I didn't go to college. I was already working by then."

"With the puppets?" asks Martin. As if he were still hopeful that this is maybe some hobby the man does on weekends, when he isn't running a hedge fund.

Gideon looking more and more miserable.

Martin returns to Gwen, telling her about his new skin doctor who's taken a mole off Jacey's back, he seriously recommends this doctor whose clients include all kinds of big names Gwen's never heard of, Gwen should go and have that spot on her face checked, he'll get Melanie to call and give her the number, the guy's office is right around the corner from Lavrinsky.

Gideon startled, displeased by this rival proprietariness (that's *his* mole, the bold little black one by her chin) which he hasn't been expecting from her stories of the absentee father.

Suddenly, they are paid up. Martin rises, pocketing his platinum card, extracting tips for waiter, maître d'hôtel, coat check girl. The women slide out of the red leather banquette, disrupting chairs in their exodus, and the three of them idle by the door, waiting for Gwen—who now needs to pee on the quarter hour. Up the short flight of three, four, five steps, and . . . out. Into the crisp Manhattan blueness. Cold spring. A rush of women in billowy fake-fur coats, of messenger boys in Lycra tights on bicycles, of office workers returning from their lunch break.

No nonsense about Which way are you going, would you like to share a cab, Jacey (who's late for a meeting with a client at the D&D building) offers her stepdaughter one of those stiff-armed martial-arts hugs that actually push you away, and a handshake version of the same for Gideon, followed by a warmer shake from Martin, he has nice hot hands, Good to meet you, Gideon. All the best. (Practically effusive in his relief to escape.) I guess Gwen'll let us know when your next uh show is on.

5

ON THEIR WAY to Madison to put Gwen on a bus, Gideon remained silent. Had Gwen told her father they were getting married, that she was pregnant? I.e., Was it Gwen's ashamed reticence that was to blame, or had it been her father's genuine intent to insult him? Speechless with rage at Martin Lewis's unconcealed assumption that Gideon was somehow after something of his. Helpless, at finding himself in a milieu in which he was regarded not as a prize, or even just blood-familiar, but a predator. An incompetent predator.

You know something, he wanted to tell Gwen's father, all the added value you've given your daughter I consider trash. Your scramble to escape your working-class background and become valedictorian of the estimable public high school (yeah, that was the golden age before you Republicans made sure *on ideological principle* that an inner-city kid could no longer get a decent education) that would wing you on to Harvard, your ascent to law school, your apotheosis as partner of This, trustee of That, and eventually some wing of New York Hospital to be named after you as mausoleum: this classic American success story, which is supposed to warm our hearts and lacrimate our eyes, *makes me sick.* What you've done your best to bury—parents who came over steerage, pious or socialist we don't know (judging from your antipathy to the left we may surmise the latter), dad who drove a baker's truck (that much Gwen remembered Katrina's once having intimated)—is the *only* thing about you I respect. (That, and perhaps Jacey, who had surprised Gideon with her maternal fierceness.)

Gwen pacing beside him, equally lost in dark thought, suddenly turned and grabbed his hand. Tight. At first Gideon didn't respond, then he squeezed back. The warm pressure like the first signs of resuscitation. "You might like my mom better," she said, with a wan grin. He twisted her a doubtful look.

Then they both started laughing. Laughing, smooching, tripping over each other. Gideon pulled her down a side street, until they came to a store whose windows were whitewashed, "Lost Our Lease," and he mashed her into its darkened doorway. His hand up her skirt and into her drawers.

Gwen laughing helplessly as his licked finger sought the vertical tunnel, shielding her with his body from the gaze of any passersby. Sticky, yielding, his. High up the dark passage there was a tiny seedling growing that was also his, and that knowledge too was obscurely exciting.

"What is this, an attempted abortion?"

"A back-alley colonic irrigation."

"Yum . . ."

"Oh my queen, my—"

"Oooo—there."

God, she loved him. Because they could have this gruelling inquisition-lunch, and all he said, giggling, was, "Your poor dad—what'd he ever do to deserve me? Man, did you see his wild eyes rolling for the exit sign? Like, I send my daughter to the best private schools and I end up with a kosher juggler for a son-in-law? This wouldna happened if you'd gone to Harvard, Gwen."

Chapter Two

GOD HELP US from getting what we want.

GIDEON BORROWED SANCHO'S VAN THAT SUNDAY, and it was done. One load of cardboard boxes, and the Vanderveer was home. It was worth the dent to his principles just to witness Gwen's appalled face when she realized that she was going to have to give up not just half a closet but a major row of bookshelves. Did he really have to have so many things, hand-to-mouth Gideon? And did his things have to be so sprawling, so dingy? (Gideon didn't realize Gwen's apartment had an aesthetic until he came to violate it.)

God help us from getting what we ask for. Friday evening, Gwen comes home to find her living room a midden of dirty socks, rancid-wet towels, cups ringed in moldy coffee, and a splayed broken-spined library book she herself is in the middle of reading (does Gideon really want to know about Stalin's dying anti-Jewish purge, the so-called Doctors' Plot?)

In the study, Gideon, wearing his bathrobe, is yakking on the telephone, just loud enough so she can't concentrate on anything else except how badly she herself needs to use that same telephone line now monopolized by Lower East Side shmoozing.

"Don't you think we might open a window in here?" She strides over to the balcony, slides open the door, stares out blankly at the Empire State Building: another thwarted loner.

Great spirits occupy themselves with virtue; small spirits with territory, said Confucius, and no doubt the punkier the territory the fiercer the little spirit's preoccupation. Gideon has a point: Gwen's never been a sharer. Her generosities have tended to be dispensed by U.S. mail or over the Internet; it's no accident her best friend lives in Singapore. Other Slavophiles she knows have a permanent turnover of ex-Muscovites camping on their sofa; Gwen, by contrast, has always come home to her apartment much as a Christian ascetic retired nightly to his coffin. And if she were asked right now, would she rather have Gideon or her study . . . well, Gideon, of course, but it's no joke changing your ways aged thirty-one and more privileged, less encumbered than a medieval king. (Hard question, to be posed to Manhattanites: would you rather have a lover or an extra room? The answer being, a lover with his own apartment.)

I have lived too long alone, Gwen thinks. I wake up on a Monday morning, and what I really want to do before I leave for the office is not make love but read the paper. Soon, under his radiant tutelage, I will soften. But did they have to come both at once, father and child? Invaded, inside and out. So what you are left with, in fact, is neither sex nor the newspaper, but your head over the toilet bowl, puking up the morning's hormones, while your Beloved squats on the bathroom floor, stroking the backs of your knees and silently imploring your forgiveness with guilty eyes.

Chapter Three

"HEY DEEN, SORRY WE'RE LATE; the FDR Drive was stuck solid. I think some visiting idiot's in town." (The New Gideon takes taxis.) "Where's the E-boy?"

"In his room," said Dina. "He's got your old room now. Can you believe it, a room of his own? Like, now he can have friends over for sleepover dates, like a regular person? So, Gwyn, how you feeling? Isn't motherhood wonderful?"

A consoling pat of Gwen's stomach. Pregnancy made your body

common property, took you down a peg or two, within the reach of advice, of infantilizing intimacies. Suddenly you were reduced from being a person who was expected to have ideas about reforming Russia's social security system, about getting the mafia out of containerized shipping in Vladivostok, to someone who was only supposed to offer hunches as to whether her baby was going to be a girl or a boy, or to listen to other women's tales of varicose veins and leaky bladder. Did sisterhood need to be so unremittingly personal, so minor? But when she complained to Gideon, said, For God's sake let's read some more Mandelstam together, let's talk about *Tristia,* about his critique of Dante, Gideon informed her that it wasn't just women who went in for body-chat, guys too liked to sit around and discuss each other's hair loss, compare workout routines. Maybe I should emigrate, she said. To another planet? Leave the husk of flesh behind.

"She's still puking day and night. We're counting the minutes till her first trimester's up."

"Did you try the ginger? Ginger and acupuncture; those are my helpful hints. I was morning-sick all nine months with Eeth."

Gwen sat down. Gideon, pulling a knitted skullcap from his jeans pocket, clapped it on his head. Two candles burning on the sideboard. Two challah loaves, under two embroidered cloths—so that they shouldn't be ashamed, Gideon explained. Bread? Ashamed? Stench of some unseasonably Eastern European mish-mush in the oven, making her crazy.

"What's for dinner, Deen?"

"I found this recipe for meatless moussaka in the Moosewood book."

"I already warned Gwen about your cooking. Kosher-meets-health-food: the unspeakable in pursuit of the inedible. We brought you some wine. Non-K, needless to say."

"No problem—our observance has somehow taken this *nosedive.* All of a sudden, I hear myself telling Ethan, Sure you can play Nintendo on Shabbos. I think it's the weather. I really would like to start studying again, take a course at Drisha, but I just don't have the time or money . . ."

Gideon handed her Gwen's last bottle of Châteauneuf du Pape (a habit she'd inherited from her father, ordering wine by the case), which Dina put away rather vaguely. "You shouldn't have. You drinking, Gwen? We got cranberry juice, seltzer . . ."

Yes, Gwen was drinking, a last-ditch way of indicating to friendly onlookers, Keep out of my face. What did it matter, anyway? The liquor didn't stay down long enough to get anywhere *near* the baby. She wouldn't mind a stiff drink this very minute, but there was evidently some encumbrance of preceding protocol.

"Eeth—you ready to make kiddush?"

Dina produced a bottle of Manischewitz, a gilt-encrusted glass. And here came Ethan from Gideon's ex-room. A skinny brown kid wearing an XXL Black Sabbath (ha-ha) T-shirt that hung down to his knees, and baggies with the crotch skirting the ankle. Work boots, unlaced. A nervous mouth full of braces. Not only his clothes but his teeth were way too big for his little silverfish body.

"Hey E-man, what's the lowdown . . ."

Gideon and Ethan hugged each other sideways, Ethan looping a weedy arm around Gideon's neck, which Gideon in a lightning flash pinned back in some mean jujitsu that broke the ice and got the two guys giggling. Fake punches, dissolving into a downright cuddle.

They assembled, standing around the kitchen table, each with her assigned booklet, dual text, plus transliteration.

"We're starting on page eleven. It goes back to front . . ."

"Oh, right."

And the three—Dina, Ethan, Gideon—poured out their voices, Dina's rich alto, Gideon's hoarse baritone, Ethan's still-crystalline soprano, in a song about angels-on-high. Gwen had nothing against angels, but something untoward was rising in her stomach. A nonangelic visitor, distinctly from on low.

Jesus Christ, here it came. The volcanic bile propulsive—Just get me through the song, I can't bolt in the middle, yes she could, yes, she'd damn well better, in fact, she'd be lucky if she made it as far as the john.

A mad lunge out of the kitchen, Dina and Gideon's big surprised eyes swivelling after her while their plaintive voices warbled on.

"Malachei Ehhhh—ehhhhhhliooooooooon . . ."

And—whhhhhh—yikes. Up and up and up. Over and over. From the kitchen a concluding wail of *"Ha-KAAAAH-dosh-BAAAAH-rookh-HOOOO."*

An instant's cleared-weather, abject, shuddering, cheek resting on the yellowed-white hexagonals of tile, and then the convulsions all over again. It made you mass-murderous. It made you hate humanity. It made you think, Why am I crouched on a dirty shag mat in a bathroom on the Lower East Side, with people singing hymns in the kitchen? What's so great about being a mammal? Why couldn't God have let women lay eggs? In which case Baby Wolkowitz would be on a shelf at home warming in the Electrolux micro-incubator . . .

Another interval in the singing, an ill-timed moment of silence. The bathroom so thin-partitioned everybody could hear her retching amplified, over the running of the taps. Including unlucky Ethan, who, despite his neutral politeness, couldn't begin to like this alien invader, this Gideon-snatcher. She hunted for someone's toothpaste, for a tube of toothpaste that didn't squirt glitter-gel.

"Sorry about that," said Gwen, emerging. Shaken, trembling. Cold sweats in a hot room.

Ethan studying his feet. As if he'd never noticed his Caterpillars were . . . unlaced. As if he were trying to calculate in his head how to tie them.

Gideon, reaching out a gorilla-arm, propelled her into his lap. "Want me to take the baby for a spell?"

"Yeah, would you mind. Maybe take it and drown it."

"Shall we proceed?" Dina, cheery.

"You up for it, sweetheart?"

"Oh, sure, there's no going back."

And Gideon assumed what was clearly his customary portion, crooning a reenactment of God's completion of the World on the Sabbath Eve, His blessing creation, His rest from His labors in birthing Us. No, not yet us, but better things: heaven and earth and those angels Gwen had found so rebarbative.

It was a tricky sight, Gideon at the head of someone else's table, the man of someone else's house. Watching him bless the wine—mother and son breaking in with their sung thankfulness for God's having chosen them—them, not her—and sanctified them—them, not her—from amongst the nations of the earth. It was tricky to see him bless the bread which Dina then broke, salted, and handed silently to each. The dark-bearded supplicant indicating, Take it, eat it. This is my body, this is my blood, which I have shed . . . And feeling with a wrench that Gideon's body and his blood—although they flowed in miniature inside her—were after all not quite as unmixedly hers as she had assumed, that they had prior, perhaps higher, fealties which she had not altogether taken into account. She remembered her dream that Dina and Ethan were really Gideon's wife and son, and suddenly wanted to cry. Christ, yes, she was that self-centered, that childish.

Now the others had completed their ritual hand-washing and were allowed to speak. Dina was telling Gideon and Gwen about Ethan's trumpet teacher, Stan Weiss, who used to play with Bill Evans and who now taught both at Mannes and at the music school Vladimir Feltsman had founded. (A nod to Gwen as she unleashed this high-power Soviet dissident name.) Last weekend she and Ethan had been to hear Stan play at the Fez.

"You getting into it, Eeth?" Meaning jazz.

Ethan pendulumed his head in a silent So-so. Personally, Ethan was into heavy metal, techno—his taste in music being a not-so-gentle revolt against the grown-ups' fey backcountriness, their communal ideology that Woody Guthrie's singing "This Land Is Your Land" or "Get Along Little Doagies" was the Last Word. But at his mother's urging, he had agreed to assay the middle ground of jazz. The clincher, Dina revealed, being that the coolest kid in Ethan's karate class—a kid so cool his name was Andre—was the son of a jazz musician. "And a ballerina," added Ethan. "But that doesn't mean I'm taking ballet."

That summer, Dina was planning to send Eeth up to Lubeck for two weeks to help out with the Mystical Circus. She wanted him to get to know Jerome again. "You know how Jerome is just like catnip to children—it's only when you're older you realize he's Hitler with a ponytail."

"Well, his kids turned out okay." Gideon, evidently feeling disloyal.

"They did? Have you seen them recently?"

"Well, not since—"

"Zeph is, like, so silent it's pathological. Someday he's gonna up and Lizzie Borden his parents. And Roxanne is her daddy's *clone*. I swear, she's doing her senior thesis on Brecht. They even wear the same shoes . . . That bucolic childhood? The home schooling, the no-preservatives? It's just too much control. Like, get real: these kids' grand-father owned a major department store, their grandmother had her own box at the Metropolitan Opera, they might legitimately feel they've missed out on something, spending their lives knee-deep in chicken shit . . ."

Gideon, still demurring. "I guess that's the price for having a genius for a father. Nothing little Gizmo here's going to suffer from."

They talked shop over the strudel—another joint project with Milena Hanak, another workshop at St. Anne's, why their *False Messiah* had never quite come together, and how they might reconfigure it. Their talk—the talk of people who have lived and worked together for much of their lives—was a slow idling river, in which Gwen floated, semi-conscious. Too feeble to try to engage the boy sitting across from her. Who abruptly rose and . . . "Mom? Can I . . ."

"Just wait until we bensh, ducky."

"Bensh" being a longer sequence of sung prayer, at the end of which all four rocked gently, eyes half shut, singing a round about the goodness of brothers' sitting around together.

And Dina? Gwen couldn't hate her, exactly. You couldn't hate someone that unhappy who still managed to be that good. She was merely irritated by Dina's assumption that a woman's job was mothering her men, who, possessive, was now complaining about how long and scraggly "Gidele's" hair was getting in back. (She had just given Ethan a haircut last weekend.) Slavic, Dina's view of the sexes: you came home from work with a bagful of groceries, you cleaned the house, cooked dinner, paid the bills, cut the men's hair. And the men were supposed to . . . what? Get drunk? Spend your money? Be cute?

After dinner, Gideon and Ethan disappeared into Ethan's room so Ethan could show Gideon how to get on-line. Leaving the two women in either corner of the ring.

Dina, smiling challengingly, a silent *You're not going to go throw up again?*

Gwen, tacitly conceding that *would* be cowardly. Nah, she could tough it out. If Jacey could win over Melanie, she could handle Dina.

"What a great boy," Gwen to Dina. "Your son is amazing. What was it like, raising him on your own? I mean, at this point, I can't imagine having a kid *with* a husband."

Dina shrugged. "Hey, no husband was the good part. Anyways, I had the Family." (She called their company the Family—ironically—like a member of the Manson cult.) "Single motherhood—well, you bribe yourself. Like, if I get through the week without referring to my ex-husband in Ethan's presence as the Asshole, then we get to go to Häagen-Dazs." Smiled at Gwen—a fat girl, daring you to join in a joke about her weight.

"Hmmmmm . . ." muttered Gwen, realizing the sally was a test she might opt to fail. Which was she supposed to ask about, the Asshole or the ice cream? Suddenly too fed up to go on.

Seeing Moby Dina with her slim olive-skinned son, you concluded it must be the Asshole genes that had triumphed. Thinking, Do I love Gideon enough to have a bald son with those funny chestnut eyes? But then Gideon, reemerging from Ethan's bedroom, grinned at Gwen, the eyes so dancing with conspiratorial merriment, with the promise that everything, even Dina, could be laughed at, that you quieted down, Gwen, and thought yes, Four of those eyes under my roof sounds like one long cosmic hoot.

Gideon stroked her belly, and Gwen shivered, happily. "Buckle up, girl, I'm gonna take you home. Your dancing days are over. I'm going to take you home and rub your back, beat you with birch sticks—isn't that how they do it in the Old Country?"

"I could stand it," said Gwen, smiling across at Dina. Who looked suddenly deflated. Empty. As if she were hungry for something to get *her* arms around. Who started talking much too fast about a client of hers, Latoya, whose boyfriend had just beaten her son Cleonce with a motorcycle chain.

"Ugly world out there, once you leave the Vanderveer," said Gideon. "C'mon, girl, you're fading, let's get you home."

Out on the street, instead of their customary ideological-pecuniary standoff over whether they were going to take the subway or a taxi, Gideon hailed the first yellow cab. In the backseat, hurtling up the Bowery, he held her so all-protectively that Gwen forgot her self-pity at being subjected to Dina's campfire scoutishness, forgot her rekindled guilt at resisting Gideon's ongoing plea that they too start staying home Friday nights, lighting candles, saying prayers . . . and zoned out.

The way a long-ago child, coming home late from Christmas revels, might have fallen asleep in the sleigh, tucked under the fur throw with her cheek against her father's overcoated breast . . . Safe . . . unutterably safe . . .

Chapter Four

I

THE MONKEY BAR, 7 p.m. on a weekday night.

Christopher, Gwen, and Christopher's Turkish boyfriend were ordering another round of martinis, having just said goodbye to Gideon, who had to get downtown for a community board meeting.

A double-date introduction, the old friends checking out each other's new squeeze. In fact, Gwen was mildly pissed by Christopher's aggressive moral equivalence, his competitive insistence on piling Yilmaz into the equation. Couldn't Christopher have had the grace to acknowledge that Gwen's future husband, father of her child, deserved more attention than this week's boy toy?

That said, Yilmaz was impressive. A sturdy twenty-six-year-old with black hair thick as a pony's, blue eyes, a big bottom, and a serene self-assurance. You took one look and knew that bully Chris had at last picked on someone his own size. Although he spoke perfect American, he let the others talk, and when Chris—annoyingly—asked Yilmaz for *his* verdict on Gideon, the boy, smiling, refused. "We have a word in Turkish, *dost,* that is an old poetic word for 'friend' and also 'beloved.' You don't want a stranger to offer judgment on your *dost.*"

"Dust?" Christopher wrinkles his nose. "That sounds rather final. Love as a crematorium."

"Isn't it Persian?" asked Gwen.

"Yes, Persian, too. All our good words are Persian or Arabic."

"I mean, when Omar Khayyam writes about God, doesn't he—"

"You seem happy enough," interrupted Christopher. Yanking Gwen away from philology, which otherwise she might rabbit on about for hours. And then quickly, "You know just because I loathed Campbell doesn't mean I have to like this one. I do reserve the right to loathe *all* your boyfriends and husbands. I mean, it might just be my position, mightn't it, that you are lucky in friends and unlucky in love . . ."

"It might," Gwen conceded.

The waitress came to ask if she could get them more drinks. A dirty-blonde, annoyed-looking. Everyone was in a bad mood tonight.

"Yes, another round of martinis, and how about a . . . what have you got to eat? Can I see the . . . well, magret of duck sounds a little ambitious. How about the *jumbo* plate of canapés? You know, I could think it was a not-very-auspicious sign that you throw up every five minutes when he's around. Look, he's been gone an hour and you haven't rushed off to the bathroom once."

"That's because I don't have any more change to give that very glowery ladies' room attendant."

"You're too stingy to throw up?"

"Don't remind her, Christopher."

Chris, by contrast, did *not* appear happy. He appeared nervous. Yilmaz had come on a six-month student visa, but already Christopher was fretting about getting him a work permit for next year. Yilmaz had worked for Turkey's largest public relations firm, and he had some experience in fashion, too. Finding Yilmaz a job was going to be no problem, Christopher assured Gwen, but he wanted to get his legal status straightened out. "I've given him his own room—I don't want him to feel cramped," Chris continued, as if Yilmaz were not there. "And if we can only get him a green card, he'll be his own man. You don't happen to know of a really first-rate immigration lawyer?"

Gwen smiled at Yilmaz, already suspecting that even if Yilmaz were sleeping on a cardboard box in an INS detention center, he'd be his own man.

Chris, reaching over to pluck the green olive from Gwen's drink, intercepted their long smile.

"Are you judging my dust?" he asked.

"God forbid," Gwen replied, and suddenly got this jolt that Yilmaz wasn't really—wasn't permanently—gay. A premonition that before he was forty, he'd be married with children, and Christopher would be this wonderful friend from his youth—a godfather of whom he'd remain gratefully fond.

2

"WHAT DID YOU DO this afternoon? I tried you about five . . ."

Over the stove, cooking tuna with pine nuts and capers. Pretending they were in Sicily, not New York on a hazy gray-white May evening. The Empire State Building unaccountably red and lurching, in the fog. Hungover-looking.

"I went out for a cup of coffee with a guy who's got a space next to ours. Have I told you the latest? Looks like we've managed to scare Steve Menkes outta buying the building." (God, it had been great: every time Menkes and his minions had come by La Merced, they'd had the building garlanded in a human chain of protesters daubed in fake blood, howling.) "Now the city's talking about selling us off at auction . . ."

"Who'd want to buy a property with thirty squatters in it?"

"That's the question. So Menkes took a pass, but, man, most city developers are not your mild-mannered squeamish types. They probably–"

Gwen stopped stirring. "Help . . ."

"What?"

"I forgot the raisins."

He rummaged in a cabinet. Gwen's kitchen had now become a place where people *ate:* the shelves were packed with couscous, olive oil, spices, honey–wholesale goods from the health food cooperative on First Street.

"No, I need golden raisins–I just bought 'em, they're . . ." She drew the sultanas out of the Fairway sack. "You're supposed to–hold on–soak 'em in boiling water for ten minutes before you put 'em in the sauce . . ."

Gideon switched on the electric kettle. "What else?"

"White wine vinegar. Do you think balsamic will do?" Gideon, who had never followed a recipe in his life, pretended to consider.

"So you had coffee with this guy. . . ?"

"We're talking about putting on some kinda Save La Merced benefit of artists in the community."

"What's he do?"

"Isaac?"

"Is that his name?"

"Isaac Hooker."

"That sounds familiar. Wasn't he some Puritan divine? Didn't he write some five-volume treatise on predestination?"

"Probably. That's before he moved to the Lower East Side and found La Merced. You think you're kidding, but this kid is definitely some kinda theological nutcase–religious atheist, he calls himself. He used to do these paintings of himself levitating. Now he makes super 8 movies . . ."

"Is he nice?"

"Yeah. A yakker. He thinks we're living at the end of the Roman Empire, too. I told him you worked in Russia–"

"Used to work in Russia," interjected Gwen, gloomily.

"He really wanted to meet you. He said when he was a kid he was like obsessed by Napoleon. He quoted me this great quote from Napoleon–he said, 'People who don't believe in God, you don't govern them. You shoot 'em.'"

Gwen, grinning, feigned being shot.

"Who, you? That's not true. God you've got no problems with; it's yourself you're not so sure about." He was hugging her now from behind, a hand on each breast, while she tried to search for a serving dish in which to put the tuna.

"So what are we going to do with this little baby of ours? You going to get dunked or what?" (Dunked meant converted, so they could have a Jewish wedding, so the baby could be born a Jew.) "If so, I think I could probably pull a rabbi out of my hat for you. Josh would be more than willing . . ." Josh was the assistant at the Pitt Street minyan—the hippie-dippy Nouveau Hasid minyan where Dina and Dan, and occasionally Gideon, davened.

"I don't know. Do we have to talk about this? I'd rather talk about Napoleon."

"Your call."

"I don't think you can change religion so easily." Defensive-sounding, voice hiking up into argumentative, maybe a little self-pitying. "I mean, just because I'm a lukewarm Protestant—"

"Your call. I'm easy, either way."

3

So GIDEON RESTED it at that. Did not press. Balked at the mere prospect of justifying his faith to you.

Thus leaving you, Gwen, with your God—underemployed, ecumenical to the point of nullity, a post-Christian Single deprived of the power to damn or save, shorn of fasts, earthquakes, and saint's-day fairs, a God that maybe was in the DNA the way vitamin A is in carrots, while Gideon kept his I-am-that-I-am close to the chest—an overbearing busybody, bustling with greasy unhealthy dishes and quaint prohibitions: intimate, stifling, borderline hysterical. Dina, bearded.

And the two strains of deity were never introduced, never left to duke it out.

Gideon, you should have been like Jacob, telling Shechem, If you want anything of me or mine, shear your foreskin and dynamite your altars, like Jesus saying, Leave your mother and father, I am your mother and father.

But instead you kept mum, passive-politely expecting her to see revelation by herself. Assented to what seemed to you a form of cultural annihilation: marriage at Gwen's mother's house in Newburyport, performed by a judge.

A wedding which to your mind, Gideon, was a wild Dionysiac three-day rite of young men stamping their bare feet in the dust, sacrificed bullocks, and ululating women with hennaed palms, was thus neutered to civil, i.e., lapsed-Episcopalian, namby-pambiness.

Chapter Five

I

"LET'S NOT TALK WEDDING. It's the most boring subject in the world, don't you think? I feel very brought down to earth by it," grumbled Gwen to her best friend Constance.

They were having lunch at the Royalton. Constance soaring, because Roger had finally gotten the word that his Singapore assignment was over. That summer, they were moving back to London. "He asked me, How long will it take you to get the house packed up? I told him, About ten minutes."

"You were pretty stoic," said Gwen. "You never really let on how much you hated it."

"Didn't I? I just sneaked outside every night and spat on the pavement. Rather reassuring to live in a country where it takes so little to be really appallingly subversive. Anyway, I'm over the moon. I couldn't care less that our house in London's let for another year, we have nowhere to live, or that it's far too late to get the children into schools for next year. We can sleep in a tent under the M4 . . . Now tell me about you. How did the meeting of the families go? You two went up to your mother's *and* . . . ? Was she a nightmare? Was he?"

Gwen frowned. "Gideon was so shy and beaming with helpfulness, it was almost too much. He spent the whole weekend hanging out the wash for my mom, talking septic tanks with Hal. He was *too* anxious to please, for my ornery vindictive tastes . . . I don't think he understands about bullies. He's such a waif, he thinks if only you're obliging enough, people are going to take you home and adopt you."

"I can see that," said Constance. "I think he's adorable, by the way. It must be nice to live with a man who moves so gracefully—you know, Roger goes crashing around like a wild boar in the underbrush, you can hear him through three floors. But Gideon—he has this Persian-miniature look, those curly jewelled eyes and long small bones . . ."

"Yeah. I guess Persian miniature's *not* what New Englanders are looking for in a son-in-law."

"No?"

"I don't know. In-laws . . . It's an impossible relation, isn't it? My own instinct is, you need to come in pretty brutal from the start, lay down the terms on which you allow 'em through the door."

"In-laws are . . . terrorists," Constance agreed.

"Right. So the answer, presumably, is counterterrorism: two eyes for an eye. But how would I know? I mean, it's no coincidence I'm marrying an orphan."

"So?"

"Oh, Hal approved of him, all right—Gideon was obviously some kind of stick to beat *me* with. You know, how did this stuck-up brat ever deserve such a right-on unassuming guy. I mean, one glance at Gid and he could see right away, Here is a man who recycles. And Gideon and Maddock honestly did hit it off—they went off and did boy stuff together, Maddock showed Gideon his motorcycle, his guns, his Meccano set, whatever—Maddock *believes* in family: if this is my husband, he's going to love him." (Unable to convey to Constance—who had always found Maddock spooky—how painfully she had been touched by her brother's warm welcome.)

"And your mother?"

"I don't know . . . I thought she liked him, at first. They had plenty to talk about—liberal politics, bleeding-heart stuff. *He* liked *her.*"

Remembering with dread how wowed Gideon was by her mother's . . . ladyishness. Her well-bred Yankee intonations, her faded jeans and Fair Isle sweater, her deceptively gawky air of being a middle-aged tomboy. He was obviously in some way scrambling to revise his impression of Gwen's abused childhood, since the eighteenth-century shingle house, the garden, the swing on the apple tree, the old family silver, answered to something so deep in him: some quite developed but never fully encountered idea of civility. Teaneck beatified.

"I thought it'd gone okay, considering I'm suddenly springing this stranger on them as father of their first grandchild. But then when Gideon went off with Maddock, I asked Katrina about having the wedding up there—and she—she kind of froze on me. Recoiled. She asked when were we thinking of . . . and she said No, we couldn't possibly do that. She said . . . you couldn't possibly organize it that fast, the garden would look a mess, April's a horrible month, it would be way too cold to have it outside even with a tent, she's working like a dog getting an exhibition together up in Kennebunk, Hal's going to be away at a conference in Sweden, we couldn't possibly do it before summer.

"It just suddenly brought out this much harder, more snobbish side I always forget about, I think of her being this unworldly person picking up driftwood on the beach, and then suddenly I get a jolt and I remember, yes, it *mattered* to her that Martin was making so much money, she married this poor boy from Milwaukee, but he'd graduated top out of Harvard Law School and he was launched on this big career. And she worshipped her father, who was a government geologist, always getting sent off to Antarctica. And I remember yes, Hal is actually a pretty distinguished scientist, at a very prestigious institution . . . She likes that—she thinks women should be wives to important men; it's the only arrangement that makes sense to her . . ."

"Parents are intolerable. What did you say?"

"Oh you know, I'm this walking hormonal powder keg at the moment. I get on the Seventy-ninth Street crosstown, I can't find the right change in my purse, and I burst into tears. So you can imagine. I totally lost it. I started snuffling and I said, all red-eyed and huffy, Fine, we'll have it at City Hall. But she wouldn't budge. She just said, It's your decision. I mean, how could I explain it to her: I don't want to wait till August, I don't want to get married with a belly big as a house, it's undignified, I'd feel like some pathetic knocked-up teenager whose dad got heavy with the boyfriend, I don't want the baby kicking the prayer book out of my hand. I want it just to be the two of us, marrying because we love each other to death, because we can't live another moment without that . . . sanctification of our love. And she's saying No, because the garden will look a mess. And then we get into this whole other separate fight because Gideon wants there to be a rabbi, too—which itself has been a nightmare, finding somebody lax enough to . . . to hitch us, I mean, but also somebody Gideon can stomach—but which means we can't get married on a Saturday, and she says it's absolutely out of the question to have a wedding on a Sunday, so I say Fine, we'll get married on a weekday, and she says, Nobody will come, and I told her, Whoever loves us will come. We don't want a lot of people. She said, Your father won't be able to come. I didn't really want to say anything, but when your parents have gone through a pretty unpleasant divorce, you have kind of mixed feelings anyway about seeing them both at your wedding . . . And then she said, Well, you'll have to do the food. You can't expect me to do kosher food. Who said anything about kosher food? I mean, yeah, so maybe we won't have a ham, but . . . Suddenly she's acting as if she's never seen a Jew in her life, as if I'm uh I don't know bringing home some untouchable species that's exotic but in a really low-class disgusting sort of way . . ."

"Is he religious?"

"He's religious the way *you're* religious. Like maybe the Jewish equivalent of baptizing your kids, going to church Christmas and Easter. Maybe a little more strenuous, but Judaism *is* a little more strenuous."

"Parents are intolerable. What are you going to do?"

"I don't know. I couldn't really say anything to Gideon—I didn't want him thinking Katrina thought he was a sap, or weak, or just not quite adequate, socially. It's such a silly cruel game to play. When he was so happy because he thought they'd . . . he kept going on about how *gracious* she'd been to him. I kind of unloaded on Maddock, who was a real lifesaver, he said, What's the big deal, you can have it at my place."

"Well, you are being a bit of a baby," said Constance, fondly. "You've chosen this man precisely *because* he's so antithetical to both your parents, to everything they understand and believe in, and now you want their approval for your rejection of them . . ."

"It's fucked-up, isn't it?"

"Mildly."

Panic settling into gloom at her recognition that Gideon, whom she'd counted on to free her from her own family, was just not bloody-minded enough to do it.

2

THIS WAS CLAUSTROPHOBIA in reverse, where what you wanted to escape was inside you. Inside, and growing. The alien corn sprouting, till there was no more room. There wasn't space for two people in one body; there'd been barely enough space for *her* in her.

Gwen had always been a fidget: one more thing she and the Gid had in common. She remembered that first day in her hotel room at the Sibirsk, his rifling through her magazines, fiddling with the remote control, and finally hanging out the window, with a skittishness unprofessional in a would-be seducer, a How-do-I-get-out-of-here look she had recognized, with an inner leap of kinship: another person who'd always be skinning out the door for a pint of milk or to put a quarter in the parking meter. Jumping into the car to drive . . . nowhere.

I've got a dybbuk inside me, Gideon, she complained, and it's growing. One of us is going to have to go.

She said, I'm going through the roof. She said, Gideon, it's inside me, eating my food and sucking up my oxygen, Gideon, I can't breathe, it's cramping my lungs, it's got its elbows jammed into my ribs, Gideon, it's slam-dancing on my bladder, I think I got a pinched nerve it's pinching, Gideon, I can't fucking stand this, Gideon, I don't want a child.

What do you want?

I want a raise. No I don't, I want to quit my job and get a travel grant to go learn Farsi. I want to go live in Isfahan for a couple of years.

Isfahan?

All this time I'm taking breathing classes I could be learning Persian. I could be reading Nizami by now . . . Gideon? Don't you think?

And he sighed, mournful, feeling sorry for her and trying not to think that if it was he who was having the baby, he wouldn't make such a song and dance about it. Feeling sorry for her (dutifully) and trying hard not to take it personally, that her not wanting his child was a not-wanting him.

How could it be, when even after she crawled back into bed after a night's groaning and puffing and pacing and puking she would still, sheepishly, slide a hand between his legs?

3

SHE WAS JEALOUS. Her jealousy was a ravening wolf, it was a newborn babe whose cry—despotic, inconsolable—tore through your nerves, and she was amazed at herself. Not ashamed, just . . . amazed.

She remembered how matter-of-course it had seemed to her when

Campbell—in one of their time-outs—had resumed sleeping with Mary Lynch, and how when they got back together again, she and Mary Lynch (whom she liked) had met quite regularly to play squash, without Gwen's ever having tormented herself unduly by picturing her lover's hands grasping those high small buttocks now encased in sweatpants, and that was how she'd thought of herself: sexually reasonable.

So who, then, was this uncaged Mrs. Rochester who wept with rage when Gideon teased the checkout girl at D'Agostino's, who lay awake at night, ravaged by thoughts of Jenny Randazzo, whom Gideon'd poked when he was . . . *fourteen* years old!!! Who wanted Dina and Dan and Andrea and, worse to admit, Ethan *dead*. Who was jealous even of his *puppets* for getting such transgressive fondling. Who cursed high heaven that she had not been there to pluck her boy as a virgin, that they'd not been betrothed like gypsies or royalty as mere toddlers. Who wished that he had never in his life had a hard-on except for her. Who raged that every spit of jizm, every last jot of spunk, had not gone to irrigating her long-hungry fields.

While Gideon, frightened by the disproportion of her sexual claim—which he understood had nothing to do with love, was in fact the enemy of love, mistrustful, vain, self-centered—said nothing. Submitted, reluctantly, to its arid totalitarian dictates while trying mutely to protect from its negations those he loved. It will pass, he told himself. When she finally learns to trust me, it will pass. He was right: it had nothing to do with him, and it passed. What he could not have foretold was that with her jealousy passed her love. From typhoon to flatline, without so much as an intervening moment of recognizing *him*. No, he was as much the unseen, unknown, unloved target as Helen of Troy.

4

ENOUGH IS WHAT SEPARATES US from the beasts.

The horse eats till its guts burst, the laboratory rat snuffs cocaine till its heart stops, but God teaches the war-weary to say, Enough bloodshed, the rich man to say, Enough wealth. Enough is a truce, enough is a feast, enough is your two feet planted in the ground, knowing here is your place in the universe.

For Gideon this was golden amplitude: his woman, with his child in her belly. A warm apartment, a wet pussy. The work of his hands. Not one dollar more. Enough was as good as sunlight, as good as gas, as good as godliness, as good as everlasting fame, world without end.

So why did he feel obscurely dissatisfied, anxious? Was it just childhood unhappiness, his mother's harrowingly melancholic legacy catching up with him?

5

WAS IT THEN, Gideon, in these early months of pregnancy, on the eve of marriage, that you belatedly realized that there was something askew between you, sexually?

That, presented with your girlfriend's comings that were vociferous and yet oddly flat, uniform as waves on a lakeshore, you had the discomfiting sense that this was not about You—that you, in fact, were less than instrumental to the whole proceeding?

This was player-piano sex.

She had some idea of you, but it wasn't you; she was in love with love, with the idea of being in love with a man who might or might not resemble you, of the eccentric generosity of her mythically descending on a common mortal.

Whereas what she managed (all unconsciously, almost indifferently) to touch in you was something that had never been touched before. That she and only she could touch. Something skinless-tender which you had only half guessed might be there, waiting to be noticed and allowed to come alive.

Chapter Six

"HOW ARE YOU FEELING, Pop?"

Martin has lost weight, to Jacey's delight, but the flesh hangs on him; his face is yellowish and puffy. He looks like a drunk, which he's not.

"Jacey says you've been under the weather."

"I'm fine, for an old geezer. Steve tells me I'm in for a new life ex-perience. I think my new life experience is having one more son getting kicked outta grade school, which for me is an old life experience."

Jacey has warned Gwen, inviting her over for dinner, that her father wants to have a talk with her. Last talk was ten years ago, after Gwen changed her mind about law school. She sits down on the study sofa, picks up a magazine.

"What's the problem?"

"With Al? He's a smart-ass, he picks fights with other kids, he's flunking two courses because he forgets his homework every day, and Jacey has turned into this Christian Science fundamentalist who will not give the kid a break by considering the appropriate treatment. Jacey just like yanks the children outta school for two weeks because she feels like being in the country, and then she wonders why Al's flunking math. She wants to take him out of Dalton, which I happen to think is a very good school. I don't think we would be doing him any kind of favor, long-term, by putting him in some touchy-feely place where the kids get to lie on the floor and eat lollipops and scream. The school is not the problem . . . I shoulda stuck to daughters, right?"

"I thought you weren't too pleased with me, either," she parries, un-characteristically ingratiating. Something about these once-a-decade talks that makes her regress.

He shrugs. "You're thirty-whatever, you're too old to care whether your father's 'pleased' or 'displeased.' I don't think you ever cared. It's not 'pleased' or 'unpleased': I admit, I'm concerned. So you're all set on this wedding, huh?"

She pauses. ("Set" as in Have-you-organized-the-caterers? or "set" as in Still-determined-to-marry-the-bum?) "Looks like."

"Well, like I say, you're a grown woman. Your mother'd had her kids by the time she was your age, so I guess you know what you're doing."

He steeples his hands; he fingers his throat and coughs.

She's damned if she's going to help him out.

"It's true I'm a little . . . concerned about your plans, Chugga. If you don't mind my butting in . . . ."

"What's the matter?" she inquires, suddenly furious.

"There's a lot in this scenario that just doesn't add up. Like, how are you people planning to live. Remember, it's not just you you have to think about. You gonna support him and the baby, or what? It makes me a little uncomfortable, Chug. You work hard already, I really woulda hoped you'd pick a fellow who could take care of you."

She looks away. She thinks, This man and I, we barely know each other. We could be riding in the same elevator and he wouldn't recognize me. She says coldly, "I guess in my own experience, Pop, money does not equal protection."

But no, Martin is not going to be guilt-tripped. He is not going to be blindsided by her insinuation that just because his first marriage didn't work out, he was in any way a deficient father; he will not falter in his certain belief that a man's job is to provide for his family, to give his children guidance at the major crossroads in their lives, not to be some kind of flat-chested auxiliary nursemaid.

"I'm being realistic, Chug," he says, patiently. (She remembers this cardinal virtue of "realism" from her father's lexicon: a readiness to make your own way in the world. People who want to change the status quo, in his book, are worse than unrealistic: they are crybabies. Martin and Gideon are not destined soulmates.) "To be crude, you're used to a certain comfort level, and I don't see you're going to get it from Mr. Wolkowitz. I mean, a baby runs you ragged. Who's going to take care of it? Are you planning to go sailing off to Russia with a newborn, or is Pulcinello going to stay home and change the diapers?"

He lifts his shoulders, fingers his throat again. Who was Brager, he asks. Why doesn't the guy have his father's name? Does she know anything whatsoever about the parents? The stepfather? Does he claim to have any kin still living? A sister? Has anybody heard from her? Has he been married before?

"Are you asking for references?" Gwen inquires.

"Aren't you? I'd want to know this shit before I hired a receptionist. I'm surprised at you, Chug—I thought you had a head on your shoulders. You're not fifteen anymore; you're about to be a mother, you gotta think about your child's welfare, too, not just your short term . . . La Vie Bohème is for single people."

"Pop," says Gwen. She places her hands on her knees, ready to terminate this session. "We're getting married in six weeks. Up at Mom's. I hope you and Jacey will come."

Martin makes a backing-off gesture, palms raised in genial surrender. "Okay, okay, I'll shut my big mouth. Enough said."

They both stand up now.

"Shit, you're as bad as your old man. Don't believe in living in sin, huh? (This really is the new age, where the parents tell the kids, For Christ's sake don't get married, just live with the guy . . .) Of course we'll come. Come to the marriage, come to the divorce, whatever. People do a lot of stupid things in their lives, otherwise my confreres and I would be in for slim pickings."

He smiles at her. Smooths his khakis, and walks over to the desk, like a doctor about to write a prescription.

"My final advice, Chug? I strongly suggest you get some kinda pre-marital agreement down on paper." (Is he about to draft her one, she wonders, incredulous. No, he's just getting a throat lozenge from a drawer of the desk. He fingers his neck again, he has a nervous cough.) "I don't think he's a greedy guy, necessarily, but money's a very emotional matter that stands in for all kinds of other things, if feelings get hurt. That's my experience."

Walking her to the door of his study, her father claps a warm hand to her shoulder. The same squeeze she has seen him give the Chinese barber Steve, the French restaurateur Gérard, but this is a No-hard-feelings squeeze, maybe more like the handshake he gives Alexander after he's creamed him at blackjack.

"You don't mind my speaking frankly with you? Of course, we all know you're going to have a wonderful marriage and be happy-ever-after, but I'm in the just-in-case business. I'm just giving you the fruits of my professional—and let's face it, personal—experience."

She flashes him a sardonic look. Relenting. "I didn't think I had enough money to attract much greed."

"You don't. What are you making, seventy, seventy-five grand?"

"Sixty-five." Ashamed not to be making more.

"Sixty-five. You don't. You got anything left in that trust your grand-father left you?"

"Nah. I cleaned it out buying the apartment."

"That was not a bad investment. I bet you've . . . let me see . . . you paid . . . remind me . . ."

"Two seventy-five."

"When did you buy it? Back in—?"

"Ninety-two."

"So you've doubled your money."

"I guess. If I were to sell it right now."

"Anyway, you're not exactly rolling in income. You need every penny you can get . . . You know Jacey and I are happy to pay for the wedding. Carte blanche. I'll write you a check, you do what you like. I paid for Courtney's wedding that lasted longer than the marriage, why shouldn't I pay for yours?" (Courtney was his stepdaughter from his second wife.)

"Thanks. But it's not looking all that big a deal. We're only inviting forty people. Mom's letting us trash the house and garden for free . . ."

He glances at his watch, ushers her into the hall. "Let's eat. All this talk makes me very . . . Jacey!" he shouts up the stairs. "So you're getting married at your mother's. Do they have any decent hotels there, or is it still that cruddy Maypole Inn?"

Jacey nips down the stairs, wearing brown suede cigarette jeans, a white T-shirt, gold locket. She gives Gwen a sympathetic hug.

"I guess we can always stay in Boston, huh, Jace . . . Where're the kids? Are we going to eat, or what? This woman is unreal," he complains to his daughter. "Ever since we got back from Paris she's decided it's, like, uncouth to sit down to dinner before nine."

"It is," says Jacey, with a wink at Gwen.

Chapter Seven

I

She is coming, my own, my sweet;
Were it ever so airy a tread,
My heart would hear her and beat,
Were it earth in an earthy bed;
My dust would hear her and beat,
Had I lain for a century dead;
Would start and tremble under her feet,
And blossom in purple and red.

Tennyson, *Maud*

PLUM ISLAND. MAY 1996.

They have pitched their circus tent (warmed by space heaters) on the beach. The path that leads to the theater is lit by flaming torches.

The almost-full moon hangs cold and pale, in a sky across which ragged clouds race.

The audience settles in the tent, Gideon and Gwen in front. Behind them, Christopher, Yilmaz, Constance (Roger's arriving tomorrow morning); Katrina and Hal; Jacey and her children (Martin's arriving later tonight); Aunt Sue and Cousin Rich and his wife Emily; Maddock and Riley. Ethan—still just young enough to fall in anonymous-indiscriminately with other children—has formed a rowdy gang with Rich and Emily's two older boys.

A ten-foot-tall bride and a ten-foot-tall groom, each borne on golden thrones.

Unearthly Music.

Elfin laughter.

Terror.

The curtain rises on a fairy tale. The bride is kidnapped on her wedding eve. Groom Orpheus summons the elements: he calls upon the North Wind and a sea dragon, who tell him his beloved's been stolen by the God of the Underworld. Orpheus descends, where he confronts the Devil (with a giant penis and a forked tail). He wins back his bride on the condition that every year, on their wedding day, he makes music in hell.

Gideon and Gwen sit alone in the front row, watching the Epithalamium that the Pants on Fireites have made for their comrade and his bride. Watching with a fascination close to fear.

Behind them, their loved ones. They can hear Aunt Sue chattering to Katrina, and Jacey hissing at Alexander to stop teasing Serena, they can hear Christopher's low comments and Constance's laughter, sniggers from the boys when the priapic Devil emerges. But they feel . . . magically alone. Outside these canvas walls is pale beach, lashed by a loud lacework of waves. Above them, the moon casts her chain-mail fishtail of light along the dark sea.

Gideon and Gwen grip each other's hands tighter, twisting their fingers together. Gwen is shivering-cold: her pale green velvet dress is too thin for the night air, and she was too vain to bring a coat. Gideon enfolds her in the sweater she's given him, a great shaggy violet-red mohair that smells like a wolfhound.

Gwen puts her cold hands under Gideon's shirt and feels the ribs beneath his warm skin. A slim Mediterranean body beached on an Atlantic coast. As Gwen moves her cold hands across his chest, Gideon shudders in something between fear and pleasure. Because what she arouses in him is always something between fear and pleasure.

On a night like this, earth and sea and sky are one blue-black-silver bowl. Demoniacal, cold, electrically alive. As if the vessels of creation had never been shattered, the world not reduced to shards.

On such a night, a son of heaven might spread his moonlit net and fish for a daughter of the earth, might scoop her away on a sea horse.

Gallop, gallop, gallant sea horse, over the sea and over the stars. Don't weep, earth-daughter. I'm going to make you queen of heaven, and our daughters will marry Orion and the Little Bear, and our sons will marry the Andromedas.

Don't cry, dust-child, I'm going to scoop you up to heaven where you can eat the Mount of Olives for an appetizer, where you can hunt with Nimrod and fish with Jonah and laugh with Sarah and drink with Noah and dance with the daughters of Shiloh, dance, dance, my bride, for every wedding night is the wedding night of Solomon and Sheba, and the seed of Abraham is, is, and ever will be countless as grains of stars in the sand, as glinting pebbles in the desert sky.

Gideon sighs and Gwen sighs. They are sick with love, and the child they have made together; like a penny thrown into a well, the baby sighs too. The stars droop and swoon in God's great sky, stars that have burned since the night Solomon peeled off the outermost of Shulamit's seven veils.

As they reemerge from the circus tent, Gwen sees a star with a green-blue tail go fuming across the sky. There are many shooting stars to be seen on a cold clear Atlantic night in May, but this star is yours alone, my bride and my groom, my sister and brother, my doves.

2

"WANNA COME BACK to my place, Gideon?"

Of course he wants to. He hasn't had nearly enough to drink, not half as much as Maddock and his friend Kid. Now that his future parents-in-law have gone to bed, he's ready to let rip.

Kid has a tangle of black curls, and a chipped front tooth permanently bared in a satyrish grin. Together, Kid and Maddock—the slim black-haired boy and the stocky blond—exude a primitive freedom. They are wearing half as many clothes as everybody else; coastal blood evidently runs hot . . .

"Where're the gals?"

Maddock's girlfriend Riley headed home hours ago in Maddock's pickup; Gideon's shivery bride was borne off just before midnight by her ladies-in-waiting, it being Christian custom that bride and groom not see each other on their wedding day; Dina, who has a migraine, has gone back to the motel with Ethan, where Maddock and Gideon and Kid now stop by to see how everybody is doing.

Elliott from the Klezmofunks who've come to play at their wedding, Josh the Pitt Street assistant rabbi, and Amnon and Hector are all congregated in Andrea and Dan's motel room drinking root beer, smoking weed, and engaged in some massive bull session about whether Brecht's plagiarisms made him any less of a genius. Dan has crawled into bed and is asleep with a pillow over his head.

"Hey guys, you wanna come on over to Maddock's place?"

"Sure," says ever-game Andrea. And now little Dan, too, rises from the dead to announce he isn't sleepy at all, only tired of hearing about Brecht, and Maddock says, "Isn't that a kid's shampoo?"

Dan and Andrea and Gideon and Elliott and Josh and Kid and Maddock pile into two cars. Leaving Amnon and Hector too stoned to budge.

Kid is driving a stripped-down Jeep that looks as if he picked it up at a U.S. Army yard sale, and so they sail across the border into New Hampshire, land of the free.

"Bet you didn't even know New Hampshire had a coastline," ventures Kid.

"I knew," replies Gideon, who is sitting up front. "We played at the Music Hall in Portsmouth one butt-freezing New Year's Eve."

"The Music Hall? That is one constipated place."

"Wasn't a barrel of laughs, was it, guys? We put on an *Orlando Furioso*, with cans of olive oil for the knights' armor. Dan, you remember the bagpipes you made for that show? We still have those bagpipes?"

"Sure. I brought 'em along for the wedding."

He's forgotten how early country people go to bed. Not a light in the cottages you pass, Chihuahua-sized deer in the front yards, mailboxes plastered in POW-MIA stickers. A ghostly night-desertedness. Boarded-up gun shops and firework stores along 1A, darkened gas stations.

They pull into a lot parked with ten, twenty trailers, and behind the trailers, Maddock and Riley's house, backing onto the marsh. It even has a name: Honeysuckle, or Sea Breeze, he can't make out the script in the darkness. Andrea and Gideon and Elliott and Josh jam into the living room and settle on the floor, furniture covered in dog hair, while Maddock and Kid, accompanied by Dan, go off to find more liquor.

3

GIDEON WANDERS OUT to the kitchen. Wondering where Kid and Maddock are expecting to rustle up liquor at 1 a.m. Thinking, I need to get more alcohol in my system, I am fading. Or maybe he's just hungry, the bridal dinner having been WASP-skimpy, and Gideon too busy to eat, trying to reassure his mother-in-law, on one side, who was fretting about her garden, while flirting with Constance, on the other.

There is an open package of Cheez Doodles sitting on the kitchen counter.

Back in the living room, Elliott—who's gone back to college to study classics—is holding forth about Aristotle's theory of tragedy. Elliott's a fine musician, but he can get a little long-winded, from living up a mountain with nobody to talk to but goats.

God, Gideon loved Cheez Doodles when he was a kid. He has the distinctest memory of unpacking his old school knapsack, in their move from Passaic to Teaneck, and squirrelled inside was a half-empty bag of Cheez Doodles, disgustingly stale, which he then proceeded to sit on the floor and scarf, one by one. Furtive, in case anyone came in and caught him. So much of a child's shame is about food . . .

Alongside the Cheez Doodles in Maddock's kitchen, a pile of magazines—biker magazines, computer magazines, *Soldier of Fortune, National Review.*

And in comes Josh, also looking hungry. Gideon hands Josh the Cheez Doodles. "Watch out, these are seriously stale. Whatsamatter, you don't want to hear any more about Greek tragedy?"

"Speaking of tragedy," says Josh, jovially. In the living room, the conversation is beginning to fragment, Andrea and Elliott arguing about whether tragedy depends on bourgeois ideas of social justice.

"Yes?"

"In my humble opinion, it's a tragedy that your wife-to-be isn't Jewish."

"Hmmmmm . . ." smiles Gideon, embarrassed. *That's* a little heavy, a bolt from the blue only slightly mitigated by Josh's dimpling facetious tone, his hand plumped on Gideon's shoulder.

"Before I met your fiancée, I thought to myself, Too bad Gid's not marrying a nice Jewish girl. But now that I've met Gwen, I can see that she has a Jewish soul."

"Hmmmmm . . ." repeats Gideon, smile fading. What *is* a Jewish soul? To him, it suggests some burden of knowledge that perhaps is merely historical, the way a once-beaten dog flinches. And Gwen, though certainly burdened with her own dark knowings, has always seemed to him in a fundamental way historically innocent . . .

A blast of cold night air and laughter as Maddock and Kid and Dan, accompanied by Maddock's bouncy Lab, burst through the kitchen door. Red-cheeked. Carrying with them a raucous townie merriment, along with cases of beer, pillaged from Maddock's partner Buddy.

"Hey guys," says Gideon.

"Think about it. You know, before the Romans, the Jews used to be a proselytizing religion."

"No kidding." An eye on Maddock. Has Maddock overheard the assistant rabbi's pronouncement that his sister has a Jewish soul? Maddock is peeling off his fleece vest, extracting beer bottles from their cardboard holster. Kid rifling through drawers for a bottle opener.

"Kiddo, what are you, like, a first-time guest here or something?" says Maddock, pointing Kid to the combined can-and-bottle-opener on the wall by the refrigerator. Thumping his skull, crossing his eyes in an idiot-face.

"You might whisper a little word of encouragement in her ear."

Gideon nods. Unencouragingly. The guy is *way* out of line. Wonders, If a pregnant Gwen were to convert, would her fetus too become Jewish at the selfsame minute she entered the ritual waters? Natch. Jewishness wasn't like baptism, it was involuntary, organic-ethnic as well as chosen. You couldn't have an un-Jewish baby in a Jewish womb, not even if the mother, God forbid, had been raped by Chetniks.

Maddock unlids three bottles of Old Brown Dog on the refrigerator door, hands some to Josh and Gid. Puts a couple of six-packs in the freezer.

"Bottoms up, boys. To the merry bridegroom . . ."

"Man, you don't look too stressed. If I was you, I'd be . . ." Kid mimes knocking knees, chattering teeth.

"That's because he knows tomorrow morning, I have the getaway car." Maddock claps Gideon on the back.

"Ha-ha-ha," laughs Gideon.

4

MADDOCK AND KID AND JOSH AND GIDEON form a new circle in a corner of the living room, joined by Elliott.

"How's business, Maddock?"

"I can't complain . . ."

"Maddock's in the roofing business."

"That sounds like the joke, How's business? Patchy."

"On the mend?"

"Ha-ha."

Gideon can't figure out what Kid does, aside from volunteer as a fireman, in which capacity he tells them about a fire in Rye last week. An old hotel, bought up by some property developer, burned to the ground.

"Toast."

"How much did he get in insurance?" Elliott asks.

"Funny you should ask."

"I'm a cynic, right?"

There is a quasi-fraternity between the New Hampshirites and Elliott, who, even if he lives in the socialist republic of Vermont, is at least not a New Yorker.

"Is Jackie coming over?" Maddock asks.

"Jackie?" Kid looks at his watch. "Jackie has probably been asleep three hours by now." His girlfriend, Kid explains, works in a shelter for battered women. "It is one horror show after another. She gets frazzled, is all. A woman came in the other day, trailing children. And there is always such *bullshit* going down. This woman's, like, pretending it's the first time her man's worked her over. She was, like, Hamburger Helper. Jackie's, like, You belong in the emergency ward. Jackie's looking over the kids, What's those scars on the girl's arm? Are those *burn* marks? And the woman's, like, Well, he's always been a good provider, he was making good money over at Pease"—Pease, Maddock interjects, is the air force base, now decommissioned—"Jackie's, like, Go on assistance. Eat at your mom's."

"That's horrible . . ." says Josh. Reproachfully, as if Kid were under the impression he'd been telling them a *nice* story.

Gideon by now sorry he'd ever asked Josh as balance to the judge. He stretches a leg which has gone to sleep. Fidgety, simultaneously excited and bored. Gwen . . . What is she doing now, at this very minute? Is she tucked up sleeping under her mother's thin quilt, or is she tiptoeing catlike around her bedroom, on her long naked golden feet, looking out at the moon? Gwen . . . his heart is yearning for her. Gwen . . . yearning, yearning.

To comfort himself, he imagines her long arms around his neck, her quick kisses, her cinnamon-spicy-bitterish-coffee smell. No one can tear them asunder. Once they are married, there will be *no* nights apart. He is peeling off her white cambric nightgown, as Solomon peeled off dancing Shulamit's veils. Kissing her small springy breasts, which are already heavier, nipples darker, laden with her coming motherhood.

Now he tries to picture Gwendolen in her wedding dress, which he has not been allowed to see. All he knows is that this unseen wedding dress cost ten thousand dollars. When Gwen saw his shock—he keeps himself deliberately ignorant of his future wife's expenditures—she explained that in fact the designer had given her a super-discount since she's been buying his clothes for years before he got famous. Gideon, a craftsman himself, finds the idea of a "famous" dressmaker absurd. Mid his shock, a naive excitement at what a ten-thousand-dollar dress might possibly look like. He wishes his mother, herself quite a clotheshorse, could be there to see his bride . . .

On the night before a wedding, the spirits of the dead visit you. Raining blessings down upon Gideon, blessings of fruitfulness, prosperity, and joy are Sonny—his own Solomon—and Paula the quick-footed dancer. Does his mother wish him joy from his bride?

The ghosts of the dead crowd around us. They wish things for us and they want things from us: a bit of our happiness, a bit of our health they want to siphon away. Scat, little ghosts. Soon enough, we will join you. Leave us our wedding nights whole, little mother, little father, don't take such a big bite from the moon-cake of our soon-to-be-wedded joy . . .

Chapter Eight

I

"Constance . . ."

They were lying in Gwen's bed, side by side. Into which Constance, who had never spent a night away from both husband and children, had crept.

Moonlight. Cold. The evening's champagne and brandy burned off, Gwen's brain still whirring kaleidoscopically.

Bare arms in the electric moonlight. Constance's arms a creamy white, star-sprinkled in freckles, Gwen's yellower. Between them, invisible, an elfin baby, likewise whirring, prodding, somersaulting in its translucent pink cage.

The women were still; the baby casually stretched: a sharp heel in the ribs, a fist in the groin. Were we its nature, its thunder and its rain?

Amazed, still, by the pain.

"Constance? My baby's kicking . . ."

"How lovely . . ." Constance put a hand, guided by Gwen's, on her stomach. A listening hand. "There, I felt it."

"Did it feel like a girl-kick or a boy-kick?"

"Have you done the trick with the ring and the thread? Shouldn't we be telling your fortune in mirrors?"

Spring by the sea, lilacs in bloom, the old house creaking. It was almost five-thirty. Half a mile away, was Gideon also lying in a strange bed, desperately excited, desperately awake?

"Or with molten silver."

"I don't dare. I don't want a fortune. I want to . . . Constance?"

"Mmmmmm. . . ."

"Do you think I'll be happy?"

Constance rolled over. Breath even. Gazing up at the stains on the bedroom ceiling. A long silence. A Constance silence. "I'm rather a dis-believer in happiness," she said at last. "I think the whole notion of hap-piness as a *right* is probably responsible for most marriages' falling apart.

It's sort of asking too much to hold your spouse accountable for your state of mind, d'you know what I mean? Some people like being married; some people don't."

"That's bad news for hardened spinsters like me."

"You might surprise yourself. It might turn out that all you really wanted in the world was *that* area of your life squared away."

"What do you think of my choice, my . . . bridegroom? Do you like him? It seems too much—marriage and parenthood in one gulp. Shouldn't you be married for years, just revel in being lovers together, before you even think of messing up your lives with children?"

Constance considered. "Yes, I do like him," she said, finally. "Didn't you know I liked him? I don't know if I would have spotted him out of all humanity and thought, Here's the one for you, but he has a wicked smile, and I should think he would keep you amused, in the long run. Why? Have you got cold feet?"

"Oh sure—ten little icicles wriggling for the next plane to Vladivostok. Can't you feel them?"

Constance reached down and put a warm hand around a foot.

"Martin's giving me a hard time about money. He thinks Gideon's too poor."

"Is he too poor?"

"He's poor enough so I had to buy my own wedding ring."

Both women laugh.

"Darling, your father's money-obsessed. Not to mention dated: if your husband doesn't make enough money, you can go out and make some yourself. At least you didn't run off with a soulful Russian—with a soulful wife and six soulful children; that would have been my prediction. I'm not convinced you respect him, but that's for you two to sort out."

"Every marriage I've seen's ended in divorce. And I'm so used to my own way."

Constance was silent for so long Gwen thought she must have fallen asleep.

"I think you have a moment when you suddenly think, This is what I want," she said, finally. "And you're willing to give up quite a lot for that, if need be. I think you have a sense of . . . you and this person, engaged in . . . this eternity-long exchange of—ah—utter trivialities. I think women on the whole marry men they find calming."

"And what do you think men want?"

"Do you know I went off with somebody else the night before—no, two nights before my wedding?"

Gwen searched her brain. "Who?"

"I'm not telling. It was good fun; I'm not a bit sorry. I did it to test my choice, really."

"I bet I know who it was."

"You're wrong. I'm not telling."

"I know you're not. And are you still . . . in love? With Roger? What have you guys been married for—five years?"

"Six, in July. Oh you know, I was born married. So was Roger. We're these two pathetically uxorious creatures who were absolutely programmed for domesticity, one of us to do the washing up while the other does the drying. He's a planner, too; he knows exactly where he wants us to be in ten years, and I find that reassuring. Otherwise, the breaking-in can be rather brutal."

"Yeah. I guess I'm about to find out."

"The looking at your husband and children and thinking, Isn't it time for them to leave? When are they going to go back to where they belong?"

"And do you ever get itchy to break out?"

"Oh, always. But you know me, I'm quite patient. I know in not very long, the children'll be gone. And as we both know, once you leave home, you never really come back. Not really . . . And I sort of want to be sure that when they do leave, there's something still between us— some flicker of suspense. So it's quite clever, really, you've married someone with such a very wicked smile. You've got something to look forward to."

"I don't know," said Gwen. "I think he just looks mischievous. I think he might be a goody-good underneath."

"That's all right, too. Because you're not."

2

JUST BEFORE DAWN, Kid and Maddock drove Gideon back to the motel. The others had headed home hours ago. Only Kid and Gideon remained, finishing off Maddock's bourbon. They talked about cars; they talked about trucks (Maddock bemoaning his ever having traded in his Toyota pickup for a Dodge. "My patriotic advice? *Don't* buy American.") They talked about storms. They talked about military hardware: for instance, whether smart bombs had proved all that smart in the Gulf War.

Every now and then Maddock or Kid would remember Gideon and say, "So you're really going through with it, huh? Remember we got the getaway car for you." And one of them would start singing "Chapel of Love." Once Maddock's girlfriend Riley came out in her nightgown and asked them would they please go sing somewhere else.

Gideon was almost too happy to speak. He felt an incredible closeness to Gwen's brother, despite his dawning certainty that the man's brains had been permanently fried by overprodigal drug use, so that what you were left with was a shell: an endearing dark blond bear with a child's not-too-active brain inside. He suspected that if he suggested this possibility to Gwen, Gwen would take offense and say no, Maddock was still in there, he was just hiding. Even though she herself—unlike Gideon—was not willing to go in there to find him.

"Maddock," said Gideon, out of the blue. "You know, your sister really loves you. You should come stay with us sometime. We'd have a ball. We can trawl Hell's Kitchen bars, there are all kinds of fun places we could go . . ."

Maddock, whom so far he had only seen so indiscriminately convivial that you imagined that if you invited him to come take a shit with you, he'd come, suddenly got the closed look that Gideon already knew from both Gwen and her father. A look that said, Have we met before? I didn't think so. "Thanks, but I grew up in New York: I already did my time. I'm not going back to that shit-pit ever."

How differently from Gwen he used language, and yet to the same end—as armor. So that was how far you could go with Maddock—a finger's length—before you reached the blank wall. And that was already farther than the nowhere you could go with Gwen's dad. These Lewises obviously stiffened with age, they did not mellow, they clenched.

And as for his bride, his Gwen-to-be, how far could you go with her? Sometimes he thought you could go to the ends of the earth and not be done, and sometimes it seemed like no, not even a finger's length. Sometimes it seemed that fending the outside off consumed her mind's best energy.

3

THIS IS THE COUNTRY: There are more people on the road at 6 a.m. than there were at 9 p.m. Gideon asks if they can take the ocean drive, and when they reach Little Boar's Head, he says, "Pull over." Maddock and Kid stay in Maddock's pickup, singing along to "You win again" on the country radio station.

Gideon climbs onto the seawall. The moon is high, a small scared-looking white wafer of a runaway, swiftly hidden by clouds. It's low tide and the sea is flat as an oil spill. Last winter's storm has cast the beach in a knee-deep ground cover of seaweed. Gideon takes off his shoes and teeters on the wall, wanting badly to run down to the ocean, but frightened to step out into this marine pasture of algae.

It's a primal fear of serpents and dragons, of slime, of slithering bloodsuckers that might leech onto your unsuspecting ankles, of being sucked down into the stenchy deep.

For the longest while, Gideon shrinks back, revolted by these snaky plumes, spirals, frizzes, and rivulets of brine, purple-black, green-black, orange-black in the dawn.

Maddock honks the horn.

Gideon hesitates once more, then forces himself to leap barefoot into the thick salad. Relieved to find it's succulent, moist underfoot. Not rancid, but young, fresh, and springy. Gideon bounds across the seaweed meadow in the gray dawn, breaking into a caper when he finally reaches the hard underfoot of sand. Running running leaping—you win again—and now the low lace of waves nips at his ankles, lazy and faint.

In a few more hours, dear God, he and his Gwen will be man and wife. He who went all his life a snot-nosed orphan will have his own wife in his bed, with a bab in her belly, not a wanderer between worlds any longer, O western wind, but home home at last.

Gideon dances before the incoming waves, alight with the familiar near-seizure of ecstasy that has visited him periodically since childhood, that comes from feeling God's majesty in the world. It's a gray day, Gideon's wedding day, big clouds and a raw wind, but suddenly he sees a streak of gold on the sea's outer rim, from a bolt of sun cracking through the broken ragged sky. The thin stripe of pink-gold is moving, moving, toward him; God's eggy finger strokes the rough sea.

When the skies close again and the sea resumes its green-gray foggy glower, Gideon understands the stripe of light, like Noah's rainbow, was meant for him as promise of conjugal joy, which of all earthly arrangements bears closest resemblance to God's relation with the world.

Throughout his wedding feast, Gideon knows, heading back toward the car, he will be no more than a mechanical husk enacting prescribed forms. Not till nighttime, when he and his bride will at last be alone in each other's arms, will he be fully returned to himself.

For the business of today—the signing of registers, the oral contract— is merely tribal-dynastic horse-trading between men, whereas the divine cleaving of Gideon to Gwen is eternal, already written in God's book.

BOOK FIVE

Chapter One

"Hello?"

"Beloved," she says.

"Hello?"

"Sweetheart, can you hear me?"

"Hello?"

Funny, she can hear him fine.

She is calling from the Hotel Yevropa in Ekaterinburg.

A less work-driven bride might not have left her new-wedded lord for three weeks, but Gwen figured it was her last big trip before the baby. (The weary dare in it, too, familiar to every career woman: the daily proving to her superiors that just because she has a stomach like a medicine ball doesn't mean her brain is equally encephalitic. Her women friends tell her she's nuts, but she still believes motherhood's not going to change her life. Soon as the brat's loose, she'll be back to her old travel schedule.)

"Hello? Hello?"

He hangs up.

She tries again.

This time the connection is better.

"Sweetheart, are you okay?" Gideon's voice is harsh with anxiety. "I got worried when I couldn't reach you today."

"Yeah, I was out in City 3."

"Are you feeling all right? How'd it go?"

She wants to tell Gideon about the godforsaken loveliness of Siberia in late summer. She and Tamara Vorashina had driven out to one of the closed warfare-cities whose regeneration they were offering to sponsor, twenty kilometers east of Ekaterinburg, formerly known as Sverdlovsk. It is harvesttime, and the landscape glimpsed from the car window seemed as if from a golden age: billows of blond crew-cut fields cropped by molten rivers; mowers chasing one another with scythes between the haycocks; white swimmers dancing around a fire to keep warm.

And then the compound.

"God, what a ruin—this futuristic ruin. You remember, Sverdlovsk is where they let loose the anthrax germs, back in the seventies. They had a hundred and fifty thousand scientists working there in Soviet days; that's a lot of orphans waiting to get adopted by North Korea and Iraq. It's going to take some doing to turn this place into Silicon Valley."

"Did they let you look around?"

"We talked to some officials, we—yeah, we wandered a bit. We met this French filmmaker, who's been there six months, making a documentary about the place. He was interesting; I took him out to dinner—"

"Did he speak English?"

"Pascal? No, but my French is . . . good enough. We went to this nightclub that absolutely didn't exist a year ago—all these kid millionaires, with their blond model wives and their bodyguards, and their bulletproof Mercedes. And meanwhile, there are these scientists who are picking through garbage cans for food, who haven't been paid their sixty-dollars-a-month pensions for a year now . . . I mean, the contrasts are completely medieval. And this isn't Moscow or St. Petersburg, this is some shit-town in the Urals, this is the city where they axed the tsar and his family! You keep thinking, These guys should really consider having a revolution . . ."

"Isn't it, like, four in the morning your time?"

"Yeah, quarter to . . ."

"You just got back?"

"Yeah."

"You were out with this French director?"

"Yeah, Pascal."

"I bet *he* gets an early start in the morning."

She hesitates, feeling the conversation is going off-track. Because—although she's had a blast this evening—in fact, what's really struck her is how much she's been changed by a mere six weeks of marriage. It's as if there is now an invisible barrier between her and other men, so that—even with her balloon-belly proclaiming her out of the fray—Gwen had found herself unable to look Pascal in the eye. Dove out of the car with insulting haste when he dropped her off at the hotel.

She is genuinely shocked by her new timidity: she never suspected, until now, that the essence of all relationships between men and women was the potential for mad fucking. That if you couldn't insinuate to a man that circumstances permitting, you might very possibly end up in bed together, then you couldn't even meet his eye. The discovery of this surviving spirit of the harem she would now be trying to describe to Gideon, were they not separated by a million miles of telephone line.

But Gideon is back in New York City, where it's 98 degrees and the air conditioner is broken. "Didn't you go to Russia to work?" he inquires. "If you want to go to nightclubs, they got nightclubs in New York. I like nightclubs, too. We could stay out till four in the morning together . . ."

"Sweetheart, I am working. It *is* work."

"Right."

A pause.

"What have *you* been up to?" she asks.

"Me? Jennings and I have been busting our guts trying to get the baby's bedroom done," his accusing voice returns. Jennings is an ex-artist turned contractor whom Gideon does carpentry work for, sometimes. Together they are converting Gwen's dressing room into the baby's room. Gideon had thought they could get away with knocking a window into the living room for air and light, but instead they've ended up hiring a third guy and making a doorway. Jennings has found them this great pair of glass doors he salvaged from a Park Avenue job . . .

"You'll like them," Gideon says. "They're *French*."

"Sweetheart . . ."

"Anyway, the place is a demolition site at the moment, but I guess it'll look okay when we're finished . . ."

"Gideon, I can't *wait*," Gwen says, conciliatory. "I am so excited to see what you guys have done. I bet it'll be gorgeous."

"I miss you," he admits, finally. "Sorry if I sound kind of pissy, but I've been working fourteen-hour days trying to finish the baby's room before you get back. Plus I get kinda worried about you. I want to be there to take care of you . . ."

She is thinking, He liked it better when I was morning-sick and at his mercy. How funny that just as I've become this waddling blimp no man wants to look at, Gideon's gotten jealous. She should be grateful, but instead she feels it's he who's put these shackles on her.

Whereas Gideon himself remains unchanged, lithe and flirtatious as ever. Does he too feel the invisible barrier between himself and other women? Does he too feel too spooked by sex's dark powers even to look Annie Dolores or Jamie Gorelick in the eye? Not likely.

"I adore you," she murmurs. "Look, it's only ten more days."

"Don't say it. Fucking eternity . . ."

But to Gwen, oddly, it's not long enough. She misses Gideon, but it's been almost six months since her last trip to Russia, and there's a lot of catching up to do. She's meeting with the ex-governor of Nizhni Novgorod, a young reformer who is a protégé of Chubais's; she is interviewing candidates for their program director in Kazan; she is having dinner with Sergei Kovalyev, who is one of the few people she trusts to tell her what's really going on in the country.

The mood in Russia has definitely shifted since the oligarchs and the IMF bought Yeltsin his reelection. There is talk of disaffection among military officers, of a coal miners' strike that turned nasty, but she has no idea how seriously to take the various grumblings of unrest.

Curious how Russia—a slave-state throughout history—to her, has always meant freedom. Even from her husband. Even lugging this twenty-five-pound belly on swollen legs, even newly disabled from looking men in the eye, she feels thrillingly free.

Chapter Two

"I HAVE TROUBLE AT WORK," said Gwen. She was lying in the bath, marinating in a chamomile stew. She couldn't lie on her back anymore, but was obliged to dock sideways. "Well, not trouble, exactly." Gwen was too lofty for trouble. "An annoyance."

She had been home nearly a month, but Gideon still tiptoed around her as if suspecting she might be the ghost of a Gwen who had actually died in an airplane crash between Ulan Bator and Bator Ulan.

Gideon, wearing only jeans, was sitting on the toilet seat. Absent-mindedly scrubbing Gwen's back with a loofah. "Maybe I should clone you," he said. "Make a Gwen-puppet to keep me company while you're nightclubbing in the Gulag. I'd have to make an accessory kit, too, with doll-sized jars of shoe polish. You wouldn't be you without the shoe polish, would you?"

"You're not listening."

"I am listening, you're having trouble at work."

"I told you Kalman's brought in this new hireling, who studied with him at Columbia? To replace Tim, who finally, thank God, has gotten the hell out. But this guy looks even worse. He's this kinda prissy bustling little know-it-all."

"What's he know?" asked Gideon. He was gradually acclimatizing himself to Gwen's attitude toward knowledge. A competitive avarice: substitute "money" for "learning," and she was her father's daughter.

"Everything I know plus. I mean Russian *and* all the Central Asian Turkic languages, *and* he spent a summer interning at the World Bank. So they've shifted Mandy to Belarus and Ukraine, and this kid's taking over Central Asia and the Caucasus. I'm supposed to be filling him in, so he's looking over my shoulder at everything I do. He thinks we need to be a lot more hard-assed about whether individual programs are working. A line-item boy. And he likes to be on the road—who doesn't, at twenty-four?—which is supposed to be great because he can do my fieldwork while I'm having the baby, which is this activity that the men seem alternately to think will take me five minutes and five years, because nobody in the office has done it before, except for the secretaries. And I don't much know, either, how long I'll be out of commission . . ."

Gideon was attending now to the parts she could no longer reach. Feet. Soaped each toe, their pads pink-wrinkly.

"I wouldn't mind if you stayed home from Chechnya for a couple of months," he said.

"I like Chechnya. I don't want Ari muscling in on my job."

"So we'll let *him* get beheaded by Muslim extortionists."

"Nah, the worst of it is I kind of like him, too. He's so transparently, thrivingly ambitious, and yet his idea of ambition is learning Tajik in three weeks or smuggling a radio transmitter into Grozny. How can I not like him?"

"That's what I asked myself when I met you," said Gideon.

"I'm not ambitious, that's the trouble. I'm going to have this baby, and it's going to turn out all I want to do in the world is sit on a park bench yakking with the other mothers about breast-feeding. And Ari's going to be running the world . . ."

"What world? Like, why is a radio transmitter more 'the world' than breast-feeding? That's what I don't understand about you career women. If men could make babies, you think they'd bother inventing radio? I mean, the Israelites invented a new religion just to muscle their way into the land of milk and honey, and meanwhile you guys got these built-in soda fountains in your chests . . ."

(Gwen, amused that Gideon, who basically spent his day sewing doll's clothes, should be so proprietarily dismissive of the "male" world.) "I still don't want him moving in on my job."

"So we'll kill him."

"Kalman likes him, and Gerald likes him, and I hear he made a good impression on Lavrinsky, too. I can't tell you how sick I am of all this Byzantine-courtier, who's-in, who's-out intrigue, who did Lavrinsky invite to Connecticut last weekend, who got a lift in his car on the way to the council . . . It's a crummy way to run an organization that's supposed to be dedicated to—"

But Gideon has gotten sidetracked by talk of breasts. "Are you going to let me taste your milk?" Hiking up her tits' unwonted weight, the nipples gone wine-dark. "Will I want to, you think, or is it taboo?"

Chapter Three

I

"I DREAMT ABOUT THE BIRTH," Gwen told her husband.

She was propped sideways in bed, pillows stuffed under knees and belly. The jackrabbit was bucking, its sinewy hind legs thumping Gwen's ribs, while its forelegs and skull rocketed hard into her groin. Yow.

She'd seen the pale day break, pacing the living room, the library, the hall, seen it hatch from pinkish-black to lavender to robin's egg.

Other insomniacs in the Manhattan darkness signalling their flame-blue-cathode wakefulness from the boxy windows of low brownstones and high towers. Invalided widows too old to sleep; young bond traders watching CNN while packing for the morning's flight to Hong Kong.

She had paced the balcony, watching the Citicorp building, across the narrow island, gleam in the dark like an iceberg with flashing red eyes. Alabaster white, white-whale white, unearthly. *Holy.* Watched it, the way you look at a mountain or the ocean. Its silvery hallowed whiteness tinging snow-pink in the dawn.

Watched the early morning sky, hugging to herself the harried oppressed mystery of these third-term nights—sleep a momentary stumbling, a dozy lighthouse glimmer, in between the long forced march dictated by the baby's kicking.

The baby. The baby was insomniac, the baby demanded action, it was a rock-star baby trashing its hotel suite, using your tenderest internal organs as springboard. You hated the unseen babe for hurting you and were proud, too, of its brutish vitality, its frenzy to grow and *be.*

Last night Gwen had tried to read a book as she paced. She'd picked a volume of Mandelstam from the shelf, figuring the drenched explosive tersity of verse might be more formally compatible than prose with her unborn offspring's zero tolerance. You could read a line, get kicked, walk, get kicked, reread. Mandelstam and his wife hadn't had any children. Nadezhda Mandelstam, she seemed to recall, had miscarried while her husband was in exile. And who wouldn't miscarry, rather than give Stalin one more perfect sacrifice?

Gideon brought her breakfast in bed and the morning papers on his way out. He had a ten o'clock meeting with the head of the drama department at Talbot College, who was looking for a director-in-residence for their next academic year.

"Here you go, ma'am."

"So the baby was born . . ." she continued.

Scrambled egg on an English muffin, the morning's prenatal vitamin alongside a glass of blood orange juice.

"Nu?"

"It turned out to be a poodle."

He looked down at her, fondly, with a trace of bewilderment. Gwen was immense now, a beehive on skinny legs, so lopsided-unsteady on her swollen feet that she had to grip the geriatric safety bar while she took a shower. It required a forklift to get her in and out of the bath . . .

She had a new walk, a new physique, new gestures for Gideon to assimilate. She waddled, potbellied, splayed-hipped. She belched; she farted. She had become uninhibitedly gross, a scabrous and malicious dog too old and sick to care. She scratched her scaly encrusted dome of a stomach—itchy as a lizard hide—she rested both hands on it like someone settling down after Thanksgiving dinner. She looked like a paunchy old man, a Halloween scarecrow, in Gideon's ex-sweatpants and a pair of unlaced sneakers; her feet too puffy to fit into her own pretty shoes. She panted as she talked, sat down on steps to catch her breath, sunk into armchairs and couldn't get up again.

Gideon had become the Greek hero whose charge was never to let go of the frenzied shape-changer. Sometimes his beloved turned crocodile, sometimes a hound dog, sometimes a cow, sometimes a foul-breathed incontinent old codger, sometimes pure demon. It was a test of his love; he was ruefully game. Whereas she just hated him, he knew, as the sick can't but hate the well. Why haven't you changed too, she wanted to know. Why are you so unencumbered, so bouncy and free, why are you just the same as you always were? Why don't *you* take the baby for a while? Furious at biology's having tripped her up, after a lifetime's unisex equality, smarting from God-the-misogynist's reminder that life *is* unfair and only so much the Civil Rights Commission can do about it. That's how people were these days—*outraged* by nature, by having to carry their own babies or not being able to carry their own babies, just because they were gay men or sixty-five-year-old businesswomen who'd forgot, *outraged* by anachronisms like disease or anybody's ever having to die ever.

Aren't you curious, she demanded accusingly, wouldn't you like to know what it feels like being pregnant, lugging a catapulting thirty pounds around your belt. No, said once-bitten Tiresias, I don't want to know. I'd take the load from you if I could, but I don't want to know. You've convinced me pretty effectively it's hell. Hadn't he traduced himself enough already, agreeing to carry around her cell phone in case she needed him? (Her need of him these days being something vengefully omnivorous as a civil war.)

"A poodle? That would save on tuition."

"I was worried Martin was going to find out and say, I told you so."

"I'd be worried, too; I'm scared shitless of dogs. Some kinda leftover shtetl thing about canine anti-Semitism."

She glanced at the headlines, reached up for a kiss that . . . pro-

longed. Hands prowling each other's bodies, searching for ways in, pleasure turning urgent, into confused excitement . . .

"Are you sure we want to have a baby, after all? I think I just want
you to myself."

He sank into the pillows beside her—the sideways jackknife being
their best bet at proximity. Her breasts, swollen as a spring river, slapping against the high hard shelf of blue-marbled belly as she groped to
meet him. Gideon, glancing at the digital clock in his feathered fall.
Twenty-seven minutes to get downtown.

"My queen, you think some poodle's gonna get in our way? I'll send
it straight to the pound . . ."

2

"Great," said Gwen. "Some money—that would be *great*."

Gwen was getting downcast at the prospect of having to support
three people indefinitely on her good-works salary. No more Walter
Steiger shoes, no more trips to London, no more lunches at the Royalton. Would Gideon mind taking a look sometime at her ob-gyn bills? It
was getting to the point—Gwen naturally having vetoed the Lavrinsky
health plan—where she wanted to ask the nurse, Do I really need a blood
test every *week*? If Gideon could contribute even a little to their family
expenses, it would be a big help . . .

"I don't think I want this job."

"Why not?"

"I'm pretty busy now fighting the eviction. Three days a week in
New Paltz just doesn't sound feasible."

"It's money. And you never know—it might turn into something
permanent."

"That's exactly what I'm scared of."

Gwen shot him a Gorgon glare, but Gideon did not shame easy.
Instead, he said, slow, deliberate, "I'll apply, sure. But I've never done
anything in my life just for money. And what's more, I don't believe
you have, either."

"I'm not sure that's something to be proud of, Gideon."

"Don't you think it's kinda presumptuous, telling somebody else
what not to be proud of in their lives?"

They didn't used to snip at each other. Or if they snipped, the tension had swiftly spun off into sexual horseplay. Now the sex had become to Gideon's mind a mite leaden, dutiful; too often tiredness or pregnancy's ailments got in the way, so that the ill will left over from their quarrels sat undissipated, reducing the next day's conversation to a sullen allotment of chores, a Where'd-he-put-the-Balducci's-catalogue, or Had-he-picked-up-more-dishwashing-liquid, or Did-he-remember-they-were-going-to-Sutton-Place-for-her-father's-birthday-dinner. No, I'd thought we were going to the Hellfire Club to fuck in a back room all night. Oh money! Oh matrimony! Oh matrimoney!

Chapter Four

I

DUE DAY PASSED, and *der Nister* was a no-show. How puzzling for Gwen, the dinner party guest who was always circling the block so as not to arrive before the hosts. How embarrassing, her failure to perform. Was she that scared, really, to cough it up?

The nurses in Dr. Landesmann's office tried to comfort her with jokes about the kid's having too good a time inside. Come *on*. Twenty-two hours a day the little squirt was corkscrewing its adamantine skull like a prisoner tunnelling its way out of the Château d'If. How could it be happy? It didn't *feel* happy. It felt bored-rigid, murderous with cabin fever. Would you be happy in a wet coffin half your size?

Her friends and relatives called. Other mothers, with an occupational tenderness for birth and its early produce. Nu? Said Dina. You still there? said Jacey. Aunt Sue. Constance. Her Cousin Emily.

"What can I say?" shrugged Gwen. "I'm cervically constipated."

In the mornings, when she waddled into Lavrinsky, her mates looked up.

"What are *you* doing here?"

"Get thee to the maternity ward."

"That kid's still in there? I thought you'd have photos by now . . ."

Sat down at a spare desk with a huff and a puff, not knowing what to do with the day since she'd already cleared the decks for maternity leave five times over.

Then, one evening when Gwen and Gideon were walking down to Carnegie Hall to meet Sasha and Irina for an Evgeny Kissin concert, the baby dropped: Gwen's high bony belly fell a good six inches, and she felt pleased as a roosting hen, dead proud that she wasn't going to be the freak-that-never-delivered.

That night, when Gideon slid sideways into her, she willed joy's now-diminished reverberations to bring on labor—this was what the paradise-haunted pair was reduced to, lovemaking because it was mechanically useful.

The almost-nightly calls from her mother, who suddenly had an *interest* in her Gwen found disconcerting.

"Should I come now?"

"No, don't come yet—we'd all just be sitting around driving each other nuts waiting."

"Has the doctor given you any idea when the baby *might* be coming?"

(Am I right in thinking your mom had two babies herself, Gideon demanded. How can she even *ask* such a medically moronic question?)

The next night, "Aunt Sue said to tell you you should get the doctor to schedule you for a C-section; that's what Patsy's daughter did."

(What, so your mom can book a cheap fare on the shuttle?)

"She's faking me out," Gwen complained. "She's making me think I can't do it."

Gideon looked exasperated. "Of course she is. That's what parents do, in the sweetest possible way. So tell her I'll give her a call once you're actually in labor. Anyway, what does *not* being able to do it mean? I simply refuse to see this *incredibly* individual and *yet* universal experience as some kind of contest."

"Why am I such a coward?"

"You're not a coward; you just got this weird idea that you shoulda been a man, so this woman-shit freaks you. You need to relax is all: your body knows what to do, if you only stop terrorizing it."

2

BRER RABBIT'S NINE DAYS LATE, and suddenly she's fed up. But, I mean, cosmically fed up. It's not coming out. Not ever, and who needs it? The kid was an accident, anyway: *she'd never wanted it.* Motherhood is not for ambitious Manhattanites. The bottom line: it takes too long.

Gideon puts his head between her legs—the tiny triangle of pubis now mammothly overshadowed by her Santa Claus belly. "I'll suck it out of you," he volunteers. "C'mon, little bugbear, your mama's tired and your papa's hungry, I'm counting to ten and then I'll smoke you out, roast you into suckling piglet for your parents' dinner."

What's most annoying is her own panting het-upness, her competitive/ingratiating straight-A eagerness to perform. All her life, Gwen's been trying to outmen the men, and now at last she's homed in on her own sex, desperate to prove herself a gal among gals. To belong. To shine. To charge into the birthing battlefield and be a hero, to add her own locker-room saga of shrugged indifference to ripped perinea and a coccyx broken in back-labor.

Forget the war stories, the hoary boasting, the I-popped-my-baby-on-my-lunch-break-and-was-back-in-the-office-by-two, My-kid-was-born-in-the-subway, I-bit-off-her-umbilical-cord-with-my-teeth. What's animating these new Amazons but a puerile resentment of their mothers' pampered generation that rested ten days in hospitals gilded as an Austro-Hungarian spa and got relieved of their babies under general anesthetic? Well, fuck that shit. Why vaunt yourself on being insensible as a ewe?

Maybe Gwen would not be brave. Fuck the fluffy slippers, the mood music, the ylang-ylang-oil lower-back rubs, the positive energy vibrating from the pulse points, the husband gelded into labor coach. Maybe she would not give birth. Maybe instead she would be the woman who, once labor started, rose and told the midwife, Bye, I'm leaving.

3

FOGGY RAIN, a ripe autumn moon. An old wives' tale that full moon and rain brought babies. Was this the foggy-full-moon night on which her phantom caller would knock to be let out? Was the free squirmer imminently to be reeled in?

She rode the Seventy-ninth Street crosstown home from work. Pressed her nose against the dripping window as the bus lunged through the Central Park transverse in the early darkness of autumn rain. Listened to the parting gush of puddles under the tunnel, the wind ripping the leaves off slick black trees.

She bought a roast Muscovy duck with plum sauce at Zabar's. Arugula, ripe Comice pears from the Korean. An autumnal birth-night feast.

The small rain was falling straight and close in a vaporous thicket of needles as she walked home, so thick a hedge that apartment buildings were curtained off, traffic lights a woozy underwater blur.

That evening, Gwen paced the apartment, looping into the baby's room, which Gideon had so handsomely reconfigured. Reading, as she walked, a book about Bolshevism she'd been asked to review for the *Slavic Quarterly*. Listening for the click of Gideon's key (ridiculous, but even now the sound of her husband's coming in the door made her almost sick with excitement). The rains had thinned now to fog, to fog, the Empire State Building's rosy crown of thorns was just now rising from the brume as she murmured to herself, Let tonight be the night, O Lord, murmured, Let my waters break.

4

TOMORROW. Tomorrow 7 a.m. Gideon and Gwendolen Wolkowitz are due at the hospital, where their baby (unluckily lodged in the latter and not the former) is to be induced.

Gwen, barricaded in her study, visited by memories of childhood constipation, her German nanny giving her one last chance to "go," and if she didn't, up went the suppository. Small wonder that a child who refused to take a shit would grow up into a woman who refused to birth her baby. If Gideon were the mother, he'd simply squat in the field . . .

She wanted to call up Constance for reassurance. Ask her, Isn't it true that childbirth is God's tough-love method of population control? Ask her, Isn't it true that induction is the electric-chair version of childbirth? Tell her, Constance, there's just no way that me and it are both gonna come out of this alive. Tell her, Constance, you know that cloisonné necklace of mine you've always liked? It's yours.

She cast inside herself for a first-aid kit of bravery. Nothing. Couldn't remember any prayers, except a snippet of one about a bedbug (really?) and one about dying before you woke, which at this point seemed like shirking.

Her mother (who had arrived that afternoon and was now installed in a room at the Empire Hotel) had never mentioned childbirth, besides maintaining that the days Gwen and Maddock were born were the two happiest days of her life. A legend her daughter now realized was proof either of Spartan heroism or of the magic of sixties-strength painkillers.

But then she looked deeper for her mother courage and struck a hard bright lode of it. Remembered Katrina, after the Belleclaire, after that shaky interval of wearing dark glasses and bumping into things and trying to send the children to school on Sundays. Remembered instead what had been too painful not to forget: Katrina's packing up Ninety-third Street, hiring a moving van, driving her kids to Newburyport. Steeling herself to learn the things Martin had previously taken care of: finding the house, buying the car, checking out the schools.

The almost bacchanalian *savagery* of her mother, that first fall and winter, as if they were Pilgrims arrived in the land of Indians, smallpox, snow. The unhappiness so wild it looked close to joy. How she'd kept *all* the lights on *all* night, like some Scandinavian winter-solstice festival, like a House of the Rising Sun. As if divorce were carnival, jubilee, leap year. As if it were finally, after a lifetime of trying to please others, Katrina's Turn. Gwen, horrified. Still friendless at boarding school, but that was nothing new: child-Gwen had had the dimmest grasp of friendship, of the possibility of deriving pleasure or inspiration from the company of others. Instead, a rather grim determination to get to her desk early. Pig-envious of those colonial orphans in Rudyard Kipling stories who *never* got sent home for holidays. Thinking—unforgivably, Pop left Mom because she was a hopeless slob . . . Now of course she saw the crazy bravery, the life force in her mother's Saturnalia.

So too this dark chill hospital-birthing-room tomorrow, this leap-year labor day would be Gwen's turn, Gwen's very own day-night-day to howl. So she too would strive to ride the pain, to drive it bucking and rocketing into some wild outerness, into some shrieking void of creation, in which fingernailed matter first catapulted blue and howling into the light. She would die a little, maybe a lot, and they would come home three.

Chapter Five

I

HE NEVER THOUGHT he would hear that scream again. Once again, it's coming from a woman in a johnny plugged to a drip, and this time it's his wife who is racked by pain, clenched, keening.

The woman in the johnny is emitting rhythmic howls of Oh Jesus or Holy shit, whatever banal execrations people spit out in their uttermost moments. She is crouching on the bed on her hands and knees, emitting this hideous wolfish keening, as the pain bears down on her, and periodically (between the spasms) she angles up toward the nurse a white screwed-up face bawling tears not of fear, but of rage. He has seen this pale twisted face of rage before, seen it in a hospital bed, too, rage and a drip, rage and the brown plastic tray of cafeteria food. Rage and a canned fruit salad (that was for him) with the maraschino weeping into the pineapple sections.

Now it seems that he has never left behind these moments of his mother's last-living, that every day since has been a wincing concealed penitential reenactment of that diabolical trajectory. Paula's wasted yellow arms, her tanned-hide of a carcass (under the johnny's wrinkled billow), the stink of her bandaged, pierced, bruised flesh are branded into his being. Her cosmic bitterness and fury; his helpless pity, grief; the shame of his final filial inadequacy—these are the set-piece emotions he's been given to live with.

He is hiding in the hall outside Gwen's hospital room, eyes fixed on a framed poster—orange flowers in a field—shuddering with sobs, trying to recover himself enough to go back in.

Earlier, before the labor started in earnest, he had fussed around Gwen, trying to hold her hand, or rub her back, or give her ice to suck on. (Those toddler-tasks intended to make the useless man feel useful.) And she had swatted him away, exasperated by his sweaty trembling neediness.

Go get a cup of coffee, counselled the nurse. Save your strength, your wife's not going anywhere.

Now time had stopped. It was . . . eight . . . ten . . . twelve hours since the labor began, and time wasn't moving. Her pain was so fierce he could not face it; he had fled as far as the hall, where he stood, listening and quaking. As long as he heard her scream, he'd know she was still alive.

A different nurse (the evening-shift nurse) struts past. "If you want to catch Dr. Landesmann, honey, she's in there with your wife." She takes a closer look. Incredulous. "You *crying*?" She is no end amused. (What could be more contemptibly pathetic than a bald man with heaving shoulders?) Men are a *riot*. Her husband didn't even show up for their last baby. He said it was boring, but she knew he was freaked. "He says, If I see what's coming *outta* there, I might not wanta go back in. I says, That's fine by me, Brian . . ." Gideon stares at her blankly, uncomprehending. She bursts out laughing again, hand over her mouth. "Go see your wife, honey, the doctor's in with her."

He hovers in the doorway of Gwen's room. (Same shit-green room they had in Teaneck, with the TV suspended from the ceiling, the table on wheels, the sink in the corner, the beige venetian blinds.) Dr. Landesmann, unfamiliar in her surgical tunic, blond hair erased by scrub cap, is just leaving, and Gideon, feeling like a guilty boy who's gotten his wife in trouble, intercepts her.

Dr. Landesmann has measured Gwen; it's ten hours into labor (Fuck me, I would have thought ten million) and Gwen's only four centimeters dilated, but on the upside, the doctor reminds him, those first few centimeters are the hardest. "I've increased the Pitocin," she says.

"Good," says Gideon, before remembering that the Pitocin is not the painkiller but the pain-inducer. They hang there a moment, listening to Gwen yowl. "Can't you give her something for the—?"

"Yeah, I think she's ready for an epidural," says the doctor on her way out.

My girl, he tries to tell his soul's beloved, my girl, let *go*. Open up those pearly gates, he commands her silently, DILATE, or else they're going to have to Caesar you.

But opening means opening to the wild storm of pain, so clamping shut, he knows, is what her cockeyed defenses are telling her, the cervical vise clutching the baby in tight from harm's way. Spit it out, mama, set the babe free.

And now, the big contractions come jolting fast in earnest, no time to catch your breath in between, it's an amusement park ride gone toxic. Buck buck bucking bronco of Gwen's possessed body trying to vomit the baby out. Now it's so bad she is vising his fingers painfully tight: you could get an electric shock from the transmitted voltage of her convulsions.

Gideon knows for sure that Gwen is dying. The baby's going to kill her, the epidural will never come, the indifferent nurses will let her die screaming, and it makes him want to die too, his two-time helplessness in the face of female pain.

Then, in a lull, a clenched mutter. "Call Mom."

"And tell her what? To come or not to come?"

His normally hyperlucid twin-soul looks flummoxed by the question, by the simultaneity of her push-pull desires, by the oncoming tidal wave of next-contraction. Tell her to come *and* not to come, to be there universal-invisible, just within her fingers' grasp for only those moments Gwen wants her. Not her *real* mother, but the dream mother, the primal earth-and-sea-and-sky mother, the sheltering Mary of strength and loving consolation now and at the moment of our death.

"You want her to come, sweetheart?" prodded Gideon.

"Call her," she shouted. "Don't you have the phone?" she shouted. (No, of course he didn't. And did he have a quarter? No.) He fled, again. Ran down the hall to the aisle of pay phones, fumbling for change. All occupied. Halted, only to be recalled by a Uniform.

"They're taking your wife into the O.R. . . ."

Why why why was his Gwen disappearing down the corridor, wheeled by nurses, a sheeted bump on the stretcher, IV at her side, a sight you'd about die before you'd want to see, your beloved, wheeled horizontal into the life-and-death house, the loudspeaker summoning the anesthesiologist *quick.*

What's happening, Gideon quavers helpless, and the nurse named Maisie, the fat one from the islands, explains. The baby's vital signs have flatlined, they're going for a C-section.

So that's the story of your birth, my sweet pea Bella, how they decided to spare you the rough usage of making the voyage solo and opted to come in and get you . . .

2

IT WAS SOMETHING WONDERFUL. The thing Gwen had unwittingly hoped for all her life. A rush, a pinch, a pressing that was the Red Sea walls of her stomach being parted. And then, as someone reached down into the rendered aisles of flesh to pull the baby aloft, she cried out. Something wonderful.

Gwen was told, "She's a girl." The child—newly she, astoundingly she—was being dangled over Gwen's head. Just as many, many years ago one Newburyport summer her Uncle Rich with burnt-sterile tweezers had extracted a splinter from her foot and held it up for her to see: There's the culprit.

To Gwen, incurious from the shifting smudge of anesthetic-turning-to-pain, the baby appeared blue-black. Angry. Eggplant-colored, eyes screwed shut against the half-light. And lanky. A lean girl, a long blood-sausage of a girl.

The girl was taken away again, and Gwen resubmerged. There were two worlds—the radiance from which the baby had been plucked, and the operating room world. Gwen wanted to go back to where the baby had come from.

Years afterwards, what she remembered was overhearing Dr. Landes-mann and Dr. Shaw as they stitched her stomach together again; two women chatting with a free-and-easy jockish camaraderie. Remembered the all-female, slang, swing, laughing birth-and-death intimacy of it, two women at the bloody cave of her, sewing and laughing.

3

WHEN THEY PUT THE BABY to her breast, Miss Girl the Miraculous knew the ropes already.

This maggot who'd spent her prior life nourished intravenously in pink darkness knew just what to do. Clamped down with the fierce might of her new-minted gums like a pro, like a nursing fool, as if she'd written the book on breast-feeding and was just demonstrating for the assembly a few of the simpler techniques, and this was the moment Gwen was supposed to begin loving her, love and milk geysering to-gether, but instead what she felt was a monumental welling-up of desire for Gideon, and also unease because the anesthesia was beginning to wear off.

Here was another undeclared reality of childbirth—that just when you were supposed to be gazing at her worshipfully, saying, She's got your chin, honey, instead you were wholly bent upon the reemerging pain. Demanding anxiously, Can I have some more morphine?

4

WHEN BABY GIRL WOLKOWITZ was one day old (still nameless, as Gideon and Gwen were deadlocked over his insistence that they call her Paula) Gwen's father and stepmother came to the hospital to visit.

Gideon had just eaten his first meal in twenty hours when he bumped into Martin—looking suddenly old in tweed suit and cashmere overcoat. Peering over his bifocals through the (bulletproof? did people shoot babies?) glass of the baby pen, trying in vain to read which one was theirs.

"The white one, presumably," Gideon heard Jacey say. Before Martin cleared his throat in warning—No, now's *not* the moment to say, What an ugly little chimp, I guess she gets her nose from the Other Side of the Family.

"So that's my little girl," said Martin, tender-foggily. (Maybe honestly not remembering anymore which ones were his.)

"No, that's *my* little girl," Gideon corrected him, smiling.

"Isn't she sweet, Mart? All that dark, dark hair. You forget how tiny they are. How's Gwen doing, Gideon?"

"Fine. Considering what a butchery it was."

"We brought her a little care package from Petrossian."

"How are *you* doing, Gideon?" Jacey asked solicitously. "You were there, right? Martin was in L.A. for Serena. Even with Al, he wouldn't come to the hospital till it was over."

"Hey, you have your work, I have mine. Why should I get in the doctor's way? He seemed to know what he was doing."

"She."

"She? I knew there was something funny about that guy."

"It must be awesome, watching your wife deliver," Jacey pursued. "I mean, it's not like the movies, is it?"

"Jacey . . ."

"They don't warn you about the gore." She was baiting her husband, on Gideon's time.

"Jacey, I just had breakfast, all right?"

"She nearly bled to death," said Gideon, slowly. "There was some kind of . . . A woman can bleed to death from her uterus in, like, fifteen minutes. It just makes you want to . . . chop it off."

"It makes you want to *what*?" asked Martin.

"Your dick. It just makes you want to chop it off."

And Martin, face frozen in disgust, turned away. Saying, "I think I'll go see how Gwen's doing." Making for the nurses' station to ask for his daughter's room number. As if a guy so in-your-face sick as Gideon wouldn't be capable of giving him directions.

BOOK SIX

Chapter One

I

OCTOBER 1996.

Home from the hospital. Home to an apartment the hushed precinct now of pink-and-blue teddy-bear mobiles, stacks of doll-sized onesies, crocheted booties slipping from a tiny red heel.

The baby days old now, eight days, nine days, ten days. Still spanking new. Still blind and furry-eared with newness, navel encrusted with the red amber of its severance, like a terrier's bobbed tail.

The strange glamour of those late autumn nights, those early winter dawns, Gwen on the rocking chair with the babe limpeted to her breast, its flaky legs tucked under one elbow, the bluish glazed-porcelain eyes searching hers, while Gwen propped open *The Rise of Bolshevism* or the fall issue of *Foreign Affairs* with one hand, reading as the baby gorged and dozed, gorged and dozed. Babies, Gwen had discovered, were equipped with one physiological improvement over the adult model: they could eat and sleep at the same time.

You read, Gwen, with a hallucinatory clarity that in other circumstances might presage some epileptic advent, a psychotic break. Your tripping-with-sleeplessness brain raked in the facts one-armed-bandit fast, the Social Revolutionaries, the Democratic Socialists, the demise of Martov, the rise of Yagoda, Brest-Litovsk and Kronstadt, mixed with whether the U.S. should buy North Korea's nukes, right breast, left breast, right, a Percocet at two, two Anaproxes at five. Hours whose insides you weren't used so routinely to seeing. Nipples scabbed and blistered from the infant's frantic rapacity. As if in a curse, your breasts dripped blood-milk. Wasn't "blood" one of the Egyptian plagues?

The baby's feeds taffied into one twenty-four-hour continuous reel. She half woke, snort-squawking into protest, you plugged her to the breast, she corked off on your lap, drunken-splayed, snoring, milk dripping from her cheeks, the ceaseless reflex of her tiny rhythmic nibbling like a minnow at the line. Your husband a distant bump beneath the covers. Crawled back frozen into bed at 7 a.m., just as the garbage trucks were clearing their throats up Amsterdam Avenue, brain still whirring with party congresses, World Bank reports, Central Asian gas deals. Baby accordioned between your sleeping bodies.

Days without horizons, without light or dark. Goofing out on this newborn hormonal brew of love and a fatigue so beyond credence that you felt omnipotent.

Gerald telephoned to find out when you were coming back to work, and you zoned out mid-conversation, reawoke thinking you were talking to your father. No one warned you, Gwen, that nursing a new baby means becoming one yourself: a bivalve whose round is miniaturized to a half-trance from which you're shaken only to feed or cry. Cry because you can't believe how tired you are. Cry because you've forgotten your book on the other side of the room and, pinned down by the nibbling mollusk and a stomach ear-to-ear grinning with stitches, you can't rise to get it. Cry because Maddock has sent a dozen yellow roses and a note scrawled "Way to Go Girl!"—an offering that makes you desperate, suddenly, for your brother to know and love your daughter as you do, because to see your tiny one in his hairy blond arms would mean a healing of wounds whose denial leaves both of you numb, half lobotomized . . . Because the love you feel for Her makes you realize how much of your energy goes into *not* loving him anymore, into pretending your shared prehistory no longer impinges on your present.

Gideon, your sole adjunct in the mystery, relives your early days of housebound love, barely leaving the apartment except to buy groceries, or to steal downtown for a few hours on company business. And you, Gwen, are uneasy in his absence, because only he understands the bone-crushing, annihilating wondrousness of your savior-girl; only he is initiate enough to spend an afternoon worrying over the color of her poop. Besides, you are still too sewn-sore to manage by yourself, to get yourself and Miss Magic through the diurnal haul, one day soon you're going to rouse yourself to take a shower and get dressed, but in the meantime you need Gideon just to keep the visitors at bay. Your mother, on her way back to Newburyport; Jacey; Christopher and Yilmaz; Irina and Sasha and their now ten-year-old son; Ari, who turns out to be baby-crazy. Gideon's colleagues: Dina, mightily amused when you confess the baby hasn't had a bath since the hospital because you're too scared of dropping her in the water. "She's tougher than you think, sweetie. C'mon, Eeth, let's give the old girl a soak . . ."

2

JACEY OFFERS SISTERLY ADVICE. Hire a maternity nurse, go back to work fast, get a good massage—you want me to send you Gigi?

"Remember, I've got loads of baby clothes for you. Didn't you know Texans are pack rats? It's something about knowing you got half a continent to clutter up, I never get rid of a *thing*: buckets and buckets of onesies from Petit Bateau that are just the *best*, velour footsies from Jacadi, party frocks with matching underpants. What else do you need? You got a changing table? I've got all the equipment; you won't have to buy a thing."

And Gwen, uncustomarily submissive, is out-of-the-blue furious at Gideon for obliging her to become, if not a supplicant to Jacey, at least a chastened recipient. Why couldn't he have thought of some of this? Why couldn't he have gone out and bought the baby a bassinet ("Can't we just put her in our bed?"). No, he hadn't so much as laid in a single undershirt, a pack of diapers. Did that seem too much to ask, she birthed the baby, he bought the diapers?

This raw resentment, which swirled in from nowhere, puzzled even you, Gwen. You were tired, you told yourself, your hormones were still ajangle. You did not know that this rage was not a passing cyclone, but a feature of the new regime. A chronic anger against the man who had been the instrument of your colonization—this unconscious brute who had made you a mother without seeming much to have been changed himself.

3

SHE WAS A BEAR CUB chased from her mother's lair. She was a baby bear, roused from nine and a half months' hibernation. She was red, red as Esau, and covered in a dark brown pelt. The dark brown hair matted on her pulsing skull, the dark brown hair fleeced her back and her shoulders and her round rosy ears, she still carried with her from the womb this prehistoric protection against the elements, from the days of cave dwellers battling lions.

Every day a little of her animalness would drop away from her, she would lose her protective fur; her eyes' cunning would soon outstrip that of her nose; toes would lose their parity with fingers; but for now, Gwen delighted in drinking in the lairish hibernal heat the pup still radiated.

Bella (after Gideon's grandma) Wolkowitz was how she'd got registered with the Authorities, but they didn't dare call her by her name. She was still too savage to be anthropomorphized by the fussy syllables: the edges of her too blurry to be hemmed in by the household-management, wildlife-control of naming. Besides, Gwen wasn't convinced she was theirs to keep, not sure enough yet to bite the tag off, fold her in the drawer, throw away the receipt.

And now that Gwen had finally met in the flesh her forty-two-week secret correspondent, those prenatal fights over whether the child should be Christian or Jew, whether they took it to church on Easter or whether it abstained from leaven for Pesach seemed madly anachronistic: here was a creature from millions of years before either Abraham or Jesus, here was a cave-cub to be wrapped in wolf skins and fed on wild honey, whose great-great-grandchild might just be lucky enough to discover fire or how to notch flint into arrowheads or chalk stampeding buffalo onto the flickery wet walls.

"I don't want to go back to work *ever*," Gwen said.

She had already bargained her leave to an extended three months, full-pay, Gerald gloomily wisecracking that she must think she was living in fucking Stockholm, next thing she was going to be demanding they set up a day care center in the boardroom and make the directors hold hands and sing Barney songs.

"I could live with your staying home," says Gideon.

"I want *you* to stay home, too."

"I thought you wanted me to suddenly become a Wall Street bond trader."

"Yeah, but if you're not going to bring home the bacon, you might as well be useful around the house."

She had intended this as a tease, but Gideon's mouth tightened and his eyes distanced, in a look she'd never seen. In Soviet Russia, you'd called this expression "internal exile," meaning, They're trying to break my spirit, but there's somewhere deep inside I've got my freedom . . .

4

GIDEON'S AT HIS DESK at La Merced.

He's ostensibly trying to put together his application for director-in-residence at Talbot, but his computer's LCD screen has conked out, and he can't seem to find a remotely current hard copy of Pants on Fire's list of attainments. In addition to which they want three references, and although every day now he's made a note to himself to put in calls to Jerome and Annie Dolores and maybe Abel Ibarra at the New Theater, in fact the last thing he feels like doing is getting on the phone to demand professional favors.

It feels like dumb torture sitting here all by himself in this big cold room five miles away from his angel daughter and her mother. He's so excited he can't bear to be alone, Hector's not coming in today, so he wanders upstairs in search of Sancho.

Carlos is in Sancho's office, which is plastered in posters of Subcomandante Marcos and Free Leonard Peltier, the radio's going, and Sancho, riding his chair on its hind legs, is talking on the phone. He is wearing a red-and-black plaid lumber jacket and a matching hat with earflaps—it's cold already—cold *inside,* outside's fine.

"Yeah, they've rescheduled. Yeah, they've—yeah, it's rescheduled for the summer—yeah, they fixed a . . . the . . . ah . . . July . . . Are you—? Yeah. Yeah. Get outta here, man. You crazy? Whaddaya think *I'd* buy this shitty building, holes in the roof, rats all over the place. I wouldn't buy this shitty building, you think *I* wanna live in a shit-house? It's a shit-house, I should know, I live here."

He hangs up. "Sit down, sit down, Gid."

"So the auction's rescheduled?"

"Yeah, I just heard back from Kitty Chow at the Department of Real Estate Services: they got us on the block, man."

"Our little Lady of Mercy," sighs Gideon.

"In there with vacant lots . . . July ten. Maurizio called, you hear that crazy sucker, he says, Why don't *you* buy the building from the city. I says to him, You think *I* wanna own a fucking cockroach-pit like this dump, what do *I* wanna own this dump for, I'm gonna invest in property I'm gonna buy myself nice and new and clean, a little three-bedroom home in Montclair."

"So what do we do this time?"

Sancho and Carlos exchange amused glances. "We do what we always do, man. We wage our war against der Führer Adolf Giuliani, we accuse him of cultural genocide, we picket City Hall—"

"I can see the posters, No Mercy to Mercy-Killers!"

"We get our media campaign mobilized, we write our petitions, we get our friends in the press writing op-ed pieces. You know anybody in TV I don't know about, Gideon, any of the reporters or producers or anybody at the local stations?"

Gideon considers.

"How about your father-in-law, Gid, he know anybody who can help us, city politicians, TV producers . . . Where'd I see his name recently, it was like in the *Post*? Does he know Betsy Gotbaum? That is a woman who could help us big-time. You think your wife's dad could fix us up a meeting with Betsy Gotbaum? All we need is to package this as, like, the kinda cultural conservation issue these Upper East Siders can get into—like, that committee that's restoring Penn Station?"

"Grand Central," Gideon corrects him.

"Whatever." Sancho is shameless. He's much more militant than Gideon, and yet he's also happy to hustle society people. He will induct anybody into his cause, he's that red-hot. Already Sancho is scrawling out a battle chart with arrows pointing to the proper divisions of communication: legal, media, arts organizations, local . . .

"You guys on-line yet, Gid?"

"Nah, I been meaning to shop around for a new computer, but . . ." ("Shop around" means call up Ethan, who can tell you why this week's best buy is the Zonar Sketch-Pad 301.) "My wife's got a laptop at home I can use." (Why, when he discusses Gwen with his colleagues, does it *still* sound as if he's talking about his mother? Is it only because she treats them as a parent might treat her son's less savory schoolmates, the ones who aren't allowed in the house? But who, of his wide-ranging acquaintance, *is* welcome home?) "That would be a help, Gideon. I been talking to Isaac, he says we need to post ourselves a web site."

Gideon is trying to pay attention, but he is not the same person he was six weeks ago. He's madly in love, utterly transformed by that mottled little squawler. His daughter keeps coming into his mind in the most improbable places, turning the piss-stinking B train at morning rush hour into this ideal vessel of commuting saints. Adorable, how she kicks her wrinkly fat legs with excitement whenever she catches you looking at her . . .

Hard as he tries to attend to Sancho's organizational pep talk, Gideon can't stop laughing from the impossibility of it, him with a baby of his own at home, not just any baby but his very own Messiah-girl.

"What about Ed Lavrinsky, man?" Sancho's asking. "Somebody told me he's, like, this big free-speech activist. You think your wife could get him to write to Giuliani?"

But Gideon is now on his feet, first pogoing up and down to warm up, then kicking his legs in a Ukrainian hat dance. "For unto us a child is born, unto us a girl is given," he sings. "And her name shall be called *Pele-yoez-el-gibor-avi-ad-sar-shalom* . . ."

"That's a mouthful, Gid, is that really what you're callin' her? I may not be able to make it to the christening . . ."

"Nah, I'm just radically underslept is all . . ." Gideon sits down again. "Have I shown you guys the pictures?"

"You shown me already," says Carlos. "You wanna show me again? Sancho, you seen these?"

Sancho eyes rapidly the photos of blob-in-bath, blob-in-snowsuit. "What can I tell you?" he sighs. "Enjoy it while it lasts. Before they start carrying concealed weapons and stealing your condoms." He returns to his chart. "Now, Gideon"—a firm but affectionate hand on Gideon's shoulder—"what we gotta do is send out another bomb campaign of letters, we print up another thousand flyers, get our kids to put 'em up all over the neighborhood, call up our friends in the media, what was the name of that Erica woman from the *Observer* who came over to talk to us last spring? You could tell her Susan Sarandon and Tim Robbins are definitely on board."

A stirring of unease as Gideon thought, If La Merced really gets sold this time, we're going to have to hit the open market and pay rent. Andrea and Dan had volunteered their apartment, but the idea of sneaking a theater into a building not zoned for commercial use felt like humiliating regression. A sudden realization that Bella had indeed changed *everything:* he didn't want to live like a student anymore, quite so hand-to-mouth precarious.

He wanted a home, not a squat, he wanted to be building something for the future that his daughter would be proud of, that one day (shivery thought) she might want to join . . .

Chapter Two

I

IT IS DEAD WRONG, the biological commonplace that humans are born uniquely defenseless, unequipped with the most rudimentary impulses of self-preservation.

The Bear Cub is a mighty hunter, remorseless in her pursuit of the Breast. Six weeks old, she can still smell dinner better than she can see it. Close-up, cornering the prey, she goes cross-eyed from concentration. As she homes in on the target, her head flicks from side to side with the same rapid jerk with which a terrier breaks a rat's neck.

Now that the unresisting breast is well and truly trapped, the gummy suction clamp secure, now that the yellow-blue milk is trickling fatly down her throat, she grunts, and wrinkles her nose in satisfaction. Victor, she can afford to toy with her captured prey, to bat the breast with her scaly paw, scrabble at it affectionately. Then, exhausted by the anxious drama of the chase, she falls asleep.

And Gwen, feeling the life-fluid drain from her, experiences a physiological sinking of the spirits, a tiny melancholy that is maybe some far cousin to that of spent men, or to the sad luxuriance of bleeding to death.

It is Thanksgiving: Gwen's first Thanksgiving with Gideon, her first Thanksgiving in her own apartment. Their first Thanksgiving as a family. The transition has not been easy. Each one of the seasonal rituals has come with some religious spat or territorial tiff or spasm of guilt at forsaking older loyalties. Their transfer of allegiance is still incomplete: no sooner are they off the hook from visiting Gwen's family (Martin and Jacey are out at a spa-ranch in Montana; Newburyport is too long and cold a hike for a newborn) than Gideon starts agitating to invite Dina and Ethan and Dan and Andrea and Hector, whose father is now in an AIDS hospice. No, says Gwen, I want it to be just us for once. What "once," grumbles Gideon. It's only ever us. Besides, she doesn't feel up to cooking turkey for seven, not to mention accommodating the abominable compounds of vegan and kosherite and preadolescent-picky among his troupe . . .

(One more fight on the horizon: the frightful subject of Bella's dietary allowances, Gideon, though an occasional bird-eater, believing more and more that meat pollutes the body, whereas to Gwen, pork is the mainstay of that sublimest of human legacies, an American childhood. Not to give her child red-striped-and-crisp-brown-fatted hickory-smoked bacon with her pancakes and maple syrup on Sunday mornings would seem famine indeed, the privations of a new Dark Age fanaticism. But this wrangle still lies ahead . . .)

Thanksgiving at the Vanderveer, three Wolkowitzes around a laden table: the sleeping Bella, impossibly sultry in a dark green velvet suit, tucked into the crook of Gwen's elbow. Gwen, still too bloated from afterbirth to fit into civilian clothes, is wearing a pair of men's pajamas, pale blue with red piping, originally from a Jermyn Street haberdasher, which she inherited from Campbell Gordon.

Is it only a year ago, she thinks, that I was eating pumpkin risotto at Calico with Campbell, trying not to flinch from the Chinese water torture of his cold pale blue-veined hands' stroking, and wondering, Am I going to have to marry this person because I can't think of a good reason not to? Thanks be to God for giving me instead *this* compact perfection, this twinkly olive-brown man-and-child. Ferocious gratitude, even though the man—her husband!—is in a sulk because his father-in-law has sent them a *ham* for Thanksgiving. (She's tried to explain it's not a deliberate insult, all Martin's done is get Melanie to reorder from the usual list, but Gideon's not buying. It would be too humiliating to concede that, actually, his father-in-law doesn't remember he exists . . .)

"Gideon," she says, reaching out for him. "Gideon, we should say a prayer."

He looks up, and a smile dawns slow, slow, slow and broad. He's lost weight in the last month: there's a slash of dimple in his cheek (bordering dark brown beard) that didn't used to be there.

"Baruch atah, Adonai," he says. "Thank you for Her—and Her." Outside the light is like a laser. A moment's blue blaze, about to crash into ultraviolet. Deep winter approaching, cold nights when Gwen and her husband and their newborn will have to snuggle under the eiderdown.

Afterwards, their first Thanksgiving will seem a raft of perfect safety, an only moment of secure joy, in the general shipwreck of their lives.

Gideon's prayer, and hers, a Roman gladiatorial Thanks-for-what-is-about-to-be-taken-away . . .

2

"SHE'S SO ALERT. Those big racing eyes of hers just don't miss a thing."

"Where's she get that from, I wonder?" Gideon.

"Alert but a genius." Gwen.

"You know, she's really fucking brilliant, isn't she?" Gideon.

"She's a goddess."

"You know what I love? Don't you love it when you play with her and she gets so wound up and overexcited she completely short-circuits?"

"And the quick way she seems to be sizing everybody up. Did you notice how she *howled* when Jacey tried to pick her up?"

"Yeah, I howl when Jacey picks me up, too."

"Did you see that little dress from Bonpoint she brought? Isn't it gorgeous?"

"Mmmm. Too bad she didn't bring the servants that go with it."

"What do you mean?"

"I mean, can you imagine trying to get a live baby into that monkey suit, let alone keeping it puke-free for an afternoon? You need a full-time Filipino to torture a kid into those million teeny hand-sewn button loops."

"I think it's beautiful; I didn't know they still had dressmakers who could do that kind of stitching."

"They don't—they have a slave shop full of Indonesian eight-year-olds losing their eyesight over a dress Bella's not going to wear even once, because Martin and Jacey forgot to send the lady's maid and the laundress that go with it . . ."

"What's the big deal, Gid? She'll wear it—once, when we go to Martin and Jacey's for Christmas. *I'll* torture her into it."

"We're not going there for Christmas. I don't know, it gives me the willies, thinking of these Third World child laborers losing their eyesight over those little hand-sewn whatnots. But don't mind me, I never had no servants, I belong to the Velcro generation."

"Just . . . cut it out, Gideon." Gwen hiking up on a shoulder, suddenly furious.

"Cut what out?"

"Just cut it out. You know, this . . . this thing you've got against Pop and Jacey. Try to be a little more magnanimous. What's it to you if they give us baby clothes? I don't notice *you* buying her any clothes."

"I don't notice her *going* anywhere. Every time I see her, she's lolling around the house in her BVDs . . ."

"I'm serious, Gideon. I want you to lay off my father. Just . . . grow up. He's my father. My parents are . . . They're irritating, but they're the only grandparents she's got . . ."

"What is this, orphan discrimination? I thought my being an orphan was my biggest asset. Anyway, I love your dad."

"I'm not asking you to love him, I'm—"

"I *love* him. He's so . . . fatherly. I love him. All I want to do is snuggle up in that little chintz love seat with him and watch ESPN all day . . ."

"I told him you were a basketball fan." Just beginning to smile.

"I like to *do* it, not watch it. Not sit on the sofa watching bigger richer handsomer people do it."

"Gideon, you know . . . He's not well."

"Nobody's well. Are you well? Am I well? The only person who's *well* is that little vampire next door."

"Is that her?" Panic—surely the child isn't waking up one bare hour after her last feed?

"No."

"It's her, Gideon." With dread.

"I don't hear anything."

"Gideon—are you going back to sleep? I can't believe it. Gideon, she's bawling. Are you going to let her . . ."

"I'm giving her a chance to get back to sleep on her own."

"Gideon, I don't *believe* you. You dare wallow in tears of grief over Third World seamstresses while your own baby's howling her—"

"She's thinking about those seamstresses, too."

"Gideon, I swear to God I hate your guts. Gideon, if you don't get up and get her this second, I swear I'm going to let Martin and Jacey send us a maternity nurse."

"Dressed up as a Virginia ham? Okay, okay, I'm getting up—later. Hey, cut it out. If you're healed enough to whack me, maybe you're strong enough to get out of bed and get the baby yourself . . . Honey, she's stopped. What did I tell you?"

But Gwen was already up, hefting, blowing, cursing. Clutching her stomach, in which she'd ripped a post-cesarean muscle. Martyr mother, humping next door, and damn, the maddening baby really had corked off again, and so had Gideon, but Gwen was too angry at Gideon to go back to sleep herself, even though it was 5:47 a.m., knowing that the second she lost consciousness the baby would resume her mewling . . . Mind cracking open with nervous fatigue, with rage at her useless husband who was so unbelievably selfish and unhelpful . . .

3

THE BEAR IS WATCHING her father take a nap. Watching him in such an emergency state of hypersuspense that her entire body wriggles with excitement.

The cycling legs are watching, her tongue is watching, her nose, mouth, ears, belly, back are watching. Her ruddy arms fist the air like a disco dancer, her ruddy legs pump fiercely. Watching for what? To be noticed, like a supplicant in a feudal-bureaucratic court. Waiting for her petition to be heard. Her petition is OPEN YOUR EYES, PICK ME UP, SHOW ME THE WORLD.

And Gideon, who is taking care of the Baby while Gwen tries to finish off her long-overdue review of *The Rise of Bolshevism*, and who has tucked her into bed with him, hoping for an hour's catnap, says, in answer to her challenging mew, Don't you want to catch a few zzz's, Baby?

But in fact he's happy to get up and sling her around the house, to let her bat at her own image in the bathroom mirror and worship its surrounding fairy-lights, to let her try to topple the bowling alley of her mother's face creams.

I know you, honey, he is thinking, I know you. You are one of us. By one of us, he means someone who gets ridiculously overexcited by the humblest manifestations of being, someone so lovestruck with the world in all its glory that its lightbulbs, its toilet paper rolls, its jars of face cream, sometimes overpower you with an agonizing joy.

How did Gideon know? He himself had not the most spectral trace-memory of a father, no blurred recollection of riding broad shoulders, of smelling aftershave or nicotine fingers, or hearing a baritone song in the dark. Until Sonny (who was really more like a grandfather, the way sixty-year-olds *were* back then) he had lived in a world that as if by Herodian decree was eerily shorn of males—there wasn't so much as an uncle or kindly neighbor in his early background to relieve the grim trinity of Mom, Sheryl, Grandma Bella.

Yet he knew, with his hands and his heart, what a baby needed from a man, how to tuck the Bella snugly in one elbow, head propped so that she could gaze around, while he talked on the phone or warmed her bottle in the microwave; he could dislodge her digestive ills with a tap; he knew when she was too hot or too cold or when the sun was shining in her eyes; blankets, at his touch, resolved themselves into velvety cocoons, free of creases and snarls. In the evenings, he put her in his bath, and there she rested, her tiny mottled nakedness spread-eagled on his hairy chest. On Sunday afternoons, he slept, wrapped around her.

To everyone but Gwen, it was obvious that Gideon was a born father, that between him and the babe was a preternatural synchronicity, an almost neural communion. When people said to Gwen, Isn't Gideon wonderful with the baby, she agreed dubiously, with a silent demurral. Because to Gwen, there was something that offended her in the proposition. Gideon's being a dream father seemed either to imply that she herself was not a dream mother—or, worse still, to take away from his absolute fealty to her. Either way, somebody—she—got shortchanged.

Chapter Three

I

"SO WHAT DO I THINK? I think we oughta double our tuberculosis budget," says Ari. "Do you realize they're now guessing they have *thirty thousand* people with treatment-resistant TB? Incurable, *highly* infectious? That's ten times more than they said five years ago. And, like, the Russian idea of treatment is still sending you to a spa for three weeks. We're talking a major culture gap . . ."

"And meanwhile male life expectancy's down to fifty-eight, because everybody's drinking paint stripper for breakfast," Gwen agrees, twisting a finger to her skull.

Ari, just back from the old USSR, is curled up on Gwen's living room sofa, having brewed them both a pot of tea. Gwen has already taken notes on his evaluations of their different offices, programs, personnel (e.g., why they don't fire that useless and unpleasant bastard Sergei Vinogradov?). He has repeated the current gossip about Yeltsin's daughter and her cronies; they have exchanged guesses about whether Russia is on the bumpy road to democratic capitalism, to becoming a rather jolly crude Eurasian bully-boy like Turkey, or whether it is hurtling toward a dangerous-for-everybody Dark Age.

"I saw your friends Bill and Jamila . . ."

Gwen had asked them to invite Ari to dinner. "How were they?"

Ari passes on the news. Bill has been promoted to bureau chief, as his boss has been transferred to Bonn; Jamila (as Gwen already knows) had another miscarriage in August, and has been told by her doctor not to try again for six months. And Gwen, listening, is impressed that Ari, who had initially struck her as a callow opportunist, turns out to be a man to whom an older woman might confide, on first meeting, her fallopian woes.

"Look at her," Ari says, suddenly, this goofy expression on his face. "She's gotten *big* since I saw her last."

Bella, as usual, has fallen asleep on the feed. When Gwen tries to extricate her nipple, clamped between the silken trap of gums, the sleeping baby jerks it back indignantly.

"So how's motherdom?" Ari is new-man enough to be unfazed by having his colleague's bare breast thirty inches away from him. "You get any reading done?"

Gwen adjusts the sleeping body so she can reach her teacup, warm her chilled hands around its porcelain middle. "Yeah, in a lunatic, four-in-the-morning sort of way. Reading newspaper classifieds upside down because I've got stuck with the baby asleep in the wrong position . . ."

Ari is a reader. Shortly after he started working at Lavrinsky—back when Gwen still hated him—they'd left the office together one evening. Gwen on the point of suggesting they go for a diplomatic drink, stop by the Bemelmans Bar and get mildly pickled, but Ari had beat her to it. You live on the Upper West Side? Let's go to the Book Ark.

Gwen'd forgotten about the Book Ark, a secondhand basement store that was a last survivor of the New York she and Ari had been born to: the New York of shabby cinemas playing Rogers and Astaire movies, Viennese tea shops frequented by elderly music teachers.

And Ari had been right. They spent an hour and a half crouched at opposite ends of the bookstore. Outside, they'd examined each other's purchases: she'd found Clarence Brown's study of Mandelstam; Bertram D. Wolfe on Trotsky; a selection of Cistercians; he'd found Womack on the Mexican revolution; an out-of-print story collection of S. Y. Agnon's; a fifty-cent copy of Machiavelli's *The Prince;* and by the time she'd put him on the M79—he lived on Second Avenue with his girlfriend, who was a fact checker at *The New Yorker*—they were friends. Real friends, not work-friends, not friends-of-convenience, not New–New York friends, but people who might ring each other's buzzer because they happened to be in the neighborhood.

"This morning I read this essay by this psychologist who has a theory about the difference between breast-feeding and bottles. (You realize this is the only subject that interests me these days; I'm thinking of starting a domestic policy quarterly entitled *Milk*)."

"What's the theory?"

"That babies who are breast-fed develop a more . . . polytheistic and, in his view, more democratic idea of the world, whereas babies who get the bottle develop a more authoritarian worldview. He says it's no coincidence that the Cold War, with its Manichean clashes of good and evil, was dreamed up by the first generation raised on formula."

"I don't know—sounds to me like another case of Blame-mom-first."

This was the kind of bullshit that really got you thinking, four-thirty on a December morning, pitch-blackness outside, pinned by the baby's feathery limbs. Suffused by a love so wild, so out-of-control, so borderless it was terrifying. Scared you might just kiss or squeeze the breath out of her. The charge of keeping this mite alive to childhood seemed a responsibility *way* beyond your capacity.

And sometimes when she sought your eyes, Gwen, clutched your finger tight, or patted your breast, you realized, This kid actually believes I'm her mother. Ha-ha-ha. And suddenly couldn't breathe for fright. She's only two minutes old, she doesn't know her knee from a chimney pot, yet she already has some kind of preconception about what a mother is, and it's ME.

2

THE BEAR IS GROWING.

Gideon likes to put her on her stomach on the floor and, flexing his palm against her heels, observe her, grunting, clearing her throat, inch like a snail, chin craning. Biology has programmed her to move; already, all unconscious, she is practicing her flight from family, her escape into the world, her search for a mate. Only her eyes—the blurry glaucous inkiness of blueberries—reveal an awareness superior to that of frogs or kittens.

Gideon, a man who finds it easier to restring a banjo or mend a roof than to work a remote control button, has finally cracked the Internet.

Which is how, on this blustery winter's afternoon, having placed his daughter in front of a floor-length mirror in the hall bathroom, he is at Gwen's computer, replying to the latest e-mail from a man named Yannick whom he's "met" through the web site Isaac Hooker has posted for La Merced. Yannick belongs to a French artists' collective called SOS that is currently occupying an unused Crédit Lyonnais office in Lille. SOS uses Situationist techniques: when the riot police storm their squat, they find a roomful of people in chicken costumes sitting on giant Styrofoam eggs and clucking.

Yannick, who writes a fairly self-serve English, knows all about Mayor Giuliani's war against the poor, black people, and other political enemies. He wants to put Gideon in touch with his American Direct Action colleagues, including an antiglobalization collective in Oregon, who are experts in nonviolent resistance. He has useful advice for minimizing the effects of tear gas.

God, Gideon loves these periods of solidarity, when suddenly he no longer feels alone, but realizes there are similar resistance movements all over the world, waging a good-humored jihad against late capitalism; it's only a question of joining forces.

"It's all thanks to you, Bear," he tells his daughter, who is grunting hard on the bathroom rug. "You give me something to work for. You scrumptious dumptious bumptious goo-ball screwball . . ." He scoops up the baby, and kisses her nose and toes and grotesquely padded bottom while she clears her throat, pretending not to notice. Love, work, Bella, joy . . .

Chapter Four

I

EIGHT A.M. IN CENTRAL PARK. Eight-oh-three, confirms the digital beacon of the Hitachi lighthouse, and thirty-eight degrees. A radiant December morning, sharp-lit, banks of snow gleaming blue in the shadows. The tall castles along Central Park West are stained pink by the rising sun. As you reach the eastern front, dog walkers are congregated on Dog Hill, exhaling frost, stomping their feet to keep warm.

By the Seventy-sixth Street entrance, a younger woman in ankle-length black mink, who resembles Jacey, is sipping from a laminated paper cup bearing a Greek coffee shop's blue-and-white frieze of crumbling Acropolis, spiky alphabet. Demotic America, which has simplified classical civilization to a coffee-cup icon.

Steam rises from the cup's lip as if from a factory funnel. "Titus!" yells the woman in black mink who looks like Jacey. "Tite!" A Labrador pretends it doesn't hear.

Gwen, reminded of Jacey, is uncomfortably reminded of her father, of whom she doesn't want to be reminded. Something is amiss with Martin. He's lost too much weight too fast this winter—his belly hangs deflated in the sausage-casing of his Egyptian cotton polo shirt. The last few times she's brought Bella over, he's seemed kind of withdrawn. She wonders whether he might not be depressed.

Gwen has tried talking to Jacey, but Jacey is no help; Jacey's delighted Martin's finally taken off some weight. And Gwen, who comes from a family where people don't meddle, is hard put to persist. She'd thought her father invulnerable. Now she suspects that his bullish rapacity, his ebullience, were merely the by-products of an immense physical vigor that is now mysteriously impaired. He's sick, she decides (he'd better be sick—if it's depression, the idea of trying to get him to a shrink is truly daunting), and her knees quake, the breath sucks away from her.

Gwen is meeting Constance for breakfast at the Carlyle. Bella, suspended in a Snugli, is zipped into Gwen's parka. The Bear's getting hefty, but Gwen relishes too much the infantine body heat against her chest. Bella, in her Snugli, is wearing a pink cashmere suit with mother-of-pearl buttons; Gwen is wearing old sweatpants of Gideon's. She still weighs twelve pounds more than she did pre-Bella, and her stomach is saggy as an elephant's hide because she doesn't have time to swim or run or play squash, and besides (except for jags of feeling strong as God) she's too damn tired.

It's only December, but already Gwen is longing for winter to be over, weary of bundling the baby into snowsuits and hats and gloves. Tired, tired. She is so tired that every bone and joint groans. She's so tired that by the time she's got Bella to bed, and should be settling down for an evening of returning phone calls, she falls asleep with her face in the soup bowl, knowing that the routine will begin again, the one o'clock feed, the 5 a.m. feed, and mounting fury at Gideon, who's "working," which means he can't be disturbed.

In six weeks, she too will be back in the office, and she's torn between separation dread and counting the hours till freedom, because what Gideon doesn't understand is that whereas taking care of a baby (even your own) is exhausting and lonely, work is exhilarating. These days, the mere glimpse of a newspaper—the reassurance that somewhere there's still a world of oil-tanker spills and civil wars and genetic engineering—is exhilarating.

She has never known such a confusion of bitter blackness (I'm too old, I never should have had a baby, I should quit my job, my marriage is a disaster, my husband's no help, he's never home, I feel like a single mother) and soaring golden ecstasy of mother love, such fatigue, resentment, self-recrimination, and claustrophobia (I'm a lousy mother, I can't do this, I wasn't made to spend my life obsessing about baby poop, if I can't escape from this screaming infant *this* minute, I am going to throw her out the window) mingling with a This-is-what-I-was-made-for, This-is-a-completeness-we-are-not-meant-to-know-on-earth . . .

Most exhausting is the terrible responsibility engendered by her conviction that if for one moment she stopped infusing the baby with her now-Jovian powers of love, if she stopped *willing* her to breathe, flourish, triumph, live, well, the child would shrivel up and die, annihilated by the world's negating indifference.

2

CONSTANCE'S FRECKLED MOON-FACE gleams around the hotel bedroom door; her white arms reach out in a sleepy-sensual embrace.

Constance in an oyster satin negligee—the kind of undergarment worn by Hollywood stars in thirties movies, that conveys a world of sexual wit that Gwen has completely blanked out on, making her feel for one moment like an adulterous boyfriend. An adulterer with a Snugli? Did motherhood not need to be so drab? Gwen, bulky and mannish as a Soviet highway repairwoman, unbundles in the hotel suite living room, knocking over a breakfast tray and a stack of foreign fashion magazines.

"Is she sleeping?"

"Her? Not likely . . ."

"Heavens, what eyes!" Constance exclaims. "She looks terribly roguish, doesn't she? (How old is she now?) I don't think I've ever seen so little a baby with such a pronounced look of . . . mirth." Constance draws the child forth from her wrapping, admiring Gwen's handiwork. "Such fingers! They're not quite yours, though, they must be—you lucky girl, my children all have Roger's hands. She's going to be a clown, there's already something fantastically humorous in her eyes, you can see she's got a wild sense of the absurd. It's wonderful having a child who's going to be funny. Tarquin was like that, too. What a dowry . . . God, put her back in the box *immediately,* or else I'm going to start wanting a third." In fact, Constance is much too happy as she is. Colonial duty dispatched, they're reinstalled in their house in Notting Hill, Tarquin is now five and a half and Ruby three and a half, which means they are both at school and are almost alarmingly independent. Her old boss has talked to her about going back to work part-time, taking on some political asylum cases. Gwen's probably read about the new immigration law the Home Office is pushing through, which is appallingly restrictive. Loathsome Labour, every bit as xenophobic as the Tories. Perhaps it's because Constance spent her formative years in America, but she simply can't see why Britain doesn't allow anyone to become British who isn't actually a convicted hatchet murderer . . . The children would be thrilled to have her back at work, she knows. Stay-at-home mothers are much too interfering, whatever the current mythology—as a certified stay-at-home mother, she *knows.*

"You look beautiful," Gwen ventures.

"Well, I suddenly feel as if I'm getting my own life back. Not quite the same life as before: nobody flirts with me anymore at parties, or tries to chat me up on the street, but not half bad. You know, we go out to dinner Saturday night, we have too much to drink, we go to bed late, I open my eyes the next morning and I suddenly realize, My God, it's ten o'clock. The children have been up for hours and are quietly watching cartoons. We're home free, at long last. And how about you, my darling—you who've only just entered the tunnel? It's hell, isn't it, producing such a prize specimen . . ."

Gwen nods. "I'm crazy about her, but sometimes I'm so tired I think maybe I'm just crazy."

"How's Gideon coping?"

"He's totally useless." Gwen starts laughing. "I mean, half the time he seems genuinely to have forgotten that we have a baby . . . He's working—in fact, he's working incredibly hard, he's got a play on at P.S. 122, he comes home after midnight, he's out of the house first thing in the morning, and he's just too tired for Bella, every time I try to hand her over so I can go pee or take a shower or make a phone call, she starts howling, and he says, She needs you. I think I'm going to murder him or else I'm going to divorce him. But murder seems quicker."

"I told you, you should have hired a maternity nurse . . ."

"I know. But Gideon was violently anti."

"Why?"

"I guess part financial—if I was going to be home anyway, what's the justification, we can't really afford to pay someone just to look after the baby while I go to the hairdresser . . ."

"I don't notice your going to the hairdresser all that much, I think you could use a little more hairdressing in your life."

"And part ideological."

"Sounds very ideological. It's the ideological part I generally haven't much use for. And has he an ideological objection to taking the baby himself?"

"I think he's jealous, too."

"You mean because *he* wants a nanny?"

They laugh. Constance picks up Bella and swings the child in the air, holds her up, up to the light, and lets her drop, so that the baby's mouth opens in amazement turning to frantic glee . . .

"You must get proper help. What are you going to do when you go back to work again?"

"I know—I've started asking around. Jacey says she has a girl for me . . . But it's going to be a major tussle." She picks up French *Vogue,* starts leafing. A blonde in gray astrakhan, a black woman in a rabbit-skin jacket with a zipper. So Jacey's dog-walking double was on the money: fur is back. She thinks how much she loves astrakhan, how much she would love a gray astrakhan coat. Then dismisses the desire. "Can we meet again before you leave? Do you want to come over for dinner tonight?"

"I'm afraid we have this particularly sticky business dinner of Roger's. It was sort of the only way I wangled myself along on this trip, that Roger has this absolute delusion I know how to talk to Mr. Bullitt and his wife . . ."

"Who are they?"

"They're from Something Bend. They're all from Something Bend. South Bend. West Bend. New Bend. Or else Something City. Indiana City. When Henry James wrote about the Ververs' building their museum back in American City, I thought it was a joke . . ."

"And tomorrow?"

"Tomorrow we're leaving *at dawn.* We have just discovered day flights. But now that we're back in London, you've no excuse not to come stay. We have a whole floor for you."

Gwen, crushed that she won't see Constance once more before she leaves, wonders why a trip to London now seems beyond-the-moon. Is it that she has become, thanks to her low-income husband, somebody who can no longer afford such pleasures, whose every penny has to be budgeted for the common good? Or is it that her campaign to prove Gideon feckless requires that she herself remain irreproachably selfless, immune to little comfort-sprees?

She has outgrown so much, she wants him to see—no more gray astrakhans for her—so he too must put away his indulgences. If she is willing to stop spending money, he must in turn start making it. Oh, you insufferable bargainers-and-negotiators, you middle-class martyrs!

3

"HELLO, TANDY?" Gideon's voice sounds self-conscious. More so because Dina, who has finally quit her job at Kings County, is sitting ten inches away.

"This is Gideon. Gideon? Gideon Wolkowitz. Yeah. Yeah. Yeah,

I'm really sorry I didn't get back to you sooner with all the paperwork. Yeah, it's been a really busy season. We've got this Hanukkah play on, over at P.S. 122, I don't know if you've—yeah . . . Jamie Gorelick has just been . . . No, I . . . No, I . . . We've had some great press, and—sure."

He glances over to Dina as the head of the Drama Department at Talbot puts him on hold. Mimics with his hand a yakking mouth.

The Hanukkah play, which he and Dina worked up in an afternoon, is wild: the mayor gets metamorphosed into a latter-day Antiochus, Emperor Rudolphicus IV Giulianices, who turns the Second Temple into a shopping mall. It's been a long time since he and Dina have worked alone together, and the result's been pure pleasure.

Dina's life has been transformed by an unlikely agent. *Years* ago, up in Lubeck, she and Ethan got ploughed into by a car that had skidded on ice. Dina injured her back; Ethan broke his arm. Now the other driver's insurance has finally paid up, and Dina has received—not quite a bonanza, but a sum she's chosen to regard as a message from God to quit her job. He hadn't fully realized how dragged down Dina had been by Kings County, till he sees her old energy flooding back.

Once again, she has time to help everybody. Prime among her causes is drippy Josh, who has been bypassed in the search to replace the departing Pitt Street rabbi. Dina is busy sounding out possible malcontents among the Pitt Street congregants to see whether they might not found their own breakaway minyan.

"Hey there." Tandy's back on the line. "No problem. Wow, that sounds like . . . Like I was saying, it's been a nuthouse season, not least because I got a newborn baby at home. Yeah . . . A girl . . . Two months . . . Bella . . . Bella . . . Yeah, it was my—no . . . She's a . . . she's a—yeah—she's a handful. Really? How old—get out of here—what did you like marry at thirteen? So these new-parent woes must seem pretty callow to you . . . Yeah, I'm a . . . I'm . . . I'm a late bloomer. It's fun, but . . . No, my wife's at home with her, for the moment. So I just wanted to check in with you and apologize for my lateness in sending in the application. Yeah, it's not too late? I've been thinking a lot about the job, what I might like to do with the kids—" Dina rolls her eyes. "I've got a lot of ideas for different kinds of—yeah, I'd love to. Sure, I think I can probably get it off in the next . . . Sure . . . You too . . . Okay, okay. I sure do. Thanks a lot, Tandy. I look forward to—bye . . ."

He turns to Dina. "Dimwit."

"I haven't heard you so insincere since we had dinner with those fascists in Warsaw. Why don't you want it?"

"Why don't I want to teach spoiled dumb rich kids? I wonder. So whaddaya think, Deen, you think we should use Karagöz puppets?"

They are talking about revamping *The False Messiah,* their old Sabbatai Zevi play, for a benefit at Ethan's school. Dina joking that it's Gideon's latent anti-Semitism that makes him even consider portraying before an impressionable Jewish audience the Jewish people's greatest rout . . .

"I have this idea of making this Grand Inquisitor-style confrontation between the vizier and Sabbatai, like, the vizier coming to Sabbatai's jail cell and tempting him into converting to Islam. With this kinda like Shakespearean jailer in the background? I was thinking it might be pretty dramatic to do it as a shadow play . . ."

"Aren't Karagöz puppets *teeny*? The old ones are made out of—"

"Yeah, camel-skin parchment. Gwen's got a friend who's just brought a bunch of antique ones back from Turkey."

"But we could make our own, any size we want."

"That auditorium is pretty big. You know something?"

"What?"

"I'm getting bugged about our housing situation."

"Mmmmmm . . ." murmurs Dina, encouragingly. "Tell me." The practiced mental health worker, easing into professional mode.

"You know, Dan and I—well, all of us—spent almost a year renovating this place. I mean, we built the theater. Remember, we got the lumber for the bleachers—"

"Yeah, from Andrea's stepfather."

"We built this workshop, we built all the shelving in Sancho's office, we made all the storage space. We put a lot of labor into getting it just so."

It eats him up, to think of some greedy developer's wrecking ball laying waste to their solid workmanship, reducing to ladders of concrete dust the space where he and Miss Gwendolen first made love . . .

"It's a dear old place," Dina agrees. "It's got this weirdly benevolent vibe to it, doesn't it, in a spook-house kinda way?"

"I got this meshuga idea."

"All your ideas are meshuga."

"Why shouldn't we buy the building ourselves? With interest rates at nothing, it shouldn't be . . . We'd just have to find a bank dumb enough to give us a mortgage. We could live here, we could work here, we could rent out space . . . You know, if Josh really is thinking of splitting from Pitt Street, starting his own shul, well, that is exactly the kind of enterprise we should be renting to . . ."

"You want to be a slum landlord. I can't believe my—"

"Am I nuts? Aren't there tax advantages to fixing up abandoned properties?"

Dina looks at him, amazed. "I never thought I'd hear the word 'tax break' come out of Gideon Wolkowitz's mouth except as the direst . . ."

"I didn't say 'tax break,' I said—"

"*Encore pire.* A euphemism."

Why couldn't he and Gwen take out a *second* mortgage on the Vanderveer, he wondered, and give the money to La Merced?

Dina is still giving him her We-got-a-live-one look. "I agree we need to lay out *all* the possibilities, and that is certainly one of the more farfetched . . . Quite honestly, Gideon? I've been wondering about going the *other* way, and calling a sabbatical for the Pantaloons, let us all stretch our legs, hitchhike to Bali for a year, discover our inner sociopath, all that jazz . . ."

"Quitter."

Dina sings back to him, " 'When the liquor first hit her/She said, "I'm no quitter/But I'm tired of living on dreams . . ." ' "

"These by you are dreams, Dina? I'd hate to know your nightmares."

Chapter Five

I

KATRINA CAME TO STAY for the week before Christmas. Gwen had wanted her to stay longer, but like her son Maddock, Katrina dreaded New York.

Once she'd had a New York life—husband, children, a home—that she thought would never end. (Gwen has little sense of the texture of her parents' life, when Martin was just starting out. Had they friends?

She doesn't remember anybody ever coming over to the apartment. Did they go out to the movies? The theater? Madison Square Garden, or were those Rangers tickets reserved for Martin's clients? She remembers her mother chiefly as a deliciously erratic homemaker, dishing out breakfasts of Nestlé Quik and Captain Crunch while her husband disappeared behind the newspaper. The paper evidently being a rabbit hole offering speedy exit from unmentionable discontents, atrocious hungers, illicit entanglements, guilt . . . Was Martin, behind the *Wall Street Journal* in the galley kitchen of their two-bedroom apartment on East Ninety-third, already dreaming of billion-dollar mergers, twenty-five acres in Connecticut, and Jacey: dark and runtier than his first wife, but someone fiercely rooting for him, who prized what they could make together, because she'd been born just as hungry and ashamed as he?)

Since leaving Manhattan, Katrina had become an inveterate country woman. She had a mess of blue jays in her garden which she sustained through the winter with lard, and a fox she knew she shouldn't feed but did. She missed the ocean when she was away, it was hard to sleep with city traffic and police sirens, she worried (with justice) about whether Hal was feeding Snark properly. Gwen fantasized about her mother's returning to find that Hal, like a sinning child from *Struwwelpeter,* had been nibbled to the bone by the bitch he'd starved.

But Bella was her first grandchild, and her daughter needed her, so Katrina came.

2

THIS TRIP, Katrina gets a sofa bed in the study, with the best goose down pillows and a comforter.

Gwen is surprised by how badly she's wanted her mother since Bella's birth, what a surfeit of validation she expects from this visit, what a healing of their own mother-daughter vicissitudes. (You were a *mean* adolescent, her mother once told her. You always tried to make me feel dumb, just like your grandfather.) What a feast of praise and baby-sitting she anticipates.

Funny how motherhood has made Gwen hunger for other women, Jacey, her mom, Aunt Sue, Constance, made her long to relax into the ribald intimacy of the harem. That's what you wanted really, not paid help, but your mother, your big sister, your aunt: your own kind. What urban professionals had improvidently divested themselves of: the ability to knock on the neighbor's door for advice, to drop off your daughter at your mom's. Gwen doesn't know by name a single person who lives in her building, except for the G. Lieberman whose invitations to the Moth Bar she is always receiving, and she can just imagine the look on his face if she tried handing him the baby.

Gideon, who knows how much Gwen's been counting on her mother's visit, is on best behavior. Even though he's frazzled, he's determined to take extra time to help out.

But as always with Gideon and her mother, despite initial goodwill, it's no go. Katrina and Gideon and Gwen all hang about in the too-small apartment, getting in each other's way. Gideon, despite his good intentions, is swiftly exasperated by Katrina's incompetence. The sight of Bella in his mother-in-law's rusty unaccustomed arms sets off an alarm bell in his brain: and no sooner has Gwen tucked Bella in Katrina's lap so she can go take a shower than Gideon comes and snatches her away, as if showing his mother-in-law by his expert solicitousness how far she herself fell short as a parent. But Gwen isn't sure she wants this battle waged on her behalf, especially not with her own daughter as proxy . . .

Meanwhile Bella, unsettled by the three adults' hysterical buzzing about whether she's too cold or too hot, hungry or tired or—"Mom, will you please just leave her ALONE!"—screams herself to sleep and starts waking again for the recently eliminated 1 a.m. feed, leaving Gwen and Gideon depressed by the unravelling of the little progress they have made.

Only toward the end of Katrina's visit does Gwen realize how far she has misjudged.

Katrina does not wish to be left alone with the baby; Katrina has never been alone with a baby in her life, and is much too old to start now. Katrina, although she has arrived with good intentions to help out, wants to see the sights. Some childish excitement at Christmas lights, at department store displays, jingling Salvation Army Santa Clauses, the tree at Rockefeller Center, survives.

On her second-to-last morning, she emerges after breakfast wearing red lipstick, a white cashmere turtleneck, and her mother's cameo brooch; she has a flush in her cheeks, she has plans and desires, although she is unwilling to voice them and wants first to be told what everyone expects her to do and how she might be most useful.

In her mind, it's twenty years since she left New York, and she's finally ready to come back. She wants to walk in Central Park, to revisit the Winslow Homers in the Metropolitan Museum, besides which, she's been so busy arranging an art show at the Old Schoolhouse that she's left all her Christmas shopping until the last minute.

She needs to buy a heated pad from Hammacher Schlemmer for Aunt Sue's sciatica, and a goat's-milk shampoo made by Crabtree & Evelyn that you can no longer find in Boston, but which Gwen has told her they have at the Apthorp Pharmacy; she wants to get an Irish cardigan for Hal; a paisley scarf for Riley. A mobile for the baby—a certain kind of mobile that she's read is both educational and biodegradable. And something for Maddock. "They don't sell dirt bikes in Manhattan," says Gwen glumly.

Katrina, although she feels guilty about having a cleaning lady three days a week, has never encountered a household without child care—even her ultracapable niece Emily had "help" with her three sons—and it clearly seems as bewildering as if Gwen had told her they'd given up using forks and knives. She keeps on thinking, poor soul, that there must be somebody to leave the baby with while she and her daughter go off to have lunch or to shop, and since there's nobody else more suitable—no strong-armed Irishwoman or Jamaican who is really "almost part of the family"—it ends up being Gideon, who is demonstrably *not* part of the family.

3

E.A.T. IS A CAFÉ on upper Madison, white-lit and parquet-tiled, as if deliberately to magnify the clamor.

Tiny tables are jammed together, narrow aisles blocked by shopping bags and fur coats, airspace invaded by jabbing elbows. Customers as trumpetingly assertive as if drowning your neighbors' conversation ensured the survival of your own. Gideon *loathes* this cynically overpriced café, whose owner's cupidity bleeds down even into the jamming of customers so cattle-car tight, and Gwen . . . well, Gwen is a watcher, and Gideon's censoriousness has made her, in reaction, only the more determined not to judge. She has chosen this lunch spot half knowing her mother too will find it immoral, but hoping she will nonetheless be amused by the excess. And because, in truth, Gwen herself, cabin-feverish, baby-bound, longs for a glimpse of the rude sleek Upper East Side throng of bumptious consumption.

So glamour-starved is Gwen that she suspects if she allowed herself out of the house alone with a credit card, it would take about ten minutes to blow six weeks' salary. (Although why, she wonders, should claustrophobia relieve itself in spending money? Is spending a form of motion?) Besides, her mother's parsimoniousness always makes her prodigal . . .

Katrina fumbles for her reading glasses. "Goodness, New York's expensive. I can't imagine what a fifteen-dollar salad tastes like," she ventures.

"Would you like to find out?"

"Are you sure you're all right for money? You know I still have a little left from Grandpa . . ."

"Thanks, Mom. We're loaded."

"I hate to give you any more expenses; you're already enough overburdened . . ."

Does that mean I've been brusque or just whiny, wonders Gwen. "We're fine. And I can't tell you how much I've enjoyed your coming. Too bad you couldn't stay for Christmas."

"Oh heavens, I know Christmas isn't exactly Gideon's thing," says Katrina. "Besides, you've already got enough on your plate."

Shit, I must have really been crabby. "I'm *fine*," Gwen repeats, crossly.

Katrina starts to speak, then silences herself, shakes her head.

"What, Mom?"

"I just wish you could get a little more help with the baby."

"Well, I can. I'm going to." Gwen thinks she's settled on a babysitter who can start in the New Year.

Her mother sighs, unconvinced. "Do you really have to go back to work so soon? It would have been nice if you could have taken some more time off. Just to rest up, I mean."

"No, I really have got to get back. Three months' leave is a *lot*, Mom."

"Yes . . ." her mother sighs. "I suppose so. Well, I worry about you. You've got a lot on your plate."

Gwen, raising her eyes from a plate which does not seem to have so much on it: one splayed kaleidoscope of raw artichoke. "What do you mean?"

"Well, I mean, if Gideon had a job, then you wouldn't–"

Gwen stares, eyebrows raised, as Katrina stabs at her three-bean salad, starts to speak, once again bites back her words. Then blurts out, "I guess I'm old-fashioned. I can see that he's certainly an attentive father, but I don't think I could live with a man who didn't work."

"Mom, he works like a *demon* . . ." She's on the point of explaining to Katrina–in case her mother's been deaf this past week–that Gideon at the moment is organizing this enormous campaign to stop the artists of La Merced from getting evicted from their home, but somehow Gideon as squatter-activist sounds a little too dingy even for her liberal mother. Whatever her worldview, a woman doesn't want an underdog for a son-in-law . . .

"Does he really? He always seems to be around the house, just–"

"He wants to be with Bella."

"Well, I guess I'm old-fashioned. And I hate to see you having to work so hard to–"

"What, you want me to be married to someone like Pop who sleeps with stewardesses and barely remembers his children's names? Is that what a good husband is, in your estimation?"

"Don't scream at me, darling. I'm certainly not setting up your father as an example of–"

Gwen takes a bite of artichoke salad, and gags. Christ–are humans really meant to digest raw thistles? Wasn't this one of the dietary mortifications that even Bernard of Clairvaux's disciples considered supererogatory? "I'm not screaming; I'm choking."

"I know you're very tired."

"I'm not tired. I mean, I am tired, but . . . Can't you see we're happy together? Doesn't that count?" Her heart is pounding so hard she can't breathe. Breathe, you dumb fuck.

"I do see you're happy together–" begins Katrina, apologetically.

"But that's not enough for you," interrupts Gwen. (Now she really is screaming, in the hopeless hope that if only she yells loud enough, her mother will be refuted.) "I'm happy in my life, I love my work, I have a lovely daughter, I'm insane about my husband, who is a GENIUS, but you still have contempt for him. Because he's an artist, and not the CEO of some–"

Now the two fur-coated women at the next table are eyeing each other, openly eavesdropping, and her mother is . . . embarrassed.

"Don't jump down my throat, darling, you're putting words in my mouth I never . . ." she says in a hushed—a hushing—voice. "Who ever said anything about. . . ? Hal doesn't . . . The men in our family have never . . . I mean, Grandpa or your Uncle Richard or Richie or . . . or . . . That's . . . I just think he should make some sort of effort to make his puppetry more of a success. I mean, I think he would feel better about *himself* if—"

"You treat him with contempt." Gwen is back to a speaking voice. "Because he isn't rich." (Because he's Jewish, because he's from the suburbs, because he has a New Jersey accent that proclaims him not from their class, because . . .) "Which is a shameful reason. You don't even say hello to him when you come into our apartment, because you're thinking, It's not his apartment, she pays the bills. You wish I were still with Campbell, whom I couldn't stand."

God, that's childish. Petulant, Miss Lewis. What self-respecting woman goes out for three years with a man she can't stand?

"That's not how I think. As you jolly well know. But I do think . . . maybe I'm a dinosaur, but I think a man should feel some sort of obligation to support his family . . . I mean, I think *he* must feel odd, making his wife go back to work when you're still nursing a newborn baby, and he's just—"

They both stare down at their plates, furious, ashamed, unable to thrash themselves free from the hook. There was a procedure to quarrels: you went farther, in the hopes of finally clearing the air, or else you retracted. But they had already gone too far to make amends, and who knew whether there was another side they could come out clean?

"I guess I think . . . I guess you don't seem happy to me. You seem at the end of your tether. I guess that's the heart of it," says Katrina finally.

And Gwen thinking, You don't know anything about the world or anything about me, searches for the waiter in silent fury and gestures for the bill.

4

GIDEON HAS INDEED BEEN WORKING like a demon. He's planning a Save La Merced night for the spring, an omnibus of Lower East Side artists that will raise some money for their war chest and draw attention to their plight.

In the meantime, he and Sancho are exploring more radical legal possibilities for La Merced. They've been to see other neighborhood activists, Peter Moglia at the Union Community Center, Mike Rivka who runs LOCO. They've presented their case to the community board and enlisted both the district leader and their municipal councilwoman in their cause.

This afternoon they have an appointment with Andrea's brother, who owns a couple of buildings in Hell's Kitchen. Bob has agreed to look around La Merced. He tours the building with a pained expression.

"The problem is, ultimately," says Sancho, "we don't know what Giuliani has in his sick little mind."

There have been other cases where the mayor has allowed community groups to buy city property for a nominal price. But that was a few years back; now real estate on the Lower East Side is going up in value.

"In addition to which, he's a vindictive suck," Gideon points out. "He knows we got our own little Rudy-puppet and skewer him every play we do—it's going to be a personal vendetta for him to shut us down."

They take a seat in Sancho's office. Bob crosses his legs, fiddles with his ballpoint pen. Puffs in and out.

"You know, if this property is seriously going to auction, well, the building's a wreck," he says finally. "You'd have to spend a fortune to repair the basic infrastructure, but the property's, like, a hundred and thirty thousand square feet? That's a lot of apartments you can fit on this site. If they got genuine developers interested, you could find yourself up against guys bidding three million dollars easy. You're much better off hitting the city with a bunch of lawsuits. If you let any potential bidders know they got thirty squatters in this building and ten different lawsuits against the city to be settled before they get their hands on the property, that could be a powerful disincentive . . ."

Sancho fires Ed Moskowitz, who's been too much of a pussyfooter, and persuades the lawyer who worked on the Community Garden Coalition to take on their cause pro bono, sock the city with some time-wasting lawsuits.

Chapter Six

I

"Looks like I got my new job," Gwen tells Gideon that night, lying on the sofa, a naked Bella tucked into her stomach, suckling while pulling her mother's hair.

Gwen has just delivered Gerald and Kalman a thousand-word memo suggesting how the institute might reassign her. If Ari can take over the bulk of her field trips, so that she'll go to Russia maybe only twice a year, then she will concentrate on making their home office more effective. She's laid out her idea for a conference on Russian corruption, which she frames as the kind of politico-philosophical debate—is criminality a more boisterous form of capitalism, or is it a parasitic killer of capitalism—that Lavrinsky gets off on. Longer-term, she's thinking of an on-line magazine that might be a little juicier than the annual report with photos of striking coal miners and dispossessed gypsies the institute currently produces.

"Mazel tov," says Gideon.

"I'm not so sure," she replies, crossly. Of *course* Gideon is relieved she's not going to be dumping him with the baby while she's in the Russian Far East six weeks a month. "Actually, it's kind of depressing, the idea of being cooped up with Kalman and Gerald and their little court intrigues. I mean, our Russian offices are pretty backbiting too, but at least the stakes are higher."

"I thought you were sweet on Gerald."

"I *was*." Why else would she have stayed in the fucking *Bush* administration? Sexual flirtation—or at least the pretense of it—being the only thing as far as Gwen can see that makes an office function. "But being ex-sweet on Gerald isn't going to keep me busy. I'm gonna feel like the war correspondent who's been pensioned off with a desk job every time I see Ari flying off to the front line."

But Bella just then gives a shuddering sigh. Gwen looks down and sees the child's fallen asleep, thick black eyelashes spread like a butterfly's wings on her flushed red cheeks, milk glistening on her lower lip,

Gwen's dark gold hair twisted tight around one fist, and she thinks, No, I could not tear myself away from her, she is all that I love, she is my very body and blood.

Gwen tries to catch her husband's eye, to make sure that he too has noticed how adorable the sleeping Bella looks, but Gideon's gaze is fixed elsewhere, unreachable.

2

GIDEON IS SORE at his wife. He is angry that she's gone and hired a nanny without consulting him. He is shocked that she has hit the market, offering top dollar to any stranger willing to rid them of their baby. (In fact, Gwen's refused to discuss how much she's offering. It's her money, she says, she isn't asking him for a penny. Even though she's always complaining to him that they're broke, a conceit that strikes Gideon as downright obscene.)

It seems to Gideon that since their child's birth, Gwen has been going behind his back, conspiring with Jacey and Martin to do things he doesn't approve of. Overruling him because she's decided, somehow, that he doesn't count.

Bella is not yet three months old. It violates Gideon's profoundest paternal instincts to think of his child alone ten hours a day with a paid stranger. He primitively wants it to be only Gwen—or him—who wipes away her poops and greases her tiny buttocks, Gwen who unlooses her breast when the babe is hungry. It seems to him, in the most private way, a privilege.

"What's wrong?" Gwen asks.

He chews on his lip awhile, then forces out the words. "I'm just not comfortable with the way you went about hiring this baby-sitter. I thought we were going to discuss it first."

Gwen tries to extricate herself from the sleeping baby, but Bella lunges for the withdrawn breast. Gwen, sighing, readjusts them both, leans back against a cushion.

"When? You're never home. Gideon, a little realism. I'm going back to work *any minute*. I'm going back because I love my job and because we need my salary. That's the bottom line."

"What do we really know about this woman? She could be a convicted child molester."

Gwen, prying loose Bella's still-nibbling lips, lifts the baby and deposits her in a nest of cushions. Fucking Gideon, who should be dis-pelling *her* absurd terrors about their child's safety. "Well, Jacey's pretty sweet on her."

"Is Jacey really the best guide? Whoever brought her kids up, it seems to me, does *not* deserve the medal of good child-rearing."

"Marguerite just baby-sat for them last year. She didn't *raise* them. But to me, she seems like a warm, intelligent woman who—"

"You mean, so Jacey basically doesn't know much about her. I don't get it, Gwen. You've always told me how much you hated being brought up by some German Nazi instead of your own mother, I don't—"

At which Gwen flips. "You want to sabotage my career by guilt-warfare?" she shouts. "*You* try taking the fucking baby for a change!"

Bella's eyelids flutter, her arms fly overhead in a startle at her mother's yell.

"The fucking baby?" Gideon repeats, genuinely shocked. "What's the problem, Gwen? All I thought was we were going to talk about it first, that you might have considered asking me before you went and hired a baby-sitter."

And yes, truth to tell, he had secretly hoped that if they postponed the nanny question long enough, they'd be able to finesse it, Gwen stay-ing home with Bella a couple of days a week, Gideon taking her down to La Merced—just the way Dina and the Family had juggled Ethan. And hadn't Ethan turned out a bright bouncing boy? "You know, this warm, caring, responsible Marguerite of yours?" he says, finally. "I didn't really share your good impression of her. She looked like kind of a pothead to me."

An island girl, with yellowish whites to her eyes. He'd only talked to her briefly, but he's surely smoked enough dope in his day to spot a fel-low adept. If Gwen is going to get a nanny, she should get a nanny, not a pothead. And what's it say about his wife's fundamental common sense, her basic gut-reliability, that she can't see this person she's chosen to take charge of their baby *is not safe*?

Chapter Seven

I

IT WAS SPRING, and the days were getting longer. When Gwen walked home from work in the evenings, the cherry trees were in blossom, the pink sky was mild, and the park was filled with young office workers, suit jackets slung over one shoulder. Couples courting. Nobody wanting to go back home quite yet. Soon she and Bella would be able to stay in the playground till dinnertime . . .

Gwen had been back at Lavrinsky since January. She had never spent so much time in their New York headquarters, and now that she was there, she realized that although it was fucked up, it was fucked up in a completely different way from how she'd previously imagined.

The fundamental problem wasn't that Gerald and Kalman each operated his own rival fief, but that the institute was so arrogantly out-of-touch with anybody else's Russian programs. There was a kind of quixotic "We're doing what the U.S. government should be doing" narcissism at work, which substituted for any effort to influence public policy.

Gwen floated a proposal that they hire a Washington liaison, charged with lobbying Congress and the State Department, the IMF, the World Bank. Only to find that in fact what Gerald wanted of her was not to reorganize the office or redefine their mission, but to do his own work for him. Thus, every day she was handed a ghostwriting assignment for Lavrinsky—an op-ed piece for the *Times,* a speech at Davos. Gwen didn't mind writing (although she lacked Gerald's shrewd flair), but ghosting made her feel still more—well, ghostly. Out of the fray.

When Ari stopped by the office and told her about Sergei Kovalyev's taking him to a meeting of Mothers-against-the-draft—the most significant protest group since Sakharov—she caught herself thinking, But I'm the one who's supposed to be hanging out with Sergei Kovalyev . . .

Instead, she found herself cutting short a meeting with a fellow from the Carnegie Endowment because her baby-sitter had a doctor's appointment. Rushing home at 5 p.m. (with a shitload of calls still to make) to find the apartment a mess and the baby squawling because she had a dirty diaper. Search me why Marguerite, who was so intelligent and attractive, who allayed Gwen's liberal guilt because she was not a "servant," but someone she herself would be quite happy to spend the day with, couldn't smell Bella's shit. But Marguerite, though doubtless impeccable with older children, was rather remiss about the nuts and bolts of baby care, and far too high-powered to be asked to dump the garbage or wash the dishes or even run to the grocery store to buy more wipes.

So there was Bella, still needing a bath and dinner and pajamas and bed, and Gwen still needing to buy food and wipes and whatever else had piled up; Mimi was back in the Philippines *again;* the dirty clothes and wet towel Gideon-the-supposed-socialist-feminist had left strewn across the floor that morning were still there; the exquisite embroidered party frock from Bonpoint (courtesy of the Third Mrs. Lewis) had impermeable tomato stains on the front because Marguerite couldn't be bothered to get out the Woolite, and her husband was never home anymore, not even on weekends . . .

And yet and yet and yet the baby was so ludicrously happy to see her mother, so convulsed by laughter when Gwen got down on her knees, picked up Bella's moccasin in her mouth, and growled like a dog, so jolly, so sportive, so resplendently *hale,* that all her domestic/professional gripes dissolved in pleasure . . .

2

JUST AS GIDEON'S ABOUT TO LEAVE THE OFFICE, the phone rings.

"Gideon?"

"Yeah?"

The voice is cold, accusing, and utterly unfamiliar to him.

"Gideon, I don't believe this."

"Who is this, please?"

"This is Tandy Kogan from Talbot."

"Hey Tandy. Did you get my application?"

"Did *you* get *my* calls? I left you, like, three messages last winter. I thought you had *died.* When I saw your package on my desk, I was, like, Gideon, this is *April.*"

"Don't remind me, I still have to file our tax returns . . ."

"HEL-LOOO, Gideon? I don't think you understand. You have royally fucked up. We closed our submissions back in January. I mean, can't you read? I thought you *wanted* this job; I thought you'd be *good* for the job. And then you don't even have the common professional decency to return my phone calls."

"So we're . . . so you found somebody else?"

"We had, like, forty applicants, all of them first-rate. And don't say you are disappointed, because I am thoroughly pissed. I was, like, asking Annie Dolores, Who is this jerk? Where does he get his sense of entitlement?"

"So I should be sending you roses, huh?"

"No, Gideon, it's your loss, not mine. We've hired a director-in-residence for next year whom I consider frankly pretty stellar. But speaking in your own interest, I think you've got a lot to learn."

Tandy hangs up. And the weird thing? He isn't even embarrassed. Sure, he's not exactly longing to confess to his wife—who asks him every couple of weeks has he heard anything back from Talbot, and to whom he couldn't quite admit he'd never got around to sending off the application—just how far he has deviated from her expectations that he do the right thing.

But flattering pampered sophomores doesn't seem to him too justifiable a mission, compared to aiding Sancho in his Reconquista of Nueva York, in his mission to expel the legions of Stargap and Bananabucks, make La Merced the Masada-that-doesn't-fall . . .

3

BABY STUDIES THE NEAR FLESH embracing her. Sticks a toasty finger up her mother's nasal passages. Prods a tiny black mole on Gwen's underarm.

"Daaaagh," she murmurs. Scrabbles at the mole harder now, trying to dislodge it and carry it away with her, as Titus's armies bore the Second Temple's candelabra. Points at the mole again.

"Daaagh!" she pronounces, fondly. A last proprietary tweak.

The intimate archaeology of infancy: Bella has tagged one of Gwen's favorite parts of her own body; a signpost that even Gideon, who imagines himself to have tracked every carnal millimeter, has overlooked. Only one of many sites that Bella the anatomical astronaut (who has poked Gwen's lungs, bladder, liver from within) alone knows, has named.

Someday Gwen's going to have to wean this child, and the thought fills her with unbearable dread. She gives herself deadlines, and then misses them, drinking in the sweetness of liquid merger, working herself up into frenzies of imminent separation. Not-weaning Bella means she can't go to Washington overnight, let alone Russia. Those succulent red lips' cannibal-avidity for human flesh, human milk is going to sideline Gwen's career. Already Gwen's forgetting what Russia smells like, losing the coast-to-coast stink—a little like formaldehyde, like hospital cafeterias—of this country that's changing almost as fast as a baby. She thinks, If only Marguerite were a little more flexible, I could bring them both, park 'em at Bill and Jamila's while I work. She thinks . . . she thinks . . .

She wonders if fatherhood appears to Gideon, too, as such iron-toothed confinement, such an inexorable grounding, a paradox of depressing joy . . .

4

"OKAY, GUYS, OKAY, you buffoons. Cut it out, enough, no more silliness. We are eating. This is serious, this is . . . chow. I mean, serious grub time . . . CUT."

There must be twenty-five people jammed into their workshop. It's the first gathering of the local participants in Save La Merced night, which they've organized for May Day—Meredith, Jamie, the Tricycle Karmanauts, Fran, Javier from Las Abuelitas, Isaac Hooker, Laura Shneerman, who performs these oral histories of retired workers from the Samuel Seward projects—Russian-Jewish garment workers, an Irish tunnel-hog who lost his legs digging the Holland Tunnel—plus a bunch of students from Rigoberta Menchú.

Gideon's been calling in a lot of chits, everybody they've ever helped out is offering their artwork, their performances, their produce, or else just two hands and a strong back. In addition to the locals, the Klezmofunks from Northfield, Vermont, and a bunch of Infernal Combusters are coming down for the occasion.

There's plenty to organize: there are fifteen potential performance spaces in the building—more, if they clear out some storage—each to be allotted to one group of artists; plus the tented basketball court where Pants on Fire is going to be holding their Mystical Circus, a show inherited from Infernal Combustion. The puppeteers are in charge of food and drink. Garden of Eden is donating the food; Andrea's father, who is part owner of a vineyard out on the North Fork, is supplying the wine at discount. Knowing the powerful thirsts of many of their associates, Gideon feels mean about charging by the glass, but Gwen has convinced him it's the only way to raise serious money.

Everybody's in high gear, giggly. Inez, a tall black-browed dancer from Bux, is chasing Amnon around a trestle table, avenging an imagined insult. Amnon, yelling overexcited Arabic curses, finally doubles back, scoops the woman in his arms, and threatens to carve her in two with a circular saw.

As for Gideon, Gideon is totally manic. Already thin, he has lost another eight, ten pounds in the last couple of months, so that his jeans now slide off his ass; his teeth look too big in his head; his beard appears a black cyclone devouring the bony promontory of his face. What's he to do? He's too excited to eat or sleep: like an angel, he lives on air and light.

Gideon, thin as a stylite, burning like an ember, is arguing with Isaac Hooker about the Future of the Left. How its scattered body parts are quietly, secretly reassembling themselves and preparing in a final insur/resurrection to rise and usher in a New Apocalypse of cooperative living . . .

"You know, Reagan was right, Reagan was right about everything, God help us; it took a senile fascist to see the light. When Reagan said 'It's morning in America,' he just didn't realize whose morning it was, that this was the blackest dawn of the socialist day, *only the foxes* realized that he was this useful idiot, this Samson bringing down simultaneously the twin towers of Soviet Communism and American capitalism, this amazing double suicide which would give rise to the phoenixlike birth of a genuine grassroots people's socialism . . ."

While he speaks, he is dishing out food on paper plates. Meeting's over, it's time to eat; Andrea's concocted this amazing tub of chili; Dan's pouring root beer into plastic cups . . .

"You're out of your mind," Isaac retorts. "This is the nation founded on a tax revolt. The only difference in the last two hundred and fifty years is this time it's single mothers, and not British aristocrats, we're tired of subsidizing."

Chili, chili, chili, slopping over the indented ridges of paper plates. The volunteers are perched on trestle tables, seated in a semicircle of folding metal chairs.

"No, no, I genuinely believe"—in fact, Gideon would be hard put to say is he joking or serious—"that this spasm of psychotic national self-ishness, this me-first tax-cut mania has peaked, and that there has never been a better time to think about an equitable redistribution of income."

"Maybe," says Andrea, "maybe if you could point out to peo-ple that the only people getting *serious* welfare in this country are corporations—"

"You are so wrong. People *do* know, and they don't care. Because unlike in Europe, you can never found an American politics based on class hatred—"

"Yeah, the only hatred here's of the lower classes," agrees Gideon.

"—people look at dot-com millionaires and they don't want to kill them, they think, I can do that, too. All it takes is the mail-order cassette that tells you how, in seven easy steps."

"Whereas we want to make the cassette that tells you how to kill the millionaires."

Gideon is *still* on the same ecstatic jag that's possessed him since Bella's birth, all fall-winter-spring, he can't remember since adolescence ever having ridden such a prolonged wave of elation. When he comes home in the evenings, his wife's already curled up in bed asleep, but he's still tripping with buzzy energy. He wants to talk, he wants to feel some kind of *connection* with this woman who wears his wedding ring. Sleep seems as intolerable a confinement as a child's nap time. Brain still racing, he tries to calm himself, to get undressed, lie down in the dark beside the shrouded bump. Most nights, after a bare half hour, he jumps out of bed again and pads out to the study to seek the computer's humming blue companionship. Checking out how many people have visited La Merced's web site that day, firing off e-mails to his friends in Direct Action: Jean-François at Espace Absurde and Yannick at SOS, Larry from Eugene, Oregon, who organizes affinity groups for non-violent protest. Sometimes he's still on-line when Bella starts crowing at 6 a.m.

And let's admit it, the aggressively taunting edge to his elation, the high-wire madness in it, comes from anger at his wife, who he knows can't *stand* him in this mood. He's angry at her for hiring the nanny, for going back to work full-time, for making him feel guilty because she's not in Russia, for withdrawing from him sexually. So he stays not overtly mad, but a kind of subterranean Vietcong-mad of trying to rile and spite her, of withdrawing his support in sneaky little ways, of jumping up and down like Squirrel Nutkin pestering Old Brown, in the hopes that if he pushes far enough, someday the great owl will pounce and *flay* him. Even his colleagues are getting irritated by Gideon's hyperness.

Lunch is over, the volunteers have disbanded, it's only Andrea and Dan and Gideon remaining, when in slouches Dina (she too has lost weight, and now has this rather winsome Janis Joplin waddle), with a young woman in tow.

"You're late," accuses Gideon. Dina, who is now running her breakaway minyan with Josh and a dropout seminarian called Avi Weissbrot, was supposed to be official minute-taker.

"Looks like I'm just on time," replies Dina. "Andy, is that vegetarian chili? Yum."

"Do you remember me?" her companion asks Gideon, lifting up her cheek to be kissed. "I came to talk to you last year."

"Emma's in the drama department at Columbia," Dina informs them. "She's doing her dissertation on the Combustibles."

Gideon doesn't have the best memory, but it's unlike him to forget someone so drop-dead gorgeous: a Jewish pearl, dark as a Yemenite, with pale green eyes.

"So we're history?" he beams. "I'da gone to college if I'd known they had girls like you. Instead I spent my formative years where the women wore Birkenstocks . . ."

Emma does a double take at this right-on puppeteer fairly Birkenstocky himself emitting such unreconstructed male chauvinisms.

"Don't give him the satisfaction of looking shocked," Dina warns, removing her knapsack and dumping it in the corner.

"You want something to eat, Emma?" Gideon asks, solicitously. "Or is your skirt too short to sit down in?"

"Gideon, go wash your mouth out with soap! He's got a new baby," Dina apologizes. "I think it's hormones. He never used to be such a misogynist, did you, Gidele?"

"Vrum-vrum," says Gideon.

"Postnatal depression, I think. Don't you, dear?"

"More like traumatic stress syndrome," says Gideon. "You ever been hit by a Scud missile? My daughter the Scud."

This graduate student is *dressed*, which he appreciates. She's wearing a comical little black-and-white Op-Art miniskirt that looks like the mobile his mother-in-law gave Bella for Christmas, and fluorescent-green plastic hoop earrings, and when she sits down, her skirt does indeed hike up crotch-high, so that she surreptitiously smooths it over her juicy thighs. Smooth, smooth, tug, tug—the delicious prudery of a woman who's worn an outfit more revealing than she has nerve for . . .

"Have we got time to talk to Emma?" asks Dina.

The others exchange glances.

"Have we got time?"

"Sure . . ."

Emma takes out a spiral stenographer's notebook, a pen. Smiles. "Okay, guys."

What she's really interested in, right now, is Jerome's activities in Latin America in the eighties. She draws them out with flatteringly earnest questions that get even Dan going—Dan, who has an autistic pack rat's gift for the total recall of mechanical minutiae. Jeez, wonders Gideon, watching Emma nod and scribble, is she really copying down how many gallons to the mile our old school bus did and how many cords of wood it took to build the bleachers in San Cristóbal during Easter 1986?

Dina sighs, feigns wiping away a tear. "All this talk about the Old Days makes me kinda . . ." She mimics a fiddle's squeak.

Gideon says, "The only thing I really miss is being on the road. I could stand to be in some Nicaraguan mountain village right now, three days' walk from electricity." He stands up. "Comrades? This interview adjourned? I gotta split."

"Where you going?"

"Oh Gid, the guy from Eagle called to say the computer's ready. Are you gonna be anywhere near Warren Street?"

"I gotta go hit up NOGA for some money. I got an appointment to see . . . Craig Silverblatt? At four. I mean, *that's* what I find frustrating about our current position"—they've been bitching a lot lately about what's wrong with where they're at—"we're kinda past the stage of being these itinerant peddlers carrying a theater in a suitcase, and yet I seem to spend all my time fundraising. I mean, either we should go *authentically* shoestring, which means leaving the city, or else we should get real and hire a full-time manager-fundraiser-booking-agent . . ."

"I.e., Dina," says Andrea.

"Nah, Deen's having way too much fun being a lady of leisure."

"Verily, by my troth," admits Dina. "Although the car-crash proceeds are dwindling apace."

"So find another car to hit you," says Gideon, unsympathetic.

"Anyway, the amount of admin's been aggravated by La Merced's demise, right?"

"Hey, demise is maybe a little—"

"Well, these are things we should definitely be talking about."

This is what he's been doing all month, fundraising. Fundraising and politicking. Leaving his comrades in charge of the home front, the artistic effects, while he rings the bell of antique clothes shops, sushi bars, tattoo galleries, explaining La Merced's plight, asking them to sign their petition, to contribute twenty bucks for an ad, show up for the party, write a letter to Giuliani.

He finds the job as exasperatingly picayune as selling Girl Scout cookies door-to-door; he's itching to get back to his own creative work, and yet, truth to tell, Gideon's a sociable animal who enjoys sweet-talking strangers, relishes the freedom of being out-of-doors, it's exhilarating in these corrupt-corporate-overmoneyed times to be reminded he belongs to a community with genuine political convictions, to meet neighbors who feel similarly disenfranchised by the multiplying manifestations of a new urban fascism, who are NOT—beneath their liberal pieties—cravenly grateful the mayor's doing the dirty work of making the Lower East Side safe for Starbucks.

Once or twice he's persuaded Ethan to join him, and when they're finished, they stop for a soda at the Red Hen, or a game of basketball with the kids from Nathan Straus. Spring light lingering past seven. There's a cute bunch of Chinese basketball players—girls and boys shyly fashion-conscious in their studded bell-bottoms and multiple nose rings, and way too dazed by hormones to concentrate on the game.

Which is just as well for Ethan, who, since he beanpoled overnight to a respectable five feet seven, now trips over his big feet. Ethan is getting sweet on girls, although he's more comfortable with computers. He's an atheist in the best Jewish tradition, proud to belong to a nation that fathered Einstein, Richard Feynman, and Glenn Gould, but he thinks the Bible's a primitive crock and there's no point wasting any more of his mom's money on teaching him ancient Near Eastern fairy tales when there's a real world of genome labelling and digital technology to be mastered. He wants to design software when he grows up, he's applying to Hunter and Bronx Science and Stuyvesant for next fall, and it's obvious to everyone he'll get into one of them.

Gideon looks at him, teasing the ball away from a bigger Chinese boy, and thinks with pride, I helped raise this kid . . .

5

IT DRIVES GWEN CRAZY that Gideon is not, as she is, attached to the baby by ropes of bleeding flesh. Gideon leaves the apartment in the morning; a smiling Bella appears mildly curious as he waves goodbye. Gwen finishes breakfast, reaches for her briefcase, and the baby, scarlet-faced, tears spurting, starts screaming like a stuck pig. At work, Gwen is still so harrowed by the memory of those outstretched arms, the grief-convulsed howls that she quite frequently slips out the door at lunch-time and darts across the park for a swift reunion. Dives into her baby's arms, vowing, Never again will we be parted . . .

And when Gideon's home, weekends? "Looking after [*sic!*]" Bella while Gwen crawls off to her bed for a shell-shocked nap? Even then, her husband does not seem to be burdened by the urge to profit from these rare snatches of togetherness, to get to know his daughter, leave his "imprint." No, Gwen comes out into the living room and finds Gideon in the study, talking to his lawyer or surfing the web on Gwen's computer, while the baby lies halfway across the living room, strapped into her rocking seat.

"Get a good rest?" he asks, welcoming smile fading as he sees Gwen's hands on furious hips.

"You're not even looking at her."

"I'm looking at you. She's fine, I'm fine. Relax. What's the problem?"

"She's going to be a sociopath if you don't interact with her a little."

"She was sleeping. We were interacting in her sleep."

"What do you mean, she never sleeps at eleven. Did you dope her up or something?"

Of course, as soon as she hears her mother, Bella raises her arms and howls.

"She was fine until you came into the room."

"Maybe I should leave."

"What's bugging you, Gwen?"

"You only see this child for a couple of hours a week. She's changing every day. You are missing this baby grow up. You don't even know what you're missing, where she's at. You are so used to seeing her *asleep* that if you ever see her awake, straightaway you want to put her to sleep again so you can get some work done."

"I'm busy," he says, mildly.

"Yeah? I'm busy, too. I mean, I would be busy, but some things come first. Some things are just more *interesting.*"

"I thought you wanted me to be working . . ."

She ignores this. "I mean, how would you like it if all I tried to do was make *you* go to sleep? How would you like it if when Constance called up and asked, How's Gideon, I said, He's a very good husband, he sleeps seven hours a night and takes a nap on weekends, I'm really getting a lot of work done? How would you like it if as soon as we were alone together, I got on the telephone or read a book over dinner?"

"You do," he said, grinning. "I like it fine. I *am* a good husband."

6

"WHY DON'T YOU EVER TAKE BELLA" has been this ax over Gideon's head, life-endangeringly nicking his neck hairs now that he's once again spending more time with Ethan. All right, why don't I, Gideon agreeably concedes, just to knock the wind out of his wife's guilt-stained sails.

Next morning, he announces, "Come on, Bear, us two are going on an adventure."

Gwen readies her daughter: a knapsack of diapers, wipes, a change of clothes, a bottle of water, a container of yogurt and mashed banana. Gwen, suspicious, inquires, "Are you going to take her in the subway? It's so *dirty* . . ."

"Would you rather I took her on my bike?" Gideon grins, which gives Gwen this somehow very raw wrenching flashback to her first glimpse of Gideon at Alice in Wonderland, riding Ethan on his crossbar—a yank of jealousy of Gideon-with-a-child, of his male tenderness, so animal-playful . . .

All day long, instead of feeling liberated, she's lost. She had planned to call up Christopher and see if he wanted to meet her at the Frick (she has a craving to see Hans Holbein the Younger's portrait of Thomas More, she can picture the shaven white stubble on his square jaw, his expression of stubborn probity.) Instead, she wanders around the apartment watering plants, scrubbing counters, doing a wash.

When Gideon and Bella get home that night, Gideon is carrying boughs of flowers and a box of sushi for Gwen's dinner, and Bella is asleep in the stroller. Gwen feels quite dog-in-the-mangerish as Gideon recounts their exploits. Of course (since Gideon's a man), everybody's taken her off his hands, Andrea and Amnon and Hector spent all morning amusing her while Gideon and Sancho met with their district councilwoman, an elderly Trotskyist who is helping them in their fight. And in the afternoon, they played with puppets (Bella almost succeeded in decapitating Mayor Giuliani, which Gideon takes as a good omen) and wound up at the Red Hen for an early supper of peanut butter and banana sandwiches and milk shakes.

"We had a ball," Gideon concludes. "She's a joy to hang with, but I'd much rather be with you. Why don't you come to work with me one day?"

He eases Gwen onto his lap, sliding a hand between her legs. She, removing his hand, rises and moves away. To do what? Wishes, too late, she hadn't. It might have been pleasant to loll on his lap like a big doll, to slip into love so loosely (how many evenings is Bella asleep by seven, and Gwen so rested?).

But she can't quite let herself. She's still too angry at Gideon for leaving her in the lurch with this baby, whose brutal need of her she finds terrifying. She is angry that far from trying to ease the burden of this neededness—by persuading the baby to need him a little, too—he guilts her for not being still more selfless. He might have the grace to admit, just once, that her own upbringing and maternal disinclinations considered, she's not doing all that bad a job. Sometimes Gwen thinks that Gideon's secret aim is to make her quit her job and stay home full-time with Bella, and that as soon as he's succeeded, he will up and leave her.

Chapter Eight

"WOLKOWITZ!" shouts Gebler. He's a big man with a powerful voice; if he hadn't married a rich woman, he could have been a circus barker. "You're not making off with any two-ton sculptures while my back is turned? I know you puppeteers have itchy fingers . . ."

Gideon has been wandering around the Aurora Foundation, waiting for Gebler to get off the phone. It's a silvery-white space-palace, over on First Street, designed by a German architect to look like some kryptonite Valhalla. He is checking out their newest exhibition: a young Australian who has marked a frieze of stenography paper with a child's crayoned crosses indicating the number of days until the New Millennium, interspersed with dark grainy Xeroxes of Mayan pyramids and of prisoners in striped pajamas . . . and is that Eichmann in the cage?

Gideon returns to Gebler's office. Gebler, perched on his desk—an Empire table with lion's paws and gilded eagles that seems to proclaim, I'm not the one around here who likes Minimalism—is pouring Scotch into two tumblers. Gideon loves hard liquor, and Gebler has just produced one of those limited-edition single-malts that are made on a peaty scrap of Off-off Hebrides where nobody lives but monks and drunks.

Gideon sips and sighs. Smoke, peat fires, bog-men, choppy North Atlantic, heaven. He sighs again, dreams of being a fisherman on a Scottish island inhabited by seven octogenarian mutes who don't talk to each other. Sighs. Sips. Suspects he has a secret vocation to become an alcoholic. Draws a pack of cigarillos from his slicker pocket, offers one to Gebler, who refuses and lights instead a Cuban cigar.

For over a week now, Gideon's been playing telephone tag with Alfred Gebler. Alfred Gebler and his wife run a foundation which, since the New York State Council on the Performing Arts stopped giving them grants, has become Pants on Fire's biggest donor. The reason that Aurora, which has permanent installations by Joseph Beuys and Richard Serra in its atrium and gives half a million dollars to world-famous artists to build Towers of Babel in the Arizona desert, even bothers to acknowledge a dinky little puppet group like Pants on Fire is that they are neighbors. Way back in the seventies when SoHo was still sweat-shop-land, back when Gary Brager-Wolkowitz was wearing an Afro and worrying simultaneously about flunking geometry and making it to second base with Laurie Kotlow, the Geblers bought an old school building on the Lower East Side and turned it into a Palace of Culture. Which gives Gideon hope that, in addition to Pants on Fire's annual grant, they might be willing to Save La Merced, a sister institution threatened with extinction.

Gebler is fiftyish, a dissolute paterfamilias who likes to goof around with young people. Gideon first met him years ago at a Christmas party at La Merced, where he wandered into Sancho's office to find Sancho and a red-bearded man in a velvet jacket smoking crack. Sancho has long since got himself a hard-ass girlfriend and cleaned up, and who knows whether Gebler still partakes?

Gebler had sounded happy to hear from him. "Even though I know you only call me up for money. Let me look at my busy diary—my social secretary has decamped for the night. You wanna have lunch next Tuesday?"

"I'm going to be out in Queens all day."

"Visiting your mom?"

"Nah, I only go where I'm paid; I'm teaching a workshop . . ."

"I've never understood about workshops: shopping's what you do when you don't feel like work. Hold on a minute—my wife gave me this electronic diary for Christmas, knowing full well I can't turn on a lightbulb by myself; I think it's a plot to keep me home at night . . . Hhhhmmm . . . hmmmm . . . hmmmm . . . I can't get out of the part that tells you all the good vintages of wine . . . Stay away from that 1995 Beaujolais, man. Hmmmm . . . hmmm . . . hmmm. I give up. What are you doing right now?" he asked finally.

"Coming to see you."

"So what are you kids up to? What's the name of the fat girl?" asks Gebler now, eyes narrowed against the blue-gray smoke.

"Dina Gribetz."

"You found her a boyfriend yet? Remember I told you I had my friend Manny from Detroit who's got this thing for big women . . ."

Gideon jiggles his foot. "I don't think she's looking to be the object of someone's mail-order perversion."

"Tell her fat girls can't be choosy."

"She's not THAT fat."

"Tell her if she doesn't lay off the Mars bars, she's gonna climb into that puppet theater one day and GET STUCK."

Gideon irritably gestures, Enough. Gideon recalls Gebler once telling him that the world was divided into Cavaliers and Roundheads. It is just such censoring gestures on Gideon's part that have evidently consigned him, in Gebler's mind, to the puritan camp.

"So what's Sancho up to?"

Sancho and Gebler have somewhere between lost touch and fallen out, both of them being men who demand an unsustainable level of loyalty. Sancho is scathing on the subject of the Geblers, who he believes took him up when they needed to get accepted on the Lower East Side, back when community activism was German and fashionable, then got bored.

"Revolution," Gideon replies. "I guess you heard this time it looks like the city really is gonna auction off La Merced. They wanna make it into condos for Wall Street suits."

"Don't I know it. When we moved in here, we were the only white people within fifty blocks. You remember Dominick's?"

"No."

"That restaurant on Avenue A? Haven't we had lunch there together? He was like this crazy *settler* serving fancy organic food in this *wasteland* of projects. He just lost his lease, because they quadrupled the rent. His space is opening up as a Christian Ibarrguengoitia boutique. First and A? Can you dig it? God bless New York. I used to be the richest person I knew. I used to be like, C'mon, guys, let's take a cab, it's on me, now I'm like, Thanks, I'd love a ride uptown in your Learjet . . ."

Gideon explains his project for Save La Merced night.

Gebler considers. "Why didn't Sancho come ask me himself?"

"Well, this is really our thing . . ."

"You know, Sancho gets up my nose. Sancho Panza. All that Hispanic nationalism is just plain narrow-minded and outta date. He should go back to Puerto Rico if he doesn't like it here."

"He's Dominican."

"He's a demagogue."

"A Dominican demagogue?"

But Gebler for once is serious. "He pretends to be this populist, but people don't buy that revolutionary Marxist bullshit, so now he's trying to blackmail Giuliani into giving him—*for the people*—what nobody wants.

You know, if New Yorkers wanted community arts centers, they'd vote for the Rainbow Coalition."

"I don't think it's democracy when . . ." (Thinking, The reason we need government support of the arts is so we don't have to suck up to people like you.)

"That's where you're wrong. It is. People on the Lower East Side need affordable housing, wouldn't you say it was somewhat *Roman* to be giving 'em circuses instead? But you know what? I'm a sucker for circuses. And you I would love to help out. Tell me more."

They discuss the planned event. Then Gebler glances at his watch. "Do you want to come along to Kicky's—I told a friend I'd meet her there."

"The topless bar?" Gideon absurdly blushes, and Gebler catches him.

"A guilty conscience. You sweet thing, I haven't seen a blush in *years*."

It's true. How long has it been since Gideon's wife has actually wanted to have sex with him? That thirsty voluptuary who sulked if he didn't stick her every morning before breakfast, whose pleasure was to find a thousand sneaky ways to make them both come, now wears pajamas to bed and feigns narcolepsy. But, God help him, his libido has not died. There is nothing more pitiful than a guy standing there with a hard-on which his wife ignores like it's some tramp at the subway corner holding out a hat. Had she expected the dick, having done its fertilizing duty, simply to drop off?

Unwanted, he catches himself making dirty jokes to the cashier at D'Agostino's, Wendy at the Red Hen, the salesgirl at Jem's. Verging-on-sleazy innuendos he never allowed himself as a proud and modest bachelor, prizing his Jewish chastity as a dowry he would one day bring his bride. Teasing strange women, testing the borders and then verging . . . over . . . Because let's face it, crazy as Gideon is about his baby daughter—wilder with love than he could ever have anticipated—being a father does not fulfill a man, no matter how much the home-fascist thinks it ought to. Does he despise Gebler because he sees his own spoiled likeness in the man's frolicsome lack of self-respect?

"So . . . Kicky's."

"They have a fresh shipment of Russian titties, Max tells me. The end of the Cold War's been great for the topless trade; those Natashas are stacked." A laughing Gebler is making salacious gestures, provoking

Gideon, who blushes all over again. Hoping to dear God he's not going to get a hard-on thinking about . . . nothing. "Come on, Wolk, it's a mixed crowd—my friend Penny who runs a gallery in Chelsea is coming with a couple of her artists . . ."

Gideon, who on second thought finds the idea of married men at a topless bar just plain depressing, shakes his head.

What's the etiquette here, is he going to have to go look at fat bare hookers to get the check? "I don't think I can, Alfred. I got a five-month-old baby at home . . ."

"Now that's what I call serious cradle-robbing." Gebler feigns a double take. "Oh, you mean you're his dad?"

"Her."

"You had a baby? Gideon! I didn't even know you were sick. Who's the luckless mother? Let me guess—you married . . . a puppet. Little Red Riding Hood?"

"Red she's not," says Gideon. "Her dad's . . . you guys probably know him—Martin Lewis?"

"Which Martin Lewis? The guy at Paramount—oh you mean, the . . . sure."

"He's a lawyer."

"Sure, I think his wife's on some board with Dolly. Holy shit, so we're talking Goldilocks."

"Well . . ."

"Goodness gracious, Gideon Goody-goo, so you're one of us now! Let me embrace you, my darling boy—I always knew you were a murderous little gold digger at heart."

"Yeah—I'm digging, I'm digging. But meanwhile . . . I'm a murderous little homeless person is what I'm about to be, if we lose our space." Gideon, naked women chased from the brain, is determined to pursue his object, undeflected.

"Why don't you ask your father-in-law to buy you La Merced for a wedding present?"

Gideon, grinning, shakes his head. "Alfred, my father-in-law is one of Rudy Giuliani's biggest supporters. Plus, he hates my guts. The only check he is writing is to take my skinny Jewish ass and get lost . . ."

Gebler chortles appreciatively. Gebler's gotten his teeth fixed since their last lunch. Everybody Gideon knows has all of a sudden gone in for the most terrifying acrylic caps and hydraulic whiteners. Dentistry being one of the many subsections of Lifestyle that's taken a magical

leap in the late nineties that Gideon—uninsured—has missed out on . . .
Gebler, stubbing out his cigar, reaches over to pat Gideon's shoulder.
"You shoulda married one of *my* daughters. Actually, I've got them auc-
tioned off to European royalty; one of them's booked for Prince Albert
of Monaco, the other one's reserved for—what's the name of the Belgian
blond with the big nose? Maybe you could take my son, he's a little shaky in his feminine-masculine articles . . . Sit down, Gideon. Your
father-in-law's brushing you off? I'll write you a check; I love you like
a son."

He takes a piece of paper, scribbles a fake check for a million dollars,
laughing.

Then, "No seriously, kiddo, I'm sure we'll help out with your benefit; I just gotta run it by the boss." The boss, of course, was his wife. Oh,
the joys of being the penniless husbands of rich women . . .

Chapter Nine

"SO IT'S DEFINITE," says Jacey. "We got the results from the biopsy . . .
And it's—yeah, it's—it's Hodgkin's."

Somehow Gwen knows this already. All year her father's seemed to
be down with the flu. Not quite so specifically known, but in a general
way. She has searched on the Internet, looking up possibilities. She already knows all about Hodgkin's lymphoma. She's braced. It could
have been worse, it could have been leukemia. It could have been . . .

Gwen and Jacey are sitting on stools in the Sutton Place kitchen,
which is the one corner of the apartment Jacey has never gotten around
to renovating, perhaps because she doesn't spend much time there herself. Consequently, the kitchen is still a dark warren of scullery and
larders, papered in yellowy wallpaper, which gives Gwen a painful clutch
in her chest because it's the same wallpaper—labelled bunches of Carrots, Parsley, Marjoram—they had in their old apartment on Ninety-
third Street, although she is certain her father has never noticed.

"Jacey, I'm so sorry." Gwen reaches over to hug Jacey tight. That's
what happens: *you* comfort *her.* Acknowledging that you're finally

grown-up enough, detached enough, for her grief to take precedence: he's by now more Jacey's husband than Gwen's father. Jacey draws in a deep gulp of breath, a quavery suppressed-sob sigh. Releases Gwen to wipe an eye, laughs at herself for crying. She loves this guy. She finds him exasperating, but he is her idea of a real man and for all his self-absorption, his inaccessibility, she finds him deeply reassuring. A rock.

"It's all right—the doctors're guessing it's only, like, stage two, which is fine. But they gotta do a CAT scan now to find out."

"How's he taking it?"

"Hey, he's a toughie. He won't talk about it, not even to me. God forbid anybody at work should find out he's not a hundred percent healthy."

"So they find out what stage he's in . . . ?"

"Yeah, and then it's, like . . . you're an outpatient. I mean, most people don't even get chemo, it's radiation, which is . . . nothing. You get zapped in the morning, you're back in the office by lunchtime. Ninety percent cure rate . . . That's what the doctors at Memorial say. I'm taking him up to Boston for a second opinion. Dana Farber is, like, the *best* . . ." (That's what had become of disease these days: for the rich, a new realm of shopping: glitzy professionals to lull your anxieties with state-of-the-art technology. God, thought Gwen, catching herself short, I've been living with a leftie too long . . .)

Gwen goes into the study, where her father's watching TV.

"Hey Chug." Barely looking up. Joe Mason, commenting on the evening's game, Yankees playing the Red Sox.

She reaches down to give him a kiss. "Pop, I'm so sorry to hear—"

Her father cuts her off with a broad swipe of his arm. "Let's talk about something more cheerful." Pudgy thumb reaching for the volume button, just in case she fails.

"Well, I wanted to thank you guys for coming last Sunday . . ."

"Hey, it was a pleasure." He and Jacey had come early to Save La Merced, brought the kids. (It evidently made it more palatable to her father that this was an event you could package as being "for children.") "How'd it go?"

"It was an enormous success."

"Looked like a good-sized crowd."

They are a little stiff, as always on the subject of Gideon.

"Yeah, it was way beyond their expectations; Gideon is really over the moon. The response has been fantastic, lots of people calling up, wanting to help out. And they got some good press, this big write-up in the *Observer* . . ." She is chattering insincerely, banally. Damn her nerves. Damn her father for not admitting to things. "Well, I've sent you the clippings; you should get them in the next couple of—"

"Good, good," said Martin, distant. Martin of course believes it is fiscally irresponsible for the city *not* to auction off its derelict property at market prices. "We gotta get him together with Mort one of these days . . ." His finger restores volume as the first inning opens, Boston up at bat. "How's the kid?"

"Glorious."

"Can she say Grandpa yet?"

"Nah, but she's got a decent crawl. Are Serena and Al home?"

"They're upstairs. Jacey bought 'em these Tamagotchis—the most annoying toy in the universe . . ."

"She got them . . . what?"

"Tamagotchis."

"Tama . . . ?"

Now he emits a rather saurian look of scorn. "What planet are you living on, Chugga: and you call yourself a mother? This is, like, the toy of the century. They sold four million in Japan. QVC sold six thousand in *four minutes* and these gizmos are not cheap, they're, like, eighteen bucks."

Red Sox out with no runs, they throw down their bats and jog for the dugout. Cut to an ad for a brokerage house. Baseball's gone upscale, she's noticed, buoyed by the all-American boom. In the old days, you only got Budweiser commercials.

"What are they?"

"They're, like, these little cyberpets with an LCD screen you keep on a key ring. They're pets, that's the gimmick, you gotta walk 'em, you gotta feed 'em, you gotta play with 'em every fifteen minutes or they stiff. The kids' school's going nuts, they're calling in the psychologist—you know they got a in-house psychologist at Dalton now—all the kids are in hysterics because they've killed their Tamagotchis . . ."

"Japanese don't believe in reincarnation?"

"Oh, reincarnation is, like, an extra eighteen bucks."

She smiles. If they were in the habit of smooching, she would give him a kiss, but they're not. Are you too gonna die, Cyberpop? Are you going to die because we forgot to walk you? His eyes are fixed on the too-bright screen. The image cuts from a young man and a young woman receiving investment advice from an elderly gray-haired man, cut to the big colonial-style house they've just bought, blond children running across the lawn, man and woman clasping each other's hands. Cut to a Day-Glo green playing field, to the pitchers' bull pen. And she sees her father's hand reach for the remote control, edge the volume deaf-man loud, too loud for conversation.

The Yankees strike out twice, no runs. Cut to a grim-faced Joe Torre slouched in the dugout. Cut to Derek Jeter, also in the dugout, spitting a long shot of chewing tobacco, leaning over to chat to a teammate, hand cupped over his mouth. Cut to Darryl Strawberry up at bat, that long-shanked tiny-headed gazelle, who dips the bat back, back, back, over his shoulder, shimmy-shimmies, just dying to fly, and . . . strikes out. Cut to an overview of the field, the Yankees jogging dugout-ward.

"I don't have too good a feeling about the Yanks this season, somehow. If I wasn't so hidebound, I'd switch to the Braves . . ."

Chapter Ten

I

"HI THERE," says Christopher. He speaks softly, like many tyrannical people. (When you lean closer to make out his words, you catch this scent of old-fashioned aftershave, of an ambiguous manliness, and feel faint. Twenty years into their friendship, Gwen still goes through days of being in love with him.) On the telephone, he's almost inaudible. In the background, the same noise of buses and sirens she hears from her own office.

"Where are you?"

"I'm feeling irresponsible. If I throw a pebble at your window, will you come downstairs?"

Gwen flushes her afternoon meeting and meets him at Karoly, where he holds her elbow tight and guides her through an exhibition of de Koonings: round-eyed squiggly blondes, their red vulva-lips snarly

with teeth. Dizzy-blonde cannibals, the paint laid on in a delirium of
hate/fascination/desire. "This is why de Kooning is the only artist in
whom you can see the direct line of descent from Titian."

"You don't say, Christopher."

Back out in the street, it's early summer, a frisky wind is ruffling the
new-green leaves of the young plane trees, the sky is blazing blue, it's
out of the question to be cooped up in a shadowy office. Looks like
she's going to miss her five o'clock meeting, too. She withdraws her
phone from her bag. "Carole? Something's come up, can you tell Gerald I won't be back?"

They wander down Madison; they drink espresso and eat mandarin
sorbets at Sant Ambroeus, where Christopher nods curtly at a colleague,
then seizes her by the elbow and steers her back out into the street. "I
don't want to be inside a moment longer . . ."

And Gwen, who has spent her lunch break at Sloan-Kettering with
her father, is equally busting for June sunlight. Madison Avenue is
gleaming, radiant-hot and cold, under the fickle brilliant hopscotch of
sun and shadow. They wander south, stopping by a Cypriot dealer of
classical antiquities ("This man is famous for hiring Turkish thugs to rob
archaeological sites . . .") to admire an alabaster woman from the Cy-
clades, a fertility goddess flawless as a date palm: a faceless morph of
breasts and pubis, surmounting curvy thighs.

"Shall I buy her?" Christopher wonders.

"Sure . . ."

He comes out carrying a small card inked in the goddess's asking
price. Wasn't that all men wanted, really—a headless body? Even Gideon
was always telling her, half seriously, If you didn't think so much, we'd
be fine . . .

They drift past windows of Ottoman calligraphy, Florentine leather,
the season's novels. Gwen eyes the posed merchandise with indiscrimi-
nate concupiscence: this lushness, this late imperial opulence, the ver-
tiginous profusion of fucking *goods* to be had. This presumably is what
Gideon calls consumerism, although it feels more like being a fox in the
chicken coop.

Gwen would rather just drool over windows; Christopher, who likes
to bully shop attendants, marches right in. "Christ, Armani's dull," he
says. "What's so great about beige?"

They pass a designer he likes: Christian Ibarrguengoitia. "French
Vogue's puffing him, but they're right: his clothes are *cut*. His grand-

mother was a seamstress for Balenciaga; he grew up making dolls' dresses out of sewing room scraps."

They enter, buzzed in by a wistful Afro-Asian girl in silver platform sneakers.

"Let's buy you something," Christopher says.

"No, I . . . I can't."

"Don't be ridiculous, I want to get you something. Don't you like these clothes?"

She stammers, looks away. "Christopher, I can't."

"Why not?" he frowns.

She rifles through a rack, lingering at an embroidered chiffon dress, then censors the impulse.

"Try it," he urges. "Is it the right size? What are you, 38?"

"I have no idea, since Bella . . ." In fact, she's finally got her figure back, perhaps even rangier than before.

She slides into a fitting room, with a rush of familiar pleasure. The evening dress is cut on the bias, snug around the hips and bottom, falling in folds like a Greek tunic, baring her shoulders. There is an apricot charmeuse undershirt, surmounted by a short sleeveless chiffon tunic of a wild luminous lavender embroidered in orange. Gwen refuses to look at the price: the dress, which is booby-trapped with the wiring reserved for the high-end items, exudes billions.

When she emerges, the salesgirl exclaims over its fit. Gwen looks at herself in the mirror and sees something queenly, almost savage, she wants back.

"Let me get it for you," says Christopher.

"I'll get it," Gwen replies. "No, really. I've been living like a hermit all year; I *feel* like splurging." She still can't look at how much the dress costs; blindly (with a recklessly festive flourish) she signs the credit card slip. Shit, she used to spend *thousands* on clothes. How bad can one dress be?

Back in the street, Gwen swings the dark green shopping bag, the dress inside snuggled in purple tissue paper. Striding down Madison Avenue, a handsome man on one arm, expensive shopping bags on the other, she thinks, This is who I fundamentally am, These are the heedless acquisitions I'm accustomed to.

At Fifty-sixth Street, Christopher steers her toward Park, and they turn into the Monkey Bar. Gwen slides into a banquette, orders a bullshot, scarfs a handful of peanuts. Meets the gaze of their nearest neighbor—a tall hollow-cheeked man who is smoking a pipe. Dutch? English? She feels a giddy impostor before this man for whom—as for Christopher—she imagines that womanhood means complexity, elegance, caprice. Perdition.

"God, it's nice to see you looking a little less desperate. I could swear the color's come back into your face."

"Do you think you can measure how much I've spent by the pinkness of my cheeks? I was desperate to bust out," she confesses. "My father's being so sick has been quite a bitch."

"It's funny, isn't it? It's much more complicated when you think you hate them. You know, for years I was wishing my father would drop dead, and then when he did—"

"I don't think Martin's going to die just yet. The trouble is Jacey, who has just . . . collapsed. She hasn't a *clue* how to handle it."

She looks up at the monkey light fixtures, the monkey wallpaper. It seems a million years ago that she first met Yilmaz here. She is a different person now; she can flaunt her Christian Ibarrguengoitia shopping bag, but she is no longer one of the elect. Politicians may court her vote with their breast cancer bills or maternity leave; automobile manufacturers may court her dollars with safety features; but that is all the attention she can expect from men, unless one day she seriously enters the labor market, in which case they will try to kill her.

"What are you up to this weekend?" Christopher asks.

"I don't know," she says. "Do you want to get together? Gideon's working, and I'd sort of been wanting to take Bella out for a treat . . ." She has an image of Christopher and Bella at the carousel in Central Park, the Plaza for tea. Do they still play Viennese waltzes in the Palm Court? She wants terribly for Christopher to get to know her daughter, to approve of her.

Christopher is wearing a tweed suit, with streaks of violet mid the browns and rusts, and a lavender-checked shirt; his cuff links—amber cameos—are outrageously pretty. "I'm going to London for the weekend; I've got an artist who's got some pictures in a show at Whitechapel."

"Is Yilmaz coming?"

"He can't leave the country till his papers come through. I'm staying at the Stafford—have I told you my discovery? They make the best martinis in the world. Constance and Roger are giving a dinner for me on Saturday night. You should come, too: it's not that expensive."

She sighs, audibly, and is embarrassed by the ferocity of her regret. "Toddlers aren't very good transatlantic companions."

"Leave the baby. What are you supposed to do this weekend, anyway?"

"Nothing. Playgrounds. What else?" She sneaks another glance at the gaunt pipe-smoking Dutchman, who gets up and . . . leaves.

"Get over it, Gwen," says Christopher, quite sharply. "It doesn't suit you to play drudge. I'm sure it would be much better for your daughter to have a mother who's *pleased* with her life. Come to London with me. You have a husband who's a whiz with the baby—let's be truthful, he's a lot better at it than you are; you've got a nanny. What's the problem? We'll have a blast and you'll feel much happier afterwards. You're so depressed you don't even know you're depressed . . ."

But she can't. She can't, because she can't imagine telling Gideon, I'm going to London this weekend and leaving you with Bella. She can't, not because it would be a dirty trick to play on him, but because they've got themselves into this hangdog game where everything she does is martyrish for the good of the child, and everything he does is martyrish for the good of the family, and nobody is allowed to have any fun.

And yet she is startled by how fiendishly badly she wants to run away to London with Christopher, and frightened by her own conviction that if she went, she would never come back, not till Bella was twenty and Gideon dead.

2

A DINGY MUNICIPAL BUILDING on Centre Street.

Outside, protesters behind blue police barricades. White sheets with red slogans. "¡Viva La Merced!" "Rudy, Don't Shut Down the Arts!" "The Lower East Side Needs Theater, not Yuppies."

Shouts that rise and dwindle. A couple of policemen survey the gathering. Office workers returning from lunch dawdle, curious, are handed flyers. A reporter from *El Pueblo* is interviewing Gideon, Sancho; someone is filming with a video camera who Gideon is convinced is an undercover cop. He catches a glimpse of Wilbur Gutierrez, who has brought his friends from the Community Garden Coalition, John and Javier from Las Abuelitas, Annie Dolores, their councilwoman, God bless her, Sancho's girlfriend with his grown son, hauling thermos flasks and a Styrofoam picnic hamper. There are probably forty, fifty people. Everybody's settling in for a long hot afternoon on the sidewalk—they are not allowed inside the building, where the city auction's slated to take place, but Carlos's got his cell phone to relay information to the street.

Gideon, Dina, Dan, Andrea, Sancho, Carlos, their lawyer Thomas Healey, all in their best clothes, crowd into the elevator. They file down the hall to Room 314, take their seats. Checking out the men in their summer suits, trying to figure out who's the enemy. Murmurs, nudges, whispers. Do you recognize that guy in the glasses—he's looking at us. I don't know, I think that's somebody from Steve Menkes's office. I thought Menkes dropped out . . . Half an hour late, the municipal auctioneer steps up to the lectern. Business begins; it's a five-borough auction. A building on Gowanus Avenue, an empty lot on Van Duisen Street that turns out to have been the attraction that's drawn the elegantly suited man Gideon imagined might be a contender for La Merced.

Minutes, stale minutes, fly-buzzing minutes. Certain items remain unsold. Sales figures, mostly, don't rise much above the asking price. Summer afternoon torpor. The air conditioner hums loudly but emits little cool. Sancho and Thomas Healey confer in noisy whispers.

At three forty-five, they come to Lot 17. The auctioneer reads aloud the terse description of La Merced. A pause, before he opens the floor to bidders.

Whereupon Thomas Healey, like the bad fairy at the christening, rises to his feet. "I'd like to mention for the record, sir, that this building is not actually for sale. Any attempts to sell it are illegal. The building currently has twelve tenant organizations that are paying rent, none of whom agree to its being sold. Whoever is ill advised enough to attempt to buy this building can expect to spend his life and fortune on lawsuits, with slim hopes of ever taking possession of the property."

A low clamor. And the two rows of La Merced's supporters, who've been posing as potential buyers, begin to chant, over and over, "Hands off La Merced! Hands off La Merced!"

It takes about two minutes for the court officers to hustle out the protesters, after which the sale is reopened. Only Sancho, Gideon, Carlos, Tom Healey, and Dan remain. The auctioneer invites bids for the former parochial school located at 235 Attorney Street.

"Ten cents!" shouts Sancho.

He is ignored.

"It's a dump," Sancho adds. "I should know, I live there."

There are sniggers. The auctioneer asks for silence.

"Four cents," yells Gideon. The auctioneer says that if there are any more interruptions, offenders will be removed. The bidding will open at $750,000.

A tall beige-suited man offers eight.

"I have a bid for eight hundred thousand dollars," says the auctioneer.

"Three cents!" yells Gideon.

The policeman appears at his side and asks him in a low voice please to come with him. Gideon goes limp and starts shouting. "Is freedom of speech a crime? Why'm I under arrest?" Two policemen seize him, one grabbing him under each arm, and drag him down the side aisle of the room, his feet are barely touching the ground.

Now everything is chaos. La Merced's remaining supporters are shouting, a heavyset man in chinos is shoving Carlos, who grabs him by the collar. More police. People have risen to their feet, are craning, jostling. Expressing puzzlement, curiosity, annoyance. "La Merced is not for sale! It's an arts center, we live there! This sale is theft!" Gideon is shouting as he's hustled down the hall and into the elevator. Somehow he's been knocked on the side of the head so his ear is buzzing. Out into the street, the protesters, seeing Gideon dragged by policemen, start shouting, catcalling. "Fascist pigs!"

Which is how he manages to spend the rest of the auction in a police station, charged with being a royal pain in the ass. It's boring being under arrest: a lot of sitting around and waiting. It's only when he makes his allotted call to Thomas Healey that he learns that the bidding was pretty brisk, the beige-suited man dropped out at 2.6, clearing the way for an agent of the Safir Brothers to acquire La Merced for 2.7 million.

"The Safir Brothers? Who own all those crappy Chinatown tenements?"

"Yup. *And* Fairleigh East—you know that development over on DeWitt?"

"Oh shit. Now you're talking low-life scum," says Gideon.

"The brother-in-law's upstate for some combination of money laundering for Colombians and tax evasion."

"Christ, I'd rather it'd been Menkes, after all."

Healey's meanwhile passed the phone to Sancho. "So how's prison, honey? You want us to come get you? Your wife's been calling; she wants to know if you gonna be home for dinner."

Sancho Panza, of course, is already geared up for guerrilla warfare, pleased to have adversaries who aren't scared of a fight.

Chapter Eleven

I

JULY 1997.

New York in its dog days. As if death were hot. As if a graveyard witch had clamped her leech-lips onto yours and were sucking the breath out. Exterminating clouds: a puff of white poison gas, and New Jersey disappears. The freezer-unit deathliness of today's commercial interiors: virtual Antarcticas of recirculated air, alternating with the pestiferous streets.

Gwen said, "I'm going to open an office in Ultima Thule, go investigate democracy in Greenland."

Bella, too, despite coloring that recalled Delacroix's *Femmes d'Alger,* wilted in the heat, sweat beading her face, howling up at Gwen angry-accusing, as if summer, like all pains, were in her mother's power to remove.

Only Gideon remained cheerful, bringing home at night mango sorbets and tangerine juices, like a hunter bearing his slain bison. Gideon was cheerful because he was about to *get out.*

Pants on Fire was hitting the road for six weeks, East Coast from Maine to Georgia, then out west to New Mexico, and a little jaunt up to Washington and Oregon, where Jerome's friend Mindy Buckett ran a marionette festival. They were taking *The Dybbuk* and *The Sad but True Story of Rumpelstiltsky,* as well as their revamped version of *The False Messiah.*

Gideon had asked Gwen to meet him out west, in Santa Fe or Seattle or Eugene, and it was just sorry-for-herself cussedness that she wouldn't. Seemed like Martyr Look was Fashion of the Year, she'd cashed in all her Prada see-through miniskirts for convict-pajamas and a hangdog scowl.

Look at him: he should be miserable, but he's not. The Safir Brothers have been broadcasting their intentions to demolish La Merced, without even a relocation bribe in the offing. Do you notice him complaining about the weather?

2

I HATE THE SUMMER, said Gwen, and there was nobody to answer but Bella. When she first moved back to the city, Gwen had thrived on New York summers from chauvinism, the way Siberians love their permafrost, the way Algis always told her, You travellers who venture here in August, you don't know the *really* beautiful time is December when it's dark by lunchtime and the snot freezes in your nostrils . . .

It was New York's repellent surfaces that had attracted her, its refusal to make any concessions to human softness, sociability, need for safety, to any sentiments but efficiency and avarice, and sometimes not even them.

She had loved it (from Massachusetts) in the late seventies when it went bankrupt, she loved it (from Ann Arbor and Moscow) in the crack-and-homeless eighties when innocent tourists got shot in the subway, and business and the middle classes "relocated." Stuck in Washington in the early 1990s, she had plotted her restoration to this city she'd left aged twelve, but which had branded itself in her equally inhospitable soul. She didn't want to live somewhere kids could ride their bikes to school and neighbors leave their doors unlocked; she was single, unattached, moneyed, she didn't want a home, she wanted . . . impact, a punch in the jaw from a howling hermit tearing along Seventy-ninth Street in a fake fur coat and nothing else, she wanted the same horror, terror, rage she carried within her mirrored in the unforgiving streets, in a subway car stinking-full of the walking dead whose yellow eyes and rotten teeth and sour breaths told you, We too are just barely scraping by, Saturday nights in the emergency room, Monday mornings waiting for the social worker . . .

Those subway advertisements for AIDS treatments, child abuse hotlines, battered-wife shelters, overnight divorces, cockroach-and-rat exterminators, cheap bail, knew their audience. New Yorkers were people who were just getting by and sometimes not.

That was then. Now she wants the world redeemed—explicable—in time for her daughter's first birthday.

3

"ARE YOU GOING TO BE HOME for the next hour?"

It's twelve. Gwen and Bella have just come back for a lunch break after a morning in Central Park. Gwen's pushed Bella in one swing after another, picked the broken glass and turds out of the sandbox, and tried to keep her daughter from eating cigarette butts or poking an index finger into the suppurating eye of a sleeping homeless person.

By noon, the baby is filthy. Her feet—through the jack-o'-lantern chinks in her jellies—*black*. It's only July, so God knows how many more weeks' heat they have left to survive. Meanwhile, Gwen dreams of icy sparkling rivers, dark forest. In short, Siberia . . .

"Sure. Why, would you like to come by?" Gwen, phone crooked between ear and shoulder, is trying to scrub the strawberry yogurt off Bella's resisting cheek. "Naaah! Naaah! Naaah!" the baby screams, simultaneously trying to hide her face, swat her mother, and grab the phone.

"I'm on my way to Quintessentials—I got to find some door-knobs for the kitchen cabinets, and I have this *mega*-batch of old toys for you—farms, play telephones, you name it. Should I drop it off with the doorman?"

"No, please, Jacey—please come up and have a cup of coffee. I'd love to talk . . ." Gwen has already arranged to pick up her father from the hospital at the end of the day—shit, that means she'll have to lug along Bella, unless by some miracle Gideon can get off early.

4

"IF YOU DON'T NEED this stuff, just tell me and I'll take it to Good-will . . ." Jacey repeats. Hungry for praise.

"What do you mean, it's a lifesaver, it's just what she needs . . ."

Gwen pours San Pellegrino. "Would you like a sandwich?"

"Thanks, I never eat lunch." Jacey pats her concave stomach.

"How's Pop? I talked to him last night, but—"

"He's driving me up the wall. You can't believe what a baby he's become—he won't let me out of his sight: if I get up to answer the phone, he's, like, Where're you going, Jace? And he never stops complaining. Thank God it's the last day of treatment. If he weren't sick, I'd—"

She'd what? How far does Jacey go in her half-ravening, half-respectable mind? Gideon doesn't even have cancer as an excuse. Are all men equally intolerable, only in different ways?

"Why don't you guys go away somewhere?" If Gwen had the money, she would. "Like that spa in Montana?"

"Honey, have you any idea what it takes just to get Martin out to Connecticut for the weekend? I mean, God forbid anybody should think he's easing off work, suspect that maybe he's had a life-threatening disease. Besides . . ."

What Jacey can't say: he is massively depressed, and she's scared to be alone with him. "Besides, I got so much work to do myself with the Pappas' apartment, which is already six weeks behind schedule because of fucking Custom Cabinets . . ."

"Oh yeah, that . . ."

The cabinet company boss, facing bankruptcy, has inconveniently put a bullet through his brain.

"How are *you* doing? You getting any sleep yet?"

"Exhausted," confesses Gwen. "I just can't seem to break her of the six a.m. feed . . ."

"You should wean her, Gwen. What is she now, like—?"

"Nine months."

"Wean her. Give yourself a break. Where's Marguerite?"

"Yeah, where's Marguerite—that's the question I find myself asking more and more often. She called up this morning for maybe the fifth time this month to say she's feeling a little sick"—Gideon shimmying out the door mid-conversation before there could be any negotiation over who stayed home from work this time—"she's leaving next month, giving herself a little vacation before she goes back to school in the fall, and I can't say I'm heartbroken . . ."

Jacey clapping the side of her head. "*That*'s what I wanted to tell you—Serena and Al's old nanny Zara? She called me up last night, she'd been looking after her grandson, now she wants to go back to work. I gave her your number, but you should call her right away, because she'll get snapped up in a second—I mean, the woman is magic, she is this black Mary Poppins"—Gwen pictures Mary Poppins in blackface, like the Virgin of Częstochowa)—"you come home, the kids are tucked in bed, she's sewed up the rip in your old jeans, she's one of these types who's always looking for something to do, like, the baby's taking a nap so she sterilizes the bottles and scrubs down the changing table, and puts in new kitchen curtains . . ."

"Sounds like bliss. Where's she from?" (The geography of "help.")

"She's from the islands."

Of course. A vision of being cradled by a big cottony bosom, the scent of dried sweat and nutmeg. Constance's theory that, screw the baby, it's *us* we want the nannies for—us, the unloved children of chilly brittle sixties mothers who held us at arm's length, frightened by our need of them.

"How much?" Gwen's just curious, that's all, to know the going rate for "magic."

"Five hundred a week, which is, like, nothing for Manhattan."

"You're kidding."

"Oh, it's nothing. That is *cheap*. Take it from me, who knows more about labor than John J. Sweeney. Believe me."

"Five hundred," Gwen murmurs. "Jacey, that is just so far out of our league, at the moment."

"Well, call her. In fact"—Jacey takes out her portable phone and electronic address book. Punches a number and leaves a message: "Zara, I'm sitting right here with my stepdaughter . . ."

"So Martin's got a couple months off treatment."

"Yeah, the doctors are pleased. They think—touch wood"—she searches the condo kitchen's laminated surfaces in vain—"this round has taken care of it. I have this dream that in a couple of years this whole episode will seem like . . . well, a bad dream. *Finito.* What are you doing this weekend?"

"Nothing. Gideon's leaving on tour next week. We're just hanging out."

"You should bring Bella out to Connecticut; I'm driving Martin out late tonight. We got Sabine, we got Martha, her daughter. You could get some rest."

And could you please tell me why Jacey knows she can get away with excluding Gwen's husband from the invitation?

5

THE FORMAL JUSTIFICATION, of course, is that because Martin is sick, he can't be troubled to make the effort. Besides, it's part of the convenient legend that Gideon is always working. And although work is normally good in the Jacey/Martin lexicon, in Gideon's case, it's not good, because he's not earning a living, he's just jerking around. Playing with puppets, playing at urban warfare, while his wife supports him.

Jacey, who once used her downtown-arts credentials to enlist Gideon in her mock struggle against Martin's fuddy-duddiness, no longer wants to know what Gwen's husband's up to. She is the vessel of Martin's unspoken disapproval, his belief that now that Gideon has a family, it's time to grow up and get a real job.

A real job means working in the Communications Industry: Martin, Gwen imagines, would like to see Gideon maybe an assistant producer at a multimedia company, or starting his own business designing children's programs for the Internet. Everybody knows these new media are hungry for product, and product is what Gideon's got coming out the wazoo, if he would only get off the said wazoo and flog it. Gideon, Martin believes, is in this field that, because baby boomers are now having their own kids, has suddenly become a hot property; he's simply too spoiled to cash in on the financial potential of Children's Entertainment.

"What a tempting invitation—I'd really love to."

"So why don't you? We're probably aiming to leave about seven . . ."

"I don't know."

"Well, the invitation's open. Like I say, we'll be there most of the month. I mean, commuting back and forth. Serena and Al are in day camp, so you'd have the place to yourself."

"I'll try—I'll have to see how—"

"I gotta run," says Jacey, glancing at her gold Rolex tank-watch. "I have a meeting with the contractor, and I've *got* to get him these doorknobs . . ."

"We're just on our way out to the park, too," replies Gwen, hastily reaching for a stack of diapers, the travel pack of wipes, a bottle of water. Where does Mimi keep all the—? Suddenly desperate not to be left alone in the apartment with the child.

With any luck, Bella will fall asleep in the stroller, allowing Gwen an hour's respite before going to pick up her dad from Sloan-Kettering. An hour in which to repossess her soul, in which to zone out. Imagines herself the one stretched out on the bench at Alice in Wonderland, and thinks it would take more than a thunderstorm to rouse her, she is that bone-weary. She needs to go to Russia is what she really needs to do. Gideon should be staying at home with Bella, and she should be in Russia.

6

GWEN IS LYING on the cold mattress, watching the man undress by the light of a naked bulb hanging from the ceiling. The man has gray hair on his chest, and blue tattoos on his arm. A lamb, a cross. His skin is white and his muscles are stringy. He strips down to his long-john bottoms and climbs into bed. She reaches over for him, and he takes her into his arms. He will not make love to her, although she feels she would like him to. He won't because she is nineteen and a virgin. No use lying about it; he knows. And approves; she's had better things to do than spread her legs.

"Your first time shouldn't be with an old jailbird," he says. "You'd be sorry afterwards." He pictures the proper first lover for Gwen: a twenty-year-old from a good family, with a degree in mathematics or engineering. She laughs; it's 1984, but he doesn't know about yuppies. Where he comes from, wealth was how much forest you owned.

He holds her, her head on his chest, and eventually, instead of feeling rebuffed, she feels unimaginably safe. His plum brandy is singing in her head, but she's not drunk. Outside the house are doubtless stationed the same two men who follow her everywhere. She's sorry to bring more secret police down on Algis, but Algis doesn't care. His landlady logs his comings and goings; the neighbor drops by for an inquiring chat; Algis's boss at the Museum of Aboriginal Peoples is regularly visited by men in brown plastic shoes. "Surveillance" is no more than white noise.

Algis holds her in his arms and sings a comic-mournful song about a man whose mother-in-law won't let him live with his wife. Gwen lies in Algis's arms in the small cold room that stinks of heating gas. She wishes they could swap memories. He's smiling, crookedly.

"What's so funny?"

"I'm remembering someone I knew in the camp, a Volga Tatar who killed his son—a three-year-old boy. He said, How can they punish me for hurting what's mine? I only took back something that belonged to me. If anybody's suffered, it's me. I thought, Here is this man who killed his son because he had a hangover and the child woke him up laughing, and here am I who has never heard his own son laugh. Are there really people in the world who believe things—people, even—belong to them?"

Gwen, who has come to Russia in part because the problem of belonging has become too acute, agrees that a person is lucky if he manages even to possess himself. Gwen knows even then that self-knowledge isn't her strong suit, but knowing's no help.

7

GIDEON TIPTOES out of Bella's bedroom, his expression solemnly reverent. "Sweet little angel," he murmurs.

It's 11 p.m. Gwen, who has only just coaxed the child to sleep, after an hour of Bella's hysterical screaming from heat exhaustion, doesn't look up from her reading.

First moment of peace since six this morning, and Gideon hasn't the wits to figure out why his wife might just rather read the *New York Review of Books* on Bakhtin's voices, while drinking a cold Dos Equis, than listen to her husband coo over how sweet their daughter looks, now that she's finally asleep.

"Did you guys have a nice day?" he asks. (Strange how he thinks someone's reading a book or paper is a perfect opportunity for conversation. The mind-set of an illiterate. Gideon himself might have considered sharing their nice day, Gwen reflects, especially as he is about to take off for six weeks.)

"Jacey came by."

"Oh yeah? How was she?"

"Fine. I think I might take Bella up to Connecticut while you're away." (As if his being "away" is much different from his being "there.")

"Do you want to?"

"Do I want to?" she repeats, exasperated. As if anything she does these days is what she *wants* to do. She throws down the *New York Re-*

view in defeat, and is even more irritated when Gideon picks it up, glancing at the cover stories.

"Well, I think Jacey needs help, and it might be good for Bella. Plus I'm pretty sick of the city."

"So do it," he says, enthusiastically.

What Gideon refuses to acknowledge is that although the heat is getting her down, the last thing in the world Gwen wants to do is be Martin and Jacey's guest. She hates their house (she thought the whole point of having her own family was never having to go to Connecticut again), but more than that, she hates being placed in this Victorian position of alms-receiver.

To Jacey and Martin, all relations are predicated on money-and-power, and she, thanks to Gideon, has teetered into the moneyless-powerless camp. Even with Martin so sick, the support she's giving Jacey falls into the category of a poor relation's due. She *hates* Gideon for leaving her at their mercy.

"So what'd Jacey have to say for herself?"

"She's got a nanny for us. A good one this time."

"Yeah? It'd be hard to find badder, short of someone selling our daughter into child prostitution rings. How much?"

He's getting cynical, her Gideon.

"Five hundred."

"A week? Nice. Maybe I should become a nanny."

"If that's what it would take to get you to spend a little time with Bella, sure, I'd pay you . . ."

"Father's daughter, huh? Only comfortable with people you pay?"

And suddenly Gwen loses it, starts shouting. "You just have no idea what this day's been like. You know how many meetings I had to cancel, how much work I've let slide, so I could sit in the playground all day and *fry*? I'm going to get fired from a job I LOVE, that I'm DYING to get back to . . . You don't want me to get a good nanny? Why couldn't you have taken her, for once?"

He says, quite coldly, "I don't understand what the big deal is, it doesn't sound to me like Auschwitz to spend your day playing in Central Park with your child."

She repeats, "Why couldn't you have taken her? If you ever took her for the day, you wouldn't be so—"

He turns away. "I spent plenty of *days* all by my lonesome looking after Ethan back when you thought a diaper was some Old Slavonic form of verse and I never thought it was that big a deal. Frankly it seemed like kind of a cinch, kind of pleasant compared to real work . . ."

And she says, wonderingly, "Isn't it strange. You did it all those years for Ethan and you never do it for Bella . . ."

Thinking, Why, why, why was I ever so dumb as to get pregnant?

He walks into the kitchen, and she—regretting not what she's said, but what she's unpardonably thought—puts down her newspaper and follows. "Have you had dinner yet?"

He's pouring himself a glass of milk. "Yeah, Andrea brought some falafel." When he finishes drinking the milk—slow and deliberate the way he places the empty glass back down on the counter; it's in such motions that you remember he's an actor—Gideon turns around and puts his arms around her. Starts massaging her lower back, stroking, doing his magic, and eventually when she's softened and melting, when the time is right to shift from nursing, from purely altruistic first aid, to love-medicine, he grabs her bottom, one apple of it in each hand, and yanks it to him hard.

"Why didn't you tell me you'd got your figure back?"

And she murmurs, joke-resisting, "But I really did want to read that piece on Bakhtin . . ."

Chapter Twelve

I

YOU THINK YOU CAN FIND the moment to talk to your father. To ask him (in between his glazed vigil of sports and Wall Street reports and news flashes from CNN, in between the oiled-by-servants routine of children's baths and suppers and bed) who his parents were, where they came from, does he have brothers and sisters still living. (Everything, in fact, he had berated you for not finding out about your husband-to-be.) But you can't. The fact that he's sick makes it all the more taboo to ask these questions which might imply you think he's dying . . .

And why and why and why does your father's being sick make you even *angrier* at your husband? Before, his mortality would have made you two cleave tighter, for who else could console you for the unconsummated sadness of your father's imminent death?

But instead, Gwen, you're madder still at Gideon, for having been so childishly jealous, for having tried to make you choose between them.

2

KATYDIDS. Stars. Votive candles guttering in the wind. The two women, alone on the porch, are a little drunk from Martha's margaritas.

"That's an amazing dress, Jacey . . ." Gwen leans over and fingers the red lace of Jacey's miniskirt. "I've been admiring it all evening."

Jacey laughs. "Martin only lets me wear it when nobody's here. I got this great pair of red patent-leather fuck-me shoes to match. This dress to me is a kinda Open Sesame, I couldn't believe it when I saw it in Donna Karan . . ."

Jacey's intonations get more southern when she drinks. "You like stories, right? Here's a story for you. When I was a girl, growing up in Lenora, Texas? One time, when my sister and I got a little money saved—my dad was *real* strict about after-school jobs, we did *not* get to lay around a pool all summer—we sent away to Frederick's of Hollywood. I ordered this red lace full-corset, with a push-up bra? Even though I was flat as a pancake, same as now.

"Evenings, we used to lock the bedroom door and dress up in our hooker gear. I had this SX-70—remember those?—which were, like, ideal for dirty pics, because you didn't have to take 'em anywhere to be developed: Lauren and I, we'd snap each other in our corsets and panties, lipstick, mascara, spread across the bed in these, like, *really* suggestive poses." She reflects. "It wasn't exactly about sexuality, it was more about getting *out* . . . and sex was the only way we could think to *get* out. Like, finding some rich guy whose car had broken down and *jumping* him. Holding a gun to his head and saying, Take me to Paris, take me to New York, hell, take me to *Houston*. And these really cheesy whore-clothes, to us girls growing up in this two-bit Baptist town, they just seemed like . . . I don't know, glamour, excitement, wealth, adventure, everything we were longing for.

"When I met your dad, he was so generous with me, so patient. I'd had a real bad first marriage, and I just wasn't ready to trust again. The life we've made together, these sweet children, it's more than I could ever have dreamed of. I just want you to know, I didn't grow up as privileged as you. I guess that's why I keep on working even when, financially, God knows I don't have to, I could be like some ladies I know and just have lunches at Le Cirque, go to the gym. Your dad is my *hero*. I went out with more shitty guys than you could believe. I came a long way fast, but I really got jerked around on the way. When he met me—she laughs—"I was a bitch. Sure I wanted him, but I wanted to get him for nothing. And your dad had so much, so dazzlingly much, to a small-town Texan girl, well, it took me years to understand that *that* was what we had in common. We were both self-made people who were wounded inside, who seemed to know everything, but who were still little kids glued to the candy store window, dreaming of this *other life* . . . Now we got it, nobody's gonna take it away . . . *Nobody, not even the Angel of Death . . .*"

She pauses, drinks fast. "So when I found out about Armanda . . ."

Armanda? Gwen feels she's missed a trick.

". . . it was like the world had come to an end. I mean, he said he was in love with her. Not that he was screwing her: that he was *in love*. That doesn't leave a person much of an *in*. My first reaction is, I grab the kids, I drive out here, it's the middle of the school week. Serena has this school play she's supposed to be rehearsing, Al's got his tutoring, the kids are, like, What's going *on,* and I don't give a shit, I don't want him touching them. We're, like, all three of us sleeping in my bed, the kids're in their pajamas all day, watching cartoons, while for all I know he's moved the slut into Sutton Place. (Even though this is not an easy time for Martin, he is right in the middle of this Time Warner takeover deal with AOL which is just, like, falling apart in his face.) And I suddenly get this revelation: This guy is worth fighting for. So maybe I'm not twenty-two years old and blond, but I've got as much love to give him as anybody. Like, instead of trying to nail his balls to the wall saying, Give me a zillion dollars to get lost, I might try to lay myself open and tell him the truth, swallow my pride and say, Sweetheart, you're all I've ever wanted in the world and *more*. We got something too good to give up."

"Hmmm," says Gwen, stiffly. "That must have been . . . difficult."

Why, she wonders, is no one able to observe this minor bylaw of family civility, that not even grown children want to hear about their parents' sex lives? Why must all of Martin's girlfriends choose grouchy Her as confessor? But Jacey is too tequila-drunk to require much in the way of sympathy . . .

"And it worked. He's not an easy man to express his deepest feelings, but it turned out he had a lot of frustration built up that was, well, totally justified. You probably think we have great sex, right? I did too. When I thought about it. But it turned out that all along, I'd been putting my kids way ahead of my husband, like, he didn't even come third, and it was time to reverse that equation, to accept that being married to Supermom is *not* the sexiest thing for a guy. So I learned to give a little, we went to Paris on our own, and it was good for me, too, to start thinking of us as lovers again."

"Hmmm," repeats Gwen. "I bet . . ." Thinking, Are we doomed? Is this what it comes back to—the ugly hangdog insatiability of male sexuality, a mindlessly repetitive cycle of self-denial, betrayal, remorse, that only stops when they get too old or sick to cheat?

Armanda, she thinks, and wants to laugh.

3

THE BEAR IS EATING DINNER. Back in their own apartment, hallelujah, the summer's heat quenched. Next week it will be September and already the leaves on the London plane trees in Central Park are turning crinkly-brown, already there's a crispness in the air. Two years ago exactly, Gwen and her best friend Constance watched a man in moth-eaten All Stars turn over in his sleep. Which means it's time to be back in Siberia, watching peroxide grandmothers sell bedroom slippers and Ping-Pong rackets. To see if it's true that the Russian economy for the first time since Count Witte was minister under Nicholas II actually stands a chance (thanks to a surge in world oil prices) of turning a profit.

The Bear whacks at a squashy lump of tomato with her paw. Chuckles speculatively. She scoops up a few strands of spaghetti, sucks them into her mouth, and watches Gwen, still chuckling.

Gwen makes as if to bite the spaghetti that is dribbling, chin-length, from Bear's mouth. Bear roars with laughter, allows her mother to gnaw off one strand. Then she fishes the remaining half-chewed spaghetti out of her mouth and stuffs it into Gwen's. Regards her mother with grave tenderness. Opens her own mouth wide, demonstrating to Gwen how to eat. Raises another handful to Gwen's lips and opens her own shark-wide, indicating that Gwen is to do the same.

There is almost nothing that makes Gwen wilder with love than her baby's determination to mother her. And this is the sick truth: she has never felt half so anchored in a safe harbor as by her daughter's protectiveness.

They are still this primal, mother and babe, this consubstantial. Two mouths, one heart. All love she has priorly known—all love be-tween man and woman, for instance—is hedged, corrupt, cowardly, self-justifying. She loved Gideon as much as she had known how to love: as one selfish, broken, and perverse adult could love another. What Gwen and the Bear share, however, is beyond love. It's organic, neurological; if it stopped for a second, both of them would die.

In less than a week, Gideon is getting back from his puppet tour, and truth to tell, she dreads his return. It is simpler when he is away. When he is *really* away—not just never home, but toothbrush-and-razors-missing, collect calls from Albuquerque and Eugene, and the bed spa-cious and cool. She cooks the Bear bacon and waffles for breakfast, takes her out to Sasha and Irina's in Red Hook, they ride on the merry-go-round in Central Park, they picnic in the Sheep's Meadow, Bella sleeps in Gwen's bed and wakes up singing.

Whereas when Gideon is around, Gwen always feels resentful. Is al-ways counting and weaselling and trading, always looking at her watch on Sunday afternoons and saying, I've looked after Bella while you slept for one hour and forty-five minutes, now I'm going to the office for one hour and forty-five minutes.

Her husband's absence has forced Gwen to become so omnipotent, so all-nurturing, that there is no longer any aperture in mother and daughter's honeyed wholeness, any chink for him to crawl through . . .

4

THEY ARE LYING NAKED in bed. Flesh to flesh, enlaced, gazing into each other's eyes. Gazing with rapt solemnity. The Other's mouth is on Gwen's breast while a hand caresses, pats, squeezes, tweaks, and dandles the free breast. One plump brown leg is wrapped around Gwen's blond thigh. The child sighs a sigh of solemn repletion and, still staring, still sucking, reaches up a toasty hand and touches Gwen's eye. The eye of the Other. The Eye. Then she unmouths the nipple, and pronounces, "Aaaaaagggghhh." And Gwen, wrapping the child's leg still tighter around her, repeats, "Eeeeeeeyyyeee." And touches the child's eye. Her glorious eye. Her curly sparkling-brown gypsy-queen eye, which is now soft, now melting with tenderness. And the baby, back to sucking at her mother's tit, pokes up one plump brown finger into her mother's mouth and chuckles, fatly, as Gwen pretends to munch it.

Tight enlaced, mother and child, naked limbs wrapped around each other, as if the child were trying to undo the mistake of birth, slide back into the welcoming womb.

O happiness. O mother and child. No wonder we imagine God as father, for how else could you account for humans' prickly unease in the universe, our inspired dissatisfaction, our hair-trigger readiness to jostle, fight. For if God were the earth's mother, there would be no earth-quakes, no droughts. We would float in the world's arms, dreamy and gay, we would suckle and we would crow, and there would be no war, no war, just a sigh of repletion.

But in the world—in our world—Hades comes to wrench Childe Persephone from her mama's arms, and the return is . . . always oc-cluded, always incomplete.

Without him, they were fine.

5

"You don't kiss the same way anymore," Gideon remarks, drawing back to look at his wife. One in the morning. His first night home from six weeks on the road, dead beat, unwashed, and horny.

"No?" She sounds genuinely stricken.

"No . . . Your mouth is kind of tense . . ."

And what he can't bring himself to say is she doesn't fuck the same way, either. Her lower lips are also tense—dry, less yielding. He can't just surge-melt into her anymore without warning, and be met by such a hot molten rush of liquidness that he doesn't know who is entering whom, that it seems as if it's her cock that's streaming-exploding inside his cunt.

Instead, he's obliged to soldier his way in against her parched resis-tance, and that same stiff-armed, pushing-you-away embrace, which he's noted in both her mother and Jacey, is what Gwen's just done with her thighs when he seeks to slide between them, fending him off, shrinking back fearfully as if, God forbid, he might hurt her.

His cock knocks at her garden gate, crying, Open to me, my sister, my dove, my perfect one, but the sister-dove's hands are no longer dripping with myrrh, her bowels no longer yearn for him, and she does not open, she remains locked-locked . . .

"Oh," she says, genuinely stricken. "I didn't know I was doing anything different."

She tries to smile, to reach for his hand in atonement, and, not finding it, ends up giving him instead a rather distant avuncular pat on the shoulder.

"I'm sorry, I didn't know . . ."

But he's shoved over to the far side of the bed, his back to her, eyes shut.

BOOK SEVEN

Chapter One

I

OCTOBER 1997.

Gwen, in her study, is chatting on the phone with Arseniy Suslov, who is in town for a five-day gathering of Lavrinsky's Russian and CIS program directors.

The institute, at Gwen's insistence, has finally hired a "personnel" consultant: a Scotswoman of high polish who helped privatize the British rail service, and now gets paid millions to tell companies how to make their employees happier and their divisions more productive.

Gwen, who can imagine how much clarity a human relations consultant might bring to her own murky life, nonetheless feels doubtful that anyone accustomed to British railway chiefs can have much insight into the perverse morass that is Russia (Dina's training in inner-city junkies would be more to the point). But Mrs. Burris's first insight—that the bosses might be considerably "motivated" by a week's spoiling in New York—has not been half bad. Gwen just hopes nobody tries to defect . . .

Through the open door, she watches her daughter twirl. Bella whirls until she topples, sprawling flat on the living room floor, arms flopped over her curly head.

Bella's first birthday was three days ago. The party was organized by her nanny Betty, including the guests: a selection of Upper West Side power babies accompanied by their power nannies. Betty is an energetic

fifty-year-old who has been in Manhattan long enough to know it's
never too young to start networking.

The nonpaid adults at Bella's birthday were Bella's parents, her step-
grandmother, and, briefly, her grandfather—who stopped by at the end
to pick up his wife. Did Bella enjoy her birthday? Moderately. She
evinced small interest in the other children, or the presents—although
the bubble wrap made her laugh—but as soon as Gideon put on some
Balkan gypsy music, then she started rocking. Twisting, twirling. Walked
over to the big pink-and-white cake perched on the coffee table, got
down on all fours, and, still rocking back and forth on her haunches,
gave it a dog-lick, dark eyes dancing up at her mother, provocative,
inviting a No. But Gwen can never say No. The girl is too winning in
her mischief.

"So you're having dinner at Ari and Patti's place. And what are you
doing later on?" Gwen asks Arseniy. (She is still a wreck from the previous night's entertainment, which began at a Brighton Beach disco called
Skandal and ended with breakfast at the Kentucky Fried Chicken on
125th Street.)

"Volodya wants to go hear James Carter at the Blue Note. Do you
know him?"

"Sounds familiar . . ."

"He came last year to St. Petersburg. He is a baby, shockingly handsome, and he does these things with the saxophone that are really rude.
You know, he spits into it and it spits back at him, it makes these noises
which are, well, embarrassing. You and your husband should come,
too."

"Maybe we will," she says. "We like being embarrassed. We're supposed to go to my father's for dinner—which is surefire embarrassment.
What time's the show?"

"The second set's at midnight. We're meeting Soloviev first at the
Mercury Lounge. Do you remember Soloviev?"

"Do I remember him? I was taught by his *mother.*"

"You don't look like such a dinosaur."

Gwen writes down Arseniy's various rendezvous. (Her other charges
are less old-fashioned bohemian, wanting only strip joints and Armani
stores. She has already taken Tamara Vorashina and her husband shopping, watched them pillage Bloomingdale's, the Sharper Image, and
Burberry's with the glazed grim rapacity of kids who weren't allowed
candy or TV at home, before heading off on their own to Macy's Herald

Square, and it's going to be fun seeing how Vladimir Levin manages to charge his night in Atlantic City to the institute. Gwen suspects it didn't take seventy years of Communism to make Russians greedy, but it sure didn't hurt.)

Next door, Bella is now practicing her knee bends while her nanny folds away ironed clothes in her bedroom dresser. Bella, one year old, is now a child. Gwen is amused by her own traces in this child—her vanity, for instance. But Gwen is even more amused by what's Gideon—the flirty taunts, the clown's grace, the luxuriant ease in her own skin. At an age when other babies still crawl, Bella practices running backwards or descending her grandfather's Sutton Place staircase, upright. She will never like to read, Gwen knows; she will be able to pitch a tent or dance on stilts before she talks, and if they are ever so benighted as to send her to school, she will run away and make her fortune as a bareback rider, a tightrope walker, the India Rubber Girl. And Gwen reassures her proleptically, It's you I love, you in your agile youness, I don't want you to be like me, all gawky and self-hating and locked up in your own fusty head.

Gwen hears the front door open, the bustle of Gideon collecting, depositing things. He sounds as if he's heading out again . . .

"Gideon? Arseniy, can you hold on please?" And, switching to English, "Gideon, are you going out?"

Her husband, poking his head around the door, looks guilty-aggrieved. "I'm just picking up some stuff from Pro-Image before it closes. I got Ethan and Dan with me."

"You remember we're going over to my dad's tonight?"

"Shit. What time?"

"About seven? Whenever the game begins . . . We're going over to my dad's to watch the World Series," she explains to Arseniy. (Hearing, with a quaver, the front door slam.) "How's that for all-American?"

2

Over dinner, Gideon has abruptly crashed.

It was an improbable game. Bottom of the eighth, score 2–0, and Bobby Bonilla suddenly hits a home run that turns the Marlins' luck. It was such a buzz, watching those slim satin-skinned Florida Dominicans and Cubans now dance up to the plate, victory in their bounce. Watching Edgar Renteria, bases loaded, bottom of the tenth, hit a long clean ball into outfield, start to run, and then, looking over his shoulder, obviously realize he's just hit the ball that's won the World Series. And so he keeps on running, leaping like a gazelle in arcs of perfect ecstasy, sailing into the air, free as the first day of creation. America, America . . .

Thrilling, until you remember that the Florida Marlins are this fly-by-night team whose creator has already broadcast his intention to sell off the value-players soon as the season's over. Maybe Gideon's getting old, but he's feeling increasingly ground down by the impermanence of things. All summer, drinking bottomless cups of coffee in West Coast diners with Direct Action coordinators, sleeping in fellow puppeteers' living rooms in Phoenix and Seattle, looking at Dina and Andrea and Dan so cozy, so dull, so familiar in their sleeping bags, their morning snuffles, their good cheer, their bad moods, he kept thinking, This may well be Pants on Fire's last tour. The Safir Brothers are threatening to start demolition next spring, and even if Gideon finds a new free home (space isn't after all the biggest problem—they could easily double up, temporarily, with Jamie Gorelick at the Lighthouse, or Fran Neuhaus), by some unhappy coincidence, a couple of the foundations that have been Pants on Fire's mainstay have suddenly said they won't be giving them any more money. Which means that even if Pants on Fire stays alive, Gideon will no longer be able to pay himself a salary.

Try explaining to his overworked wife that his unlucrative job has suddenly devolved into a full-time hobby. And Gwen, meanwhile, keeps asking couldn't he at least put in a little for the rent, or the cleaning lady, or the telephone bill, which is jammed with his Internet excursions to Lille and Antwerp and Eugene, Oregon. As it is, Gideon doesn't know how he's going to be able to pay October's credit card bills, except by the old expedient of borrowing from Visa to pay MasterCard . . .

Jacey raises her glass of Merlot to Gideon. Clinks, with a grin.

"Happy days."

"*Salud y pesetas,*" replies Gideon, emptying his glass a little too fast. Jeez, he hadn't realized how nervous going over to Sutton Place made him.

"Gideon, we haven't seen you in *months,*" complains Jacey. "This time of year, it seems like we're booked every night from Labor Day till Christmas. I've barely seen the children this week, you know what I mean, Martin? We went to this Dalton fundraiser last night . . ."

"Speaking of which, Chugga, I wrote them a big check in your name." Martin, sour because he bet on the Indians, has barely spoken all evening.

Gwen frowns. "Why? I hated Dalton."

"You never know," says Martin. "It's changed a lot since your day. Besides, it's not too early to start thinking about where you'd like to send the kid."

"I've always been drawn by the idea of home schooling," Gideon remarks, amiably.

"Of course, there are also some excellent girls' schools," Martin pursues, as if his son-in-law hadn't spoken.

"Or there's also the Ringling Brothers circus school," smiles Gideon. Reaching for the bottle to pour himself another glass.

"I think it's still a ways down the road," says Gwen, shooting her husband a warning glance.

"Well, I would start looking into it if I were you," replies Martin. "This is not the seventies where you had to pay parents to keep their kids in the city. Nowadays you need all the strings you can pull."

Gideon is no longer smiling. Gideon has the strangest feeling that his father-in-law has been slipping Gwen money behind his back, money for the nanny, money for music class. He has a vision of being in ever-deeper hock to this man he despises for privileges he reviles. He puts down his fork and leans forward. "You know something? It just happens I have pretty strong feelings about education. No way is Bella *ever* going to set foot in an Upper East Side private school."

Funny how fast the mood has turned.

"No?" inquires Martin, coldly. "Are you people thinking of leaving New York?"

"Don't put it past us. We're thinking of all kinds of things . . ."

"Like moving to Mars?"

Jacey laughs. "Martin . . . Martin has this old-fashioned faith in the power of American education, which I always find kinda sweet."

"I don't have any faith whatsoever in the power of American public school education."

"But Martin, they're right, Bella's only a year old."

"In England, they sign 'em up at birth," says Martin, grimly.

"Yeah, in England they also beat them with leather straps . . ."

"Cool," says Gideon.

Uneasy laughter.

"How about some . . . pudding, *sir*?" Jacey fakes an English accent. "Pudding, glorious pudding. Isn't that what they say?"

Chapter Two

I

THE SAD CITY, worn and tired.

For of course New York's not all blazing Christian Ibarrguengoitia boutiques and Upper East Side private schools, not unmixedly the shining citadel of the New Economic Paradigm that its publicists would have you believe.

The sad city, in the autumn rain, in rush hour. The prewar city, wizened and decrepit: a sad dingy manufacturing city, the city Edward Hopper and George Bellows painted. You see it on Madison in the Twenties, Park Avenue South: tall rows of bedraggled office buildings, low-ceilinged, their fluorescent grids revealing men in shirtsleeves, secretaries in high heels whose soles turn to cardboard mush in the rain. Businesses which sell sportswear, stationery. PARK FAST. Early Bird Specials, the Deauville Hotel, a boy in a red baseball jacket waiting outside a Mamma Mia pizzeria, joined by his mother in a monkey-fur coat. Steam rising from the grates of office buildings, pouring up from manhole covers, and the smoggy suffocating smell the steam gives off.

Rush hour in the city, rush hour in the rain, stuck in a taxi in the tunnel under Park Avenue South. The yellow gleam of the taxis, the red bloom of their backlights. Gideon is riding uptown with Alfred Gebler.

Gebler, annoyed, says, "I gather you haven't been following the changes."

Gideon glances sideways, inquiring.

"Well, it's been in the papers every day for the past . . . There was a cover story in *New York* magazine last month. You're not exactly plugged in, are you? Our lawsuit."

"Your . . ."

"Our *demise*."

"No, I hadn't really been following. That's terrible. What's happened?"

Gebler draws a finger across his throat and makes a rattling noise.

"In short? A palace coup. We got sued by half our board and Aurora's parent foundation for supposed violations of our own charter in how we've financed our art acquisitions. It was pretty ugly. I won't bore you with the details, but the upshot is, the bad guys won. As they always do. We've been given a new board, and a brave new mission to . . . contract. We're selling off our collection at rock-bottom prices. You wanna buy a Jasper Johns for sixty thousand dollars?"

"Sure."

"Well, too bad, you're thirty years too late."

"Alfred, I'm really sorry. What a tragedy for modern art. God, what evil times we're living in." Gideon puts his head in his hands, rocks back and forth. He is . . . overcome. "To have your life's creation snatched away from you just like that? It's inhuman, it's crushing. God, I can't tell you how sorry I am."

Gebler says, "C'mon, Gideon, don't let it sweat you, man. It's not *that* terrible. I mean, we still have a private collection worth a zillion dollars, we are not genuinely worthy of your socialist-populist Marxist-Zapatista-Brechtian-Stalinist pity . . ."

And Gideon says, "I'm sorry for both of us . . . Because . . . because . . ." He can hardly say it lest his voice break. "Because we're going under, too. We are drowning, and I can't think how to save us, we don't have a fucking dime for next . . . Every last little bit of funding we used to get by on has just, like, magically vanished. And the Safir Brothers are demolishing La Merced . . ."

He can't believe he's losing it like this in front of Gebler, whom he barely knows, but the strain of the eviction battle, of days in which one more last hope falls through (the Chillingworth Foundation's mysteriously relocated to Cincinnati, where it's concentrating on local good works; the VICO has just stopped its program for performing arts, and now Aurora!), of scrambling and hiding his panic under a show of bravado is suddenly too much for him; he hasn't slept for weeks; he's got this tic in his eye that keeps twitching; his mouth is bitter and his stomach rumbling so loud surely Gebler can hear it; he is falling apart, he is about to crack; and there is no one he can talk to, not even his colleagues, because he feels like such a fool, having lost their home and their financing in this boom when even Mirko, the Vanderveer super, has made so much money in the stock market that he's thinking of opening a café in Dubrovnik. And every time he tries to rally his mates for one more effort, remind them that they know how to produce plays for nothing, that it'll be years before they're actually evicted from La Merced, he can feel that they are in the nicest possible way planning their separate futures, trying to break it to him gently, Gideon, it's time to let go . . .

"So you'll find something else to keep your sticky little fingers busy," Gebler retorts. "Something more remunerative. Or else you can make like me and live off your wife."

"What are you guys going to do?"

Gebler raises his palms, indicating Buddhist indifference. Then opens his mouth wide and trumpets, " 'I-will-survive!' Well, we're fairly fancy-free. Our daughters are both out of college; Leopold, ignorant of the fact that he is not technically Jewish, is living in some kinda Hasidic ashram in Jerusalem. I have this vision of Dolly ending up in a wig, picking cabbages—well, not cabbages—with her Uzi by her side in some settlement in fucking Samaria. (You know, my wife is this zealot, and now that modern art's abandoned us, stay tuned to what her next religion's gonna be.) Now Orthodoxy I could *not* survive."

Gideon, trying to calm himself, looks out the window. Drums his fingers on the door. They are out of the tunnel now, they are driving up Park, past the Waldorf-Astoria, where his wife as a teenager used to come down from prep school to attend Christmas balls. "Have you ever thought of leaving New York? I mean, I feel more and more this is not the same city I moved to . . ."

"Leave the city?" Gebler stares. "You know something? (You don't know yet, but you will.) You look at your kid: at four, she's on the top of the world; at fourteen, she's sulky; at twenty-two, she's going through some spiritual-professional meltdown; at twenty-three she's got a boyfriend you can't stand; at twenty-five, she decides she's a lesbian, but she's *your child*. I was born here. Where'm I gonna move to? Pittsburgh? Los Angeles? *The country?*"

"I could stand the country . . ."

Gebler draws back and looks at him hard. "To tell you the truth, Gideon, I've never liked puppets—they're creepy. I just thought *you* were a nice boy. I'm glad you didn't marry the fat girl, that was a wise career move . . ."

Gideon sighs, a sigh that escapes as an involuntary groan.

Gebler pats his knee. "Why don't you try sculpture? You look like you could be handy with a blowtorch. Just look at puppets as an unfortunate phase you grew out of."

2

THE RAIN HAS STOPPED, and now a soft purple-gray fog, infinitely moist and forgiving, shrouds the cityscape in its warm breath. Gideon hunches over his plate of now-cold spaghetti, gazing out at the fog. The mutability of New York, that just as you are ready to renounce it, touches you with a forgotten tenderness . . .

"Are you finished?" His wife, having cleared their plates, reaches for the newspaper. Dinner officially over, they can go their separate ways.

"Gwen . . . ?"

"Mmmmmmmm." She's already behind the gray-rag curtain of the *Wall Street Journal*. Gideon imagines pursuing Gwen through a paper theater, chasing her past ten-foot-tall paper screens of stock market listings. Why does she hate him so much?

"Gwen, it looks like we're not getting our grant from Aurora next year."

Gwen puts down her newspaper. "Yeah, I've been reading about that battle. I'd forgotten that they were your supporters. What is it, it's pharmaceutical money?"

"Yeah, this Chicago company that makes nothing you ever heard of. And I guess they figured Greek goddesses made prettier cover than acne cream."

"Roman," says Gwen, automatically. "It was Eos who was the Greek goddess of the dawn. How much were you getting from them?"

"Oh, it's scary. It was, like, more than half our operating budget. But, you know, we were neighbors. And they felt kinda beholden to us: they used to run these after-school programs that we kinda picked up the slack on. I mean, that's how we met Hector . . . I somehow thought we could count on them forever . . ."

"So what are you going to do?" Her tone is curious, detached. If he were her neighbor at a dinner party, she would evince a warmer concern.

He shrugs. Angry because the way their dynamic works, it's he who has to reassure her. "We'll find a way out. Either we'll come up with the scratch somewhere else, or—I don't know . . . We'll go underground. Disband, temporarily. We're talking about all kinds of possibilities." He's babbling, from irritable fatigue, trying to guess what she's thinking. But Gwen doesn't speak. Speak, goddamn it, but she doesn't, she gazes into space, a frown on her face that tells him nothing.

"That's rough," she says, finally. "You really think you might close down the company?"

He shrugs again, then is annoyed at himself for having repeated the same lame gesture. She's making him nervous. "That's certainly one of the options we're considering . . ."

Gwen stares into the middle distance as a passenger gazes out the window of an airplane. Is she worrying about money? Is she dreading having to tell people that, in this era of full employment, her husband's managed to lose his job—some New York wolf-pack fear of failure, of having to admit to her friends that she's married a man who, it turns out, is not On the Edge, but a never-been on his way down-and-out. You give off a scent of blood, and they're at your throat.

"And if you closed the company, what would you do . . . you'd . . . find other work . . . ?"

Gideon shrugs a third time. So it's the money she minds. Money, and having him conveniently out of the house. Isn't a wife supposed to be a helpmeet who in tough times is there to remind you an artist's career is always phoenix-cyclical, and that since you're the biggest genius since Meyerhold, any minute the rest of the world's going to wake up and think so, too? Isn't your beloved supposed to say, Screw the loss of short-term income, we've got our love to keep us warm? She might even, God forbid, have thought to say, Never mind, honey, I'll sell some stocks; we'll get a second mortgage on the apartment; we'll ask my daddy for a loan.

Chapter Three

"HEY EETH. Are you all on your lonesome?"

Ethan, in tracksuit bottoms and no shirt, nods. Suddenly he has a masculine physique: bony chest, brawn in the upper arms. Does Ethan work out?

"Did I wake you?"

Sunday at one, and Gideon's rung the bell of Rivington Street. Thinking, I need to talk to Dina or I'll die . . .

"Mom's out."

"Will she be back soon? Do you know where she's gone?"

"She was meeting Avi."

For a second, Gideon's weary mind draws a blank. All he can think of is Ari, Gwen's colleague at Lavrinsky, who lives with the fact checker from *The New Yorker.* Then he clicks—Avi Weissbrot, the dropout seminarian with whom Dina and Josh are running their new minyan. Avi Weissbrot, who, with blond beard and pink cheeks, looks somewhere between a Hasid and a Swiss milkmaid, but actually comes from some prominent San Francisco family. His uncle, Gideon now remembers, is the lawyer in charge of the German slave labor case.

Gideon sits down at the kitchen table. He watches Ethan extract Pop-Tarts from the toaster. Ethan offers one to Gideon. "Cinnamon? Or strawberry sprinkle?"

"Yum. No thanks . . ."

The kitchen looks cozy. Somebody's painted the walls this funky high-gloss pale yellow. There's new black-and-white linoleum on the floor that evokes a bygone idea of metropolitan elegance. There's a homemade poppy-seed cake under a bell jar he doesn't remember. Even though the apartment's small, it feels like a place Ethan's friends might enjoy coming to. Even though the Vanderveer is by contrast big, it is not a place Gideon imagines that Bella's friends would ever enjoy coming to . . .

Ethan, who has now pulled on a purple Grateful Dead T-shirt that once belonged to Gideon but that doesn't look ridiculously too big for the kid, is making himself and Gideon tall glasses of chocolate milk. He offers Gideon some poppy-seed cake.

Gideon, after saying no, realizes he's ravenous.

"I'm glad I caught you," he smiles. "I haven't had chocolate milk in *years.*"

It's no joke, trying to meet up with Ethan these days. First of all, the E-boy himself is as busy as only a modern-day thirteen-year-old can be. And then somehow, every time Gideon mentions to Gwen that he's planning to pick up Ethan from school, or take him out for Sunday brunch, she seems to put a spanner in the works. Last time, she'd guilt-tripped him into bringing along Bella so she could let the nanny off early. A disaster. They'd met at the Café Lalo, after Ethan's trumpet lesson, but Gideon and Ethan had not been able to exchange a word, so distracted was Gideon by his screaming toddler's knocking over wait-

resses, or trying to dart out the door into traffic. He'd come home angry
at himself, angry at his daughter, angry at his wife and unable to tell
her why.

"So Dina's minyan's really taken off, huh? I thought their
High Holidays were pretty impressive. Your mom woulda made a great
rabbi . . ."

Ethan, who since Gideon moved out of Rivington Street has developed zits, as well as biceps, nods.

"Do you go every week?"

"No way," Ethan grins slyly. "It's bad enough having to go to Josh
for bar mitzvah lessons."

"Yeah, I certainly remember bar mitzvah lessons as one of the blots
on an extremely blotted adolescence. And we don't even know enough
rich people to make it seriously pay off. You better hand over the guest
list to your grandparents."

Ethan picks up a second Pop-Tart and devours it in two gulps, standing up. He licks his fingers. "What a scam. It's kinda weird: I've been an
atheist as long as I can remember, but it still *means* something to me,
you know what I'm saying? I mean, I'm not just going through with it to
please my mom."

"You got any friends at school who are religious?"

Ethan has just begun his first year at Stuyvesant. "Nah. My friend
Chris is a Buddhist, but that's not a religion, that's, like, try not to
squash ants if you can help it. But if I ever get married, I wouldn't mind
if my wife was observant, as long as she didn't expect me to do anything
too freaky about it . . ."

Gideon is amused. Ethan, almost without Gideon's noticing, has
slipped across the border to young man. It's a relief to be on the firm
ground of the masculine world, even just for an hour. He knows that if
he wants to make Ethan really happy, he'll ask him his opinion about
makes of stereo, or whether he thinks Microsoft's finally gotten the bugs
out of its Internet provider. Gideon, who now has his own child, gets
the funniest little twinge of wishing Ethan was his, too. He wants in the
worst way to have a son.

He ventures, instead, "So your mom . . . she seems well, doesn't
she?"

"Yeah, Mom's great," replies Ethan, firmly. "It was great she quit
her job." One more nice thing about the boy: he's *for* his mother; he
doesn't just love her or need her, he's rooting for her. They chat about

school, about music, about computers, about sports. Ethan confides that he's been trying to make his own music. Andre's dad works at a recording studio, and sometimes he lets the boys fool around with the equipment . . .

Then the phone rings. Gideon lingers, hoping it's Dina.

"Hey, what's happening?" says Ethan, and Gideon can tell from his shy shuffle that it's a girl. Catching sight of the kitchen clock, Gideon jumps up. Gwen's going to be hitting the roof: she's asked him to take Bella for the afternoon while she finishes off a Lavrinsky speech, and he hasn't even seen Dina yet. He must see Dina, he feels. She is the only person who can give him a lucid opinion about whether he is wasting his time trying to hold Pants on Fire together.

He puts a hand on Ethan's shoulder, indicates that he's leaving. Ethan makes a Wait gesture. "Leah, can you hold on? I got a friend who's just—"

Ethan stands up; the two men hug. Gideon massages Ethan's shoulder. "If I headed over to Twelfth Street, you think I could still catch your mom?"

Gideon, you see, has been assuming all this time that Dina and Avi Weissbrot are just hanging out with Josh, taking down the sukkah or discussing next week's parsha . . .

Ethan pauses. An unwilling look on his face, as if in the strangest way, his instinct is to cover up. "Uh—actually, she and Avi are at the opera." Gideon must have looked amazed. "They've gone to see *Rigoletto.*"

Well, Gideon thinks, once he's reached the safety of the street, I've spent half my life with Dina, but I never thought to ask her to the opera. He recalls his friend's slimmer figure, her look of glossy well-being, and concludes, *Yashar Koach,* Avi, for intuiting that that forsaken tree might yet bear sweetest fruit.

Chapter Four

I

CHRISTOPHER D'AURILHAC owns a house in Chelsea—a tall rose-brick house, opposite the seminary.

Inside, the small rooms are painted saffron, vermilion, rose. Gideon admires with a professional eye how creamily the paint's been laid on, how immaculate the finish.

"Yes," agrees Christopher. "The boy who does my painting's in the Biennale. He's a much better housepainter than artist."

Gwen's friends know how to live.

Gideon wonders what Christopher makes of Gwen's executive suite at the Vanderveer, and decides he must figure she's too brainy to bother with a private life. Or maybe too bluestocking to allow herself mere prettiness. Or maybe (as Gideon formerly suspected) one more reaction against an artistic mother?

"You don't have any photographs," he observes.

"No, hardly any. There are a couple of Lynn Davis icebergs in my dressing room," Christopher replies. "I have a rather un-New York squeamishness about mixing business and home."

Instead, there's a small Flemish Nativity in oils. A seventeenth-century Spanish portrait of a nun.

"An ancestress," Christopher lets on.

"Direct?" Gideon inquires.

"Hush your mouth," says Christopher. "The women in my family are chaste, and the men are brave."

"That's not what your mom tells me."

A Biedermeier sideboard, next to a zebra rug. An alabaster Cycladic fertility goddess.

"She an ancestress, too?"

"No, actually I bought her with Gwen a couple of months ago." (Giving Gideon a stab in his gut. He too would have liked to have been able to buy expensive beautiful things with Gwen . . .)

"Come meet our friends," says Christopher, leading Gideon into the library.

Gwen is sitting on a sofa with a long-legged blonde loaded in gold whom she seems already to know.

"Molly Kellaway, Gideon Wolkowitz. This is Gwen's husband," Chris explains, still holding Gideon by the arm.

"Gwen, you're *married*?! My God, I can't believe it!" beams the blonde, grabbing Gwen's arm so that husband and wife are pinioned in matching grips. *Why* can't she believe it, Gideon wonders. Why *wouldn't* you be able to believe a thirty-three-year-old woman was married? (Unless, for example, you had spotted her very recently in the arms of someone else? Or engaged in a particularly sordid orgy?)

"I've even got a child," Gwen coolly confirms. Thus leaving Gideon out of the equation.

On the opposite sofa is an older woman whom Christopher introduces as Agnes. A very talented sculptor, he adds. Gideon has just taken a seat beside the woman, who he discovers lives and works in a renovated synagogue several blocks from La Merced, when a sorrowful person in a gray uniform and white apron announces dinner.

Christopher and his guests pass through French doors into the dining room, where he seats them around an oval fruitwood table, inlaid in marquetry, that is one of the loveliest things Gideon has ever seen outside of a museum. (He can't quite decide which would rankle sorer: to learn that the table was another legacy from Christopher's pious Franco-Spanish ancestors or that Gwen had helped him pick it . . .)

Over dinner, there is general chatter about the summer, which in Christopher's case seems to have dawdled into early October. Christopher, Molly, and Yilmaz are recently returned from Turkey, where Christopher rented a house on the coast. A beautiful old stone house in a former Greek village near the Dardanelles.

"Why didn't you come?" Yilmaz asks Gideon. "It's paradise for children—we had seven of my nephews and nieces."

"Paradise?" grumbles Christopher. "Calling your family paradise— well, maybe paradise by the standards of a Hezbollah suicide bomber, but I must say I have more celibate visions. Paradise is where the Izzik family *isn't*."

Molly explains how they'd had to pretend to Yilmaz's relatives that Molly was Yilmaz's girlfriend. "Luckily, they're very traditional, there was no problem about Yilmaz and me not sharing a bedroom. I'm very jealous of you and Gwen having a baby," she now confesses to Gideon. "I'm *dying* to have a baby."

"Molly—you better find a husband first," warns her host.

"I'd like a love-baby," coos Molly.

"Molly, I don't think you would. I think you'd like a husband—a rich one, preferably. I'm trying to talk her into marrying Yilmaz," Christopher explains to the others.

"Yes, it would be great for him because he could become an American citizen, and it would be great for him so his family would never figure out that he was gay, but I can't quite see why it would be great for me . . ." ponders Molly, all smiles. "Except of course that you're so adorable," she adds, half apologetically. "If I were going to marry for love, of course I'd want to marry you . . ."

"But it's much easier to find a husband once you've been married already. Men are such sheep: if one's been in, they all want to follow," retorts Christopher.

"I've got a boyfriend," Molly explains to the table. "He's sweet, but—I see Yilmaz and Chris together, and I know something's missing."

(A second dick, thinks Gideon uncharitably. A *bigger* asshole.)

Her suitor, Molly continues, is a divorced venture capitalist with teenage children, who lives out in Denver and is absolutely crazy about her. "I guess he's a little boring. Is that too awful to say? But he's sweet and incredibly generous." She holds out her wrist into the lamplight. "See, he gave me this watch."

"It's Bulgari," Christopher informs them. "It's hideous, but it must have cost him ten grand. Why don't you sell it?"

"I just don't like him all that much—I guess that's what it comes down to."

"Have you met him?" Gwen asks Christopher, in a low voice. He makes a face, leans over. They exchange words that are brusque, almost indifferent—an incivility which Gideon somehow finds much more intimate, more inadvertently revealing than a caress.

They are coconspirators, he thinks, and is suddenly absolutely certain that Gwen confides in Christopher. It makes him feel desperately exposed, to suspect that this man whom he hates—who hates him—his enemy—knows something about Gideon's own fate that he himself does not yet know. She has talked to him about wanting to leave me, Gideon thinks. And he's invited us here tonight, knowing how proud Gwen is, to make me look like a jerk in front of her friends.

"What I want to know is, if I break up with Davis, do I have to give back the watch?"

"Of course you do—you have to offer to. I mean, he'd look pretty petty if he said yes. The polite thing would be just to send it to him, so he can't refuse."

"Are you sure?" ponders Agnes. "It's not like an engagement ring. When I left my husband," she confides, "I threw my wedding ring into the Tiber."

"How could you?" wonders Molly. "You could have given it to charity. To some poor girl for a dowry . . ."

"Well, I thought it had kind of a curse on it. He wasn't a very nice man."

"What is this, Saint Nicholas? Girls don't have dowries anymore," Chris chides Molly affectionately.

"Didn't your daddy give you a dowry?" Molly turns to Gwen.

"Molly, what a question. Gwen's virtue is her dowry . . ."

Gideon mock coughs.

Molly is still examining her own wrist. "Do you really think it's ugly? I don't think it's all that ugly."

Christopher shrugs. "I've never liked Bulgari."

She picks up his wrist. "So you've got a tank watch—is it Cartier? Well, that's classic."

Everybody now compares watches. Yilmaz is wearing an old Rolex watch of Chris's; Agnes has a Swatch; Gwen is wearing a Swiss Army watch.

"Surprise, surprise," teases Christopher. "Miss Gwendolen being one of the more militaristic people of our acquaintance. Aren't the Swiss a little too passive for you? I see you more in an Israeli storm trooper's watch . . ."

The conversation moves from jewelry to gossip about people they (except Gideon) know, including a South African college friend of Molly and Chris's who has just committed suicide in a hotel on the Rue de Rivoli. Suicide leads to murder, and they wind up eating homemade caramel ice cream with lace cookies, chattering about celebrity murders, above all, the still-unsolved case of a child beauty queen found murdered in her parents' basement in Denver. Molly, thanks to her boring boyfriend's living in that city, is able to supply them with forensic details they otherwise would never have known.

Gideon is depressed. Almost unbearably depressed by the chasm between the high culture to which Christopher's beautiful possessions bear witness and the trashiness of his guests' conversation. What's the point of having ancestors who were guillotined in the French Revolution if all you talk is tabloid porn?

"Did you read that piece in the *New York Review of Books* about gay marriage?" Agnes asks Christopher, suddenly.

"Did you see it?" she asks the others.

Christopher frowns. "Yes. I think it's rather missing the point. I mean, most of us are so shell-shocked from what we've witnessed of other people's marriages . . . What's the point of gay marriage—so there can be gay adultery and gay divorce and gay child abuse and gay delinquent fathers? Why multiply the damage?"

"Well, I thought he pretty well demolished the reasons *against.* That if having children is the only justification, then widows and widowers shouldn't be allowed to—"

"Why *shouldn't* men marry men and women marry women?" Molly asks, suddenly, with a passionate conviction that makes everybody laugh.

"You think you'd double your chances, Molly?" Chris teases.

"No, I think it's nonsense to say that some gay couple who've been together—like Giovanni and Ted—for forty years shouldn't have the same rights as—"

Christopher shrugs. "It's not a question of legal rights, we're talking—"

"I mean, if you and Yilmaz are still together in five, ten years, wouldn't you want to—"

"Me, marry a Muslim?" inquired Christopher. "You must be joking."

Gideon looks across the table at Gwen. He tries to catch her eye, to elicit some, however quiet, repudiation of the other women's consensus. But she nods in seeming agreement. Jesus, he thinks, is that how little marriage means to her, that no travesty of its sacred import, including Molly's cynical chatter about rich husbands, offends her? Could the Bible have put it clearer, that men and women are to cleave to each other, become one sacred flesh, while same-sex intercourse is classed along with bestiality and idol-worship?

"What about you, Gideon? As the only married man amongst us," says Molly. "Don't you think gays should be allowed to marry?"

He feels his heart pounding, certain he's being set up. "Sure," he says, finally. "And monkeys should be allowed to vote."

There is a moment's pall, then first Yilmaz, then everyone else bursts out laughing.

2

ON THE TAXI RIDE HOME, husband and wife are silent. It's past midnight. They are both very tired—still more tired knowing that Bella, who wakes up in the night when anyone other than Gwen puts her to bed, is sure to start squawking in about three hours.

The Sikh driver, who is driving too fast, runs a second red. Gwen, banging on the partition, reprimands him.

"Did you hate them all?" she asks, at last. She is furious at Gideon. Furious at how he'd sat all evening, yellow, wizened, sunk deep inside himself, not even pretending to listen. Sighing loudly. It hurt her pride, that he should make it clear to her friends how cataclysmically unhappy he is. And then his final unprovoked assault . . . No wonder they never go out together.

"No, I didn't mind Molly. She at least can't help it, she really was born without frontal lobes. It's the other ones who would rather die before letting you know they actually graduated from the world's finest universities . . ."

"You mean Christopher."

"How can *you* stand it?"

"I didn't think it was boring. But I guess I knew most of the people they were talking about." Thinking, I would have had a blast if you hadn't been there.

"You didn't think it was boring, talking about this year's Bulgari watch and next year's Rolodex?"

"Rolex."

"Excuse *me*. Look, my dad was an appliance salesman. My stepfather owned a sporting goods store. Do you think he went out to dinner with his friends and their wives and talked retail all night? I mean, let's just put to one side the crassness of how much these toys cost, would you think it was amusing—would they think it was amusing—if I'd talked all evening about whether Black & Decker circular saws are better than Sears'?"

Gwen doesn't reply.

Gideon is now shaking with rage. His wife's refusal to answer, her superior put-upon expression, drives him wild. "Tell me something. Before we got together, did you ever go out with anyone who had less than ten million dollars?"

She looks out the window, annoyed. "Yeah, the first boy I slept with was straight out of reform school. His dad was the caretaker of a motel on Route 1, and his mom was an Abenaki Indian. We used to have sex in one of the cabins, and I liked him a lot, better than anyone else I went out with for years after. Does that make you feel better?"

Gideon goes even paler. "Is this slumming too?" he asks, in a low trembling voice.

"No," she says, very calmly. "You're the one who thinks you're slumming. You think you picked me out of the gutter, morally. And you think I ought to be grateful."

Gideon chews on his beard. For the rest of the drive home, and for their ride up in the elevator, he says nothing. But after they have sent Betty back to Queens in a cab, he goes into the study and closes the door.

She can hear from the squeaks and shuffles that he's pulled out the sofa bed and is settling down to sleep. Only then does Gwen realize how much she counts, no matter how nasty she's been to him, on his warm lithe body beside her all night.

Chapter Five

I

THE A TRAIN is uncustomarily quiet as Gideon rides uptown from meeting Annie Dolores for a drink. In Gideon's car, there is a girl with thick glasses, in a navy green parochial-school blazer and ruler-straight cornrows her mama must have risen at 6 a.m. to braid: hair that, like geranium pots in a tenement window, proclaims to a menacing world, This child is held precious.

The bespectacled girl is bent over her homework. Gideon, craning, watches the inky loops, the painstaking crossings-out. What will she be when she grows up, he wonders, a nurse, a clerical worker? That solemnity, that breathless cursiveness, her mother's overseeing, paying off someday into a government job, church on Saturday nights. (And he knows, just knows, from the contrary flick of her eyes' whites, that *his* girl, Miss Mischief, will never be that sedulous, that she's always gonna kick against the traces.)

Annie Dolores has told Gideon he's got to do the math: add up how much money Pants on Fire has left in its account, offset against it their monthly running expenses, figure out how much they can expect to get next year, and where they can cut costs. He can't. It's reached the point where he knows he better call up Jennings. Jennings has carpentry jobs coming out of his ears: there are four million Manhattanites renovating their apartments this winter, commissioning built-in desks and filing cabinets for their home offices, and Jennings would be happy to put him on a crew, but this is just what Gideon doesn't want to do . . .

The schoolgirl finishes her homework, slips the binder back in her knapsack, and closes her eyes. Next to the schoolgirl is a paint-dusted blond worker in quilted overalls, Polish, probably (it's he who's made Gideon think just now of Jennings), who gets off at Fourteenth Street to change for the train to Woodside or Jackson Heights. A mustachioed lug wearing a jacket labelled "Madison Square Security Corporation" sits down in his place, and Gideon knows well the comfort, on a cold evening, of a subway seat that's been warmed by someone else's butt.

Everybody looks tired. Everybody is coming off shifts, or starting shifts. Everybody is going home, and home is a long way from work, because in New York nobody can afford to live less than an hour from where the money is made.

Working New York. Real-life New York, which nowadays is the New York of the Boroughs, Manhattan being just a stage set for arbitrageurs and UN ambassadors. The mayoral election is in less than a week, but Ruth Messinger has already blown it. She has been too calculating, too craven to come out and say, This so-called boom is a shell game. What's hidden under the "shells" is not the money, but the moneyless.

Last winter, five homeless men burned to death under the boardwalk in Brighton Beach. Last spring, the "last" major shantytown was evicted from a coal storage lot under Penn Station so that Donald Trump's tower city could get built (the deal he cut with the city was that his new project would contain a riverside park; but, of course, he's omitted the park).

What's so remarkable about the nineties, Gideon reflects, is not that poverty or homelessness have become acceptable, but that the abyss has so widened between prosperous and poor that the middle classes have quite sincerely forgotten about Them. This is what Giuliani brilliantly understood: that his commission was, all discreetly, to make Them disappear.

That thousands of families are locked in filthy stinking detention centers in Queens for the crime of wanting to become Americans, to share in our freedom and prosperity, is not known. If our fellow consumers—I mean, citizens—knew, of course they would storm City Hall, but as it is, they're too busy taking their children to speech therapy and ballet lessons, developing allergies to dairy products and wheat, worrying about the lead level in their bedroom paint: I'm lactose-intolerant, I can't eat gluten, has become an acceptable line of conversation among people who once read Rilke and Kierkegaard.

This, Gideon thinks, is the truth we all need to be hammering home. When the media flatter and shirk, *we* become the media; our little bits of felt and string and glue and papier-mâché and poster paint, our hands, are all that's left to tell the truth. It makes him feel that Pants on Fire has *no right* in these dangerous perjured times just to lie down and die . . .

2

SHUDDERING FLUORESCENCE, the tube lights flickering off and on as the train howls through the tunnel. He thinks of all the great American music about trains—one of the finest, in fact, about this very A train. Without trains, there'd be no American music. Remembering with a wrench in the gut—this definitely hurts too much to think about—Gwen's telling him she first fell in love with him when she discovered he knew all thirty-seven verses to "Casey Jones." And when'd you fall out of love with me, ma'am? Is Bella too gonna find she's "got another poppa on the Salt Lake Line"?

Next to Gideon is a pimply young man who is underlining in red Magic Marker on a large-print copy of *Los Actos de los Apostoles*. On his other side, a young black woman fifty pounds too fat, with purple lipstick and a purple scarf, is reading horoscopes of TV celebrities.

Thirty-fourth Street. A pissed-off-looking Chinese grandmother gets on the train, dangling hot-pink furry monkeys. Nobody looks up. Gideon stops her to buy one; she regards him with cold black eyes that say, Sucker. All the women in the world, his daughter included, seem to look at him with those eyes that say, Sucker. But little girls don't mind having pushover dads, and Bella surely will dance her Indian war dance of glee when he presents her with the monkey on a string.

Children are happy, or else they fake happiness. Children get very good at faking. The best thing they are at faking is being children—grown-ups' idea of children, that is: carefree. Not powerless beings perpetually on the verge of an almost unbearable anxiety.

Gideon, too, used to be okay at faking happiness, for his daughter's sake—he's an actor, he can fake anything, but now he no longer has the heart for it. And besides, Bella appears genuinely impervious to her parents' bitterness, to the wretched blight caused by her arrival. Bella is fine. Even Gwen, in her own way, is fine. In the old days, Gwen used to mock Gideon for being a joiner. Now she's joined the ultimate sisterhood of working mothers (this cabal of women who sit around the office bitching about their useless husbands) and it's he who's found himself . . . alone.

He has a diminished passion for his work, because his wife despises it; he feels alienated from his colleagues. When Gwen makes fun of Dina or Dan, he defends them, but her judgment nonetheless corrodes. With the result that everything he has made and stood for now seems tinny, strident, cheap. A kind of shrill childish flailing against the serious things in the world—the things that count in her eyes, like money, success, and power. Like nodding sycophantically through dinner table conversations about Bulgari watches and tabloid pedophile murders.

He is caught between worlds, which leaves him all the more at Gwen's mercy. She doesn't want him, it seems, but first she's going to strip him of whatever others might regard as assets.

And if he is a disappointment to Gwen, she—he is coming to feel, in his bleaker moments—is not the wife for him.

3

WHAT SHE LACKS, so oddly for a career philanthropist, is generosity. The recognition that Gideon's professional life, too, might spill over the edges of nine-to-five, might require him to bring home half a dozen hungry talkative strangers, and that all this takes is an extra packet of spaghetti, a couple more bottles of wine.

Gwen might have figured they have so much, they can afford to have Dina and Ethan over once in a while for Sunday lunch. She might have realized, if they didn't pay orphan Hector, they could at least feed him. But for Gwen and Gideon, "his" has never devolved into "theirs"; she has forced him to assume his work obligations single-handed, to ensure that they don't cut into "her" time. He can't have his friends over at night because she needs to read the newspaper.

Don't you see how good it could be for Bella, to grow up in this loud adoring theater family—a useful complement to Sutton Place or Newburyport? Don't you get it, Gwen? Unlike you, I got no mother, no father to offer my child: this is what's mine to give her.

4

HE'S THINKING, Why don't we ever go *out*, we have this full-time nanny, we should go hear music, we should go to clubs, she's got this fucking money, we should spend it. But we don't, because any time with me by definition is downtime, home drudgery; if she goes out, it's gonna be with someone *fun* like Christopher, and am I unfairly cynical in suspecting that for my wife, being fun by definition means being rich?

He's thinking, Why don't we talk anymore, even if we have to sit home every evening, we got tongues and ears and brains, we're not deaf-mutes.

But when he tries asking her what she's reading or thinking—I KNOW there are salty-prickly quick thoughts frisking around her head same as before, I know she hasn't really been witched into a working-mother robot grindingly fixated on play groups and career moves—she won't let him in. *Pit'chi li,* but she won't.

5

THERE'S A MORE topical bitterness: Bella's birthday, three weeks ago.

Gideon had had this scheme of making Bella a puppet show down at La Merced; Andrea could bake her killer chocolate cake; presents afterwards. But Gwen had vetoed the idea: she couldn't ask her sick father to haul down to the Lower East Side to that cold space. (That cold space where I first pulled down your drawers and ate your pussy; we used to know good ways to keep warm, my honey.)

And Gideon couldn't fight her, because if he let himself get too upset, she'd accuse him of projecting onto Bella the little comforts and spoilings *he* craved. (Because he as a kid had never had a birthday party. Because, when he finally got old enough to arrange one for himself—Jenny Randazzo was giving him a sweet-seventeen—well, the week before, his mom had finally died . . .)

So Gideon shut up. Instead, Gwen had laid on this sterile set piece at the Vanderveer, at once overpriced and perfunctory—a bought cake, Little Mermaid plates and napkins—importing the nanny's friends, strange children who meant nothing to Bella, as if she had no one of her own. And Gideon thought, Why am I here, Gwen? I am so irrelevant, so extraneous to this event. The balloon man has more place in this room than I do. Why am I here?

There is a rule in mafia assassinations: if you intend to kill someone, first you need to isolate him. And Gideon, in particular, was becoming dangerously isolated.

6

READING THE WHIZZ of blue mosaic station names. Reading the advertisements and trying not to burst out laughing or groaning or coughing, biting down hard to suppress his terrible anxiety because . . . his fear that his . . . Idiot. Calm yourself, man. Just because your wife no longer wants to fuck you doesn't mean you're entitled to fall apart. Pathetic, that he seemed to have no core of essential being to see him through this ordeal, this hellish uncertainty, this time when they *should be so happy.* Kid's first birthday, clear sailing ahead: a joint accomplishment to be proud of. We made her, this brave charming swaggerer. Any moment you'll be getting your own life back, Gwen; she all too soon won't need you quite so strangulation-tight, maybe one day she'll sleep through the night; maybe one day you'll even wean her. Don't throw me away when you're about to need me again. Or have Gwen's needs changed?

When Gideon looks at his wife—so tired and so angry, so hollow-eyed, so haggard—he still wells up with tenderness for her; even in her harsh vengefulness he *knows* her, and with his veins and heart and bowels he yearns for her. There is no phase of her anger he doesn't understand from within, doesn't, God help him, even root for and strangely applaud, but she, blind woman, will not know him.

She has whittled him down to a crude utilitarian hieroglyph of the Bad Father, who either will or won't change Bella's diapers, feed her dinner, give her a bath, get up for her in the night: he is reduced to a mute checklist of services either rendered or malevolently withheld, and her assessment is cold as a parking meter: just because he took Bella to the park all Sunday gives him no credit on Monday. And if he obeys— if he suppresses his young man's energies, his thirst, his impatience, his broad-cast desire, into becoming a nursing father—will she then love him? Hell, no. Once she's won—broken him down, harried him into doing for the baby all that a mother should do—although, yes, his wife is less *raging*, expresses a contemptuously insincere thanks, she is really no better pleased. On the contrary, she finds him, predictably, unmanned.

Useless conundrum: she resents you for being a man, and she despises you once she's shamed you out of being a man. In short, there is no percentage whatsoever in doing what she says she wants you to do.

Worse still, some part of Gideon suspects that she's goading him in the very hopes that if she pushes far enough (i.e., insanely criminally too far), he will finally lose his temper and smack her. That what she wants, quite simply, is a fight—not snotty needling words, but honest fists. This kinda scenario: he whacks her, she bites him, he whacks her harder, and they end up, panting, bruised, fucking. But he can't. Taming of the Shrew has always left him cold, he finds the notion of treating a woman as child-to-be-mastered utterly degrading to both parties, a total turnoff . . .

7

THE MUFFLED LOUDSPEAKER announces that this stop is Columbus Circle, which is where Gideon changes for the number 1. But he doesn't change. The schoolgirl in the green blazer scuttles out of the car, but Gideon remains. He's so breathless, so weak he feels if he stood up, he would black out. His legs are trembling violently, he feels as if he's going to be sick, the doors start to close but he does not move.

A long black arm glides through the closing doors, the doors jerk, they close, they spring open again, there's laughter, the doors spring open one last time at the Columbus Circle station, and a gang of five, six young men jumps onto the car. There's the *bing-bing* of closing doors, and the train moves off. Next stop, Harlem. The train is now rocketing with a speed that proclaims they're in for a long, long ride, not a brake in sight from 59th to 125th. And Gideon experiences the strangest exhilaration. His trembling limbs relax, he feels deliciously suffused with languor, as if he's just come.

The boys are dressed in baggy jeans and Tommy Hilfiger windbreakers, the clean-preppy look that's hit the inner city—they are jostling each other, they guffaw, they swing from the metal hoops. The other passengers stiffen into wariness, but to Gideon, the kids' high spirits are innocently infectious. He wonders where they've come from and where they're going, and wishes he could come, too. The tallest has a crew cut, his small high ears cling close to his skull, and Gideon, gazing up at him, is overcome by the warmest affection for this twenty-year-old whom he'll never see again. The young man's got the straight back and long clean limbs of a self-respecting athlete, a whole healthy animal, which makes Gideon feel by contrast housebound, fussy, stale. That he's even thinking of punching his wife means it's time to get out of the house. He thinks of Edgar Renteria, leaping across outfield, free as a gazelle, and his body quivers, yearns.

Now the train is slowing down for 125th and Gideon'd better get out if he doesn't want to land in the Bronx (no thonks), and instead of thinking he'll just nip around to the southbound track, he wonders, Who do I know uptown?

Gideon, in the 125th Street subway station, which is radiant, dear God, with vibrant lissome life: a girl in leopard-skin tights and patent-leather platforms, a man in a long leather coat and red sunglasses. His heart's pounding—the world is all around him, jostling, glimmering-bright and everywhere. There's no reason to cower in your mean little condo with the heat dimmed down low—the world is bursting bursting.

I don't want to go home, he thinks. I am not half defeated enough to sneak into that loveless bed, those sheets that are too immaculate to bear, that no longer, that maybe will nevermore, reek of Us. I do not consent to this excommunication, this slow live burial.

He's got eighteen dollars in his pocket and a MetroCard. When there's all this bursting life to be seized, why slink home to someone's ignoring back, why shrivel up and die by begrudged inches?

Gideon, running up the stairs, skipping two at a time, surfaces into the crisp navy blue air, a stream of red taillights, the dancing neon martini glass of a bar sign, police siren, car radios. Gideon surfaces into the screaming night-brightness—a long-legged man dangling a pink monkey from a stick.

Chapter Six

I

THERE WAS NOTHING more offensive to nature or good sense than a middle-aged "new father," thought Gwen, sitting in the sandbox, 9 a.m. on a Friday morning, watching the gray-haired man in the suede bomber jacket build sand castles with his three-year-old.

The father, exasperated by the crumbling ruins, the sand hovels his son was erecting, offered coaching. Until—unable to *bear* that any kid of his should be developing such substandard real estate—the fifty-year-old launched his hostile takeover bid, snatched the spade and bucket away from the child.

"Here, watch me, Jake, this is how you build a castle . . ."

Too absorbed to notice that his son, dispossessed, now crouched listless, his drool-gaze fastened on some distant object, on a luckier child (the charge of a nanny sitting on a far bench) who was being allowed to play with his own toys.

There was nothing more ridiculous than a middle-aged new father. Unless it was a middle-aged new mother. And this, really, was the problem, thought Gwen: that people were not having babies as they were meant to, when they were twenty and hard and gay and carelessly selfish, but were dawdling until they were forty, and soft and pompous and anxiously selfish.

Here they were, in the almost deserted Diana Ross Playground Friday morning in late November (Betty's morning off). Bella was wearing a rose tweed coat with a rose velvet collar that once belonged to her half-aunt Serena; Gwen was wearing sweatpants that once belonged to her half-husband Gideon Wolkowitz; both women were scowling on the verge of tears.

Gwen was angry because she'd had a telephone interview to do that morning, which Bella had done her best to sabotage, and Bella was angry because Gwen had yelled at her all the way to the park, and they both were exhausted because Gwen had jammed Bella, kicking and screaming, into clothes just to get the two of them out of the house, because if you hung around indoors all morning in your pajamas, you'd surely murder each other.

Gwen was wondering why Gideon was still comatose in bed when she'd told him three times she was supposed to do a BBC radio interview at eight, and why his sleep always took precedence over her work, and why she'd had to handle Bella's screaming tantrum while trying to talk coherently about Russia's health crisis, whereas Gideon's telephone shmoozing with Dan or Dina had to be sacredly guarded from any infantine incursions. Why wouldn't he just admit outright he wanted to destroy her career and make her as idle and wretchedly unemployable as he?

She was wondering why if she wanted to bust out of the house—even under some sanctimonious pretext, such as their having run out of diapers—she was expected to haul the baby too, whereas Gideon, unexplained, unnegotiated, unexcused, was simply out-of-there. And why was he always *there*, hovering, underfoot, needy, just when she'd finally managed to rock Bella to sleep and was desperate to be alone, and why was he always not-there when she needed him to help with Bella?

Often it occurred to Gwen these days how much simpler and more harmonious life would be if she were married to the nanny and not to her husband.

"Forget I'm a man," Gideon had said to her, not long ago. Kindly. In one of their ever-rarer truces. "Forget that I'm a man and you're a woman. No more balls, no more cunt, no more who changes the diapers or takes out the garbage. Let me be a . . . tumbleweed, you be a sewing machine. All right, you want me to be the sewing machine? A poplar tree, a grain of sand, whatever. Or let's both be sand. So long as we love. The rest is bullshit. Idle devilry."

Gwen had laughed, uneasily, and allowed him to kiss her. "But that's not it," she'd then protested, breaking free. "It's . . ." But she couldn't say. Something deeper. Older. Some anger that wasn't at root inspired by him, she occasionally suspected, that was . . . against herself, perhaps? Of whom he was now, poor soul, a hostage satellite. "It's . . ." But she couldn't say. She didn't know. And she did, after all, have so much pretext: he was so childish, so useless.

"Ma-ma!" An imperious crow, Bella indicating the three twigs she'd planted in the sand, and Gwen applauded, admired, wondered, burrowing her face into the child's sugarplum cheeks, covering her dimpled hands with kisses, hugging her tight in guilty penitence for everything she'd been thinking, and everything she had yet to think and everything she had left unthought.

2

SUNDAY AFTERNOON. Pants on Fire is putting on a children's Hanukkah workshop: it's listed in the *New York Press, The Village Voice,* and even *Time Out.* Nineteen children show up (ages 5–10), with their parents: Gideon and Andrea and Dan and Amnon and Dina (accompanied by Avi Weissbrot) sit them down on the floor before boxes of construction paper, elastic, feathers, glitter, childproof staple gun, scissors, glue.

After they make their masks and costumes, they will perform a short play, with the children as the victorious Maccabees, and the Pantaloons as Roman baddies.

Gwen brings Bella. Bella's too young to know what's happening, but she runs in wobbly, ever-tightening circles, cantering like a pony and clicking her tongue, until she falls down, banging her head against a filing cabinet. Emits a philosophical "Ow." Eventually, she gets overexcited and tries to tear apart the older children's paper masks and costumes. Gwen draws her into a corner of the workshop, where Bella, seizing a breast from inside Gwen's sweater, settles down to suckle while still observing the older children, big-eyed.

It's been months since Gwen's seen Gideon at work, and even in these reduced nursery-circumstances, she gets a surge of sad fondness for his old merriment, his patience, his lack of self-consciousness as he capers, in a Roman helmet with a pink feather plume. The avid wolfish gleam of his dog-teeth between dark beard as he looks over his shoulder to grin at Bella.

Why can't he always be like this, she wonders, and not so censorious, so sorry-for-himself? But this is the trap of love-gone-wrong: you withdraw your love, and your lover, feeling unloved, acts only the more unlovable . . .

"Okay, Bear, time to split," says Gwen, rising, the child in her arms, limbs asprawl.

And Gideon, who hasn't looked at his wife all afternoon, now swings around abruptly. "You going home already?"

"I said I'd take her to Sutton Place for an early dinner."

Gideon looks as if he's been slapped.

3

UPTOWN, SERENA, wearing a pink furry miniskirt, with frosted pink lipstick and blue eye shadow, takes Bella by the hand and leads her toward her bedroom, which is plastered in posters of the Spice Girls and Leonardo DiCaprio. Music is blasting.

"Kids only," says Serena, giggling.

Gwen hesitates; Bella's already dropping, she fell asleep for a few minutes in the cab uptown.

"Is Martin home?" she asks. (Gwen never knows what to call their common parent: oddly enough, "your father" is what springs most naturally to her lips.)

"I don't know—I haven't seen him."

"Bella, you want to go with Serena?" Bella is enchanted: music, makeup, a big girl to make much of her. Following Serena into the bedroom, she shouts, "Yee! Yeee! Yeeee!"

Gwen wanders into the kitchen, where she finds her father on the telephone. "Yeah, yeah, Milt already said he'd . . . Melanie, I just . . . Melanie, I just want to . . . No, that's not true . . . No, he said he'd have it delivered to my desk by Friday . . . Melanie, that is just not true. Why are you sticking up for that little cocksucker?" He waves to his daughter that he'll be off the phone soon. "No, Melanie, don't ask him, tell him. That's an order. No, I am not being out of line, I am—fine . . . Melanie, I got Chugga sitting here with me; I do not want to . . ." To Gwen, now, "Melanie says she's going to kill you if you don't deliver her some baby pictures *tomorrow*."

"I did already, Pop: I gave you a batch from Bella's birthday party . . ."

Gwen takes a seat at the counter. Her father is dipping into a container of low-cholesterol, low-fat salmon-flavored tofu spread as he talks. He holds the tofu spread on a bagel chip in one hand and with the other reaches into the overhead cabinet, from which he pulls a jumbo pack of Halloween candy corn. Offers it to his daughter, who shakes her head.

"Jacey, of course, says I'm not allowed to eat candy corn, which is my favorite food in the entire world." (Martin, like his granddaughter, lives in a cozy harem of monitoring females.)

"Mine, too. Only the white tips, though."

"No, Melanie, I am not . . ."

"You keep your secretary working on Sundays?"

Martin frowns at her. "What's Sunday? Is that some holiday I never heard of? Anyway, secretaries are not unionized . . . *yet*. That's why we have Secretary's Day once a year, to fool 'em with flowers. Melanie, are you–? This woman is such a ball-buster . . ."

She wanders upstairs, and this time bumps into Jacey, who has just come out of the bedroom, plucked eyebrows dug deep into a frown. She indicates for Gwen to follow.

Gwen sits on the chaise longue by the picture window, which faces east. Below, the dark glimmering river. The low roar of traffic on the FDR Drive. Across the East River–a canal, not a river–spread the flat-lands of Queens, a landscape lowland Flemish, in which the highest points are church steeples. Outside, the glimmering humming night-city, cars and taxis racing south to Battery Park and north to the Tribor-ough Bridge, and high up here, two women in a rose chintz bedroom. One frowning, biting her nails, the other one thinking, nervous, Should I go check on Bella? What if she wants me, and can't find me?

"It's come back again," says Jacey.

"What? Oh shit. Same place?"

"No, it's it's in the uh the uh the uh they think it may have spread, like, to the abdomen. The doctors at Memorial are recommending chemotherapy, but I want to seriously examine the other options first . . . Martin is . . . Martin won't talk about it. Martin is in, like, total denial. Hodgkin's? We did that. That was *last* year. Sometimes I see the advantage of having a ten-second attention span . . ."

4

THAT NIGHT, after Bella, hysterically overtired, has first screamed and then sung herself to sleep, Gwen, tamed by this lick of mortality's whip, allows her husband to comfort her.

Gideon, who still has green glitter in his eyebrows, strokes her heavy hair out of her eyes, tries to pin it back behind her ears, but it falls forward again. He sighs.

"I'm scared," she says.

"Of course you're scared . . ."

"I'm scared shitless," she repeats. And finally, "I'm scared *shitless* of my father's dying." She looks at him, wondering for a moment whether he thinks if Martin dies, there'll be money for them. Well, there won't.

Gideon takes his wife in his arms. She allows him to hold her, while she draws long shaky breaths. (But somehow his body no longer reassures her: it seems flimsy, a boy's body, unreliable.)

"Breathe, sweetheart. Breathe *into* the place where you feel that fear, where you feel that pain." He holds her what seems like hours, until with a groan, she reaches to turn out the bedroom light.

Gideon lies awake until he hears his wife's breath soften into sleep. Once in the middle of the night, she shouts, "Stop!" But she rolls over again, without waking up. By the next morning, she has already left for work, and Betty and Bella and Mimi are in the kitchen.

Gideon phones Gwen twice during the day, but she is away from her desk, and doesn't return his calls. And when he gets home that evening, she doesn't look up from her reading.

Chapter Seven

THEY ARE SITTING in Katz's Delicatessen. December afternoon, fiveish. Rain smearing the bleary windows. It's always raining on East Houston Street. Gideon, suddenly ravenous, is devouring a pastrami sandwich. He hasn't eaten red meat (well, gray) in years. The others drinking Celray, Dr. Brown's Black Cherry.

"So what's the plan, Stan?" Dina inquires, jocosely.

Gideon, who has just come from meeting Fran Neuhaus, finds the question irritating. "What's the plan? I don't know what you're planning, that's the problem."

"What do you—"

"You guys . . . I don't get it, I don't get what's going on with you, I feel like I'm fighting this battle all alone. I mean, here we are, we have this chance really to make a difference politically, Giuliani's won with a landslide, we are the opposition, somebody's gotta fight this fight to re-claim our city.

"The way I see it, this is our chance: let's face it, we haven't had it so good since Reagan. The face of evil. This is the time to arm, we should be putting on plays *every week,* regular, like a newspaper column, we should be putting on plays about police racism, about the persecution of illegal immigrants, about the criminalization of poverty, the censor-ship of the media by big business. Globalization, genetic engineering, the end of democracy, you name it. I talked to Fran and she said sure, we could use her space. She was really enthusiastic, and . . . this would cost *no* money. I don't understand why you want to hand Giuliani this victory on a silver plate."

A sigh from Andrea. "You know, Gideon, I don't want to sound like a party pooper, but you know, it's not all about Giuliani. Politics is great, but we're also a theater. We got theatrical issues, and also personal issues to . . . It's a—it's a puppet company, remember?"

"Everything's political—remember?" says Gideon, stubbornly.

"Everything's political, so maybe it's time to make a *political* choice to . . . I think—I don't want to speak for anyone else, but I think for some of us, it seems like the timing is—we have each separately reached this point where . . ."

"Well, it's been what, like, nine years?" Dan offers.

"Ten in March," says Dina.

"We need to maybe renew ourselves, explore other possibilities."

"You want to surrender that easy, the first moment that—"

"This isn't surrender, this is growth," says Andrea. "I feel kinda stale, like we've been rehashing the same old shit for too long."

"I don't feel that," says Gideon. "There was nothing stale about the Abner Louima play, I was just showing Fran the video: it's hair-raising; I think it's one of the greatest things we've ever done. So does Jerome. He wants us to teach it to them. Do you feel we're stale, Dan?"

Dan finds this conversation very difficult. His cheeks have gone bright red from the eczema. "Truthfully? I've been thinking I'd like to be spending more time on my music."

"What does that mean?"

"I've been talking to Elliott about taking the Klezmofunks somewhere new, maybe joining them full-time. They just lost their other fiddler—"

"You mean move up to *Vermont*?"

"Whatever. I mean, we'd definitely need some way of sustaining ourselves financially, but—"

"You really want to leave New York?"

"Well, every time Dan and I talk about having a kid, we come up against the fucking *finances* of it," Andrea intercedes.

"And I'm not sure it's the only place there's interesting music happening. *Or* theater. Anyways, when Elliott asked me, I told him I couldn't tell him anything until *we* got our future settled."

"I mean, no way we're gonna break up Pants on Fire unless we're all agreed it's a good time to take a breather," Andrea adds.

"And what're you gonna do, Andy, you're going to be the farm wife, cooking for the boys? How do *you* fit into this? I thought you wanted to go back to school."

Andrea just laughs. "It's . . . it's, you know, it's Dan's call. I mean, I was the one who dragged him away from Boston, this time it's his call. I'd be pretty happy to quit Legal Aid, I've always liked living in the country." She mimics milking a cow, including the piss of squirting milk.

They all laugh, except for Gideon.

"Dina?"

Dina won't look at him.

"Dina's got something she needs to talk to us about," Andrea says.

"Dina? Dina is not a woman I generally think of as tongue-tied . . ."

Dina still won't look up. Gideon takes her by the chin. Her dark eyes are filled with tears.

"My God, Deen, what is it?"

But then she starts smiling.

"What?" he demands. "What? What does everybody know that I don't know? What is this, a conspiracy, a palace coup?"

Dina, smiling, looks around the dingy cafeteria, with its greasy hot plates. "This by you is a palace? I'd hate to see your idea of a hovel."

"What is it, Dina?" he repeats, drumming his fingers now. Chewing on his beard. "I am not going to play guessing games. What have you been keeping from me?"

"I'm in the dark too," says Dan.

"Women, will you please enlighten us dumb beasts?"

"Well, thanks a lot, Andrea, this is not really how I meant to introduce this subject, but—"

"What?!"

"It looks like Avi and I are going to get married."

Stunned silence.

Then, "Dina, I had no idea you—"

"Yeah, we've been . . . we've been going out—I don't know, no time at all. Eight months? But it feels *right*."

"You look really happy," smiles Andrea.

"Yeah. It's been amazing, the most amazing meeting of minds that has just been, like, completely"—Dina raises hooked fingers—"karmic."

"So you guys get along?" Gideon asks, trying not to let his voice sound resentful, judging.

"It's . . . it's . . . I'm, like, speechless. So you know how serious that is. Our first date? We went to hear *The Magic Flute* at Lincoln Center? Afterwards, we end up sitting by the fountain all night, talking, and when the sun comes up, we jump into the fountain. I felt like Anita Ekberg in *La Dolce Vita*. He is this really intense, really idealistic person. You know, he left JTS because he thought the rabbinical leadership of the Conservative movement was totally bankrupt, morally, but he couldn't face going Orthodox because of their position on women. At first, I thought he was too naive, but now I see he's got this amazing determination, too. I hadn't realized how cynical I'd become, how *tired:* he makes me look *forward* to things. Anyways, I don't know how long we would have gone on like this, but suddenly his brother-in-law calls up and is, like, Look, I'm starting up my own software company, we got a backer, you want to join me?"

"So?"

"Well, his sister and brother-in-law live in San Francisco, and he left San Francisco because he comes from this totally overpowering family, and he felt if he was ever going to make something of himself independently, he'd have to do it elsewhere, but . . . this offer is just too good to be true, I mean, he'd just left Dell to go to rabbinical school because he found the corporate hierarchy was, like, too stifling, and here comes this chance to—"

"Sounds like a pretty naively idealistic line of work, Dina."

"Well, he's got me saying, Go for it, Avi. And he's, like, What about the minyan? What about us? And I'm trying to be supportive, I'm, like, Well, Josh 'n' I'll manage without you, and we'll e-mail, and we'll still . . . and suddenly he's, like, I'm not going back unless you come with me, and I'm, like, Me on the West Coast? And he's, like, *Us.*"

The others are smiling, nodding, Andrea's got her hand on Dina's knee. Dan, red-cheeked, gets up, leans over the table, and gives Dina a long hug. When they finally part, both have tears in their eyes.

"You deserve it, darlin' . . ."

Gideon can no longer contain himself. "I can't believe this," he bursts out. "What about Ethan? Have you given a moment's thought to your son? I mean, he's had all these disastrous upheavals in his life, including me moving out, he's just started a new school which is intensely competitive and where he's *flourishing,* and you're–"

"Gideon," says Andrea, "what–what is wrong with you? Why are you guilt-tripping Dina about this? Ethan's–I mean, when has Dina ever thought about anything *but* Ethan?"

"Ethan's really into the idea. I mean, he loves Avi, he loves software, he's already asking if they can give him a summer job–for Ethan, it's, like, pig heaven."

"You are going to transplant this kid who's at this really crucial crossroads in his life to this city you know nothing about, where you've spent what, like, three nights in your life, where you don't have a friend of your own, to be at the mercy of this guy you barely know, and who apparently has very good reason to have left the city, too . . ."

"So we'll hate it together. If it doesn't work out, we'll come back. I mean, no way I'm giving up the lease on Rivington Street . . ."

"Gideon, relax. What is your problem, what–"

"I can't believe you are even considering doing this to your son."

"Look, Gideon. I . . . It's true Ethan's at a very important point in his life–intellectually, socially. Sexually, God help him. And I am really proud of how well prepared he is for all these big changes."

"Prepared? That is just male swagger. He is terrified . . . Nobody can be prepared."

"Ethan is making his own life. He's got a lot of friends; he's getting–"

"Who you're planning to rip him away from . . ."

"He's getting interested in girls," Dina continues. "Girls are getting interested in him. He's kinda geeky, our E-man, but he's a boy girls like. The ones who call up, they sound *our* age. There's this number from Stuy called Shana who's got this voice like Mae West. What really worries me is . . . I was so young when I had him. What really worries me is his maybe feeling he has to stay at home to look after me–that he is somehow not free to develop, to go out in the world because *I'm* lonely and unhappy.

"Like, why do you think I finally quit my job? So I got this windfall from Allstate, but, let's face it . . . Because I suddenly thought, a teenage son, college tuition coming up, this is a really good time to throw away my only source of income? I just was sick of contaminating him with my own misery. I thought it was more important for him to see me happy, free, finding something to do I believe in. Even if we were broke. And that applies to my personal life, too."

"Listen, I don't think you understand diddly-squat about adolescent male psychology. I think you're ascribing a kind of altruism that's just about a million miles from . . . I can tell you, I've been there, the last thing an adolescent male is interested in—can handle—wants—is his single mother's *sexual satisfaction*."

"Gideon, you are reducing this to the crudest possible—" Andrea protests.

"That's okay." Dina raises her hands, palms toward Gideon. "Devil's advocate? There is nothing you're telling me that I haven't accused myself of."

"Yeah, but you're still veiling this in some self-sacrificial I'm-doing-this-for-my-son."

"Bullshit!" explodes Andrea.

"Not really. I'm doing it for me."

"And Ethan?"

"They have schools in San Francisco, too. Supposedly. They have girls. Supposedly. They have Jews. Supposedly."

He looks at her suspiciously. "You're not thinking of having more children?"

"Gideon, you sound like, is she thinking of um joining Hitler Youth."

"A year ago? The idea of having another child would have been about that appealing. I mean, I was, like, Take me to the glue factory . . . But you know? Quitting Kings County has been so energizing, I had no idea how much of my energy was being sapped by those horrible bureaucratic-administrative wars, all that hatred and opposition and intrigue."

"Aren't you on the old side?"

"I'm thirty-six. Avi's thirty-three. *Baruch Ha Shem,* we'll manage."

"And what about your minyan? What does Josh think about all this?"

"Gideon, like I say, I've been living in New York thirteen years. Of course I have a *life* here, of course there's things I've *made* that I'm gonna be uprooting. It'd be pretty pathetic if there *weren't* anything I'd miss—or that might miss me—after all these years . . ."

Gideon sighs. He shoves back his chair, lays his head in his hands. Everybody is against him. Andrea is glaring at him, Dan won't look his way, and Dina's good humor makes him feel even more in the wrong. He sighs, raises his head. Looks out the window. Blackness. Blackness, and rain. His sneakers are soaking wet, his socks are wet. He feels as if he's coming down with a cold.

"When are you thinking of moving?"

"Avi's going out there for some meetings, but, like, this is starting up your own business, maybe it will all fall through . . . If this backer's for real, Avi's brother-in-law wants to start right away. I definitely wouldn't move till the summer—we'd take Ethan for a week or so to check out schools, meet Avi's folks, but we wouldn't *move* till the summer . . ."

Gideon broods. "And us?" he murmurs, consciously echoing Avi's usage.

"You know, Gideon"—she's got tears in her eyes again—"I love you like my own soul, you dumb shmuck. We're family. Nothing can ever change that. But I can't help feeling—and I'm just speaking for myself here, I'd like to know what the rest of you guys think—that you are pulling the company in a different direction. Like, we started out, we were doing the Mystical Circus, we were thinking of reviving some Yiddish classics, *Breindele Cossack* and what have you, we weren't aiming to blow up City Hall. I feel, aside from our geographical-economic issues of rent and space and budget, that you are trying to take us somewhere the rest of us don't necessarily belong. Sancho is, like . . . fine. He's a revolting misogynist, but he's fine. I'm grateful, La Merced was a godsend, but I don't especially trust him. The man is a zealot and that was great as long as our interests happened to overlap, but I don't necessarily see that Hispanic separatism is Pants on Fire's central crusade. I think it's a good time to stop and reevaluate honestly where we all want to go. Individually and/or collectively."

"Hhmmmm," Gideon replies. His tone is thoughtful, now. "Hhhmmmmm. So that's how it is. Huh. So we're closing down."

He glances at his comrades, whose faces are suddenly anxious with concern for him. Dan, embarrassed, shifts.

Letting out a heavy sigh, Gideon shoves away his plate. "What are we going to do with all our stuff? We got costumes, puppets, material, tools? The computer . . ."

"You should keep 'em," says Andrea.

"I should keep 'em? What is this, a consolation prize? No, they're worth money, we should sell 'em. We should sell 'em and divide the money."

"No, no, you should keep 'em. Somebody needs to hang on to them."

"What for?"

"This has happened before; this is not the final goodbye."

"And you're going to keep performing, right?"

"You mean, solo?"

"No, there's still Sally and Hector and Amnon and . . . all our friends in the community–Fran, Annie. Jamie. So Dan and Dina and I go off and do our own thing for a couple of years. It's happened before. But you know how it goes, in a year or so, Dina'll call up and say, We hate San Francisco, there's no theater scene, we're moving back east and Avi wants to become a puppeteer too, because it pays better than software. Pants on Fire–it's like the Burning Bush: 'And the pants were not consumed.' We'll get back together again, one form or another, when the time's right . . ."

Gideon's chewing on his beard, wanting to be consoled, wanting to be inconsolable. He hefts another sigh. Andrea puts an arm around him, and to his embarrassment, his eyes fill with tears and his throat chokes up.

BOOK EIGHT

Chapter One

I

APRIL 1998.

"My God, Gwendolen Lewis, you look like a . . . like a school-teacher. I feel as if it's Mademoiselle Hérault come to give me a home tutorial." Christopher's gaze sweeps down to the magenta stilettos. "Hmmmm . . . maybe a governess dressed by Karl Lagerfeld."

Gwen has just been shown by Marie-Claude into the library of the house on Seminary Row—a small room painted malachite-green, walled in leather-bound volumes which Chris inherited from his French grandparents.

A crackly fire—it's *cold*, for April. An alabaster fireplace topped in a bronze Empire clock, invitations—to gallery openings, to dinners—ranged on the mantelpiece; irises in vases around the room.

And Christopher, convalescing from monster bronchitis, looking indeed like a French schoolboy, in dark blue pleated corduroys, is curled on the sofa by the fire, a book in his hand.

Clatter-clatter-clatter of leather soles on the staircase: in rushes Yilmaz, rosy, smiling, smelling of Christopher's aftershave.

"Why are you running?" Christopher sounds cross.

"I am . . ."—Yilmaz checks his watch—"fourteen minutes behind schedule. I am very lazy, I am someone who *hates* to be in a hurry," he explains, kissing Gwen. Yilmaz now does public relations for a young Anglo-Iranian designer who is opening a New York boutique. "So, the solution is always to be early."

"He makes *me* look lackadaisical," Chris confirms. "You forget, Turks ruled an empire. This boy has generations of civil servants in the blood . . ."

"That's not true, I'm a peasant. I have goatherds in the blood." Yilmaz stands back, hands on hips, regarding Christopher with a mock frown. "The color's better today. For a month, Gwen, he was yellow."

"That's just because of all the disgusting homeopathic brews you were trying to poison me with," grumbles Christopher. "Are you going to be home for dinner?"

Yilmaz bends to give Christopher a warm kiss full on the lips. "Yes, but don't we have the—"

"Oh God, that's right. The horrific Mrs. Shelton's supposed to come over." A client from Los Angeles. "But that's just for a drink . . ."

Yilmaz is out the door, with a muffled slam. Just as Marie-Claude, in black dress and white apron, announces lunch.

Christopher leads Gwen into the dining room, where two places are laid, and an open bottle of Burgundy awaits. "What's Gideon up to?"

Gwen, not wanting to say that Gideon is up to nothing, instead finds herself fabricating Gideon's doings into a "story": her unemployed husband, under the spell of Sancho, this Dostoevskian agent provocateur, is conspiring to overthrow the mayor, organizing marches on City Hall, raising barricades on Stanton Street.

Christopher shakes his head. "I don't know," he says, "I find your husband rather unsettling. He's got this sweetness that I feel is very genuine, combined with a bitter streak that seems way disproportionate to—"

"I know," she says. "It can get a little outta control."

"In any case, his politics are beyond me. The American left is so *whiny*. It seems to me fairly elemental that this city cannot survive without a tax base. If you drive business, the middle classes, out of New York by keeping it a roach-infested slum—which is what his friend Sancho is doing—who, exactly, is supposed to be funding the performing arts? Farmers from upstate?"

"Exactly."

"Last time I talked to Gideon, he was very high on the French—you know that old line, Why can't our government support the arts the way Europeans do. I told him, If that's your model, you'd better start kissing Giuliani's ass, because that's how France works: good old patronage. Anyway, *you* look all right. A little less wan."

"I'm better. Motherhood's getting manageable."

"Ha, just you wait. How's the girl?"

"Glorious. Wicked. She's a terrible tease. She won't talk. I'm longing for her to talk . . ."

"How old is she?"

"A year and a half."

"Isn't that young?"

"Oh no, everybody else's children—especially the girls—are composing sonnets by this age. She knows I want her to, so she won't. Sometimes I hear her practicing in her crib, trying out words, but as soon as she hears me coming, she clams up."

Gwen doesn't divulge her secret theory—that the reason Bella won't speak is that all she hears from her parents are words of hatred, accusation. That for her, silence is nonviolence.

Marie-Claude reappears carrying a cheese soufflé. Gwen, pausing to admire, plunges the serving fork and spoon into the golden dome of its high toasty crust. Inside, molten goo. "And how have you been, Christopher, aside from sick? I've missed you. It's the worst thing about being a mother; I never see my friends. I didn't know I had any friends till I had a baby, and lost them."

"Oh, I'm limping along. I've been much less grumpy since I gave in and started reading Proust all over again. You know, I'd finished *Le Temps Retrouvé* last summer in Assos, and I'd thought, Don't be so pathetic, you've got to find something new . . ."

He helps himself to cheese soufflé. An enormous helping. Christopher's greed being one of his enduring strengths: a large appetite for food, money, *things*.

"Where're you at?"

"Oh, right at the beginning."

"Have you gotten to Aunt Léonie yet?"

"Oh sure . . ."

"Where she keeps reminding herself"—they both are laughing now—" 'Remember to tell them that I didn't sleep a wink all night, not a wink . . .' "

"Sure. You know, it was the one great thing my father gave me, who was otherwise a fairly perfunctory presence in my life . . ."

"What?"

"French," says Chris, chasing the remaining soufflé-melt with a crust of bread.

In fact, it seems to Gwen, it's Chris's American mother who is due the praise, having kept him on at the lycée even after Hubert decamped. Every time Gwen sees those crocodiles of French girls and boys marching to Central Park in navy blue duffel coats and balaclavas, she thinks of Christopher, and wonders if their paths ever crossed, aged eight, nine . . .

Green salad.

"God, I would love to be spending my mornings by the fire, reading Proust."

"You should make the effort to read him in French. I would never have the nerve, for instance, to try to talk to you about *The Possessed*—I know, by your lights, I haven't read it."

"No, you haven't."

"His language is not that difficult."

"At the moment? I'd rather learn Persian than try to read Proust in French."

"Oh come *on*. Don't be ridiculous," Christopher snaps. "I feel as if we have been having the same conversation—as if I've been trying to teach you the same thing—since we were sixteen. If Yilmaz wants to learn Persian, fine, it's part of his Ottoman inheritance. But you . . . you've got this rather indiscriminating hankering after the exotic, the merely other—and *that's* what I find lazy. I mean, why eat Burmese take-out when you can eat like this"—to illustrate, he forks another mouthful, straight from the dish, of the now-solidified soufflé—"cheese, milk, eggs, butter, flour. A green salad. It's so simple. Why buy some CD of saz players sitting in a yurt when there are probably seven Beethoven quartets you've never heard in your life? Am I being pretentious? Of course I am. I'm pretentious in my sleep. But I feel as if you're toying with things that you get tired of before you begin to understand them . . . from some kind of tourism that just isn't good enough. Even Russia, which you've really set your mind to, well, so what? Russia is this karaoke culture, this tenth-rate veneer of civilization overlying a vast barbarism, a country that's just lost its fifteen minutes of geostrategic significance. If you come to understand Russia, you have learned *nothing* of *any* significance."

Gwen grimaces, indicating disagreement. Wonders if Christopher, ominously, is including her husband among her exotic hankerings. Is Passaic exotic?

"That's simply not true; can you imagine nineteenth-century literature, or twentieth-century music, without—"

"Oh, get real—the only Russian *culture* is concentration camps and secret police."

Gwen gives up. It's like arguing with an octogenarian: you could *never* get Chris to change his mind or even listen. "Let me get this straight, Monsieur d'Aurilhac. I am being lectured against exoticism—"

"No, you're—"

"—by someone who lives with . . . a Turk?"

"Sweetheart, I really had exhausted the fifty states, not to mention the European Union, by the time—"

"Anyway," she says, inconsequently, "if I were to stick to my own culture, I'd be eating corn pone. And my father's family did come from Russia . . ."

"Yes, I imagine they were made to feel *very* much at home there, too."

"It *is* my—"

"Oh, that's just ethnic reductivism. A sentimental perversion you and I can live without . . . You know as well as I do that *our* Culture, *our* Inheritance, is Anglo-Continental. Nineteenth-century Englishmen lived on a nasty dank foggy little island, but they didn't sit around saying, Basically, we're Pictish savages who painted themselves blue, they said, We are the inheritors of Homer and Virgil: classical Mediterranean civilization is ours . . ."

"Well, so their reaching to the Mediterranean isn't any more of a stretch than my going for the Caspian."

"Yes, you donkey, it's a stretch *upwards*. What I'm sick of is your cultural slumming. Why don't you pick on a civilization your own size?"

There's something about Christopher's harangue that she finds so comforting that instead of arguing, she leans back, smiling. "Maybe I need you to show me Europe again."

"Really? Most memories I have are of us not talking because you've behaved so abominably." Christopher, still too revved up to stop flailing.

"Are you thinking of Amsterdam?"

"I'm thinking of Amsterdam"—where they'd spent a bleak wintry week in a pension—"*and* Venice. *And* that summer in Brittany you were so rude to my cousins . . ."

"Maybe I've grown up."

"Maybe I'm an elephant."

"You are. Do you think we'll be able to go to Europe together again someday?"

"Of course we will. Why not?" says Christopher, stoutly. Understanding, she believes in retrospect, that what her coded question signifies is, If I extricate myself from my marriage, will you be there to pick up the pieces?

When she tells her husband that night—in a now-rare burst of confidence—what a wonderful day she's spent with Christopher, Gideon presses his lips tight and drums his fingers. What exactly was so great about this lunch, he presses. I don't know, she trails off, it was so nice to talk about Proust again . . .

Gideon rolls his eyes—at the preciousness, she imagines, of these two trust-fund dilettantes sitting around smugly vaunting what big books they've read. And Gwen, shamed silent, hates him. Wonders why she yoked herself to a semiliterate with no culture deeper than bluegrass, whose prejudices are so banally copied, so *rote*.

2

THIS WAS THE TRUTH. She had made a mistake, born of an unadmitted terror at being left on the shelf. Gideon had been a fuck, not a life's-choice.

If only she'd met him a few years earlier, they could have spent a week in bed and parted affably. She could imagine how such restraint might have played itself out: the sly fond tweak of semirecidivism provoked by periodic flyers from Pants on Fire, to be put aside—along with solicitations from anti-land-mine campaigners and newsletters from her senator—and then junked.

If she'd married, someone to tease her *real* husband about—a merry old fling. Gideon the impoverished carnyman. Her Siberian sweetmeat, he of the lightning tongue, the deliciously insinuating cock. If only she'd had more self-respect, she'd have let him go, thought, So what if I never marry? Maybe I'll meet someone when I'm sixty, maybe I won't; I have enough *inside* to keep me resolute, useful, serene . . .

Instead of which she'd taken Gary-Gideon Wolkowitz-Brager farther than he was ever meant to go and had discovered that underneath the sweet talk was someone brittle, hysterical, dishonest.

She thought, with a grip of dread, Even if we make it through the ordeal of child-rearing, even if we survive Bella's babyhood, this is not a man who's going to wear well, whom I will feel pleased to have ended up with, long winter nights by the fire . . .

3

WE LIVE IN THIS SEXUALLY LIBERATED AGE in which the truth is supposed to make us free. But how many people tell the truth about their *real* sexual lives? Writers write about sex under the pretense that since it happens, we should write about it, just as Jonathan Swift wrote about shitting and farting, but what they write is a lie. What you read about in books is rhapsodies of orgasmic fulfillment. What you see on the screen is flawless young bodies mingling in the cool delirium of a first encounter.

What you don't read about is most people's experience, Gideon reflects, which is not getting any, or getting turned down, or its being made tragicomically clear to you that although you've bullied your wife into sex, she'd rather be watching the news.

What they don't tell you about is sexual frustration (how you never want to do it at the same time, or if you do, that's when your kid needs a drink of water); sexual humiliation (you make a move, she turns you down, or complies insincerely or indifferently, so you feel like you're begging for a favor); sexual boredom (when you're frantically trying to visualize the last person who excited you and you suddenly wonder whom she's thinking of, obviously not quite hard enough, and you imagine a whole city of wedded beds, each with two ghosts floating above it); or outright sexual failure (you can't make her come, or by the time you get there, your cock has shrivelled into a dead mouse). Or all of the above.

Why can't someone have the honesty to express one man's desperation because his wife still drives him wild, but she has frozen him out, for reasons he is way too fucked up and demoralized to fathom, so that when she finally finally invites him to have a look in, he's in such pain he can't even kiss her on the mouth . . .

4

NOW IT'S GWEN'S TURN to be working like a dog, unbotherably, irreproachably busy, and he's expected to not ask any questions, not make any sexual-emotional demands. He complies. Every night he cooks the dinner he's bought, because of course he has nothing else to do all day.

He had figured the one great thing about being out of work was he'd get to spend time with Bella, who is now old enough to be taken places and taught things. He had foreseen expeditions, treats—the city was a fortune hunt of hidden secrets: they would ride on ferries, have picnics in the Botanical Garden, go to Carnival in Flushing Meadow.

But it turned out nannies didn't appreciate parents' kidnapping their charges: since Betty was *there*, meter ticking away ten dollars an hour, ten hours a day, Gideon was not encouraged to disrupt their busy schedule. It was more important for Bella's developmental socialization that she interact with her peer group—i.e., that the nannies congregate in Dick Snyder's penthouse duplex and yak all day—than that father and daughter be together.

So Gideon, sad because Bella, whom he'd wanted to take to Annie Dolores's for tea, is instead borne off to meet Mallory and Hunter and their nannies for Story Hour at Barnes & Noble, is left to grumble about why every thing Queen Betty plans has some corporate tie-in, enlarges some multinational shark's share of the market. Whatever happened to playing in the park?

5

NOTHING ENDURED in this city. That's why they called it "New" York. Because nothing got a chance to be old. Everything here was born a week ago and gone in a month.

It wasn't as if you were a citizen of Athens or Jerusalem or Cairo, or even "Old" York, which was already a mature enough civilization seven hundred years ago to be murdering its Jews (that's what civilization meant in Gwen's beloved Europe: being advanced enough to have adopted the pogrom): New York, by contrast, was a tent city of arrivals and departures, of spectacular bust-ups, fire-sale clearances. You prospered, you moved somewhere with a yard and good schools. You foundered, it was potter's field.

People blew across its harsh pocked surface like dust bunnies, vacated its tight-packed spaces QT. You went to the Little Bombay movie theater: boarded up. You went to Lupe's East L.A. Kitchen where you used to be able to stuff yourself for ten dollars; the space it last month occupied was now a day spa. Your address book shifted like the announcement board in Penn Station: an automated shuttle of moves and foreclosures, of buyouts leveraged and unleveraged. The scorched-earth

decimation of an elaborate civilization that a thousand years ago required Hunnish invasions was now done decorously by the Gap.

Why should Pants on Fire be any different?

So too someone Gideon hadn't talked to in a year would call up to
see what they were performing this spring and find not only that the
company had folded, its members relocated to Vermont, California,
and hell, but that even the building was dust—where last year there were
artist's spaces, a dance studio, a puppet company, a theater, a film lab
was the substandard-cement-and-wonky-steel undergarment of an ugly-
as-a-monkey's-ass high-rise beckoning a new Noah's arkload of trans-
planted midwesterners.

What once had been a family was now a job lot of orphaned wards:
a single mother, an abandoned child, a divorced father. An ache of am-
putated limbs, of court orders, custody battles. People sleeping on other
people's sofas, and then moving on.

Was there a law that said things should stay the same?

6

ALL WEEK Betty's been in a tizzy about a birthday party Bella's been invited to. The birthday girl is Zoe, whose nanny is the alpha nanny of
Betty's and hence Bella's set. Zoe lives on Central Park West. Her parents are both in television. They are older people, Betty confides: he has
grown children from an earlier marriage.

"Here," says Gwen, searching through her wallet and producing two
twenties, a ten. "Is that enough? I'm sorry I don't have time right now to
get Zoe a present myself. Could you get a birthday card, too, Betty?"

Gideon ironically chants the names of the unknown children in
Bella's set—Courtney, Brittany, Mallory, Kylie, Hunter, Zoe, Jack, Jake,
ZEKE. A mantra of infantine upward mobility.

"Don't you find it a little disquieting we don't know a single one of
these kids *or* their parents?" he inquires.

Gwen pretends she doesn't. She is on the point of suggesting that if
he finds it disquieting, he should go along to one of their play groups,
but, realizing Betty would flip, thinks better of it. "I think I'd find it
more disquieting *knowing* the parents."

"How much did you give her for that kid's birthday present?"
Gideon demands, after Bella and Betty are gone.

"I . . ." Gwen stalls. She is already embarrassed about how much she gave Betty. Was it a kind of indirect showing-off, a trying to impress, that she's willing to spend on a child she'll never meet an amount it takes Betty five hours to earn? Or was it revenge against Gideon, a reminder that this is the scale of lavishness she's grown up on? Meaningless, in any event.

"Look," she says, propitiatory. "Sasha and Irina asked us over for lunch on Sunday. I'd thought I'd say no, I'm so tired out by the weekends, but maybe we should go . . ."

Sasha and Irina are about her only friends (except for Constance, whose wiggly bottom he unabashedly has the hots for) whom Gideon deems to have acceptable values. Of course, if you are a family of three, surviving in New York on a music teacher's salary of eighteen grand a year, it's hard to have *bad* values, according to Gideon's lights . . .

Chapter Two

I

SPRING 1998.

Manhattan's knife-edged light and shadow. In the shade, it's cave-cold; in the sunlight, you're aflame. The light glitters, flickers, trembles, cascades. Moves on, fickle, fast. The blue so clean it burns.

In the changeable spring sunlight, the mirrored towers' silvery-green bellies glint, undulate in diaphanous speckles like fish scales, like chain mail. The city is a sea of leaping dolphins. Fish-tailed mermaids. Barnacled shipwrecks, coruscating.

Midtown Manhattan in the spring sunlight: the seedy reaches of Fifth Avenue in the Forties, electronics stores, tobacconists, souvenir shops. Hustle, bargain, haggle, scam. A three-card-monte player on the corner of Forty-third attracting a small crowd of curious onlookers, and up past Forty-fifth, Forty-sixth, Forty-seventh, where Hasidic men—as short and stout, as short and spindly, as short and red-cheeked, as short and pale as people from the seventeenth century—pour forth from enclosed arcades.

Gideon is out walking with Bella. They've come from the public library, where the child's checked out three books on her first library card and barked "Woo-woo!" at the stone lions.

Now as they reach Fifty-seventh Street, Bella riding on her father's shoulders, they cross east to Madison. The new clean safe city, all-American, a mall of multimedia chain stores selling brand-name trinkets for middle-class tourists.

Gideon is chattering to his daughter about how heavy she's become, almost too heavy to lug around town on his shoulders, and maybe it's time to put a child seat on his bike for her, and would she like that and did she think Mommy would let him. "Ma-ma!" says Bella enthusiastically, drumming her feet.

Walking up Madison Avenue, the girl on his shoulders, her ankles in his fists, her hands stroking his skull—"You know, Bella-boop, can you believe Daddy used to have *hair* on his head, curly hair just like you? I know that's like telling you the Sahara used to be ocean, but it's God's truth . . ." Madison and Fifty-eighth, Madison and Fifty-ninth, Sixtieth.

Once more they have entered a different city, as distinct as if there'd been border guards checking identity papers. Now the stores are smaller, more burnished, exquisite, they are colonial outposts of empires based in Milan, London, Brussels, Geneva.

In the windows are aggressively whimsical glad rags: a pair of hot-pink platform jellies, a pair of silver-and-lavender jogging pants of a fabric that looks like nylon but costs a billion yen.

Here the streets are patrolled by privately paid security guards—a militia for the rich, uniformed in this obscenely preppy gear of khaki pants and blazers, as if they're Princeton boys on vacation, and not a Latin American–style death squad. Do they carry guns? Would he care to find out? This private militia reveals the ruthlessness of New York entrepreneurs in smashing any potential threat to a happy business climate, to the rule of lifestyle, fitness, feeling good. Easy Money, Mad Money, for everyone but him, whom it makes . . . Mad.

Gideon wonders how best to convey to Bella, whose grandfather is cramming her—sedating her!—with the poisoned candies of corporate America (the commodification of childhood is another subject altogether, Big Business's inspired realization that Kids "R" Money), his own violent disagreement with the mores of their time.

I hate your new moons and your feasts; I am wearied by the smell of your burnt offerings. Let judgment run down as waters, and righteousness as a mighty stream.

How to make his child ethically whole, how to make her respect honest work—the work of her own hands and others'?

How do you live in permanent opposition without becoming a sour wacko, a blowhard?

They pass the new Calvin Klein building, the new Armani building—they pass other spanking-new temples of commerce, each of them clean as capped teeth, luminous white, polished white! How is the faithful city become a harlot! Suddenly Madison Avenue—which when Gideon first came to New York was still a crumbling strip of sooty pigeon-haunted brownstones housing stationery stores and hamburger joints—resembles some Italian Renaissance fresco of the Ideal City, except that in place of Virtuous Government is the Nasdaq index . . .

There is nothing supporting the neoclassical pillars and porticoes of this fantastical edifice but a bull market, no traditional skills, no real value, nothing but marketing, promotion. So Madison Avenue in one century has come full circle—from the brain-house of advertising to the living fulfillment of the ad . . .

As he's walking, unfolding his beliefs to Bella, who companionably retorts "Da" or "Ba" or "Yeeeee!" or sings a little droning saga (he keeps meaning to tape one of her wordless chanties) or tries to hurl herself off his shoulders in her pursuit of the praline seller's cart, a woman stops him. "Gideon . . . ?"

She is strikingly beautiful. You had high school fantasies that such women would stop you on the street, "Gideon . . . ?" Women you'd never seen before. Then by the time it happens, you have a kid in bulging diapers on your shoulders.

"I was just meaning to call you up. This is so weird—I swear, I was going to call you *this week.*"

Gideon gives the damsel his absentminded-professor flourish, culminating in a droopy-kneed camel's bow that plops his daughter down onto the sidewalk. Howls of protest. "Ta-yee!" shrieks Bella, raising her arms to him tragically. "Ta-yee!"

Now the baby sags her legs, feigning someone who is too fatigued-beyond-endurance to stand up. "Ta-yee!"

"Carry yourself, sweetheart. Better yet, why don't you carry me?"

He still doesn't have a clue who this young woman is.

She's smiling, a dimple in each cheek. She has straight black hair in a Cleopatra bob, and green eyes, and a mouth that's machine-made perfect, the upper lip as full as the bottom, and yet eminently kissable.

"Do you remember, I came to interview you a couple of times. I'm Emma Rogan. I'm doing this dissertation—"

"Oh yeah, on Jerome," he says. Bella's distracting him again, lifting her arms, pulling at his legs, demanding "Ta-yee, ta-yee." Finally flinging herself flat on the sidewalk in her extravagant grief.

"What an adorable girl," says Emma, bending down to examine Bella.

"Look who's talking."

She blushes, which he appreciates.

"What are you doing in this neighborhood?" Hiking Bella up into his arms, just to keep the kid quiet.

"I was visiting my dad."

"Jeez, I didn't know that anybody but Egyptian mummies lived on the Upper East Side."

"Actually, he's a doctor—it's his office . . ."

"Which way you going? I'll walk you a few blocks."

They start walking, south now, Bella cradled in her father's arms.

"I haven't been to this neighborhood for years," says Gideon. "Madison Avenue kinda spooks me—all these boutiques, it's European-style materialism, you know what I mean, it's somehow colder than American greed . . ."

She smiles politely, obviously puzzled. Which only makes him want to gabble faster.

"I feel like it isn't even New York anymore. Half of it's Middle America, look at that Eddie Bauer store—I mean, what is a mail-order store doing on Madison Avenue?—and the rest is this European invasion. I mean, fifty years ago, it was Jewish philosophers and scientists, it was Einstein and Hannah Arendt who were coming here from Europe, now it's Giorgio Armani boutiques, and what does that say about us?"

She squinches up her eyes. "I never heard anybody romanticizing the Holocaust before. Isn't it better Europeans are coming here, because everybody loves their clothes, than they're coming here to flee Hitler?"

"Ha-ha-ha. What you don't realize, Miss Rogan, is that our worship of image makes another Holocaust *that* much more likely . . ."

She makes a face that says, Bullshit.

Why's he burdening this beautiful girl with his own darkness?

"Where do you live, Miss Rogan? Or—may I presume to call you . . . Emma? Are you on your way somewhere?"

"Actually," she says, "I was just heading over to Lex to catch the subway . . ."

They stop, Gideon fiddling with Bella's curls. "So you were going to call me, huh?"

"Yeah, I was looking over my notes, and there were still a few things I wanted to follow up on, before I go back to Lubeck. What's your schedule like, the next couple of weeks? Could we meet sometime and talk?"

"Sure, I'm all tongue. Why don't you—why don't you give me your number?"

She hunts in vain for something to write with.

"Look in my pocket, I got a pen . . ." Gideon's hands are full of Bella. She gingerly withdraws the pen from his trousers pocket, scribbles her number.

"Da!" shouts Bella, imperious. Wriggling out of his arms, having spotted an ice cream cart. "Da!"

"Da?" repeats Emma.

"Her mom's a Slavicist."

2

GWEN IS INDEED A SLAVICIST. That evening, after dinner, Gideon's lying on the sofa listening to his wife talking on the phone, he's not quite sure who to, probably Irina. He's stretched out, half asleep, listening to the darts and flurries of Gwen's Russian.

And it's funny, she's a different person in Russian. She talks in this deep guttural tumble, then suddenly her voice will hike up high-high. She's laughing a growly laugh as she speaks, and it's obvious to Gideon that she's *funnier* in Russian. A different person: rougher, less guarded, more sincere, there's a burry warmth in her voice.

No wonder she loves Russia: it's her Russian *self* she prefers. He has this sudden revelation that he might like her better in Russian and she might like him better, too. It was no coincidence that they fell in love in Novosibirsk—if he could only find and cleave to Gwen's Russian double, as opposed to her New York persona, uptight, superficial, obsessed by success and status, they might be able to save themselves.

When she hangs up, he reaches over to stroke her thigh, to run his finger up between her legs. But Gwen mimes ostentatious fatigue. Too tired to be touched. "I'm just about ready for bed . . ." She rises, clearing away dirty glasses, newspapers.

He's thinking bitterly, *She's not too tired to go get a haircut after work, or talk on the phone to Irina for an hour. Is it me that she's tired of?*

"I don't think this city is good for us," he says.

"Oh yeah?" Gwen frowns, glancing at the headlines of the newspaper she is about to throw away. So frantic with work these days she doesn't get to look at the papers till midnight. She hasn't really taken in what Gideon's just said, merely registered his plaintive intonation: a voice that can't bear the sound of itself.

Gwen is organizing a conference on Russian corruption and criminality which will take place over a three-day weekend next October. She has made her wish list of speakers and begun to invite them, to sketch out the topics of panels and lectures. Kalman's approved the budget, which at first seemed pharaonic but now she realizes must pay for flights, hotel rooms, honoraria, a venue.

She is extremely nervous and extremely excited. It's a shitload of organization of a kind she's not much versed in, although luckily she's got Mandy and Carole to help her. If she pulls it off, if the conference gets good press, Lavrinsky will be pleased, she will doubtless get the much-delayed raise, and she will have contributed something useful to people's understanding of how Russia's democratic-capitalist revolution has gone wrong. But it's only six months away, which is . . . nothing.

"What's wrong with the city? I find it kinda charming at the moment . . ."

"That's what you say, but look at you: you're totally stressed out, you got circles under your eyes like a raccoon. And so does Bella. She is way overtired *all the time* because Betty loads her with this high-pressure competitive Manhattan social life."

Gideon is on his feet now, pacing. She watches him. He has a new gesture of pressing his hands in on either side of his head, as if his skull were a helmet that no longer fit. He stops now, and stares at his feet.

"Sometimes I'm in the subway, watching rats squirming around on the tracks? And I think, Why'm I bringing up my child in this insane asylum, ambulances and sirens screaming all night, and toxic gases we're breathing, and police brutality, race hatred on the streets. Any kid growing up here might as well be some Sarajevan war orphan. Unless you are *so* insulated by money as to be a different kind of sociopath . . ."

"I don't know," she counters. (Useless trying to argue with Gideon in these moods.) "I think it's quite a *good* place to bring up a child . . . I mean, you haven't been to Lucy Moses with Bella, but it's wonderful."

"Money."

"No, not money—the older kids' school's run by Vladimir Feltsman, it's a public school for kids who are talented in music. Most of the other parents are Russian immigrants . . . I think the city's got a density of culture that for a child is—"

"You call it culture? I call it a rat race. I call it blood money. You look at these kids who come over with their nannies, you look at Jacey's kids, I see white faces, hollow eyes. These are two-year-olds, six-year-olds whose every waking hour is crammed with—it's like this Victorian lady's regime. Piano, dancing, fencing. *Bullshit.* Is that culture? It's parents driving their kids like Olympic athletes because they're so hopped-up competitive themselves. Whose every poop has got to be productive so they can grow up to throw poor people out of their tenements for a living. So the kids don't notice that they never see their own parents from one week to the next. I see children—"

"Who are you talking about?"

"I'm talking Serena, I'm talking Alexander, who are this truly fucked-up combination of overobserved and underprotected, overstimulated and underloved."

"I don't think Serena and—"

"You think I don't listen? You think you're the only one who takes Bella to the playground?" His voice is shrill now. "I sit in the playground and I listen to these mothers obsessing about how come Caleb knows his alphabet and Wally doesn't and how they're taking Yahoo to the speech therapist for her lisp? I listen and I'm appalled. You want to know what this New York culture's doing? It is cheating kids of a childhood. They might as well be sending them down the coal mine these kids are so . . . hurled into adulthood."

"I know what you mean, but do you think it's any—"

"And the parents? The children are adults and the parents are *babies*. You got no idea how perverse this is. When we went out to your dad's for Easter? I was looking at Jacey and her kids and I'm thinking, Something's wrong with this picture. Then I realize. The children are wearing black and the adults are wearing shorts. I promise you, the result will be a generation of dangerous defectives, of sociopaths who are *not* going to be as soft in their unforgivingness of *us*."

"You think it'd be any different in the country?"

"I think we'd have more control over the poison she was fed. I think—you know what I think? I think it might be good for us, simply on an aesthetic level, to restore our souls. I think, we're living in the richest portion of the richest nation known to God, why not take our money and buy some tranquillity and beauty? For the price of this apartment, we could buy a hundred acres in upstate New York, an eighteenth-century farmhouse, a stream."

"You're thinking of Lubeck."

"Whatever. Or Dan and Andrea, moving up to Vermont. I think they're not so dumb. I think there might just be an outside chance they're onto something. I think, well, Andrea's been trying to have a baby for over a year now and maybe working a shitty job at Legal Aid and living a block away from St. Vincent's with ambulance sirens twenty-four hours a day is not the most conducive thing to productivity, whether creative or . . . biological. Sometimes it makes me very uncomfortable, thinking of Bella's lungs getting fucked up with that poison from all these cars and buses and . . . and people's envy and greed and unhappiness. And what for? These bad values—I don't like the toy guns in the stores, the . . . We should leave. It's not good for us, we never have time for each other."

She looks at him, weary, guarded. "What are we going to do in the country?"

"Look after our child. Talk. Read books. Plant a garden. Play music. Love each other."

"What would we do for money, I mean. They use money in the country, too, don't they? I've been thinking I really need to ask for a raise . . ."

"I don't want you to have to work so hard. I could do carpentry. We wouldn't need so much."

"But I . . ." She thinks of humoring him, then feels too impatient. "I like my work."

"So we can move to Russia. Live out in some log cabin in the taiga? It didn't sound so bad, what you used to tell me about your museum-guard buddy—keeping bees, pickling your own cucumbers, brewing your own moonshine. I could get into that: Siberian survivalism . . ."

"Oh yeah?" She smiles now, despite herself. "Now you're talking. If you really want to get away from ecological poison and bad values, yeah, Russia's definitely the place." And then, nervously, "But I . . . I think we can get . . . um . . . teach her good values wherever we are."

"I don't think so," he says. He is lying on his back on the sofa, staring at the ceiling. His eyes are empty and black. Flat, opaque. Just say it: Dead. His skin looks chalky.

She imagines them leaving the city—her, Gideon, and the child, in a last-ditch scramble to save themselves. Imagines them in a farmhouse in the Catskills, the Adirondacks, the White Mountains, no job to escape to, no streets, no city lights, no friends. And it fills her with dread. She remembers her father saying, when he first started chemotherapy and was told to take time off work, "The worst thing for a marriage is a husband at home, having lunch with his wife every day."

"The country . . ." she mutters. "So you can home-school her, like Jerome did? Doesn't that strike you as maybe dangerously controlling?"

Tone so unintentionally contemptuous he flares back. "Yeah, it's true I wouldn't mind reasserting some kinda control over what kind of lies my child gets taught. (That's hard for you to understand, seeing as you don't believe in *anything*.)

"Your dad stuffing Bella with Barbie dolls and Disney videos makes me sick: it's a kind of rape of her imagination, it's neural genocide. And his bullying us *already* about which twenty-thousand-dollar-a-year private school we're signing her up for, yeah, it does make me think kinda fondly of Jerome and—"

"He's just being realistic about how the world actually works."

"What's so great about the world?"

"He wants her to get a good start . . ."

"What's so great about a world that kills Jews?" he persists.

She stares. "I'm sorry—do they kill Jews at Brearley?"

"Where the U.S. government sues South Africa in order to deny them the same access to AIDS drugs we have? That—what kind of world is that? What's a head start mean, a head start killing Jews, a world head start denying AIDS drugs to—"

"Here we go again," she says. "Do you mind if I read the paper?" She moves away from her husband, whose unhappiness stinks like a wound, and she thinks, He's insane. One of us has got to be out in the world, earning a living, or else Bella will be sunk. She can't grow up in this sickly bitter cocoon. I've got to work harder, because I don't love him anymore, because I'm scared to be shut up alone with him.

But even now, some flick inside Gwen knows the only reason Gideon is threatening to move them to rural Russia and home-school their daughter is because when he ran his hand up her thigh, she ignored it. That all she has to do to make the dead eyes dance with mischief, to make him stop ranting about poisonous belief systems, is to take him in her arms, and let him kiss her and tickle her clit until she laughs and comes.

But this knowledge is too hard to admit, because at the moment she is so overwhelmed by nervous exhaustion that she thinks she would rather kill him than make love, in fact she wants to murder him just for making her feel sexually guilty when she's so fucking exhausted. She wonders, which has priority: his desperation for sex or her desperation to be left alone?

Chapter Three

I

"WHAT ARE YOU DOING TODAY?" Bolting a cup of coffee, grabbing an apple on her way to work.

He shrugs, sullen. As if it's her fault he doesn't have anything to do.

"There's a directors' meeting this afternoon. Do you think you could be here five-thirtyish, when Betty brings Bella back?"

"Back from where?"

"I told you already, she's got a birthday party at three."

"Whose birthday party?"

"Zoe's."

"Who's Zoe? Do we know Zoe?"

Gwen is running late, antsy to get going, especially as Bella has fallen back to sleep in their bed. She's desperate to slip out of the house *now* while Bella's safely unconscious, to evade the separation-psychodrama of her daughter's clutching her knees and howling . . .

"She's part of the gang."

"I don't think Bella should go *anywhere* this afternoon. She's way too tired."

Rage bubbling up in Gwen. A murderous fury out of nowhere. She paces. Throws things into her briefcase. Papers, proposals. Address book. "Okay, fine. *You* tell Betty you don't want Bella to go to Zoe's birthday party."

"What's the big deal, Gwen? I don't get why we are totally burning out our child in order to keep the nanny amused. I mean, isn't it a little bizarre that Betty can't see for herself Bella's tired? Maybe it's time to think of what's best for Bella, is she stressed, does she maybe need a day at home, just looking at picture books, in whose interest is she being dragged to the houses of people we don't even know?"

Gwen seizes the present Betty's bought—a Noah's ark, wrapped in royal blue paper with a pink ribbon—and slams it down in front of Gideon on the kitchen counter.

"Here. *You* tell Betty you don't want Bella going to Zoe's birthday party. *You* take this birthday present *back* to West Side Kids, Amsterdam and I think Eighty-third, Eighty-fourth, northwest corner, *you* get a store credit. Buy yourself something nice. And maybe you can arrange Bella's days from now on. I told you Annie Dolores left a message the other day?"

He nods.

"Did you ever get in touch with her?"

An inscrutable gesture.

"You didn't call her back?"

He blows out his breath. Sighs. Raises his hands as if to push her away. "I need a little more time to think, to figure out where I'm going next. I'm not ready to—"

"Look, I don't think she was proposing marriage, it was just—"

"Yeah, right, it was another workshop out at St. Anne's? Well, what's the point of that? You know, busting my ass for carfare and a donut?"

She stares. Any day now, she is going to *murder* this person. "You know what New York's like. People need to be reminded you exist . . ."

He stares back at her. "Do I?"

2

THERE WERE MOMENTS when Gwen remembered that there were other ways of being, besides their petty warfare, their bickering, their undermining, their one-upping, their ignoring: a parallel realm of domestic plenty, contentment, amused teasing. When she remembered that *they had so much.*

She thought of the book of the *Iliad* that sometimes she found dead dull and sometimes she found heartbreaking: where Thetis goes to Mount Olympus to request a new shield for her son, to replace the one captured by the Trojans when they killed Patroclus, and Hephaestus forges Achilles the most glorious shield ever made.

On Achilles' shield is engraved a world intricate as a peach-pit Nativity. In one corner is harvest season, with mowers romping in the hay; in another there's a wedding feast, with musicians piping, and bride and groom and their guests revelling under the poplars by a big lazy river; in another, young men are running and jumping while spectators cheer. How amply, how luxuriantly Homer delineates this Otherworld which exists in miniature on Achilles' chased-gold shield: the jovial august realm of peacetime, with its natural rhythms of weddings and games and harvests. He tantalizes us with this vision of *how things might be,* because this mirror world is not the world of the *Iliad,* its code is not that to which Achilles (who already carries his death within him) is plighted: Achilles will only ever know the burning of crops, the slaughter of heroes, the sacking of cities, the dividing of spoil, an early descent into darkness. Achilles is vowed to turn harvest to famine, young brides into widows, to create a generation who will never know their fathers and whose mothers are slaves at the enemy's loom.

We know what we are missing. It is the sign carved on our palms, the Might-Have-Been World of Natural Rightness. We hear its diminishing echo: the sound of a bride, the sound of her boy, the sound of happiness, the sound of joy: the sound of the babe snort-guzzling as she, dozing, still tipples at her mama's breast. Achilles admires the handiwork of his new shield, which his mother has brought him back from the netherworld, but he knows that by tomorrow sundown, its bright chased gold will be deep grimed in Trojan brains and Trojan entrails, and that in another few days it will be his own bier . . .

3

INHUMAN WOMAN. If he had proposed to her that henceforth they stop brushing their teeth, she would pronounce him a dangerous lunatic. But for her to have imposed this unilateral embargo on lovemaking, to render it unthinkably grasping for him even to want to kiss her mouth or stroke her hair, this appeared to her too self-evident to discuss.

He watched her squinched away on what had become inviolably *her* side of the bed, clothed (as if for the office) in a suit of pajamas buttoned to the chin, and asked himself what many a husband has asked, in an anguish of self-loathing. Does she *want* me to sleep with another woman? The tears ran down his cheeks at the thought that he might be forced to prowl and cheat, when all he yearned for was her.

He hadn't *needed* to get married to feel solid and palpable in the world, he hadn't hungered to perpetuate the House of Wolkowitz: for him, marriage was a cleaving of souls sealed by the eternal union of two bodies, and anything less was a desolating fraud. It was a declaration of survivalist satiety: a This is my cunt, these are my belly and my breasts, my dark gold hair, my gray eyes, my husky laughter, this is all I ever need.

After all, let's be honest: for a man, monogamy was about as natural an act as ballet dancing—almost harder than chastity, since it might be easier to gouge out your eyes than to fix your conscious gaze forever on one point. It was as if, entering into the marital state, he had been obliged to cauterize a universal drive, to lay the fear of God in his marrow that "if you so much as raise your hat to another woman, you will burn in hell forever." He had accepted the creed that she was the walled garden within which he would find everlasting delight. And now it was as if God three thousand years after Sinai was telling Israel, Oh, you know the one about no-adultery? I was kidding. And here, you wanna bite of my ham sandwich?

That was how he felt: a chump, royally swindled.

4

THIS CITY DEVOURS YOUR HEART.

He remembered coming to it with Jenny Randazzo in the late seventies, off the bus from Teaneck, like teenage pilgrims on hajj. He remembered their haunting the Carnegie Hall Cinema for Bertolucci movies; shoplifting Allen Ginsberg from the New Yorker bookstore; taking the A train down to the Blue Note to hear John Lee Hooker croak "One Bourbon, One Scotch, One Beer."

Walking barefoot through the streets, thinking that there were prophets throughout history who had preached humility, lovingkindness, and that here was the New Jerusalem where such burning ideas might catch fire, where he himself, with a few friends, could propagate the mystery of revolutionary love, with his poor makeshift materials, his puppets, his shoe-box theater on his back. His broken hoarse voice, his clumsy charm.

That was all he'd ever wanted, in the way of payback—not fame, awards, commissions, national coverage. Not his own TV show. Not even transcendent greatness. Just a little brotherly love. It was enough to play basketball on summer evenings with the kids on his block, to have the neighbors come freely in and out of his apartment, everybody looking after each other's children, helping each other out.

And now. And now . . . And now he found himself slipping in the street, losing his balance, while people pushed past him, aggressively impatient. Cursing under their breath. They would trample you underfoot if you fell. Busy people with capped teeth and silicone breasts and lifted faces and surrogate children, who were in a hurry to get to work, to sales conferences, to the gym. Even to prayer meetings, for there were churches and synagogues on Wall Street, too, that preached tax-deductible giving. They did not heed the twin Testaments' call to feed the hungry and clothe the naked, to shelter widows and orphans, to succor the downtrodden. They had different gods—younger ones, who slouched on paper thrones high above Times Square—teenage gods, clothed and unclothed in Calvin Klein underpants and Calvin Klein undershirts, who hung out in limp friezes of five and six, moony, slack-jawed, affectless. And what a nightmare, really—to be the subjects of teenage deities. Amoral, fidgety, narcissistic, illiterate.

Slot-machine city, which ate up your money and spat you out. Where you couldn't afford to get old, let alone sick, because, like most of your fellow citizens, you had no health insurance. I must not get sick, he thought over and over. In the past, he had felt childishly hardy, invulnerable. Now he was seized by mysterious stomach pains and chest pains, now he had watches in the night when he couldn't breathe, when his fingers started to tingle and his arms went numb, when he thought he was going to pass out. And sometimes in the subway when the doors were closing, when the doors closed and sprang open again and snapped shut once more, his chest went tight and he was afraid he was going to scream, but he had no breath. It was then that he remembered that his mother was no older than he when she began her long day's dying. And he thought, I won't live to be old. And when I die, Gwen (whom he had always imagined at his side) will not be there. She will not even know.

He thought of moving to the country with Bella, maybe even to Vermont. Dan and Andrea, *Baruch Ha Shem*, would soon have their baby; they could raise their children together. He and Bella would rent a house where he'd have a carpentry shop in the garage, and she could run barefoot in the summers, play outdoors till dark.

Which did a child more good: Suzuki lessons and speech therapy, or having her father at home, doing honest work within earshot? In a couple of years, she'd be going to school, and he'd be there to welcome her in the afternoons, to fix her milk and cookies, to ask her about her day. He would have time and quiet and space enough to slow down and *listen* to her.

This was the direction his thoughts led him when he was calm, when it seemed, briefly, there might after all be a way of slipping his neck free from the noose. Other times, the city's slippery sides closed in on him, and he gasped from animal panic. Gideon was a simple organism: if he were no longer loved—if he had never been loved, then he would simply turn his face to the wall.

Chapter Four

I

SATURDAY MORNING. Eight forty-five. The far side of your bed has had time to get cold. Bear's crib is empty. Nobody in the kitchen. Stroller gone. No note, Gideon. No lipstick kiss on the bathroom mirror. No sign of life. At first you feel unutterably abandoned, then relieved. Should you try to find them in the playground? But Central Park is *big*, and you already know that should you succeed, you will be rewarded for your ingenious fidelity by your wife's cold shoulder because *you* should have been the one who got up with Bella in the morning. Besides, she's got this gang of Russian biddies she likes to gossip with. Relax.

You shower, make a cup of coffee, turn on the cartoon channel. (But cartoons make Gideon panicky-sad, recalling lonely mornings in Passaic waiting for his mother to wake up.)

Nine forty-eight.

And then, on impulse, you rifle through your jeans.

No.

Reach into the drawer, try the pockets of another pair of jeans.

Look again, Gideon. *There*, on the back of a nail salon flyer, is the number.

Is it too early on a weekend morning to call a single girl? Maybe she's got some guy in bed with her.

Nine fifty-six. You go out to the kitchen, pick up the phone. Hang up. Reheat your coffee.

Pick up. Dial.

This time it rings once, and a sleepy voice answers. You hang up.

It's Saturday morning and it's still only ten o'clock . . .

Saturday morning. The apartment is so quiet it spooks you. All you can hear are the mourning doves, who are mourning . . . whom?

You climb into a pair of black jeans that are not too dirty, a white shirt that's passably white. Now begins the great key-hunt. Where did Bella-the-magpie, Mistress of All Keys, last dump your set of keys, or has Gwen taken them away from you?

2

ON THE CORNER of Amsterdam and Seventy-ninth, under the melancholy red-brown Deco sign of Last Pharmacy, Gideon hesitates.

He wants to go, but on the other hand, he doesn't want to sink even lower in his own estimation by announcing to himself, I'm going to shul this morning, and then weaselling out. Falling into the slime of other Manhattanites who have no holy days, no respect, who live in bland profanity, neutered Jews to whom the Sabbath has been denatured into "weekend," a day to buy bagels and smoked salmon from Barney Greengrass, magazines at Barnes & Noble, a pair of chinos at Ralph Lauren, not to fall on your face before your God.

There's a fork in the road. Hell or shul. Starbucks or Shaarei Tzedek. He's been mulling it over for weeks now, sick of drifting along Amsterdam or Broadway on a Saturday morning, seeing observant Jews—dark-suited husbands with their dark-suited sons, hatted women with their long-skirted daughters—and feeling by contrast flimsy, like someone who doesn't know the difference between things.

Jewishness, once his salvation, his pride, he has dropped, like so many of his older European kin who, despite their pains not to irritate Gentile wives or neighbors with any primitive or unpatriotic demonstrations of faith, were nonetheless butchered, burned, and gassed . . .

There's a synagogue down the block—a hippieish synagogue, charismatic, an uptown cousin to Pitt Street that he had been to once with

Ethan, for Noah Liebman's bar mitzvah. That he's been meaning to check out again.

Which is how, at noon, Gideon finds himself holding hands with two men, kicking up his heels, and carolling *"Dai-dai-dai . . ."*

3

THE SYNAGOGUE OF OHELEI YA'AKOV was a small pink-and-turquoise room bedizened in kabalistic runes and palm prints evidently meant to recall the delirium of a shrine in Safed.

To Gideon, it resembled a Lower East Side bodega selling green plantains and voodoo oil. A bodega with a screen down the middle, gentlemen on one side, ladies on the other, and children streaming fluid and scuttery between the two sexual landmasses.

Baruch atah, Adoshem, ha mavdil ben zachar u nekevah.

When Gideon arrived, a plump-faced young man with blue-black cheeks had just begun reading that week's haftarah, which was taken from the Book of Samuel.

4

SOMEDAY, GWEN, I want to tell you about David and his first wife Michal. Michal was King Saul's daughter, and as you know, everybody in that family—Saul, his son Jonathan, his daughter Michal—broke their hearts over David.

They loved this ballsy little upstart, knowing that he was destined to unthrone them all: they were the Ancient Régime, chivalrous, haughty, borderline manic-depressive. But the shepherd with the harp was God's boy. The next new thing.

So David married Michal, the boss's daughter, and she, like her brother Jonathan, risked her neck to save his life. But once David ousted her dad, no way Michal was going to last . . .

The morning's reading told of how young King David, having established Jerusalem as his capital, recaptures the Ark of the Tabernacle from the Philistines.

All Israel runs to join the Victory Parade, at whose head David is prancing—all except Michal, who watches from the palace window her husband "leaping and dancing before the Lord, and she despised him in her heart."

When David comes home, his queen frostily compliments him on having bared his ass in front of serving girls.

And David retorts, I may be vile in your eyes, and I plan to make myself even viler in my own, but with serving girls and with God—who chose me over your father to rule His people—will I always find honor.

Poor king's daughter, who thinks grace lies in a long face. Poor pride, unable to bear it that God should have a soft spot for shameless rascals who like to get down and dirty. Cold woman, jealous of her husband's high spirits . . .

5

AND NO SOONER were the gates of the ark closed, and the Torah scrolls locked in their stalls, than the men of the synagogue clapped their hands and started singing, capering before the Lord. And Gideon, too, found himself leaping before the Lord.

The rabbi, a tall fat man with a red-gold beard, grabbed one of Gideon's hands, and the haftarah reader seized the other hand. Away they pranced, up and down the crowded aisle. The women on their side of the *mehitsah* were singing and clapping, too. (And was there one who watched her husband, leaping and capering before the Lord and, in her heart, despised him?)

And what's pitiful is the *relief* Gideon feels, the crushing burden that's rolling off him, in the exultancy of surging motion, the raw searing beauty of the shouted tunes. Sweat's pouring off him, the white shirt is wet through, and his heart is pounding with love.

Oh God in heaven, the tears are rolling down his cheeks, he is chastised Ephraim, he is harlot Israel, he was lost and now he is found, and God's grace is nearly crushing his chest in, and even though his fellow congregants are irritating and the rabbi strikes him as a phony, Gideon feels this radiant warmth from his hand that is almost . . . holy—all he wants is to jump and prance in this shouting crowd of young men in white shirts, to hold hot hands with the rabbi and be borne aloft in the sea of brotherhood . . .

His people. My people. Mine, all of you, for sicker for poorer, in rain and in sludge, in the desert and in the Bronx. We were a pain in the ass under Pharaoh, we were a pain in the ass at Sinai, we were a pain in the ass in Toledo, in Mainz, in Nineveh and in Rheims, and here we are still, a pain in the ass on West End Avenue.

Mi k'mochah? Who is like you, God? No one, luckily.

Who is like us? No one, luckily. A nation of nudges. Our neighbors drive us out, they burn, they profane, they pillage, but the glorious stiff-necked persistence of this whiny crumb of a people, this fractious mite, won't give up. This flea-bitten God-bitten remnant.

This scrap.

My people.

Me and mine.

You can't take this away from me, Gwen. I will go up in flames, with the crowns beneath each sacred letter flaring gold-and-black, and I will not murmur.

But why must these moments be so fleeting? If only he could hang on to this good joy, if only he could maintain the habit of faith, then everything else that's slipped away from him wouldn't matter—his Christian wife, his pagan daughter—he's even been on the point of telling Gwen, Fine, baptize her, better she should have a false religion than none—the sins that are on his mind, on the tip of his tongue to commit . . .

Let this moment let this moment let this moment last . . .

6

WE ARE LIVING in an age of antilove.

I am talking primarily of romantic love, which has gone to shit, but also of blood-love, despite our official cult of Family Values.

This is very strange, because so many other intervening passions have receded: our brightest souls don't run for office or go to war or feed the hungry or preach God's word to infidels.

There has been a wholesale defilement to private life, only to find that there is nothing there, because we have made nothing.

A flickering blue electronic hearth, a stack of takeout menus by the phone in the darkened kitchen, your—not lover, God forbid, but—partner calling to say she's working late.

We have forsaken love, and entered into "relationships." The difference between a love affair and a "relationship" is not just semantic but radical. Love you pour yourself into unchecked, a flood of vulnerability and sacrifice, strong as death, terrible as an army with banners. Abandon control, all ye who enter here.

Whereas a relationship is a contractual arrangement, subject to renegotiation, dependent on each party's continued satisfaction. A hotel has a relationship with a garbage hauler, a contractor has a relationship with a roofer, but once the cock enters into a "relationship" with the pussy, love flies out the window.

And the result is a bloodless scoreboarding: does she get along with your friends, how good's the sex, does he talk about his feelings. Sexuality being something that's not in every glance, every smile, every wriggle of the toe, every FIGHT, but another multilateral treaty—I'll fuck if you do the dishes—another improving activity, another thing to "work on."

We know how to work and we know how to keep fit, but we don't know how to lose ourselves in love.

7

SUNDAY MORNING Gwen came home from a run in the park.

Bella was sitting on Gideon's lap in the kitchen, howling. She had evidently been howling awhile. Her red face was swollen, her cheeks snotted with tears.

"What's happened?"

"She cut her foot," said Gideon, staring at his wife, in her shorts and sweaty T-shirt: a vision of harlot-health, a worshipper of the Fitness God.

Gwen was not the same woman he had fallen for, a mere two and a half years ago. Her body had cast off childbearing's blubber, but had come back smoother in its movements. She had lost the proud lunging gawkiness of her young womanhood for a more banal efficiency.

Gideon hasn't told Gwen about going to shul last week. It's something he wants to keep to himself until he's sure it's genuinely sustainable. Besides, he knows (even if she doesn't say so) she will think it's merely a symptom of his unhappiness, a time-wasting diversion from finding work. Or perhaps an oblique reproach of *her*.

"Oh Baby," Gwen bent to kiss Bella and pick her up from Gideon's lap, but instead of raising her arms as she usually did, Bella shrank from her mother and began howling louder.

"What happened?"

"Did you break something?" Gideon countered. "She stepped on this fucking enormous spike of glass . . ."

"Oh hell—yeah, I broke a bottle of V8 this morning. I thought I'd got all the pieces . . ."

Gideon glared at her, shaking his head. "This one was, like, the size of a . . . What were you, like, waiting for Mimi to get in on Monday and clean it up?"

"I'm sorry. Did you get it all out?"

"Let's hope so."

All that day, Baby played theatrical sufferer, refusing to walk. And Gideon's chivalric protection of his little lady, his carrying the child around the house, bandaged foot dangling, got under Gwen's skin.

It was Father and Daughter against Mother, she had been obscurely cast out, and what's more, she felt half relieved to be free. In three weeks, she was leaving for Russia; she had all her appointments fixed up, the people she needed for the conference next fall. She was staying with Bill and Jamila for five nights, another two days in St. Petersburg with the Rezniks. And two nights with Constance on her way back through London, her visit happily coinciding with her goddaughter Ruby's birthday.

Excitement alternating with anguish at the idea of being parted from Bella. Periodically, Gwen—realizing she couldn't bear to leave the child—schemed to see if she couldn't bring her. But Gideon objected. It just didn't make sense, Gwen would be working night and day, it wasn't fair to dump Bella with strangers. (I could bring Betty, Gwen argued. Yeah, for an extra thousand dollars. Thinking, You could bring me, too.) Reminding her, in a rare moment of tough-mindedness, Look, don't be amateurish. Serious professionals don't bring along their kids on a business trip. Besides, there were too many weird diseases floating around Russia these days . . .

Gideon wanted Bella with him, and that was good. Since Pants on Fire had closed down, he'd been taking more of an interest in his daughter, and that was . . . good. It was good because it left Gwen more time for work, which she needed, and it was good for Bella. Wasn't it?

Now that the trip was fixed, she felt like a balloon on a long long string, half yanked, half free. She watched Gideon and Bella, who now were both crouched under the living room table, Bella in her father's lap. Two babes in the woods of the Upper West Side. He was telling her, as he often did, a story about a naughty little girl named Iddabella who was scared of nothing—not tigers, not kings—and who got into the most flamboyant scrapes. And every time he drew breath, Bella demanded "Muh?"

Gwen, gathering scattered toys from the living room floor, sweeping away old coffee cups, breakfast plates, newspapers, felt a pang. What life's-blood stories did she have to feed into the girl child's narrative veins—the 1998 budget for their library program in Rostov?

8

GWEN IS LEAVING for a two-week trip to Russia, taking Bella with her. It is all arranged: not only Bill and Jamila's nanny Zarife, a buxom Azeri with grown children of her own, but Zarife's nineteen-year-old sister are going to be looking after Bella while Gwen is working.

Gideon, convinced that Gwen and Bella are never coming back, pretends that they're not leaving. He ignores their preparations: Gwen's calling the airline to request the bulkhead seat and the infant bassinet; ordering the car which will take them to the airport; packing their suitcases; leaving money for Mimi while she's gone.

Gideon blackly watches his wife pack supplies whose overabundance seems to confirm his conviction that this isn't a business trip but a kidnapping.

The morning of their flight, Gwen asks Betty to take Bella out to the park for a last ramble while Gwen packs a knapsack for the airplane—books and toys, diapers, wipes, juice.

"Do you want to say goodbye to Daddy?" Gwen asks.

Gideon shakes his head in a preemptive No and escapes to the study. He scrunches up on the sofa, pretending to read the *Village Voice*, blocking his ears against the departing peals of Bella's giggling pronouncements as Betty bundles her out the door. "Just get Tony to ring up, and I'll be right down," he hears his wife say. If he were a decent husband and father, he would be taking his family to the airport, but he would rather fry: he wants in no way to be seen as backing his wife's criminal irresponsibility in dragging their baby daughter to this war zone.

He hears the shuffle of Gwen's suitcase across the living room floor, he hears the study door open, but he doesn't look up, he is suddenly panicked by the certainty that he will never see her again. Without Bella as hostage, he doesn't stand a chance.

His throat's choked, he can't look up, doesn't acknowledge her dropped kiss, her subdued goodbye. He is paralyzed by fear. Only when he hears the *bing* of the elevator does he go running barefoot into the building hall, but by then the elevator door has closed.

She is gone. Gone! And he didn't even say goodbye to Bella!

He lets out an involuntary cry, a werewolf howl that he tries to smother into a cough, and ends up choking as the other elevator disgorges—not a repentant Gwen, but a small stout Central American woman with a Scottie, who glances at him disapprovingly.

9

HIS WIFE WANTS TO LEAVE HIM, Gideon knows.

She wants him to leave her. She has made a psychoeconomic calculation, a "guesstimate." She has asked herself, Am I better off with him or without him? This was how people thought nowadays.

Gwen has looked at her husband, looked at their child, weighed her options, and calculated, Time to switch horses. She's thought, The nanny's more use to me than the husband; I'll get the nanny to sleep in. I feel like a single mother anyway, I might as well get the good of it. (What was the good of it, he wondered. Being able to date other guys? And something truly sick in him would almost rather she had the hots for *somebody* than that her lust was a riverbed run dry.) She's figured they'd be better off without him, she and Bella, since she feels like a single mother anyway (these pampered self-righteous career women who've marginalized their adoring husbands just love bandying about this phrase), so she's going to take the baby and run.

He says, in the quiet of the empty apartment, "Who are you kidding, sweetheart? You don't like being alone any more than I do. Ten minutes after you throw me out, you're gonna be trawling for my replacement, if you haven't found him already. Every time I walk in the door, it's Gideon, I can't get the printer to work, Gideon, could you get the air conditioner up from storage. Who's gonna install your air conditioner when I'm gone?"

Chapter Five

I

THE HOUSES ALONG ELGIN CRESCENT, in west London, back onto a communal garden the size of a city block. It's in one of these white stucco houses, with a glassed-in conservatory leading to the larger garden, that Constance and Roger live.

Constance and Roger both come from big families, with a comfortable mixture of new money and old blood running through the generations. The house is tall, three stories of rooms with threadbare Persian carpets and overstuffed sofas with griffon-clawed feet and portraits of Constance's great-grandmother—an American heiress married to a prime minister's grandson. ("Can't you just tell she slept with him, from the way he paints her?")

There is a mixture of college-student beanbag chairs and fine eighteenth-century sideboards that attests to owners who are used to good things but not very interested in them. (When her mother-in-law comes to stay, Constance complains, she is always going about removing coffee cups from the inlaid surfaces of tables . . .)

Gwen is standing before a library bookshelf. She feels, after Russia, so overdosed on current events that she's hungering for reading matter ancient as Herodotus or scrupulous as Pascal. Constance and Roger's books, for the most part, come in sets. There are hunting novels and Church Fathers and leather-bound copies of Johnson's *Rambler* or the *Edinburgh Quarterly,* Constance's father's Persian poets, Goethe in Gothic script. She takes a red-and-gold volume of Kipling out into the conservatory and settles down on a wicker chaise longue to read about the young Kipling and his new bride holing up in an unheated shack in Maine . . .

Gwen is exhausted from her Russian trip. The atmosphere in the country was so thick, so unhealthy, so steamy with rumor, violent crimes, ill-gotten wealth, you just knew something was about to explode. This is how Russia must have felt in the 1880s, she thinks, when every week there was a new assassination attempt upon the tsar.

The happy surprise was Bella, who, pleased to be fed boiled candies by old ladies in the Metro and to have internationally respected economists get down on their knees to play horsey with her, had appeared to recognize that this barbarous land was, in some mystery of blood-belonging, hers too.

Only once Bella had shown herself an adoptive Slav could Gwen admit how she'd feared that her daughter might recoil from Russia's alienness, might object to hearing her mother speak a strange language. (Irina's American-raised son Alexei now throws a fit when his parents speak their native tongue, like General Franco's ordering Basques and Catalans, Speak Christian!)

2

TODAY IS RUBY'S BIRTHDAY. Ruby is now five years old. Gwen, from the conservatory, watches Ruby's party guests fan across the communal garden on a fortune hunt.

Dark gray clouds race through the sky. The stormy light brings out the garden greens vividly—it's weather that makes you feel *alive*, Constance claims, a climate that produces Tarquin's Viking-red hair, Ruby's peachy skin.

Tonight, after Ruby's birthday tea, Constance and Roger are taking Gwen out to dinner at the River Cafe.

I could live in this city; it's civilized, thinks Gwen, wishing they weren't going back to New York the next day.

There are seven children at Ruby's birthday—three girls from school, plus her brother, a boy cousin, and Bella, who is so excited she runs around in circles until she falls over, laughing.

Ruby is wearing a long mirror-sequined Indian patchwork dress, with Doc Martens. Ruby and Tarquin's cousin Clement is wearing a raw silk Nehru jacket with matching breeches. The children's names are equally ornate: there is an Apollonia, a Thea, and a Cosima.

Constance, who has come indoors to get her camera, declares: "God, you can't imagine how I wish I'd called my babies Tom and Jane. There's nothing so mortifying as being at the tail end of a trend. Besides, when it comes to tea, one feels like some sort of papal/imperial protocol person—Diocletian surely can't sit next to Augustine . . ."

She lingers a moment beside Gwen. The two women stare into the garden, watching the children dart, in search of party favors hidden in the crooks of mulberry trees and in rose beds. Bella, too young to spot spoils, has silently attached herself to Ruby.

Gwen feels relieved, watching Ruby and her friends, so reasonable, so self-possessed, even in their frantic greed for sweets. "So this is all you have to do—survive till your child's fifth birthday, then you're home free," she says. "No more worrying about their swallowing bleach or electrocuting themselves . . ."

"No," says Constance, thoughtfully. "The anxieties are different. Now it's more like Tarquin coming out in spots the night before a school interview. These children are so conscientious, *that's* what's terrifying. You sort of want to say, Go smoke some dope or something. Why don't you listen to the Grateful Dead *instead* of practicing the piano . . ."

Roger, stepping out into the conservatory, comes up behind Constance and draws her to him, clasping her hands across her chest in his. He speaks in her ear, low, smiling. "You won't believe it, darling—Mirjana's just cancelled."

"No!!!" returns Constance, with a kind of guffaw. "What is it this time?" she asks, twisting around to give him a look. "This is our second-string nanny," she explains to Gwen, "who is *such* a weed."

"She was a bit vague. Her period?"

"God, I hadn't heard that one since gym class. And I've already promised Eva she could go home at six . . . Didn't I tell you Mirjana would cancel?"

"You did," Roger confirms, smiling at his wife. "Never mind, I'm quite happy to stay home and baby-sit."

Their complicit amusement stands in such contrast to the weaselly penury of Gwen's own home life that she quite gapes. Too far left behind for envy. No, in truth, desperately envious.

"Mumma! Mumma!" Ruby, followed by Bella, has come running inside, panting. "I can't get the—I can't get this to open." She's carrying a toy parachute whose ties have become knotted.

"Try your godmother—she's got much nimbler fingers than me."

Gwen untangles the parachute quickly, handing it back to Ruby, who is fidgeting to get back to the sacking of the garden, the accumulation of spoils, which is continuing without her.

Gwen catches hold of Bella, who is running after Ruby, and hugs her daughter from behind, in unconscious emulation of Roger's husbandly gesture, trying to tuck the child's tangled curls away from her chocolate-smeared cheek. God, how she loves the small furnace of her daughter's sanguine heat. Bella, flailing to get back outside, shouts "Dop! Dop!" and succeeds in breaking free.

3

CENTRAL PARK a smutty-sooty purple-gray. The hazy bloom on the trees, heavy-hanging, musky, soporific. A rolling recklessness, lax bravado in those who remain in its embrace after darkness has fallen. Bladers, lovers, drinkers. The lake turns to a lagoon. Oriental droopiness. Lamplight electrifying the mad monochromity of greens.

Man and woman, coming up the hill from the Bethesda Fountain. He is wearing suspenders, a madras shirt, a battered straw hat, like Huckleberry Finn. He is goofing and clowning for the girl, goofing for love. He jumps up into the air as if to shoot a basket, and grabs hold of the branch of a plane tree. Now he swings from the branch, playing ape, one-armed, and with the other hand scratches his ear, his armpit. And drops. The girl shakes her head, with a chiding smile. She is a black-haired girl with pale green eyes. She is wearing a pale blue sleeveless sundress. She is exquisite, and there is some perverse dissonance between the fat lips and the demure manner that is driving him wild.

She is Emma Rogan. She's telling him her impressions of Jerome and Bridey, her problems with her thesis supervisor, and he's not listening to a word.

At the beginning of the evening, she was wearing crimson lipstick, and now her lipstick is all smeared and his own lips sting, that's how hard they've been kissing, that's how hard you kiss when you know you mustn't fuck and he's had a hard-on for the last two hours and she knows it, little Cleopatra . . .

When they met for a drink, Gideon warned her that he was already a little drunk. (Using drunkenness as carnival license.) Are you celebrating, she had asked, smiling uncertainly. Yeah, I'm celebrating, my family's outta town, I'm celebrating.

There is something prim and shockable about this Emma that he can't resist, that he suspects is generational. Her generation is very prim.

"I can't talk here," he says now, "the outside's just too distracting, I grew up in downtown Passaic, nature makes me tongue-tied. Come over to my house, and I'll show you my videos of taking Infernal Combustion on tour. I got this amazing tape of us doing a *Harrowing of Hell* at night down by the river, fifty people, with torches, in Czechoslovakia . . ."

She hesitates.

"Red Rover, Red Rover, let Emma come over."

Hesitates a beat longer.

"Come on," he says, "one glimpse of my apartment you'd never dream of sleeping with me, it's got toddler's toys all over the place. I mean, you couldn't fool around with a guy who's got Barbie dolls on the floor, wouldn't it just be like totally transgressively taboo?"

And she looks at him with a wry look of, Just how drunk is he?

"Come over," he said, "I'll play you the video, we won't even hold hands in the scary part."

4

"PEOPLE THINK young children are boring," says Constance.

Dinner at the River Cafe, where Gwen and Gideon dined the night they discovered that she was pregnant. The rain has blown over. It's a gentle lingering midsummer's evening. On the Thames, crews glide past. As they stroll from the river to the restaurant, Gwen spots the first evening star and wishes . . . doesn't know what to wish for. Wishes Bella will always be as happy as she was that afternoon, tumbling after the bigger girls, candy-stained, speechless with excitement.

"But it's not that they're boring—it's that they are so ruthlessly *un-*boring that they force you to become boring on their behalf."

"Trivial," Gwen agrees.

"Having a seven-year-old in your care is rather like being married to Isaac Newton or Stephen Hawking: here is this creature who is so monstrously consumed by the existential problems of how do you make a map of the brain, and what's the quickest way out of the Milky Way, that he is absolutely incapable of wiping his own bottom.

"That's why I can't see the point of being married to famous people—it's so obvious they save all their brilliance for their work, or for their public, and you're the one left holding the bedpan.

"Except that luckily your babies don't have anybody more important than you to talk to. It's the opposite of romantic love, where you love your lover from some kind of narcissistic thrill because you love the self you are with him. Well, I've never met a mother who doesn't loathe the person her children have made her become—this foul-tempered *drudge* who only thinks about wet socks and eating up your carrots. And yet you worship them, because although they've made you stupid, they themselves are so impossibly brilliant, these little vampires who've sucked dry your last brain cell, leached the last autonomous bit of laughter or youth out of you."

Gwen has stopped listening. "Constance, I'm in a jam."

"You do seem rather . . . somber these days, beyond the normal working-mother madness."

"I hate my husband."

She's said it.

Constance looks up. "Do you really? What a relief to hear it said."

"Yeah, I hate his guts."

"So do I. Mine, I mean. Yours I find rather adorable. I suspect all women hate their husbands, much of the time."

"No, this is worse than the usual . . . buildup of domestic resentment. It's not only that I don't want to sleep with him—although that, in our case, is pretty catastrophic—I don't believe in him anymore. I think he's fake. A hollow man."

"Now this is beginning to sound serious."

"And I hate myself for seeing through him. And for telling you this. Because it's so disloyal, to turn against him when he's down on his luck. But what am I supposed to do—wait till he finds a job so I can divorce him? I guess I should go to a shrink, right, pay some neutral professional to unload this on? It's less of a betrayal that way . . ."

Constance considers. "Do you know something bizarre? How old is Bella now—I am fairly certain that in about six months all this will pass. Of course you want to murder him now, you are the mother of a small child and you probably haven't slept in two years, and he's doubtless lying there like a snoring corpse, expecting you to get up every time she has a nightmare. Husbands' uses are not very obvious at this stage. They were intended biologically to be off fighting the Crusades during this messy sleepless part, because the inadmissible truth is you don't really hate your husband, you hate the child, who after all is the one who's ruining your life. But since you've decided on second thought not to commit infanticide, but to be some sort of maternal saint, then you've got no one to blame but your husband. But later on, you'll see. You think he's a creep, but I bet she won't. And who knows, very likely in not too long you'll want another baby."

"I won't. One's terrifying enough. I look at her sleeping and I think, I can't believe she's still *alive.*"

"Hang on, and then you'll find he's very handy at keeping your firstborn occupied, who by this time will be old enough for you to hate *her* for all the dreadful things the new baby's done to you—I'm quite serious, I spent the first eighteen months of Ruby screaming at Tarquin because she wouldn't sleep. The only reason I didn't hate Roger is he wasn't in the same country as me long enough to hate. Anyway, Gideon's a resourceful boy, you know he'll start working fairly soon."

"I don't think he'll start working. I think he's flipped out. And the fact that I'm the one who's driven him insane doesn't make me any more forbearing."

"May I ask the obvious question?"

"You mean . . ."

"Is there somebody else?"

"Yes." Gwen starts laughing again. "There's somebody else—who . . ." She's laughing too hard almost to proceed. "There's somebody else who—who is incontinent and pretty monosyllabic, as far as conversation goes and is in any event *female,* but I love the guts out of her, and I think our life would be a whole lot better if I had her to myself. I mean, hauling Bella around Russia, I realized, it's doable. If I can handle her in Russia on my own, I can do it."

"Yes, but . . . raising a child isn't really a survival test—she's probably better off with two parents, and preferably ten grandparents and twenty aunts and uncles and a large staff, who are *not* being tested to the outer limits of their endurance. You think it's going to be easier, without the useless husband, but it won't. Instead of screaming at him, you'll be screaming at Bella all day. Because, to be perfectly honest, children are even more useless than men. Anyway, they like them. Children—they do like their fathers."

Gwen pries a finger of melting wax from the candle. Hot. "Constance . . . This isn't—I'm not expressing myself quite . . . It's over. It's no longer a—it's over. I don't love him anymore, and I don't think it's fair to him, to live with him without loving him. I mean, I can see it's killing him. I mean it, Constance, this is no longer just a question of who changes the diapers, this is . . . reaching the end."

"I hear you." Constance draws a cigarette from her bag. Leans over, lights it from the candle flame. Inhales, blows out. They both sit in silence, thinking.

"And do you have a sense of a life without him?" she asks, finally.

"Beyond the simple Then-at-least-I-wouldn't-have-two-babies-to-look-after?"

Gwen reaches out a hand to pry another wax stalactite loose from the dripping candle. "Yes. Of her and me together. Beyond that, no."

Chapter Six

I

WHEN GWEN GETS BACK from work, the apartment is dark, the stroller is gone. That's right, she remembers, it's Wednesday, when Betty takes Bella over to Hunter's house for Sing-along.

She picks up the portable phone to dial her father, wanders into the kitchen, turns on the light, and—OOOhhhh!

"Christ, you gave me a scare. Why are you—are you all *right*?"

It's Gideon, sitting on a stool. Alone in the dark. Immobile, head in his hands. Now she's really scared. "What's wrong? Tell me, Gideon. What's happened?"

He doesn't answer.

"What is it?" She goes over to him and puts a hand on his shoulder. He gives a great shuddering sigh.

"*Speak*. Tell me." But he won't look up, won't speak.

She goes into the bedroom to put down her things. She turns on the light. And sees the Christian Ibarrguengoitia shopping bag, with the evening dress she'd bought with Christopher spread out on the bed.

She stands frozen. It's a curious thing to have bought and then squirrelled away in its bag, all these months—over a year ago!—in the back of the closet: an evening dress of a truly Byzantine opulence, still resting in its violet tissue. Porphyrogenitos.

She smooths the wrinkles. Hears Gideon behind her, and turns. Gideon's face is oddly contorted, he is biting his lip. He looks so pale she is frightened. She has been "found out," like a child caught in a lie, she who is used to being terribly, terribly right.

Has he seen the price tag, she wonders. How has he interpreted her buying so outlandish a dress when he's out of work, when she guilt-trips him mercilessly about their empty bank accounts, his credit card debts?

He says, "Put it on . . ."

"What?"

"Put the dress on."

Frightened, she slips out of her work clothes, wriggles into the dress—which has no zipper, no buttons, no snaps, which is made of deliciously clinging sheaths of chiffon and satin. She smooths it over her hips. And stands, defiant. She catches a glimpse of herself in the mirror—eyes flashing like an animal's, points of her nipples pressing tight against the fabric. She looks half crazed. Her husband's tic-twitching bloodshot eyes are fixed on her. His hand spin-gestures, Turn around. She swirls for him. A ghoulish parody of their old play, his former lustful delight in her elegance.

It's not the dress's price that pains him, she realizes, but that it is an acquisition with no referent to their common life, a dress she has bought and secretly stowed away for her future life, a life without him: her trousseau for her *next* husband.

Only when she takes off the dress and hangs it in the closet, slips into a T-shirt and jeans, does he speak.

"How's Cash?" he inquires.

Cash is his nickname for Campbell, whom he used (theoretically) to like.

"I don't know. Fine. Why? I think he's still seeing Mary Lynch."

"Is he? And who are *you* seeing?"

2

THAT NIGHT, after Bella's asleep, Gwen lies in bed reading Ailred of Rievaulx's treatise on Spiritual Friendship, from the Cisterian book she bought that long-ago afternoon with Ari. Gideon is sitting out on the balcony. She waits for him to come to bed. She is simultaneously dropping with fatigue and jumpy. She waits. Finally she goes out onto the balcony.

"Are you coming to bed soon?"

Gideon is sitting on the deck chair, a tall glass of whiskey in his hand. He is uncharacteristically immobile. Staring out at the city. The marvellous jewelled night-city, humming, alive. Him dead, the city alive. He doesn't answer.

"Gideon . . . ?"

He turns and she sees with surprise, a little fear, that he is so drunk he can hardly sit upright.

"What do you care?"

She stands there, uncertain. He takes hold of her nightgown. Gives it a hard yank upward. Looks at her bare thighs, her belly. Puts his hand on her pubis, grabs it hard, so that he pulls the hairs. She flinches, silent. His hand drops.

"What do you care? You don't want me in bed."

"I can't sleep till you come . . ."

"Oh, am I keeping you up? Go to sleep, go to sleep, I won't keep you up any longer." He stumbles to his feet and crosses the living room.

"Gideon . . ."

He's gone.

3

WHAT GWEN DOESN'T KNOW is that Gideon, too, has an outfit he's concealing from his wife. Gideon has excavated from his "trousseau" of cardboard boxes a prayer shawl of Sonny's, which he's supplemented with a pair of tefillin bought from a store on Allen Street.

He feels way too self-conscious actually to carry the prayer shawl to synagogue, and the tefillin he hasn't a clue how to put on: he has stared once or twice in dismay at the junkie-style straps, but when he's ready— if he's ever ready—he will learn, there are plenty of other aspiring born-agains wandering around this city, not knowing how to put on tefillin, and convoys of Lubavitcher lying in wait to show 'em. The paths of those seeking Zion are pleasant, shady, well-trodden . . .

Why does he hide these things from Gwen? Because, with one snide word, she would make his hunger for Jewish practice—which he himself doesn't yet trust, which is still only a tiny newborn red and squawling thing liable to stop breathing any minute—seem meretricious. Like everything about him. What he wants to tell her, preemptively, is this: Just because my motives are weak and vile, just because I'm a foxhole Jew, doesn't mean the religion itself isn't noble.

Gwen has been concealing an evening dress she means to wear without Gideon; Gideon is concealing a prayer shawl and phylacteries he means to wear without Gwen. The things about themselves they prize the other finds unacceptable. They no longer have common passions, except their daughter, about whom they cannot agree.

4

FOR GWEN AND GIDEON, the world was such a minefield that there was now *nothing* they could mention without risking a limb.

Not politics, not books, not her father's health, not Russia, not theater, not nothing. They were gagged, both of them. Inflamed, *raging*, inwardly. Frosty-mute, on the surface.

He looked across at his wife as they lay in bed at night, reading. Silently begging, challenging her to say something. Say something to me about what's inside you. Tell me what you've done today, who's come to see you in the office. When they first got together, she'd liked to talk about the weather—to dissect the quality of the light, the grain of the clouds, the trees in Central Park. He hadn't paid much attention. In the mornings, she used to want to tell him her dreams. He had teased her about the boringness of weather; he, who never remembered what he dreamt, had faked yawns when she tried to tell him her dreams. He would forfeit the remaining days of his life to have her back in his lap, stuttering and backtracking and trailing off, in her efforts to recount her sleeping mind's psychomachy.

He heard Gwen and Mimi laughing in the kitchen; he heard Gwen chatter on the telephone to her friends. All he knew now about his wife's travails at work, her opinion of Starr's investigation of President Clinton, even her plans for the summer, was what he managed to eavesdrop.

Their own commerce had been reduced to a clipped surly apportioning of chores. She would ask him in the morning, Was he going to be home at five, as Betty had a doctor's appointment, and he would say he didn't know. (Oh yeah? Where *might* he be? Sitting in the Utopia, reading *Time Out*?) You mean, so he couldn't bestir himself to be there to let Betty off work? Evidently not. Well, in that case, she would try to leave the office early. If he *was* going out, would he please try to remember to buy some garbage bags. Get a lot, she continued, so *I* don't have to go to the store in a week. Get the heavy-duty ones, get a hundred, if you could.

With that loving injunction, she was out the door. Leaving Gideon trapped in the apartment—God, he hated the apartment!—with these alien females: this Mimi, this Betty. Even his daughter, dressed in Polly Pocket sneakers and a Beauty and the Beast sun hat, was becoming a stranger to him, a vessel of enemy values.

He had discovered by chance that Betty had been taking Bella to Catholic mass, and although he had asked Gwen to tell her not to, he suspected that she continued to do so, with Gwen's allowance. That was how amoral Gwen was at heart—she believed in *nothing*. The reason Gwen let Bella be taken to Catholic mass, Gideon was convinced, was that she knew that he had begun going to shul again. If Gwen had conceieved a passionate desire to take their daughter to St. John the Tightass, Gideon would have been—well, livid, but he could at least respect it. But to allow the nanny to indoctrinate the child in a religion that was neither of theirs, well, that was truly cynical. Let her be sacrificed to Moloch, why don't you, Gwen?

He was getting the feeling about Bella that a mother bird gets after a human has touched her nest.

And what you don't know, Gwen, you who obsess about garbage bags to avoid your real problems, is that Gideon too is going to spend his morning obsessing about garbage bags. Wondering why his wife has asked him to buy so crazily many garbage bags, wondering who in the world could need a hundred garbage bags, and finding the chilling answer. She wants him to buy enough garbage bags to tide her over *after he has left*. Have you worked out my eviction day, my lovely? If I happened to find your Filofax, would I see the fateful jubilee rubricated: Gideon moves out. But what if Gideon doesn't move out, my honey, what if I would prefer not to? After all, it wasn't my idea to move in. Do you ever think of this, dear, how you pleaded and manipulated and connived to overcome my instinct of self-preservation, my sense of duty, how you swore you'd love me forever if only I left Dina and Ethan. You said, Come live with me, you're all I've ever wanted, I'll love you till the day I die.

Now a bare two and a half years later, you are in such a tearing mad rush to be shut of me you're like the sailor in the lifeboat chopping off the fingers of the drowning man. The man's your husband, honey, he's the father of your child. Have you no shame? *I* don't. I will cling, I will cling. You can cut off my fingers and I will still hang on with the stumps of my hands. A changeable woman shouldn't ask home a squatter.

If you want your freedom (what does it mean when your wife speaks of freedom? Freedom to fornicate? Freedom to destroy someone new's peace of mind? Freedom to reprogram your child, to unhinge her sturdy mind, to make her the baby-sitter's Catholic foundling? Freedom to leave your husband homeless?), *you* get out. But the child stays with me. I don't consider it a necessary part of her holistic development to walk in on her mama getting butt-fucked by strange men.

5

HE REMEMBERED their early days. When he saw Bella sitting on her mother's lap, feeding Gwen tidbits, giggling throatily while Gwen pretended to hijack her daughter's spoonful of peas.

He would mutter, jealous, "Why don't you ever put her in the high chair? This way, she just makes a mess over both of you." Thinking, Baby, where you are, that's where I once was. Where I am now, that's where you too one day will be. Disenthroned, because where you think she sees you, she sees only herself: wonder-mother. When she persuades you—against your reason, your sanity, your own life's experience—that you're the sun, moon, stars, her eternal all-beloved godling? It's all about HER. You don't exist. It's all about her giving you yourself just so she has the power to take it away again.

But chuckling brown baby girl doesn't yet know the score. Deluded poppet believes she really *is* the sun and the moon. One day, soon or not so soon, her mama is going to take her love away, and then Bella will discover that without that love, she's nothing. A tear-drenched cringing ashamed wad of nothing.

Chapter Seven

I

A SUNDAY AFTERNOON HEAVINESS.

Bella, who's fallen asleep beside her, rises from their joint doze much too soon and much too perky. Gwen tries to sit up, but feels as if she's moving through an element thick as water. It's a queasy torpor she remembers too well.

"Bear? Will you give me a moment?" The child, astride her mother, tries to pry open Gwen's eyelids.

"Bear-pie? Will you give me a minute to wake up?"

"Nah! Nah! Nah!" shouts the child, furious. Unable to bear the exclusion implied by her mother's unconsciousness. Tugging an arm. "Up! Up! UUUUUUUhhhhhPPPPP!!!!"

Gwen makes it to the bathroom sink just in time. Blugghhhhhhhh. And . . . panic. Good God, what day of the month was it? And last month it was the . . . twelfth? The fifteenth? When had she and Gid . . . ? Was it . . . ? Thinking over their last act of nonlove, when he had come into the bathroom—already with a hard-on like a policeman's billy club—and grabbed her without a word, it seemed to her imbecile that a congress so stony, so strangled, so gratingly devoid of tenderness or an intended future, might have borne fruit, might hock them to . . . Good God, let it not be true. When she thought of people—adoring anchored couples, hungering for a baby of their own, who, after years of barren "trying," were now enrolled in in vitro clinics, or wait-listed for Chinese foundlings . . . Telling her traitor-body, Bleed.

2

FOR DAYS she kept it to herself, mind slamming from wall to wall. Mind slamming. What to do.

Slamming from one intolerable course of action, of inaction, to another. There was . . . she was increasingly certain, although she was too chicken, too paralyzed to get a pregnancy test . . . there was a protobaby in her body. Already it had a head and tail. It was growing. If she didn't do something about it, it would be too late. And she would be unable to act.

The fetus (that's what you called it when you were considering abortion), the baby (that's what you called it when you were considering birth) was forcing a decision on her. It demanded, Do you believe in your marriage, do you believe you and this man have a future together. Its existence was a horrible mistake; its survival would be a renewal of vows. And she didn't. So she must act quickly, without fudging. You couldn't murder a man's child and then decide you wanted after all to live with him and possibly make another. Conversely, you couldn't bring a baby into the world whom you'd willfully be depriving of a father.

Her now two-weeks-late period was running them out of time. She woke in the middle of the night, and wanted to jump out of her skin. She felt intolerably invaded, seized by the compulsion to expel the baby from her stomach, the man from her house. Veering, slamming. Slamming from wall to wall. Back and forth, back and forth. Battering against impossibles. Thinking, I'll leave him and have the baby. If we divorce, it'll be better for Bella if there's two of them. *Wanting* the baby, her mad body wanting it. Thinking, I don't have to tell him, I can just take Bella away and have the baby. Thinking, I couldn't: it's his, too. Then not thinking. Waking in the night, in the morning suffused by a heavy dread whose cause she could not for a moment identify, then remembering . . .

One morning Gideon walked in on her, doubled over the john.

"So it's true," he said.

3

SHE COMES OUT in the middle of the night. Again, he is sitting on the balcony. Again, he is very drunk. He looks at her and he screams, "What is to become of me?"

She won't meet his stare.

He rises to his feet. "You want me to jump? You want me to jump, to save your conscience? So you can tell Bella her daddy was schizo? You want me to jump? Is that what you are silently commanding me, day in, day out, do I read you right, am I being very obtuse, or are you telling me, Don't hang around, don't wimp out . . . just . . . jump. And what would you do, if I jumped, would you keep the kid or would you flush it? Is that what you're hoping for, a twofer?"

He has clambered up onto the railing of the balcony, and is crouched, holding on to her orange tree for balance. Then he raises himself, precarious. Wobbling on the edge, still hanging on to a skinny branch. Throwing out an arm for balance. He glares down at her—a look of wild hate.

If he goes, the tree goes with him. If the branch breaks, he's dead.

"If I promise to do the decent thing and jump, will you promise you won't murder my baby? But you're not exactly a promise-keeper, are you?"

He is balanced upright on the railing now. The metal ledge is perhaps six inches wide. From the Mystical Circus, he is experienced at walking a balance beam. But now he is tottering.

She holds out a hand to help him down. He draws back, still glaring. Loses his balance. Backyards below. Fencing. Concrete pavement. Metal walkways. Six stories below. Concrete. Then leaps. And lands, catlike. On the balcony.

He glares at her, panting, trying to catch his breath. Breathe, he used to tell her. Breathe. Breathe/don't breathe/hold your breath/die.

Her heart is racing.

His heart is racing.

"What is to become of me?" he repeats. "Just tell me that. *What am I to do with this fucking love?*"

She doesn't answer.

4

NEW YORK THE INEXORABLE.

Gideon awoke shrieking, clutching strangulation-tight Gwen's resistant body. Inched back, sullen but still shaking, to his (soon-to-be-ex) side of the bed. What was it? A nightmare about . . . burnt babies . . . about stoking up a fire in a cold country house that was supposedly Constance's parents' house, and finding . . . in the hearth, a mound of babies' skeletons. White ashes. A mound of baby-fine hair. Some editorial consciousness in him interjecting. But they don't *cremate* unborn fetuses . . . iyyyiiiyiiii.

That evening, Ari and his fiancée had come over to dinner—a farce, their entertaining, but Gwen for her own impenetrable reasons of social vanity would not spare him this last humiliation—Ari and his fiancée were getting married in the fall, so G&G were supposed to dust off the wedding china and pose as a simulacrum of family bliss.

Gideon had drunk a tall glass of Jack Daniel's, barely watered, while putting Bella to bed, and when he came out, they were hovering around the dinner table, waiting for him.

Everybody smiling, expectant.

"Is she asleep?" asked Gwen.

He leaned over, toward Ari and Patti. "Did Gwen tell you she's pregnant?"

Man, you have to take your satisfactions where you can. A shot of pure meanness to be derived from the exquisite discomfort of his wife's double-take—she, who got her Ph.D. in treason.

Ari, God bless him, beamed in genuine delight.

"You're having a baby, Gwen, mazel tov," spreading wide-embracing arms. "When's it due?"

But Gwen was looking at her plate. "This is your show, Gideon, I don't even . . ."

"Yeah, when?" echoed Gideon. "When, Gwen?"

"When what?" she muttered.

"When are you aborting it, Gwen? You made a date yet or you want to draw it out to a really cool *late*-term abortion? Incidentally, Ari, it's not your kid, is it, because I don't honestly see how it can be mine."

Horror. Horror in the silence. Horror in the stupid malignity of Gideon's bearded grin. Horror in Ari's decent confusion. He is staring down at the table, but when he finally raises his face, Gideon sees, no, he's not confused: he's enraged. All of a sudden you know this is a kid with a temper. He may have gone to Ethical Culture, he may give his fiancée shiatsu massages and wear an apron when he cooks, but there are two fists on his lap that are just itching to bloody Gideon's nose. Patti knows this about her intended, too: she rises. "Ari, let's just go. Listen," she says. "I don't even *know* you guys. I don't know what you're playing at, but I feel like this is something you should be working out on your own . . ."

Impressive, how quick she grabbed their his-and-her briefcases and hustled her boyfriend out of the house, before this unexpectedly pugnacious New Man could haul back and slug his host. Maybe that's what Gideon needed, at this point, to get decked by a boy half his height.

Maybe Gideon hadn't been so far off the mark, after all. Maybe Ari was sweet on Gwen. Maybe Gwen was sweet on Ari.

And there was the tajine on the table, the plates, the water glasses untouched. Only a couple of white damask napkins scattered. He and Gwen alone, alone at last, their sleeping child—their first contraceptive fuck-up—next door.

So this was his payback for the mean trick: a head full of burnt babies, of baby ash.

He was no King David, he. He was barely even a dirty rascal.

He put a hand on her sleeping shoulder.

"Gwen?"

Even in her sleep, she shuddered free of him.

"Gwen? Gwen?"

Now he was sobbing.

"Gwen?"

She squinted back over her shoulder.

"WHAT!?"

"Gwen? I'm scared, Gwen, I don't want you to leave me, I don't want you to take Bella away, for God's sake, don't leave me!" He was sobbing, sobbing, sobbing, beard wet with tears.

She looked at him and she allowed him to bury his wet face in her arms. She held him, saying nothing, but she held him nonetheless, and eventually he felt her body soften and yield. He didn't dare speak, didn't dare say, Please let's stay together, let's have this child who will be the fruit of our reconciliation, whose conception in this haunted time of war is a sign from God, but he felt forgiveness in her arms and shoulders and legs and breast.

Dear heart, let's bury this bitter pointless enmity, when the truth is we love each other madly . . .

Chapter Eight

I

THEIR LAST GOOD DAY TOGETHER. (Not that Gideon accepts the notion that they will ever have "good days" apart.)

Sunday in late June.

The Siege of Paris is being performed by the Piccolo Teatro, which has been brought over, as part of an Italian arts festival at NYU, along with Nanni Moretti movies and cooking classes.

Has Gideon ever told you, Gwen, how much he loves Sicilian marionettes? The first time, aged nineteen, he sat on a wooden floor in the bombed-out Old City of Palermo and watched one of these old-fashioned adventures of Charlemagne's knights battling the Saracens, he felt drunk with pride.

It was a sense of revealed kinship, a This-is-the-world-and-this-is-where-I-belong that was comparable to what Gwen at the same age felt sitting around a Moscow kitchen table sharing a bottle of vodka with three men who'd lost their health and teeth and any hopes of old age in Magadan.

At heart, Gideon is an aesthete: he would trade the dictatorship of the proletariat any day for a prancing knight in gilded armor. These Sicilian plays—plundered from *Orlando Furioso,* mostly, and patched together for saints' days—are just plain beautiful: the ocher-and-lavender backdrops of fountains and palaces are beautiful; the mustachioed boy knights in glittery armor are beautiful; the devils and sorceresses even more so. There's no politics in it, no hectoring: it's sheer bravura, sheer charm. And he loves it.

Today is no different. The Piccolo Teatro is a family business: father, mother, son, and daughter, all of whom Gideon has known not well but for years.

The Ragusas have taken an old story about a virtuous knight taking shelter in the castle of a sorcerer who tries to kill him in his sleep. It's a nothing little fairy tale cobbled together (and mangled) from diverse legends, but there is a wizard and a devil and a sorceress-princess, and to hear the children's roars and shrieks, to see the wonder-terror-glee on their faces as they dive into their mothers' laps to hide from the wizard and then leap up dolphinlike to peek, and watch Bella, who has gone solemn with mystery—is to be reminded why Gideon and the Ragusas and Jerome and Fran and Annie all keep banging away at this archaic and unremunerative line of work.

When the curtain comes down, Bella whispers, "Muh?" and Gwen, smiling, seconds, "More?"

Gideon hoists Bella onto his shoulders and leads Gwen by the hand backstage. Gideon and the Ragusas hug and kiss; they talk idiot Italian, idiot English; Tonino and Anna and their father make much of Bella, who goes coy and tries to burrow herself between her mother's boobs; Tonino pulls out photographs of *his* two daughters. Gideon makes a plan to meet the Ragusas tomorrow for lunch: he will pick them up at the NYU apartment where they are staying.

For an hour, showing Bella and Gwen this thing he loves, Gideon forgets what his wife is doing to them.

Even Gwen is touched by his high spirits. Listening to Gideon's lavishly ungrammatical Italian, watching him flail his arms in exuberant mime, she gets a flash both of why she once loved him and of why they cannot be parents together.

2

THE NEXT MORNING, Gwen lay in.

It was Gideon who got up when Bella at six climbed into their bed. He changed the child's diaper and brushed her teeth and dressed her and took her out to breakfast at the Utopia so that Gwen, in her early pregnancy torpor, could go back to sleep.

When she next awoke, it was ten o'clock, and she felt rested. She fixed herself coffee, cast an eye over the newspaper, watered the plants on the balcony, decided to put in a wash.

She emptied the laundry hamper in the bathroom, which they rarely used because its metal lid stuck. There was a pair of underpants in it she didn't recognize. They were little-girlish underpants, but in a woman's size, white nylon with pink-and-blue rosebuds. They were badly stained in the crotch. She took them out of the hamper and looked at them. Then she sat down on the bed.

3

YES, HE HAD. Yes, he was. For how long? Oh, a while. What did they do? He met her for a drink, he took her out to dinner. Places Gwen didn't know, places near the girl's apartment. So they could hurry home and—yes. So he was dating? And they'd done it. That's what people did, when they'd been dating awhile, right—they had sex. So they'd done it. Yes. Where? No, he—where? Here? Yes. In this apartment? Yes. In our bed? Yes, in our bed, and . . . all over. In his workshop? Yes.

And who was she? Was she the woman who had called up one evening to speak to him but didn't want to leave a message?

And were there others?

He has never imagined her finding out. He's been so angry at her that he's felt entirely justified in fucking Emma. All the wrong is on her side: it's she who has forced him to stray.

Still, her reaction disquiets him. Instead of yelling, she goes pale. As soon as she's asked her questions and he's answered, she excuses herself, politely. Locks herself in the bathroom and comes out dressed, except she's buttoned the buttons wrong.

Gideon is sitting on the bed. He hasn't moved. He watches her searching through her drawers for something she's unable to find. She gives up, she goes out into the living room, then dives back into the bathroom, a roar of taps.

She comes out, whiter still.

"Are we done?" she asks. "Have we got anything more to discuss?"

"No," he says.

Gideon watches his wife get ready for work.

She is wearing a gray linen sailor dress, and he thinks to himself, with a surge of sympathy, No, you shouldn't wear that beautiful dress because you will never want to wear it again. Just as she will never be able to wear the orange-and-purple evening dress that caused him such pain, or the green crocodile shoes that were his pickup bait in long-ago Novosibirsk. He is wreaking havoc on her wardrobe: he has already seen with a certain remorse how her love for clothes has deserted her.

She is a splendid woman. He has almost forgotten how splendid she is: tall as a man, broad-shouldered, erect, with a nose like a ship's prow, and large heavy-lidded Minerva eyes that gaze so gravely at you.

Now that she is battered, humbled by early pregnancy, she is almost more beautiful to him than in their beginning. He looks at her and thinks, She will age well. She will be a lean straight-backed old woman, and the good bones of her face, her beaky nose, will show through. She won't go spongy in her old age, she will be proud as a mountain peak.

But unfortunately, at a fateful moment, he has forgotten to take her pride into account. That unholy pride, the first thing he'd spotted, across the Siberian market. Haughty Michal, who never shares a bed with King David after she's seen him dancing bare-assed before serving girls. Proud woman, who refuses to accept that God, the preeminent antinomian, loves two-faced scoundrels, raucous self-degradation. Gwen's pride means Gideon's fall. Gideon can bare his ass to all the serving girls he pleases, but he won't be there to see Gwen's upright old age.

Meanwhile, his wife (who is all that he loves in the world) is clumsied, confused. Greenish-white-faced, she's losing things—Filofax, keys—and then forgetting what she's looking for. He watches her pick up a tiny red sweatshirt of Bella's and try to fold it, smoothing the wrinkles, rubbing at a spot.

He watches her get down on her hands and knees in search of the partner to a striped Bella sock. She goes next door to put away the clothes in Bella's drawer, and comes back still carrying the lone sock, which she then stuffs into her dress pocket. An amulet, he wonders, or absentmindedness?

She is so clumsy it's like watching somebody who's had a stroke learn to move. His defiant sense of vindication dissolves into pity for her—this woman who is pregnant, and does not know what to do.

Gideon, by contrast, knows exactly what to do. Although the thrill of a new romance has been deliciously restorative, still he understands that he's got to stop seeing this Emma, who is not cut out for the part of mistress, who has no understanding whatsoever of the basic rules of dating married men.

This is his proposition: he will give up the girl, and they will put their bitterness behind them and start again. He says it. He says, "I've just about ended it already. I'm not going to see her anymore."

She answers, "I don't care what you do. So long as you leave. I'd like you to leave now, as soon as possible." She glances at her watch again, as if she really thinks he might be out of there by noon. "You can keep on seeing the woman, you can marry the woman, you can do whatever you like. But I expect you to leave."

4

TOO EASY, Gideon, did you have to make it easy for her? Dumb dick, that's what they do to you, they are so fucking obvious. You long to be a patient devious person, but the panting peeing wriggly little puppy between your legs always goes and gives the game away. Did you ever hear of a subtle dick, a dick with a long-term strategy, that thought beyond its next square meal, its any-port-in-a-storm urgencies?

He seizes her wristwatch to see what time it is and she flinches away. Late.

"I don't know about that," he says. "Look, I gotta go meet the Ragusas now, we'll talk about it later, okay?"

Somehow at this crucial point he's misfiring.

Chapter Nine

I

WHEN SHE GOT TO WORK, it was lunchtime. The office was empty except for Trish and Carole, who were sitting in the conference room eating sandwiches in tinfoil.

Gwen—catching sight of ridged pickle, yellow mustard—ducked into the bathroom, where she puked up once more the yellow bile of *him*. Washed harshly, cold water and institutional liquid soap. Her face in the mirror: a frightened child's face, with wrinkles. You've learned nothing, she told herself. You are as ignorant of the world as your own mother, and such ignorance is not touching, it's an abomination against nature, which gave us the wits to understand ourselves, if we only would.

"Hey Trish?" She was by habit (perhaps in reaction to her father's coercive overfamiliarity as boss) solicitous of the clerical staff, conscious that everybody else's lives were shittier than hers. Today she mistrusted her own courtesies, which reeked of condescension.

"Yeah?"

"I have to finish something on a tight deadline. Is there anywhere I can hole up?"

"Why don't you go into Kalman's office?"

Kalman was in Budapest.

"Do you mind taking my calls? Even if somebody says it's an emergency."

Kalman's office, like its owner, was small and stuffy. Gwen opened the window, shut the door, and put her head on the desk, like a child at school not feeling well. She remembered the clunky wooden desks at Dalton, their yellow varnished lids scored thick in vows and curses, "Down with math!" "Emily sucks!" How solid, how consoling the desk felt against her cheek as she'd taken a breather from the British Corn Laws. Rainy winter afternoons—French class, with its thumbtacked posters of Loire châteaux and the Roman amphitheater at Nîmes—when the radiators clicked and hissed, and the room stank of wet wool, and the great clock's hands stopped moving. When the days before summer vacation, the years before adulthood, seemed slave-long, slow-drawled eternity. Soon Gwen's daughter would be school-age, and she'd need a firmer backing to her life than this parental flimflam of cheating and undermining, in order to go out into the world each morning hardy, unencumbered.

Kalman's desk was beige Formica, metallic to the touch. Nobody had ever carved her boxy imprecations into its synthetic finish.

Gwen raised her head and looked out the window. White sky of early summer heat wave. Smoggy, unavailing. Heat makes you sicker. Dumb bunny, getting pregnant in June. Looked north, at the blue-and-white crosstown bus charging Fifth Avenue, at the men selling Russian dolls on blankets by the Metropolitan Museum; west, into Central Park. Gwen could see the beginning of the path that led down, under the tunnel and up a small slope and down again to Alice in Wonderland, where she had first laid eyes on the nameless one. Who had tupped another woman in Gwen's bed. Slipped his rearing red-brownness between another's portals.

Had she been wet? Had he excited her, teased her, led her on, gotten her strung up tight as a bowstring, had he fingered her, sucked her, eaten her, till she begged for it? Did she realize, as Gideon unveiled himself, The man has a beautiful cock. A funny-looking face, but an exquisite cock, that knew moreover how to move in a woman's body. Did she too know how to move, Gwen's successor? (Gwen having been given to understand by Gideon that, in her own case, enthusiasm had to substitute for a certain native adroitness.) Had he let out that same dying cry as he junked inside her? Had he fucked her three times the first night in his laughing pride?

Did she too—the twinkie, Gwen's replacement, twenty-three, he had told her, as if gloating, a *kid*—marvel and feel cured, somehow, by the good yeasty smell of his spunk, clean as sourdough, as its viscousness trickled yellow down her thigh . . .

What did it mean, when you were twenty-three, to sleep in a married man's bed? Anything? What if she got pregnant, too, or was she a twenty-three-year-old who knew the ropes? Did this woman even *like* Gideon, Gwen wondered.

Now that they were truly finished, now that there was nothing left but to make him go, she could begin to mourn a little the spread and conjugated attributes of his perjured trueness. Of their befouled ex-love.

Her stomach was seizing up again, the taste of bile resurging. She wanted (what else did she want these days?) to go to sleep. She wanted not to be so dull, so frightened. She remembered the long pale ears of a skin doctor she had consulted as a teenager for her eczema. She remembered the frayed *Yankee* magazines in Dr. Whittaker's Newburyport office; she remembered the name of the receptionist, which was Julie. Something inherited from her father, the compulsion, half feudal, half ingratiating, to remember other people's secretaries and doormen's names, to play Sugar Plum Fairy to the uniformed world. She could remember the telephone number of her old accountant, the genealogies of Aunt Sue's long-dead dogs. She thought of eating oysters the first time with Christopher one Easter in Brittany. Too proud to admit she was sickened by the idea of raw mollusks, quailing, as she tried to pry loose the slippery gray lace of their fluid flesh. Poor creatures, whose sole attribute was to cling—how wanton it had seemed to rip them living from their homes. How they shrank from exposure, which was death. The adolescent's permanent dilemma—between doing what appalls you and looking like a jerk. She had swallowed them—half a dozen—and excused herself. She had *never* had a mite of courage.

Interrupting these random reminiscences, like a news bulletin on a reel of digital ticker tape, her dismal discovery. GIDEON SLEEPS WITH OTHER WOMAN. SENATE DEFEATS $560 BILLION TOBACCO BILL; DOW JONES SURGES 150 POINTS.

She couldn't even work out the basic chronology. Did this mean Gideon had slept with Gwen and her replacement simultaneously? When he had surprised her in the bathroom, was he leftover excited? Excited by Gwen's unknowing humiliation? (Had he thought about his wife's being unprotected as he'd stabbed at her from behind, a sore scrabbling fuck, the *worst* in fact of their entire career? What kind of changeling could spring from such harsh soil?)

She tried to think of impressive places she had been, of Garni, a Roman temple in Armenia carved from ocher-purple stone. Behind the temple was a bush covered in rags that her friend Sarkis had explained were handkerchiefs tied by women praying to have babies. A cultic throwback that under Soviet rule amounted to political subversion. Did your mama tie handkerchiefs to get you, Gwen had asked, half teasing. My father sacrificed a ram when I was born, answered long-lashed Sarkis, shy with pride. Back then, wanting to have a child had seemed to Gwen as alien a compulsion as tying rags to bushes. (Now she is crying, because, God help her, she feels this baby in her, feels this baby in her, feels the minor turbulences, its small churning wake, and *wants* it, her bowels, her womb, her heart yearn for it.) She remembered standing on the steps of the temple staring at the bush, and smoking. When she visited Garni—that first year in Russia—she smoked. She smoked cheap Russian cigarettes, cheap Bulgarian cigarettes, cheap North Korean cigarettes. She had started smoking because it was a good way to meet strangers. Maybe it was time to take up cigarettes again.

Dear God. For now she had to turn her mind—bend it, twist it—from the Armenian peasant women knotting strips of flowered head scarf, from Sarkis's father (a science teacher!) slitting the curly ram's throat in thanks for his lusty son, to her own despicable predicament. Of course, she needed to call back the clinic she'd been recommended—not by Dr. Landesmann, but by her previous gynecologist, from before her marriage—and see if the Wednesday slot was still available.

An abortion. What did it entail? She knew nothing. As a teenager, a college student, she had been the only person of her acquaintance who had never got knocked up. She had remained stolidly chaste throughout boarding school, throughout a year in Russia. (Throughout several nights in Algis's cold basement cot.) And had given up the equivocal goods, finally, in a cabin of the Ocean Breeze Motel, to Maddock's friend Byron Beale—having decided she meant to do it, and then got drunk enough to see it through.

Byron, a hollow-cheeked starveling, half Indian, with one walleye, who already had a three-year-old son, had played her like a snake charmer, and left her bewildered, bowlegged, but strangely delighted.

Why? Why was she so late, so clumsy?

Why, you dumb fuck? Don't you know by now?

Because she'd lived with her mother after her father left, that's why. Which was like living in a train wreck, among lumps of flesh, splintered glass, crumpled metal. (Which also is why she can never feelingly hate Hal.) Because she had seen what happened when men and women came together. Because she didn't want to leave any—what did smarmy Francis Bacon call them?—any "hostages to fortune." Because she was so damned determined never to be left.

I don't know what to expect, she thought. (Desolation. A cosmic emptiness, of your own wicked making. For to kill a baby after having borne one was an altogether darker business: you *knew* what you were killing . . .) Did you walk out of it whole, or would she need a couple of days off work? Would she be able to take care of Bella by herself?

I'll ask Betty to sleep over, she decided, say I've got the flu. People do get the flu. Especially people whose husbands are moving out do tend to be in not so florid health. Oh *fuck.*

She would flush the fetus, day after tomorrow, and Gideon would be gone by the end of the week. Then she would start smoking again. She would go to one of those old-fashioned tobacconists on Sixth Avenue, where you could buy anything, Lucky Strikes, Gitanes. This is how she would spend her evenings, after Gideon was gone, after Bella was asleep, sitting on the balcony, smoking and reading.

Mesrop, she said aloud. Mesrop. She was thinking of Garni again, of her June in Yerevan—not a city, but a roasted nut, wrote Mandelstam—reading a yellowed grammar book she'd picked up in the market, trying to commit to memory an alphabet cursive to the point of scoliosis. Mesrop was the name of the priest who, according to legend, had brought Armenia its alphabet (he had two more in his pack: one for the Circassian Albanians, and one for Georgia—Medea's proud nephews), along with Orthodox Christianity.

An alphabet was a handsome present: an abacus on which to string your prayers and purchases. This, too, was what the Phoenicians had done, a thousand years earlier: trawled the Mediterranean, the Atlantic even, hawking alphabets, olive oil, spices, notions (among them the extraterritorial mono-God). Were these Semitic merchants and priests then the software programmers of Asia Minor: was the *aleph-bet-gimel* no more sacred, God-laden a cargo than Windows?

Her brain was an arsenal of useless information, she could rearrange its stockpiles infinitely. She would have the abortion, she would raise her daughter. Forget she ever met the man (who had turned the world ashen). She would blot out the mistake of him; she would take other lovers, or none. Bring up her daughter unsapped by his wheedling hypocrisies. She would sleep alone, and not let anyone touch what he had touched.

And once Martin got better (or worse) she could leave. Move back to Russia with Bella, if she liked. Rent out her New York condo for forty-five hundred a month, ask Mikhail Becker to find her a nice apartment in Moscow. Tell Lavrinsky, I'm going to run your Russian offices from Russia for a change. (Or not.) She could see their Moscow life: her and Jamila taking their daughters to the baths. A bosomy Azeri to look after Bella, and in a couple of years, school. Bella would learn Cyrillic letters before Latin! And Gwen, too, could accumulate new languages. She would learn Armenian, learn Georgian, which were blocks of the Caucaso-Iranian language group. Two new trophy alphabets. More word-candy to wolf, to hoard, in order to flush out the acrid nagging memory of Clown Wolkowitz and his paranoid-sanctimonious harangues—the adulterer hiding behind his starchy-new prayer shawl. No more covert bullying, no more trying to remake her, no more sickly overwatchfulness of Bella.

Time was opening up before her: not a screaming wilderness, but purposeful. She would have free time now, without a husband. Long days, serene spacious nights. Her daughter, to herself. (And yet something in her unable still to call the clinic. Unable.)

2

"WHAT'S HER NAME?" Gwen inquires, glacially polite. Having volunteered, once she's back on her feet, to take Bella away for a few days until he's packed up and gone. (Gone where?)

Gideon, who is only just beginning to plumb the extent of his predicament, is panicked. He *hates* Emma now that he realizes what she's brought down on him, hates her as if she were the paid agent of a sting operation, he is filled with a hysterical revulsion. He cannot bring himself to say her name. Why does Gwen want to know?

"Rogan," he mutters, finally. "Emma Rogan."

"Ro-gaine?" repeats Gwen, incredulous. "Miss *Rogaine*? So she's going to make your hair grow back, is that it?"

"I thought you wanted me to."

She cannot grasp what he means.

"I thought you wanted me to leave you in peace, just go away and take care of that side of things for myself . . ."

3

FOR THE CRUELEST part is that she who once was a Boadicea, a Pol Pot of sexual jealousy, does not *really* mind his having cheated. She's said it herself: his having fucked another woman is just a "symptom" of their general bankruptcy. Oh, her damnable pride minds, her legalistic pedantry objects to this infraction of the conjugal contract, but her cunt does not rage, does not weep, turn to salt or stone or pus at the stinking-to-high-heaven treason of it. Her cunt is silent. If it still talks, it doesn't talk to him. A man's inactive member is a despicable thing: a shrivelled, rank, dangling dishrag, a bit of useless hose; a woman's, unused, doesn't shame her. It is sealed. Secret. Unknowable. It's hers, inviolate.

4

GWEN IS LOCKED TIGHT. She will not talk. She expresses no mitigating grief.

She is acting as people do when there's something terribly violent they must do, against others' wills: she's got a tunnel-vision compulsion to rid herself of Gideon and his baby fast, and beyond that, nothing. The effort these twin expulsions require leaves no room for reason. Otherwise, she's performing her job and household chores admirably, coming home with groceries, opening her mail, attending to their daughter, as if *nothing has happened*, as if *nothing is about to happen*.

Gideon watches his wife, who, pretending to be a roaring lion, is now on all fours, pursuing Bella. But Bella, though shrieking with terri-fied excitement, is still too much a baby to be able to conceive of so counterintuitive an act as running *away* from one's mother: When a growling Gwen tries to chase her, Bella, instead of fleeing, runs *to* the lion and clings to it.

Gideon watches his wife, who has now rolled over on her back on the floor, pretending to be a friendly lion, while Bella bounces on her stomach, and thinks, Something is not connecting.

5

ANOTHER RECOVERY ROOM.

And voices. Chatter. Laughter.

The voices are talking about parties, and talking about boys, and talking about whose house they're going to that night.

These voices are not the doctors' voices.

She has surfaced to consciousness in a room full of white-cloth tables, on which other women are lying. They are lying on their backs, scattered, and everybody is surfacing to consciousness at different moments, because they have all had the same—procedure, you call it.

They are women who were pregnant who did not want their babies. Who are now no longer pregnant. A tall Dispoz-All filled with babies?

But the other women—her fellow patients, Gwen sees—are *girls*. There are two friends—who, strangely, must have found themselves pregnant simultaneously and gone for an abortion together, as you might go for a facial.

They are young black girls, loud, merry—fourteen-, fifteen-year-old girls—who have got knocked up, probably, by fellow fifteen-year-olds. They do not bear the sinful knowledge that Gwen bears: they have no idea yet what it might mean instead to carry a baby to term, to birth your baby, to suckle your baby, and once they've grown up and had children of their own, Gwen feels sure, they will never dream of aborting one.

A rip of pain. More pain, in spasms.

All she wants in the world is to have her own living girl in her arms, her rosy-brown bear cub, wriggling safe in her arms.

6

"I'M SORRY," says Gideon.

"I'm sorry, too," she says. They both know it's truly over. She will not let Bella out of her sight, she is going to hold her tight until Gideon and his cardboard boxes are out the door.

And now Gideon, pale, says, defeated, "I'll do whatever you say."
His anger is crushed.

He is going to move into his workshop in La Merced, he has everything he needs there—a mini-fridge, a gas hob. (Gwen offers the sofa bed, but he refuses, with the faintest curl of scorn. She will need it for her "second husband," as he calls Betty: the one permanently consigned to sleeping in the study. She offers him money, but again he refuses; he has borrowed money from Sancho. If he needs more, he will sell his tools. She even offers him her computer so he can stay on-line. Nice try, Gwen.)

Such a short time ago, Gideon borrowed Sancho's van to move his boxes into Gwen's apartment, and now he's borrowing Sancho's van to move them back out. Only this time it's not Dina and Ethan, it's his own flesh and blood that he's being torn away from, and as for what he will do about living without his daughter, that doesn't bear thinking of.

This time he has no work, no colleagues, no theater, only airless space, and imminent eviction.

He will surely kill himself, one night, in the big empty school with the mice and the bats, but if he doesn't kill himself he will . . . live . . .

Chapter Ten

I

THE LAST DAY THEY LIVED TOGETHER. A Saturday in late July. A breezy day, unseasonably brisk, when the high summer skies were the guileless blue-swirled-with-white of marbles. Newly washed, limitless, innocent and bold. They went out to the park early, while the dew still gleamed in the grassy hollows, the three of them, Mary, Joseph, and infant Jesus pushing her own Maclaren stroller. Mary and Joseph's bodies racked, their brains poisoned-fried from the previous night's all-nighter.

This was their circular journey, from sleepless nights of love to sleepless nights of recrimination, tears, yells, loathing, pleas. The sometimes furtive, sometimes sadistic ripping apart of what had been so tightly joined for eternity and a day. You could see the tic of nervous fatigue in the corner of Joseph's bloodshot eye, new scowl-wrinkles of defensive grief scoring Mary's brow. And Jesus? Oblivious. Crowing, yodelling, impishly triumphant, as if her parents' writhing contorted self-destruction made more room, more love for her.

They wandered eastward, in their Flight from Egypt, keeping time with baby Jesus's divagations, her hariscupatory reading of twigs and bottle tops and fragments of burst balloon; they alighted in a glade of empty playground, and there Gideon curled up on a bench, just as in Gwen's first sighting of the man-tramp who would be her mortal enemy, her loving jailer. And so thoroughly beaten was he that he fell asleep. Lay down and slept, remembering Zion.

Did you dream, Joseph? Did you dream of stars bowing down to you, did you dream of sheaves of wheat and the fat and lean cows? His estranged wife watched him as he slept, wondering what he could dream of. Wondering did he find a tiny glade of green, a moment's reprieve. If God brought dreams, he did. Her own brain a searing desert: oh you could not touch it; it was too too hot.

She closed her eyes and entered deep within the dry earth of herself. She thought about the sacking of cities, about the rebirth of rivers, about the dissolution of bones in earth, she thought about the tomb of the Scythian princess whose excavation Lavrinsky had helped fund. Buried with her horses and chariot and jewelry and servants in a surrounding semicircle. Are you that Scythian, Gwen? Do you want your horses and serving maids killed with you? She opened her eyes and there was Gideon, lying open-eyed. His eyes immense and dark-lidded. His lips parched, and through the parched lips, croaking words.

"Who's going to look after you two when I'm gone?"

She turned her head away.

Now Bella, holding arms aloft to a swing, summoned her daddy, imperious. Gideon uncoiled his long body (which still *moved* Gwen, months after she'd come to hate all it housed) and ambled over to his daughter. Gwen sat in the speckled sun and she watched the man push the child on her swing—the spectator of a life that was hers for only a moment longer. If anybody saw Gwen, he would think her a fond mother on the point of urging a sun hat or a sip of juice on her daughter, of reminding her husband to put sunscreen on his nose, of bundling her small family home for lunch. Gwen watched and she thought of all the men—her father, Gideon's father—who had similarly sat and watched, knowing that unbeknownst to the watched ones, the next day you would be far away. Thinking, This is the last time.

2

THIS WAS THE LAST TIME. This was the last time he would see her slouch on the pot, daydreaming as she peed. This was the last time he would watch her scrub her face, scowling with an ambivalent self-love at her own image in the mirror. (Her own transcendent image. Large eyes like the gray-green sea. If he'd seen her for the first time tonight, would he have fallen in love with her all over again? Or had she, tall tyrant, merely overawed him into believing her flawless as Aphrodite? Might he not, at a virgin sighting, find her mannish, hard?)

This was the last time he would see her scuff off her white velvet slippers, or watch the round pink of her heels disappear between the sheets quick as mice. This was the last time he would lie beside her in the dark—he who had imagined their bones mulching together in one grave, imagined overhead the graven legend attesting to their progenitive prowess, their sexual valor. Their steadfastness. Had imagined them aged eighty and still hot rabbits, his withered balls slapping her withered ass on their nightly caper. This was the last time he would hear the worried little grunts and canine whimpers of Gwen asleep. (And even at this late date he could not suppress the desire to protect her from her demons.) Thinking that the next man who watched over her nightmares and hoped to vanquish them would not be he.

Was love—or that spook-house of mirrors Gwen mistook for love—progressive? Four ruined husbands on, might she happen upon the One? A thistle of a man, too indigestible to be chewed up? But then, recollecting that his successors would not just be bedmates to his wife but usurper-fathers foisted on his daughter, he felt wild at the injustice.

This was the last time. Jolting upright in bed, clutching the pillow to his chest in order to stop his hands, to stop his hands, to stop his hands from wringing her neck . . . his fingers were plucking at the pillow, his fingers were possessed by a terrible anxiety, his body was too alive for someone who no longer had any use for it.

From now on, he was going to have to subdue his body, to bleed away its strength a little each day, he was going to have to become an old man early, or else his body's vigor would be too terrible, his body which was still surging with the terrible hunger of love, the habit of love. Still aching to protect his two women.

This now unhusbanded unfathered body was going to have to be retrained into sullen sloth, into lone selfishness. He was going to be an old man alone.

He padded next door to look at Bella sleeping in her barred cage, in the high heat of late babyhood. Long black ringlets tumbled damp across her flushed face, arms flung wide in crucifixion-surrender. Mouth wet and quivering with sweet whistling exhalations, thick black eyelashes quivering with the passing storm of dreams.

Why were you so obedient, so beaten-abject, Gideon, another Jewish lamb trotting docile to the slaughter?

You could have scooped up your sleeping daughter in your arms and spirited her away. You could have dropped her over the balcony and listened to the delayed smack of her six-story fall, better yet, you could have jumped with her in your arms, like someone escaping a fire, and known that only by your double deaths would the child's mother come close to feeling the terror she was causing you.

You looked down at your daughter, you stroked her almond-furred cheek, her hot naked brown foot, which twitched away, as from a fly. And closed her bedroom door.

You dressed quietly, you edged toward the front door, still waiting for the reprieve of Gwen's sleepy "Gideon?" Listened to the sound of her breathing, wondering whether she was awake and feigning sleep, waiting for you to go.

Opened the front door, and hovered. Hesitating over whether or not to take your key. Pocketing it, and then leaving it, taking it, leaving it. Taking it. Opened the door, paused. And let the heavy metal door swing shut.

This is the last time.

BOOK NINE

Chapter One

I

HE WOULD NEVER KNOW. And she, who knew, must stop knowing. Because it didn't bear thinking about, those still-dark mornings when Bella
dove into her parents' bed half asleep, and then, thrashing free of
Gwen's embrace, searched the neighboring sheets. "Da? Da?" as if her
father were playing hide-and-seek. Those afternoons when Bella, arriving home from the park, trotted from room to room in search of her father. Her gay imperiousness turning to unease. An uncertain smile, a
crestfallen laugh intended to propitiate the gods of absence.

2

THAT LANGUAGE—the last language which Gwen had acquired—must be
forgotten. The language of their amazed complicity, their safety in each
other. The language her husband called "Gwiddish," a scurrilous scato-
logical demotic tongue of alley-God and gutters, a kitchen-bedroom-
bathroom vernacular peculiar to their love.

All those faded slangs and stilted intonations that Gwen had
acquired from boarding school, her first Russian teacher, from Constance, those sayings lifted from Gideon's grandmother, from Sonny,
from Dina, from Jenny Randazzo, from Jerome, had been poured into
their household kitty. And now must be liquidated. (Only in retrospect

did Gwen see that what had drawn them together was their moral incoherence: two shape-shifters who had calculated, Together we can add up to one person. One person, being Bella. One, but not two.) So that Gwen, when she lovingly called her Bella *"vilde chaye"* was barely conscious of echoing Bella Gradner's chiding of her grandson Gary. And Gideon, when he complained of feeling "peckish," was ignorant of borrowing Constance's mother's usage. (And had he called Emma Rogan's clitoris, too, the names of oysters? Did it never strike Gwen as revealing, Gideon's calling his wife's privates by the name of a thing his religion considered unclean, an abomination?)

The language must die. First she would purge from her consciousness its vocabulary—the way he (and she, trained mimic) said, "Come again?"; the way he (and ingratiating she) said, "Count me out." Or, "I kid you not." Or, "Hold your horses." Or, *"Takke."* Or (an early favorite of hers), *"Hass v ha-leela!"* Or, "Say," as in "Say, Gwen, what's the big idea?" Or, in a squawky voice (this one rather tiresome), "Now Mr. Punch, shall I cook the dinner while you mind the baby? Or will you mind the dinner while I cook the baby?"

In the end, all would be suppressed. (Only a few strongholds of emphasis might remain, a hidden syntax leaching deep into her unutterable soil.) The language that was theirs would be no longer spoken. A dead language, extinct as Mountain Tat, no longer a matter even for filial piety to disinter.

3

How DO YOU kill off love? How do man and wife dissolve their plighted union? How do you never again kiss a mouth that once was your thirsty sustenance, sunder yourself from flesh which once was yours, how do you disown your life's blood, your all-in-one, your mawkish searingly true heart?

Do you expel your beloved as villagers from a Balkan war, house afire, identity papers confiscated at the border? Or in stumbling intervals, with many a remorseful reversion, mixed message, still more crushing arousal of hope?

There were the books she sent him, the letters they exchanged, there were the 3 a.m. phone calls, there was the night he invited her to the Czech Marionette Theater's *Rasselas*—and they went, both dressed up ghoulish-chic, he in his raw silk wedding suit, and afterwards he came back to her bed, back for one last ghostly night, both of them crying (knowing that never again would they feel anything so deep, so right as him-in-her), and he sneaked out of the house before Bella should awaken.

And sat on the stoop next to the Vanderveer, bawling his eyes out, doorman Tony—a father of young children himself—pretending not to see.

4

GIDEON HAS BECOME obsessed by money—specifically, by the economics of Gwen's kicking him out.

He's going to have to find a lawyer to have this thing done he doesn't want to happen, and that lawyer will have to be paid. And will he be hauled before a family court (inhuman paradox) and commanded to pay his rich wife child support? Has he—in vengeance/self-punishment for having been an unloved son—willed himself into that bogeyman of his own childhood, the delinquent father? (If your daddy cared about you, *he'd* buy you tap shoes, but he doesn't give us a dime, not so much as a birthday phone call to see how you're doing.)

There is nothing in any of the life-choices he has made that render him either financially or emotionally able to withstand this thing Gwen is inflicting on him.

And now Gideon understands how truly fucked he is. He has always suspected that New York was this big talker whose bluff you could call. Hop on a bus, and six weeks out of the city, the addiction of Centrality would be kicked, and you'd suddenly realize, I don't *need* to see crack-hookers before breakfast to feel alive: porcupines and mockingbirds are nice, too. I can live cheap and honestly elsewhere, maybe even do some good in the world. How many of the ideas that improve people's lives are actually being discovered in Manhattan?

But this is the gallows humor of family breakup. Your wife kicks you out and yet you cannot go, she declares herself free of you and yet you are never free of her—*because she's got the kid.* If you want your child to remain yours in any sense, you are chained to her whim, obliged to bankroll two separate establishments in a city where you can no longer afford to take a piss.

The other Pantaloons, meanwhile, are fleeing. (Had they so hated being together, to scatter with such impressive haste?) Amnon's found an internship at MTV; Dan and Andrea have rented an apartment in downtown Northfield, but are trying to get a mortgage for a house near Elliott's, with a loan from Andy's dad.

And Gideon is *glad*. He hadn't counted on the humiliation factor: he is sleeping on the office couch, bathing out of a cold-water sink, and he doesn't much feel like having his ex-colleagues tiptoeing around him with sandwiches and long faces, asking how his daughter's handling it.

Dina is in town till the end of July, packing up Rivington Street, which she's illegally subletting for fifteen hundred dollars a month to a couple who work in advertising. But Gideon finds Dina insufferable these days, so babble-mouthed is she with the brilliance of her future husband, the excitement of her new life.

The resourceful Avi Weissbrot has found them an apartment within the catchment zone of a public school that's supposedly strong in science. And Dina is looking into the possibility of teaching theater to— what was the euphemism?—juvenile offenders, a prospect that the Pantaloons had often discussed.

When, massaging Gideon's hunched shoulders, Dina, out of the kindness of her oozing heart, offers, "Why don't you move to San Francisco with us, Gid? You'd love it. The light reminds me of Jerusalem, it's so clear you kinda get this feeling of a country that's still somehow in the making, where everything's possible," Gideon barely prevents himself from snarling, I've got a child—remember? (Besides, it's precisely the illusion that everything's possible that makes nothing stick. If only his wife had been afflicted with a little more Old World pessimism, she'd have known adultery is just something you get through, in a marriage.)

Hector and the neighborhood kids show up a couple of times, then don't come back: it was the *fun* of Pants on Fire that attracted them, and Gideon these days, silent, unwashed, red-eyed, liable to shout, is . . . not fun.

Sancho still comes by with news from the front, but Gideon no longer cares. The war's over; big business won, and he doesn't have the gumption to be like that rabbinical enclave that kept the faith throughout the Roman occupation.

Most of their neighbors, too, seem to have vacated La Merced. The place is a ghost town. At night, when being alone threatens to turn him werewolf-mad, he wanders down the halls, turning locked knobs.

No one.

There is the studio which belonged to the dance group Bux, but where are they? Summering in Saratoga Springs?

(Later, he was to wonder what stopped him *then,* those nights, from jumping off the roof, from slitting his throat. What? It would have been better. But low as he was that summer, he still had that variant of hope which is simply a grim wanting to see what comes next.)

5

GIDEON HAS HIS ROUTINES. If he finds himself calm enough in daylight hours, he marshalls his nerve to leave La Merced. (Always a residual fear that he'll come back to find the door under a police seal.) Inches down the block in the infernal white heat, hoping his neighbors—the old men on folding chairs with radios, the ladies in housecoats and slippers, with their poodles—won't recognize him.

He goes to the bodega to buy Twinkies and Cherry Coke and Cheez Doodles, he goes to the liquor store, the post office. And home. And home. And home. Someday he really oughta get out, go to the Russian Baths, the movies. Catch some pussy.

There are days on end when he won't talk to Sancho or Carlos, who get on his nerves. Last week someone from the Safir Brothers came by, an acne-scarred kid in a white permanent-press shirt still pleated from its box, who said, Listen, sign this paper saying you'll drop all lawsuits and be out of here by such and such a date. Otherwise, the police are coming in to get you. Sancho had laughed—this was the moment he was waiting for, but Gideon? Gideon wasn't in the mood for a fight. If he were in the mood for a fight, he'd still be living in the Vanderveer.

Picture Gideon. Five-thirty a.m., he's dribbled into a shivery restless doze, after a night's drinking, writing Gwen, drinking, writing Gwen (she's screening her calls, so he's reduced to letters), having drunk so much and howled so much he can't even jerk off to get to sleep, and in his half-trance he thinks he's "home," he can see out of one hairline-fractured eyelid the inky lightening before sunrise. He's thinking, No point trying to go back to sleep, any minute Bear's going to come bounding into the bed, yelling "Up! Up! Up!" small warm body on his chest, trying to peel open her father's shut eyes. Then he remembers where he is.

6

HE IS DREAMING of absolution, of total love, a pussy warm as toast, a clit you can ring like a bell—hers and none other—that sings to him, sings, Home is the sailor home from the sea, that sings him the sad songs of his childhood, long arms tight around his throat and her lovely deep voice strafing his ear, the ladylike sonority of her, my Siberian husky, my . . . heart murmur my endless night my Jack the Ripper my oblivion my end . . . my rat escaping the sinking ship of our love my little coward my turn tail trustless Tokyo Rose my dear traitor . . . my death . . .

He awakens into a sizzling afternoon, the radio still humming and a voice saying that the stock market's crashed, and Asia's down the tubes. He thinks, Oh good.

Chapter Two

I

MARTIN JOEL LEWIS, in front of the television.

"Watching" is the wrong verb for our relation to the screen, suggesting as it does a guard's alertness.

Martin Lewis, plugged into the television, inert but for a thumb clicking the remote control: college basketball, weather, stock reports, home shopping. The announcers hysterical-chirpy; the colors saturated like North African sweetmeats; Martin Lewis, inert as a mollusk, soaking up the noise, the color. Squat paunchy body, sports-clothed, hunched in on itself. Martin Lewis, inert.

He's finished chemotherapy, but his skin is still the jaundiced yellow of a cancer patient. When Gwen takes him to Memorial, the small children, teenagers, young mothers in the waiting room are all the same pinched sallow, some hairless, some not. (Now that Gwen knows the look, she spots it all over town, finds herself gulping at the sight of a yellow-skinned ten-year-old with no eyebrows being helped onto a see-saw by his parents.) Her father refuses to acknowledge his compatriots, buries himself in papers, as if his professional importance will save him. And the doctors do indeed feel confident that this round has success-fully zapped the little mites.

The dark gleam of the home entertainment center, its recessed light-ing like that of an airport cocktail lounge: confidential, anonymous. Insulated from the upstairs squeals, where Alexander is trying to skate over Serena's Barbie dolls, and Serena trying to wrench the skates off his feet. The children get on his nerves, Jacey says, he doesn't want to see them. Wincing, he fends them off, yells for Jacey or Sabine or Martha to take them away. Gwen hasn't brought Bella over for months.

A freckled hand sneaks a salted almond, the eyes poached, unmov-ing. Flicks channels, lingering over commercials. Sighs heavily. "How you doing, Chug?"

"Fine," says Gwen.

"Did you get the—the thing I sent you?"

"Yes, I did—thank you." Not sure what he means: the newspaper clipping about Russian oil companies, the red patent-leather Betty Boop knapsack for Bella.

She is sorry for her father, who obviously feels like shit, and yet she kind of hates him too, suspecting that the moment he feels any better, he'll go beetling off to the newest Armanda, that the only thing that's keeping him uxorious, housebound is sheer physical debility . . .

"How's your conference shaping up?"

"Okay, so far." She makes as if to touch wood. "We've got a good mix." The Russian journalist who'd crusaded against the loans-for-shares deal; an ex-deputy finance minister who takes the quixotic line that the IMF shouldn't lend Russia any more money. An antimafia prosecutor, who has been investigating Russian organized crime's spread into America, Europe, Asia. "And it looks pretty sure that Larry Summers is going to make it . . ."

Her father nods. "Great. How's the kid?"

"Fine. I worry about her, but she seems fine."

Not wanting to tell him about Bella's nightmares, when Gwen comes in to find the baby standing upright in her crib, tearstained face a mask of screaming horror.

"She's little. Kids forget."

Meaning, she and Maddock were too old? Kids forget what? That they ever lived with a father and a mother who loved each other? If such a thing had been true—had once been the child's unthinking possession—was it better to forget it?

He reaches again for the remote control, shifts the curaçao-blue to gray. Presses MUTE.

"You got a lawyer yet?"

"Nope."

"You need a lawyer. The guy's gonna want some money."

"I don't know . . ."

"You don't know. The Gideon Wolkowitzes of this world, they have a sense of entitlement. Injured entitlement. I know the type, believe me. Your money to him is just like comfort food and he's gonna need a lotta comforting . . ."

"I don't think so, Pop."

"You don't know."

2

CAN YOU HEAR ME?

Can you hear me?

Can you hear me?

3

FOR A WHILE, after moving out, I prowled the streets with the worst kinda itch between my legs, this permanent hard-on. Jerking off three times a night, and feeling NO relief. I watched women in the subway who had big hard nipples poking through their summer dresses and jutting rears, bodies slick with sweat, and I laughed at the dirty day.

Then I thought maybe drink was more total.

What do you think, Gwen? What's your idea of totality?

4

"So WHAT HAPPENED?" asked Dan.

It had to be Dan, didn't it? Dan, who was so nonmammalian calm, so uncognizant of human intrigue and turmoil, that he could ask, without inhibiting scruples, "What happened?"

As if Gideon's wife's throwing him out of the house were a naturalistic curiosity.

Dan was back in New York for two days, loading up their last possessions in the Honda Civic they'd bought from a neighbor. Dan, who showed up without warning, had suggested an early dinner at Ratner's, but Gideon had wanted to drink, so they'd shimmied through to Lansky's.

Gideon, hands trembling. (He wondered would they tremble too much to do puppets.) His voice didn't sound like his voice anymore: it was strained by tears, higher-pitched; his sarcasms came across whiny.

When he saw himself in the mirror, he looked wizened, red-rimmed. He had a permanent summer cold, and stomach cramps that wouldn't go away. He'd had the runs for months now, and blood in his shit. Yet if you waited for the body to disintegrate, it took its sweet time. He could wait fifty years.

"I guess she didn't want me in there, with her."

"In where?"

"In her bottle."

"Explain," said Dan, gamely. Willing to follow, if it was sensibly explained.

"I married a scorpion," said Gideon. "Anything that gets caught in the bottle with her, she kills."

He hunched over farther, slurped up the melted ice at the bottom of his Scotch.

"How's Bella taking it? I guess she's too little to understand, right?"

"Oh, even mama scorpions don't kill their babes. But I don't think it's going to be too healthy, growing up in that bottle. No, not too healthy. If I could get custody of her . . ."

He hunches over, pauses, slurps more ice. "So I'm one of the suitors who failed. You know, like in the Greek myths where you get a challenge to . . . kill the monster. The Hydra, the Medusa, the . . . Minotaur. I didn't. I didn't manage to extricate the scorpion out of her bottle. I failed. She killed me. So . . . maybe the next hero on . . . or the fiftieth hero from now will manage to kill the beast, to turn the scorpion back into a lovely princess. I didn't know she thought love was progressive . . ."

"Is that what she says?"

"She doesn't say anything. I mean, anything true. She doesn't know the first thing about herself. She can't admit what she's done. She looks at Bella . . . screaming out for reassurance, for everything to go back to before. And she says Bella's doing fine. Just a little stressed from her play group. She says it would be better for Bella not to see me for a while."

"That's fucked up."

"She says that, and then if I'm ten minutes late picking up Bella she screams at me. In front of the child. Sometimes I've thought she's making me crazy on purpose, so I'll get mad enough to do it."

"Do what?"

"Kill her," says Gideon. Crunching up the peanuts now. Scooping them up in handfuls. Thirsty. Wanting another drink. Things wore off too fast. Waving to the bartender. "Sometimes I think she's asking me to kill her. Or kill myself. Kill us all. I think she thinks I'm nuts enough to kill us all."

"Don't get too crazy," said Dan. "You want to be able to still see your daughter." That was Dan—practical.

"True," nodded Gideon. He blew out. Breathed in. Forced his body to stop rocking back and forth, hunching over. Forced himself to sit up, stay still. Conquered the impulse to jump up and run, to . . . jump. "You know what I'd really like? I'd really like to move to the country with Bella. She's not a . . . she's not a city girl. She's a little fox."

"She's a riot," agreed Dan. He reflects. Dan was a problem-solver, that was part of why they'd been so good together, Gideon saying, I want the Virgin of La Merced flying down from heaven, Dan calculating the size pulley and the length of wire required.

"You wanna join us up in Northfield?"

"Thanks, I appreciate it, but . . ."

"Well, you're welcome to."

"Thanks."

"How about Lubeck? You ever think about going up to Lubeck? If you're thinking of getting back to the country for a while, I know Jerome could use some—"

"Nah, that'd be as bad as moving back in with your mom, after the divorce."

"You know, Peter's left, Roxanne's left . . ."

Gideon didn't say anything for a minute. "I can't face Jerome, I can't face going back into that whole scene. It's so fucked, so hothouse . . ."

"Well, think about it."

"I got enough to think about that already makes me nuts without . . ."

But he was thinking about it. He was picturing the hayloft in the big red barn where the puppeteers slept, taking turns over who went downstairs to put more wood in the stove. Thought of staggering outside for a midnight piss and seeing the big wilderness of salty stars overhead, the steep forested crags. Hearing nocturnal hunters: an owl's shriek; wild dogs' howling. One spring they'd had to scare away a black bear that got too friendly. What was tempting was Bella *in that place* he'd never persuaded Gwen to go, which was what might today make it tolerable—here was something of himself, pre-Gwen, that he loved. "Peter left?"

"Yeah, he went back to school."

"Jesus, Jerome must be on the secret payroll of Graduate Schools of America . . ."

5

ARE YOU READING ME, my Miss Darling Gwen?

Those first few weeks, the reception was so clear I could talk to you in my head. I talked, and you chattered back, I heard your husky-sweet voice trembling with your old dark fervor, I could have sworn I knew what you were doing and feeling every minute of the day—now she's meeting Christopher for a drink and she's trying to tell him what went wrong between us (God, I wish you'd tell me, sweetheart), now she's having dinner with one of her ugly lonely-heart women friends or some poor widower Slav in need of a meal (that bucked me up some, remembering the *kindness* of you, the gruff generosity, you were never much of a provider, but you know how to listen and that cheered me up, believing insanely that there might be some of that kindness left for me). And in my deludedness I thought, I can help her, she still needs me, she is all that I love in the world and I want her with all my heart to prosper, to flourish, to triumph, to heal, even if that means without me. If a mother was told, For your sick child to get well, she must be taken away from you and you will never see her again, wouldn't that mother gladly accept the sacrifice?

Then the weeks passed, and I realized, of course, that you didn't want my help. With your powerful wad of daddy-inherited spite, you wanted me ground into the dirt, subjugated. In short, dead.

Why, I wondered. What did I do to become your enemy? And then I understood. I had to die in order to leave you an innocent brave widow-lady, free to start afresh. So our daughter wouldn't grow up and reproach you someday for having denied her a fairly serviceable and adoring father. (Did you ever think how much I could have taught her? How to play the banjo, how to build a bookcase, how to plant a garden or change a tire, how to pray to God in the language of her fathers, how to love? But these minor skills are nothing, compared to the arid totality of your pride . . .) You needed to be everything to her, so that if she ever balked, or showed an inclination to become her own woman, you could threaten to take that everything away.

6

DO YOU READ ME, sister? Do you read me? This is the last time. This is the last time. This is the last time you will ever hear from me again. This is the last . . .

Chapter Three

MOSQUITOES, MARSH GRASS, the slam of screen doors, the childhood smells of fried clams and suntan lotion. Maddock in his Ray-Bans and feed cap, singing along to country radio as they cruise Ocean Boulevard in his pickup.

It's August, and Gwen has finally cracked, in a piddling sort of way. Every day she was dragging herself into the office and . . . sitting. Mail, telephone messages piling up, and suddenly she felt too listless to pick up the phone.

So this is when you found out whose name you cry in the night. When she hit rock-bottom, it was Maddock she wanted. Always.

Maddock's cottage is three rooms. Gwen and Bella and Maddock's dog Blooper are sleeping in the living room, which is separated from Maddock and Riley's bedroom by an inch of plywood. Riley, who gets off work after midnight, can't much enjoy being roused by her boy-friend's niece's 6 a.m. reveille, but both Maddock and Riley prove un-failingly generous with the little they've got, quick to make room for awkward guests.

Having arrived, Gwen discovers it's as much as she can do to hustle Bella to the beach, where together they paddle in rock pools, collect broken shells and legless crabs. Here Gwen can flatline, watching a cargo ship low on the horizon, waiting to unload in Portsmouth Harbor. Not think. Not be swamped by unuseful regret. Not think.

At noon, she hauls Bella across Ocean Boulevard to the Sandpiper. Bella throwing fits over an imaginary black spot on her grilled cheese sandwich, or over being forced to come in from the beach, or prevented from tearing off her bathing suit in the coffee shop, or from bringing in-side large bucketfuls of sand. Gwen's child-days are largely tantrum-management. It's the age. Anyway, tantrums over bathing suits are less epic than tantrums over snowsuits.

This evening, Gwen and Maddock are stretched out in the late sum-mer grass drinking rum and Coke. Through the open window they can hear the small rumble of Bella's snoring, from her bed of cushions on the living room floor.

"Sweet little girl," says Maddock, fondly. Gwen can see the glow of his cigarette in the dark. Hers (she only smokes after Bella's asleep) an answering beam.

"Didn't there used to be more stars on summer nights, when we were children?"

"Light-pollution. I got a telescope inside, but there's too much light from the highway. We should take it down to the beach some night."

"You have a telescope?" She is surprised.

"Yeah, it's pretty old and crappy. I stole it, years ago."

Gwen thinks of their New York days of shoplifting candies and doorknobs. Telescopes are *big*. "From a store?"

"Nope, I broke into someone's house."

Gwen reflects. "I forgot about that," she says. "Your robbery days."

"Well, it wasn't exactly banks or 7-Elevens; it was more like skinning up drainpipes into people's bedrooms and walking off with a bottle of Percodan."

"When was it—my last year at Milton?"

"It was the winter before I moved out west. After I got kicked out of Thorndale. Me and a friend I won't name. We targeted vacation homes;

we'd break a window, fix ourselves a drink, watch TV, walk off with a radio or some golf trophy. The telescope. Something we could carry on foot."

"Why'd you do it?"

"Boredom. Winters here are *long*. Maybe a little jealous to see how other people lived—you know, regular mom-and-pop families. Most of my friends were worse off than us—like, nothing to eat in the house, their dads belting them. I wanted to see how normal people lived; whether they slept in twin beds or double, what kinda pills they had in the bathroom chest. Most people don't leave shit in the house when they pack up for the season—one time all we walked away with was a medical dictionary."

"Was it Byron Beale?" she asks. "Your partner in crime?"

"Not telling."

"What's happened to Byron? You still see him?"

Silence. Maddock rolls over and stubs out his cigarette. "I wondered if you were ever going to ask that question. Nothing happened. He's still around."

"Is he working?"

"Yeah, he keeps the grounds at the Okateague Club. He lives with a girl who's one of the Costello sisters—Jessie, one of the little ones."

"They have kids?"

"They got custody of his son, who's, like, sixteen now. He asks me about you, sometimes."

A sudden image of Byron Beale's stomach roped in a scar from a burst appendix, because his mom wouldn't believe he had a pain. More scars, across his shoulders, legs, back. So Maddock had known that she and Byron Beale had sneaked off together. And been disturbed, by her utilitarian heartlessness. *I wondered if you were ever going to ask that question.*

"Hey, did you see that?"

They both exclaim over the shooting star, its tail fizzy-bright, that streaks almost to earth.

"So you guys—you and your nameless friend—got caught?"

"Uncle Rich saved my hide, as per usual. We got greedy. *I* got greedy. We hit a house on Meredith Road, and I took this fishing rod that was like brand-new top-of-the-line. I didn't even know whose house it was. Anyways, one of those old farts on Parker River saw me with this three-hundred-dollar rod and figured I didn't get it for Christmas: the police came around, asking questions. It turned out the guy owned, like, this big lobster house in Newick. Uncle Rich took me over there—with the rod—to apologize, the guy said, Lose the kid, and I won't press charges. Send him to boot camp: I don't want to see the punk till he's got a buzz cut and found God. It was beautiful fishing gear, too." Maddock pauses. "I wasn't a highflyer like you. If I couldn't scrape by decently, I figured I might as well take the low road."

"I wasn't a highflyer, either."

"Nah, but at least you understood if you made your grades, people would leave you alone."

"Mmmmm. Maybe." She assents, vaguely, not wanting to admit that in fact she'd gone straight-A for the same reason Maddock robbed houses: just another stupid ineffective way of begging for love. "Anyway, it looks as if the low road's more lucrative . . ."

He and Riley have driven her out to their property—twenty-five acres of woodland up by Durham, with some good old trees. Maddock's shown her the plans—a four-bedroom house with a steam room. They intend to start building next spring. Gwen impressed to discover her brother's been hoarding his money all these years for something *big*.

"Nah," he says, dismissive. "The economy's picked up some, that's all. Ten years ago, things were *not* pretty around here. Course, I've probably bought at the top of the market . . ."

Gwen thinks about the previous day, when they drove down to Newburyport to visit Katrina and Hal. Aunt Sue, along with Emily and her three sons, met them for a picnic on Plum Island. Everybody over the age of eleven knew even in August the water was too cold to swim; only the boys plunged in and out of the surf briefly, blue-lipped.

Katrina hanging on to Bella's hand as the child, yelling, strained to follow.

"My, she's willful," said her grandmother. "Just like someone else I know."

Gwen has never managed to patch up relations with her mother, after the disastrous Christmas visit. They talk on the phone every couple of months, Gwen mails off photographs of Bella, her mother recently sent an announcement of a group exhibition at an old firehouse in Haverhill, but the rapprochement never seems to take: each gesture is jolty, forced, as if starting from scratch and leading nowhere; every joke ends up barbed.

When they met this time, on the front drive of Addison Road,

Gwen could feel Katrina steel herself to embrace her daughter, hear the welcoming voice blurry with suppressed resentment. Her mother clearly believes Gwen was the aggressor in their clash; Gwen must have said one of those things people can never forgive. That Gwen's marriage has fallen through only appears to make her mother the crosser.

She was trying, Gwen thinks now. The strain of the effort was visible: it made the cords stand out on her neck. Katrina tried—valiantly—to praise and cuddle Bella, who had no idea who the faded blond lady was. "She's *enormous!* I feel as if my own grandchild's a stranger!"

But for all Katrina's determination—she had baked Gwen's childhood favorite, butterscotch brownies; she had laid in coffee, in three indigestible flavors—Gwen understood for the first time that things will never really be okay. They get each other's backs up, it's a question of an almost physical antipathy.

Gwen watches Maddock—who calls their mother "Ma" or "doll," whose cottage is walled in Katrina's driftwood sculptures, her watercolors, who sits over lunch with one arm flung around Katrina's neck—and realizes that by contrast, Gwen has always made their mother feel unloved, as if her firstborn were perpetually sitting in big-eyed judgment.

"You know," Gwen says now, staring up at the pooling stars. "It's been great, us getting to talk again. About the only good thing to come of my marital shipwreck . . ."

"I'm sorry about you guys."

"Yeah. You liked him, right?"

A pause. "He's a likable guy. And you two made yourselves a lovely little girl. That's something, anyway."

Thinking of the second child she'd pulled the plug on. "Well, we're not getting back together to make another one."

"I understand."

"I didn't do him much good."

"Don't run yourself down. If it's over, you got to keep your nerve."

She says slowly, "I make a lot of trouble for everybody, not knowing what I want . . ."

Maddock reaches out a hand in the dark. "You're a strong girl, honey. I'm sure having the kid to think of will make things clearer for you. You're doing a great job with her, you can't be all that bad news . . ."

There are katydids in the darkness, motorcycle-roars as a gang of

Hell's Angels rumble past. She knows from the quiver in his palm that the apparent effortlessness of Maddock's generosity is mere showmanship. Your sister calls up wanting shelter from her ended marriage, and all of a sudden what you thought was your own happy life is shot to smithereens, leaving pure pain.

Maddock's cell phone rings: Riley, saying the last customer has just paid up. Maddock hauls himself upright, plucking dead grass from his clothes. In a moment, he'll be gone to pick up Riley from Hemingway's, and she'll be left with this insufferable remorse. A sleeping child, a heavy conscience.

It doesn't seem enough anymore to feel horribly in the right. "Do you think we're doomed to repeat things? I think of Mom and Pop, this idiot cycle of family breakups . . ."

Maddock, shaking the pins and needles from one leg, considers. "Honestly? I don't see much resemblance. Although sometimes on a bad day, I've thought this country would be a lot healthier if they banned divorce instead of tobacco." He puts his weight on the cramped foot. Takes a step, wobbly, laughing. "You know one thing for sure? If Riley and I ever get that far, that girl better know, Divorce is not an option. You cheat on me, you try to walk out, it's the chain saw."

Chapter Four

I

Dear Gwen,

Thanks for your birthday call.

I hadn't expected to be quite so free by the time I was thirty-five.

I went over to Dina's to celebrate. High old times. More cardboard boxes. I thought maybe my former colleagues might gang together to hire me a brace of whores for the night. I thought you might jump out of the cake.

You didn't.

Ethan gave me a book about artificial language.

The author writes about the first translating computer, which was programmed to translate from English to Russian. They started with proverbs.

Trial run: the programmer feeds the computer, "Out of sight, out of mind."

The computer answers in Russian: "Blind, insane."

I guess in this story you're the American, I'm the Russian.

You will think I am still being sorry for myself, which maybe is a leftover cultural tic.

In the same book, the guy writes that they now know British cryptographers were intercepting the German army's telexes from Russia documenting the beginnings of the Holocaust. And when someone wondered, Shouldn't we be stopping this, an unnamed British diplomat said, "The last thing we want to be bothering about is a lot of wailing Jews."

I quite agree; in fact, it's always been part of Jews' exasperating versatility that even mid-wail they can see why the unmarked world doesn't want to be bothered.

See—I've gone back to reading books again, so things can't be all that bad. In fact, since you took your love away—I mean, since you recommended that I leave—my cultural life is a lot tonier. I've almost become a bluestocking in my spare time. I miss your stockings too, although I don't remember any blue ones.

Your sometime friend, g.

2

LATE SUMMER STORM, a sulfurous wind. Leaves clattering across the pavement like tiny skeletons, and Zion says, "The Lord has forsaken me, and my Lord has forgotten me." Can a woman forget her suckling child? But we know from the siege of Jerusalem that women can *eat* their suckling babes, that this will and *must* occur precisely in order to expedite the business of redemption.

And God, recognizing this maternal propensity, admits, "Yea, a mother may forget her suckling child [forget, i.e., crunch its frail spine and ribs and skull between her newly capped chompers, as if her babe were a sardine, a shrimp, a fragrant crunchy songbird] yet I will not for-get [i.e., devour] thee. Behold, I have GRAVEN thee upon the palms of my hands [God's palms!], thy walls are always before me."

What, holy fuck, what are we to make of this, this mutilation, this theogonic circumcision? *God the bloody bridegroom has carved our name upon the palms of His hands.*

Gideon too has a knife. He is a workman, all workmen have knives. He has a bowie knife he carries in his belt loop, or in his pocket, or sometimes hangs up on the grid in his workshop. He gets out his bowie knife now—it's dawn enough so he doesn't need to turn on his lamp to see—and practices. A "G" on his right palm—slicing, hacking through the mottled nervous flesh where once his lifeline and fateline also sang her name—her "G," gyno-gismo-geiser-gush—and his "G." G is for Gary. He should go back to his slave name, he knows, he is no longer a Gideon—i.e., a warrior—but a Gary. Are there tribal rites for *un*initiation, unmanning?

He tries to carve a "G" on his left—but (being a lefty) doesn't make much headway. Good goring, bad lettering. Concludes that God, unlike him, must—no surprise—be ambidextrous.

It's stinging and messy, the blood is spurting, pooling, running down his wrists, and mucking up the blanket, but he goes back to his Jerusalem Bible, because now comes the part where it says that the res-urrected Zion will have kings as her nursing fathers, and even though Gideon knows himself no king, no, not even a five-and-dime-store rook, he can see pretty plainly they are talking about him, the nursing father. A role he didn't choose, that was thrust upon him in some horrendous Ovidian metamorphosis. Gwen has milk, and he has blood, but he can feed their baby off his blood, like a pelican.

3

JEROME ON THE LINE.

Dog-day haze. Heavy. Airless.

Jerome isn't a person who calls.

Every time the phone rings, Gideon jumps, thinking it's going to be Gwen. Thinking, so many times it hasn't been Gwen, the mathematical odds are this time it's *got* to be.

It isn't. Ever.

How many weeks since he took her to *Rasselas,* since they lay together naked in their old marriage bed? His palms are still bandaged.
His right hand has become infected. The simplest movements—dressing
himself, opening a bag of potato chips—are prohibitively clumsy and
painful.

"Gidele, have I ever done you a favor?"

"No."

"I've never been the littlest teeniest help to you in life?"

"Well, maybe as an object lesson to me in how *not* to treat my
employees . . ."

"Thanks a lot, Gideon. Enough with the wheedling. No more Mr.
Nice Guy, no more flattery. I need your help: Dan said you might be
available this fall? Peter's left, I need somebody to take the company on
tour."

"I thought Dan said you were going to do it."

"God forbid. I'm meeting everybody at the end, in Budapest. Bridey
and I are taking a little trip on our own, a sentimental journey. I got a
twinge, I thought maybe it was time to go weep over the ancestral
shtetl."

"I always thought you were a *yekke.*"

"Oh, my mother's family were Berliners, but my father's family was
from Bessarabia."

"No kidding."

"Have I never told you about my grandparents?"

"I'd forgotten." Liar.

"Oh, my grandfather was a famous comedian in Mogulesco's
troupe. My grandmother sneaked out of the house to see them: she
came from a pious family. My grandfather, who was already married,
persuaded her to run away with the troupe. And my grandmother became a singer. You can't imagine the furor when they first put respectable Jewish girls on the stage—she was one of the first. Before, it was
completely Elizabethan, young men in falsettos playing the women's
parts. My grandmother was an enormous star—it was she who got them
to America, before the war . . ."

Gideon's heard the story a million times verbatim, but the telephone is company. It's a talking telephone: an animist idol from which
sentences burble, gush, and cackle. Don't leave me, don't hang up, he
tells the phone, keep talking. He is suddenly frightened to be alone any
longer in this room—the room where he first pulled down his wife's
woollen tights and ate her golden-ripe pussy. Where he first tasted her

salt-sweets. That he will never taste again. Next time he starts cutting, he doesn't know where he'll stop . . .

Besides, there's something in Jerome's rich fruity voice, his seasoned egotism, that Gideon finds comforting.

"So you want somebody to take the company on tour," he says. "When?"

"Starting September third, for two months."

Maybe it's not such a bad idea, being out of town when La Merced finally gets the ax. But where will he go afterwards?

"You know, Jerome, I'm not sixteen anymore."

"That's good news," says Jerome's voice.

"I'm a father now who's supposedly gotta kick in with a little support for his uh . . . family."

"I understand, believe me, that's why I thought—"

"You try to slave-labor me, I'm bringing charges to Dina's uncle-in-law . . ."

"Gideon, what do you take me for?"

"I take you for a rich stingy bastard. What are you paying tour managers these days?"

"Gideon, you and I know each other far too well to—"

"That's the trouble, I know you far too well."

"Gideon, we can write a contract. We can give you an advance, we can make it legal, whatever you like . . ."

"I'm telling you, Jerome, the only way I'm interested in taking the company on tour is for a lot of money."

"I understand, I hear you, Gideon. A lot of money I'm not promising you, but you certainly will be paid."

"No—you're not hearing me. A *lot* of money."

4

I AM READING that book of Rumi you gave me last Valentine's Day. (Remember your hurt feelings that I didn't read it straightaway? It never occurred to me, you had so persuasively broken down my initial mistrust, that we would not have years in which to dawdle over each other's findings.) So now I'm telling you too late, into a vacuum. How much I, too, love Rumi. (Isn't that a sign that we were, after all, meant for each other?)

I am rereading the introduction, where it describes Rumi's lost love,

Shams of Tabriz, who wandered the world in search of someone "who will endure me," for which prize, he swears to God, he will give his very head. He is searching, like the Song of Songs, for the Beloved. The Friend. The *Dost*–do you remember how you used to call me your *Dost?*

One day, in Konya, he is introduced to Rumi, then thirty-seven years old, who at the sight of Shams falls to the floor in an epileptic seizure of recognition. And for four years they know this ecstatic communion. Four years, my sweetheart. We barely had three.

Shams cannot bear it. He cannot bear the accusing, soul-rending trueness of Rumi's love. From time to time, he vanishes, goes off on subterranean benders.

But Rumi will not let him off the hook. Each time, Rumi leaves his wife, his children, his disciples, his *medresa,* in search of the absconded *Dost,* and brings him home. Each return is more partial, more perturbed. Until one time, Shams disappears, and this time, he don't come back no more no more no more no more. He has vanished without a trace, forever.

Conspiracy theorists suggest that Rumi's jealous disciples murdered the little cunt, but my guess is Shams just went too deep. And Rumi? Does he crack up? Rumi is at heart balanced, detached. A pragmatist. In the end, the bereft Lover concludes that the Beloved, in fact, lies within. I am my own Other.

Nice try, Rumi. Like, what else is a philosopher to do when he gets jilted, but make a philosophy of abandonment? But count me out; I don't buy it, not by a long shot. I say, hire your hit men and kill that Shams. Flush him out of the bolt-hole where he's shacked up with his wine and his boy, and kill. Did he not vow to God he would give his head for someone who'd endure him? Did you not endure? Take his head, Rumi, take the head of the unendurer. And then chop off your own. Ashes to ashes, *dost* to *dost.* No love, no earth, no life.

5

THE EARTH IS THE LORD's, but the abominations that you commit on it are your own.

Gideon hears noises in the night and he thinks it's the Safir Brothers' thugs come to get him. He gets up, with his knife. It's a rat or it's a Safir. He hears noises and he thinks it's Martin Lewis come to get him. He hears skittering-rustling noises. Of people running. People hiding. He hears noises and he follows. One night he ends up on the roof, shouting. By the time he wakes up, the voices have gone. Martin Safir Martin Brothers Martin Martin Martin Safir. Get me! Get me!

He opens his eyes and finds somebody standing over him.

Daylight. Heat. The muzzy buzz of a fly. The muzzy buzz of a fly that is drowning in a glass of Scotch. Day. Heat. His blanket damp with sweat. The person is gone.

He closes his eyes.

Opens.

Day. Heat. This time he's being handed something.

A man.

A paper to sign.

No.

Divorce or eviction.

No.

A paper to sign, signing away his rights to his wife and daughter, signing away his rights to his bed. His rights to his head.

No.

He waves the paper away.

No.

Another day.

No.

Another man bending over him, this time large, and a smell coming off him as he bends close that is animal-stable familial. A smell of horses, of hay, of clean sweat. Not a suave cheap city-lawyerly smell: this is a country smell as good as his own twenty-one-month-old daughter smells, as clean as a child that still suckles its mother's milk. It smells like the smell of your own blood, the way Esau sniffs Jacob and then puts down his weapon and weeps. The man is big—he looks like an angel, if you can imagine a 210-pound angel with blond sideburns and glasses.

At first, Gideon thinks it's the rabbi from Ohelei Yaakov, but then he recognizes his old work-neighbor Isaac.

Gideon rubs his eyes, gives a doglike shake that is mostly shudder. He's cold. His old sweat is damp-cold. He sits up.

"Here's some coffee," says Isaac.

It's Isaac, his neighbor.

A laminated cup of takeout coffee by his head. A doughnut, crinkly, with white icing that's got smushed all over the wax-paper wrapping.

"French cruller," Isaac explains. "The sugar's a jump start."

Gideon, wrapping a blanket around himself like a homeless person, warms his hands on the paper coffee cup.

He is shivering, shivering.

It's August and he can tell from the white-wavy filter of the light that it shouldn't be cold, but the room faces east, and the morning light has been and gone already. He hates east. North, west, south, anything but. He's not a morning-boy. He had rather the sun never came than that it had been and gone by the time he opens his eyes . . . Glory departed.

That's always been his problem. Why fight for a east-facing room?

He wolfs down the cruller.

"There's a whole bag of 'em."

He downs another. Better, better. "Is it cold in here or is it me?" He's warming up.

"It's you," says Isaac. Who is perched on the foot of Gideon's bed, wearing a piss-yellow T-shirt that says in red letters "Ostrich Brothers' Autos, Ashuelot, N.H."

Don't leave, Gideon wills him. *Don't leave.*

"Ashuelot," he says. "Wherzat?"

"New Hampshire. My homeland."

"You still have family there?" Don't leave, is the subliminal text. Don't leave.

"Nope. A graveyard full of Hookers, but nobody still kicking. My mom moved when she remarried. My brother's in San Francisco, he works in software."

Isaac by now has found the packet of Bustelo, the Turkish pot, figured out how to light the hob. If he's making more coffee, it means he's planning to stay. *Stay.*

"Shit, is there anybody alive today who isn't doing software in San Francisco? You ever meet Dina?"

Dina has gone. She still calls Gideon almost daily, just to make sure he hasn't died in the night. What he hears in her officiously cheery long-distance voice is guilt at their lots having so unexpectedly reversed. She would give him a little of her happiness if she could: women can handle solitude better than men, who have to erect some religion around it not to lose their minds. When Dina's husband walked out on her, Dina didn't loll in a dirty bed bawling, she got her kid dressed and fed every morning and off to day care, she went to work. Yeah, Gideon answers himself, But if it was Michael Pinto'd walked out on me, I'd be dancing the Hokey Pokey, too . . .

"Dina? I think so. You ready for more coffee?"

"Cups are down below," says Gideon, hunching over, he knows it's high summer but nobody's told his body, his teeth are still chitter-chattering, conducting their own independent monkey-conversation from the rest of him.

Isaac pours them each a cup. Little yellow cups, relics from Andrea's stepmother. Ridiculously dainty demitasses, each of which has been broken and glued back together in five places.

Gideon bolts the hot coffee fast to ingest a little warmth.

"So you get back up to New Hampshire much?"

"Some. I've got friends I visit."

"You ever think of moving back?"

Isaac shakes his head. "New Hampshire's home. You know about home. 'Home is where the hatred is.' "

"Honestly? I don't. I never had much of a home; I came from one of those families that moved every six weeks. And then—"

"Then you became a travelling player," ventures Isaac, genially.

"*Takke.* I wouldn't know what to do with a home if it hit me on the head. You still living out on Long Island?" He wants to talk; he hasn't talked to a live soul since dropping off Bella last week. If Isaac's come to see him, it means he can bear him. I would give my very head for some-one who'll endure me . . .

The reason men like men is because men aren't picky; they're not so judgmental as women. You put two guys in front of a TV set with a cou-ple of six-packs, they're fine.

He remembers Gwen's fury the first time he turned on the TV in front of her. How she sulked and flounced, called him a hypocrite, and yes, Gwen, TV is the great lobotomizer, but sometimes a person needs to tune out. You don't have much of a feel for ordinary life, Gwen, you have this willed idea of perfection that sometimes can strike a partner as a little rigid.

"Decidedly. I can't move any closer to the city: I made a resolution not to read books during the working day; my only excuse is trains and buses. If I lived any closer, I might have to do some real work." (Isaac, Gideon remembers, has one of those paying jobs that if you're smart take about an hour of your day.)

"And what are you up to? I haven't seen you around for a while." I was loved and now I am not. If I am not loved, I am not going to live.

"A lot of nonsense. I've just formed this . . . this filmmakers' cooperative. Nonfilmmakers' uncooperative. A bunch of babies like me, who love Pasolini and have this suspicion that film is the perfect vehicle for polemics. We've got a founding manifesto that we pool everything we earn, and that we make a movie a month . . ."

"Cool," says Gideon. Nodding too hard and unable to stop nodding.

Suddenly he is absolutely certain that Isaac Hooker is working up his nerve to ask him if he needs a place to live. And Gideon hates him for it. What gives this big lunk the right to think he can invite home like a pound puppy a grown man, father of a family, a neighbor from work whom he barely knows? He remembers that this person described himself as a Christian atheist, which after all is the worst of all worlds: sanctimonious authoritarianism unmitigated by any larger sense of awe.

"And you? Sancho told me you're—"

"Yeah, I'm living here now. The hunchback of La Merced."

Gideon, snuffling, rises. Wraps a winding-sheet around his waist. Picks up their coffee cups, dumps them in the sink. Spits into the sink. Man, he's repulsive. Wonders where the toothpaste has got to. He hasn't brushed his teeth in he can't remember how long.

This afternoon at three he's supposed to pick up Bella, which means it's time to start getting himself presentable. Children have delicate noses. He's not yet sure which way to go, up or down, more coffee or more Scotch—not the kind of Scotch he likes—he's got a fifth of cheap shit stashed in the file cabinet. Which he buys from an Indian store on Clinton Street that hasn't heard about Lower East Side gentrification: there's a caged window like a subway token booth, through which you shove your money and receive the goods. Won't they get a surprise next year when their rent quintuples, and they learn they're now expected to pay five grand a month for the privilege of living next door to investment bank trainees.

"What time's it?"

Gideon turns over the alarm clock. Twenty to one? Two hours to pull himself together in.

"Twenty to one?" repeats Isaac. "I'd better split. I'm going out to Dushan's; he's got a studio in Gowanus now."

"Do-what?"

"Remember Dushan? He's doing these Stations of the Cross. You want to come?"

"I can't," says Gideon. "I gotta pick up my daughter."

But mentioning Bella is making him lose it, so he wipes his nose on the sheet and thinks, More coffee. Nobody cries on coffee.

Isaac is still lingering. "So what do you think of Sancho's Eviction Day plans?"

"I haven't really been—"

"Sounds to me like Waco staged by the Theater of the Absurd. Lot of television cameras, and people throwing flowers at the police."

"Cool," says Gideon. "But I don't think I'll be here by then. I don't know where I'm going, but I need to get out . . ."

"You know," Isaac says. And here it comes, because Gideon, mangy hound, has given him the opening. "If you're looking for a place to live, I have an extra room. It's peaceful. You'd have a room to yourself, you and three thousand books . . ."

"Thanks," Gideon replies. "I am definitely reviewing all applications for assistance and advice."

"Think about it. It's a nice old house, biking distance to the beach; I got the top floor."

"Thanks," repeats Gideon, "but I think I should be making my toilette now."

Galvanized, suddenly, by anger.

He runs the tap full blast in the hopes that eventually the trickle of brownish-orange will turn at least tepid. Where did I put the soap? Wondering was his blanket too funky, too blood-encrusted to use for a towel.

He's got to get clean, somehow.

Last couple of times, the Bear's been shy with him. When Betty hands her over, she's clung to the older woman, crying. Then, by the end of the day, when Gideon's dropping her back home, it's Gideon she doesn't want to let go. Wraps her arms and legs around him as if he's a palm tree she's shinnying, buries her face in his knee, with a deep shaky sigh to break your heart.

Chapter Five

I

"So Russia's in total free fall," says Martin, coming out onto the porch, followed by his granddaughter, who is eating an oatmeal raisin cookie. "Looks like your pal Lavrinsky's about to lose a fortune."

A hot blue day, one of the last best August days, in whose clarity a hopeful eye can see the cusp of autumn. Broad green sloping lawn, across which a crew-cut youth is driving a mowing machine. Below, the splashes of children: Alexander and his weekend guest Jack, doing cannonballs into the swimming pool, inundating Serena and her friend Charlotte. Angry shrieks.

"Have you heard anything new?" Gwen, in a white piqué summer dress already smeared in ketchup from Bella's lunch, takes her daughter in her arms.

"Mama!" Bella, struggling free, yanks at her mother's hand. Bella, who has finished her cookie, wants another.

"Sssshhhhh," murmurs Gwen, wiping the crumbs from the child's chin. A sugary goatee. An unappeasable hunger for more.

"Well, President Clinton's flown over there to hold Yeltsin's hand!"

Father and daughter laugh. Gwen has already seen the television news footage of Yeltsin greeting Clinton, two fat buffoons with W. C. Fields noses, the drunk and the lech propping each other up . . .

"Mama, Mama, Mama . . ." begs Bella. Tugging.

"What's happening?" Jacey asks.

"Basically, there's no government," says Gwen. "Yeltsin's fired his prime minister and his cabinet, the ruble's lost forty percent of its value in a week, the banks have all gone bust, and there's no government. I don't know who Clinton thinks he's going to see . . . Russia's got no prime minister, we've got no president."

"Mama! Mama!" cries Bella, more insistently. Getting ready to belly flop into a mini-seizure of thwarted gluttony.

"It's kind of ironic," says Jacey. Jacey, in mirrored glasses, is resting on a deck chair after a game of doubles with some friends at the club. "America and Russia in meltdown at the same time."

"Mama? Mama? *MA-MA!*"

"It's kind of fatal, is what it is," Martin says, irritably. "There are things to be *done* in the world, like fixing the Asian economy. And here nobody's home, because the president's too busy perjuring himself. It would be a great moment for somebody to start a world war." On a lovely summer day like this, Gavril Princip assassinated the Archduke Franz Ferdinand . . .

"Well, that's your hero Kenneth Starr's fault," Jacey retorts. "It wasn't exactly Clinton's idea to get impeached."

"Ma-ma! Ma-ma! Ma-ma!"

"SSSShhhh, honey. Wait."

"Jacey, we happen to have a Constitution in this country. I'm sorry, but lying under oath is—"

"I think it's a KGB plot," says Gwen.

"Mama," screams Bella, tugging hard, hard on her mother's hand. "Mama! Mama!"

"Ssssshhhhh," murmurs Gwen, finger on her lips. "Just a moment, honey . . ."

"Mama! Mama!" Bella tugs, tugs, tugs harder on her seated mother's hand. Each time, she loses her grip and tumbles onto her bottom. Howls from irritation. Then seizes hold of the maternal hand and pulls again. It's a hard life being a baby.

"Sweetheart, you wanna come down to the pool with me?" says Jacey, holding out a hand.

"No, I think it's another cookie she wants, but she's had enough . . ."

"It's time for Serena's tennis lesson," Jacey tells Martin. "I don't suppose *you* feel like running her down to the—"

Martin looks evasive.

"I didn't think so."

"Mama! Mama! Mama!"

"Ssssssshhhhh . . ."

"What *are* your plans for this lovely afternoon, Martin, you gonna plug into CNN again?"

"Mama! Mama!"

"Nah. Honestly? I gotta shitload of work . . ." Martin has some color back in his face. Jacey has told Gwen that the impeachment business has given him a new lease on life. He's well enough to be back at work on the Yippee Time Warner deal. Martin's being better means Jacey is hopping mad at him from all the months when she wasn't allowed to get angry because he was supposedly dying of cancer. Anyone who didn't know Jacey would imagine she regarded her husband's recovery as a massive gyp.

"You wanna come down to the pool with me, honey?" Jacey is heading down the flagstone steps to where Serena and Charlotte are sunbathing. "Gwen, you want me to take Bella to the club? She might enjoy watching the tennis . . ."

"Nah! Nah! Nah!" screams Bella. Now, giving up on forcibly towing her mother inside to the cookie jar, she flings herself flat. Pounds fists, hammers feet. Tries her damnedest to turn blue. Gwen cannot take her daughter's tantrums seriously. She could be taking lessons, they are such exquisite illustrations of the form.

"What's the matter, sweetheart?" demands Martin.

"She's screaming because she wants another cookie, Pop."

"You want a cookie, sweetheart? I'll get you a cookie."

"I don't want her to have any more cookies."

"What's the matter, these are health food cookies, Sabine makes them, they're just oatmeal and—"

"She's had enough already, Pop, I don't want her getting sick."

Martin stands up, smoothing down his shirt where he's begun to get his belly back.

"What are you doing this afternoon, Gwen?" asks Jacey.

"Me?" Gwen grins. "I'm watching Russia sink. I'm gonna sail out my little boat and watch the big ship go down . . ."

Jacey puts on a sympathetic face. This was supposed to be Gwen's three-day vacation. Instead, she's spent the last thirty-six hours between the computer and the telephone, sending off e-mails, listening to Russian news stations on the Internet. Talking to the office. Today she's been checking up on her friends in Moscow, St. Petersburg, the provinces, who are waiting to see if their savings and investments have just become worthless.

"We'll survive," shrugged her friend Masha, who's an importer-exporter, "but last night Alex Tarielashvili came over." (Alex was unlucky enough to have opened a wine bar six months ago, catering to the new rich.) "He's wondering with how many of his vital organs he's going to have to pay off the criminals who put up the money. You know that's what the mafia is doing these days, they don't just kill you: they sell your liver and kidneys. Suicide is looking like his *best* option. It's sad, he has a six-month-old daughter . . ."

Gwen gets up to find Bella a cookie, a bribe to silence the kid so she can make a couple more phone calls in peace. It's funny, she's had this inkling it was going to come any minute. What was it, last week George Soros published his letter in the *Financial Times* demanding a devaluation of the ruble? And the next day, crash.

From the pool area rises an amplified yowl from Serena, who *hates* tennis, who *loathes* tennis, who doesn't see why she should be made to go to her tennis lesson when she's got her friend Charlotte staying.

Gwen thinks, Nothing has any meaning. The world is made of plaster. Ingratiating worthlessness.

Her small daughter, who is still lying on the ground, cocks her head, astounded by the sound of a half-grown-up child's tears.

The disjunction between mowed lawn and extorted kidneys, between tennis lessons and her broken Gideon, is too jarring.

Everything she bet on was wrong.

But the alternative is worse.

There is no alternative: it's all garbage, fancy garbage or unadorned garbage. The same gussied-up dreck. Same spilled jizm.

Her cell phone rings. She glances at her watch, working out time differences. No, it's a 212 call, from a number she doesn't recognize. Hoping it's not Gideon on a rant.

"Hey Gwendolen, what's up? You at the country club sipping mint juleps?" Gerald, who's been giving her a hard time about her summer of ease.

"Almost. Country clubs I can't do, it brings out the nonexistent Jew in me. But there does happen to be an Olympic-sized pool within spitting distance . . ."

She watches Serena being led indoors, like a prisoner on the way to the dock. Serena, slim and long-legged in her gold-hooped bikini, almost as tall as her mother, has Jacey's brown skin paired with streaky golden hair, now plastered slick across her small skull. Perfect prepubescent beauty, marred by an expression of rabid petulance.

"I got Paul Kravitz from the *Wall Street Journal* wants Lavrinsky to write an op-ed piece on the crisis. You want to do it?"

"When's it due?"

"Tomorrow."

"How long?"

"Eight hundred words. You want his number? You can talk to him yourself."

"Sure."

"Any more news from Rubleville? Who's prime minister this afternoon?"

"I think it's Molotov," says Gwen. "Speaking of mint juleps. Have I got any news? Not much, it's just not a country anymore, that's all."

"It's a pretty large noncountry . . ."

"A large robbed grave. It's not going to be a country for what? Decades. Maybe never. Russia is predictable. The question I want to know is, are we out of a job?"

Gerald laughs. Gerald can afford to laugh. Gerald's never liked Russia: he was happy to bring it to its knees and rather bored by having to help it up again. It will always be the enemy, and not nearly as worthy an enemy as, say, Germany.

If Lavrinsky decides that he's lost enough money and his programs aren't working, Gerald won't much blame him: it's no fun losing money. Besides, Gwen has reason to believe, Gerald, along with Lavrinsky, thinks it's time for a third party in American politics. Gwen would not be surprised to learn that Gerald was going to go work for Steve Forbes's next presidential campaign . . .

2

THE DAY THE U.S. stock market crashed because of Asia—no, pardon me: in our era of endless economic growth, we no longer have crashes, just "corrections"—I thought, Maybe you will lose all your money, and I thought, maybe your daddy will lose all his money, and maybe Lavrinsky will lose all his money, and then you will come back to me. Because I'll be like the blind man who can see in the night, who can teach you how to see with the heart's inward eye. We can teach our daughter to glean birds' eggs and wild sorrel in Central Park, and our laughter will keep us warm, and we will not want. We will no longer be giants, but very, very small. Not Herods, but the little doves, the remnants of Zion, who are saved because they hide in the cleft of the rock.

The day Russia crashed, I thought, Wheeee. Because here is a girl who doesn't like sick people, here is a girl who only likes the rich. She got tired of me because I was a loser, and now she will get tired of Russia too, since it's going to be poor forever. I thought, Who will be your next project, widow-spider-woman?

3

CRISP AUTUMN DAY, as sparkly—after three days' rain—as if God had bathed the city with His own hands. In Central Park, the grass is newly washed silk, the earth underneath delicious rich muck. Fall is the season of beginnings.

When they reach the cherry grove overhanging the toy-boat pond, mother and child break into a downhill canter.

Gwen, behind, delights in her daughter's prowess: how she shoots free of the maternal grasp and streaks down the hill, sturdy little legs splaying sideways.

Gwen knows she should teach her daughter caution, but instead she encourages Bella's wildnesses, thrilled silly to have produced a child who has less sense than a fox of traffic, high windows, electrical sockets. People talk of courting danger: well, danger had never been so thoroughly beguiled.

Bella races all the way to the boat pond, where for one panicked instant Gwen—too far behind—thinks the baby's not going to stop. Caught, on the brink, by an elderly gentleman, who pins her, flailing, by the hood of her sweatshirt, till Gwen—simultaneously frightened, angry, and *impressed*—catches up.

Just before her mother can bawl her out, Bella, grinning, kisses Gwen's knees, and is off again. Stops once more to look into the water.

"Ba?" she inquires, teasingly. "Ba" means bath. She wants to swim. She makes a show of pulling off her sweatshirt, of plunging in. "No!" yells Gwen. Being the mother of a nearly two-year-old makes you feel very Soviet. There are days on end when *"Nyet"* is all Gwen gets to say.

She's a fish, Gwen's Bella, a mermaid, magnetically attracted to glittering surfaces, glint, slither, flux. Next summer she'll be old enough to swim. Gwen plans to take her to stay for several weeks with Christopher and Yilmaz, who are renting the same house in Assos. Bella will learn to paddle in the great Aegean, like Thetis, daughter of Nereus. But for now she's stranded at the pebbly rim of the model-boat pond. Where her mother first laid eyes on her father, a thousand and three years ago.

Gwen had always imagined telling Bella the story of her parents' encounter: how Gwen, sitting on a bench with Bella's unofficial god-mother Constance, had mistaken her future husband for a tramp. Gwen used to think of Ulysses' homecoming when she remembered her husband-in-disguise. But nowadays, when Gideon shows up for his "visitations" in the same sweatpants he sleeps in, the alcohol vaporing from every pocked pore, her mistake seems a more malevolent foreshadowing of fate.

Today there are real tramps—realer than Gideon—by the boat pond: a swollen-faced man with a topknot who wears a Japanese kimono, a red-chapped lady who, like a fisherman with his net, is laying out her undergarments to dry on a sunny bench, before whom Bella stands in fascination. Gwen reclaims her child just before she seizes one of the lady tramp's ranged stockings.

They wander in search of other children. A few nannies by Alice in Wonderland—Vietnamese, Caribbean. A Russian mother on a bench, her small daughter by her side. Gwen can spot the Slavs a city block away, because their children are dressed like circus poodles, in neurotically unseasonable clothes. If she sees a pale sausage wearing tartan wool overalls and matching tartan hair bows in July, her mama's from Stavropol.

This particular mother Gwen already knows. Gwen, with a New Yorker's inveteracy for networking, has concluded that since Bella will not allow her to use playground time to read the newspaper or make phone calls, chatting to captive Russians is the most efficient dual use she can manage.

"Kag'dila?" Gwen inquires of the pale depressed woman in an Hermès scarf whose husband is in "bizniz." Occasionally Gwen has tried to find out more about the husband's particular line of business, but mostly she must content herself with acquiring a new annex, a back porch to her Russian fluency: toilet training, inner ear infections, preschool. The vocabulary of anxiety, of fear. Of fussing. Of transferred ambition. Of fatigue deep as shell shock.

Bella, however, has no interest in underwriting her mother's professional Slavicism: she's already deemed three-year-old Nadezhda a wuss. Having robbed her of her Petits Beurres, she's agitating to move onto swings and monkey bars, to other children who have tricycles and dolls' strollers to steal.

And Nadezhda's mother, though homesick for her mother tongue, is too preoccupied by her single offspring's constipation to discuss Russia, even the great topic of the hour, which must have put quite a dent in the family "bizniz."

For maternity, as Gwen has discovered, although universal, is not social. Although identical, it is not shareable. It is deeply deeply narrowing. You see it, this morning as Gwen and Bella ascend to the Seventy-sixth Street playground. There is a gang of happy nannies, knitting, gossiping, laughing, whooping in the sunlight. And then there is this scattering of solitary women, muttering into cell phones. The mothers. *Un*happy, preoccupied. Each positively harrowed by her own private calvary of boredom, depression, exhaustion. Blanched women with deep lines in their foreheads, dark circles under their eyes, who have already lost their temper four times that morning, and will regain it six more times before dark. Professional women who once lived in the world and earned a cheering paycheck, and whose energies and cunning are now spent, bankrupted even, on unsuccessfully cajoling another person into putting on her shoes. With the same expenditure of energy and cunning, you could win autonomy for the Turkish Kurds or negotiate a new trans-Caucasian gas pipeline. Or you could lie in bed with drawn curtains, making up for the last seven hundred nights of butchered sleep and brain drain.

Poor mothers, thinks Gwen, who, almost out the other side, feels omnipotent. Bella now regularly sleeps through the night; she is learning (with immense satisfaction) to pee in a pot, and although she's restless and stubborn and headstrong, she's an only girl, which means Gwen can take her to Christopher's for Sunday lunch, to museum exhibitions, to Sasha and Irina's for the day.

Gwen has come into the clear, where her two lives no longer glare and squabble. It feels like permanent jubilee, to come home from a brainstorming session on the Russian economy and be assailed by a shrieking-with-glee baby wanting to ride on your back—jubilee, equally, to flee the triviality of child-life into the high-adrenaline world of IMF bailouts, civil war, currency flight. Secure in Betty, who has promised to remain at least till next summer, Gwen quite often will say, "Why don't you take Monday off? I'll stay home with the girl."

Besides, there are the "visitation" hours when Bella is with her father, and Gwen, trying to bribe herself with bachelor pleasures that now seem hollow, realizes that without this child her life is *nothing*.

Do you think sometimes, Gwen, of what went wrong?

Gwen is a practiced hand at *not* thinking, a person to whom systematic forgetting appears mental hygiene. When Constance or Christopher or Gerald or Jacey initially pressed her, she said only that it was her fault, that she was impossible to live with, a person horribly selfish and controlling who was better off alone, who should not be "with" someone (excepting Bella, with whom mysteriously she manages never to get cross except by design). If Gideon's share of the blame was impelled by some darker impulse to self-destruct, well, that's for him to figure out.

When she sees her husband on drop-offs or pickups, she sees a fallen man who fills her with sorrow. A broken man, whom she has not helped, whom she is all too conscious of having left worse off than when they met. (Whereas she, because of Bella, is better off.) And although she is convinced of his ultimate resilience, they two have nothing more to say to each other. Something is broken in each of them that can never be mended, and they can no more come together than go back to the womb—the cord that bound them in their amniotic love is cut, and it is time to learn to breathe.

The sunlight in the playground has shifted, leaving the sandbox in a Dantesque state of icy darkness. Gwen moves her daughter over to the now-glittering slide and sees that her friend Galya has come through the playground gate. Galya, short-legged, with a long black braid, is a Georgian Jewish mathematics graduate, one of the few ex-Soviet playground mothers with a little spunk, and a son naughty enough to handle Bella.

"So?" demands Gwen.

"SO?" retorts Galya, with a face of theatrical disgust.

"SO?"

"Are you asking me about the economy or about our clown president or about this week's prime minister who is the paid servant of Gazprom?"

"All."

"Don't ask. Better we should talk about our families and where we won't go on vacation next summer. It's a KGB plot to make people beg for Communism again."

"Well, listen, it's great for me," says Gwen. "First of all, I'm about to be unemployed because Lavrinsky's fed up with losing money in Russia. Second of all, I'm giving this conference next month on Russian criminality, which suddenly seems a pretty topical subject . . ."

"Why don't you give yourself an easy assignment that doesn't take so much work," suggests Galya. "Why don't you give a conference instead on Russian honesty or Russian intelligence? But maybe you don't want to be like the Greek philosopher Diogenes, searching with his flashlight for nobody . . ."

"Ma-ma! Ma-ma!" Bella approaches, opening and closing her outstretched hand to indicate that Gwen is to come climb the slide with her.

"I don't know," shrugs Gwen as she is dragged across the playground, far from people she might want to talk to. "I'm considering moving *back* to Russia. I didn't much like it the year it was rich."

4

GWEN DREAMS THAT she is sewing buttons on Bella's dress. It's a beautiful old nightdress—the white cambric nightgown in which Gwen slept the night before her wedding, which in real life she bought with Christopher at a street market in Saint-Nazaire, but which in the dream is Bella-sized.

She's sewing buttons on the nightdress *while* Bella is wearing it. The child is uncharacteristically still. Until, examining her handiwork, Gwen realizes that she has been piercing her daughter's flesh with the needle, sewing the girl's flesh to the fabric with each stitch.

The torn flesh of Bella's chest is sewn tight to the white cloth, and the girl is not making a sound. Only an odd little smile on her face. Her eyes are open, but she is dead . . .

And Gwen, in her dream, starts screaming, and awakens, midscream. She switches on her bedside light. It's 3:47. The days are fine, but the nights are tricky. At first, it was Bella's nightmares. Then Gideon would call up, 3, 4 a.m., hysterical-accusing, slobbering-gibbering drunk. Now Gwen unplugs her telephone, switches off the cell phone; now Bella is sleeping the nights through. But these days it's Gwen who awakens, rigid with terror . . .

There's a Hebrew song Gideon used to sing Bella that runs through Gwen's head. In English it went, "The whole world is a narrow bridge, and the thing is not to be scared."

This saying by some Hasidic mystic (which could equally well be pre-Socratic, Confucian) had charmed her, with its humorous reversal of one's accepted conception of the world as a great wide-open place. She had pictured the bridge as a medieval pontoon from a Chinese watercolor or a Japanese woodcut, suspended in the river fog, with vendors selling caged songbirds and grasshoppers, and fat merchants crossing on donkeys.

These nights, the words reel through her brain, over and over, and now the-bridge-that-is-the-world seems more of a frayed rope ladder strung rickety across the abyss, over which you crawled, on hands and knees. And the claustrophobic insecurity of the bridge urged you to jump, because a person with guts or self-respect would say, I want to get off this narrow bridge, I don't consent to crawl.

There are moments in the night when she thinks, I cannot do this. I cannot bring up my child alone. I cannot face the day.

There are moments when she thinks, I've fucked up so badly I don't even deserve custody of this girl. There are moments when she too agrees, When she grows up, she won't forgive me.

5

THEN ONE EVENING, when Gideon drops off Bella, he tells Gwen, "I'm moving out of the city."

The relief seeps all across her body. "For good?"

"Probably. I'm going back up to Lubeck for a while."

She doesn't know what to say. Anything she says, he jumps on. Anything she doesn't say, he jumps on. But this evening, he appears to be in a more benign mood. He sits down on the sofa at her invitation, after Bella's gone to sleep.

"What are you going to do?" she asks.

"I'm going to look after the place while everybody's on tour. There's a cottage that used to be Bridey's parents' I'm going to live in. Jerome figures there's enough odd jobs to keep me busy. I can stay there through the winter, anyways, till I figure out what to do next."

There's something Gideon wants from her. His voice is soft, polite. "I was thinking maybe I could start taking Bella for weekends. I'll have Jerome's car, I can drive her back and forth . . ."

Gwen considers. She hates the idea. She hates everything about it. "Weekends. You mean, every weekend? Every other weekend?"

"Or during the week, if that suits you better."

"You mean for a night, two nights at a time?" She hates the idea. She and Bella have never spent a night apart.

"Yeah, it's kind of a long trip to make sense for less than two nights."

She hesitates. She hates it. So this is the price of having Gideon at a safe distance. Having her daughter unsafe. Is she allowed to say no?

"What is it, two and a half, three hours' drive? You know," she says, "forgive me, but I don't think I'd feel too happy about having Bella in a car with you these days . . ."

He sighs. "I'm not going to drive drunk, if that's what you mean. Believe me, I'm as concerned for her safety as you are. I *want* her to feel happy and safe with me, it's in my own interest . . ."

She bites back every answer that might provoke a wrangle she's not up for. "Isn't there a train? Or a bus, or something? And how would I know if she was up there for a couple of days, she'd be all right?"

She wants in the worst way to cry, but she can't, not in front of him. "You'd have to show me, Gideon. You'd really have to show me you were in okay shape to . . . There isn't somewhere you can stay in the city? Look, you can stay *here* with her—I'll move over to my father's, or Christopher's. It just . . . it just makes me nervous, these days. Why don't you two stay here, in the apartment?"

Every ounce of self-control Gideon possesses has been summoned to get him through this conversation. Gwen has never heard her husband so reasonable.

"I think that would be more destabilizing for her. I need to take her somewhere that's mine—that she and I can have together, our own place. We'll have this cottage, where she can keep some of her toys, her clothes. Where she's got her own bed. Where we can make things together, that she'll find waiting for her."

He's obviously planned thoroughly this idea which appalls her. She sighs, feeling cornered. "You have to show me, Gideon. You're going to have to talk me through this one."

He nods. On his face is an expression of calm control that she knows is pure acting.

What is he planning, really?

Chapter Six

Who is like you, God?

No one.

Who is like you, God?

No one. Compared to you, our lives are broken glass. Compared to you, our highest hopes are a black hole.

Who is like you, God? You are great; we are dried scumbags discarded beneath a bridge. But even though we stink, we are yours. So please, God, take pity on us, and inscribe us for a healthy prosperous year.

The congregation has regathered after Yizkor. It is pouring rain. There must be a hundred and fifty people crammed into the tiny pink-and-turquoise sanctuary of Ohelei Yaakov, Jews in their holiday best, woozy with fasting, keyed up with the gabby alarm of Judgment Day. Dripping wet. Gideon, glaring, burning, radioactive, warning his neighbors, Do not touch me.

Back in August (shortly after their night at *Rasselas*), Gideon had ordered a family ticket for the High Holidays: one step in his sneaky scheme to recapture his family. He'd had this inciting revelation that he had failed Gwen by neither giving her enough of himself nor exacting enough from her. He'd thought of Gwen's friend Ari, who'd insisted that his Irish Catholic girlfriend convert to Judaism before they even discussed marriage, and he'd decided, I'll tell Gwen, Cut off your hair and wear a hat, I'm going to make a Jewish wife of you, and together we'll search the paths of righteousness. In his insane optimism (engendered, he now realizes, by the fluke of having slept once more with his wife, having buried his semen an unforeseen time in her sealed womb), he had called up Ohelei Yaakov and ordered a family ticket for the High Holidays, even though he could ill afford the $175 sedan to Forgiveness, on the wager that they'd be back together by the end of September. (As if his expulsion were merely a test, proving to Gwen that their dybbukry was indeed soul-destined, foreordained, irreversible.)

And now this envelope marked "The Gideon Wolkowitz Family"

taunts him. He feels horribly light, horribly shorn, a luftmensch-Niobe in this crowd of stocky husbands and plump wives with teeming broods. Gideon, who is tall enough to peer into the women's section, sees young mothers in floppy hats; humpbacked liver-speckled grandmothers with brooches and veils; slouchy teen hipsters in hooded sweatshirts, black maxiskirts, white platform sneakers, lissome stalk-slender beauties, old enough to flirt but too young to marry.

In Gideon's section, the grizzled *makhers*—developers, lawyers, brokers in penitential Nikes and New Balances—huddle in twos and threes. There are men of Gideon's age—i.e., in the bloom of loudmouthed, thrusting, self-important parenthood. (For surely forty is the most pompous age of man.) There are young men yeshiva-wan, bobbing and droning in prayer; young men with Jersey Shore tans and pumped-up muscles; there are downy-lipped adolescents, hanging on to wisecracking fathers; reedy-voiced ten-year-olds still shuttling between the women's section and the men's.

Jews, Jews, Jews. Jews chatting, Jews praying, Jews bored and daydreaming, Jews checking out the opposite sex over the fence. *Gmar tov, gmar tov.* Rich Jews, struggling Jews, Jews with too many children, Jews in search of business, Jews in search of a marriage partner. Jews in tennis shoes, Jews in kittel. Today their fate will be sealed, by sundown the Book of Judgment will be closed.

Wives and husbands meet at the border of the *mehitzah,* exchange children, strategies, admonitions; men shmooze. How's business, Dave? *Baruch Ha Shem,* no layoffs yet. So where you living now? The West Side is this . . . Riverdale is that. Aw, I think Clinton's gonna skin through this one fine. The *last* thing the Republicans want is Al Gore in the canary seat . . . Ironically, the project on Water Street has been held up by . . . And can you believe they sprang this new supervisor on us the week before we . . .

The brightest sparks of each epoch and each encampment of the long Judaic drama have given their best to the day's passion. Medieval wonderboys—"ben So-and-so" and "ibn Such-and-such"—from provincial towns in Catalonia and the Rhineland have bled their jewels into the liturgy, into fevered acrostics, willfully hermetic—Moses, Jacob, Isaac, encoded as the Meek One, the Perfect One, the One Who Was Bound.

Such cults of hiddenness, of bondage, of exile and sacrifice! Such flaming tales of martyrdom, obscenely gory, of medieval saints who were uncomplainingly flayed and charred! They set you an example, Gideon. You thought, My turn next.

But hard as he tries to concentrate on the text, to give himself over to heartfelt repentance and to prayer, Gideon finds himself distracted by the nagging volubility of the masculine chatter. So, Mike, I'm thinking of buying Ruchi a computer. You got anything to recommend . . . My health? Don't ask. You shouldn't know from . . . SSSSSSHHHHH-HHH . . .

Abominable, his prayer mates' shallow fatuous self-preoccupation, their inability to stop smart-alecking and bragging and complaining even under the shadow of the guillotine, in this holiest most horrible moment, when judgment is falling. Who will be strangled who will be stoned who will be eaten by ravening beasts. When their sins are screaming scarlet, their lies, their chicaneries, their frauds, their concealments, their complicity in murder, their bad-mouthing, their rejoicing in others' discomfiture their fleecing the innocent their tax evasions their running to do evil their blindness to social injustice their refusal to feed the starving to clothe the naked to comfort windows and orphans. Widows.

There are no windows in the room, Gideon realizes, plenty of widows but no windows, no air, no air, only a ceiling fan circulating stale breath, stale bodies. The aisles are jammed tight, there is probably no working fire exit. At the rear, leading to the foyer and the street, a mass of dawdlers, mothers of footloose toddlers, courting singles, block the exit. You could not get out of here alive.

Gideon has been fasting not merely since the previous sundown but since the previous morning, and what had he eaten then? A bag of Cheez Doodles. He has not eaten anything but dyed-orange deep-fried artificial-cheese puffs in . . . weeks. He has a permanent pain in his stomach, nagging cramps, he is shitting blood, he is so weak—so weakened by sin!—he can barely drag himself down a city block. His body, which has polluted itself, is a worthless sac of bloody shit.

Tomorrow he is leaving leaving tomorrow he is leaving. Making himself leave *Them* is the hardest thing he has yet had to do. He is ripping himself away from Them because living for those ten minutes each week at drop-offs and pickups, in which he lays eyes on his once-beloved, is worse than not living. It will not happen, he now understands from their last meeting, she will not change her mind, he will never be allowed home. Judgment is sealed.

Tomorrow Dan and Andrea, who are back in the city for the High Holidays, will drive him and his cardboard boxes up to Lubeck. And after they leave, Gideon will stay on, alone. Lubeck awaits him like the prison of his past, the fatal family home. A place where he has been very happy, with a happiness that is irrecoverable, and also virulently unhappy, with a wild black howling unhappiness that now seems his maternal legacy, his recurrent lot. (And who knows what he'll do in a month's time, when Jerome and Bridey and the crew return, because being resubmitted to Jerome's conniving twisted will seems a truly annihilating regression . . .)

Gideon tries to catch up with the cantor, who is cantering through the siddur, skipping many pages at a time and then doubling back. Gideon clings to the mane of the liturgy, trying to keep his mount, but each time that his mind wanders, he loses his place, the runaway horse gallops away, and he has to wait until a familiar text recurs in order to scramble back on.

Now he sees that his fellow congregants are once again beating their chests in the Ashamnu, and he too falls in, relieved to be able to fold his own misdoings into the communal lot.

We have lied, we have stolen, we have borne false witness, we have been stiff-necked. Again and again, in a continuous reel, the message rolls around: You are everything, we are nothing, we are whores, you are our john—I mean, our wronged husband, and Gideon too pounds his chest, thinking, The president of the United States is being impeached by Congress for lying under oath about masturbating all over the blue Gap dress of an overweight Jewish hussy, and I am being divorced by my wife for not lying under oath about getting my ashes hauled by an underweight Jewish hussy, there is nothing but robbery and stinking idol-worship and hatred under the sun, and an obscene disparity in lots, for some, starvation, slaughter, epidemic, while others wallow in goatish gut-busting offshore plenty . . .

For three months now, off and on, he has cursed his wife for driving him to fornication, he has fantasized about sending a letter bomb to Emma Rogan, or waiting outside her building and seizing her by the throat and squeeze-squeezing, his hands are itching to squeeze, he has dreamed of dismembering her with a meat cleaver because it is ALL HER FAULT, because if she had not, from calculating malice, stuffed her stinking sperm-slimed panties in his wife's laundry hamper (he has thought many, many times how hard Emma would have had to pry loose the stuck metal lid in order to deposit them there), then his wife would not have aborted their baby, then their reconciliation would have taken, G&G&B would be all three in one warm adoring embrace, his wife with a big belly, heavy with their second child, their worst worry, Was Bella going to feel displaced by her new sibling?

The woman killed my baby, she has made our daughter an only child. She was sent like a KGB mole to entrap me. Because I was giving off vibes that I wasn't getting sex from my wife, she was sent like Job's plagues, and I—no prophet—was too measly-vindictive to resist. I fell. And because I fell, we all fell. All fallen, all three of us, Gwen, Bella, me. Fallen. Because of the woman, we are fallen. And if he hadn't slept with the woman, they would be together . . . And if President Clinton hadn't slept with the woman, if she hadn't danced in her ungainly hefty-heifer nakedness before him, reamed his cigar up her fat pussy, oh shame-sodden shit-eating Shulamit, the United States too would be greatly un-defiled, not a land of cringing hyena-whoredom.

Gideon tries once again to find his place in the siddur, but (in his impatience, he'd grabbed an old prayer book which doesn't have the same page numberings as his neighbors') he is lost. He sits and listens, until he realizes that they have entered a new still more fateful portion of the service.

The cantor has just begun reciting the "Ameetz Koach": a History of the World, culminating in the high priest's temple sacrifice on Atonement Day. It's an amazing piece of work. You, Gwen, who are into eso-teric types like Khlebnikov, should really take a look at the Ameetz Koach, a text kaleidoscopically condensed and refracted as if written by a particularly absinthe-doped French Symbolist.

Gideon zips through the English version of how the priest is kept awake by the elders for the nights preceding Yom Kippur lest he unwit-tingly pollute himself in his sleep. (Gideon can remember his own snig-gering wonderment, as a filthy-minded adolescent, that so much of the Holiest Day should be preoccupied with secrecies and perversions of sexuality, including the high priest's wet dreams!)

The cantor, who sings the story seemingly in one breath, has a voice at once nasal and sweet, repulsive and pleasing. It's not hard to believe that the singer himself is the high priest, abstaining from sleep's impuri-ties, bathing and anointing and girding himself in his white robes, ex-pelling the scapegoat who carries Israel's sins, withdrawing alone to the inner sanctum, and reemerging, radiant as Moses, to ensure the com-munity's survival for another year.

Only Gideon, listening, feels intolerably impure. The weight of his own sin is pressing down on his skull, threatening to splinter his temples, to crush his brain.

Once again, the congregation is on its knees, creakily prostrating themselves, pressing their heads to the ground, and suddenly Gideon is seized by such a violence of self-loathing at his failure once again to make himself loved that he bangs his head against the linoleum floor, God smash my worthlessness crush and annihilate me, explode this fetid sac to smithereens, he wants to shatter his skull into shards, immolate himself into Eastern European ashes, he wants to flay his own hide because he is no longer willing to pollute this already poisoned earth, he is banging banging his forehead against the dusty linoleum, he is choking, choking, his beard eats the dust, he wants to lick until he strangles, he wants to DIE DIE DIE . . .

There is an aggravated buzzing above him. Devilry. Somebody helps him to his feet, somebody gently sits him down. He closes his eyes. He doesn't want to know his meddlesome repriever. If he keeps his eyes closed, he can dream it's tall Gwen with ten-foot wings who's bearing him back to their wedded bed.

A voice intolerably male asks if he's all right.

Gideon says irritably, "I'm fine, I'm fine."

The long day won't die. The gates of repentance won't close. The long long day has turned to stone. Immobile. He has a sudden flash—the long day's waiting, the being supported by helpful assistants—of Gwen in labor, the orange-flowered poster in the hospital corridor—dear God, he'd thought it was the worst moment in his life, his wife in so much pain and him helpless, he hadn't known it was the best!

BOOK TEN

Chapter One

I

"RUSSIA'S FIRST ORDER of business is tax collection. You get these empires, Gazprom, Oneximport, Sibneft, Gusinsky's complex of media, banks, whatever—*that basically do not pay their taxes.* The public treasury is *empty* because the largest corporations in the country are tax cheats. In 1994, the Finance Ministry figured Russia lost five billion dollars just in tax breaks, plus anywhere from fifteen to twenty billion in capital flight. This is a fiscal problem, this is also a problem of civic morale. If you—"

"That's certainly the conventional wisdom, Mike," says Eugene Kolchuk. "Unfortunately, it happens to be one of the very few pieces of conventional wisdom that do not stand up to reality."

The audience chuckles. Eugene Kolchuk, five feet five with a boxer's squashed face behind black glasses, grins back, baring buckteeth with a gap you could squeeze through. Kolchuk was born in Odessa. Though he came to the U.S. as a small boy, he still exudes that port city's roustabout showmanship.

"Fact," Kolchuk continues: "Thirty-one percent of Russia's GDP comes from revenue. In the United States, it's thirty-four. Tax collection obviously is not Russia's defining problem."

"And in your view, Eugene, the cause of the Russian crisis is . . . ?" Gerald intervenes.

"Crisis? What crisis?"

A snort of laughter from Mike Kaplan and Ludovic Sanders, the other two members of the panel.

"There is no crisis. What we're seeing is a combination of some Soviet-style reactions by the Russian treasury—like capital control has ever solved anything—and short-term panic among Western banks and investors, who suddenly realize their newfound partners are not playing by the same rules as the FDIC. But the Russian economy is fundamentally sound—"

"If you mean, Eugene, that the country's got a potentially fabulous wealth in oil, gold, nickel, natural gas, I'm with you. So does much of sub-Saharan Africa. But unfortunately, postcolonialism, there doesn't seem to be much correlation between natural resources and a country's comfort level. In the—"

"Remember this: two years ago, the ruble was not even convertible. In another eighteen months, two years, I predict that Russia will be seeing positive growth."

"How much do you wanna bet, Eugene? Do you want to make it rubles?" Gerald, who is moderator, inquires.

"For a number of reasons. The—"

Gwen is sitting in the second-to-last row of the audience in the Renaissance Room at the Hotel Siena, Day Two of the Lavrinsky Institute's conference on the New Russia.

It's an impressive turnout for a Saturday morning. She sees many of the same journalists from yesterday afternoon's session: Jim Beck from the *Washington Post,* Laurie Weiner from the *Wall Street Journal,* James Munro from the *Financial Times,* and a kid who introduces herself as Charlene Grossman from *Newsweek.* And a reporter from *La Repubblica,* who is covering the conference, has asked Gwen for an interview.

Dee-dee-dee. Gwen's new cell phone, which sings "London Bridge Is Falling Down." Or is it "Mary Had a Little Lamb"?

Eugene Kolchuk is still gesticulating. If history hadn't intervened, he might have grown up to be an Odessan bookie, a boxer, a character actor. Instead, he is a resident scholar at the Hoover Institution.

Men hate listening to other men talk. Ludovic Sanders, a mild-mannered blond with tiny octagonal glasses, has gone pink with irritation; Michael Kaplan, who wears a crosshatched gray-black wig, feigns magisterial amusement.

". . . Falling down, falling down . . ." the phone bleeps. (Little lamb, little lamb?) Her new cell phone tells you who's calling before you pick up. This perk is almost worth the tune.

"And the third reason is . . ." Kolchuk is counting off on square fingers.

An upstate area code, which means it's Gideon calling. Bad timing, but a relief: Bella is spending the weekend up in Lubeck. Gwen has just survived (more or less) their first night apart.

It was unreasonably wrenching, yesterday morning, helping Bella (wearing her red patent-leather Betty Boop knapsack strapped across her front) into Gideon's waiting taxi. Gwen pressed her nose against the window, blew Bella a kiss. The child, hugging the knapsack like a baby, blew her mother back a tentative kiss—blew, as you blow out a candle. The cab pulled away, and Gwen felt her heart plummet.

Being with Bella demands a capability that leaves no room for inner collapse. So long as Bella is there, Gwen's had to make everything royally all right, and the daily battle of dressing-teeth-brushing-feeding-bathing-story-reading-sleep has proved redemption-by-normality. This was what people didn't tell you about having a child: the child made you strong so you in turn could make her free.

It was brutal, peeking into the baby's room last night, sitting on Bella's brand-new little-girl's bed (no bars) this morning and thinking, She is all I love. Even mid-conference, the missing-her is raw. Gwen needs to remind herself that it's good for the girl to spend a few days with her father. That Gideon, too, needs the child.

Besides, Gwen's running frantic this weekend, coping with faulty microphone systems, delayed flights and missed connections, lunch seating plans, and last-minute interference from Lavrinsky. There won't be a moment to breathe till Sunday night, when her girl will be returned to her.

2

UNTIL GIDEON MOVED UP TO LUBECK, she had not realized how jumpy he'd made her. How, each time she left the Vanderveer or came home at night, she'd half-consciously expected him to be lurking in wait.

Gideon still calls every day, ostensibly to speak to Bella. (The schizophrenic disjunction of trying to tune out her ex-partner's recriminations while telling Bella cheerfully, "It's Daddy, honey, would you like to say hello?" Overhearing his telephone voice mutate from a shriek to a coo.)

Yet she believes he's been calmer since he left the city. Not better: Gideon will never allow her to think he's any better, he would sooner disembowel himself on the podium of the Hotel Siena's Renaissance Room than allow the minutest relaxation of her atrocious culpability, her crime.

But—this is the catch—he nonetheless needs her to think him stable enough to look after Bella for three days—a feat he certainly wasn't capable of *before* they broke up. She has fought, she has fought, she has fought—it kills her to let go of the girl—but finally she's surrendered. Everybody tells her she's got to allow Bella's father "access": Galya recounts how for years her ex-husband showed up two, three hours late, or not at all, for his monthly appointments with their son, before moving to Germany without telling them. You're lucky your daughter has a father who wants her, is the message.

Even so, Gwen's done a little detective work. She has tracked down Andrea in Vermont, called to say, Look, I know I'm the last person you want to hear from, but have you seen Gideon lately, and how did he seem to you, because for God's sake I've got to know the truth.

And Andrea, caught by surprise, too nice to freeze out this woman Pantaloons consider poison, confirms that Gideon is indeed saner. She and Dan went to stay with him last week: he's done a lot of work around the farm, he's reshingling the roof on the main house. He is dead excited about Bella's visit: he's strung up a hammock behind the cottage; he was even talking about building a tree house for her.

Gwen, hating herself, clears her throat. "And is he—is he still drinking a lot?"

A moment's silence. "I'd say he has it under control. We were with him four nights, it wasn't . . . out of hand."

In the end, Gwen's only stipulation has been that he not drive the two round-trips, a thousand miles in a weekend, but leave his car at the station and take Bella back and forth on the bus. (It's stamina, she feels, that's never been his strong suit.)

Gwen wiggles past seated people and ducks into the corridor, but she's lost the connection. She presses the call-back code. "Gideon?"

3

W HEN G IDEON PICKED UP B ELLA from the Vanderveer, she had seemed to him a little sad. Once or twice, she had asked, "Mama? Mama? Mama coming?" and although Gideon had explained that this was *their* adventure, when they got off the bus at Holcombe, Bella was obviously expecting her mother to be waiting for them.

He asked her if she needed to pee, and she said No, but when they arrived at the farm, he'd found that both her overalls and the car seat were sopping.

After this uncertain start, however, Bella's spirits improved. She had darted around the cottage, excited by the clatter of her shoes on the wooden floorboards; she lay down in her little bed (on which he'd already placed her giant Babar) and pretended to be asleep, snoring merrily and ordering him to lie down beside her and also pretend to be asleep. (Whereupon she tugged at him, shouting "Up-up!" A pity; Gideon wouldn't have minded drifting off to eternity, side by side with his girl.)

She was eager to explore the farm. He had taken her down to the brook, with its ford of stepping-stones. (Bella mightily amused when her father lost his balance and got drenched to the knee.) Together they had climbed up into the loft of the barn, and he had shown her the remaining stalls in the stable that was now their workshop; she had hidden in the woodshed. He led her to the hammock he had strung from two fir trees, and watched her wind herself tight in its rope coils and then scream with alarmed laughter as it deposited her with a bump in the grass. He had taken her around the big house, where she had installed herself in the playroom, riding Roxanne's old rocking horse, scattering cribbage pegs across the floor. Climbed up on a sofa to reach the cuckoo clock, which she'd succeeded in dismantling without, however, persuading the cuckoo to emerge from its sanctum.

In the white-cold hour before the sun dipped down behind Mount Temaquit, they gathered kindling from the woodshed. And Gideon, watching his daughter stagger under the weight of the branches he'd given her, was impressed as always by how serious and purposeful she became once you set her to a task.

After supper, she fell asleep on the sofa. And Gideon, having deposited Bella in her box bed (warmed by electric blanket), stayed up the rest of the night, raging against the feelings his daughter had unloosed.

4

"GIDEON? I missed your call."

"What's the matter," crackles Gideon's voice. "Were you with a lover?"

This is his new tone with her: a joshing that keeps hiking up into a more out-of-control rage. And she wills herself to endure his nasty jokes, because . . . he's in torment. Because he's Bella's father. Because Bella's *there*.

"Can, can I call you—"

"Who's the lucky prick, is it Cash?"

"Is it what?" Why has he got Campbell on the brain? "No, I'm in the middle of the—"

"Whatever happened to the dear old chap? He hasn't been downsized, I hope."

"Gideon, I'm in the middle of a panel. Can I call you back in—"

Marion Esterhazy, coming out of the ladies' room, looks at Gwen curiously as she goes into the conference hall.

"Sorry, I guess I'm jealous, that's all."

"What?" The reception is ricocheting from a static razz to eerie clarity. Gwen, anxious about the panel, even more anxious about Bella. How does their day look, if Gideon's already trashed at eleven? Holy shit, why'd she ever let the girl go? Didn't he promise her he'd keep things safe, the fucking *liar*?

"Yeah, I'm jealous someone else managed to live with you all those years and get away alive. Avoid the mortal coils of matrimony. I guess Campbell'll be one nervous guy, hearing you're back on the warpath . . . Yeah?" he shouts, suddenly. "Honey, I'm on the phone with Mommy— I'll be down in a sec . . ."

She glances at her watch, peeks back inside. There's still fifteen minutes left to go. "You sound a little sloshed."

"A little sloshed?" he repeats, laughing. "Did I hear you right? I guess that's a fair description."

A pause. "I was thinking. Do you remember when I used to call you from work, or on the road, and I'd ask you to feel yourself, to touch your clitoris, your vulva . . . ?"

Oh God. Dear God. God help us. They are alone, him and Bella, up in the mountains, and he is raving-drunk. Has he been drinking all morning, or is he still tanked up from last night's drunk? Oh *Jesus*. She's calculating, Is there someone I can call to go check on Bella?

She has a sudden vision of Gideon their first fall, so adroitly coaxing *Thanks/No Thanks* teen-jaguars, recalcitrant Zapatas, and plumed serpents through tight spaces. Gideon in his midnight-blue wedding suit, chestnut eyes sparkling as he encircled her waist for the first dance, the Klezmofunks tweedling madly. Their daughter still a tadpole in her belly. He was a fine dancer, that man. He knew just how to hold you, so that it felt like somewhere between fucking and flying. Where is that man now? Where is that baby?

"How's Bella, Gideon? Is she okay?"

"What's it to you? Well, what I wanted to know is, did you really do it?"

She wonders is there some grown-up who can pluck Bella from Gideon's unsteady hands, keep her safe till Gwen can come and get her. Pray to God Bella's little enough not to be much disturbed by her father's being so out-of-control.

"Where are you, Gideon? Are you guys up at the main house? Is Zeph around?"

This is a stretch of terror you have to get through. Get through and then you're safe. Your daughter will be back in your arms. Safe. You will never allow Gideon to have her again. Remembering Bella's lips the first weeks of her birth, smooth as boiled candy, as wet paint in the can. Now her child's sweet mouth is striped by dryness, chapped, like other people's. She pictures Bella's cherubic mouth, "blowing" her mother a kiss through the taxicab window.

"Never mind. Tell me this. This is my million-dollar question. Did you really touch your clitoris, did you really make yourself come, when I was sweet-talking you on the phone, or was it a lie like everything else? Were you faking?"

"Gideon, this is not the—"

"Answer my question."

"This is not the moment."

She is thinking, Do I ask the police to go make sure everything's okay? But he'll never forgive me, it'll go on the records. Are there police in Lubeck? What's the nearest town? She needs a New York State map. There's . . . Holcombe?

She says, "I think maybe I'd better come on up there. Are you guys all alone? Is there anybody else around? Is Zeph still there?" But she doesn't know where "there" is, or what good Zeph's being there might do.

"No way," Gideon's voice has gone panicky. "I don't want you setting foot here. No trespassing, Gwen. You are not wanted."

"I think I should come, just to make sure you guys are . . ."

It's going to take her what, three, four hours? Forever to get out of the conference, rent a car, buy a map, find her way upstate. And whom can she deputize—does she dare ask Gerald to take over, to make her excuses? (Remembering that Lavrinsky has told her he's bringing by Stanford Krauss after lunch, whom he wants Gwen to meet.)

She needs to speak to Bella, badly. She needs to spirit herself over the telephone wires, infuse her child with magic courage, an amulet of protecting love . . .

"No way. I got another—another day and a half, that's the deal."

"I don't think you sound in too good shape, Gideon. It's not a question of rights, it's a question of safety." You promised me, Gideon, you double-crossing worm.

"Don't you come anywhere near here," his voice repeats. "The only way I can stand it is because you've never set eyes here. You just scoot now, Gwen, you go back and queen-bee it over your little conference, you just go back to sucking the dicks of those—"

"I want to talk to the girl." (She doesn't want to say Bella's name, as if it might jinx the child.) "I'm a little uncomfortable, I'm a long way away and I don't know what's happening."

"*You're* uncomfortable? Everything I have, you've poisoned." His voice is no longer accusing; it's almost matter-of-fact.

"Talk to me, Gwen," he says. "I don't want to see you, I just want to hear your voice so I can . . . Talk to me, tell me what you're thinking."

"What I'm thinking?" She's trying to bite down her tearful panic, to keep her mind from wheeling into orbit, where's the nearest car rental, but it's a two-and-a-half-hour drive even if you know your way, she's got to get a map, and Gideon's sure not going to give her directions to the farm. Can she sic the police on her own husband?

"I'm thinking . . . I'm thinking, I've got this panel going on two yards away that's about to end, and I've got to get up on that platform and introduce the next speakers . . ."

"I'll let you go," he says, sadly. "Gwen . . ."

"I'm thinking—I'm thinking, I'm thinking, I need to speak to Bella."

"Gwen . . ."

"Could you"—she's good and crying now, crying from sheer fear—"could you put Bella on the phone, please, Gid?"

She is crying, but she'd better quit crying before her daughter gets on the line, her daughter whose phone conversations consist of heavy breathing. She's thinking, If I can just hear that moist foggy breath on the line that is comforting as a horse's velvet-nosed snort, then I will be strong enough to do what I need to do, to get out of here and get her back, if I can only hear her—hold her—on the line.

"She's fine, she's fine," says Gideon. Impatiently/irritably, meaning, He's not, meaning, He's the one she should be worrying about.

"What's she doing?"

"She's playing on the rocking horse, we're about to have pancakes . . . You know, she's a lot nicer kid without you, Gwen. You really haven't done her a favor by spoiling her rotten."

A pause.

"Can I speak to her, please?"

"Hold on," he says. "Let me go . . ."

Gwen, heart pounding, peers into the conference room.

Gideon's heavy breath comes back on the line, as if his mouth's too close to the receiver. Gideon's breath like an anonymous caller. Heavy breathing, a snuffle. Not Bella, Gideon.

"Is she there, Gideon? Can you put her on?"

"Let me go get her," he says, heavily. A crash as he lets the phone drop. The reception once again is eerily clear. Noise of Gideon clattering downstairs.

Gwen, waiting to speak to her daughter, ducks back into the conference hall.

Gerald appears to be winding up the panel, summarizing the speakers' positions. Gwen looks up at Gerald in his gray flannel suit, so suave, so practiced. He projects protective capabilities that she's never tested, that she suspects are merely an illusion of his being six feet three and weighing 220 pounds. She is about to find out.

"So we have just heard Mike Kaplan questioning why we should pour any more money into a—what was your phrase, Mike? A criminal-syndicalist state," says Gerald. "And Ludovic Sanders, who thinks Russia today is a bigger danger than under Communism, because these are gangsters who are dealing in plutonium. And Eugene Kolchuk, who wants—am I right, Eugene—to create a free market in nuclear weapons?"

"Now you malign me," says Eugene. "I am perverse, but I am not that perverse. Although maybe this is not such a bad idea." Everybody laughs.

"My own view? I am not going to sit here and tell you our taxpayers' money can reform the Russian economy, or even, properly monitored, can stay out of the bad guys' Swiss bank accounts," Kolchuk continues. "Some of you have already heard me argue that organized crime in Russia is a healthy thing, because it breaks the government's monopoly on corruption, that gangsterism too is a primitive form of capitalism.

"Today I'm going to try another line. Call me a cynic. But *if*–having persuaded Russia to abandon Communism and unilaterally disband its empire, abandon its satellites, its African, Middle Eastern, Latin American, and Southeast Asian clients, and switch to democratic capitalism–*without* a drop of blood, compared to how many dead white European males did it take to topple the Ottoman Empire, or the Axis? (And incidentally, if there were victory celebrations all over the land of America the day Communism fell, bottles of champagne opened, toasts to our dissident friends, telegrams of thanks from our European allies for years of free defense, nobody invited me.) *If then* we in the West had refused to help Russia rebuild its infrastructure and reform its economy, well, then we would rightly go down as the sorest winners in history. And any disasters that ever happened to Russia or that Russia ever wreaked on the rest of the world could rightly be blamed on our mean-spirited shortsighted penny-pinching. In brief? We had to feed them *billions*."

More laughter.

"I'm not questioning the billions, Eugene," says Ludovic. "I suppose I'm questioning the *unmonitored* billions. Jeffrey Sachs and a lot of other economists talked about a Marshall Plan for Russia–"

"Of course. The trouble with a Marshall Plan is Russia in 1991 was not occupied Germany 1945. This is a sovereign state with which we have been allied in two world wars, with which in fact we have never fought a war, which has voluntarily and peacefully voted out a regime we didn't like."

"That's disingenuous–we're not at war with Thailand or Malaysia or Brazil, either–"

"In no way were we in a position to send in the OSS and say, Hey fellows, we're de-Communizing you, like it or not . . ."

"But Eugene, basically, you're talking about giving the Russian oligarchy a sixty-billion-dollar tip. Now, under the Cold War, we made that bargain with the Devil, we were basically happy to pay into anti-Communist dictators' retirement funds. But today . . ."

On the phone there is silence. Staticky silence. *CFDTYYEREXD-Serserwwefdteyiouiohwjjkgiwytyw.* Silence. A roar of static.

"Gideon!" she says into the receiver. Softly.

It's no good, the connection's broken. Gideon! Gideon! Gideon! There is no human sound now, only a muffled roar, like the roar of a waterfall, the roar of the sea. Gideon has let the phone drop and he has gone away, and she is left hanging in the roaring void, without having spoken to her daughter, without having received the reassurance of that muggy breathing. She can't even disconnect and try again . . .

"Well, gentlemen," says Gerald, leaning back, big arms folded. "I think it's time to open the debate to questions from the floor." There's already a lineup of geeks at the microphone.

"May I remind you all to keep your questions brief. And keep them questions. No pronunciamentos, please. And in the meantime, I'd like to thank these three gentlemen for their lively participation."

Applause drowning out the staticky roar of the telephone, and Gwen, poised in the doorway, wringing her hands, seized by an animal grief . . .

Chapter Two

I

SHE HAD FALLEN into the stream, their mermaid-babe. It preyed on her parents later: that Bella had slipped into wateriness so readily, as if they hadn't given her enough appetite for earth. As if their rancor had taken it away.

Her escape had been quick. A mere eight minutes of telephone talk before Gideon, who'd brought Bella up to the main house to make pancakes and call her mother, noticed the quiet, and grappled for the lost thread of his child's whereabouts. Tumbled downstairs to find the dominoes, the cribbage set, the playing cards fanned across the floor, the rocking horse still shuddering on its wire springs.

The playroom door wide-open. (If he hadn't just removed it for the winter, Gideon would have been alerted by the screen door's slam.) Ran

outside, shouting, to find Bella. Up to the hammock. Back to their cottage. Then, dreadful, down to the brook. Screaming her name. He didn't
see anything at first, and then, just above the ford, a bundled glow of
sodden pink, of shiny scarlet, one red rubber boot further downstream.

The ineffable simultaneities: Saturday morning, October 1998, while
her mother, in the corridor of the Hotel Siena, was listening to a short
bespectacled scholar predict that the Russian economy would be back
into positive growth within two years, her not-yet-two-year-old daughter
was lying face downward in a knee-deep tributary of the Manapattox
River, the life slipping out of her as the water flooded into her nose, her
mouth, her lungs.

For you, Gideon, the moment you have been put on earth and
will be kept in hell to replay. The moment of spotting her, of slipping, splashing down into the dammed eddy where she is beached,
the moment of hoicking her out, of trying to rip her free from the tangle of branches. Turning her over, trying to push out of his way the
knapsack that is strapped across her chest. Her dripping clothes as heavy
as cement. Her head hanging horribly limp. On her face there is a
blue bruise, a goose egg that stretches from the temple to her eye. There
is a long scratch across her other cheek, which as he carries her out of
the water (slipping, falling down to his knees in the stream, hoisting
himself—and her—aloft again) starts to bleed. He plops down in the
muddy grave of the bank, and he lays her body across his knees, he
clutches convulsively tight to his chest that inhuman cold-wetness,
he begins to howl. But there is no reviving her, Gideon, there is no Bella
anymore in that body, no matter how you try to pump breath back
down her throat, no matter how you blow and storm.

2

OFTEN, her parents would retrace the child's journey into the world.
Her journey to the underworld. Bella, alone in the basement playroom
while her father quarrels with her mother on the kitchen phone, decides
to go on an adventure. Loads her red patent-leather Betty Boop knapsack full of trophies: a Chinese checkers set, a lusterware ashtray, a
wooden nutcracker.

Reaches on her tiptoes, unlatches the door, sets off on her solitary excursion. It's a crackling cold October morning. The leaves are

crimson-scarlet-orange-gold, the sky is almost violet-blue. Knapsack hanging around her neck, she marches. Perhaps she intended to go to the stable or up to the hammock, and then remembers the brook: the forbidden spot she's drawn to, because she's a little fish. She leans over the brink into the dark brown flood, sparkly, flickering. And, arms overloaded, trips (they found later the slip-tread of her boot soles on a patch of muddy bank, like a doll-sized tractor). The weighted knapsack entangling her arms so that she can't break her fall, can't save herself, but is pinned, facedown in the water.

3

THE THOUGHTS that come into your head. Thinking, But I never gave her breakfast!

He'd mixed the pancake batter in Bridey's kitchen while Bella played in the basement, and if only he'd had the self-restraint to sit the child down to breakfast before calling Gwen. (Maliciously cognizant that this time she would be obliged to take his call; this time, he had the bait!)

You imagine the other way, the path you missed by this error in sequencing. The picture carved on Achilles' shield. In this golden engraving, your bear cub is perched atop a cushion at the breakfast table, sedated by maple syrup, while you, watching, talk on the phone. Bella, sticky, crows her sagas of merriment and wonder, her munching and dripping accompanied by satisfied humming, interspersed with inquiries about the "huss" that used to live in the stable, the "er-er" in the henhouse. Words she would now never outgrow.

You spend a peaceable weekend; you deliver her back to her mother Sunday night. She comes up for more weekends. She grows up, you make a home for her.

But you didn't eat your breakfast, Bella . . . Which means you don't get to grow up.

4

GIDEON, sitting with Zeph Drexler in a row of poured-plastic chairs in the hospital basement, outside the morgue, hears noises. The *bing-bing* of the elevator. Soothing murmurs, a shuffle. Someone coming down the corridor. A moan. Someone who can't walk. More encouraging murmurs; more shuffling. Strangled sobs that rise into a high keening. And then they come around the corner, this nurse-and-patient pair: a tiny brisk woman supporting a tall woman who is oddly stooped, askew, who keeps collapsing at the knees. Shuddering, convulsing. Who shuffles a couple of steps and then, clawing at her face, begins again to moan. The smaller woman has her charge underneath the armpit while she bends double, half gagging, half moaning.

"Here we are, darling," urges Jacey. "You can do it." Now Gideon's wife keels back upright, head tilted back. As she approaches Gideon, he sees her eyes are screwed tight shut and her mouth is hanging open . . .

5

THE DAYS AND NIGHTS that followed were lightless, jumbled, altered by the sedatives both parents had been pumped with.

That first night without Bella, the first night of their new life, their interminable life of sinful loss. (Yes, there is a hell and it's right here, and it doesn't end, it doesn't really matter if you're alive or dead. Hell is being without her, knowing you caused her wrongful death.)

There were the summits: ghostly gatherings back at Lubeck, and then in Newburyport, where previously unacquainted friends or estranged relatives congregated in cold rooms at odd hours, discussing—with you, without you—what was to be done. Jacey; Maddock; Dan, Andrea; Katrina with Aunt Sue. Jerome and Bridey, who'd flown back immediately.

It was Sue, of course, who took charge, cajoling Katrina into acknowledging Gideon because he was the child's father, her daughter's lawful husband, who offered him a room in her house for the funeral. Maddock, who was peacemaker in those leaden discussions—mirror-mockery of Gwen and Gideon's wedding wrangles—of where their baby's body (rosy-brown flesh now turned irreversibly to corpse) was to be buried, extracting Gideon's consent to his daughter's resting in Episcopalian soil (Aunt Sue having ceded her spot next to Uncle Rich). Maddock, again, who after the unbearable funeral drove his sister back to New York and stayed with her a good ten days in her apartment (which she was now scared to be in), sleeping not in the study, but in

Bella's bed. Wanting Gwen—the many times each night she wandered into her daughter's old room—to find instead *him*: hairy, snoring, temporary but real.

Someone (not Maddock) had taken Bella's clothes and toys away, when Gwen wasn't looking. Someone had spirited away this treasure, which might prove to Gwen in distant days that she had once possessed the sun and the moon and a bundle of stars in a girl who smelled like cinnamon toast, who liked to lick your cheek and eat her own snot, and sing on the pot as she swung her legs merrily. Merrily down the stream . . . facedown . . . life is but . . . life is but . . . facedown.

Chapter Three

AFTER OVERSEEING the Lavrinsky Institute's disbandment of its Russian offices, Gwendolen Lewis stayed on in Moscow.

A visitor to Russia in the spring of 1999 might have imagined the country was reeling from a massive military defeat: old people were freezing to death in their bed-sits; syphilis, cholera, tuberculosis were raging; glue-sniffing orphans slept in train stations; eighteen-year-old boys were mutilating themselves so as not to be drafted; a young woman with a degree in computer science told Gwen her best hope was to become a prostitute in the West.

Gwen felt like a nurse at the front. She rented two rooms in a nineteenth-century building near the Arbat; and she did piecework translating for the mayor's office, acting as a freelance consultant to foreign businesses and charities.

She had made enough money from selling her New York apartment to live on savings. There was certainly no money in Russia: it was back to the barter system.

Sometimes for days on end she did not speak English; sometimes for days on end she did not speak. There was a life that was running in her head—her imaginary, remembered, and projected life with her daughter—that was too compelling to interrupt.

She did not want daily events loud or vivid enough to dispel such images as her last sight of Bella: her child's blowing her a goodbye kiss through the taxi window, blowing with a silent puff, as you blow out a candle.

When they threatened to grow faint (the sounds of an almost two-year-old child are not loud, no louder than that exhaled kiss) she resorted to magic: unpacking her few things, a tiny striped sock she had found stashed in the back of her drawer, a pack of Polaroids, the small pink polar fleece. She whispered the names she carried with her.

But whether you want to or not, you heal. Regularly you tear off the scab, but the body is remorseless in its self-curing.

For several years into her new Muscovite life, Gwen did not touch anybody. She carried it before her, the fending-off legend, Don't come near me, for I let my daughter die. Then she quietened and allowed someone into her bed. Someone who didn't ask questions, guessed more. Someone who traced the scar across her lower abdomen, but asked nothing. Someone already self-contained enough to tolerate her polite evasion of his existence.

There was plenty not to tell. That night—maybe a month after the drowning—that Gideon had come down from Vermont to visit her and they had slept once more in their marital bed: two crushed killers who, in their wretchedness, had tried to couple—in the mad idea that Bella's spirit, so newly fled, might be willing to reenter Gwen's body and be born again. But Gideon had been unable, and then, when he was wretched-able, Gwen had been too convulsed by tears, too undone, almost, to let him in, and yet what a good idea it had nonetheless seemed.

How she'd reckoned, I should die quickly, so I can still catch her—and then realized, Not so easy; it's not your merry prattling gypsy-tot who awaits you on the other side. Your two babies, whom you killed, are dead, and will always be dead. It's judgment that awaits, because you have done things for which you will be damned: sinned against your husband, sinned against the infants God gave you, sinned against life itself.

Curious, how people reacted to a child's death, to the hatchet-drop of "tragedy." The friends who were too scared to see you, the New England relatives—Rich and Emily, Hal—who patted your arm but didn't dare mention it. Distant acquaintances who had intervened with ancient ritual kindness, Gail Lefever, Gwen's best friend from fourth grade, who suddenly called every week and made her come to dinner. And Gwen had *come*. People old-fashioned enough to be acquainted with the habits of mourning, like knowing embroidery or the waltz. People she made use of, and didn't see again after she decided to close up. Years you blanked out. Intonations. Vows. Instincts: what that womb, those arms, those breasts were made for.

Her friends urged her to see a shrink, and she went once, to a gray young man, wondering if she might not be able to stir some sense out of the muck in her head. But she had looked at his wolfish body, which had never been full with a child; and she had come up against this in-compatible difference: that his science did not recognize the notion of sin, except as a pathology.

Her proposed solution, which was to lead a life of penance, devot-ing her days to an impossible atonement—a solution which had been conventional wisdom throughout human history and which still under-lay our prison system—was as alien to his training as tar and feathers. When she saw they spoke different languages, she told him that she hadn't slept in four months, and he wrote her a prescription, which she never filled.

That winter Gwen had tried to quit her job, but Gerald, kind-gruff, wouldn't let her, had reminded her that when all else failed, there was al-ways the office. And then, by the following spring, no office.

Epilogue

GIDEON AND GWEN are sitting opposite each other at the Café Galactica.

Gideon is in Moscow for an arts festival arranged by Roman Grinspan. Gideon has gained a certain renown in the last couple of years: he directed a puppet sequence in a production of *L'Incoronazione di Poppaea* that premiered at Santa Fe and then toured Europe. Now he has a one-man show, in which he stands on a chair with a marionette of himself as "Gary Brager" and conducts a bitter-comic monologue—about politics, the stock market, Islamic terrorism, his grandmother, the Jews. Somebody sent Gwen clippings of a review. Gwen keeps up, from a distance, with her old friends. It's the first warm day of the year: they have chosen a table in the window of the café.

Gideon, who now calls himself Brager, is not entirely the same man. Up close, Gwen would think him fifteen years older. His now close-cropped beard is mostly white; he has three vertical frown-marks dug deep between his brows, and a polite titter, in the place of his old raspy belly laugh. He looks drawn, grizzled, saintly . . . beautiful, still. With his bald head and his gray-white beard, he appears an old man. But when he walks, the same long-legged lope expresses an optimism that is surely more than physiological.

Their child would now be six-and-a-half years old, and if she'd lived, they would presumably have arrived at some truce over her schooling. She would be able to read and write, she might know how to tell time on a clock with hands, she would have her own circle of friends. Maybe she would have grown gentle enough only to like princesses and ballet. She would have ideas about what she wanted to be when she grew up. She would know how to swim. They would have had an extra fifteen hundred days of her.

Gideon's looking at Gwen when she's not looking. Then his eyes slip away. "So you've been living in Moscow . . ."

Gwen nods.

"How is it?"

"Fine." She considers how to give a reckoning that is neither too clipped nor too revealing. "I spent a year and a half in Grozny—well, shuttling back and forth between here and Grozny. But now I'm here."

Gwen works for Memorial, which is a human rights group composed of former dissidents and prisoners of the Gulag, who are trying to maintain a liberal opposition to the current regime.

"It's draining—I believe in what we're doing, but you feel it's not the direction the country is going in—it's a relic of something good that's over."

And you, Gideon? Gideon lives out in Fort Greene. He's living with a woman he's about to marry, which is what he's come to tell you, Gwen. I thought you should know. (She's grateful: she knows it took guts for him to call Jacey and track her down.)

Gideon's fiancée is called Laura Shulevitz; she teaches at UVA; her subject is biblical anthropology. She commutes between Brooklyn and Charlottesville. He tells her a little about the woman's field, and Gwen pores over his words, nodding. She doesn't feel entitled to ask him much about his wife-to-be, such as how old she is, or has she been married before, and does she have children already, and does she want them. She studies what Gideon's already told her, feeling it would sound flippant to offer good wishes. There is in fact so little they can say that conversation soon dries up.

Each is too immersed in his own internal monologue—in the reel of imaginary conversations they conduct with each other, the daily liturgy of inquiry, avowal, speculation, remorse—to break through into live sounded speech.

Gideon looks out the window. He gazes out the window so long he seems to have forgotten that Gwen's there. Gwen examines her ex-husband as he stares out the window, quite unconscious of her presence. As if he's so used to dreaming her he now can't tell her from his dream. She sees that he's begun looking at something. His body is alert as a hunting dog's, even his crooked nose seems to be pointing, and his face quivers with a sympathetic curiosity. She looks out the window and sees he's watching an acrobat on the corner, who is now standing on his hands, an umbrella gripped in his bare feet.

And although Gwen still lives with what she and Gideon did (to the two children God gave them, and to each other) like lead in the chest, although a large portion of her freedom of mind and emotional range are gone—something cursed and uncured in her thinks, It would always have happened. Wherever and however we met, we would have come together. In whatever age or whatever country, we would have found each other . . .

Hector they called the horse-breaker, she reflects, and when you've broken a horse, you've got a ride, but break your lover, and all that's left is your own arid will, a bed turned to rocky soil that will never take the plough.

A NOTE ON THE TYPE

This book was set in Garamond. The fonts are based on types first cut by Claude Garamond (c. 1480–1561). Garamond was a pupil of Geoffroy Tory and is believed to have followed the Venetian models, although he introduced a number of important differences, and it is to him that we owe the letter we now know as "old style." He gave to his letters a certain elegance and feeling of movement that won their creator an immediate reputation and the patronage of Francis I of France.

Composed by Creative Graphics
Allentown, Pennsylvania
Printed and bound by Berryville Graphics,
Berryville, Virginia